The Greatest
Short Stories of
ANTON CHEKHOV

Translated by Constance Garnett

CLASSICS

Reprint 2023

FiNGERPRINT! CLASSiCS
An imprint of Prakash Books India Pvt. Ltd

113/A, Darya Ganj,
New Delhi-110 002
Email: info@prakashbooks.com/sales@prakashbooks.com

 Fingerprint Publishing
 @FingerprintP
 @fingerprintpublishingbooks
www.fingerprintpublishing.com

ISBN: 978 93 8971 710 5

"My mother and father are the only people on the whole planet for whom I will never begrudge a thing. Should I achieve great things, it is the work of their hands; they are splendid people and their absolute love of their children places them above the highest praise. It cloaks all of their shortcomings, shortcomings that may have resulted from a difficult life."

— Letter to his cousin,
M.M. Chekhov (July 29, 1877)

Believed to be one of the greatest short story writers in the history of literature, Anton Pavlovich Chekhov was born on January 29, 1860 in Taganrog, a port on the Sea of Azov in southern Russia. Grandson of a serf, and son of a grocery store owner, he came from humble beginnings but rose in popularity as a playwright and short story writer.

His father, Pavel Yegorovich Chekhov, was not one to spare the rod when it came to disciplining his children, though he claimed to be a devout orthodox Christian. Chekhov's mother was a labourer and did sewing part-time, but still made time to entertain him and her other children with tales of her travels in Russia.

Chekhov went to Greek School in Taganrog, where he was held back for a year for failing an examination in ancient Greek. He received a good education there—thorough but unimaginative. Problems occurred when Chekhov's father went bankrupt. This happened in 1876. The family fled to Moscow so Pavel could have a fresh start, and, more importantly, avoid debtor's prison. Anton Chekhov was left behind to sell the family's possessions and joined his family after three years. During these three years, he paid for his own education by doing odd jobs, such as tutoring, selling goldfinches, selling his sketches to newspapers, etc., and whatever extra cash remained, he sent it to his family. Once he moved to Moscow, he wasted no time in enrolling in a medical university. He graduated as a doctor in 1884.

Medicine was Chekhov's lawful wife, but literature was his mistress (as he once said). Being a doctor was his main profession, but it didn't fetch him enough money. He treated the poor free of charge. In order to support his family, he began to write humorous sketches and vignettes of contemporary Russian life under a pseudonym. His freelance journalism and comic writings had made him immensely popular in the Russian public and literary circles by 1888. Over time, Chekhov also wrote about serious subject matters, such as human misery and despair. His fascination with such subjects predominated his later writings.

In 1887, Chekhov moved away from writing humorous tidbits and got *The Lottery Ticket*, one of Chekhov's most well-known short stories, published. A year later, his story, *Steppe*, was published in a leading literary review, and in the same year, he received the Pushkin Prize for literary excellence. The story was autobiographical, describing the journey in Ukraine through the eyes of a child, inspired from Chekhov's own trip to the place. During this time, Chekhov was also commissioned to write a play. He wrote his first full-length play, *Ivanov*, in a fortnight. Russian drama saw its high point when Chekhov's plays came out. He wrote fourteen plays, of which four were critically acclaimed—*The Seagull* (written in 1895), *Uncle Vanya* (written in 1897), *The Three Sisters* (written in 1900), and *The Cherry Orchard* (written in 1903). They were lauded for aptly portraying realism—how people behave and act in real life, and what it means to be a human. His writings mainly portrayed bourgeoisie values such as kindness, politeness, sobriety, paying one's debts, and avoiding self-pity, amongst others.

Chekhov was garnering praise as a writer and a playwright. His writings were based on what later came to be known as 'Chekhov's Gun.' The idea was to have only the things that are relevant to the narrative.

> "Remove everything that has no relevance to the story. If you say in the first chapter that there is a rifle hanging on the wall, in the second or third chapter it absolutely must go off. If it's not going to be fired, it shouldn't be hanging there."

Along with praise, Chekhov was attracting criticism for holding no fixed political or social views. This backlash didn't change his style or content of writing though—he remained unpolitical. He was undeterred by the remarks of his contemporary, the renowned writer Leo Tolstoy, who said to Chekhov, "You know I cannot abide Shakespeare, but your plays are even worse." Tolstoy, however, praised Chekhov's short stories. He even had a list of the stories that he put under 'first quality' and 'second quality,' and then bound them in a book.

In 1892, Chekhov bought a country estate in the old village of Melikhovo. He lived in this seemingly unremarkable village for a short period of time—only seven years—but this period of his life proved to be the most fruitful for his creativity. It was here that he wrote the stories that created a stir in Russia—'Peasants' (1897), which is a story based on Chekhov's stay at Melikhovo, 'The Black Monk' (1894), 'An Anonymous Story' (1893), 'The Student' (1894) which was Chekhov's favourite story, 'Gooseberries' (1898), 'About Love' (1898), and various others. Since he was a doctor, he communicated with the Russian peasantry in the village. Chekhov then portrayed this peasantry without sentimentalizing it, as was the convention till then. Chekhov wrote *The Seagull* during this period. It was not received well at first. Chekhov could not bear to see his play being hissed off the stage, so he left in the second act. But the play was later revived by the Moscow Art Theatre. It was a success and re-established Chekhov as a dramatist.

Though Chekhov's literary works were being lauded, tragedy befell his family when his father died in 1897. The next year, Chekhov suffered a lung hemorrhage and was diagnosed with tuberculosis. So, he, with his mother and sister, moved to Yalta, a city in southern Russia. The move to this villa aided Chekhov with his illness, but it was completely cut off from the intellectual life of Moscow. Also, Chekhov had to move at a time when his plays had started attracting attention. He entertained guests such as Leo Tolstoy and Maxim Gorky, yet Chekhov was always relieved to leave the villa and travel.

It was during his stay in Yalta that he wrote one of his most famous short stories, 'The Lady with the Dog.' Vladimir Nobokov claimed it to be the greatest short story ever written. Readers conjecture that this story, in a way, described the author's relationship with his wife. In 1901, Chekhov got married to Olga Knipper, the leading lady of the Moscow Art Theatre, the star of his plays. Due to Knipper's acting career and Chekhov's deteriorating health, they were forced to stay apart—she mostly stayed at the theatre, and he at the villa. Even in such condition, their love for each other remained as strong as ever. Their marriage came to an end with Chekhov's untimely death in 1904, but during the three years that they were together, they exchanged as many as four hundred letters.

Chekhov's death has been a subject of interest for many. Allegedly, Chekhov, on the day that he died, spoke in German, although he didn't know the language. The words he uttered were *'Ich sterbe'* (I'm dying). He breathed his last on July 15, 1904.

Though already well-known in the Russian public, Anton Chekhov became famous internationally after World War I, when Constance Garnett translated his works. Forty years after his death, *Complete Works and Letters of A.P. Chekhov* was published—a book in twenty volumes that presented Chekhov's work on a scholarly level for the first time. His works have also been adapted for screen and continue to be read and celebrated even today.

Contents

The Death of a Government Clerk

[First published with the subtitle 'The Incident' in
Oskolki (*Fragments*), a Russian literary weekly, on July 2, 1883.
Published in *Motley Stories* (1886) without the subtitle.
Collected in *Love and Other Stories* (1922).]

One fine evening, a no less fine government clerk called Ivan Dmitritch
Tchervyakov was sitting in the second row of the stalls, gazing through an
opera glass at the *Cloches de Corneville*. He gazed and felt at the acme of bliss.
But suddenly. . . . In stories one so often meets with this "But suddenly."
The authors are right: life is so full of surprises! But suddenly his face
puckered up, his eyes disappeared, his breathing was arrested . . . he took
the opera glass from his eyes, bent over and . . . "Aptchee!!" he sneezed
as you perceive. It is not reprehensible for anyone to sneeze anywhere.
Peasants sneeze and so do police superintendents, and sometimes even
privy councillors. All men sneeze. Tchervyakov was not in the least
confused, he wiped his face with his handkerchief, and like a polite man,
looked round to see whether he had disturbed any one by his sneezing.
But then he was overcome with confusion. He saw that an old gentleman
sitting in front of him in the first row of the stalls was carefully wiping
his bald head and his neck with his glove and muttering something to
himself. In the old gentleman, Tchervyakov recognised Brizzhalov, a
civilian general serving in the Department of Transport.

"I have spattered him," thought Tchervyakov, "he is not the head of
my department, but still it is awkward. I must apologise."

Tchervyakov gave a cough, bent his whole person forward, and whispered in the general's ear.

"Pardon, your Excellency, I spattered you accidentally. . . ."

"Never mind, never mind."

"For goodness sake excuse me, I . . . I did not mean to."

"Oh, please, sit down! let me listen!"

Tchervyakov was embarrassed, he smiled stupidly and fell to gazing at the stage. He gazed at it but was no longer feeling bliss. He began to be troubled by uneasiness. In the interval, he went up to Brizzhalov, walked beside him, and overcoming his shyness, muttered:

"I spattered you, your Excellency, forgive me . . . you see . . . I didn't do it to. . . ."

"Oh, that's enough . . . I'd forgotten it, and you keep on about it!" said the general, moving his lower lip impatiently.

"He has forgotten, but there is a fiendish light in his eye," thought Tchervyakov, looking suspiciously at the general. "And he doesn't want to talk. I ought to explain to him . . . that I really didn't intend . . . that it is the law of nature or else he will think I meant to spit on him. He doesn't think so now, but he will think so later!"

On getting home, Tchervyakov told his wife of his breach of good manners. It struck him that his wife took too frivolous a view of the incident; she was a little frightened, but when she learned that Brizzhalov was in a different department, she was reassured.

"Still, you had better go and apologise," she said, "or he will think you don't know how to behave in public."

"That's just it! I did apologise, but he took it somehow queerly . . . he didn't say a word of sense. There wasn't time to talk properly."

Next day Tchervyakov put on a new uniform, had his hair cut and went to Brizzhalov's to explain; going into the general's reception room he saw there a number of petitioners and among them the general himself, who was beginning to interview them. After questioning several petitioners the general raised his eyes and looked at Tchervyakov.

"Yesterday at the *Arcadia*, if you recollect, your Excellency," the latter began, "I sneezed and . . . accidentally spattered . . . Exc. . . ."

"What nonsense. . . . It's beyond anything! What can I do for you," said the general addressing the next petitioner.

"He won't speak," thought Tchervyakov, turning pale; "that means that he is angry. . . . No, it can't be left like this. . . . I will explain to him."

When the general had finished his conversation with the last of the petitioners and was turning towards his inner apartments, Tchervyakov took a step towards him and muttered:

"Your Excellency! If I venture to trouble your Excellency, it is simply from a feeling I may say of regret! . . . It was not intentional if you will graciously believe me."

The general made a lachrymose face, and waved his hand.

"Why, you are simply making fun of me, sir," he said as he closed the door behind him.

"Where's the making fun in it?" thought Tchervyakov, "there is nothing of the sort! He is a general, but he can't understand. If that is how it is I am not going to apologise to that *fanfaron* any more! The devil take him. I'll write a letter to him, but I won't go. By Jove, I won't."

So thought Tchervyakov as he walked home; he did not write a letter to the general, he pondered and pondered and could not make up that letter. He had to go next day to explain in person.

"I ventured to disturb your Excellency yesterday," he muttered, when the general lifted enquiring eyes upon him, "not to make fun as you were pleased to say. I was apologising for having spattered you in sneezing. . . . And I did not dream of making fun of you. Should I dare to make fun of you, if we should take to making fun, then there would be no respect for persons, there would be. . . ."

"Be off!" yelled the general, turning suddenly purple, and shaking all over.

"What?" asked Tchervyakov, in a whisper turning numb with horror.

"Be off!" repeated the general, stamping.

Something seemed to give way in Tchervyakov's stomach. Seeing nothing and hearing nothing he reeled to the door, went out into the street, and went staggering along. . . . Reaching home mechanically, without taking off his uniform, he lay down on the sofa and died.

Joy

[First published in 1883.
Collected in *The Schoolmaster and Other Stories* (1921).]

It was twelve o'clock at night.

Mitya Kuldarov, with excited face and ruffled hair, flew into his parents' flat, and hurriedly ran through all the rooms. His parents had already gone to bed. His sister was in bed, finishing the last page of a novel. His schoolboy brothers were asleep.

"Where have you come from?" cried his parents in amazement. "What is the matter with you?

"Oh, don't ask! I never expected it; no, I never expected it! It's . . . it's positively incredible!"

Mitya laughed and sank into an armchair, so overcome by happiness that he could not stand on his legs.

"It's incredible! You can't imagine! Look!"

His sister jumped out of bed and, throwing a quilt round her, went in to her brother. The schoolboys woke up.

"What's the matter? You don't look like yourself!"

"It's because I am so delighted, Mamma! Do you know, now all Russia knows of me! All Russia! Till now only you knew that there was a registration clerk called Dmitry Kuldarov, and now all Russia knows it! Mamma! Oh, Lord!"

Mitya jumped up, ran up and down all the rooms, and then sat down again.

"Why, what has happened? Tell us sensibly!"

"You live like wild beasts, you don't read the newspapers and take no notice of what's published, and there's so much that is interesting in the papers. If anything happens it's all known at once, nothing is hidden! How happy I am! Oh, Lord! You know it's only celebrated people whose names are published in the papers, and now they have gone and published mine!"

"What do you mean? Where?"

The papa turned pale. The mamma glanced at the holy image and crossed herself. The schoolboys jumped out of bed and, just as they were, in short nightshirts, went up to their brother.

"Yes! My name has been published! Now all Russia knows of me! Keep the paper, mamma, in memory of it! We will read it sometimes! Look!"

Mitya pulled out of his pocket a copy of the paper, gave it to his father, and pointed with his finger to a passage marked with blue pencil.

"Read it!"

The father put on his spectacles.

"Do read it!"

The mamma glanced at the holy image and crossed herself. The papa cleared his throat and began to read: "At eleven o'clock on the evening of the 29th of December, a registration clerk of the name of Dmitry Kuldarov . . ."

"You see, you see! Go on!"

". . . a registration clerk of the name of Dmitry Kuldarov, coming from the beershop in Kozihin's buildings in Little Bronnaia in an intoxicated condition . . ."

"That's me and Semyon Petrovitch. . . . It's all described exactly! Go on! Listen!"

". . . intoxicated condition, slipped and fell under a horse belonging to a sledge-driver, a peasant of the village of Durikino in the Yuhnovsky district, called Ivan Drotov. The frightened horse, stepping over Kuldarov and drawing the sledge over him, together with a Moscow merchant of the second guild called Stepan Lukov, who was in it, dashed along the street and was caught by some house-porters. Kuldarov, at first in an unconscious condition, was taken to the police station and there examined by the doctor. The blow he had received on the back of his head . . ."

"It was from the shaft, papa. Go on! Read the rest!"

". . . he had received on the back of his head turned out not to be serious. The incident was duly reported. Medical aid was given to the injured man. . . ."

"They told me to foment the back of my head with cold water. You have read it now? Ah! So you see. Now it's all over Russia! Give it here!"

Mitya seized the paper, folded it up and put it into his pocket.

"I'll run round to the Makarovs and show it to them. . . . I must show it to the Ivanitskys too, Natasya Ivanovna, and Anisim Vassilyitch. . . . I'll run! Goodbye!"

Mitya put on his cap with its cockade and, joyful and triumphant, ran into the street.

In the Graveyard

[First published in October 1884.
Collected in *The Schoolmaster and Other Stories* (1921).]

"The wind has got up, friends, and it is beginning to get dark. Hadn't we better take ourselves off before it gets worse?"

The wind was frolicking among the yellow leaves of the old birch trees, and a shower of thick drops fell upon us from the leaves. One of our party slipped on the clayey soil, and clutched at a big grey cross to save himself from falling.

"Yegor Gryaznorukov, titular councillor and cavalier . . ." he read. "I knew that gentleman. He was fond of his wife, he wore the Stanislav ribbon, and read nothing. . . . His digestion worked well. . . . life was all right, wasn't it? One would have thought he had no reason to die, but alas! fate had its eye on him. . . . The poor fellow fell a victim to his habits of observation. On one occasion, when he was listening at a keyhole, he got such a bang on the head from the door that he sustained concussion of the brain (he had a brain), and died. And here, under this tombstone, lies a man who from his cradle detested verses and epigrams. . . . As though to mock him his whole tombstone is adorned with verses. . . . There is someone coming!"

A man in a shabby overcoat, with a shaven, bluish-crimson countenance, overtook us. He had a bottle under his arm and a parcel of sausage was sticking out of his pocket.

"Where is the grave of Mushkin, the actor?" he asked us in a husky voice.

We conducted him towards the grave of Mushkin, the actor, who had died two years before.

"You are a government clerk, I suppose?" we asked him.

"No, an actor. Nowadays it is difficult to distinguish actors from clerks of the Consistory. No doubt you have noticed that. . . . That's typical, but it's not very flattering for the government clerk."

It was with difficulty that we found the actor's grave. It had sunken, was overgrown with weeds, and had lost all appearance of a grave. A cheap, little cross that had begun to rot, and was covered with green moss blackened by the frost, had an air of aged dejection and looked, as it were, ailing.

". . . forgotten friend Mushkin . . ." we read.

Time had erased the *never*, and corrected the falsehood of man.

"A subscription for a monument to him was got up among actors and journalists, but they drank up the money, the dear fellows . . ." sighed the actor, bowing down to the ground and touching the wet earth with his knees and his cap.

"How do you mean, drank it?"

That's very simple. They collected the money, published a paragraph about it in the newspaper, and spent it on drink. . . . I don't say it to blame them. . . . I hope it did them good, dear things! Good health to them, and eternal memory to him."

"Drinking means bad health, and eternal memory nothing but sadness. God give us remembrance for a time, but eternal memory— what next!"

"You are right there. Mushkin was a well-known man, you see; there were a dozen wreaths on the coffin, and he is already forgotten. Those to whom he was dear have forgotten him, but those to whom he did harm remember him. I, for instance, shall never, never forget him, for I got nothing but harm from him. I have no love for the deceased."

"What harm did he do you?"

"Great harm," sighed the actor, and an expression of bitter resentment overspread his face. "To me he was a villain and a scoundrel—the Kingdom of Heaven be his! It was through looking at him and listening to him that I became an actor. By his art he lured me from the parental home, he enticed me with the excitements of an actor's life, promised me all sorts of things—and brought tears and sorrow. . . . An actor's lot is a bitter one! I have lost youth, sobriety, and the divine semblance. . . . I haven't a half-penny to bless myself with, my shoes are down at heel,

18

my breeches are frayed and patched, and my face looks as if it had been gnawed by dogs. . . . My head's full of freethinking and nonsense. . . . He robbed me of my faith—my evil genius! It would have been something if I had had talent, but as it is, I am ruined for nothing. . . . It's cold, honoured friends. . . . Won't you have some? There is enough for all. . . . B-r-r-r. . . . Let us drink to the rest of his soul! Though I don't like him and though he's dead, he was the only one I had in the world, the only one. It's the last time I shall visit him. . . . The doctors say I shall soon die of drink, so here I have come to say goodbye. One must forgive one's enemies."

We left the actor to converse with the dead Mushkin and went on. It began drizzling a fine cold rain.

At the turning into the principal avenue strewn with gravel, we met a funeral procession. Four bearers, wearing white calico sashes and muddy high boots with leaves sticking on them, carried the brown coffin. It was getting dark and they hastened, stumbling and shaking their burden. . . .

"We've only been walking here for a couple of hours and that is the third brought in already. . . . Shall we go home, friends?"

Small Fry

[First published in *Oskolki* (*Fragments*), a Russian literary
weekly, in March 1885. Collected in *Motley Stories* (1886).
First published in English in 1918 as a part of the
collection *The Schoolmistress and Other Stories*.]

"Honoured Sir, Father and Benefactor!" a petty clerk called Nevyrazimov
was writing a rough copy of an Easter congratulatory letter. "I trust that
you may spend this Holy Day even as many more to come, in good health
and prosperity. And to your family also I . . ."

The lamp, in which the kerosene was getting low, was smoking and
smelling. A stray cockroach was running about the table in alarm near
Nevyrazimov's writing hand. Two rooms away from the office Paramon
the porter was for the third time cleaning his best boots, and with such
energy that the sound of the blacking-brush and of his expectorations was
audible in all the rooms.

"What else can I write to him, the rascal?" Nevyrazimov wondered,
raising his eyes to the smutty ceiling.

On the ceiling he saw a dark circle—the shadow of the lampshade.
Below it was the dusty cornice, and lower still the wall, which had once
been painted a bluish muddy colour. And the office seemed to him such
a place of desolation that he felt sorry, not only for himself, but even for
the cockroach.

"When I am off duty I shall go away, but he'll be on duty here all his
cockroach-life," he thought, stretching. "I am bored! Shall I clean my boots?"

And stretching once more, Nevyrazimov slouched lazily to the
porter's room. Paramon had finished cleaning his boots. Crossing himself

with one hand and holding the brush in the other, he was standing at the open windowpane, listening.

"They're ringing," he whispered to Nevyrazimov, looking at him with eyes intent and wide open. "Already!"

Nevyrazimov put his ear to the open pane and listened. The Easter chimes floated into the room with a whiff of fresh spring air. The booming of the bells mingled with the rumble of carriages, and above the chaos of sounds rose the brisk tenor tones of the nearest church and a loud shrill laugh.

"What a lot of people!" sighed Nevyrazimov, looking down into the street, where shadows of men flitted one after another by the illumination lamps. "They're all hurrying to the midnight service. . . . Our fellows have had a drink by now, you may be sure, and are strolling about the town. What a lot of laughter, what a lot of talk! I'm the only unlucky one, to have to sit here on such a day: And I have to do it every year!"

"Well, nobody forces you to take the job. It's not your turn to be on duty today, but Zastupov hired you to take his place. When other folks are enjoying themselves you hire yourself out. It's greediness!"

"Devil a bit of it! Not much to be greedy over—two roubles is all he gives me; a necktie as an extra. . . . It's poverty, not greediness. And it would be jolly, now, you know, to be going with a party to the service, and then to break the fast. . . . To drink and to have a bit of supper and tumble off to sleep. . . . One sits down to the table, there's an Easter cake and the samovar hissing, and some charming little thing beside you. . . . You drink a glass and chuck her under the chin, and it's first-rate. . . . You feel you're somebody. . . . Ech h-h! . . . I've made a mess of things! Look at that hussy driving by in her carriage, while I have to sit here and brood."

"We each have our lot in life, Ivan Danilitch. Please God, you'll be promoted and drive about in your carriage one day."

"I? No, brother, not likely. I shan't get beyond a 'titular,' not if I try till I burst. I'm not an educated man."

"Our General has no education either, but . . ."

"Well, but the General stole a hundred thousand before he got his position. And he's got very different manners and deportment from me, brother. With my manners and deportment one can't get far! And such a scoundrelly surname, Nevyrazimov! It's a hopeless position, in fact. One may go on as one is, or one may hang oneself . . ."

He moved away from the window and walked wearily about the rooms. The din of the bells grew louder and louder. . . . There was no need to stand by the window to hear it. And the better he could hear the bells and the louder the roar of the carriages, the darker seemed the muddy walls and the smutty cornice and the more the lamp smoked.

"Shall I hook it and leave the office?" thought Nevyrazimov.

But such a flight promised nothing worth having. . . . After coming out of the office and wandering about the town, Nevyrazimov would have gone home to his lodging, and in his lodging it was even grayer and more depressing than in the office. . . . Even supposing he were to spend that day pleasantly and with comfort, what had he beyond? Nothing but the same grey walls, the same stop-gap duty and complimentary letters. . . .

Nevyrazimov stood still in the middle of the office and sank into thought. The yearning for a new, better life gnawed at his heart with an intolerable ache. He had a passionate longing to find himself suddenly in the street, to mingle with the living crowd, to take part in the solemn festivity for the sake of which all those bells were clashing and those carriages were rumbling. He longed for what he had known in childhood—the family circle, the festive faces of his own people, the white cloth, light, warmth . . .! He thought of the carriage in which the lady had just driven by, the overcoat in which the head clerk was so smart, the gold chain that adorned the secretary's chest. . . . He thought of a warm bed, of the Stanislav order, of new boots, of a uniform without holes in the elbows. . . . He thought of all those things because he had none of them.

"Shall I steal?" he thought. "Even if stealing is an easy matter, hiding is what's difficult. Men run away to America, they say, with what they've stolen, but the devil knows where that blessed America is. One must have education even to steal, it seems."

The bells died down. He heard only a distant noise of carriages and Paramon's cough, while his depression and anger grew more and more intense and unbearable. The clock in the office struck half-past twelve.

"Shall I write a secret report? Proshkin did, and he rose rapidly."

Nevyrazimov sat down at his table and pondered. The lamp in which the kerosene had quite run dry was smoking violently and threatening to go out. The stray cockroach was still running about the table and had found no resting-place.

"One can always send in a secret report, but how is one to make it up? I should want to make all sorts of innuendoes and insinuations, like Proshkin, and I can't do it. If I made up anything I should be the first to get into trouble for it. I'm an ass, damn my soul!"

And Nevyrazimov, racking his brain for a means of escape from his hopeless position, stared at the rough copy he had written. The letter was written to a man whom he feared and hated with his whole soul, and from whom he had for the last ten years been trying to wring a post worth eighteen roubles a month, instead of the one he had at sixteen roubles.

"Ah, I'll teach you to run here, you devil!" He viciously slapped the palm of his hand on the cockroach, who had the misfortune to catch his eye. "Nasty thing!"

The cockroach fell on its back and wriggled its legs in despair. Nevyrazimov took it by one leg and threw it into the lamp. The lamp flared up and spluttered.

And Nevyrazimov felt better.

A Malefactor

[First published in *Peterburgskaya Gazeta* (*St. Petersburg Gazette*),
a Russian newspaper, in August 1885, with the subtitle
'A Little Scene.' Collected in *Motley Stories* (1886).
Published in English in *The Witch and Other Stories* (1918).]

An exceedingly lean little peasant, in a striped hempen shirt and patched drawers, stands facing the investigating magistrate. His face overgrown with hair and pitted with smallpox, and his eyes scarcely visible under thick, overhanging eyebrows have an expression of sullen moroseness. On his head there is a perfect mop of tangled, unkempt hair, which gives him an even more spider-like air of moroseness. He is barefooted.

"Denis Grigoryev!" the magistrate begins. "Come nearer, and answer my questions. On the seventh of this July the railway watchman, Ivan Semyonovitch Akinfov, going along the line in the morning, found you at the hundred-and-forty-first mile engaged in unscrewing a nut by which the rails are made fast to the sleepers. Here it is, the nut! . . . With the aforesaid nut he detained you. Was that so?"

"Wha-at?"

"Was this all as Akinfov states?"

"To be sure, it was."

"Very good; well, what were you unscrewing the nut for?"

"Wha-at?"

"Drop that 'wha-at' and answer the question; what were you unscrewing the nut for?"

"If I hadn't wanted it I shouldn't have unscrewed it," croaks Denis, looking at the ceiling.

"What did you want that nut for?"

"The nut? We make weights out of those nuts for our lines."

"Who is 'we'?"

"We, people. . . . The Klimovo peasants, that is."

"Listen, my man; don't play the idiot to me, but speak sensibly. It's no use telling lies here about weights!"

"I've never been a liar from a child, and now I'm telling lies . . ." mutters Denis, bJlinking. "But can you do without a weight, your honour? If you put live bait or maggots on a hook, would it go to the bottom without a weight? . . . I am telling lies," grins Denis. . . . "What the devil is the use of the worm if it swims on the surface! The perch and the pike and the eel-pout always go to the bottom, and a bait on the surface is only taken by a shillisper, not very often then, and there are no shillispers in our river. . . . That fish likes plenty of room."

"Why are you telling me about shillispers?"

"Wha-at? Why, you asked me yourself! The gentry catch fish that way too in our parts. The silliest little boy would not try to catch a fish without a weight. Of course anyone who did not understand might go to fish without a weight. There is no rule for a fool."

"So you say you unscrewed this nut to make a weight for your fishing line out of it?"

"What else for? It wasn't to play knuckle-bones with!"

"But you might have taken lead, a bullet . . . a nail of some sort. . . ."

"You don't pick up lead in the road, you have to buy it, and a nail's no good. You can't find anything better than a nut. . . . It's heavy, and there's a hole in it."

"He keeps pretending to be a fool! as though he'd been born yesterday or dropped from heaven! Don't you understand, you blockhead, what unscrewing these nuts leads to? If the watchman had not noticed it the train might have run off the rails, people would have been killed—you would have killed people."

"God forbid, your honour! What should I kill them for? Are we heathens or wicked people? Thank God, good gentlemen, we have lived all our lives without ever dreaming of such a thing. . . . Save, and have mercy on us, Queen of Heaven! . . . What are you saying?"

"And what do you suppose railway accidents do come from? Unscrew two or three nuts and you have an accident."

Denis grins, and screws up his eye at the magistrate incredulously.

"Why! how many years have we all in the village been unscrewing nuts, and the Lord has been merciful; and you talk of accidents, killing people. If I had carried away a rail or put a log across the line, say, then maybe it might have upset the train, but . . . pouf! a nut!"

"But you must understand that the nut holds the rail fast to the sleepers!"

"We understand that. . . . We don't unscrew them all . . . we leave some. . . . We don't do it thoughtlessly . . . we understand. . . ."

Denis yawns and makes the sign of the cross over his mouth.

"Last year the train went off the rails here," says the magistrate. "Now I see why!"

"What do you say, your honour?"

"I am telling you that now I see why the train went off the rails last year. . . . I understand!"

"That's what you are educated people for, to understand, you kind gentlemen. The Lord knows to whom to give understanding. . . . Here you have reasoned how and what, but the watchman, a peasant like ourselves, with no understanding at all, catches one by the collar and hauls one along. . . . You should reason first and then haul me off. It's a saying that a peasant has a peasant's wit. . . . Write down, too, your honour, that he hit me twice—in the jaw and in the chest."

"When your hut was searched they found another nut. . . . At what spot did you unscrew that, and when?"

"You mean the nut which lay under the red box?"

"I don't know where it was lying, only it was found. When did you unscrew it?"

"I didn't unscrew it; Ignashka, the son of one-eyed Semyon, gave it me. I mean the one which was under the box, but the one which was in the sledge in the yard Mitrofan and I unscrewed together."

"What Mitrofan?"

"Mitrofan Petrov. . . . Haven't you heard of him? He makes nets in our village and sells them to the gentry. He needs a lot of those nuts. Reckon a matter of ten for each net."

"Listen. Article 1081 of the Penal Code lays down that every wilful damage of the railway line committed when it can expose the traffic on that line to danger, and the guilty party knows that an accident must be caused by it . . . (Do you understand? Knows! And you could not help knowing what this unscrewing would lead to . . .) is liable to penal servitude."

"Of course, you know best. . . . We are ignorant people. . . . What do we understand?"

"You understand all about it! You are lying, shamming!"

"What should I lie for? Ask in the village if you don't believe me. Only a bleak is caught without a weight, and there is no fish worse than a gudgeon, yet even that won't bite without a weight."

"You'd better tell me about the shillisper next," said the magistrate, smiling.

"There are no shillispers in our parts. . . . We cast our line without a weight on the top of the water with a butterfly; a mullet may be caught that way, though that is not often."

"Come, hold your tongue."

A silence follows. Denis shifts from one foot to the other, looks at the table with the green cloth on it, and bJlinks his eyes violently as though what was before him was not the cloth but the sun. The magistrate writes rapidly.

"Can I go?" asks Denis after a long silence.

"No. I must take you under guard and send you to prison."

Denis leaves off bJlinking and, raising his thick eyebrows, looks inquiringly at the magistrate.

"How do you mean, to prison? Your honour! I have no time to spare, I must go to the fair; I must get three roubles from Yegor for some tallow! . . ."

"Hold your tongue; don't interrupt."

"To prison. . . . If there was something to go for, I'd go; but just to go for nothing! What for? I haven't stolen anything, I believe, and I've not been fighting. . . . If you are in doubt about the arrears, your honour, don't believe the elder. . . . You ask the agent . . . he's a regular heathen, the elder, you know."

"Hold your tongue."

"I am holding my tongue, as it is," mutters Denis; "but that the elder has lied over the account, I'll take my oath for it. . . . There are three of us brothers: Kuzma Grigoryev, then Yegor Grigoryev, and me, Denis Grigoryev."

"You are hindering me. . . . Hey, Semyon," cries the magistrate, "take him away!"

"There are three of us brothers," mutters Denis, as two stalwart soldiers take him and lead him out of the room. "A brother is not responsible for a brother. Kuzma does not pay, so you, Denis, must answer for it. . . . Judges indeed! Our master the general is dead—the Kingdom of Heaven be his—or he would have shown you judges. . . . You ought to judge sensibly, not at random. . . . Flog if you like, but flog someone who deserves it, flog with conscience."

The Huntsman

[First published in the Russian newspaper *Peterburgskaya Gazeta* (*St. Petersburg Gazette*) in August 1885. Collected in *Motley Stories* (1886). Published in English in *The Witch and Other Stories* (1918).]

A sultry, stifling midday. Not a cloudlet in the sky. . . . The sun-baked grass had a disconsolate, hopeless look: even if there were rain it could never be green again. . . . The forest stood silent, motionless, as though it were looking at something with its treetops or expecting something.

At the edge of the clearing a tall, narrow-shouldered man of forty in a red shirt, in patched trousers that had been a gentleman's, and in high boots, was slouching along with a lazy, shambling step. He was sauntering along the road. On the right was the green of the clearing, on the left a golden sea of ripe rye stretched to the very horizon. He was red and perspiring, a white cap with a straight jockey peak, evidently a gift from some open-handed young gentleman, perched jauntily on his handsome flaxen head. Across his shoulder hung a game-bag with a blackcock lying in it. The man held a double-barrelled gun cocked in his hand, and screwed up his eyes in the direction of his lean old dog who was running on ahead sniffing the bushes. There was stillness all round, not a sound . . . everything living was hiding away from the heat.

"Yegor Vlassitch!" the huntsman suddenly heard a soft voice.

He started and, looking round, scowled. Beside him, as though she had sprung out of the earth, stood a pale-faced woman of thirty with a sickle in her hand. She was trying to look into his face, and was smiling diffidently.

"Oh, it is you, Pelagea!" said the huntsman, stopping and deliberately uncocking the gun. "H'm! . . . How have you come here?"

"The women from our village are working here, so I have come with them. . . . As a labourer, Yegor Vlassitch."

"Oh . . ." growled Yegor Vlassitch, and slowly walked on.

Pelagea followed him. They walked in silence for twenty paces.

"I have not seen you for a long time, Yegor Vlassitch . . ." said Pelagea looking tenderly at the huntsman's moving shoulders. "I have not seen you since you came into our hut at Easter for a drink of water . . . you came in at Easter for a minute and then God knows how . . . drunk . . . you scolded and beat me and went away . . . I have been waiting and waiting . . . I've tired my eyes out looking for you. Ah, Yegor Vlassitch, Yegor Vlassitch! you might look in just once!"

"What is there for me to do there?"

"Of course there is nothing for you to do . . . though to be sure . . . there is the place to look after. . . . To see how things are going. . . . You are the master. . . . I say, you have shot a blackcock, Yegor Vlassitch! You ought to sit down and rest!"

As she said all this Pelagea laughed like a silly girl and looked up at Yegor's face. Her face was simply radiant with happiness.

"Sit down? If you like . . ." said Yegor in a tone of indifference, and he chose a spot between two fir trees. "Why are you standing? You sit down too."

Pelagea sat a little way off in the sun and, ashamed of her joy, put her hand over her smiling mouth. Two minutes passed in silence.

"You might come for once," said Pelagea.

"What for?" sighed Yegor, taking off his cap and wiping his red forehead with his hand. "There is no object in my coming. To go for an hour or two is only waste of time, it's simply upsetting you, and to live continually in the village my soul could not endure. . . . You know yourself I am a pampered man. . . . I want a bed to sleep in, good tea to drink, and refined conversation. . . . I want all the niceties, while you live in poverty and dirt in the village. . . . I couldn't stand it for a day. Suppose there were an edict that I must live with you, I should either set fire to the hut or lay hands on myself. From a boy I've had this love for ease; there is no help for it."

"Where are you living now?"

"With the gentleman here, Dmitry Ivanitch, as a huntsman. I furnish his table with game, but he keeps me . . . more for his pleasure than anything."

"That's not proper work you're doing, Yegor Vlassitch. . . . For other people it's a pastime, but with you it's like a trade . . . like real work."

"You don't understand, you silly," said Yegor, gazing gloomily at the sky. "You have never understood, and as long as you live you will never understand what sort of man I am. . . . You think of me as a foolish man, gone to the bad, but to anyone who understands I am the best shot there is in the whole district. The gentry feel that, and they have even printed things about me in a magazine. There isn't a man to be compared with me as a sportsman. . . . And it is not because I am pampered and proud that I look down upon your village work. From my childhood, you know, I have never had any calling apart from guns and dogs. If they took away my gun, I used to go out with the fishing-hook, if they took the hook I caught things with my hands. And I went in for horse-dealing too, I used to go to the fairs when I had the money, and you know that if a peasant goes in for being a sportsman, or a horse-dealer, it's goodbye to the plough. Once the spirit of freedom has taken a man you will never root it out of him. In the same way, if a gentleman goes in for being an actor or for any other art, he will never make an official or a landowner. You are a woman, and you do not understand, but one must understand that."

"I understand, Yegor Vlassitch."

"You don't understand if you are going to cry. . . ."

"I . . . I'm not crying," said Pelagea, turning away. "It's a sin, Yegor Vlassitch! You might stay a day with luckless me, anyway. It's twelve years since I was married to you, and . . . and . . . there has never once been love between us! . . . I . . . I am not crying."

"Love . . ." muttered Yegor, scratching his hand. "There can't be any love. It's only in name we are husband and wife; we aren't really. In your eyes I am a wild man, and in mine you are a simple peasant woman with no understanding. Are we well matched? I am a free, pampered, profligate man, while you are a working woman, going in bark shoes and never straightening your back. The way I think of myself is that I am the foremost man in every kind of sport, and you look at me with pity. . . . Is that being well matched?"

31

"But we are married, you know, Yegor Vlassitch," sobbed Pelagea.

"Not married of our free will. . . . Have you forgotten? You have to thank Count Sergey Paylovitch and yourself. Out of envy, because I shot better than he did, the Count kept giving me wine for a whole month, and when a man's drunk you could make him change his religion, let alone getting married. To pay me out he married me to you when I was drunk. . . . A huntsman to a herd-girl! You saw I was drunk, why did you marry me? You were not a serf, you know; you could have resisted. Of course it was a bit of luck for a herd-girl to marry a huntsman, but you ought to have thought about it. Well, now be miserable, cry. It's a joke for the Count, but a crying matter for you. . . . Beat yourself against the wall."

A silence followed. Three wild ducks flew over the clearing. Yegor followed them with his eyes till, transformed into three scarcely visible dots, they sank down far beyond the forest.

"How do you live?" he asked, moving his eyes from the ducks to Pelagea.

"Now I am going out to work, and in the winter I take a child from the Foundling Hospital and bring it up on the bottle. They give me a rouble and a half a month."

"Oh. . . ."

Again a silence. From the strip that had been reaped floated a soft song which broke off at the very beginning. It was too hot to sing.

"They say you have put up a new hut for Akulina," said Pelagea.

Yegor did not speak.

"So she is dear to you. . . ."

"It's your luck, it's fate!" said the huntsman, stretching. "You must put up with it, poor thing. But goodbye, I've been chattering long enough. . . . I must be at Boltovo by the evening."

Yegor rose, stretched himself, and slung his gun over his shoulder; Pelagea got up.

"And when are you coming to the village?" she asked softly.

"I have no reason to, I shall never come sober, and you have little to gain from me drunk; I am spiteful when I am drunk. Goodbye!"

"Goodbye, Yegor Vlassitch."

Yegor put his cap on the back of his head and, clicking to his dog, went on his way. Pelagea stood still looking after him. . . . She saw his

32

moving shoulder-blades, his jaunty cap, his lazy, careless step, and her eyes were full of sadness and tender affection. . . . Her gaze flitted over her husband's tall, lean figure and caressed and fondled it. . . . He, as though he felt that gaze, stopped and looked round. . . . He did not speak, but from his face, from his shrugged shoulders, Pelagea could see that he wanted to say something to her. She went up to him timidly and looked at him with imploring eyes.

"Take it," he said, turning round.

He gave her a crumpled rouble note and walked quickly away.

"Goodbye, Yegor Vlassitch," she said, mechanically taking the rouble.

He walked by a long road, straight as a taut strap. She, pale and motionless as a statue, stood, her eyes seizing every step he took. But the red of his shirt melted into the dark colour of his trousers, his step could not be seen, and the dog could not be distinguished from the boots. Nothing could be seen but the cap, and . . . suddenly Yegor turned off sharply into the clearing and the cap vanished in the greenness.

"Goodbye, Yegor Vlassitch," whispered Pelagea, and she stood on tiptoe to see the white cap once more.

A Dead Body

[First published in September 1885.
Included in the collection *The Horse-Stealers and Other Stories* (1921).]

A still August night. A mist is rising slowly from the fields and casting an opaque veil over everything within eyesight. Lighted up by the moon, the mist gives the impression at one moment of a calm, boundless sea, at the next of an immense white wall. The air is damp and chilly. Morning is still far off. A step from the by road which runs along the edge of the forest a little fire is gleaming. A dead body, covered from head to foot with new white linen, is lying under a young oak tree. A wooden ikon is lying on its breast. Beside the corpse almost on the road sits the "watch"—two peasants performing one of the most disagreeable and uninviting of peasants' duties. One, a tall young fellow with a scarcely perceptible moustache and thick black eyebrows, in a tattered sheepskin and bark shoes, is sitting on the wet grass, his feet stuck out straight in front of him, and is trying to while away the time with work. He bends his long neck, and breathing loudly through his nose, makes a spoon out of a big crooked bit of wood; the other—a little scraggy, pock-marked peasant with an aged face, a scanty moustache, and a little goat's beard—sits with his hands dangling loose on his knees, and without moving gazes listlessly at the light. A small campfire is lazily burning down between them, throwing a red glow on their faces. There is perfect stillness. The only sounds are the scrape of the knife on the wood and the crackling of damp sticks in the fire.

"Don't you go to sleep, Syoma . . ." says the young man.

"I . . . I am not asleep . . ." stammers the goat-beard.

34

"That's all right. . . . It would be dreadful to sit here alone, one would be frightened. You might tell me something, Syoma."

"You are a queer fellow, Syomushka! Other people will laugh and tell a story and sing a song, but you—there is no making you out. You sit like a scarecrow in the garden and roll your eyes at the fire. You can't say anything properly . . . when you speak you seem frightened. I dare say you are fifty, but you have less sense than a child. Aren't you sorry that you are a simpleton?"

"I am sorry," the goat-beard answers gloomily.

"And we are sorry to see your foolishness, you may be sure. You are a good-natured, sober peasant, and the only trouble is that you have no sense in your head. You should have picked up some sense for yourself if the Lord has afflicted you and given you no understanding. You must make an effort, Syoma. . . . You should listen hard when anything good's being said, note it well, and keep thinking and thinking. . . . If there is any word you don't understand, you should make an effort and think over in your head in what meaning the word is used. Do you see? Make an effort! If you don't gain some sense for yourself you'll be a simpleton and of no account at all to your dying day."

All at once a long drawn-out, moaning sound is heard in the forest. Something rustles in the leaves as though torn from the very top of the tree and falls to the ground. All this is faintly repeated by the echo. The young man shudders and looks enquiringly at his companion.

"It's an owl at the little birds," says Syoma, gloomily.

"Why, Syoma, it's time for the birds to fly to the warm countries!"

"To be sure, it is time."

"It is chilly at dawn now. It is co-old. The crane is a chilly creature, it is tender. Such cold is death to it. I am not a crane, but I am frozen. . . . Put some more wood on!"

Syoma gets up and disappears in the dark undergrowth. While he is busy among the bushes, breaking dry twigs, his companion puts his hand over his eyes and starts at every sound. Syoma brings an armful of wood and lays it on the fire. The flame irresolutely licks the black twigs with its little tongues, then suddenly, as though at the word of command, catches them and throws a crimson light on the faces, the road, the white linen with its prominences where the hands and feet of the corpse raise it, the ikon. The "watch" is silent. The young man bends his neck still lower and sets to work with still more nervous haste. The goat-beard sits motionless as before and keeps his eyes fixed on the fire. . . .

"Ye that love not Zion . . . shall be put to shame by the Lord." A falsetto voice is suddenly heard singing in the stillness of the night, then slow footsteps are audible, and the dark figure of a man in a short monkish cassock and a broad-brimmed hat, with a wallet on his shoulders, comes into sight on the road in the crimson firelight.

"Thy will be done, O Lord! Holy Mother!" the figure says in a husky falsetto. "I saw the fire in the outer darkness and my soul leapt for joy. . . . At first I thought it was men grazing a drove of horses, then I thought it can't be that, since no horses were to be seen. 'Aren't they thieves,' I wondered, 'aren't they robbers lying in wait for a rich Lazarus? Aren't they the gypsy people offering sacrifices to idols? And my soul leapt for joy. 'Go, Feodosy, servant of God,' I said to myself, 'and win a martyr's crown!' And I flew to the fire like a light-winged moth. Now I stand before you, and from your outer aspect I judge of your souls: you are not thieves and you are not heathens. Peace be to you!"

"Good evening."

"Good orthodox people, do you know how to reach the Makuhinsky Brickyards from here?"

"It's close here. You go straight along the road; when you have gone a mile and a half there will be Ananova, our village. From the village, father, you turn to the right by the riverbank, and so you will get to the brickyards. It's two miles from Ananova."

"God give you health. And why are you sitting here?"

"We are sitting here watching. You see, there is a dead body. . . ."

"What? what body? Holy Mother!"

The pilgrim sees the white linen with the ikon on it, and starts so violently that his legs give a little skip. This unexpected sight has an overpowering effect upon him. He huddles together and stands as though rooted to the spot, with wide-open mouth and staring eyes. For three minutes he is silent as though he could not believe his eyes, then begins muttering:

"O Lord! Holy Mother! I was going along not meddling with anyone, and all at once such an affliction."

"What may you be?" enquires the young man. "Of the clergy?"

"No . . . no. . . . I go from one monastery to another. . . . Do you know Mi . . . Mihail Polikarpitch, the foreman of the brickyard? Well, I am his nephew. . . . Thy will be done, O Lord! Why are you here?"

"We are watching . . . we are told to."

"Yes, yes . . ." mutters the man in the cassock, passing his hand over his eyes. "And where did the deceased come from?"

"He was a stranger."

"Such is life! But I'll . . . er . . . be getting on, brothers. . . . I feel flustered. I am more afraid of the dead than of anything, my dear souls! And only fancy! while this man was alive he wasn't noticed, while now when he is dead and given over to corruption we tremble before him as before some famous general or a bishop. . . . Such is life; was he murdered, or what?"

"The Lord knows! Maybe he was murdered, or maybe he died of himself."

"Yes, yes. . . . Who knows, brothers? Maybe his soul is now tasting the joys of Paradise."

"His soul is still hovering here, near his body," says the young man. "It does not depart from the body for three days."

"H'm, yes! . . . How chilly the nights are now! It sets one's teeth chattering. . . . So then I am to go straight on and on? . . ."

"Till you get to the village, and then you turn to the right by the riverbank."

"By the riverbank. . . . To be sure. . . . Why am I standing still? I must go on. Farewell, brothers."

The man in the cassock takes five steps along the road and stops.

"I've forgotten to put a kopeck for the burying," he says. "Good orthodox friends, can I give the money?"

"You ought to know best, you go the round of the monasteries. If he died a natural death it would go for the good of his soul; if it's a suicide it's a sin."

"That's true. . . . And maybe it really was a suicide! So I had better keep my money. Oh, sins, sins! Give me a thousand roubles and I would not consent to sit here. . . . Farewell, brothers."

The cassock slowly moves away and stops again.

"I can't make up my mind what I am to do," he mutters. "To stay here by the fire and wait till daybreak. . . . I am frightened; to go on is dreadful, too. The dead man will haunt me all the way in the darkness. . . . The Lord has chastised me indeed! Over three hundred miles I have come on foot and nothing happened, and now I am near home and there's trouble. I can't go on. . . ."

"It is dreadful, that is true."

"I am not afraid of wolves, of thieves, or of darkness, but I am afraid of the dead. I am afraid of them, and that is all about it. Good orthodox brothers, I entreat you on my knees, see me to the village."

"We've been told not to go away from the body."

"No one will see, brothers. Upon my soul, no one will see! The Lord will reward you a hundredfold! Old man, come with me, I beg! Old man! Why are you silent?"

"He is a bit simple," says the young man.

"You come with me, friend; I will give you five kopecks."

"For five kopecks I might," says the young man, scratching his head, "but I was told not to. If Syoma here, our simpleton, will stay alone, I will take you. Syoma, will you stay here alone?"

"I'll stay," the simpleton consents.

"Well, that's all right, then. Come along!" The young man gets up, and goes with the cassock. A minute later the sound of their steps and their talk dies away. Syoma shuts his eyes and gently dozes. The fire begins to grow dim, and a big black shadow falls on the dead body.

Oh! The Public

[First published on November 30, 1885.
Collected in *The Schoolmaster and Other Stories* (1921).]

"Here goes, I've done with drinking! Nothing . . . n-o-thing shall tempt me to it. It's time to take myself in hand; I must buck up and work. . . . You're glad to get your salary, so you must do your work honestly, heartily, conscientiously, regardless of sleep and comfort. Chuck taking it easy. You've got into the way of taking a salary for nothing, my boy—that's not the right thing . . . not the right thing at all. . . ."

After administering to himself several such lectures Podtyagin, the head ticket collector, begins to feel an irresistible impulse to get to work. It is past one o'clock at night, but in spite of that he wakes the ticket collectors and with them goes up and down the railway carriages, inspecting the tickets.

"T-t-t-ickets . . . P-p-p-please!" he keeps shouting, briskly snapping the clippers.

Sleepy figures, shrouded in the twilight of the railway carriages, start, shake their heads, and produce their tickets.

"T-t-t-tickets, please!" Podtyagin addresses a second-class passenger, a lean, scraggy-looking man, wrapped up in a fur coat and a rug and surrounded with pillows. "Tickets, please!"

The scraggy-looking man makes no reply. He is buried in sleep. The head ticket-collector touches him on the shoulder and repeats impatiently: "T-t-tickets, p-p-please!"

The passenger starts, opens his eyes, and gazes in alarm at Podtyagin.

"What? . . . Who? . . . Eh?"

"You're asked in plain language: t-t-tickets, p-p-please! If you please!"

"My God!" moans the scraggy-looking man, pulling a woebegone face. "Good Heavens! I'm suffering from rheumatism. . . . I haven't slept for three nights! I've just taken morphia on purpose to get to sleep, and you . . . with your tickets! It's merciless, it's inhuman! If you knew how hard it is for me to sleep you wouldn't disturb me for such nonsense. . . . It's cruel, it's absurd! And what do you want with my ticket! It's positively stupid!"

Podtyagin considers whether to take offence or not—and decides to take offence.

"Don't shout here! This is not a tavern!"

"No, in a tavern people are more humane . . ." coughs the passenger. "Perhaps you'll let me go to sleep another time! It's extraordinary: I've travelled abroad, all over the place, and no one asked for my ticket there, but here you're at it again and again, as though the devil were after you. . . ."

"Well, you'd better go abroad again since you like it so much."

"It's stupid, sir! Yes! As though it's not enough killing the passengers with fumes and stuffiness and draughts, they want to strangle us with red tape, too, damn it all! He must have the ticket! My goodness, what zeal! If it were of any use to the company—but half the passengers are travelling without a ticket!"

"Listen, sir!" cries Podtyagin, flaring up. "If you don't leave off shouting and disturbing the public, I shall be obliged to put you out at the next station and to draw up a report on the incident!"

"This is revolting!" exclaims "the public," growing indignant. "Persecuting an invalid! Listen, and have some consideration!"

"But the gentleman himself was abusive!" says Podtyagin, a little scared. "Very well. . . . I won't take the ticket . . . as you like. . . . Only, of course, as you know very well, it's my duty to do so. . . . If it were not my duty, then, of course . . . You can ask the stationmaster . . . ask anyone you like. . . ."

Podtyagin shrugs his shoulders and walks away from the invalid. At first he feels aggrieved and somewhat injured, then, after passing through two or three carriages, he begins to feel a certain uneasiness not unlike the pricking of conscience in his ticket-collector's bosom.

"There certainly was no need to wake the invalid," he thinks, "though it was not my fault. . . .They imagine I did it wantonly, idly. They don't know that I'm bound in duty . . . if they don't believe it, I can bring the stationmaster to them." A station. The train stops five minutes. Before the third bell, Podtyagin enters the same second-class carriage. Behind him stalks the stationmaster in a red cap.

"This gentleman here," Podtyagin begins, "declares that I have no right to ask for his ticket and . . . and is offended at it. I ask you, Mr. Stationmaster, to explain to him. . . . Do I ask for tickets according to regulation or to please myself? Sir," Podtyagin addresses the scraggy-looking man, "sir! you can ask the stationmaster here if you don't believe me."

The invalid starts as though he had been stung, opens his eyes, and with a woebegone face sinks back in his seat.

"My God! I have taken another powder and only just dozed off when here he is again . . . again! I beseech you have some pity on me!"

"You can ask the stationmaster . . . whether I have the right to demand your ticket or not."

"This is insufferable! Take your ticket . . . take it! I'll pay for five extra if you'll only let me die in peace! Have you never been ill yourself? Heartless people!"

"This is simply persecution!" A gentleman in military uniform grows indignant. "I can see no other explanation of this persistence."

"Drop it . . ." says the stationmaster, frowning and pulling Podtyagin by the sleeve.

Podtyagin shrugs his shoulders and slowly walks after the stationmaster.

"There's no pleasing them!" he thinks, bewildered. "It was for his sake I brought the stationmaster, that he might understand and be pacified, and he . . . swears!"

Another station. The train stops ten minutes. Before the second bell, while Podtyagin is standing at the refreshment bar, drinking seltzer water, two gentlemen go up to him, one in the uniform of an engineer, and the other in a military overcoat.

"Look here, ticket-collector!" the engineer begins, addressing Podtyagin. "Your behaviour to that invalid passenger has revolted all who witnessed it. My name is Puzitsky; I am an engineer, and this gentleman is a colonel. If you do not apologise to the passenger, we shall make a complaint to the traffic manager, who is a friend of ours."

"Gentlemen! Why of course I . . . why of course you . . ." Podtyagin is panic-stricken.

"We don't want explanations. But we warn you, if you don't apologise, we shall see justice done to him."

"Certainly I . . . I'll apologise, of course . . . To be sure. . . ."

Half an hour later, Podtyagin having thought of an apologetic phrase which would satisfy the passenger without lowering his own dignity, walks into the carriage. "Sir," he addresses the invalid. "Listen, sir. . . ."

The invalid starts and leaps up: "What?"

"I . . . what was it? . . . You mustn't be offended. . . ."

"Och! Water . . ." gasps the invalid, clutching at his heart. "I'd just taken a third dose of morphia, dropped asleep, and . . . again! Good God! when will this torture cease!"

"I only . . . you must excuse . . ."

"Oh! . . . Put me out at the next station! I can't stand any more. . . . I . . . I am dying. . . ."

"This is mean, disgusting!" cry the "public," revolted. "Go away! You shall pay for such persecution. Get away!"

Podtyagin waves his hand in despair, sighs, and walks out of the carriage. He goes to the attendants' compartment, sits down at the table, exhausted, and complains:

"Oh, the public! There's no satisfying them! It's no use working and doing one's best! One's driven to drinking and cursing it all. . . . If you do nothing—they're angry; if you begin doing your duty, they're angry too. There's nothing for it but drink!"

Podtyagin empties a bottle straight off and thinks no more of work, duty, and honesty!

A Blunder

[First published in January 1886.
Collected in *Love and Other Stories* (1922).]

Ilya sergeitch peplov and his wife Kleopatra Petrovna were standing at the door, listening greedily. On the other side in the little drawing room a love scene was apparently taking place between two persons: their daughter Natashenka and a teacher of the district school, called Shchupkin.

"He's rising!" whispered Peplov, quivering with impatience and rubbing his hands. "Now, Kleopatra, mind; as soon as they begin talking of their feelings, take down the ikon from the wall and we'll go in and bless them. . . . We'll catch him. . . . A blessing with an ikon is sacred and binding . . . He couldn't get out of it, if he brought it into court."

On the other side of the door this was the conversation:

"Don't go on like that!" said Shchupkin, striking a match against his checked trousers. "I never wrote you any letters!"

"I like that! As though I didn't know your writing!" giggled the girl with an affected shriek, continually peeping at herself in the glass. "I knew it at once! And what a queer man you are! You are a writing master, and you write like a spider! How can you teach writing if you write so badly yourself?"

"H'm! . . . That means nothing. The great thing in writing lessons is not the hand one writes, but keeping the boys in order. You hit one on the head with a ruler, make another kneel down. . . . Besides, there's nothing in handwriting! Nekrassov was an author, but his handwriting's a disgrace, there's a specimen of it in his collected works."

"You are not Nekrassov. . . ." (A sigh). "I should love to marry an author. He'd always be writing poems to me."

"I can write you a poem, too, if you like."

"What can you write about?"

"Love—passion—your eyes. You'll be crazy when you read it. It would draw a tear from a stone! And if I write you a real poem, will you let me kiss your hand?"

"That's nothing much! You can kiss it now if you like."

Shchupkin jumped up, and making sheepish eyes, bent over the fat little hand that smelt of egg soap.

"Take down the ikon," Peplov whispered in a fluster, pale with excitement, and buttoning his coat as he prodded his wife with his elbow. "Come along, now!"

And without a second's delay Peplov flung open the door.

"Children," he muttered, lifting up his arms and blinking tearfully, "the Lord bless you, my children. May you live—be fruitful—and multiply."

"And—and I bless you, too," the mamma brought out, crying with happiness. "May you be happy, my dear ones! Oh, you are taking from me my only treasure!" she said to Shchupkin. "Love my girl, be good to her. . . ."

Shchupkin's mouth fell open with amazement and alarm. The parents' attack was so bold and unexpected that he could not utter a single word.

"I'm in for it! I'm spliced!" he thought, going limp with horror. "It's all over with you now, my boy! There's no escape!"

And he bowed his head submissively, as though to say, "Take me, I'm vanquished."

"Ble-blessings on you," the papa went on, and he, too, shed tears. "Natashenka, my daughter, stand by his side. Kleopatra, give me the ikon."

But at this point the father suddenly left off weeping, and his face was contorted with anger.

"You ninny!" he said angrily to his wife. "You are an idiot! Is that the ikon?"

"Ach, saints alive!"

What had happened? The writing master raised himself and saw that he was saved; in her flutter the mamma had snatched from the wall the portrait of Lazhetchnikov, the author, in mistake for the ikon. Old Peplov and his wife stood disconcerted in the middle of the room, holding the portrait aloft, not knowing what to do or what to say. The writing master took advantage of the general confusion and slipped away.

Anyuta

[First published in *Oskolki* (*Fragments*),
a Russian literary and art weekly, on March 5, 1886.
Edited and included in the collection *Motley Stories* (1886).
Collected in *The Darling and Other Stories* (1916).]

In the cheapest room of a big block of furnished apartments Stepan Klotchkov, a medical student in his third year, was walking to and fro, zealously conning his anatomy. His mouth was dry and his forehead perspiring from the unceasing effort to learn it by heart.

In the window, covered by patterns of frost, sat on a stool the girl who shared his room—Anyuta, a thin little brunette of five-and-twenty, very pale with mild grey eyes. Sitting with bent back she was busy embroidering with red thread the collar of a man's shirt. She was working against time. . . . The clock in the passage struck two drowsily, yet the little room had not been put to rights for the morning. Crumpled bed-clothes, pillows thrown about, books, clothes, a big filthy slop-pail filled with soap-suds in which cigarette ends were swimming, and the litter on the floor—all seemed as though purposely jumbled together in one confusion. . . .

"The right lung consists of three parts . . ." Klotchkov repeated. "Boundaries! Upper part on anterior wall of thorax reaches the fourth or fifth rib, on the lateral surface, the fourth rib . . . behind to the spina scapulæ . . ."

Klotchkov raised his eyes to the ceiling, striving to visualise what he had just read. Unable to form a clear picture of it, he began feeling his upper ribs through his waistcoat.

"These ribs are like the keys of a piano," he said. "One must familiarise oneself with them somehow, if one is not to get muddled over them. One must study them in the skeleton and the living body. . . . I say, Anyuta, let me pick them out."

Anyuta put down her sewing, took off her blouse, and straightened herself up. Klotchkov sat down facing her, frowned, and began counting her ribs.

"H'm! . . . One can't feel the first rib; it's behind the shoulder-blade. . . . This must be the second rib. . . . Yes . . . this is the third . . . this is the fourth. . . . H'm! . . . yes. . . . Why are you wriggling?"

"Your fingers are cold!"

"Come, come . . . it won't kill you. Don't twist about. That must be the third rib, then . . . this is the fourth. . . . You look such a skinny thing, and yet one can hardly feel your ribs. That's the second . . . that's the third. . . . Oh, this is muddling, and one can't see it clearly. . . . I must draw it. . . . Where's my crayon?"

Klotchkov took his crayon and drew on Anyuta's chest several parallel lines corresponding with the ribs.

"First-rate. That's all straightforward. . . . Well, now I can sound you. Stand up!"

Anyuta stood up and raised her chin. Klotchkov began sounding her, and was so absorbed in this occupation that he did not notice how Anyuta's lips, nose, and fingers turned blue with cold. Anyuta shivered, and was afraid the student, noticing it, would leave off drawing and sounding her, and then, perhaps, might fail in his exam.

"Now it's all clear," said Klotchkov when he had finished. "You sit like that and don't rub off the crayon, and meanwhile I'll learn up a little more."

And the student again began walking to and fro, repeating to himself. Anyuta, with black stripes across her chest, looking as though she had been tattooed, sat thinking, huddled up and shivering with cold. She said very little as a rule; she was always silent, thinking and thinking. . . .

In the six or seven years of her wanderings from one furnished room to another, she had known five students like Klotchkov. Now they had all finished their studies, had gone out into the world, and, of course, like respectable people, had long ago forgotten her. One of them was living in Paris, two were doctors, the fourth was an artist, and the fifth was said to be already a professor. Klotchkov was the sixth. . . . Soon he, too, would finish his studies and go out into the world. There was a fine future before him, no doubt, and Klotchkov probably would become a great man, but the present was anything but bright; Klotchkov had no tobacco and no tea, and there were only four lumps of sugar left. She must make haste and finish her embroidery, take it to the woman who had ordered it, and with the quarter rouble she would get for it, buy tea and tobacco.

"Can I come in?" asked a voice at the door.

Anyuta quickly threw a woollen shawl over her shoulders. Fetisov, the artist, walked in.

"I have come to ask you a favour," he began, addressing Klotchkov, and glaring like a wild beast from under the long locks that hung over his brow. "Do me a favour; lend me your young lady just for a couple of hours! I'm painting a picture, you see, and I can't get on without a model."

"Oh, with pleasure," Klotchkov agreed. "Go along, Anyuta."

"The things I've had to put up with there," Anyuta murmured softly.

"Rubbish! The man's asking you for the sake of art, and not for any sort of nonsense. Why not help him if you can?"

Anyuta began dressing.

"And what are you painting?" asked Klotchkov.

"Psyche; it's a fine subject. But it won't go, somehow. I have to keep painting from different models. Yesterday I was painting one with blue legs. 'Why are your legs blue?' I asked her. 'It's my stockings stain them,' she said. And you're still grinding! Lucky fellow! You have patience."

"Medicine's a job one can't get on with without grinding."

"H'm! . . . Excuse me, Klotchkov, but you do live like a pig! It's awful the way you live!"

"How do you mean? I can't help it. . . . I only get twelve roubles a month from my father, and it's hard to live decently on that."

"Yes . . . yes . . ." said the artist, frowning with an air of disgust; "but, still, you might live better. . . . An educated man is in duty bound to have taste, isn't he? And goodness knows what it's like here! The bed not made, the slops, the dirt . . . yesterday's porridge in the plates . . . Tfoo!"

"That's true," said the student in confusion; "but Anyuta has had no time today to tidy up; she's been busy all the while."

When Anyuta and the artist had gone out Klotchkov lay down on the sofa and began learning, lying down; then he accidentally dropped asleep, and waking up an hour later, propped his head on his fists and sank into gloomy reflection. He recalled the artist's words that an educated man was in duty bound to have taste, and his surroundings actually struck him now as loathsome and revolting. He saw, as it were in his mind's eye, his own future, when he would see his patients in his consulting room, drink tea in a large dining room in the company of his wife, a real lady. And now that slop-pail in which the cigarette ends were swimming looked incredibly disgusting. Anyuta, too, rose before his imagination—a plain, slovenly, pitiful figure . . . and he made up his mind to part with her at once, at all costs.

When, on coming back from the artist's, she took off her coat, he got up and said to her seriously:

"Look here, my good girl . . . sit down and listen. We must part! The fact is, I don't want to live with you any longer."

Anyuta had come back from the artist's worn out and exhausted. Standing so long as a model had made her face look thin and sunken, and her chin sharper than ever. She said nothing in answer to the student's words, only her lips began to tremble.

"You know we should have to part sooner or later, anyway," said the student. "You're a nice, good girl, and not a fool; you'll understand. . . ."

Anyuta put on her coat again, in silence wrapped up her embroidery in paper, gathered together her needles and thread: she found the screw of paper with the four lumps of sugar in the window, and laid it on the table by the books.

"That's . . . your sugar . . ." she said softly, and turned away to conceal her tears.

"Why are you crying?" asked Klotchkov.

He walked about the room in confusion, and said:

"You are a strange girl, really. . . . Why, you know we shall have to part. We can't stay together for ever."

She had gathered together all her belongings, and turned to say goodbye to him, and he felt sorry for her.

"Shall I let her stay on here another week?" he thought. "She really may as well stay, and I'll tell her to go in a week;" and vexed at his own weakness, he shouted to her roughly:

"Come, why are you standing there? If you are going, go; and if you don't want to, take off your coat and stay! You can stay!"

Anyuta took off her coat, silently, stealthily, then blew her nose also stealthily, sighed, and noiselessly returned to her invariable position on her stool by the window.

The student drew his textbook to him and began again pacing from corner to corner. "The right lung consists of three parts," he repeated; "the upper part, on anterior wall of thorax, reaches the fourth or fifth rib. . . ."

In the passage some one shouted at the top of his voice: "Grigory! The samovar!"

The Witch

[First published in the Russian newspaper *Novoye Vremya* on
March 8, 1886. Republished in the collection *The Twilight* (1887).
Collected in *The Witch and Other Stories* (1918).]

It was approaching nightfall. The sexton, Savely Gykin, was lying in his
huge bed in the hut adjoining the church. He was not asleep, though it
was his habit to go to sleep at the same time as the hens. His coarse red
hair peeped from under one end of the greasy patchwork quilt, made up
of coloured rags, while his big unwashed feet stuck out from the other.
He was listening. His hut adjoined the wall that encircled the church
and the solitary window in it looked out upon the open country. And
out there a regular battle was going on. It was hard to say who was being
wiped off the face of the earth, and for the sake of whose destruction
nature was being churned up into such a ferment; but, judging from the
unceasing malignant roar, someone was getting it very hot. A victorious
force was in full chase over the fields, storming in the forest and on the
church roof, battering spitefully with its fists upon the windows, raging
and tearing, while something vanquished was howling and wailing. . . .
A plaintive lament sobbed at the window, on the roof, or in the stove. It
sounded not like a call for help, but like a cry of misery, a consciousness
that it was too late, that there was no salvation. The snowdrifts were
covered with a thin coating of ice; tears quivered on them and on the
trees; a dark slush of mud and melting snow flowed along the roads and
paths. In short, it was thawing, but through the dark night the heavens
failed to see it, and flung flakes of fresh snow upon the melting earth
at a terrific rate. And the wind staggered like a drunkard. It would not

51

let the snow settle on the ground, and whirled it round in the darkness at random.

Savely listened to all this din and frowned. The fact was that he knew, or at any rate suspected, what all this racket outside the window was tending to and whose handiwork it was.

"I know!" he muttered, shaking his finger menacingly under the bedclothes; "I know all about it."

On a stool by the window sat the sexton's wife, Raissa Nilovna. A tin lamp standing on another stool, as though timid and distrustful of its powers, shed a dim and flickering light on her broad shoulders, on the handsome, tempting-looking contours of her person, and on her thick plait, which reached to the floor. She was making sacks out of coarse hempen stuff. Her hands moved nimbly, while her whole body, her eyes, her eyebrows, her full lips, her white neck were as still as though they were asleep, absorbed in the monotonous, mechanical toil. Only from time to time she raised her head to rest her weary neck, glanced for a moment towards the window, beyond which the snowstorm was raging, and bent again over her sacking. No desire, no joy, no grief, nothing was expressed by her handsome face with its turned-up nose and its dimples. So a beautiful fountain expresses nothing when it is not playing.

But at last she had finished a sack. She flung it aside, and, stretching luxuriously, rested her motionless, lacklustre eyes on the window. The panes were swimming with drops like tears, and white with short-lived snowflakes which fell on the window, glanced at Raissa, and melted. . . .

"Come to bed!" growled the sexton. Raissa remained mute. But suddenly her eyelashes flickered and there was a gleam of attention in her eye. Savely, all the time watching her expression from under the quilt, put out his head and asked:

"What is it?"

"Nothing. . . . I fancy someone's coming," she answered quietly.

The sexton flung the quilt off with his arms and legs, knelt up in bed, and looked blankly at his wife. The timid light of the lamp illuminated his hirsute, pock-marked countenance and glided over his rough matted hair.

"Do you hear?" asked his wife.

Through the monotonous roar of the storm he caught a scarcely audible thin and jingling monotone like the shrill note of a gnat when it wants to settle on one's cheek and is angry at being prevented.

"It's the post," muttered Savely, squatting on his heels.

Two miles from the church ran the posting road. In windy weather, when the wind was blowing from the road to the church, the inmates of the hut caught the sound of bells.

"Lord! fancy people wanting to drive about in such weather," sighed Raissa.

"It's government work. You've to go whether you like or not."

The murmur hung in the air and died away.

"It has driven by," said Savely, getting into bed.

But before he had time to cover himself up with the bedclothes he heard a distinct sound of the bell. The sexton looked anxiously at his wife, leapt out of bed and walked, waddling, to and fro by the stove. The bell went on ringing for a little, then died away again as though it had ceased.

"I don't hear it," said the sexton, stopping and looking at his wife with his eyes screwed up.

But at that moment the wind rapped on the window and with it floated a shrill jingling note. Savely turned pale, cleared his throat, and flopped about the floor with his bare feet again.

"The postman is lost in the storm," he wheezed out glancing malignantly at his wife. "Do you hear? The postman has lost his way! . . . I . . . I know! Do you suppose I . . . don't understand?" he muttered. "I know all about it, curse you!"

"What do you know?" Raissa asked quietly, keeping her eyes fixed on the window.

"I know that it's all your doing, you she-devil! Your doing, damn you! This snowstorm and the post going wrong, you've done it all—you!"

"You're mad, you silly," his wife answered calmly.

"I've been watching you for a long time past and I've seen it. From the first day I married you I noticed that you'd bitch's blood in you!"

"Tfoo!" said Raissa, surprised, shrugging her shoulders and crossing herself. "Cross yourself, you fool!"

"A witch is a witch," Savely pronounced in a hollow, tearful voice, hurriedly blowing his nose on the hem of his shirt; "though you are my wife, though you are of a clerical family, I'd say what you are even at confession. . . . Why, God have mercy upon us! Last year on the Eve of the Prophet Daniel and the Three Young Men there was a snowstorm, and what happened then? The mechanic came in to warm himself. Then on St. Alexey's Day the ice broke on the river and the district policeman turned up, and he was chatting with you all night . . . the damned brute! And when he came out in the morning and I looked at him, he had rings under his eyes and his cheeks were hollow! Eh? During the August fast there were two storms and each time the huntsman turned up. I saw it all, damn him! Oh, she is redder than a crab now, aha!"

"You didn't see anything."

"Didn't I! And this winter before Christmas on the Day of the Ten Martyrs of Crete, when the storm lasted for a whole day and night—do you remember?—the marshal's clerk was lost, and turned up here, the hound. . . . Tfoo! To be tempted by the clerk! It was worth upsetting God's weather for him! A drivelling scribbler, not a foot from the ground, pimples all over his mug and his neck awry! If he were good-looking, anyway—but he, tfoo! he is as ugly as Satan!"

The sexton took breath, wiped his lips and listened. The bell was not to be heard, but the wind banged on the roof, and again there came a tinkle in the darkness.

"And it's the same thing now!" Savely went on. "It's not for nothing the postman is lost! Blast my eyes if the postman isn't looking for you! Oh, the devil is a good hand at his work; he is a fine one to help! He will turn him round and round and bring him here. I know, I see! You can't conceal it, you devil's bauble, you heathen wanton! As soon as the storm began I knew what you were up to."

"Here's a fool!" smiled his wife. "Why, do you suppose, you thickhead, that I make the storm?"

"H'm! . . . Grin away! Whether it's your doing or not, I only know that when your blood's on fire there's sure to be bad weather, and when there's bad weather there's bound to be some crazy fellow turning up here. It happens so every time! So it must be you!"

To be more impressive the sexton put his finger to his forehead, closed his left eye, and said in a sing-song voice:

"Oh, the madness! oh, the unclean Judas! If you really are a human being and not a witch, you ought to think what if he is not the mechanic, or the clerk, or the huntsman, but the devil in their form! Ah! You'd better think of that!"

"Why, you are stupid, Savely," said his wife, looking at him compassionately. "When father was alive and living here, all sorts of people used to come to him to be cured of the ague: from the village, and the hamlets, and the Armenian settlement. They came almost every day, and no one called them devils. But if anyone once a year comes in bad weather to warm himself, you wonder at it, you silly, and take all sorts of notions into your head at once."

His wife's logic touched Savely. He stood with his bare feet wide apart, bent his head, and pondered. He was not firmly convinced yet of the truth of his suspicions, and his wife's genuine and unconcerned tone quite disconcerted him. Yet after a moment's thought he wagged his head and said:

"It's not as though they were old men or bandy-legged cripples; it's always young men who want to come for the night. . . . Why is that? And if they only wanted to warm themselves—But they are up to mischief. No, woman; there's no creature in this world as cunning as your female sort! Of real brains you've not an ounce, less than a starling, but for devilish slyness—oo-oo-oo! The Queen of Heaven protect us! There is the postman's bell! When the storm was only beginning I knew all that was in your mind. That's your witchery, you spider!"

"Why do you keep on at me, you heathen?" His wife lost her patience at last. "Why do you keep sticking to it like pitch?"

"I stick to it because if anything—God forbid—happens tonight . . . do you hear? . . . if anything happens tonight, I'll go straight off tomorrow morning to Father Nikodim and tell him all about it. 'Father Nikodim,' I shall say, 'graciously excuse me, but she is a witch.' 'Why so?' 'H'm! do you want to know why?' 'Certainly. . . .' And I shall tell him. And woe to you, woman! Not only at the dread Seat of Judgment, but in your earthly life you'll be punished, too! It's not for nothing there are prayers in the breviary against your kind!"

Suddenly there was a knock at the window, so loud and unusual that Savely turned pale and almost dropped backwards with fright. His wife jumped up, and she, too, turned pale.

"For God's sake, let us come in and get warm!" they heard in a trembling deep bass. "Who lives here? For mercy's sake! We've lost our way."

"Who are you?" asked Raissa, afraid to look at the window.

"The post," answered a second voice.

"You've succeeded with your devil's tricks," said Savely with a wave of his hand. "No mistake; I am right! Well, you'd better look out!"

55

The sexton jumped on to the bed in two skips, stretched himself on the feather mattress, and sniffing angrily, turned with his face to the wall. Soon he felt a draught of cold air on his back. The door creaked and the tall figure of a man, plastered over with snow from head to foot, appeared in the doorway. Behind him could be seen a second figure as white.

"Am I to bring in the bags?" asked the second in a hoarse bass voice.

"You can't leave them there." Saying this, the first figure began untying his hood, but gave it up, and pulling it off impatiently with his cap, angrily flung it near the stove. Then taking off his greatcoat, he threw that down beside it, and, without saying good evening, began pacing up and down the hut.

He was a fair-haired, young postman wearing a shabby uniform and black rusty-looking high boots. After warming himself by walking to and fro, he sat down at the table, stretched out his muddy feet towards the sacks and leaned his chin on his fist. His pale face, reddened in places by the cold, still bore vivid traces of the pain and terror he had just been through. Though distorted by anger and bearing traces of recent suffering, physical and moral, it was handsome in spite of the melting snow on the eyebrows, moustaches, and short beard.

"It's a dog's life!" muttered the postman, looking round the walls and seeming hardly able to believe that he was in the warmth. "We were nearly lost! If it had not been for your light, I don't know what would have happened. Goodness only knows when it will all be over! There's no end to this dog's life! Where have we come?" he asked, dropping his voice and raising his eyes to the sexton's wife.

"To the Gulyaevsky Hill on General Kalinovsky's estate," she answered, startled and blushing.

"Do you hear, Stepan?" The postman turned to the driver, who was wedged in the doorway with a huge mailbag on his shoulders. "We've got to Gulyaevsky Hill."

"Yes . . . we're a long way out." Jerking out these words like a hoarse sigh, the driver went out and soon after returned with another bag, then went out once more and this time brought the postman's sword on a big belt, of the pattern of that long flat blade with which Judith is portrayed by the bedside of Holofernes in cheap woodcuts. Laying the bags along the wall, he went out into the outer room, sat down there and lighted his pipe.

"Perhaps you'd like some tea after your journey?" Raissa inquired.

"How can we sit drinking tea?" said the postman, frowning. "We must make haste and get warm, and then set off, or we shall be late for the mail train. We'll stay ten minutes and then get on our way. Only be so good as to show us the way."

"What an infliction it is, this weather!" sighed Raissa.

"H'm, yes. . . . Who may you be?"

"We? We live here, by the church. . . . We belong to the clergy. . . . There lies my husband. Savely, get up and say good evening! This used to be a separate parish till eighteen months ago. Of course, when the gentry lived here there were more people, and it was worth while to have the services. But now the gentry have gone, and I need not tell you there's nothing for the clergy to live on. The nearest village is Markovka, and that's over three miles away. Savely is on the retired list now, and has got the watchman's job; he has to look after the church. . . ."

And the postman was immediately informed that if Savely were to go to the General's lady and ask her for a letter to the bishop, he would be given a good berth. "But he doesn't go to the General's lady because he is lazy and afraid of people. We belong to the clergy all the same . . ." added Raissa.

"What do you live on?" asked the postman.

"There's a kitchen garden and a meadow belonging to the church. Only we don't get much from that," sighed Raissa. "The old skinflint, Father Nikodim, from the next village celebrates here on St. Nicolas' Day in the winter and on St. Nicolas' Day in the summer, and for that he takes almost all the crops for himself. There's no one to stick up for us!"

"You are lying," Savely growled hoarsely. "Father Nikodim is a saintly soul, a luminary of the Church; and if he does take it, it's the regulation!"

"You've a cross one!" said the postman, with a grin. "Have you been married long?"

"It was three years ago the last Sunday before Lent. My father was sexton here in the old days, and when the time came for him to die, he went to the Consistory and asked them to send some unmarried man to marry me that I might keep the place. So I married him."

"Aha, so you killed two birds with one stone!" said the postman, looking at Savely's back. "Got wife and job together."

Savely wriggled his leg impatiently and moved closer to the wall. The postman moved away from the table, stretched, and sat down on the mailbag. After a moment's thought he squeezed the bags with his hands, shifted his sword to the other side, and lay down with one foot touching the floor.

"It's a dog's life," he muttered, putting his hands behind his head and closing his eyes. "I wouldn't wish a wild Tatar such a life."

Soon everything was still. Nothing was audible except the sniffing of Savely and the slow, even breathing of the sleeping postman, who uttered a deep prolonged "h-h-h" at every breath. From time to time there was a sound like a creaking wheel in his throat, and his twitching foot rustled against the bag.

Savely fidgeted under the quilt and looked round slowly. His wife was sitting on the stool, and with her hands pressed against her cheeks was gazing at the postman's face. Her face was immovable, like the face of some one frightened and astonished.

"Well, what are you gaping at?" Savely whispered angrily.

"What is it to you? Lie down!" answered his wife without taking her eyes off the flaxen head.

Savely angrily puffed all the air out of his chest and turned abruptly to the wall. Three minutes later he turned over restlessly again, knelt up on the bed, and with his hands on the pillow looked askance at his wife. She was still sitting motionless, staring at the visitor. Her cheeks were pale and her eyes were glowing with a strange fire. The sexton cleared his throat, crawled on his stomach off the bed, and going up to the postman, put a handkerchief over his face.

"What's that for?" asked his wife.

"To keep the light out of his eyes."

"Then put out the light!"

Savely looked distrustfully at his wife, put out his lips towards the lamp, but at once thought better of it and clasped his hands.

"Isn't that devilish cunning?" he exclaimed. "Ah! Is there any creature slyer than womenkind?"

"Ah, you long-skirted devil!" hissed his wife, frowning with vexation. "You wait a bit!"

And settling herself more comfortably, she stared at the postman again.

It did not matter to her that his face was covered. She was not so much interested in his face as in his whole appearance, in the novelty of

58

this man. His chest was broad and powerful, his hands were slender and well formed, and his graceful, muscular legs were much comelier than Savely's stumps. There could be no comparison, in fact.

"Though I am a long-skirted devil," Savely said after a brief interval, "they've no business to sleep here. . . . It's government work; we shall have to answer for keeping them. If you carry the letters, carry them, you can't go to sleep. . . . Hey! you!" Savely shouted into the outer room. "You, driver. What's your name? Shall I show you the way? Get up; postmen mustn't sleep!"

And Savely, thoroughly roused, ran up to the postman and tugged him by the sleeve.

"Hey, your honour, if you must go, go; and if you don't, it's not the thing. . . . Sleeping won't do."

The postman jumped up, sat down, looked with blank eyes round the hut, and lay down again.

"But when are you going?" Savely pattered away. "That's what the post is for—to get there in good time, do you hear? I'll take you."

The postman opened his eyes. Warmed and relaxed by his first sweet sleep, and not yet quite awake, he saw as through a mist the white neck and the immovable, alluring eyes of the sexton's wife. He closed his eyes and smiled as though he had been dreaming it all.

"Come, how can you go in such weather!" he heard a soft feminine voice; "you ought to have a sound sleep and it would do you good!"

"And what about the post?" said Savely anxiously. "Who's going to take the post? Are you going to take it, pray, you?"

The postman opened his eyes again, looked at the play of the dimples on Raissa's face, remembered where he was, and understood Savely. The thought that he had to go out into the cold darkness sent a chill shudder all down him, and he winced.

"I might sleep another five minutes," he said, yawning. "I shall be late, anyway. . . ."

"We might be just in time," came a voice from the outer room. "All days are not alike; the train may be late for a bit of luck."

The postman got up, and stretching lazily began putting on his coat.

Savely positively neighed with delight when he saw his visitors were getting ready to go.

"Give us a hand," the driver shouted to him as he lifted up a mailbag.

The sexton ran out and helped him drag the post-bags into the yard. The postman began undoing the knot in his hood. The sexton's wife gazed into his eyes, and seemed trying to look right into his soul.

"You ought to have a cup of tea . . ." she said.

"I wouldn't say no . . . but, you see, they're getting ready," he assented. "We are late, anyway."

"Do stay," she whispered, dropping her eyes and touching him by the sleeve.

The postman got the knot undone at last and flung the hood over his elbow, hesitating. He felt it comfortable standing by Raissa.

"What a . . . neck you've got! . . ." And he touched her neck with two fingers. Seeing that she did not resist, he stroked her neck and shoulders.

"I say, you are . . ."

"You'd better stay . . . have some tea."

"Where are you putting it?" The driver's voice could be heard outside. "Lay it crossways."

"You'd better stay. . . . Hark how the wind howls."

And the postman, not yet quite awake, not yet quite able to shake off the intoxicating sleep of youth and fatigue, was suddenly overwhelmed by a desire for the sake of which mailbags, postal trains . . . and all things in the world, are forgotten. He glanced at the door in a frightened way, as though he wanted to escape or hide himself, seized Raissa round the waist, and was just bending over the lamp to put out the light, when he heard the tramp of boots in the outer room, and the driver appeared in the doorway. Savely peeped in over his shoulder. The postman dropped his hands quickly and stood still as though irresolute.

"It's all ready," said the driver. The postman stood still for a moment, resolutely threw up his head as though waking up completely, and followed the driver out. Raissa was left alone.

"Come, get in and show us the way!" she heard.

One bell sounded languidly, then another, and the jingling notes in a long delicate chain floated away from the hut.

When little by little they had died away, Raissa got up and nervously paced to and fro. At first she was pale, then she flushed all over. Her face was contorted with hate, her breathing was tremulous, her eyes gleamed with wild, savage anger, and, pacing up and down as in a cage, she looked like a tigress menaced with red-hot iron. For a moment she stood still and looked at her abode. Almost half of the room was filled up by the bed, which stretched the length of the whole wall and consisted of a dirty feather-bed, coarse grey pillows, a quilt, and nameless rags of various sorts. The bed was a shapeless ugly mass which suggested the shock of hair that always stood up on Savely's head whenever it occurred to him to oil it. From the bed to the door that led into the cold outer room stretched the dark stove surrounded by pots and hanging clouts. Everything, including the absent Savely himself, was dirty, greasy, and smutty to the last degree, so that it was strange to see a woman's white neck and delicate skin in such surroundings.

Raissa ran up to the bed, stretched out her hands as though she wanted to fling it all about, stamp it underfoot, and tear it to shreds. But then, as though frightened by contact with the dirt, she leapt back and began pacing up and down again.

When Savely returned two hours later, worn out and covered with snow, she was undressed and in bed. Her eyes were closed, but from the slight tremor that ran over her face he guessed that she was not asleep. On his way home he had vowed inwardly to wait till next day and not to touch her, but he could not resist a biting taunt at her.

"Your witchery was all in vain: he's gone off," he said, grinning with malignant joy.

His wife remained mute, but her chin quivered. Savely undressed slowly, clambered over his wife, and lay down next to the wall.

"Tomorrow I'll let Father Nikodim know what sort of wife you are!" he muttered, curling himself up.

Raissa turned her face to him and her eyes gleamed.

"The job's enough for you, and you can look for a wife in the forest, blast you!" she said. "I am no wife for you, a clumsy lout, a slug-a-bed, God forgive me!"

"Come, come . . . go to sleep!"

"How miserable I am!" sobbed his wife. "If it weren't for you, I might have married a merchant or some gentleman! If it weren't for you, I should love my husband now! And you haven't been buried in the snow, you haven't been frozen on the highroad, you Herod!"

Raissa cried for a long time. At last she drew a deep sigh and was still. The storm still raged without. Something wailed in the stove, in the chimney, outside the walls, and it seemed to Savely that the wailing was within him, in his ears. This evening had completely confirmed him in his suspicions about his wife. He no longer doubted that his wife, with the aid of the Evil One, controlled the winds and the post sledges. But to add to his grief, this mysteriousness, this supernatural, weird power gave the woman beside him a peculiar, incomprehensible charm of which he had not been conscious before. The fact that in his stupidity he unconsciously threw a poetic glamour over her made her seem, as it were, whiter, sleeker, more unapproachable.

"Witch!" he muttered indignantly. "Tfoo, horrid creature!"

Yet, waiting till she was quiet and began breathing evenly, he touched her head with his finger . . . held her thick plait in his hand for a minute. She did not feel it. Then he grew bolder and stroked her neck.

"Leave off!" she shouted, and prodded him on the nose with her elbow with such violence that he saw stars before his eyes.

The pain in his nose was soon over, but the torture in his heart remained.

Easter Eve

[First published in the Russian newspaper *Novoye Vremya*, March 1886.
Collected in *The Bishop and Other Stories* (1919).]

I was standing on the bank of the River Goltva, waiting for the ferry-boat from the other side. At ordinary times the Goltva is a humble stream of moderate size, silent and pensive, gently glimmering from behind thick reeds; but now a regular lake lay stretched out before me. The waters of spring, running riot, had overflowed both banks and flooded both sides of the river for a long distance, submerging vegetable gardens, hayfields and marshes, so that it was no unusual thing to meet poplars and bushes sticking out above the surface of the water and looking in the darkness like grim solitary crags.

The weather seemed to me magnificent. It was dark, yet I could see the trees, the water and the people. . . . The world was lighted by the stars, which were scattered thickly all over the sky. I don't remember ever seeing so many stars. Literally one could not have put a finger in between them. There were some as big as a goose's egg, others tiny as hempseed. . . . They had come out for the festival procession, every one of them, little and big, washed, renewed and joyful, and everyone of them was softly twinkling its beams. The sky was reflected in the water; the stars were bathing in its dark depths and trembling with the quivering eddies. The air was warm and still. . . . Here and there, far away on the further bank in the impenetrable darkness, several bright red lights were gleaming. . . .

A couple of paces from me I saw the dark silhouette of a peasant in a high hat, with a thick knotted stick in his hand.

"How long the ferry-boat is in coming!" I said.

"It is time it was here," the silhouette answered.

"You are waiting for the ferry-boat, too?"

"No I am not," yawned the peasant—"I am waiting for the illumination. I should have gone, but to tell you the truth, I haven't the five kopecks for the ferry."

"I'll give you the five kopecks."

"No; I humbly thank you. . . . With that five kopecks put up a candle for me over there in the monastery. . . . That will be more interesting, and I will stand here. What can it mean, no ferry-boat, as though it had sunk in the water!"

The peasant went up to the water's edge, took the rope in his hands, and shouted; "Ieronim! Ieron—im!"

As though in answer to his shout, the slow peal of a great bell floated across from the further bank. The note was deep and low, as from the thickest string of a double bass; it seemed as though the darkness itself had hoarsely uttered it. At once there was the sound of a cannon shot. It rolled away in the darkness and ended somewhere in the far distance behind me. The peasant took off his hat and crossed himself.

"Christ is risen," he said.

Before the vibrations of the first peal of the bell had time to die away in the air a second sounded, after it at once a third, and the darkness was filled with an unbroken quivering clamour. Near the red lights fresh lights flashed, and all began moving together and twinkling restlessly.

"Ieron—im!" we heard a hollow prolonged shout.

"They are shouting from the other bank," said the peasant, "so there is no ferry there either. Our Ieronim has gone to sleep."

The lights and the velvety chimes of the bell drew one towards them. . . . I was already beginning to lose patience and grow anxious, but behold at last, staring into the dark distance, I saw the outline of something very much like a gibbet. It was the long-expected ferry. It moved towards us with such deliberation that if it had not been that its lines grew gradually more definite, one might have supposed that it was standing still or moving to the other bank.

"Make haste! Ieronim!" shouted my peasant. "The gentleman's tired of waiting!"

The ferry crawled to the bank, gave a lurch and stopped with a creak. A tall man in a monk's cassock and a conical cap stood on it, holding the rope.

"Why have you been so long?" I asked jumping upon the ferry.

"Forgive me, for Christ's sake," Ieronim answered gently. "Is there no one else?"

"No one. . . ."

Ieronim took hold of the rope in both hands, bent himself to the figure of a mark of interrogation, and gasped. The ferry-boat creaked and gave a lurch. The outline of the peasant in the high hat began slowly retreating from me—so the ferry was moving off. Ieronim soon drew himself up and began working with one hand only. We were silent, gazing towards the bank to which we were floating. There the illumination for which the peasant was waiting had begun. At the water's edge barrels of tar were flaring like huge camp fires. Their reflections, crimson as the rising moon, crept to meet us in long broad streaks. The burning barrels lighted up their own smoke and the long shadows of men flitting about the fire; but further to one side and behind them from where the velvety chime floated there was still the same unbroken black gloom. All at once, cleaving the darkness, a rocket zigzagged in a golden ribbon up the sky; it described an arc and, as though broken to pieces against the sky, was scattered crackling into sparks. There was a roar from the bank like a faraway hurrah.

"How beautiful!" I said.

"Beautiful beyond words!" sighed Ieronim. "Such a night, sir! Another time one would pay no attention to the fireworks, but today one rejoices in every vanity. Where do you come from?"

I told him where I came from.

"To be sure . . . a joyful day today. . . ." Ieronim went on in a weak sighing tenor like the voice of a convalescent. "The sky is rejoicing and the earth and what is under the earth. All the creatures are keeping holiday. Only tell me kind sir, why, even in the time of great rejoicing, a man cannot forget his sorrows?"

I fancied that this unexpected question was to draw me into one of those endless religious conversations which bored and idle monks are so fond of. I was not disposed to talk much, and so I only asked:

"What sorrows have you, father?"

"As a rule only the same as all men, kind sir, but today a special sorrow has happened in the monastery: at mass, during the reading of the Bible, the monk and deacon Nikolay died."

"Well, it's God's will!" I said, falling into the monastic tone. "We must all die. To my mind, you ought to rejoice indeed. . . . They say if anyone dies at Easter he goes straight to the kingdom of heaven."

"That's true."

We sank into silence. The figure of the peasant in the high hat melted into the lines of the bank. The tar barrels were flaring up more and more.

"The Holy Scripture points clearly to the vanity of sorrow and so does reflection," said Ieronim, breaking the silence, "but why does the heart grieve and refuse to listen to reason? Why does one want to weep bitterly?"

Ieronim shrugged his shoulders, turned to me and said quickly:

"If I died, or anyone else, it would not be worth notice perhaps; but, you see, Nikolay is dead! No one else but Nikolay! Indeed, it's hard to believe that he is no more! I stand here on my ferry-boat and every minute I keep fancying that he will lift up his voice from the bank. He always used to come to the bank and call to me that I might not be afraid on the ferry. He used to get up from his bed at night on purpose for that. He was a kind soul. My God! how kindly and gracious! Many a mother is not so good to her child as Nikolay was to me! Lord, save his soul!"

Ieronim took hold of the rope, but turned to me again at once.

"And such a lofty intelligence, your honour," he said in a vibrating voice. "Such a sweet and harmonious tongue! Just as they will sing immediately at early matins: 'Oh lovely! oh sweet is Thy Voice!' Besides all other human qualities, he had, too, an extraordinary gift!"

"What gift?" I asked.

The monk scrutinized me, and as though he had convinced himself that he could trust me with a secret, he laughed good-humouredly.

"He had a gift for writing hymns of praise," he said. "It was a marvel, sir; you couldn't call it anything else! You would be amazed if I tell you about it. Our Father Archimandrite comes from Moscow, the Father Sub-Prior studied at the Kazan academy, we have wise monks and elders, but, would you believe it, no one could write them; while Nikolay, a simple monk, a deacon, had not studied anywhere, and had not even any outer appearance of it, but he wrote them! A marvel! A real marvel!" Ieronim clasped his hands and, completely forgetting the rope, went on eagerly:

"The Father Sub-Prior has great difficulty in composing sermons; when he wrote the history of the monastery he worried all the brotherhood and drove a dozen times to town, while Nikolay wrote canticles! Hymns of praise! That's a very different thing from a sermon or a history!"

"Is it difficult to write them?" I asked.

"There's great difficulty!" Ieronim wagged his head. "You can do nothing by wisdom and holiness if God has not given you the gift. The monks who don't understand argue that you only need to know the life of the saint for whom you are writing the hymn, and to make it harmonize with the other hymns of praise. But that's a mistake, sir. Of course, anyone who writes canticles must know the life of the saint to perfection, to the least trivial detail. To be sure, one must make them harmonize with the other canticles and know where to begin and what to write about. To give you an instance, the first response begins everywhere with 'the chosen' or 'the elect.' . . . The first line must always begin with the 'angel.' In the canticle of praise to Jesus the Most Sweet, if you are interested in the subject, it begins like this: 'Of angels Creator and Lord of all powers!' In the canticle to the Holy Mother of God: 'Of angels the foremost sent down from on high,' to Nikolay, the Wonder-worker—'An angel in semblance, though in substance a man,' and so on. Everywhere you begin with the angel. Of course, it would be impossible without making them harmonize, but the lives of the saints and conformity with the others is not what matters; what matters is the beauty and sweetness of it. Everything must be harmonious, brief and complete. There must be in every line softness, graciousness and tenderness; not one word should be harsh or rough or unsuitable. It must be written so that the worshipper may rejoice at heart and weep, while his mind is stirred and he is thrown into a tremor. In the canticle to the Holy Mother are the words: 'Rejoice, O Thou too high for human thought to reach! Rejoice, O Thou too deep for angels' eyes to fathom!' In another place in the same canticle: 'Rejoice, O tree that bearest the fair fruit of light that is the food of the faithful! Rejoice, O tree of gracious spreading shade, under which there is shelter for multitudes!'"

Ieronim hid his face in his hands, as though frightened at something or overcome with shame, and shook his head.

"Tree that bearest the fair fruit of light . . . tree of gracious spreading shade. . . ." he muttered. "To think that a man should find words like those! Such a power is a gift from God! For brevity he packs many thoughts into one phrase, and how smooth and complete it all is! 'Light-radiating torch to all that be . . .' comes in the canticle to Jesus the Most Sweet. 'Light-radiating!' There is no such word in conversation or in books, but you see he invented it, he found it in his mind! Apart from the smoothness and grandeur of language, sir, every line must be beautified in every way, there must be flowers and lightning and wind and sun and all the objects of the visible world. And every exclamation ought to be put so as to be smooth and easy for the ear. 'Rejoice, thou flower of heavenly growth!' comes in the hymn to Nikolay the Wonder-worker. It's not simply 'heavenly flower,' but 'flower of heavenly growth.' It's smoother so and sweet to the ear. That was just as Nikolay wrote it! Exactly like that! I can't tell you how he used to write!"

"Well, in that case it is a pity he is dead," I said; "but let us get on, father, or we shall be late."

Ieronim started and ran to the rope; they were beginning to peal all the bells. Probably the procession was already going on near the monastery, for all the dark space behind the tar barrels was now dotted with moving lights.

"Did Nikolay print his hymns?" I asked Ieronim.

"How could he print them?" he sighed. "And indeed, it would be strange to print them. What would be the object? No one in the monastery takes any interest in them. They don't like them. They knew Nikolay wrote them, but they let it pass unnoticed. No one esteems new writings nowadays, sir!"

"Were they prejudiced against him?"

"Yes, indeed. If Nikolay had been an elder perhaps the brethren would have been interested, but he wasn't forty, you know. There were some who laughed and even thought his writing a sin."

"What did he write them for?"

"Chiefly for his own comfort. Of all the brotherhood, I was the only one who read his hymns. I used to go to him in secret, that no one else might know of it, and he was glad that I took an interest in them. He would embrace me, stroke my head, speak to me in caressing words as to

68

a little child. He would shut his cell, make me sit down beside him, and begin to read. . . ."

Ieronim left the rope and came up to me.

"We were dear friends in a way," he whispered, looking at me with shining eyes. "Where he went I would go. If I were not there he would miss me. And he cared more for me than for anyone, and all because I used to weep over his hymns. It makes me sad to remember. Now I feel just like an orphan or a widow. You know, in our monastery they are all good people, kind and pious, but . . . there is no one with softness and refinement, they are just like peasants. They all speak loudly, and tramp heavily when they walk; they are noisy, they clear their throats, but Nikolay always talked softly, caressingly, and if he noticed that anyone was asleep or praying he would slip by like a fly or a gnat. His face was tender, compassionate. . . ."

Ieronim heaved a deep sigh and took hold of the rope again. We were by now approaching the bank. We floated straight out of the darkness and stillness of the river into an enchanted realm, full of stifling smoke, crackling lights and uproar. By now one could distinctly see people moving near the tar barrels. The flickering of the lights gave a strange, almost fantastic, expression to their figures and red faces. From time to time one caught among the heads and faces a glimpse of a horse's head motionless as though cast in copper.

"They'll begin singing the Easter hymn directly," said Ieronim, "and Nikolay is gone; there is no one to appreciate it. . . . There was nothing written dearer to him than that hymn. He used to take in every word! You'll be there, sir, so notice what is sung; it takes your breath away!"

"Won't you be in church, then?"

"I can't; . . . I have to work the ferry. . . ."

"But won't they relieve you?"

"I don't know. . . . I ought to have been relieved at eight; but, as you see, they don't come! . . . And I must own I should have liked to be in the church. . . ."

"Are you a monk?"

"Yes . . . that is, I am a lay-brother."

The ferry ran into the bank and stopped. I thrust a five-kopeck piece into Ieronim's hand for taking me across and jumped on land. Immediately a cart with a boy and a sleeping woman in it drove creaking onto the ferry.

Ieronim, with a faint glow from the lights on his figure, pressed on the rope, bent down to it, and started the ferry back. . . .

I took a few steps through mud, but a little farther walked on a soft freshly trodden path. This path led to the dark monastery gates, that looked like a cavern through a cloud of smoke, through a disorderly crowd of people, unharnessed horses, carts and chaises. All this crowd was rattling, snorting, laughing, and the crimson light and wavering shadows from the smoke flickered over it all. . . . A perfect chaos! And in this hubbub the people yet found room to load a little cannon and to sell cakes. There was no less commotion on the other side of the wall in the monastery precincts, but there was more regard for decorum and order. Here there was a smell of juniper and incense. They talked loudly, but there was no sound of laughter or snorting. Near the tombstones and crosses people pressed close to one another with Easter cakes and bundles in their arms. Apparently many had come from a long distance for their cakes to be blessed and now were exhausted. Young lay brothers, making a metallic sound with their boots, ran busily along the iron slabs that paved the way from the monastery gates to the church door. They were busy and shouting on the belfry, too.

"What a restless night!" I thought. "How nice!"

One was tempted to see the same unrest and sleeplessness in all nature, from the night darkness to the iron slabs, the crosses on the tombs and the trees under which the people were moving to and fro. But nowhere was the excitement and restlessness so marked as in the church. An unceasing struggle was going on in the entrance between the inflowing stream and the outflowing stream. Some were going in, others going out and soon coming back again to stand still for a little and begin moving again. People were scurrying from place to place, lounging about as though they were looking for something. The stream flowed from the entrance all round the church, disturbing even the front rows, where persons of weight and dignity were standing. There could be no thought of concentrated prayer. There were no prayers at all, but a sort of continuous, childishly irresponsible joy, seeking a pretext to break out and vent itself in some movement, even in senseless jostling and shoving.

The same unaccustomed movement is striking in the Easter service itself. The altar gates are flung wide open, thick clouds of incense float in the air near the candelabra; wherever one looks there are lights, the gleam and splutter of candles. . . . There is no reading; restless and lighthearted singing goes on to the end without ceasing. After each hymn the clergy change their vestments and come out to burn the incense, which is repeated every ten minutes.

I had no sooner taken a place, when a wave rushed from in front and forced me back. A tall thick-set deacon walked before me with a long red candle; the grey-headed archimandrite in his golden mitre hurried after him with the censer. When they had vanished from sight the crowd squeezed me back to my former position. But ten minutes had not passed before a new wave burst on me, and again the deacon appeared. This time he was followed by the Father Sub-Prior, the man who, as Ieronim had told me, was writing the history of the monastery.

As I mingled with the crowd and caught the infection of the universal joyful excitement, I felt unbearably sore on Ieronim's account. Why did they not send someone to relieve him? Why could not someone of less feeling and less susceptibility go on the ferry? 'Lift up thine eyes, O Sion, and look around,' they sang in the choir, 'for thy children have come to thee as to a beacon of divine light from north and south, and from east and from the sea. . . .'

I looked at the faces; they all had a lively expression of triumph, but not one was listening to what was being sung and taking it in, and not one was 'holding his breath.' Why was not Ieronim released? I could fancy Ieronim standing meekly somewhere by the wall, bending forward and hungrily drinking in the beauty of the holy phrase. All this that glided by the ears of the people standing by me he would have eagerly drunk in with his delicately sensitive soul, and would have been spell-bound to ecstasy, to holding his breath, and there would not have been a man happier than he in all the church. Now he was plying to and fro over the dark river and grieving for his dead friend and brother.

The wave surged back. A stout smiling monk, playing with his rosary and looking round behind him, squeezed sideways by me, making way for a lady in a hat and velvet cloak. A monastery servant hurried after the lady, holding a chair over our heads.

I came out of the church. I wanted to have a look at the dead Nikolay, the unknown canticle writer. I walked about the monastery wall, where there was a row of cells, peeped into several windows, and, seeing nothing, came back again. I do not regret now that I did not see Nikolay; God knows, perhaps if I had seen him I should have lost the picture my imagination paints for me now. I imagine the lovable poetical figure solitary and not understood, who went out at nights to call to Ieronim over the water, and filled his hymns with flowers, stars and sunbeams, as a pale timid man with soft mild melancholy features. His eyes must have shone, not only with intelligence, but with kindly tenderness and that hardly restrained childlike enthusiasm which I could hear in Ieronim's voice when he quoted to me passages from the hymns.

When we came out of church after mass it was no longer night. The morning was beginning. The stars had gone out and the sky was a morose greyish blue. The iron slabs, the tombstones and the buds on the trees were covered with dew There was a sharp freshness in the air. Outside the precincts I did not find the same animated scene as I had beheld in the night. Horses and men looked exhausted, drowsy, scarcely moved, while nothing was left of the tar barrels but heaps of black ash. When anyone is exhausted and sleepy he fancies that nature, too, is in the same condition. It seemed to me that the trees and the young grass were asleep. It seemed as though even the bells were not pealing so loudly and gaily as at night. The restlessness was over, and of the excitement nothing was left but a pleasant weariness, a longing for sleep and warmth.

Now I could see both banks of the river; a faint mist hovered over it in shifting masses. There was a harsh cold breath from the water. When I jumped on to the ferry, a chaise and some two dozen men and women were standing on it already. The rope, wet and as I fancied drowsy, stretched far away across the broad river and in places disappeared in the white mist.

"Christ is risen! Is there no one else?" asked a soft voice.

I recognized the voice of Ieronim. There was no darkness now to hinder me from seeing the monk. He was a tall narrow-shouldered man of five-and-thirty, with large rounded features, with half-closed listless-looking eyes and an unkempt wedge-shaped beard. He had an extraordinarily sad and exhausted look.

"They have not relieved you yet?" I asked in surprise.

"Me?" he answered, turning to me his chilled and dewy face with a smile. "There is no one to take my place now till morning. They'll all be going to the Father Archimandrite's to break the fast directly."

With the help of a little peasant in a hat of reddish fur that looked like the little wooden tubs in which honey is sold, he threw his weight on the rope; they gasped simultaneously, and the ferry started.

We floated across, disturbing on the way the lazily rising mist. Everyone was silent. Ieronim worked mechanically with one hand. He slowly passed his mild lustreless eyes over us; then his glance rested on the rosy face of a young merchant's wife with black eyebrows, who was standing on the ferry beside me silently shrinking from the mist that wrapped her about. He did not take his eyes off her face all the way.

There was little that was masculine in that prolonged gaze. It seemed to me that Ieronim was looking in the woman's face for the soft and tender features of his dead friend.

A Day in the Country

[First published on May 19, 1886.
Collected in *The Cook's Wedding and Other Stories* (1922).]

Between eight and nine o'clock in the morning.

A dark leaden-coloured mass is creeping over the sky towards the sun. Red zigzags of lightning gleam here and there across it. There is a sound of faraway rumbling. A warm wind frolics over the grass, bends the trees, and stirs up the dust. In a minute there will be a spurt of May rain and a real storm will begin.

Fyokla, a little beggar-girl of six, is running through the village, looking for Terenty the cobbler. The white-haired, barefoot child is pale. Her eyes are wide open, her lips are trembling.

"Uncle, where is Terenty?" she asks every one she meets. No one answers. They are all preoccupied with the approaching storm and take refuge in their huts. At last she meets Silanty Silitch, the sacristan, Terenty's bosom friend. He is coming along, staggering from the wind.

"Uncle, where is Terenty?"

"At the kitchen gardens," answers Silanty.

The beggar-girl runs behind the huts to the kitchen gardens and there finds Terenty; the tall old man with a thin, pock-marked face, very long legs, and bare feet, dressed in a woman's tattered jacket, is standing near the vegetable plots, looking with drowsy, drunken eyes at the dark storm cloud. On his long crane-like legs he sways in the wind like a starling-cote.

"Uncle Terenty!" the white-headed beggar-girl addresses him. "Uncle, darling!"

Terenty bends down to Fyokla, and his grim, drunken face is overspread with a smile, such as come into people's faces when they look at something little, foolish, and absurd, but warmly loved.

"Ah! servant of God, Fyokia," he says, lisping tenderly, "where have you come from?"

"Uncle Terenty," says Fyokia, with a sob, tugging at the lapel of the cobbler's coat. "Brother Danilka has had an accident! Come along!"

"What sort of accident? Ough, what thunder! Holy, holy, holy. . . . What sort of accident?"

"In the count's copse Danilka stuck his hand into a hole in a tree, and he can't get it out. Come along, uncle, do be kind and pull his hand out!"

"How was it he put his hand in? What for?"

"He wanted to get a cuckoo's egg out of the hole for me."

"The day has hardly begun and already you are in trouble. . . ." Terenty shook his head and spat deliberately. "Well, what am I to do with you now? I must come . . . I must, may the wolf gobble you up, you naughty children! Come, little orphan!"

Terenty comes out of the kitchen garden and, lifting high his long legs, begins striding down the village street. He walks quickly without stopping or looking from side to side, as though he were shoved from behind or afraid of pursuit. Fyokla can hardly keep up with him.

They come out of the village and turn along the dusty road towards the count's copse that lies dark blue in the distance. It is about a mile and a half away. The clouds have by now covered the sun, and soon afterwards there is not a speck of blue left in the sky. It grows dark.

"Holy, holy, holy . . ." whispers Fyokla, hurrying after Terenty. The first raindrops, big and heavy, lie, dark dots on the dusty road. A big drop falls on Fyokla's cheek and glides like a tear down her chin.

"The rain has begun," mutters the cobbler, kicking up the dust with his bare, bony feet. "That's fine, Fyokla, old girl. The grass and the trees are fed by the rain, as we are by bread. And as for the thunder, don't you be frightened, little orphan. Why should it kill a little thing like you?"

As soon as the rain begins, the wind drops. The only sound is the patter of rain dropping like fine shot on the young rye and the parched road.

"We shall get soaked, Fyolka," mutters Terenty. "There won't be a dry spot left on us. . . . Ho-ho, my girl! It's run down my neck! But don't be frightened, silly. . . . The grass will be dry again, the earth will be dry again, and we shall be dry again. There is the same sun for us all."

A flash of lightning, some fourteen feet long, gleams above their heads. There is a loud peal of thunder, and it seems to Fyokla that something big, heavy, and round is rolling over the sky and tearing it open, exactly over her head.

"Holy, holy, holy . . ." says Terenty, crossing himself. "Don't be afraid, little orphan! It is not from spite that it thunders."

Terenty's and Fyokla's feet are covered with lumps of heavy, wet clay. It is slippery and difficult to walk, but Terenty strides on more and more rapidly. The weak little beggar-girl is breathless and ready to drop.

But at last they go into the count's copse. The washed trees, stirred by a gust of wind, drop a perfect waterfall upon them. Terenty stumbles over stumps and begins to slacken his pace.

"Whereabouts is Danilka?" he asks. "Lead me to him."

Fyokla leads him into a thicket, and, after going a quarter of a mile, points to Danilka. Her brother, a little fellow of eight, with hair as red as ochre and a pale sickly face, stands leaning against a tree, and, with his head on one side, looking sideways at the sky. In one hand he holds his shabby old cap, the other is hidden in an old lime tree. The boy is gazing at the stormy sky, and apparently not thinking of his trouble. Hearing footsteps and seeing the cobbler he gives a sickly smile and says:

"A terrible lot of thunder, Terenty. . . . I've never heard so much thunder in all my life."

"And where is your hand?"

"In the hole. . . . Pull it out, please, Terenty!"

The wood had broken at the edge of the hole and jammed Danilka's hand: he could push it farther in, but could not pull it out. Terenty snaps off the broken piece, and the boy's hand, red and crushed, is released.

"It's terrible how it's thundering," the boy says again, rubbing his hand. "What makes it thunder, Terenty?"

"One cloud runs against the other," answers the cobbler. The party come out of the copse, and walk along the edge of it towards the darkened road. The thunder gradually abates, and its rumbling is heard far away beyond the village.

"The ducks flew by here the other day, Terenty," says Danilka, still rubbing his hand. "They must be nesting in the Gniliya Zaimishtcha marshes. . . . Fyolka, would you like me to show you a nightingale's nest?"

"Don't touch it, you might disturb them," says Terenty, wringing the water out of his cap. "The nightingale is a singing-bird, without sin. He has had a voice given him in his throat, to praise God and gladden the heart of man. It's a sin to disturb him."

"What about the sparrow?"

"The sparrow doesn't matter, he's a bad, spiteful bird. He is like a pickpocket in his ways. He doesn't like man to be happy. When Christ was crucified it was the sparrow brought nails to the Jews, and called 'alive! alive!'"

A bright patch of blue appears in the sky.

"Look!" says Terenty. "An ant-heap burst open by the rain! They've been flooded, the rogues!"

They bend over the ant-heap. The downpour has damaged it; the insects are scurrying to and fro in the mud, agitated, and busily trying to carry away their drowned companions.

"You needn't be in such a taking, you won't die of it!" says Terenty, grinning. "As soon as the sun warms you, you'll come to your senses again. . . . It's a lesson to you, you stupids. You won't settle on low ground another time."

They go on.

"And here are some bees," cries Danilka, pointing to the branch of a young oak tree.

The drenched and chilled bees are huddled together on the branch. There are so many of them that neither bark nor leaf can be seen. Many of them are settled on one another.

"That's a swarm of bees," Terenty informs them. "They were flying looking for a home, and when the rain came down upon them they settled. If a swarm is flying, you need only sprinkle water on them to make them settle. Now if, say, you wanted to take the swarm, you would bend the branch with them into a sack and shake it, and they all fall in."

Little Fyokla suddenly frowns and rubs her neck vigorously. Her brother looks at her neck, and sees a big swelling on it.

"Hey-hey!" laughs the cobbler. "Do you know where you got that from, Fyokia, old girl? There are Spanish flies on some tree in the wood.

The rain has trickled off them, and a drop has fallen on your neck—that's what has made the swelling."

The sun appears from behind the clouds and floods the wood, the fields, and the three friends with its warm light. The dark menacing cloud has gone far away and taken the storm with it. The air is warm and fragrant. There is a scent of bird-cherry, meadowsweet, and lilies-of-the-valley.

"That herb is given when your nose bleeds," says Terenty, pointing to a woolly-looking flower. "It does good."

They hear a whistle and a rumble, but not such a rumble as the storm clouds carried away. A goods train races by before the eyes of Terenty, Danilka, and Fyokla. The engine, panting and puffing out black smoke, drags more than twenty vans after it. Its power is tremendous. The children are interested to know how an engine, not alive and without the help of horses, can move and drag such weights, and Terenty undertakes to explain it to them:

"It's all the steam's doing, children. . . . The steam does the work. . . . You see, it shoves under that thing near the wheels, and it . . . you see . . . it works. . . ."

They cross the railway line, and, going down from the embankment, walk towards the river. They walk not with any object, but just at random, and talk all the way. . . . Danilka asks questions, Terenty answers them. . . .

Terenty answers all his questions, and there is no secret in Nature which baffles him. He knows everything. Thus, for example, he knows the names of all the wild flowers, animals, and stones. He knows what herbs cure diseases, he has no difficulty in telling the age of a horse or a cow. Looking at the sunset, at the moon, or the birds, he can tell what sort of weather it will be next day. And indeed, it is not only Terenty who is so wise. Silanty Silitch, the innkeeper, the market-gardener, the shepherd, and all the villagers, generally speaking, know as much as he does. These people have learned not from books, but in the fields, in the wood, on the river bank. Their teachers have been the birds themselves, when they sang to them, the sun when it left a glow of crimson behind it at setting, the very trees, and wild herbs.

Danilka looks at Terenty and greedily drinks in every word. In spring, before one is weary of the warmth and the monotonous green of the fields, when everything is fresh and full of fragrance, who would not want to hear about the golden may-beetles, about the cranes, about the gurgling streams, and the corn mounting into ear?

The two of them, the cobbler and the orphan, walk about the fields, talk unceasingly, and are not weary. They could wander about the world endlessly. They walk, and in their talk of the beauty of the earth do not notice the frail little beggar-girl tripping after them. She is breathless and moves with a lagging step. There are tears in her eyes; she would be glad to stop these inexhaustible wanderers, but to whom and where can she go? She has no home or people of her own; whether she likes it or not, she must walk and listen to their talk.

Towards midday, all three sit down on the river bank. Danilka takes out of his bag a piece of bread, soaked and reduced to a mash, and they begin to eat. Terenty says a prayer when he has eaten the bread, then stretches himself on the sandy bank and falls asleep. While he is asleep, the boy gazes at the water, pondering. He has many different things to think of. He has just seen the storm, the bees, the ants, the train. Now, before his eyes, fishes are whisking about. Some are two inches long and more, others are no bigger than one's nail. A viper, with its head held high, is swimming from one bank to the other.

Only towards the evening our wanderers return to the village. The children go for the night to a deserted barn, where the corn of the commune used to be kept, while Terenty, leaving them, goes to the tavern. The children lie huddled together on the straw, dozing.

The boy does not sleep. He gazes into the darkness, and it seems to him that he is seeing all that he has seen in the day: the storm clouds, the bright sunshine, the birds, the fish, lanky Terenty. The number of his impressions, together with exhaustion and hunger, are too much for him; he is as hot as though he were on fire, and tosses from, side to side. He longs to tell someone all that is haunting him now in the darkness and agitating his soul, but there is no one to tell. Fyokla is too little and could not understand.

"I'll tell Terenty tomorrow," thinks the boy.

The children fall asleep thinking of the homeless cobbler, and, in the night, Terenty comes to them, makes the sign of the cross over them, and puts bread under their heads. And no one sees his love. It is seen only by the moon which floats in the sky and peeps caressingly through the holes in the wall of the deserted barn.

The Chemist's Wife

[First published on June 21, 1886.
Collected in *The Duel and Other Stories* (1916).]

The little town of B——, consisting of two or three crooked streets, was sound asleep. There was a complete stillness in the motionless air. Nothing could be heard but far away, outside the town no doubt, the barking of a dog in a thin, hoarse tenor. It was close upon daybreak.

Everything had long been asleep. The only person not asleep was the young wife of Tchernomordik, a qualified dispenser who kept a chemist's shop at B——. She had gone to bed and got up again three times, but could not sleep, she did not know why. She sat at the open window in her nightdress and looked into the street. She felt bored, depressed, vexed . . . so vexed that she felt quite inclined to cry—again she did not know why. There seemed to be a lump in her chest that kept rising into her throat . . . A few paces behind her Tchernomordik lay curled up close to the wall, snoring sweetly. A greedy flea was stabbing the bridge of his nose, but he did not feel it, and was positively smiling, for he was dreaming that everyone in the town had a cough, and was buying from him the King of Denmark's cough drops. He could not have been wakened now by pinpricks or by cannon or by caresses.

The chemist's shop was almost at the extreme end of the town, so that the chemist's wife could see far into the fields. She could see the eastern horizon growing pale by degrees, then turning crimson as though from a great fire. A big broad-faced moon peeped out unexpectedly from behind bushes in the distance. It was red (as a rule when the moon emerges from behind bushes it appears to be blushing).

Suddenly in the stillness of the night there came the sounds of footsteps and a jingle of spurs. She could hear voices.

"That must be the officers going home to the camp from the Police Captain's," thought the chemist's wife.

Soon afterwards two figures wearing officers' white tunics came into sight: one big and tall, the other thinner and shorter . . . They slouched along by the fence, dragging one leg after the other and talking loudly together. As they passed the chemist's shop, they walked more slowly than ever, and glanced up at the windows.

"It smells like a chemist's," said the thin one. "And so it is! Ah, I remember . . . I came here last week to buy some castor oil. There's a chemist here with a sour face and the jawbone of an ass! Such a jawbone, my dear fellow! It must have been a jawbone like that Samson killed the Philistines with."

"M'yes," said the big one in a bass voice. "The pharmacist is asleep. And his wife is asleep too. She is a pretty woman, Obtyosov."

"I saw her. I liked her very much . . . Tell me, doctor, can she possibly love that jawbone of an ass? Can she?"

"No, most likely she does not love him," sighed the doctor, speaking as though he were sorry for the chemist. "The little woman is asleep behind the window, Obtyosov, what? Tossing with the heat, her little mouth half open . . . and one little foot hanging out of bed. I bet that fool the chemist doesn't realise what a lucky fellow he is . . . No doubt he sees no difference between a woman and a bottle of carbolic!"

"I say, doctor," said the officer, stopping. "Let us go into the shop and buy something. Perhaps we shall see her."

"What an idea—in the night!"

"What of it? They are obliged to serve one even at night. My dear fellow, let us go in!"

"If you like . . ."

The chemist's wife, hiding behind the curtain, heard a muffled ring. Looking round at her husband, who was smiling and snoring sweetly as before, she threw on her dress, slid her bare feet into her slippers, and ran to the shop.

On the other side of the glass door she could see two shadows. The chemist's wife turned up the lamp and hurried to the door to open it, and now she felt neither vexed nor bored nor inclined to cry, though her heart was thumping. The big doctor and the slender Obtyosov walked in. Now she could get a view of them. The doctor was corpulent and swarthy; he wore a beard and was slow in his movements. At the slightest motion his tunic seemed as though it would crack, and perspiration came on to his face. The officer was rosy, clean-shaven, feminine-looking, and as supple as an English whip.

"What may I give you?" asked the chemist's wife, holding her dress across her bosom.

"Give us . . . er-er . . . four pennyworth of peppermint lozenges!"

Without haste the chemist's wife took down a jar from a shelf and began weighing out lozenges. The customers stared fixedly at her back; the doctor screwed up his eyes like a well-fed cat, while the lieutenant was very grave.

"It's the first time I've seen a lady serving in a chemist's shop," observed the doctor.

"There's nothing out of the way in it," replied the chemist's wife, looking out of the corner of her eye at the rosy-cheeked officer. "My husband has no assistant, and I always help him."

"To be sure . . . You have a charming little shop! What a number of different . . . jars! And you are not afraid of moving about among the poisons? Brrr!"

The chemist's wife sealed up the parcel and handed it to the doctor. Obtyosov gave her the money. Half a minute of silence followed . . . The men exchanged glances, took a step towards the door, then looked at one another again.

"Will you give me two pennyworth of soda?" said the doctor.

Again the chemist's wife slowly and languidly raised her hand to the shelf.

"Haven't you in the shop anything . . . such as . . ." muttered Obtyosov, moving his fingers, "something, so to say, allegorical . . . revivifying . . . seltzer-water, for instance. Have you any seltzer-water?"

"Yes," answered the chemist's wife.

"Bravo! You're a fairy, not a woman! Give us three bottles!"

The chemist's wife hurriedly sealed up the soda and vanished through the door into the darkness.

"A peach!" said the doctor, with a wink. "You wouldn't find a pineapple like that in the island of Madeira! Eh? What do you say? Do you hear the snoring, though? That's his worship the chemist enjoying sweet repose."

A minute later the chemist's wife came back and set five bottles on the counter. She had just been in the cellar, and so was flushed and rather excited.

"Sh-sh! . . . quietly!" said Obtyosov when, after uncorking the bottles, she dropped the corkscrew. "Don't make such a noise; you'll wake your husband."

"Well, what if I do wake him?"

"He is sleeping so sweetly . . . He must be dreaming of you. . . . To your health!"

"Besides," boomed the doctor, hiccupping after the seltzer-water, "husbands are such a dull business that it would be very nice of them to be always asleep. How good a drop of red wine would be in this water!"

"What an idea!" laughed the chemist's wife.

"That would be splendid. What a pity they don't sell spirits in chemist's shops! Though you ought to sell wine as a medicine. Have you any *vinum gallicum rubrum*?"

"Yes."

"Well, then, give us some! Bring it here, damn it!"

"How much do you want?"

"*Quantum satis* . . . Give us an ounce each in the water, and afterwards we'll see . . . Obtyosov, what do you say? First with water and afterwards *per se* . . ."

The doctor and Obtyosov sat down to the counter, took off their caps, and began drinking the wine.

"The wine, one must admit, is wretched stuff! *Vinum nastissimum!* Though in the presence of . . . er . . . it tastes like nectar. You are enchanting, madam! In imagination I kiss your hand."

"I would give a great deal to do so not in imagination," said Obtyosov. "On my honour, I'd give my life."

"That's enough," said Madame Tchernomordik, flushing and assuming a serious expression.

"What a flirt you are, though!" the doctor laughed softly, looking slyly at her from under his brows. "Your eyes seem to be firing shot: piff-paff! I congratulate you: you've conquered! We are vanquished!"

The chemist's wife looked at their ruddy faces, listened to their chatter, and soon she, too, grew quite lively. Oh, she felt so gay! She entered into the conversation, she laughed, flirted, and even, after repeated requests from the customers, drank two ounces of wine.

"You officers ought to come in oftener from the camp," she said; "it's awful how dreary it is here. I'm simply dying of it."

"I should think so!" said the doctor indignantly. "Such a peach, a miracle of nature, thrown away in the wilds! How well Griboyedov said, 'Into the wilds, to Saratov!' It's time for us to be off, though. Delighted to have made your acquaintance . . . very. How much do we owe you?"

The chemist's wife raised her eyes to the ceiling and her lips moved for some time.

"Twelve roubles forty-eight kopecks," she said.

Obtyosov took out of his pocket a fat pocket-book, and after fumbling for some time among the notes, paid.

"Your husband's sleeping sweetly . . . He must be dreaming," he muttered, pressing her hand at parting.

"I don't like to hear silly remarks . . ."

"What silly remarks? On the contrary, it's not silly at all . . . Even Shakespeare said: 'Happy is he who in his youth is young.'"

"Let go of my hand."

At last after much talk and after kissing the lady's hand at parting, the customers went out of the shop irresolutely, as though they were wondering whether they had not forgotten something.

She ran quickly into the bedroom and sat down in the same place. She saw the doctor and the officer, on coming out of the shop, walk lazily away a distance of twenty paces; then they stopped and began whispering together. What about? Her heart throbbed, there was a pulsing in her temples, and why she did not know . . . Her heart beat violently as though those two whispering outside were deciding her fate.

Five minutes later the doctor parted from Obtyosov and walked on, while Obtyosov came back. He walked past the shop once and a second time . . . He would stop near the door and then take a few steps again. At last the bell tinkled discreetly.

"What? Who is there?" the chemist's wife heard her husband's voice suddenly. "There's a ring at the bell, and you don't hear it," he said severely. "Is that the way to do things?"

He got up, put on his dressing gown, and staggering, half asleep, flopped in his slippers to the shop.

"What . . . is it?" he asked Obtyosov.

"Give me . . . give me four pennyworth of peppermint lozenges."

Sniffing continually, yawning, dropping asleep as he moved, and knocking his knees against the counter, the chemist went to the shelf and reached down the jar.

Two minutes later the chemist's wife saw Obtyosov go out of the shop, and, after he had gone some steps, she saw him throw the packet of peppermints on the dusty road. The doctor came from behind a corner to meet him . . . They met and, gesticulating, vanished in the morning mist.

"How unhappy I am!" said the chemist's wife, looking angrily at her husband, who was undressing quickly to get into bed again. "Oh, how unhappy I am!" she repeated, suddenly melting into bitter tears. "And nobody knows, nobody knows . . ."

"I forgot fourpence on the counter," muttered the chemist, pulling the quilt over him. "Put it away in the till, please . . ."

And at once he fell asleep again.

A Trifle from Life

[First published on September 29, 1886.
Collected in *The Party and Other Stories* (1917).]

A well-fed, red-cheeked young man called Nikolay Ilyitch Belyaev, of thirty-two, who was an owner of house property in Petersburg, and a devotee of the racecourse, went one evening to see Olga Ivanovna Irnin, with whom he was living, or, to use his own expression, was dragging out a long, wearisome romance. And, indeed, the first interesting and enthusiastic pages of this romance had long been perused; now the pages dragged on, and still dragged on, without presenting anything new or of interest.

Not finding Olga Ivanovna at home, my hero lay down on the lounge chair and proceeded to wait for her in the drawing room.

"Good evening, Nikolay Ilyitch!" he heard a child's voice. "Mother will be here directly. She has gone with Sonia to the dressmaker's."

Olga Ivanovna's son, Alyosha—a boy of eight who looked graceful and very well cared for, who was dressed like a picture, in a black velvet jacket and long black stockings—was lying on the sofa in the same room. He was lying on a satin cushion and, evidently imitating an acrobat he had lately seen at the circus, stuck up in the air first one leg and then the other. When his elegant legs were exhausted, he brought his arms into play or jumped up impulsively and went on all fours, trying to stand with his legs in the air. All this he was doing with the utmost gravity, gasping and groaning painfully as though he regretted that God had given him such a restless body.

"Ah, good evening, my boy," said Belyaev. "It's you! I did not notice you. Is your mother well?"

Alyosha, taking hold of the tip of his left toe with his right hand and falling into the most unnatural attitude, turned over, jumped up, and peeped at Belyaev from behind the big fluffy lampshade.

"What shall I say?" he said, shrugging his shoulders. "In reality mother's never well. You see, she is a woman, and women, Nikolay Ilyitch, have always something the matter with them."

Belyaev, having nothing better to do, began watching Alyosha's face. He had never before during the whole of his intimacy with Olga Ivanovna paid any attention to the boy, and had completely ignored his existence; the boy had been before his eyes, but he had not cared to think why he was there and what part he was playing.

In the twilight of the evening, Alyosha's face, with his white forehead and black, unblinking eyes, unexpectedly reminded Belyaev of Olga Ivanovna as she had been during the first pages of their romance. And he felt disposed to be friendly to the boy.

"Come here, insect," he said; "let me have a closer look at you."

The boy jumped off the sofa and skipped up to Belyaev.

"Well," began Nikolay Ilyitch, putting a hand on the boy's thin shoulder. "How are you getting on?"

"How shall I say! We used to get on a great deal better."

"Why?"

"It's very simple. Sonia and I used only to learn music and reading, and now they give us French poetry to learn. Have you been shaved lately?"

"Yes."

"Yes, I see you have. Your beard is shorter. Let me touch it. . . . Does that hurt?"

"No."

"Why is it that if you pull one hair it hurts, but if you pull a lot at once it doesn't hurt a bit? Ha, ha! And, you know, it's a pity you don't have whiskers. Here ought to be shaved . . . but here at the sides the hair ought to be left. . . ."

The boy nestled up to Belyaev and began playing with his watch-chain.

"When I go to the high school," he said, "mother is going to buy me a watch. I shall ask her to buy me a watch-chain like this. . . . Wh-at a lo-ket! Father's got a locket like that, only yours has little bars on it and his has letters. . . . There's mother's portrait in the middle of his. Father has a different sort of chain now, not made with rings, but like ribbon. . . ."

"How do you know? Do you see your father?"

"I? M'm . . . no . . . I . . ."

Alyosha blushed, and in great confusion, feeling caught in a lie, began zealously scratching the locket with his nail. . . . Belyaev looked steadily into his face and asked:

"Do you see your father?"

"N-no!"

"Come, speak frankly, on your honour. . . . I see from your face you are telling a fib. Once you've let a thing slip out it's no good wriggling about it. Tell me, do you see him? Come, as a friend."

Alyosha hesitated.

"You won't tell mother?" he said.

"As though I should!"

"On your honour?"

"On my honour."

"Do you swear?"

"Ah, you provoking boy! What do you take me for?"

Alyosha looked round him, then with wide-open eyes, whispered to him:

"Only, for goodness' sake, don't tell mother. . . . Don't tell any one at all, for it is a secret. I hope to goodness mother won't find out, or we should all catch it—Sonia, and I, and Pelagea. . . . Well, listen . . . Sonia and I see father every Tuesday and Friday. When Pelagea takes us for a walk before dinner we go to the Apfel Restaurant, and there is father waiting for us. . . . He is always sitting in a room apart, where you know there's a marble table and an ashtray in the shape of a goose without a back. . . ."

"What do you do there?"

"Nothing! First we say how-do-you-do, then we all sit round the table, and father treats us with coffee and pies. You know Sonia eats the meat-pies, but I can't endure meat-pies! I like the pies made of cabbage and eggs. We eat such a lot that we have to try hard to eat as much as we can at dinner, for fear mother should notice."

"What do you talk about?"

"With father? About anything. He kisses us, he hugs us, tells us all sorts of amusing jokes. Do you know, he says when we are grown up he is going to take us to live with him. Sonia does not want to go, but I agree. Of course, I should miss mother; but, then, I should write her letters! It's a queer idea, but we could come and visit her on holidays—couldn't we? Father says, too, that he will buy me a horse. He's an awfully kind man! I can't understand why mother does not ask him to come and live with us, and why she forbids us to see him. You know he loves mother very much. He is always asking us how she is and what she is doing. When she was ill he clutched his head like this, and . . . and kept running about. He always tells us to be obedient and respectful to her. Listen. Is it true that we are unfortunate?"

"H'm! . . . Why?"

"That's what father says. 'You are unhappy children,' he says. It's strange to hear him, really. 'You are unhappy,' he says, 'I am unhappy, and mother's unhappy. You must pray to God,' he says; 'for yourselves and for her.'"

Alyosha let his eyes rest on a stuffed bird and sank into thought.

"So . . ." growled Belyaev. "So that's how you are going on. You arrange meetings at restaurants. And mother does not know?"

"No-o. . . . How should she know? Pelagea would not tell her for anything, you know. The day before yesterday he gave us some pears. As sweet as jam! I ate two."

"H'm! . . . Well, and I say . . . Listen. Did father say anything about me?"

"About you? What shall I say?"

Alyosha looked searchingly into Belyaev's face and shrugged his shoulders.

"He didn't say anything particular."

"For instance, what did he say?"

"You won't be offended?"

"What next? Why, does he abuse me?"

"He doesn't abuse you, but you know he is angry with you. He says mother's unhappy owing to you . . . and that you have ruined mother. You know he is so queer! I explain to him that you are kind, that you never scold mother; but he only shakes his head."

"So he says I have ruined her?"

"Yes; you mustn't be offended, Nikolay Ilyitch."

Belyaev got up, stood still a moment, and walked up and down the drawing room.

"That's strange and . . . ridiculous!" he muttered, shrugging his shoulders and smiling sarcastically. "He's entirely to blame, and I have ruined her, eh? An innocent lamb, I must say. So he told you I ruined your mother?"

"Yes, but . . . you said you would not be offended, you know."

"I am not offended, and . . . and it's not your business. Why, it's . . . why, it's positively ridiculous! I have been thrust into it like a chicken in the broth, and now it seems I'm to blame!"

A ring was heard. The boy sprang up from his place and ran out. A minute later a lady came into the room with a little girl; this was Olga Ivanovna, Alyosha's mother. Alyosha followed them in, skipping and jumping, humming aloud and waving his hands. Belyaev nodded, and went on walking up and down.

"Of course, whose fault is it if not mine?" he muttered with a snort. "He is right! He is an injured husband."

"What are you talking about?" asked Olga Ivanovna.

"What about? . . . Why, just listen to the tales your lawful spouse is spreading now! It appears that I am a scoundrel and a villain, that I have ruined you and the children. All of you are unhappy, and I am the only happy one! Wonderfully, wonderfully happy!"

"I don't understand, Nikolay. What's the matter?"

"Why, listen to this young gentleman!" said Belyaev, pointing to Alyosha.

Alyosha flushed crimson, then turned pale, and his whole face began working with terror.

"Nikolay Ilyitch," he said in a loud whisper. "Sh-sh!"

Olga Ivanovna looked in surprise at Alyosha, then at Belyaev, then at Alyosha again.

"Just ask him," Belyaev went on. "Your Pelagea, like a regular fool, takes them about to restaurants and arranges meetings with their papa. But that's not the point: the point is that their dear papa is a victim, while I'm a wretch who has broken up both your lives . . ."

"Nikolay Ilyitch," moaned Alyosha. "Why, you promised on your word of honour!"

"Oh, get away!" said Belyaev, waving him off. "This is more important than any word of honour. It's the hypocrisy revolts me, the lying! . . ."

"I don't understand it," said Olga Ivanovna, and tears glistened in her eyes. "Tell me, Alyosha," she turned to her son. "Do you see your father?"

Alyosha did not hear her; he was looking with horror at Belyaev.

"It's impossible," said his mother; "I will go and question Pelagea." Olga Ivanovna went out.

"I say, you promised on your word of honour!" said Alyosha, trembling all over.

Belyaev dismissed him with a wave of his hand, and went on walking up and down. He was absorbed in his grievance and was oblivious of the boy's presence, as he always had been. He, a grown-up, serious person, had no thought to spare for boys. And Alyosha sat down in the corner and told Sonia with horror how he had been deceived. He was trembling, stammering, and crying. It was the first time in his life that he had been brought into such coarse contact with lying; till then he had not known that there are in the world, besides sweet pears, pies, and expensive watches, a great many things for which the language of children has no expression.

The Orator

[First published on November 29, 1886.
Collected in *The Schoolmaster and Other Stories* (1921).]

One fine morning the collegiate assessor, Kirill Ivanovitch Babilonov, who had died of the two afflictions so widely spread in our country, a bad wife and alcoholism, was being buried. As the funeral procession set off from the church to the cemetery, one of the deceased's colleagues, called Poplavsky, got into a cab and galloped off to find a friend, one Grigory Petrovitch Zapoikin, a man who though still young had acquired considerable popularity. Zapoikin, as many of my readers are aware, possesses a rare talent for impromptu speechifying at weddings, jubilees, and funerals. He can speak whenever he likes: in his sleep, on an empty stomach, dead drunk, or in a high fever. His words flow smoothly and evenly, like water out of a pipe, and in abundance; there are far more moving words in his oratorical dictionary than there are beetles in any restaurant. He always speaks eloquently and at great length, so much so that on some occasions, particularly at merchants' weddings, they have to resort to assistance from the police to stop him.

"I have come for you, old man!" began Poplavsky, finding him at home. "Put on your hat and coat this minute and come along. One of our fellows is dead, we are just sending him off to the other world, so you must do a bit of palavering by way of farewell to him . . . You are our only hope. If it had been one of the smaller fry it would not have been worth troubling you, but you see it's the secretary . . . a pillar of the office, in a sense. It's awkward for such a whopper to be buried without a speech."

"Oh, the secretary!" yawned Zapoikin. "You mean the drunken one?"

"Yes. There will be pancakes, a lunch . . . you'll get your cab-fare. Come along, dear chap. You spout out some rigmarole like a regular Cicero at the grave and what gratitude you will earn!"

Zapoikin readily agreed. He ruffled up his hair, cast a shade of melancholy over his face, and went out into the street with Poplavsky.

"I know your secretary," he said, as he got into the cab. "A cunning rogue and a beast—the kingdom of heaven be his—such as you don't often come across."

"Come, Grisha, it is not the thing to abuse the dead."

"Of course not, *aut mortuis nihil bene*, but still he was a rascal."

The friends overtook the funeral procession and joined it. The coffin was borne along slowly so that before they reached the cemetery they were able three times to drop into a tavern and imbibe a little to the health of the departed.

In the cemetery came the service by the graveside. The mother-in-law, the wife, and the sister-in-law in obedience to custom shed many tears. When the coffin was being lowered into the grave the wife even shrieked "Let me go with him!" but did not follow her husband into the grave, probably recollecting her pension. Waiting till everything was quiet again Zapoikin stepped forward, turned his eyes on all present, and began:

"Can I believe my eyes and ears? Is it not a terrible dream this grave, these tear-stained faces, these moans and lamentations? Alas, it is not a dream and our eyes do not deceive us! He whom we have only so lately seen, so full of courage, so youthfully fresh and pure, who so lately before our eyes like an unwearying bee bore his honey to the common hive of the welfare of the state, he who . . . he is turned now to dust, to inanimate mirage. Inexorable death has laid his bony hand upon him at the time when, in spite of his bowed age, he was still full of the bloom of strength and radiant hopes. An irremediable loss! Who will fill his place for us? Good government servants we have many, but Prokofy Osipitch was unique. To the depths of his soul he was devoted to his honest duty; he did not spare his strength but worked late at night, and was disinterested, impervious to bribes . . . How he despised those who to the detriment of the public interest sought to corrupt him, who by the seductive goods of this life strove to draw him to betray his duty! Yes, before our eyes

Prokofy Osipitch would divide his small salary between his poorer colleagues, and you have just heard yourselves the lamentations of the widows and orphans who lived upon his alms. Devoted to good works and his official duty, he gave up the joys of this life and even renounced the happiness of domestic existence; as you are aware, to the end of his days he was a bachelor. And who will replace him as a comrade? I can see now the kindly, shaven face turned to us with a gentle smile, I can hear now his soft friendly voice. Peace to thine ashes, Prokofy Osipitch! Rest, honest, noble toiler!"

Zapoikin continued while his listeners began whispering together. His speech pleased everyone and drew some tears, but a good many things in it seemed strange. In the first place they could not make out why the orator called the deceased Prokofy Osipitch when his name was Kirill Ivanovitch. In the second, everyone knew that the deceased had spent his whole life quarrelling with his lawful wife, and so consequently could not be called a bachelor; in the third, he had a thick red beard and had never been known to shave, and so no one could understand why the orator spoke of his shaven face. The listeners were perplexed; they glanced at each other and shrugged their shoulders.

"Prokofy Osipitch," continued the orator, looking with an air of inspiration into the grave, "your face was plain, even hideous, you were morose and austere, but we all know that under that outer husk there beat an honest, friendly heart!"

Soon the listeners began to observe something strange in the orator himself. He gazed at one point, shifted about uneasily and began to shrug his shoulders too. All at once he ceased speaking, and gaping with astonishment, turned to Poplavsky.

"I say! He's alive," he said, staring with horror.

"Who's alive?"

"Why, Prokofy Osipitch, there he stands, by that tombstone!"

"He never died! It's Kirill Ivanovitch who's dead."

"But you told me yourself your secretary was dead."

"Kirill Ivanovitch was our secretary. You've muddled it, you queer fish. Prokofy Osipitch was our secretary before, that's true, but two years ago he was transferred to the second division as head clerk."

"How the devil is one to tell?"

"Why are you stopping? Go on, it's awkward."

Zapoikin turned to the grave, and with the same eloquence continued his interrupted speech. Prokofy Osipitch, an old clerk with a clean-shaven face, was in fact standing by a tombstone. He looked at the orator and frowned angrily.

"Well, you have put your foot into it, haven't you!" laughed his fellow clerks as they returned from the funeral with Zapoikin. "Burying a man alive!"

"It's unpleasant, young man," grumbled Prokofy Osipitch. "Your speech may be all right for a dead man, but in reference to a living one it is nothing but sarcasm! Upon my soul what have you been saying? Disinterested, incorruptible, won't take bribes! Such things can only be said of the living in sarcasm. And no one asked you, sir, to expatiate on my face. Plain, hideous, so be it, but why exhibit my countenance in that public way! It's insulting."

Who Was to Blame?

[First published on December 20, 1886.
Collected in *The Cook's Wedding and Other Stories* (1922).]

As my uncle Pyotr Demyanitch, a lean, bilious collegiate councillor, exceedingly like a stale smoked fish with a stick through it, was getting ready to go to the high school, where he taught Latin, he noticed that the corner of his grammar was nibbled by mice.

"I say, Praskovya," he said, going into the kitchen and addressing the cook, "how is it we have got mice here? Upon my word! yesterday my top hat was nibbled, today they have disfigured my Latin grammar. . . . At this rate they will soon begin eating my clothes!

"What can I do? I did not bring them in!" answered Praskovya.

"We must do something! You had better get a cat, hadn't you?"

"I've got a cat, but what good is it?"

And Praskovya pointed to the corner where a white kitten, thin as a match, lay curled up asleep beside a broom.

"Why is it no good?" asked Pyotr Demyanitch.

"It's young yet, and foolish. It's not two months old yet."

"H'm. . . . Then it must be trained. It had much better be learning instead of lying there."

Saying this, Pyotr Demyanitch sighed with a careworn air and went out of the kitchen. The kitten raised his head, looked lazily after him, and shut his eyes again.

The kitten lay awake thinking. Of what? Unacquainted with real life, having no store of accumulated impressions, his mental processes could only be instinctive, and he could but picture life in accordance with the conceptions that he had inherited, together with his flesh and blood, from his ancestors, the tigers (*vide* Darwin). His thoughts were of the nature of daydreams. His feline imagination pictured something like the Arabian desert, over which flitted shadows closely resembling Praskovya, the stove, the broom. In the midst of the shadows there suddenly appeared a saucer of milk; the saucer began to grow paws, it began moving and displayed a tendency to run; the kitten made a bound, and with a thrill of bloodthirsty sensuality thrust his claws into it.

When the saucer had vanished into obscurity a piece of meat appeared, dropped by Praskovya; the meat ran away with a cowardly squeak, but the kitten made a bound and got his claws into it. . . . Everything that rose before the imagination of the young dreamer had for its starting-point leaps, claws, and teeth . . . The soul of another is darkness, and a cat's soul more than most, but how near the visions just described are to the truth may be seen from the following fact: under the influence of his daydreams the kitten suddenly leaped up, looked with flashing eyes at Praskovya, ruffled up his coat, and making one bound, thrust his claws into the cook's skirt. Obviously he was born a mouse catcher, a worthy son of his bloodthirsty ancestors. Fate had destined him to be the terror of cellars, storerooms and cornbins, and had it not been for education . . . we will not anticipate, however.

On his way home from the high school, Pyotr Demyanitch went into a general shop and bought a mouse-trap for fifteen kopecks. At dinner he fixed a little bit of his rissole on the hook, and set the trap under the sofa, where there were heaps of the pupils' old exercise-books, which Praskovya used for various domestic purposes. At six o'clock in the evening, when the worthy Latin master was sitting at the table correcting his pupils' exercises, there was a sudden "klop!" so loud that my uncle started and dropped his pen. He went at once to the sofa and took out the trap. A neat little mouse, the size of a thimble, was sniffing the wires and trembling with fear.

"Aha," muttered Pyotr Demyanitch, and he looked at the mouse malignantly, as though he were about to give him a bad mark. "You are cau—aught, wretch! Wait a bit! I'll teach you to eat my grammar!"

Having gloated over his victim, Poytr Demyanitch put the mouse-trap on the floor and called:

"Praskovya, there's a mouse caught! Bring the kitten here!

"I'm coming," responded Praskovya, and a minute later she came in with the descendant of tigers in her arms.

"Capital!" said Pyotr Demyanitch, rubbing his hands. "We will give him a lesson. . . . Put him down opposite the mouse-trap . . . that's it. . . . Let him sniff it and look at it. . . . That's it. . . ."

The kitten looked wonderingly at my uncle, at his armchair, sniffed the mouse-trap in bewilderment, then, frightened probably by the glaring lamplight and the attention directed to him, made a dash and ran in terror to the door.

"Stop!" shouted my uncle, seizing him by the tail, "stop, you rascal! He's afraid of a mouse, the idiot! Look! It's a mouse! Look! Well? Look, I tell you!"

Pyotr Demyanitch took the kitten by the scruff of the neck and pushed him with his nose against the mouse-trap.

"Look, you carrion! Take him and hold him, Praskovya. . . . Hold him opposite the door of the trap. . . . When I let the mouse out, you let him go instantly. . . . Do you hear? . . . Instantly let go! Now!"

My uncle assumed a mysterious expression and lifted the door of the trap. . . . The mouse came out irresolutely, sniffed the air, and flew like an arrow under the sofa. . . . The kitten on being released darted under the table with his tail in the air.

"It has got away! got away!" cried Pyotr Demyanitch, looking ferocious. "Where is he, the scoundrel? Under the table? You wait . . ."

My uncle dragged the kitten from under the table and shook him in the air.

"Wretched little beast," he muttered, smacking him on the ear. "Take that, take that! Will you shirk it next time? Wr-r-r-etch. . . ."

Next day Praskovya heard again the summons.

"Praskovya, there is a mouse caught! Bring the kitten here!"

After the outrage of the previous day the kitten had taken refuge under the stove and had not come out all night. When Praskovya pulled him out and, carrying him by the scruff of the neck into the study, set him down before the mouse-trap, he trembled all over and mewed piteously.

"Come, let him feel at home first," Pyotr Demyanitch commanded. "Let him look and sniff. Look and learn! Stop, plague take you!" he shouted, noticing that the kitten was backing away from the mouse-trap.

"I'll thrash you! Hold him by the ear! That's it. . . . Well now, set him down before the trap. . . ."

My uncle slowly lifted the door of the trap . . . the mouse whisked under the very nose of the kitten, flung itself against Praskovya's hand and fled under the cupboard; the kitten, feeling himself free, took a desperate bound and retreated under the sofa.

"He's let another mouse go!" bawled Pyotr Demyanitch. "Do you call that a cat? Nasty little beast! Thrash him! thrash him by the mousetrap!"

When the third mouse had been caught, the kitten shivered all over at the sight of the mousetrap and its inmate, and scratched Praskovya's hand. . . . After the fourth mouse my uncle flew into a rage, kicked the kitten, and said:

"Take the nasty thing away! Get rid of it! Chuck it away! It's no earthly use!"

A year passed, the thin, frail kitten had turned into a solid and sagacious tom-cat. One day he was on his way by the back yards to an amatory interview. He had just reached his destination when he suddenly heard a rustle, and thereupon caught sight of a mouse which ran from a water-trough towards a stable; my hero's hair stood on end, he arched his back, hissed, and trembling all over, took to ignominious flight.

Alas! sometimes I feel myself in the ludicrous position of the flying cat. Like the kitten, I had in my day the honour of being taught Latin by my uncle. Now, whenever I chance to see some work of classical antiquity, instead of being moved to eager enthusiasm, I begin recalling, *ut consecutivum*, the irregular verbs, the sallow grey face of my uncle, the ablative absolute. . . . I turn pale, my hair stands up on my head, and, like the cat, I take to ignominious flight.

Love

[First published in 1886.
Collected in *Love and Other Stories* (1922).]

"Three o'clock in the morning. The soft April night is looking in at my windows and caressingly winking at me with its stars. I can't sleep, I am so happy!

"My whole being from head to heels is bursting with a strange, incomprehensible feeling. I can't analyse it just now—I haven't the time, I'm too lazy, and there—hang analysis! Why, is a man likely to interpret his sensations when he is flying head foremost from a belfry, or has just learned that he has won two hundred thousand? Is he in a state to do it?"

This was more or less how I began my love letter to Sasha, a girl of nineteen with whom I had fallen in love. I began it five times, and as often tore up the sheets, scratched out whole pages, and copied it all over again. I spent as long over the letter as if it had been a novel I had to write to order. And it was not because I tried to make it longer, more elaborate, and more fervent, but because I wanted endlessly to prolong the process of this writing, when one sits in the stillness of one's study and communes with one's own daydreams while the spring night looks in at one's window. Between the lines I saw a beloved image, and it seemed to me that there were, sitting at the same table writing with me, spirits as naïvely happy, as foolish, and as blissfully smiling as I. I wrote continually, looking at my hand, which still ached deliciously where hers had lately pressed it, and if I turned my eyes away I had a vision of the green trellis of the little gate. Through that trellis Sasha gazed at me after I had said goodbye to her. When I was saying goodbye to Sasha I was thinking of nothing and was simply admiring her figure as every decent man admires a pretty woman; when I saw through the trellis two big eyes, I suddenly, as though by inspiration, knew that I was in love, that it was all settled between us, and fully decided already, that I had nothing left to do but to carry out certain formalities.

It is a great delight also to seal up a love letter, and, slowly putting on one's hat and coat, to go softly out of the house and to carry the treasure to the post. There are no stars in the sky now: in their place there is a long whitish streak in the east, broken here and there by clouds above the roofs of the dingy houses; from that streak the whole sky is flooded with pale light. The town is asleep, but already the water-carts have come out, and somewhere in a faraway factory a whistle sounds to wake up the work-people. Beside the postbox, slightly moist with dew, you are sure to see the clumsy figure of a house porter, wearing a bell-shaped sheepskin and carrying a stick. He is in a condition akin to catalepsy: he is not asleep or awake, but something in between.

If the boxes knew how often people resort to them for the decision of their fate, they would not have such a humble air. I, anyway, almost kissed my postbox, and as I gazed at it I reflected that the post is the greatest of blessings.

I beg anyone who has ever been in love to remember how one usually hurries home after dropping the letter in the box, rapidly gets into bed and pulls up the quilt in the full conviction that as soon as one wakes up in the morning one will be overwhelmed with memories of the previous day and look with rapture at the window, where the daylight will be eagerly making its way through the folds of the curtain.

Well, to facts. . . . Next morning at midday, Sasha's maid brought me the following answer: "I am delited be sure to come to us to day please I shall expect you. Your S."

Not a single comma. This lack of punctuation, and the misspelling of the word 'delighted,' the whole letter, and even the long, narrow envelope in which it was put filled my heart with tenderness. In the sprawling but diffident handwriting I recognised Sasha's walk, her way of raising her eyebrows when she laughed, the movement of her lips . . . But the contents of the letter did not satisfy me. In the first place, poetical letters are not answered in that way, and in the second, why should I go to Sasha's house to wait till it should occur to her stout mamma, her brothers, and poor relations to leave us alone together? It would never enter their heads, and nothing is more hateful than to have to restrain one's raptures simply because of the intrusion of some animate trumpery in the shape of a half-deaf old woman or little girl pestering one with questions. I sent an answer by the maid asking Sasha to select some park or boulevard for a rendezvous. My suggestion was readily accepted. I had struck the right chord, as the saying is.

Between four and five o'clock in the afternoon I made my way to the furthest and most overgrown part of the park. There was not a soul in the park, and the tryst might have taken place somewhere nearer in one of the avenues or arbours, but women don't like doing it by halves in romantic affairs; in for a penny, in for a pound—if you are in for a tryst, let it be in the furthest and most impenetrable thicket, where one runs the risk of stumbling upon some rough or drunken man. When I went up to Sasha she was standing with her back to me, and in that back I could read a devilish lot of mystery. It seemed as though that back and the nape of her neck, and the black spots on her dress were saying: Hush! . . . The girl was wearing a simple cotton dress over which she had thrown a light cape. To add to the air of mysterious secrecy, her face was covered with a white veil. Not to spoil the effect, I had to approach on tiptoe and speak in a half whisper.

From what I remember now, I was not so much the essential point of the rendezvous as a detail of it. Sasha was not so much absorbed in the interview itself as in its romantic mysteriousness, my kisses, the silence of the gloomy trees, my vows. . . . There was not a minute in which she forgot herself, was overcome, or let the mysterious expression drop from her face, and really if there had been any Ivan Sidoritch or Sidor Ivanitch in my place she would have felt just as happy. How is one to make out in such circumstances whether one is loved or not? Whether the love is 'the real thing' or not?

From the park I took Sasha home with me. The presence of the beloved woman in one's bachelor quarters affects one like wine and music. Usually one begins to speak of the future, and the confidence and self-reliance with which one does so is beyond bounds. You make plans and projects, talk fervently of the rank of general though you have not yet reached the rank of a lieutenant, and altogether you fire off such high-flown nonsense that your listener must have a great deal of love and ignorance of life to assent to it. Fortunately for men, women in love are always blinded by their feelings and never know anything of life. Far from not assenting, they actually turn pale with holy awe, are full of reverence and hang greedily on the maniac's words. Sasha listened to me with attention, but I soon detected an absent-minded expression on her face, she did not understand me. The future of which I talked interested her only in its external aspect and I was wasting time in displaying my plans and projects before her. She was keenly interested in knowing which would be her room, what paper she would have in the room, why I had an upright piano instead of a grand piano, and so on. She examined carefully all the little things on my table, looked at the photographs, sniffed at the bottles, peeled the old stamps off the envelopes, saying she wanted them for something.

"Please collect old stamps for me!" she said, making a grave face. "Please do."

Then she found a nut in the window, noisily cracked it and ate it.

"Why don't you stick little labels on the backs of your books?" she asked, taking a look at the bookcase.

"What for?"

"Oh, so that each book should have its number. And where am I to put my books? I've got books too, you know."

"What books have you got?" I asked.

Sasha raised her eyebrows, thought a moment and said:

"All sorts."

And if it had entered my head to ask her what thoughts, what convictions, what aims she had, she would no doubt have raised her eyebrows, thought a minute, and have said in the same way: "All sorts."

Later I saw Sasha home and left her house regularly, officially engaged, and was so reckoned till our wedding. If the reader will allow me to judge merely from my personal experience, I maintain that to be engaged is very dreary, far more so than to be a husband or nothing at all. An engaged man is neither one thing nor the other, he has left one side of the river and not reached the other, he is not married and yet he can't be said to be a bachelor, but is in something not unlike the condition of the porter whom I have mentioned above.

Every day as soon as I had a free moment I hastened to my fiancée. As I went I usually bore within me a multitude of hopes, desires, intentions, suggestions, phrases. I always fancied that as soon as the maid opened the door I should, from feeling oppressed and stifled, plunge at once up to my neck into a sea of refreshing happiness. But it always turned out otherwise in fact. Every time I went to see my fiancée I found all her family and other members of the household busy over the silly trousseau. (And by the way, they were hard at work sewing for two months and then they had less than a hundred roubles' worth of things). There was a smell of irons, candle grease, and fumes. Bugles scrunched under one's feet. The two most important rooms were piled up with billows of linen, calico, and muslin and from among the billows peeped out Sasha's little head with a thread between her teeth. All the sewing party welcomed me with cries of delight but at once led me off into the dining room where I could not hinder them nor see what only husbands are permitted to behold. In spite of my feelings, I had to sit in the dining room and converse with Pimenovna, one of the poor relations. Sasha, looking worried and excited, kept running by me with a thimble, a skein of wool or some other boring object.

"Wait, wait, I shan't be a minute," she would say when I raised imploring eyes to her. "Only fancy that wretch Stepanida has spoilt the bodice of the barège dress!"

And after waiting in vain for this grace, I lost my temper, went out of the house and walked about the streets in the company of the new cane I had bought. Or I would want to go for a walk or a drive with my fiancée, would go round and find her already standing in the hall with her mother, dressed to go out and playing with her parasol.

"Oh, we are going to the Arcade," she would say. "We have got to buy some more cashmere and change the hat."

My outing is knocked on the head. I join the ladies and go with them to the Arcade. It is revoltingly dull to listen to women shopping, haggling, and trying to outdo the sharp shopman. I felt ashamed when Sasha, after turning over masses of material and knocking down the prices to a minimum, walked out of the shop without buying anything, or else told the shopman to cut her some half rouble's worth.

When they came out of the shop, Sasha and her mamma with scared and worried faces would discuss at length having made a mistake, having bought the wrong thing, the flowers in the chintz being too dark, and so on.

Yes, it is a bore to be engaged! I'm glad it's over.

Now I am married. It is evening. I am sitting in my study, reading. Behind me on the sofa Sasha is sitting, munching something noisily. I want a glass of beer.

"Sasha, look for the corkscrew . . ." I say. "It's lying about somewhere."

Sasha leaps up, rummages in a disorderly way among two or three heaps of papers, drops the matches, and without finding the corkscrew, sits down in silence . . . Five minutes pass—ten . . . I begin to be fretted both by thirst and vexation.

"Sasha, do look for the corkscrew," I say.

Sasha leaps up again and rummages among the papers near me. Her munching and rustling of the papers affects me like the sound of sharpening knives against each other . . . I get up and begin looking for the corkscrew myself. At last it is found and the beer is uncorked. Sasha remains by the table and begins telling me something at great length.

"You'd better read something, Sasha," I say.

She takes up a book, sits down facing me and begins moving her lips . . . I look at her little forehead, moving lips, and sink into thought.

"She is getting on for twenty . . ." I reflect. "If one takes a boy of the educated class and of that age and compares them, what a difference! The boy would have knowledge and convictions and some intelligence."

But I forgive that difference just as the low forehead and moving lips are forgiven. I remember in my old Lovelace days I have cast off women for a stain on their stockings, or for one foolish word, or for not cleaning their teeth, and now I forgive everything: the munching, the muddling about after the corkscrew, the slovenliness, the long talking about nothing that matters; I forgive it all almost unconsciously, with no effort of will, as though Sasha's mistakes were my mistakes, and many things which would have made me wince in old days move me to tenderness and even rapture. The explanation of this forgiveness of everything lies in my love for Sasha, but what is the explanation of the love itself, I really don't know.

Misery

[First published in the Russian newspaper *Peterburgskaya Gazeta* (*St. Petersburg Gazette*) in 1886. Collected in *The Schoolmistress and Other Stories* (1918). The story is considered one of Chekhov's best stories. It has also been translated as 'Heartache.']

"To whom shall I tell my grief?"

The twilight of evening. Big flakes of wet snow are whirling lazily about the street lamps, which have just been lighted, and lying in a thin soft layer on roofs, horses' backs, shoulders, caps. Iona Potapov, the sledge-driver, is all white like a ghost. He sits on the box without stirring, bent as double as the living body can be bent. If a regular snowdrift fell on him it seems as though even then he would not think it necessary to shake it off. . . . His little mare is white and motionless too. Her stillness, the angularity of her lines, and the stick-like straightness of her legs make her look like a halfpenny gingerbread horse. She is probably lost in thought. Anyone who has been torn away from the plough, from the familiar grey landscapes, and cast into this slough, full of monstrous lights, of unceasing uproar and hurrying people, is bound to think.

It is a long time since Iona and his nag have budged. They came out of the yard before dinnertime and not a single fare yet. But now the shades of evening are falling on the town. The pale light of the street lamps changes to a vivid colour, and the bustle of the street grows noisier.

"Sledge to Vyborgskaya!" Iona hears. "Sledge!"

Iona starts, and through his snow-plastered eyelashes sees an officer in a military overcoat with a hood over his head.

"To Vyborgskaya," repeats the officer. "Are you asleep? To Vyborgskaya!"

In token of assent Iona gives a tug at the reins which sends cakes of snow flying from the horse's back and shoulders. The officer gets into the sledge. The sledge-driver clicks to the horse, cranes his neck like a swan, rises in his seat, and more from habit than necessity brandishes his whip. The mare cranes her neck, too, crooks her stick-like legs, and hesitatingly sets of. . . .

"Where are you shoving, you devil?" Iona immediately hears shouts from the dark mass shifting to and fro before him. "Where the devil are you going? Keep to the r-right!"

"You don't know how to drive! Keep to the right," says the officer angrily.

A coachman driving a carriage swears at him; a pedestrian crossing the road and brushing the horse's nose with his shoulder looks at him angrily and shakes the snow off his sleeve. Iona fidgets on the box as though he were sitting on thorns, jerks his elbows, and turns his eyes about like one possessed as though he did not know where he was or why he was there.

"What rascals they all are!" says the officer jocosely. "They are simply doing their best to run up against you or fall under the horse's feet. They must be doing it on purpose."

Iona looks as his fare and moves his lips. . . . Apparently he means to say something, but nothing comes but a sniff.

"What?" inquires the officer.

Iona gives a wry smile, and straining his throat, brings out huskily: "My son . . . er . . . my son died this week, sir."

"H'm! What did he die of?"

Iona turns his whole body round to his fare, and says:

"Who can tell! It must have been from fever. . . . He lay three days in the hospital and then he died. . . . God's will."

"Turn round, you devil!" comes out of the darkness. "Have you gone cracked, you old dog? Look where you are going!"

"Drive on! drive on! . . . ," says the officer. "We shan't get there till tomorrow going on like this. Hurry up!"

The sledge-driver cranes his neck again, rises in his seat, and with heavy grace swings his whip. Several times he looks round at the officer, but the latter keeps his eyes shut and is apparently disinclined to listen. Putting his fare down at Vyborgskaya, Iona stops by a restaurant, and again sits huddled up on the box. . . . Again the wet snow paints him and his horse white. One hour passes, and then another. . . .

Three young men, two tall and thin, one short and hunchbacked, come up, railing at each other and loudly stamping on the pavement with their goloshes.

"Cabby, to the Police Bridge!" the hunchback cries in a cracked voice. "The three of us . . . twenty kopecks!"

Iona tugs at the reins and clicks to his horse. Twenty kopecks is not a fair price, but he has no thoughts for that. Whether it is a rouble or whether it is five kopecks does not matter to him now so long as he has a fare. . . . The three young men, shoving each other and using bad language, go up to the sledge, and all three try to sit down at once. The question remains to be settled: Which are to sit down and which one is to stand? After a long altercation, ill-temper, and abuse, they come to the conclusion that the hunchback must stand because he is the shortest.

"Well, drive on," says the hunchback in his cracked voice, settling himself and breathing down Iona's neck. "Cut along! What a cap you've got, my friend! You wouldn't find a worse one in all Petersburg. . . ."

"He-he! . . . he-he! . . ." laughs Iona. "It's nothing to boast of!"

"Well, then, nothing to boast of, drive on! Are you going to drive like this all the way? Eh? Shall I give you one in the neck?"

"My head aches," says one of the tall ones. "At the Dukmasovs' yesterday Vaska and I drank four bottles of brandy between us."

"I can't make out why you talk such stuff," says the other tall one angrily. "You lie like a brute."

"Strike me dead, it's the truth! . . ."

"It's about as true as that a louse coughs."

"He-he!" grins Iona. "Me-er-ry gentlemen!"

"Tfoo! the devil take you!" cries the hunchback indignantly. "Will you get on, you old plague, or won't you? Is that the way to drive? Give her one with the whip. Hang it all, give it her well."

Iona feels behind his back the jolting person and quivering voice of the hunchback. He hears abuse addressed to him, he sees people, and the feeling of loneliness begins little by little to be less heavy on his heart. The hunchback swears at him, till he chokes over some elaborately whimsical string of epithets and is overpowered by his cough. His tall companions begin talking of a certain Nadyezhda Petrovna. Iona looks round at them. Waiting till there is a brief pause, he looks round once more and says:

"This week ... er ... my ... er ... son died!"

"We shall all die," says the hunchback with a sigh, wiping his lips after coughing. "Come, drive on! drive on! My friends, I simply cannot stand crawling like this! When will he get us there?"

"Well, you give him a little encouragement ... one in the neck!"

"Do you hear, you old plague? I'll make you smart. If one stands on ceremony with fellows like you one may as well walk. Do you hear, you old dragon? Or don't you care a hang what we say?"

And Iona hears rather than feels a slap on the back of his neck.

"He-he! ...." he laughs. "Merry gentlemen.... God give you health!"

"Cabman, are you married?" asks one of the tall ones.

"I? He he! Me-er-ry gentlemen. The only wife for me now is the damp earth.... He-ho-ho!.... The grave that is! ... Here my son's dead and I am alive.... It's a strange thing, death has come in at the wrong door.... Instead of coming for me it went for my son...."

And Iona turns round to tell them how his son died, but at that point the hunchback gives a faint sigh and announces that, thank God! they have arrived at last. After taking his twenty kopecks, Iona gazes for a long while after the revelers, who disappear into a dark entry. Again he is alone and again there is silence for him.... The misery which has been for a brief space eased comes back again and tears his heart more cruelly than ever. With a look of anxiety and suffering Iona's eyes stray restlessly among the crowds moving to and fro on both sides of the street: can he not find among those thousands someone who will listen to him? But the crowds flit by heedless of him and his misery.... His misery is immense, beyond all bounds. If Iona's heart were to burst and his misery to flow out, it would flood the whole world, it seems, but yet it is not seen. It has found a hiding-place in such an insignificant shell that one would not have found it with a candle by daylight....

Iona sees a house-porter with a parcel and makes up his mind to address him.

"What time will it be, friend?" he asks.

"Going on for ten.... Why have you stopped here? Drive on!"

Iona drives a few paces away, bends himself double, and gives himself up to his misery. He feels it is no good to appeal to people. But before five minutes have passed he draws himself up, shakes his head as though he feels a sharp pain, and tugs at the reins. . . . He can bear it no longer.

"Back to the yard!" he thinks. "To the yard!"

And his little mare, as though she knew his thoughts, falls to trotting. An hour and a half later Iona is sitting by a big dirty stove. On the stove, on the floor, and on the benches are people snoring. The air is full of smells and stuffiness. Iona looks at the sleeping figures, scratches himself, and regrets that he has come home so early. . . .

"I have not earned enough to pay for the oats, even," he thinks. "That's why I am so miserable. A man who knows how to do his work . . . who has had enough to eat, and whose horse has had enough to eat, is always at ease. . . ."

In one of the corners a young cabman gets up, clears his throat sleepily, and makes for the water bucket.

"Want a drink?" Iona asks him.

"Seems so."

"May it do you good. . . . But my son is dead, mate. . . . Do you hear? This week in the hospital. . . . It's a queer business. . . ."

Iona looks to see the effect produced by his words, but he sees nothing. The young man has covered his head over and is already asleep. The old man sighs and scratches himself. . . . Just as the young man had been thirsty for water, he thirsts for speech. His son will soon have been dead a week, and he has not really talked to anybody yet. . . . He wants to talk of it properly, with deliberation. . . . He wants to tell how his son was taken ill, how he suffered, what he said before he died, how he died. . . . He wants to describe the funeral, and how he went to the hospital to get his son's clothes. He still has his daughter Anisya in the country. . . . And he wants to talk about her too. . . . Yes, he has plenty to talk about now. His listener ought to sigh and exclaim and lament. . . . It would be even better to talk to women. Though they are silly creatures, they blubber at the first word.

"Let's go out and have a look at the mare," Iona thinks. "There is always time for sleep. . . . You'll have sleep enough, no fear. . . ."

He puts on his coat and goes into the stables where his mare is standing. He thinks about oats, about hay, about the weather. . . . He cannot think about his son when he is alone. . . . To talk about him with someone is possible, but to think of him and picture him is insufferable anguish. . . .

"Are you munching?" Iona asks his mare, seeing her shining eyes. "There, munch away, munch away. . . . Since we have not earned enough for oats, we will eat hay. . . . Yes . . . I have grown too old to drive. . . . My son ought to be driving, not I. . . . He was a real cabman. . . . He ought to have lived. . . ."

Iona is silent for a while, and then he goes on:

"That's how it is, old girl. . . . Kuzma Ionitch is gone. . . . He said goodbye to me. . . . He went and died for no reason. . . . Now, suppose you had a little colt, and you were own mother to that little colt. . . . And all at once that same little colt went and died. . . . You'd be sorry, wouldn't you? . . ."

The little mare munches, listens, and breathes on her master's hands. Iona is carried away and tells her all about it.

Vanka

[First published in the 'Christmas Stories' section of
Peterburgskaya Gazeta (*St. Petersburg Gazette*), a Russian literary and political
newspaper, on December 25, 1886 (old style; new style: January 7, 1887).
Collected in *The Cook's Wedding and Other Stories* (1922).]

Vanka Zhukov, a boy of nine, who had been for three months apprenticed
to Alyahin the shoemaker, was sitting up on Christmas Eve. Waiting till
his master and mistress and their workmen had gone to the midnight
service, he took out of his master's cupboard a bottle of ink and a pen
with a rusty nib, and, spreading out a crumpled sheet of paper in front of
him, began writing. Before forming the first letter he several times looked
round fearfully at the door and the windows, stole a glance at the dark
ikon, on both sides of which stretched shelves full of lasts, and heaved a
broken sigh. The paper lay on the bench while he knelt before it.

"Dear grandfather, Konstantin Makaritch," he wrote, "I am writing
you a letter. I wish you a happy Christmas, and all blessings from God
Almighty. I have neither father nor mother, you are the only one left me."

Vanka raised his eyes to the dark ikon on which the light of his
candle was reflected, and vividly recalled his grandfather, Konstantin
Makaritch, who was night watchman to a family called Zhivarev. He was a
thin but extraordinarily nimble and lively little old man of sixty-five, with
an everlastingly laughing face and drunken eyes. By day he slept in the
servants' kitchen, or made jokes with the cooks; at night, wrapped in an
ample sheepskin, he walked round the grounds and tapped with his little
mallet. Old Kashtanka and Eel, so-called on account of his dark colour and
his long body like a weasel's, followed him with hanging heads. This Eel

was exceptionally polite and affectionate, and looked with equal kindness on strangers and his own masters, but had not a very good reputation. Under his politeness and meekness was hidden the most Jesuitical cunning. No one knew better how to creep up on occasion and snap at one's legs, to slip into the storeroom, or steal a hen from a peasant. His hind legs had been nearly pulled off more than once, twice he had been hanged, every week he was thrashed till he was half dead, but he always revived.

At this moment grandfather was, no doubt, standing at the gate, screwing up his eyes at the red windows of the church, stamping with his high felt boots, and joking with the servants. His little mallet was hanging on his belt. He was clasping his hands, shrugging with the cold, and, with an aged chuckle, pinching first the housemaid, then the cook.

"How about a pinch of snuff?" he was saying, offering the women his snuff-box.

The women would take a sniff and sneeze. Grandfather would be indescribably delighted, go off into a merry chuckle, and cry:

"Tear it off, it has frozen on!"

They give the dogs a sniff of snuff too. Kashtanka sneezes, wriggles her head, and walks away offended. Eel does not sneeze, from politeness, but wags his tail. And the weather is glorious. The air is still, fresh, and transparent. The night is dark, but one can see the whole village with its white roofs and coils of smoke coming from the chimneys, the trees silvered with hoar frost, the snowdrifts. The whole sky spangled with gay twinkling stars, and the Milky Way is as distinct as though it had been washed and rubbed with snow for a holiday. . . .

Vanka sighed, dipped his pen, and went on writing:

"And yesterday I had a wigging. The master pulled me out into the yard by my hair, and whacked me with a boot-stretcher because I accidentally fell asleep while I was rocking their brat in the cradle. And a week ago the mistress told me to clean a herring, and I began from the tail end, and she took the herring and thrust its head in my face. The workmen laugh at me and send me to the tavern for vodka, and tell me to steal the master's cucumbers for them, and the master beats me with anything that comes to hand. And there is nothing to eat. In the morning they give me bread, for dinner, porridge, and in the evening, bread again; but as for tea, or soup, the master and mistress gobble it all up themselves. And I am put to sleep in the passage, and when their wretched brat cries I get no sleep at all, but have to rock the cradle. Dear grandfather, show the divine mercy, take me away from here, home to the village. It's more than I can bear. I bow down to your feet, and will pray to God for you for ever, take me away from here or I shall die."

Vanka's mouth worked, he rubbed his eyes with his black fist, and gave a sob.

"I will powder your snuff for you," he went on. "I will pray for you, and if I do anything you can thrash me like Sidor's goat. And if you think I've no job, then I will beg the steward for Christ's sake to let me clean his boots, or I'll go for a shepherd-boy instead of Fedka. Dear grandfather, it is more than I can bear, it's simply no life at all. I wanted to run away to the village, but I have no boots, and I am afraid of the frost. When I grow up big I will take care of you for this, and not let anyone annoy you, and when you die I will pray for the rest of your soul, just as for my mammy's."

"Moscow is a big town. It's all gentlemen's houses, and there are lots of horses, but there are no sheep, and the dogs are not spiteful. The lads here don't go out with the star, and they don't let anyone go into the choir, and once I saw in a shop window fishing-hooks for sale, fitted ready with the line and for all sorts of fish, awfully good ones, there was even one hook that would hold a forty-pound sheat-fish. And I have seen shops where there are guns of all sorts, after the pattern of the master's guns at home, so that I shouldn't wonder if they are a hundred roubles each. . . . And in the butchers' shops there are grouse and woodcocks and fish and hares, but the shopmen don't say where they shoot them."

"Dear grandfather, when they have the Christmas tree at the big house, get me a gilt walnut, and put it away in the green trunk. Ask the young lady Olga Ignatyevna, say it's for Vanka."

Vanka gave a tremulous sigh, and again stared at the window. He remembered how his grandfather always went into the forest to get the Christmas tree for his master's family, and took his grandson with him. It was a merry time! Grandfather made a noise in his throat, the forest crackled with the frost, and looking at them Vanka chortled too. Before chopping down the Christmas tree, grandfather would smoke a pipe, slowly take a pinch of snuff, and laugh at frozen Vanka. . . . The young fir trees, covered with hoar frost, stood motionless, waiting to see which of them was to die. Wherever one looked, a hare flew like an arrow over the snowdrifts. . . . Grandfather could not refrain from shouting: "Hold him, hold him . . . hold him! Ah, the bob-tailed devil!"

When he had cut down the Christmas tree, grandfather used to drag it to the big house, and there set to work to decorate it. . . . The young lady, who was Vanka's favourite, Olga Ignatyevna, was the busiest of all. When Vanka's mother Pelageya was alive, and a servant in the big house, Olga Ignatyevna used to give him goodies, and having nothing better to do, taught him to read and write, to count up to a hundred, and even to dance a quadrille. When Pelageya died, Vanka had been transferred to the servants' kitchen to be with his grandfather, and from the kitchen to the shoemaker's in Moscow.

"Do come, dear grandfather," Vanka went on with his letter. "For Christ's sake, I beg you, take me away. Have pity on an unhappy orphan like me; here everyone knocks me about, and I am fearfully hungry; I can't tell you what misery it is, I am always crying. And the other day the master hit me on the head with a last, so that I fell down. My life is wretched, worse than any dog's. . . . I send greetings to Alyona, one-eyed Yegorka, and the coachman, and don't give my concertina to anyone. I remain, your grandson, Ivan Zhukov. Dear grandfather, do come."

Vanka folded the sheet of writing-paper twice, and put it into an envelope he had bought the day before for a kopeck. . . . After thinking a little, he dipped the pen and wrote the address:

To grandfather in the village.

Then he scratched his head, thought a little, and added: *Konstantin Makaritch.* Glad that he had not been prevented from writing, he put on his cap and, without putting on his little greatcoat, ran out into the street as he was in his shirt. . . .

The shopmen at the butcher's, whom he had questioned the day before, told him that letters were put in postboxes, and from the boxes were carried about all over the earth in mailcarts with drunken drivers and ringing bells. Vanka ran to the nearest postbox, and thrust the precious letter in the slit. . . .

An hour later, lulled by sweet hopes, he was sound asleep. . . . He dreamed of the stove. On the stove was sitting his grandfather, swinging his bare legs, and reading the letter to the cooks. . . .

By the stove was Eel, wagging his tail.

The Lottery Ticket

[First published on March 9, 1887.
Collected in *The Wife and Other Stories* (1918).]

Ivan Dmitritch, a middle-class man who lived with his family on an income of twelve hundred a year and was very well satisfied with his lot, sat down on the sofa after supper and began reading the newspaper.

"I forgot to look at the newspaper today," his wife said to him as she cleared the table. "Look and see whether the list of drawings is there."

"Yes, it is," said Ivan Dmitritch; "but hasn't your ticket lapsed?"

"No; I took the interest on Tuesday."

"What is the number?"

"Series 9,499, number 26."

"All right . . . we will look . . . 9,499 and 26."

Ivan Dmitritch had no faith in lottery luck, and would not, as a rule, have consented to look at the lists of winning numbers, but now, as he had nothing else to do and as the newspaper was before his eyes, he passed his finger downwards along the column of numbers. And immediately, as though in mockery of his scepticism, no further than the second line from the top, his eye was caught by the figure 9,499! Unable to believe his eyes, he hurriedly dropped the paper on his knees without looking to see the number of the ticket, and, just as though some one had given him a douche of cold water, he felt an agreeable chill in the pit of the stomach; tingling and terrible and sweet!

"Masha, 9,499 is there!" he said in a hollow voice.

His wife looked at his astonished and panic-stricken face, and realised that he was not joking.

"9,499?" she asked, turning pale and dropping the folded tablecloth on the table.

"Yes, yes . . . it really is there!"

"And the number of the ticket?"

"Oh, yes! There's the number of the ticket too. But stay . . . wait! No, I say! Anyway, the number of our series is there! Anyway, you understand. . . ."

Looking at his wife, Ivan Dmitritch gave a broad, senseless smile, like a baby when a bright object is shown it. His wife smiled too; it was as pleasant to her as to him that he only mentioned the series, and did not try to find out the number of the winning ticket. To torment and tantalize oneself with hopes of possible fortune is so sweet, so thrilling!

"It is our series," said Ivan Dmitritch, after a long silence. "So there is a probability that we have won. It's only a probability, but there it is!"

"Well, now look!"

"Wait a little. We have plenty of time to be disappointed. It's on the second line from the top, so the prize is seventy-five thousand. That's not money, but power, capital! And in a minute I shall look at the list, and there—26! Eh? I say, what if we really have won?"

The husband and wife began laughing and staring at one another in silence. The possibility of winning bewildered them; they could not have said, could not have dreamed, what they both needed that seventy-five thousand for, what they would buy, where they would go. They thought only of the figures 9,499 and 75,000 and pictured them in their imagination, while somehow they could not think of the happiness itself which was so possible.

Ivan Dmitritch, holding the paper in his hand, walked several times from corner to corner, and only when he had recovered from the first impression began dreaming a little.

"And if we have won," he said—"why, it will be a new life, it will be a transformation! The ticket is yours, but if it were mine I should, first of all, of course, spend twenty-five thousand on real property in the shape of an estate; ten thousand on immediate expenses, new furnishing . . . travelling . . . paying debts, and so on. . . . The other forty thousand I would put in the bank and get interest on it."

"Yes, an estate, that would be nice," said his wife, sitting down and dropping her hands in her lap.

"Somewhere in the Tula or Oryol provinces. . . . In the first place we shouldn't need a summer villa, and besides, it would always bring in an income."

And pictures came crowding on his imagination, each more gracious and poetical than the last. And in all these pictures he saw himself well-fed, serene, healthy, felt warm, even hot! Here, after eating a summer soup, cold as ice, he lay on his back on the burning sand close to a stream or in the garden under a lime tree. . . . It is hot. . . . His little boy and girl are crawling about near him, digging in the sand or catching ladybirds in the grass. He dozes sweetly, thinking of nothing, and feeling all over that he need not go to the office today, tomorrow, or the day after. Or, tired of lying still, he goes to the hayfield, or to the forest for mushrooms, or watches the peasants catching fish with a net. When the sun sets he takes a towel and soap and saunters to the bathing-shed, where he undresses at his leisure, slowly rubs his bare chest with his hands, and goes into the water. And in the water, near the opaque soapy circles, little fish flit to and fro and green water-weeds nod their heads. After bathing there is tea with cream and milk rolls. . . . In the evening a walk or *vint* with the neighbours.

"Yes, it would be nice to buy an estate," said his wife, also dreaming, and from her face it was evident that she was enchanted by her thoughts.

Ivan Dmitritch pictured to himself autumn with its rains, its cold evenings, and its St. Martin's summer. At that season he would have to take longer walks about the garden and beside the river, so as to get thoroughly chilled, and then drink a big glass of vodka and eat a salted mushroom or a soused cucumber, and then—drink another. . . . The children would come running from the kitchen garden, bringing a carrot and a radish smelling of fresh earth. . . . And then, he would lie stretched full length on the sofa, and in leisurely fashion turn over the pages of some illustrated magazine, or, covering his face with it and unbuttoning his waistcoat, give himself up to slumber.

The St. Martin's summer is followed by cloudy, gloomy weather. It rains day and night, the bare trees weep, the wind is damp and cold. The dogs, the horses, the fowls—all are wet, depressed, downcast. There is nowhere to walk; one can't go out for days together; one has to pace up and down the room, looking despondently at the grey window. It is dreary!

Ivan Dmitritch stopped and looked at his wife.

"I should go abroad, you know, Masha," he said.

And he began thinking how nice it would be in late autumn to go abroad somewhere to the South of France . . . to Italy . . . to India!

"I should certainly go abroad too," his wife said. "But look at the number of the ticket!"

"Wait, wait! . . ."

He walked about the room and went on thinking. It occurred to him: what if his wife really did go abroad? It is pleasant to travel alone, or in the society of light, careless women who live in the present, and not such as think and talk all the journey about nothing but their children, sigh, and tremble with dismay over every farthing. Ivan Dmitritch imagined his wife in the train with a multitude of parcels, baskets, and bags; she would be sighing over something, complaining that the train made her head ache, that she had spent so much money. . . . At the stations he would continually be having to run for boiling water, bread and butter. . . . She wouldn't have dinner because of its being too dear. . . .

"She would begrudge me every farthing," he thought, with a glance at his wife. "The lottery ticket is hers, not mine! Besides, what is the use of her going abroad? What does she want there? She would shut herself up in the hotel, and not let me out of her sight. . . . I know!"

And for the first time in his life his mind dwelt on the fact that his wife had grown elderly and plain, and that she was saturated through and through with the smell of cooking, while he was still young, fresh, and healthy, and might well have got married again.

"Of course, all that is silly nonsense," he thought; "but . . . why should she go abroad? What would she make of it? And yet she would go, of course. . . . I can fancy . . . In reality it is all one to her, whether it is Naples or Klin. She would only be in my way. I should be dependent upon her. I can fancy how, like a regular woman, she will lock the money up as soon as she gets it. . . . She will hide it from me. . . . She will look after her relations and grudge me every farthing."

Ivan Dmitritch thought of her relations. All those wretched brothers and sisters and aunts and uncles would come crawling about as soon as they heard of the winning ticket, would begin whining like beggars, and fawning upon them with oily, hypocritical smiles. Wretched, detestable people! If they were given anything, they would ask for more; while if they were refused, they would swear at them, slander them, and wish them every kind of misfortune.

Ivan Dmitritch remembered his own relations, and their faces, at which he had looked impartially in the past, struck him now as repulsive and hateful.

"They are such reptiles!" he thought.

And his wife's face, too, struck him as repulsive and hateful. Anger surged up in his heart against her, and he thought malignantly:

"She knows nothing about money, and so she is stingy. If she won it she would give me a hundred roubles, and put the rest away under lock and key."

And he looked at his wife, not with a smile now, but with hatred. She glanced at him too, and also with hatred and anger. She had her own daydreams, her own plans, her own reflections; she understood perfectly well what her husband's dreams were. She knew who would be the first to try and grab her winnings.

"It's very nice making daydreams at other people's expense!" is what her eyes expressed. "No, don't you dare!"

Her husband understood her look; hatred began stirring again in his breast, and in order to annoy his wife he glanced quickly, to spite her at the fourth page on the newspaper and read out triumphantly:

"Series 9,499, number 46! Not 26!"

Hatred and hope both disappeared at once, and it began immediately to seem to Ivan Dmitritch and his wife that their rooms were dark and small and low-pitched, that the supper they had been eating was not doing them good, but lying heavy on their stomachs, that the evenings were long and wearisome. . . .

"What the devil's the meaning of it?" said Ivan Dmitritch, beginning to be ill-humoured. "Wherever one steps there are bits of paper under one's feet, crumbs, husks. The rooms are never swept! One is simply forced to go out. Damnation take my soul entirely! I shall go and hang myself on the first aspen tree!"

Typhus

[First published on March 23, 1887.
Collected in *The Party and Other Stories* (1917).]

A young lieutenant called Klimov was travelling from Petersburg to Moscow in a smoking carriage of the mail train. Opposite him was sitting an elderly man with a shaven face like a sea captain's, by all appearances a well-to-do Finn or Swede. He pulled at his pipe the whole journey and kept talking about the same subject:

"Ha, you are an officer! I have a brother an officer too, only he is a naval officer. . . . He is a naval officer, and he is stationed at Kronstadt. Why are you going to Moscow?"

"I am serving there."

"Ha! And are you a family man?"

"No, I live with my sister and aunt."

"My brother's an officer, only he is a naval officer; he has a wife and three children. Ha!"

The Finn seemed continually surprised at something, and gave a broad idiotic grin when he exclaimed "Ha!" and continually puffed at his stinking pipe. Klimov, who for some reason did not feel well, and found it burdensome to answer questions, hated him with all his heart. He dreamed of how nice it would be to snatch the wheezing pipe out of his hand and fling it under the seat, and drive the Finn himself into another compartment.

"Detestable people these Finns and . . . Greeks," he thought. "Absolutely superfluous, useless, detestable people. They simply fill up space on the earthly globe. What are they for?"

121

And the thought of Finns and Greeks produced a feeling akin to sickness all over his body. For the sake of comparison he tried to think of the French, of the Italians, but his efforts to think of these people evoked in his mind, for some reason, nothing but images of organ-grinders, naked women, and the foreign oleographs which hung over the chest of drawers at home, at his aunt's.

Altogether the officer felt in an abnormal state. He could not arrange his arms and legs comfortably on the seat, though he had the whole seat to himself. His mouth felt dry and sticky; there was a heavy fog in his brain; his thoughts seemed to be straying, not only within his head, but outside his skull, among the seats and the people that were shrouded in the darkness of night. Through the mist in his brain, as through a dream, he heard the murmur of voices, the rumble of wheels, the slamming of doors. The sounds of the bells, the whistles, the guards, the running to and fro of passengers on the platforms, seemed more frequent than usual. The time flew by rapidly, imperceptibly, and so it seemed as though the train were stopping at stations every minute, and metallic voices crying continually:

"Is the mail ready?"

"Yes!" was repeatedly coming from outside.

It seemed as though the man in charge of the heating came in too often to look at the thermometer, that the noise of trains going in the opposite direction and the rumble of the wheels over the bridges was incessant. The noise, the whistles, the Finn, the tobacco smoke—all this mingling with the menace and flickering of the misty images in his brain, the shape and character of which a man in health can never recall, weighed upon Klimov like an unbearable nightmare. In horrible misery he lifted his heavy head, looked at the lamp in the rays of which shadows and misty blurs seemed to be dancing. He wanted to ask for water, but his parched tongue would hardly move, and he scarcely had strength to answer the Finn's questions. He tried to lie down more comfortably and go to sleep, but he could not succeed. The Finn several times fell asleep, woke up again, lighted his pipe, addressed him with his "Ha!" and went to sleep again; and still the lieutenant's legs could not get into a comfortable position, and still the menacing images stood facing him.

At Spirovo he went out into the station for a drink of water. He saw people sitting at the table and hurriedly eating.

"And how can they eat!" he thought, trying not to sniff the air, that smelt of roast meat, and not to look at the munching mouths—they both seemed to him sickeningly disgusting.

A good-looking lady was conversing loudly with a military man in a red cap, and showing magnificent white teeth as she smiled; and the smile, and the teeth, and the lady herself made on Klimov the same revolting impression as the ham and the rissoles. He could not understand how it was the military man in the red cap was not ill at ease, sitting beside her and looking at her healthy, smiling face.

When after drinking some water he went back to his carriage, the Finn was sitting smoking; his pipe was wheezing and squelching like a golosh with holes in it in wet weather.

"Ha!" he said, surprised; "what station is this?"

"I don't know," answered Klimov, lying down and shutting his mouth that he might not breathe the acrid tobacco smoke.

"And when shall we reach Tver?"

"I don't know. Excuse me, I . . . I can't answer. I am ill. I caught cold today."

The Finn knocked his pipe against the window-frame and began talking of his brother, the naval officer. Klimov no longer heard him; he was thinking miserably of his soft, comfortable bed, of a bottle of cold water, of his sister Katya, who was so good at making one comfortable, soothing, giving one water. He even smiled when the vision of his orderly Pavel, taking off his heavy stifling boots and putting water on the little table, flitted through his imagination. He fancied that if he could only get into his bed, have a drink of water, his nightmare would give place to sound healthy sleep.

"Is the mail ready?" a hollow voice reached him from the distance.

"Yes," answered a bass voice almost at the window.

It was already the second or third station from Spirovo.

The time was flying rapidly in leaps and bounds, and it seemed as though the bells, whistles, and stoppings would never end. In despair Klimov buried his face in the corner of the seat, clutched his head in his hands, and began again thinking of his sister Katya and his orderly Pavel, but his sister and his orderly were mixed up with the misty images in his brain, whirled round, and disappeared. His burning breath, reflected from the back of the seat, seemed to scald his face; his legs were uncomfortable; there was a draught from the window on his back; but, however wretched he was, he did not want to change his position. . . . A heavy nightmarish lethargy gradually gained possession of him and fettered his limbs.

When he brought himself to raise his head, it was already light in the carriage. The passengers were putting on their fur coats and moving about. The train was stopping. Porters in white aprons and with discs on their breasts were bustling among the passengers and snatching up their boxes. Klimov put on his great-coat, mechanically followed the other passengers out of the carriage, and it seemed to him that not he, but some one else was moving, and he felt that his fever, his thirst, and the menacing images which had not let him sleep all night, came out of the carriage with him. Mechanically he took his luggage and engaged a sledge-driver. The man asked him for a rouble and a quarter to drive to Povarsky Street, but he did not haggle, and without protest got submissively into the sledge. He still understood the difference of numbers, but money had ceased to have any value to him.

At home Klimov was met by his aunt and his sister Katya, a girl of eighteen. When Katya greeted him she had a pencil and exercise book in her hand, and he remembered that she was preparing for an examination as a teacher. Gasping with fever, he walked aimlessly through all the rooms without answering their questions or greetings, and when he reached his bed he sank down on the pillow. The Finn, the red cap, the lady with the white teeth, the smell of roast meat, the flickering blurs, filled his consciousness, and by now he did not know where he was and did not hear the agitated voices.

When he recovered consciousness he found himself in bed, undressed, saw a bottle of water and Pavel, but it was no cooler, nor softer, nor more comfortable for that. His arms and legs, as before, refused to lie comfortably; his tongue stuck to the roof of his mouth, and he heard the wheezing of the Finn's pipe. . . . A stalwart, black-bearded doctor was busy doing something beside the bed, brushing against Pavel with his broad back.

"It's all right, it's all right, young man," he muttered. "Excellent, excellent . . . goo-od, goo-od . . . !"

The doctor called Klimov "young man," said "goo-od" instead of "good" and "so-o" instead of "so."

"So-o . . . so-o . . . so-o," he murmured. "Goo-od, goo-od . . . ! Excellent, young man. You mustn't lose heart!"

The doctor's rapid, careless talk, his well-fed countenance, and condescending "young man," irritated Klimov.

"Why do you call me 'young man'?" he moaned. "What familiarity! Damn it all!"

And he was frightened by his own voice. The voice was so dried up, so weak and peevish, that he would not have known it.

"Excellent, excellent!" muttered the doctor, not in the least offended. . . . "You mustn't get angry, so-o, so-o, so-s. . . ."

And the time flew by at home with the same startling swiftness as in the railway carriage. The daylight was continually being replaced by the dusk of evening. The doctor seemed never to leave his bedside, and he heard at every moment his "so-o, so-o, so-o." A continual succession of people was incessantly crossing the bedroom. Among them were: Pavel, the Finn, Captain Yaroshevitch, Lance-Corporal Maximenko, the red cap, the lady with the white teeth, the doctor. They were all talking and waving their arms, smoking and eating. Once by daylight Klimov saw the chaplain of the regiment, Father Alexandr, who was standing before the bed, wearing a stole and with a prayer book in his hand. He was muttering something with a grave face such as Klimov had never seen in him before. The lieutenant remembered that Father Alexandr used in a friendly way to call all the Catholic officers "Poles," and wanting to amuse him, he cried:

"Father, Yaroshevitch the Pole has climbed up a pole!"

But Father Alexandr, a light-hearted man who loved a joke, did not smile, but became graver than ever, and made the sign of the cross over Klimov. At night-time by turn two shadows came noiselessly in and out; they were his aunt and sister. His sister's shadow knelt down and prayed; she bowed down to the ikon, and her grey shadow on the wall bowed down too, so that two shadows were praying. The whole time there was a smell of roast meat and the Finn's pipe, but once Klimov smelt the strong smell of incense. He felt so sick he could not lie still, and began shouting:

"The incense! Take away the incense!"

There was no answer. He could only hear the subdued singing of the priest somewhere and some one running upstairs.

When Klimov came to himself there was not a soul in his bedroom. The morning sun was streaming in at the window through the lower blind, and a quivering sunbeam, bright and keen as the sword's edge, was flashing on the glass bottle. He heard the rattle of wheels—so there was no snow now in the street. The lieutenant looked at the ray, at the familiar furniture, at the door, and the first thing he did was to laugh. His chest and stomach heaved with delicious, happy, tickling laughter. His whole body from head to foot was overcome by a sensation of infinite happiness and joy in life, such as the first man must have felt when he was created and first saw the world. Klimov felt a passionate desire for movement, people, talk. His body lay a motionless block; only his hands stirred, but that he hardly noticed, and his whole attention was concentrated on trifles. He rejoiced in his breathing, in his laughter, rejoiced in the existence of the water-bottle, the ceiling, the sunshine, the tape on the curtains. God's world, even in the narrow space of his bedroom, seemed beautiful, varied, grand. When the doctor made his appearance, the lieutenant was thinking what a delicious thing medicine was, how charming and pleasant the doctor was, and how nice and interesting people were in general.

"So-o, so, so . . . Excellent, excellent! . . . Now we are well again. . . . Goo-od, goo-od!" the doctor pattered.

The lieutenant listened and laughed joyously; he remembered the Finn, the lady with the white teeth, the train, and he longed to smoke, to eat.

"Doctor," he said, "tell them to give me a crust of rye bread and salt, and . . . and sardines."

The doctor refused; Pavel did not obey the order, and did not go for the bread. The lieutenant could not bear this and began crying like a naughty child.

"Baby!" laughed the doctor. "Mammy, bye-bye!"

Klimov laughed, too, and when the doctor went away he fell into a sound sleep. He woke up with the same joyfulness and sensation of happiness. His aunt was sitting near the bed.

"Well, aunt," he said joyfully. "What has been the matter?"

"Spotted typhus."

"Really. But now I am well, quite well! Where is Katya?"

"She is not at home. I suppose she has gone somewhere from her examination."

The old lady said this and looked at her stocking; her lips began quivering, she turned away, and suddenly broke into sobs. Forgetting the doctor's prohibition in her despair, she said:

"Ah, Katya, Katya! Our angel is gone! Is gone!"

She dropped her stocking and bent down to it, and as she did so her cap fell off her head. Looking at her grey head and understanding nothing, Klimov was frightened for Katya, and asked:

"Where is she, aunt?"

The old woman, who had forgotten Klimov and was thinking only of her sorrow, said:

"She caught typhus from you, and is dead. She was buried the day before yesterday."

This terrible, unexpected news was fully grasped by Klimov's consciousness; but terrible and startling as it was, it could not overcome the animal joy that filled the convalescent. He cried and laughed, and soon began scolding because they would not let him eat.

Only a week later when, leaning on Pavel, he went in his dressing gown to the window, looked at the overcast spring sky and listened to the unpleasant clang of the old iron rails which were being carted by, his heart ached, he burst into tears, and leaned his forehead against the window-frame.

"How miserable I am!" he muttered. "My God, how miserable!"

And joy gave way to the boredom of everyday life and the feeling of his irrevocable loss.

In Passion Week

[First published on March 30, 1887.
Collected in *The Cook's Wedding and Other Stories* (1922).]

"Go along, they are ringing already; and mind, don't be naughty in church or God will punish you."

My mother thrusts a few copper coins upon me, and, instantly forgetting about me, runs into the kitchen with an iron that needs reheating. I know well that after confession I shall not be allowed to eat or drink, and so, before leaving the house, I force myself to eat a crust of white bread, and to drink two glasses of water. It is quite spring in the street. The roads are all covered with brownish slush, in which future paths are already beginning to show; the roofs and sidewalks are dry; the fresh young green is piercing through the rotting grass of last year, under the fences. In the gutters there is the merry gurgling and foaming of dirty water, in which the sunbeams do not disdain to bathe. Chips, straws, the husks of sunflower seeds are carried rapidly along in the water, whirling round and sticking in the dirty foam. Where, where are those chips swimming to? It may well be that from the gutter they may pass into the river, from the river into the sea, and from the sea into the ocean. I try to imagine to myself that long terrible journey, but my fancy stops short before reaching the sea.

A cabman drives by. He clicks to his horse, tugs at the reins, and does not see that two street urchins are hanging on the back of his cab. I should like to join them, but think of confession, and the street urchins begin to seem to me great sinners.

"They will be asked on the day of judgment: 'Why did you play pranks and deceive the poor cabman?'" I think. "They will begin to defend themselves, but evil spirits will seize them, and drag them to fire everlasting. But if they obey their parents, and give the beggars a kopeck each, or a roll, God will have pity on them, and will let them into Paradise."

The church porch is dry and bathed in sunshine. There is not a soul in it. I open the door irresolutely and go into the church. Here, in the twilight which seems to me thick and gloomy as at no other time, I am overcome by the sense of sinfulness and insignificance. What strikes the eye first of all is a huge crucifix, and on one side of it the Mother of God, and on the other, St. John the Divine. The candelabra and the candlestands are draped in black mourning covers, the lamps glimmer dimly and faintly, and the sun seems intentionally to pass by the church windows. The Mother of God and the beloved disciple of Jesus Christ, depicted in profile, gaze in silence at the insufferable agony and do not observe my presence; I feel that to them I am alien, superfluous, unnoticed, that I can be no help to them by word or deed, that I am a loathsome, dishonest boy, only capable of mischief, rudeness, and tale-bearing. I think of all the people I know, and they all seem to me petty, stupid, and wicked, and incapable of bringing one drop of relief to that intolerable sorrow which I now behold.

The twilight of the church grows darker and more gloomy. And the Mother of God and St. John look lonely and forlorn to me.

Prokofy Ignatitch, a veteran soldier, the church verger's assistant, is standing behind the candle cupboard. Raising his eyebrows and stroking his beard he explains in a half-whisper to an old woman: "Matins will be in the evening today, directly after vespers. And they will ring for the 'hours' tomorrow between seven and eight. Do you understand? Between seven and eight."

Between the two broad columns on the right, where the chapel of Varvara the Martyr begins, those who are going to confess stand beside the screen, awaiting their turn. And Mitka is there too—a ragged boy with his head hideously cropped, with ears that jut out, and little spiteful eyes. He is the son of Nastasya the charwoman, and is a bully and a ruffian who snatches apples from the women's baskets, and has more than once carried off my knuckle bones. He looks at me angrily, and I fancy takes a spiteful pleasure in the fact that he, not I, will first go behind the screen. I feel boiling over with resentment, I try not to look at him, and, at the bottom of my heart, I am vexed that this wretched boy's sins will soon be forgiven.

In front of him stands a grandly dressed, beautiful lady, wearing a hat with a white feather. She is noticeably agitated, is waiting in strained suspense, and one of her cheeks is flushed red with excitement.

I wait for five minutes, for ten . . . A well-dressed young man with a long thin neck, and rubber goloshes, comes out from behind the screen. I begin dreaming how, when I am grown up, I will buy goloshes exactly like them. I certainly will! The lady shudders and goes behind the screen. It is her turn.

In the crack, between the two panels of the screen, I can see the lady go up to the lectern and bow down to the ground, then get up, and, without looking at the priest, bow her head in anticipation. The priest stands with his back to the screen, and so I can only see his grey curly head, the chain of the cross on his chest, and his broad back. His face is not visible. Heaving a sigh, and not looking at the lady, he begins speaking rapidly, shaking his head, alternately raising and dropping his whispering voice. The lady listens meekly as though conscious of guilt, answers meekly, and looks at the floor.

"In what way can she be sinful?" I wonder, looking reverently at her gentle, beautiful face. "God forgive her sins, God send her happiness." But now the priest covers her head with the stole. "And I, unworthy priest . . ." I hear his voice, ". . . by His power given unto me, do forgive and absolve thee from all thy sins . . ."

The lady bows down to the ground, kisses the cross, and comes back. Both her cheeks are flushed now, but her face is calm and serene and cheerful.

"She is happy now," I think to myself, looking first at her and then at the priest who had forgiven her sins. "But how happy the man must be who has the right to forgive sins!"

Now it is Mitka's turn, but a feeling of hatred for that young ruffian suddenly boils up in me. I want to go behind the screen before him, I want to be the first. Noticing my movement he hits me on the head with his candle, I respond by doing the same, and, for half a minute, there is a sound of panting, and, as it were, of someone breaking candles . . . We are separated. My foe goes timidly up to the lectern, and bows down to the floor without bending his knees, but I do not see what happens after that; the thought that my turn is coming after Mitka's makes everything grow blurred and confused before my eyes; Mitka's protruding ears grow large, and melt into his dark head, the priest sways, the floor seems to be undulating . . .

The priest's voice is audible: "And I, unworthy priest . . ."

Now I too move behind the screen. I do not feel the ground under my feet, it is as though I were walking on air . . . I go up to the lectern which is taller than I am. For a minute I have a glimpse of the indifferent, exhausted face of the priest. But after that I see nothing but his sleeve with its blue lining, the cross, and the edge of the lectern. I am conscious of the close proximity of the priest, the smell of his cassock; I hear his stern voice, and my cheek turned towards him begins to burn . . . I am so troubled that I miss a great deal that he says, but I answer his questions sincerely in an unnatural voice, not my own. I think of the forlorn figures of the Holy Mother and St. John the Divine, the crucifix, my mother, and I want to cry and beg forgiveness.

"What is your name?" the priest asks me, covering my head with the soft stole.

How light-hearted I am now, with joy in my soul!

I have no sins now, I am holy, I have the right to enter Paradise! I fancy that I already smell like the cassock. I go from behind the screen to the deacon to enter my name, and sniff at my sleeves. The dusk of the church no longer seems gloomy, and I look indifferently, without malice, at Mitka.

"What is your name?" the deacon asks.

"Fedya."

"And your name from your father?"

"I don't know."

"What is your papa's name?"

"Ivan Petrovitch."

"And your surname?"

I make no answer.

"How old are you?"

"Nearly nine."

When I get home I go to bed quickly, that I may not see them eating supper; and, shutting my eyes, dream of how fine it would be to endure martyrdom at the hands of some Herod or Dioskorus, to live in the desert, and, like St. Serafim, feed the bears, live in a cell, and eat nothing but holy bread, give my property to the poor, go on a pilgrimage to Kiev. I hear them laying the table in the dining room—they are going to have supper, they will eat salad, cabbage pies, fried and baked fish. How hungry I am! I would consent to endure any martyrdom, to live in the desert without my mother, to feed bears out of my own hands, if only I might first eat just one cabbage pie!

"Lord, purify me a sinner," I pray, covering my head over. "Guardian angel, save me from the unclean spirit."

The next day, Thursday, I wake up with my heart as pure and clean as a fine spring day. I go gaily and boldly into the church, feeling that I am a communicant, that I have a splendid and expensive shirt on, made out of a silk dress left by my grandmother. In the church everything has an air of joy, happiness, and spring. The faces of the Mother of God and St. John the Divine are not so sorrowful as yesterday. The faces of the communicants are radiant with hope, and it seems as though all the past is forgotten, all is forgiven. Mitka, too, has combed his hair, and is dressed in his best. I look gaily at his protruding ears, and to show that I have nothing against him, I say:

"You look nice today, and if your hair did not stand up so, and you weren't so poorly dressed, everybody would think that your mother was not a washerwoman but a lady. Come to me at Easter, we will play knuckle bones."

Mitka looks at me mistrustfully, and shakes his fist at me on the sly.

And the lady I saw yesterday looks lovely. She is wearing a light blue dress, and a big sparkling brooch in the shape of a horseshoe. I admire her, and think that, when I am grown up, I will certainly marry a woman like that, but remembering that getting married is shameful, I leave off thinking about it, and go into the choir where the deacon is already reading the 'hours.'

A Happy Ending

[First published on July 25, 1887.
Collected in *The Horse-Stealers and Other Stories* (1921).]

Lyubov Grigoryevna, a substantial, buxom lady of forty who undertook matchmaking and many other matters of which it is usual to speak only in whispers, had come to see Stytchkin, the head guard, on a day when he was off duty. Stytchkin, somewhat embarrassed, but, as always, grave, practical, and severe, was walking up and down the room, smoking a cigar and saying:

"Very pleased to make your acquaintance. Semyon Ivanovitch recommended you on the ground that you may be able to assist me in a delicate and very important matter affecting the happiness of my life. I have, Lyubov Grigoryevna, reached the age of fifty-two; that is a period of life at which very many have already grown-up children. My position is a secure one. Though my fortune is not large, yet I am in a position to support a beloved being and children at my side. I may tell you between ourselves that apart from my salary I have also money in the bank which my manner of living has enabled me to save. I am a practical and sober man, I lead a sensible and consistent life, so that I may hold myself up as an example to many. But one thing I lack—a domestic hearth of my own and a partner in life, and I live like a wandering Magyar, moving from place to place without any satisfaction. I have no one with whom to take counsel, and when I am ill no one to give me water, and so on. Apart from that, Lyubov Grigoryevna, a married man has always more weight in society than a bachelor. . . . I am a man of the educated class, with money, but if you look at me from a point of view, what am I? A man with no kith and kin, no better than some Polish priest. And therefore I should be very desirous to be united in the bonds of Hymen—that is, to enter into matrimony with some worthy person."

"An excellent thing," said the matchmaker, with a sigh.

"I am a solitary man and in this town I know no one. Where can I go, and to whom can I apply, since all the people here are strangers to me? That is why Semyon Ivanovitch advised me to address myself to a person who is a specialist in this line, and makes the arrangement of the happiness of others her profession. And therefore I most earnestly beg you, Lyubov Grigoryevna, to assist me in ordering my future. You know all the marriageable young ladies in the town, and it is easy for you to accommodate me."

"I can...."

"A glass of wine, I beg you...."

With an habitual gesture the matchmaker raised her glass to her mouth and tossed it off without winking.

"I can," she repeated. "And what sort of bride would you like, Nikolay Nikolayitch?"

"Should I like? The bride fate sends me."

"Well, of course it depends on your fate, but everyone has his own taste, you know. One likes dark ladies, the other prefers fair ones."

"You see, Lyubov Grigoryevna," said Stytchkin, sighing sedately, "I am a practical man and a man of character; for me beauty and external appearance generally take a secondary place, for, as you know yourself, beauty is neither bowl nor platter, and a pretty wife involves a great deal of anxiety. The way I look at it is, what matters most in a woman is not what is external, but what lies within—that is, that she should have soul and all the qualities. A glass of wine, I beg. . . . Of course, it would be very agreeable that one's wife should be rather plump, but for mutual happiness it is not of great consequence; what matters is the mind. Properly speaking, a woman does not need mind either, for if she has brains she will have too high an opinion of herself, and take all sorts of ideas into her head. One cannot do without education nowadays, of course, but education is of different kinds. It would be pleasing for one's wife to know French and German, to speak various languages, very pleasing; but what's the use of that if she can't sew on one's buttons, perhaps? I am a man of the educated class: I am just as much at home, I may say, with Prince Kanitelin as I am with you here now. But my habits are simple, and I want a girl who is not too much a fine lady. Above all, she must have respect for me and feel that I have made her happiness."

"To be sure."

"Well, now as regards the essential. . . . I do not want a wealthy bride; I would never condescend to anything so low as to marry for money. I desire not to be kept by my wife, but to keep her, and that she may be sensible of it. But I do not want a poor girl either. Though I am a man of means, and am marrying not from mercenary motives, but from love, yet I cannot take a poor girl, for, as you know yourself, prices have gone up so, and there will be children."

"One might find one with a dowry," said the matchmaker.

"A glass of wine, I beg. . . ."

There was a pause of five minutes.

The matchmaker heaved a sigh, took a sidelong glance at the guard, and asked:

"Well, now, my good sir . . . do you want anything in the bachelor line? I have some fine bargains. One is a French girl and one is a Greek. Well worth the money."

The guard thought a moment and said:

"No, I thank you. In view of your favourable disposition, allow me to enquire now how much you ask for your exertions in regard to a bride?"

"I don't ask much. Give me twenty-five roubles and the stuff for a dress, as is usual, and I will say thank you . . . but for the dowry, that's a different account."

Stytchkin folded his arms over his chest and fell to pondering in silence. After some thought he heaved a sigh and said:

"That's dear. . . ."

"It's not at all dear, Nikolay Nikolayitch! In old days when there were lots of weddings one did do it cheaper, but nowadays what are our earnings? If you make fifty roubles in a month that is not a fast, you may be thankful. It's not on weddings we make our money, my good sir."

Stytchkin looked at the matchmaker in amazement and shrugged his shoulders.

"H'm! . . . Do you call fifty roubles little?" he asked.

"Of course it is little! In old days we sometimes made more than a hundred."

"H'm! I should never have thought it was possible to earn such a sum by these jobs. Fifty roubles! It is not every man that earns as much! Pray drink your wine. . . ."

The matchmaker drained her glass without winking. Stytchkin looked her over from head to foot in silence, then said:

"Fifty roubles. . . . Why, that is six hundred roubles a year. . . . Please take some more . . . With such dividends, you know, Lyubov Grigoryevna, you would have no difficulty in making a match for yourself. . . ."

"For myself," laughed the matchmaker, "I am an old woman."

"Not at all. . . . You have such a figure, and your face is plump and fair, and all the rest of it."

The matchmaker was embarrassed. Stytchkin was also embarrassed and sat down beside her.

"You are still very attractive," said he; "if you met with a practical, steady, careful husband, with his salary and your earnings you might even attract him very much, and you'd get on very well together. . . ."

"Goodness knows what you are saying, Nikolay Nikolayitch."

"Well, I meant no harm. . . ."

A silence followed. Stytchkin began loudly blowing his nose, while the matchmaker turned crimson, and looking bashfully at him, asked:

"And how much do you get, Nikolay Nikolayitch?"

"I? Seventy-five roubles, besides tips. . . . Apart from that we make something out of candles and hares."

"You go hunting, then?"

"No. Passengers who travel without tickets are called hares with us."

Another minute passed in silence. Stytchkin got up and walked about the room in excitement.

"I don't want a young wife," said he. "I am a middle-aged man, and I want someone who . . . as it might be like you . . . staid and settled and a figure something like yours. . . ."

"Goodness knows what you are saying . . ." giggled the matchmaker, hiding her crimson face in her kerchief.

"There is no need to be long thinking about it. You are after my own heart, and you suit me in your qualities. I am a practical, sober man, and if you like me . . . what could be better? Allow me to make you a proposal!"

The matchmaker dropped a tear, laughed, and, in token of her consent, clinked glasses with Stytchkin.

"Well," said the happy railway guard, "now allow me to explain to you the behaviour and manner of life I desire from you. . . . I am a strict, respectable, practical man. I take a gentlemanly view of everything. And I desire that my wife should be strict also, and should understand that to her I am a benefactor and the foremost person in the world."

He sat down, and, heaving a deep sigh, began expounding to his bride-elect his views on domestic life and a wife's duties.

A Story without a Title

[Written in December 1887. First published under the title
'Fairy tale' in the Russian newspaper *Novoye Vremya* on January 1, 1888.
Collected in *The Horse-Stealers and Other Stories* (1921).]

In the fifth century, just as now, the sun rose every morning and every
evening retired to rest. In the morning, when the first rays kissed the dew,
the earth revived, the air was filled with the sounds of rapture and hope;
while in the evening the same earth subsided into silence and plunged into
gloomy darkness. One day was like another, one night like another. From
time to time a storm cloud raced up and there was the angry rumble of
thunder, or a negligent star fell out of the sky, or a pale monk ran to tell
the brotherhood that not far from the monastery he had seen a tiger—
and that was all, and then each day was like the next.

The monks worked and prayed, and their Father Superior played on
the organ, made Latin verses, and wrote music. The wonderful old man
possessed an extraordinary gift. He played on the organ with such art
that even the oldest monks, whose hearing had grown somewhat dull
towards the end of their lives, could not restrain their tears when the
sounds of the organ floated from his cell. When he spoke of anything,
even of the most ordinary things—for instance of the trees, of the wild
beasts, or of the sea—they could not listen to him without a smile or
tears, and it seemed that the same chords vibrated in his soul as in the
organ. If he were moved to anger or abandoned himself to intense joy,
or began speaking of something terrible or grand, then a passionate
inspiration took possession of him, tears came into his flashing eyes,
his face flushed, and his voice thundered, and as the monks listened to

him they felt that their souls were spellbound by his inspiration; at such marvellous, splendid moments his power over them was boundless, and if he had bidden his elders fling themselves into the sea, they would all, every one of them, have hastened to carry out his wishes.

His music, his voice, his poetry in which he glorified God, the heavens and the earth, were a continual source of joy to the monks. It sometimes happened that through the monotony of their lives they grew weary of the trees, the flowers, the spring, the autumn, their ears were tired of the sound of the sea, and the song of the birds seemed tedious to them, but the talents of their Father Superior were as necessary to them as their daily bread.

Dozens of years passed by, and every day was like every other day, every night was like every other night. Except the birds and the wild beasts, not one soul appeared near the monastery. The nearest human habitation was far away, and to reach it from the monastery, or to reach the monastery from it, meant a journey of over seventy miles across the desert. Only men who despised life, who had renounced it, and who came to the monastery as to the grave, ventured to cross the desert.

What was the amazement of the monks, therefore, when one night there knocked at their gate a man who turned out to be from the town, and the most ordinary sinner who loved life. Before saying his prayers and asking for the Father Superior's blessing, this man asked for wine and food. To the question how he had come from the town into the desert, he answered by a long story of hunting; he had gone out hunting, had drunk too much, and lost his way. To the suggestion that he should enter the monastery and save his soul, he replied with a smile: "I am not a fit companion for you!"

When he had eaten and drunk he looked at the monks who were serving him, shook his head reproachfully, and said:

"You don't do anything, you monks. You are good for nothing but eating and drinking. Is that the way to save one's soul? Only think, while you sit here in peace, eat and drink and dream of beatitude, your neighbours are perishing and going to hell. You should see what is going on in the town! Some are dying of hunger, others, not knowing what to do with their gold, sink into profligacy and perish like flies stuck in honey. There is no faith, no truth in men. Whose task is it to save them? Whose work is it to preach to them? It is not for me, drunk from morning till

139

night as I am. Can a meek spirit, a loving heart, and faith in God have been given you for you to sit here within four walls doing nothing?"

The townsman's drunken words were insolent and unseemly, but they had a strange effect upon the Father Superior. The old man exchanged glances with his monks, turned pale, and said:

"My brothers, he speaks the truth, you know. Indeed, poor people in their weakness and lack of understanding are perishing in vice and infidelity, while we do not move, as though it did not concern us. Why should I not go and remind them of the Christ whom they have forgotten?"

The townsman's words had carried the old man away. The next day he took his staff, said farewell to the brotherhood, and set off for the town. And the monks were left without music, and without his speeches and verses. They spent a month drearily, then a second, but the old man did not come back. At last after three months had passed the familiar tap of his staff was heard. The monks flew to meet him and showered questions upon him, but instead of being delighted to see them he wept bitterly and did not utter a word. The monks noticed that he looked greatly aged and had grown thinner; his face looked exhausted and wore an expression of profound sadness, and when he wept he had the air of a man who has been outraged.

The monks fell to weeping too, and began asking him with sympathy why he was weeping, why his face was so gloomy, but he locked himself in his cell without uttering a word. For seven days he sat in his cell, eating and drinking nothing, weeping and not playing on his organ. To knocking at his door and to the entreaties of the monks to come out and share his grief with them he replied with unbroken silence.

At last he came out. Gathering all the monks around him, with a tear-stained face and with an expression of grief and indignation, he began telling them of what had befallen him during those three months. His voice was calm and his eyes were smiling while he described his journey from the monastery to the town. On the road, he told them, the birds sang to him, the brooks gurgled, and sweet youthful hopes agitated his soul; he marched on and felt like a soldier going to battle and confident of victory; he walked on dreaming, and composed poems and hymns, and reached the end of his journey without noticing it.

But his voice quivered, his eyes flashed, and he was full of wrath when he came to speak of the town and of the men in it. Never in his life had he seen or even dared to imagine what he met with when he went into the town. Only then for the first time in his life, in his old age, he saw and understood how powerful was the devil, how fair was evil and how weak and faint-hearted and worthless were men. By an unhappy chance the first dwelling he entered was the abode of vice. Some fifty men in possession of much money were eating and drinking wine beyond measure. Intoxicated by the wine, they sang songs and boldly uttered terrible, revolting words such as a God-fearing man could not bring himself to pronounce; boundlessly free, self-confident, and happy, they feared neither God nor the devil, nor death, but said and did what they liked, and went whither their lust led them. And the wine, clear as amber, flecked with sparks of gold, must have been irresistibly sweet and fragrant, for each man who drank it smiled blissfully and wanted to drink more. To the smile of man it responded with a smile and sparkled joyfully when they drank it, as though it knew the devilish charm it kept hidden in its sweetness.

The old man, growing more and more incensed and weeping with wrath, went on to describe what he had seen. On a table in the midst of the revellers, he said, stood a sinful, half-naked woman. It was hard to imagine or to find in nature anything more lovely and fascinating. This reptile, young, long-haired, dark-skinned, with black eyes and full lips, shameless and insolent, showed her snow-white teeth and smiled as though to say: "Look how shameless, how beautiful I am." Silk and brocade fell in lovely folds from her shoulders, but her beauty would not hide itself under her clothes, but eagerly thrust itself through the folds, like the young grass through the ground in spring. The shameless woman drank wine, sang songs, and abandoned herself to anyone who wanted her.

Then the old man, wrathfully brandishing his arms, described the horse races, the bullfights, the theatres, the artists' studios where they painted naked women or moulded them of clay. He spoke with inspiration, with sonorous beauty, as though he were playing on unseen chords, while the monks, petrified, greedily drank in his words and gasped with rapture. . . .

After describing all the charms of the devil, the beauty of evil, and the fascinating grace of the dreadful female form, the old man cursed the devil, turned and shut himself up in his cell. . . .

When he came out of his cell in the morning there was not a monk left in the monastery; they had all fled to the town.

Sleepy

[First published in the Russian newspaper *Peterburgskaya Gazeta*
(*St. Petersburg Gazette*) in January 1888. Revised and collected in
Moody People (1890). Collected in *The Cook's Wedding and Other Stories* (1922).
Also translated as 'Sleepyhead' by R. E. C. Long.]

Night. Varka, the little nurse, a girl of thirteen, is rocking the cradle in which the baby is lying, and humming hardly audibly:

> *"Hush-a-bye, my baby wee,*
> *While I sing a song for thee."*

A little green lamp is burning before the ikon; there is a string stretched from one end of the room to the other, on which baby-clothes and a pair of big black trousers are hanging. There is a big patch of green on the ceiling from the ikon lamp, and the baby-clothes and the trousers throw long shadows on the stove, on the cradle, and on Varka. . . . When the lamp begins to flicker, the green patch and the shadows come to life, and are set in motion, as though by the wind. It is stuffy. There is a smell of cabbage soup, and of the inside of a boot-shop.

The baby's crying. For a long while he has been hoarse and exhausted with crying; but he still goes on screaming, and there is no knowing when he will stop. And Varka is sleepy. Her eyes are glued together, her head droops, her neck aches. She cannot move her eyelids or her lips, and she feels as though her face is dried and wooden, as though her head has become as small as the head of a pin.

"Hush-a-bye, my baby wee," she hums, "while I cook the groats for thee. . . ."

A cricket is churring in the stove. Through the door in the next room the master and the apprentice Afanasy are snoring. . . . The cradle creaks plaintively, Varka murmurs—and it all blends into that soothing music of the night to which it is so sweet to listen, when one is lying in bed. Now that music is merely irritating and oppressive, because it goads her to sleep, and she must not sleep; if Varka—God forbid!—should fall asleep, her master and mistress would beat her.

The lamp flickers. The patch of green and the shadows are set in motion, forcing themselves on Varka's fixed, half-open eyes, and in her half slumbering brain are fashioned into misty visions. She sees dark clouds chasing one another over the sky, and screaming like the baby. But then the wind blows, the clouds are gone, and Varka sees a broad high road covered with liquid mud; along the high road stretch files of wagons, while people with wallets on their backs are trudging along and shadows flit backwards and forwards; on both sides she can see forests through the cold harsh mist. All at once the people with their wallets and their shadows fall on the ground in the liquid mud. "What is that for?" Varka asks. "To sleep, to sleep!" they answer her. And they fall sound asleep, and sleep sweetly, while crows and magpies sit on the telegraph wires, scream like the baby, and try to wake them.

"Hush-a-bye, my baby wee, and I will sing a song to thee," murmurs Varka, and now she sees herself in a dark stuffy hut.

Her dead father, Yefim Stepanov, is tossing from side to side on the floor. She does not see him, but she hears him moaning and rolling on the floor from pain. "His guts have burst," as he says; the pain is so violent that he cannot utter a single word, and can only draw in his breath and clack his teeth like the rattling of a drum:

"Boo—boo—boo—boo. . . ."

Her mother, Pelageya, has run to the master's house to say that Yefim is dying. She has been gone a long time, and ought to be back. Varka lies awake on the stove, and hears her father's "boo—boo—boo." And then she hears someone has driven up to the hut. It is a young doctor from the town, who has been sent from the big house where he is staying on a visit. The doctor comes into the hut; he cannot be seen in the darkness, but he can be heard coughing and rattling the door.

"Light a candle," he says.

"Boo—boo—boo," answers Yefim.

Pelageya rushes to the stove and begins looking for the broken pot with the matches. A minute passes in silence. The doctor, feeling in his pocket, lights a match.

"In a minute, sir, in a minute," says Pelageya. She rushes out of the hut, and soon afterwards comes back with a bit of candle.

Yefim's cheeks are rosy and his eyes are shining, and there is a peculiar keenness in his glance, as though he were seeing right through the hut and the doctor.

"Come, what is it? What are you thinking about?" says the doctor, bending down to him. "Aha! have you had this long?"

"What? Dying, your honour, my hour has come. . . . I am not to stay among the living."

"Don't talk nonsense! We will cure you!"

"That's as you please, your honour, we humbly thank you, only we understand. . . . Since death has come, there it is."

The doctor spends a quarter of an hour over Yefim, then he gets up and says:

"I can do nothing. You must go into the hospital, there they will operate on you. Go at once . . . You must go! It's rather late, they will all be asleep in the hospital, but that doesn't matter, I will give you a note. Do you hear?"

"Kind sir, but what can he go in?" says Pelageya. "We have no horse."

"Never mind. I'll ask your master, he'll let you have a horse."

The doctor goes away, the candle goes out, and again there is the sound of "boo—boo—boo." Half an hour later someone drives up to the hut. A cart has been sent to take Yefim to the hospital. He gets ready and goes. . . .

But now it is a clear bright morning. Pelageya is not at home; she has gone to the hospital to find what is being done to Yefim. Somewhere there is a baby crying, and Varka hears someone singing with her own voice:

"Hush-a-bye, my baby wee, I will sing a song to thee."

Pelageya comes back; she crosses herself and whispers:

"They put him to rights in the night, but towards morning he gave up his soul to God. . . . The Kingdom of Heaven be his and peace everlasting. . . . They say he was taken too late. . . . He ought to have gone sooner. . . ."

Varka goes out into the road and cries there, but all at once someone hits her on the back of her head so hard that her forehead knocks against a birch tree. She raises her eyes, and sees facing her, her master, the shoemaker.

"What are you about, you scabby slut?" he says. "The child is crying, and you are asleep!"

He gives her a sharp slap behind the ear, and she shakes her head, rocks the cradle, and murmurs her song. The green patch and the shadows from the trousers and the baby-clothes move up and down, nod to her, and soon take possession of her brain again. Again she sees the high road covered with liquid mud. The people with wallets on their backs and the shadows have lain down and are fast asleep. Looking at them, Varka has a passionate longing for sleep; she would lie down with enjoyment, but her mother Pelageya is walking beside her, hurrying her on. They are hastening together to the town to find situations.

"Give alms, for Christ's sake!" her mother begs of the people they meet. "Show us the Divine Mercy, kind-hearted gentlefolk!"

"Give the baby here!" a familiar voice answers. "Give the baby here!" the same voice repeats, this time harshly and angrily. "Are you asleep, you wretched girl?"

Varka jumps up, and looking round grasps what is the matter: there is no high road, no Pelageya, no people meeting them, there is only her mistress, who has come to feed the baby, and is standing in the middle of the room. While the stout, broad-shouldered woman nurses the child and soothes it, Varka stands looking at her and waiting till she has done. And outside the windows the air is already turning blue, the shadows and the green patch on the ceiling are visibly growing pale, it will soon be morning.

"Take him," says her mistress, buttoning up her chemise over her bosom; "he is crying. He must be bewitched."

Varka takes the baby, puts him in the cradle and begins rocking it again. The green patch and the shadows gradually disappear, and now there is nothing to force itself on her eyes and cloud her brain. But she is as sleepy as before, fearfully sleepy! Varka lays her head on the edge of the cradle, and rocks her whole body to overcome her sleepiness, but yet her eyes are glued together, and her head is heavy.

"Varka, heat the stove!" she hears the master's voice through the door.

So it is time to get up and set to work. Varka leaves the cradle, and runs to the shed for firewood. She is glad. When one moves and runs about, one is not so sleepy as when one is sitting down. She brings the wood, heats the stove, and feels that her wooden face is getting supple again, and that her thoughts are growing clearer.

"Varka, set the samovar!" shouts her mistress.

Varka splits a piece of wood, but has scarcely time to light the splinters and put them in the samovar, when she hears a fresh order:

"Varka, clean the master's goloshes!"

She sits down on the floor, cleans the goloshes, and thinks how nice it would be to put her head into a big deep golosh, and have a little nap in it. . . . And all at once the golosh grows, swells, fills up the whole room. Varka drops the brush, but at once shakes her head, opens her eyes wide, and tries to look at things so that they may not grow big and move before her eyes.

"Varka, wash the steps outside; I am ashamed for the customers to see them!"

Varka washes the steps, sweeps and dusts the rooms, then heats another stove and runs to the shop. There is a great deal of work: she hasn't one minute free.

But nothing is so hard as standing in the same place at the kitchen table peeling potatoes. Her head droops over the table, the potatoes dance before her eyes, the knife tumbles out of her hand while her fat, angry mistress is moving about near her with her sleeves tucked up, talking so loud that it makes a ringing in Varka's ears. It is agonising, too, to wait at dinner, to wash, to sew, there are minutes when she longs to flop on to the floor regardless of everything, and to sleep.

The day passes. Seeing the windows getting dark, Varka presses her temples that feel as though they were made of wood, and smiles, though she does not know why. The dusk of evening caresses her eyes that will hardly keep open, and promises her sound sleep soon. In the evening visitors come.

"Varka, set the samovar!" shouts her mistress. The samovar is a little one, and before the visitors have drunk all the tea they want, she has to heat it five times. After tea Varka stands for a whole hour on the same spot, looking at the visitors, and waiting for orders.

"Varka, run and buy three bottles of beer!"

She starts off, and tries to run as quickly as she can, to drive away sleep.

"Varka, fetch some vodka! Varka, where's the corkscrew? Varka, clean a herring!"

But now, at last, the visitors have gone; the lights are put out, the master and mistress go to bed.

"Varka, rock the baby!" she hears the last order.

The cricket churrs in the stove; the green patch on the ceiling and the shadows from the trousers and the baby-clothes force themselves on Varka's half-opened eyes again, wink at her and cloud her mind.

"Hush-a-bye, my baby wee," she murmurs, "and I will sing a song to thee."

And the baby screams, and is worn out with screaming. Again Varka sees the muddy high road, the people with wallets, her mother Pelageya, her father Yefim. She understands everything, she recognises everyone, but through her half sleep she cannot understand the force which binds her, hand and foot, weighs upon her, and prevents her from living. She looks round, searches for that force that she may escape from it, but she cannot find it. At last, tired to death, she does her very utmost, strains her eyes, looks up at the flickering green patch, and listening to the screaming, finds the foe who will not let her live.

That foe is the baby.

She laughs. It seems strange to her that she has failed to grasp such a simple thing before. The green patch, the shadows, and the cricket seem to laugh and wonder too.

The hallucination takes possession of Varka. She gets up from her stool, and with a broad smile on her face and wide unbDlinking eyes, she walks up and down the room. She feels pleased and tickled at the thought that she will be rid directly of the baby that binds her hand and foot. . . . Kill the baby and then sleep, sleep, sleep. . . .

Laughing and winking and shaking her fingers at the green patch, Varka steals up to the cradle and bends over the baby. When she has strangled him, she quickly lies down on the floor, laughs with delight that she can sleep, and in a minute is sleeping as sound as the dead.

The Bet

[Written in December 1888. First published in
No. 4613 issue of *Novoye Vremya*, a Russian newspaper,
on January 1, 1889, titled 'Fairy tale.' The story was revised
and included in *Chekhov's Collected Works* published by
Adolf Marks with the title 'The Bet.']

It was a dark autumn night. The old banker was walking up and down his study and remembering how, fifteen years before, he had given a party one autumn evening. There had been many clever men there, and there had been interesting conversations. Among other things they had talked of capital punishment. The majority of the guests, among whom were many journalists and intellectual men, disapproved of the death penalty. They considered that form of punishment out of date, immoral, and unsuitable for Christian States. In the opinion of some of them the death penalty ought to be replaced everywhere by imprisonment for life.

"I don't agree with you," said their host the banker. "I have not tried either the death penalty or imprisonment for life, but if one may judge *a priori*, the death penalty is more moral and more humane than imprisonment for life. Capital punishment kills a man at once, but lifelong imprisonment kills him slowly. Which executioner is the more humane, he who kills you in a few minutes or he who drags the life out of you in the course of many years?"

"Both are equally immoral," observed one of the guests, "for they both have the same object—to take away life. The State is not God. It has not the right to take away what it cannot restore when it wants to."

Among the guests was a young lawyer, a young man of five-and-twenty. When he was asked his opinion, he said:

"The death sentence and the life sentence are equally immoral, but if I had to choose between the death penalty and imprisonment for life, I would certainly choose the second. To live anyhow is better than not at all."

A lively discussion arose. The banker, who was younger and more nervous in those days, was suddenly carried away by excitement; he struck the table with his fist and shouted at the young man:

"It's not true! I'll bet you two millions you wouldn't stay in solitary confinement for five years."

"If you mean that in earnest," said the young man, "I'll take the bet, but I would stay not five but fifteen years."

"Fifteen? Done!" cried the banker. "Gentlemen, I stake two millions!"

"Agreed! You stake your millions and I stake my freedom!" said the young man.

And this wild, senseless bet was carried out! The banker, spoilt and frivolous, with millions beyond his reckoning, was delighted at the bet. At supper he made fun of the young man, and said:

"Think better of it, young man, while there is still time. To me two millions are a trifle, but you are losing three or four of the best years of your life. I say three or four, because you won't stay longer. Don't forget either, you unhappy man, that voluntary confinement is a great deal harder to bear than compulsory. The thought that you have the right to step out in liberty at any moment will poison your whole existence in prison. I am sorry for you."

And now the banker, walking to and fro, remembered all this, and asked himself: "What was the object of that bet? What is the good of that man's losing fifteen years of his life and my throwing away two millions? Can it prove that the death penalty is better or worse than imprisonment for life? No, no. It was all nonsensical and meaningless. On my part it was the caprice of a pampered man, and on his part simple greed for money. . . ."

Then he remembered what followed that evening. It was decided that the young man should spend the years of his captivity under the strictest supervision in one of the lodges in the banker's garden. It was agreed that for fifteen years he should not be free to cross the threshold of the lodge, to see human beings, to hear the human voice, or to receive letters and newspapers. He was allowed to have a musical instrument and books, and was allowed to write letters, to drink wine, and to smoke. By the terms of the agreement, the only relations he could have with the outer world were by a little window made purposely for that object. He might have anything he wanted—books, music, wine, and so on—in any quantity he desired by writing an order, but could only receive them through the window. The agreement provided for every detail and every trifle that would make his imprisonment strictly solitary, and bound the young man to stay there *exactly* fifteen years, beginning from twelve o'clock of November 14, 1870, and ending at twelve o'clock of November 14, 1885. The slightest attempt on his part to break the conditions, if only two minutes before the end, released the banker from the obligation to pay him two millions.

For the first year of his confinement, as far as one could judge from his brief notes, the prisoner suffered severely from loneliness and depression. The sounds of the piano could be heard continually day and night from his lodge. He refused wine and tobacco. Wine, he wrote, excites the desires, and desires are the worst foes of the prisoner; and besides, nothing could be more dreary than drinking good wine and seeing no one. And tobacco spoilt the air of his room. In the first year the books he sent for were principally of a light character; novels with a complicated love plot, sensational and fantastic stories, and so on.

In the second year the piano was silent in the lodge, and the prisoner asked only for the classics. In the fifth year music was audible again, and the prisoner asked for wine. Those who watched him through the window said that all that year he spent doing nothing but eating and drinking and lying on his bed, frequently yawning and angrily talking to himself. He did not read books. Sometimes at night he would sit down to write; he would spend hours writing, and in the morning tear up all that he had written. More than once he could be heard crying.

In the second half of the sixth year the prisoner began zealously studying languages, philosophy, and history. He threw himself eagerly into these studies—so much so that the banker had enough to do to get him the books he ordered. In the course of four years some six hundred volumes were procured at his request. It was during this period that the banker received the following letter from his prisoner:

"My dear Jailer, I write you these lines in six languages. Show them to people who know the languages. Let them read them. If they find not one mistake I implore you to fire a shot in the garden. That shot will show me that my efforts have not been thrown away. The geniuses of all ages and of all lands speak different languages, but the same flame burns in them all. Oh, if you only knew what unearthly happiness my soul feels now from being able to understand them!" The prisoner's desire was fulfilled. The banker ordered two shots to be fired in the garden.

Then after the tenth year, the prisoner sat immovably at the table and read nothing but the Gospel. It seemed strange to the banker that a man who in four years had mastered six hundred learned volumes should waste nearly a year over one thin book easy of comprehension. Theology and histories of religion followed the Gospels.

In the last two years of his confinement the prisoner read an immense quantity of books quite indiscriminately. At one time he was busy with the natural sciences, then he would ask for Byron or Shakespeare. There were notes in which he demanded at the same time books on chemistry, and a manual of medicine, and a novel, and some treatise on philosophy or theology. His reading suggested a man swimming in the sea among the wreckage of his ship, and trying to save his life by greedily clutching first at one spar and then at another.

* * *

The old banker remembered all this, and thought:

"Tomorrow at twelve o'clock he will regain his freedom. By our agreement I ought to pay him two millions. If I do pay him, it is all over with me: I shall be utterly ruined."

Fifteen years before, his millions had been beyond his reckoning; now he was afraid to ask himself which were greater, his debts or his assets. Desperate gambling on the Stock Exchange, wild speculation and the excitability which he could not get over even in advancing years, had by degrees led to the decline of his fortune and the proud, fearless, self-confident millionaire had become a banker of middling rank, trembling at every rise and fall in his investments. "Cursed bet!" muttered the old man, clutching his head in despair. "Why didn't the man die? He is only forty now. He will take my last penny from me, he will marry, will enjoy life, will gamble on the Exchange; while I shall look at him with envy like a beggar, and hear from him every day the same sentence: 'I am indebted to you for the happiness of my life, let me help you!' No, it is too much! The one means of being saved from bankruptcy and disgrace is the death of that man!"

It struck three o'clock, the banker listened; everyone was asleep in the house and nothing could be heard outside but the rustling of the chilled trees. Trying to make no noise, he took from a fireproof safe the key of the door which had not been opened for fifteen years, put on his overcoat, and went out of the house.

It was dark and cold in the garden. Rain was falling. A damp cutting wind was racing about the garden, howling and giving the trees no rest. The banker strained his eyes, but could see neither the earth nor the white statues, nor the lodge, nor the trees. Going to the spot where the lodge stood, he twice called the watchman. No answer followed. Evidently the watchman had sought shelter from the weather, and was now asleep somewhere either in the kitchen or in the greenhouse.

"If I had the pluck to carry out my intention," thought the old man, "suspicion would fall first upon the watchman."

He felt in the darkness for the steps and the door, and went into the entry of the lodge. Then he groped his way into a little passage and lighted a match. There was not a soul there. There was a bedstead with no bedding on it, and in the corner there was a dark cast-iron stove. The seals on the door leading to the prisoner's rooms were intact.

When the match went out the old man, trembling with emotion, peeped through the little window. A candle was burning dimly in the prisoner's room. He was sitting at the table. Nothing could be seen but his back, the hair on his head, and his hands. Open books were lying on the table, on the two easy chairs, and on the carpet near the table.

Five minutes passed and the prisoner did not once stir. Fifteen years' imprisonment had taught him to sit still. The banker tapped at the window with his finger, and the prisoner made no movement whatever in response. Then the banker cautiously broke the seals off the door and put the key in the keyhole. The rusty lock gave a grating sound and the door creaked. The banker expected to hear at once footsteps and a cry of astonishment, but three minutes passed and it was as quiet as ever in the room. He made up his mind to go in.

At the table a man unlike ordinary people was sitting motionless. He was a skeleton with the skin drawn tight over his bones, with long curls like a woman's and a shaggy beard. His face was yellow with an earthy tint in it, his cheeks were hollow, his back long and narrow, and the hand on which his shaggy head was propped was so thin and delicate that it was dreadful to look at it. His hair was already streaked with silver, and seeing his emaciated, aged-looking face, no one would have believed that he was only forty. He was asleep. . . . In front of his bowed head there lay on the table a sheet of paper on which there was something written in fine handwriting.

"Poor creature!" thought the banker, "he is asleep and most likely dreaming of the millions. And I have only to take this half-dead man, throw him on the bed, stifle him a little with the pillow, and the most conscientious expert would find no sign of a violent death. But let us first read what he has written here. . . ."

The banker took the page from the table and read as follows:

"Tomorrow at twelve o'clock I regain my freedom and the right to associate with other men, but before I leave this room and see the sunshine, I think it necessary to say a few words to you. With a clear conscience I tell you, as before God, who beholds me, that I despise freedom and life and health, and all that in your books is called the good things of the world.

"For fifteen years I have been intently studying earthly life. It is true I have not seen the earth nor men, but in your books I have drunk fragrant wine, I have sung songs, I have hunted stags and wild boars in the forests, have loved women. . . . Beauties as ethereal as clouds, created by the magic of your poets and geniuses, have visited me at night, and have whispered in my ears wonderful tales that have set my brain in a whirl. In your books I have climbed to the peaks of Elburz and Mont Blanc, and from there I have seen the sun rise and have watched it at evening flood the sky, the ocean, and the mountain-tops with gold and crimson. I have watched from there the lightning flashing over my head and cleaving the storm clouds. I have seen green forests, fields, rivers, lakes, towns. I have heard the singing of the sirens, and the strains of the shepherds' pipes; I have touched the wings of comely devils who flew down to converse with me of God. . . . In your books I have flung myself into the bottomless pit, performed miracles, slain, burned towns, preached new religions, conquered whole kingdoms. . . .

"Your books have given me wisdom. All that the unresting thought of man has created in the ages is compressed into a small compass in my brain. I know that I am wiser than all of you.

"And I despise your books, I despise wisdom and the blessings of this world. It is all worthless, fleeting, illusory, and deceptive, like a mirage. You may be proud, wise, and fine, but death will wipe you off the face of the earth as though you were no more than mice burrowing under the floor, and your posterity, your history, your immortal geniuses will burn or freeze together with the earthly globe.

"You have lost your reason and taken the wrong path. You have taken lies for truth, and hideousness for beauty. You would marvel if, owing to strange events of some sorts, frogs and lizards suddenly grew on apple and orange trees instead of fruit, or if roses began to smell like a sweating horse; so I marvel at you who exchange heaven for earth. I don't want to understand you.

"To prove to you in action how I despise all that you live by, I renounce the two millions of which I once dreamed as of paradise and which now I despise. To deprive myself of the right to the money I shall go out from here five hours before the time fixed, and so break the compact. . . ."

When the banker had read this he laid the page on the table, kissed the strange man on the head, and went out of the lodge, weeping. At no other time, even when he had lost heavily on the Stock Exchange, had he felt so great a contempt for himself. When he got home he lay on his bed, but his tears and emotion kept him for hours from sleeping.

Next morning the watchmen ran in with pale faces, and told him they had seen the man who lived in the lodge climb out of the window into the garden, go to the gate, and disappear. The banker went at once with the servants to the lodge and made sure of the flight of his prisoner. To avoid arousing unnecessary talk, he took from the table the writing in which the millions were renounced, and when he got home locked it up in the fireproof safe.

The Princess

[First published on March 26, 1889.
Collected in *The Duel and Other Stories* (1916).]

A carriage with four fine sleek horses drove in at the big so-called Red Gate of the N—Monastery. While it was still at a distance, the priests and monks who were standing in a group round the part of the hostel allotted to the gentry, recognised by the coachman and horses that the lady in the carriage was Princess Vera Gavrilovna, whom they knew very well.

An old man in livery jumped off the box and helped the princess to get out of the carriage. She raised her dark veil and moved in a leisurely way up to the priests to receive their blessing; then she nodded pleasantly to the rest of the monks and went into the hostel.

"Well, have you missed your princess?" she said to the monk who brought in her things. "It's a whole month since I've been to see you. But here I am; behold your princess. And where is the Father Superior? My goodness, I am burning with impatience! Wonderful, wonderful old man! You must be proud of having such a Superior."

When the Father Superior came in, the princess uttered a shriek of delight, crossed her arms over her bosom, and went up to receive his blessing.

"No, no, let me kiss your hand," she said, snatching it and eagerly kissing it three times. "How glad I am to see you at last, holy Father! I'm sure you've forgotten your princess, but my thoughts have been in your dear monastery every moment. How delightful it is here! This living for God far from the busy, giddy world has a special charm of its own, holy Father, which I feel with my whole soul although I cannot express it!"

The princess's cheeks glowed and tears came into her eyes. She talked incessantly, fervently, while the Father Superior, a grave, plain, shy old man of seventy, remained mute or uttered abruptly, like a soldier on duty, phrases such as:

"Certainly, Your Excellency. . . . Quite so. I understand."

"Has Your Excellency come for a long stay?" he inquired.

"I shall stay the night here, and tomorrow I'm going on to Klavdia Nikolaevna's—it's a long time since I've seen her—and the day after tomorrow I'll come back to you and stay three or four days. I want to rest my soul here among you, holy Father. . . ."

The princess liked being at the monastery at N——. For the last two years it had been a favourite resort of hers; she used to go there almost every month in the summer and stay two or three days, even sometimes a week. The shy novices, the stillness, the low ceilings, the smell of cypress, the modest fare, the cheap curtains on the windows—all this touched her, softened her, and disposed her to contemplation and good thoughts. It was enough for her to be half an hour in the hostel for her to feel that she, too, was timid and modest, and that she, too, smelt of cypress-wood. The past retreated into the background, lost its significance, and the princess began to imagine that in spite of her twenty-nine years she was very much like the old Father Superior, and that, like him, she was created not for wealth, not for earthly grandeur and love, but for a peaceful life secluded from the world, a life in twilight like the hostel.

It happens that a ray of light gleams in the dark cell of the anchorite absorbed in prayer, or a bird alights on the window and sings its song; the stern anchorite will smile in spite of himself, and a gentle, sinless joy will pierce through the load of grief over his sins, like water flowing from under a stone. The princess fancied she brought from the outside world just such comfort as the ray of light or the bird. Her gay, friendly smile, her gentle eyes, her voice, her jests, her whole personality in fact, her little graceful figure always dressed in simple black, must arouse in simple, austere people a feeling of tenderness and joy. Every one, looking at her, must think: "God has sent us an angel. . . ." And feeling that no one could help thinking this, she smiled still more cordially, and tried to look like a bird.

After drinking tea and resting, she went for a walk. The sun was already setting. From the monastery garden came a moist fragrance of freshly watered mignonette, and from the church floated the soft singing of men's voices, which seemed very pleasant and mournful in the distance. It was the evening service. In the dark windows where the little lamps glowed gently, in the shadows, in the figure of the old monk sitting at the church door with a collecting-box, there was such unruffled peace that the princess felt moved to tears.

Outside the gate, in the walk between the wall and the birch trees where there were benches, it was quite evening. The air grew rapidly darker and darker. The princess went along the walk, sat on a seat, and sank into thought.

She thought how good it would be to settle down for her whole life in this monastery where life was as still and unruffled as a summer evening; how good it would be to forget the ungrateful, dissipated prince; to forget her immense estates, the creditors who worried her every day, her misfortunes, her maid Dasha, who had looked at her impertinently that morning. It would be nice to sit here on the bench all her life and watch through the trunks of the birch trees the evening mist gathering in wreaths in the valley below; the rooks flying home in a black cloud like a veil far, far away above the forest; two novices, one astride a piebald horse, another on foot driving out the horses for the night and rejoicing in their freedom, playing pranks like little children; their youthful voices rang out musically in the still air, and she could distinguish every word. It is nice to sit and listen to the silence: at one moment the wind blows and stirs the tops of the birch trees, then a frog rustles in last year's leaves, then the clock on the belfry strikes the quarter. . . . One might sit without moving, listen and think, and think. . . .

An old woman passed by with a wallet on her back. The princess thought that it would be nice to stop the old woman and to say something friendly and cordial to her, to help her. . . . But the old woman turned the corner without once looking round.

Not long afterwards a tall man with a grey beard and a straw hat came along the walk. When he came up to the princess, he took off his hat and bowed. From the bald patch on his head and his sharp, hooked nose the princess recognised him as the doctor, Mihail Ivanovitch, who had been in her service at Dubovki. She remembered that some one had told her that his wife had died the year before, and she wanted to sympathise with him, to console him.

"Doctor, I expect you don't recognise me?" she said with an affable smile.

"Yes, Princess, I recognised you," said the doctor, taking off his hat again.

"Oh, thank you; I was afraid that you, too, had forgotten your princess. People only remember their enemies, but they forget their friends. Have you, too, come to pray?"

"I am the doctor here, and I have to spend the night at the monastery every Saturday."

"Well, how are you?" said the princess, sighing. "I hear that you have lost your wife. What a calamity!"

"Yes, Princess, for me it is a great calamity."

"There's nothing for it! We must bear our troubles with resignation. Not one hair of a man's head is lost without the Divine Will."

"Yes, Princess."

To the princess's friendly, gentle smile and her sighs the doctor responded coldly and dryly: "Yes, Princess." And the expression of his face was cold and dry.

"What else can I say to him?" she wondered.

"How long it is since we met!" she said. "Five years! How much water has flowed under the bridge, how many changes in that time; it quite frightens one to think of it! You know, I am married. . . . I am not a countess now, but a princess. And by now I am separated from my husband too."

"Yes, I heard so."

"God has sent me many trials. No doubt you have heard, too, that I am almost ruined. My Dubovki, Sofyino, and Kiryakovo have all been sold for my unhappy husband's debts. And I have only Baranovo and Mihaltsevo left. It's terrible to look back: how many changes and misfortunes of all kinds, how many mistakes!"

"Yes, Princess, many mistakes."

The princess was a little disconcerted. She knew her mistakes; they were all of such a private character that no one but she could think or speak of them. She could not resist asking:

"What mistakes are you thinking about?"

"You referred to them, so you know them . . ." answered the doctor, and he smiled. "Why talk about them!"

"No; tell me, doctor. I shall be very grateful to you. And please don't stand on ceremony with me. I love to hear the truth."

"I am not your judge, Princess."

"Not my judge! What a tone you take! You must know something about me. Tell me!"

"If you really wish it, very well. Only I regret to say I'm not clever at talking, and people can't always understand me."

The doctor thought a moment and began:

"A lot of mistakes; but the most important of them, in my opinion, was the general spirit that prevailed on all your estates. You see, I don't know how to express myself. I mean chiefly the lack of love, the aversion for people that was felt in absolutely everything. Your whole system of life was built upon that aversion. Aversion for the human voice, for faces, for heads, steps . . . in fact, for everything that makes up a human being. At all the doors and on the stairs there stand sleek, rude, and lazy grooms in livery to prevent badly dressed persons from entering the house; in the hall there are chairs with high backs so that the footmen waiting there, during balls and receptions, may not soil the walls with their heads; in every room there are thick carpets that no human step may be heard; every one who comes in is infallibly warned to speak as softly and as little as possible, and to say nothing that might have a disagreeable effect on the nerves or the imagination. And in your room you don't shake hands with any one or ask him to sit down—just as you didn't shake hands with me or ask me to sit down. . . ."

"By all means, if you like," said the princess, smiling and holding out her hand. "Really, to be cross about such trifles. . . ."

"But I am not cross," laughed the doctor, but at once he flushed, took off his hat, and waving it about, began hotly: "To be candid, I've long wanted an opportunity to tell you all I think. . . . That is, I want to tell you that you look upon the mass of mankind from the Napoleonic standpoint as food for the cannon. But Napoleon had at least some idea; you have nothing except aversion."

"I have an aversion for people?" smiled the princess, shrugging her shoulders in astonishment. "I have!"

"Yes, you! You want facts? By all means. In Mihaltsevo three former cooks of yours, who have gone blind in your kitchens from the heat of the stove, are living upon charity. All the health and strength and good looks that is found on your hundreds of thousands of acres is taken by you and your parasites for your grooms, your footmen, and your coachmen. All these two-legged cattle are trained to be flunkeys, overeat themselves, grow coarse, lose the 'image and likeness,' in fact. . . . Young doctors, agricultural experts, teachers, intellectual workers generally—think of it!—are torn away from their honest work and forced for a crust of bread to take part in all sorts of mummeries which make every decent man feel ashamed! Some young men cannot be in your service for three years without becoming hypocrites, toadies, sneaks. . . . Is that a good thing? Your Polish superintendents, those abject spies, all those Kazimers and Kaetans, go hunting about on your hundreds of thousands of acres from morning to night, and to please you try to get three skins off one ox. Excuse me, I speak disconnectedly, but that doesn't matter. You don't look upon the simple people as human beings. And even the princes, counts, and bishops who used to come and see you, you looked upon simply as decorative figures, not as living beings. But the worst of all, the thing that most revolts me, is having a fortune of over a million and doing nothing for other people, nothing!"

The princess sat amazed, aghast, offended, not knowing what to say or how to behave. She had never before been spoken to in such a tone. The doctor's unpleasant, angry voice and his clumsy, faltering phrases made a harsh clattering noise in her ears and her head. Then she began to feel as though the gesticulating doctor was hitting her on the head with his hat.

"It's not true!" she articulated softly, in an imploring voice. "I've done a great deal of good for other people; you know it yourself!"

"Nonsense!" cried the doctor. "Can you possibly go on thinking of your philanthropic work as something genuine and useful, and not a mere mummery? It was a farce from beginning to end; it was playing at loving your neighbour, the most open farce which even children and stupid peasant women saw through! Take for instance your—what was it called?—house for homeless old women without relations, of which you made me something like a head doctor, and of which you were the patroness. Mercy on us! What a charming institution it was! A house was built with parquet floors and a weathercock on the roof; a dozen old women were collected from the villages and made to sleep under blankets and sheets of Dutch linen, and given toffee to eat."

The doctor gave a malignant chuckle into his hat, and went on speaking rapidly and stammering:

"It was a farce! The attendants kept the sheets and the blankets under lock and key, for fear the old women should soil them—'Let the old devil's pepper-pots sleep on the floor.' The old women did not dare to sit down on the beds, to put on their jackets, to walk over the polished floors. Everything was kept for show and hidden away from the old women as though they were thieves, and the old women were clothed and fed on the sly by other people's charity, and prayed to God night and day to be released from their prison and from the canting exhortations of the sleek rascals to whose care you committed them. And what did the managers do? It was simply charming! About twice a week there would be thirty-five thousand messages to say that the princess—that is, you—were coming to the home next day. That meant that next day I had to abandon my patients, dress up and be on parade. Very good; I arrive. The old women, in everything clean and new, are already drawn up in a row, waiting. Near them struts the old garrison rat—the superintendent with his mawkish, sneaking smile. The old women yawn and exchange glances, but are afraid to complain. We wait. The junior steward gallops up. Half an hour later the senior steward; then the superintendent of the accounts' office, then another, and then another of them . . . they keep arriving endlessly. They all have mysterious, solemn faces. We wait and wait, shift from one leg to another, look at the clock—all this in monumental silence because we all hate each other like poison. One hour passes, then a second, and then at last the carriage is seen in the distance, and . . . and . . ."

The doctor went off into a shrill laugh and brought out in a shrill voice:

"You get out of the carriage, and the old hags, at the word of command from the old garrison rat, begin chanting: 'The Glory of our Lord in Zion the tongue of man cannot express . . .' A pretty scene, wasn't it?"

The doctor went off into a bass chuckle, and waved his hand as though to signify that he could not utter another word for laughing. He laughed heavily, harshly, with clenched teeth, as ill-natured people laugh; and from his voice, from his face, from his glittering, rather insolent eyes it could be seen that he had a profound contempt for the princess, for the home, and for the old women. There was nothing amusing or laughable in all that he described so clumsily and coarsely, but he laughed with satisfaction, even with delight.

"And the school?" he went on, panting from laughter. "Do you remember how you wanted to teach peasant children yourself? You must have taught them very well, for very soon the children all ran away, so that they had to be thrashed and bribed to come and be taught. And you remember how you wanted to feed with your own hands the infants whose mothers were working in the fields. You went about the village crying because the infants were not at your disposal, as the mothers would take them to the fields with them. Then the village foreman ordered the mothers by turns to leave their infants behind for your entertainment. A strange thing! They all ran away from your benevolence like mice from a cat! And why was it? It's very simple. Not because our people are ignorant and ungrateful, as you always explained it to yourself, but because in all your fads, if you'll excuse the word, there wasn't a ha'p'orth of love and kindness! There was nothing but the desire to amuse yourself with living puppets, nothing else. . . . A person who does not feel the difference between a human being and a lap-dog ought not to go in for philanthropy. I assure you, there's a great difference between human beings and lap-dogs!"

The princess's heart was beating dreadfully; there was a thudding in her ears, and she still felt as though the doctor were beating her on the head with his hat. The doctor talked quickly, excitedly, and uncouthly, stammering and gesticulating unnecessarily. All she grasped was that she was spoken to by a coarse, ill-bred, spiteful, and ungrateful man; but what he wanted of her and what he was talking about, she could not understand.

"Go away!" she said in a tearful voice, putting up her hands to protect her head from the doctor's hat; "go away!"

"And how you treat your servants!" the doctor went on, indignantly. "You treat them as the lowest scoundrels, and don't look upon them as human beings. For example, allow me to ask, why did you dismiss me? For ten years I worked for your father and afterwards for you, honestly, without vacations or holidays. I gained the love of all for more than seventy miles round, and suddenly one fine day I am informed that I am no longer wanted. What for? I've no idea to this day. I, a doctor of medicine, a gentleman by birth, a student of the Moscow University, father of a family—am such a petty, insignificant insect that you can kick me out without explaining the reason! Why stand on ceremony with me! I heard afterwards that my wife went without my knowledge three times to intercede with you for me—you wouldn't receive her. I am told she cried in your hall. And I shall never forgive her for it, never!"

The doctor paused and clenched his teeth, making an intense effort to think of something more to say, very unpleasant and vindictive. He thought of something, and his cold, frowning face suddenly brightened.

"Take your attitude to this monastery!" he said with avidity. "You've never spared any one, and the holier the place, the more chance of its suffering from your loving-kindness and angelic sweetness. Why do you come here? What do you want with the monks here, allow me to ask you? What is Hecuba to you or you to Hecuba? It's another farce, another amusement for you, another sacrilege against human dignity, and nothing more. Why, you don't believe in the monks' God; you've a God of your own in your heart, whom you've evolved for yourself at spiritualist séances. You look with condescension upon the ritual of the Church; you don't go to mass or vespers; you sleep till midday. . . . Why do you come here? . . . You come with a God of your own into a monastery you have nothing to do with, and you imagine that the monks look upon it as a very great honour. To be sure they do! You'd better ask, by the way, what your visits cost the monastery. You were graciously pleased to arrive here this evening, and a messenger from your estate arrived on horseback the day before yesterday to warn them of your coming. They were the whole day yesterday getting the rooms ready and expecting you. This morning your advance-guard arrived—an insolent maid, who keeps running across the courtyard, rustling her skirts, pestering them with questions, giving orders. . . . I can't endure it! The monks have been on the lookout all day, for if you were not met with due ceremony, there would be trouble! You'd complain to the bishop! 'The monks don't like me, your holiness; I don't know what I've done to displease them. It's true I'm a great sinner, but I'm so unhappy!' Already one monastery has been in hot water over you. The Father Superior is a busy, learned man; he hasn't a free moment, and you keep sending for him to come to your rooms. Not a trace of respect for age or for rank! If at least you were a bountiful giver to the monastery, one wouldn't resent it so much, but all this time the monks have not received a hundred roubles from you!"

Whenever people worried the princess, misunderstood her, or mortified her, and when she did not know what to say or do, she usually began to cry. And on this occasion, too, she ended by hiding her face in her hands and crying aloud in a thin treble like a child. The doctor suddenly stopped and looked at her. His face darkened and grew stern.

"Forgive me, Princess," he said in a hollow voice. "I've given way to a malicious feeling and forgotten myself. It was not right."

And coughing in an embarrassed way, he walked away quickly, without remembering to put his hat on.

Stars were already twinkling in the sky. The moon must have been rising on the further side of the monastery, for the sky was clear, soft, and transparent. Bats were flitting noiselessly along the white monastery wall.

The clock slowly struck three quarters, probably a quarter to nine. The princess got up and walked slowly to the gate. She felt wounded and was crying, and she felt that the trees and the stars and even the bats were pitying her, and that the clock struck musically only to express its sympathy with her. She cried and thought how nice it would be to go into a monastery for the rest of her life. On still summer evenings she would walk alone through the avenues, insulted, injured, misunderstood by people, and only God and the starry heavens would see the martyr's tears. The evening service was still going on in the church. The princess stopped and listened to the singing; how beautiful the singing sounded in the still darkness! How sweet to weep and suffer to the sound of that singing!

Going into her rooms, she looked at her tear-stained face in the glass and powdered it, then she sat down to supper. The monks knew that she liked pickled sturgeon, little mushrooms, Malaga and plain honey-cakes that left a taste of cypress in the mouth, and every time she came they gave her all these dishes. As she ate the mushrooms and drank the Malaga, the princess dreamed of how she would be finally ruined and deserted— how all her stewards, bailiffs, clerks, and maid-servants for whom she had done so much, would be false to her, and begin to say rude things; how people all the world over would set upon her, speak ill of her, jeer at her. She would renounce her title, would renounce society and luxury, and would go into a convent without one word of reproach to any one; she would pray for her enemies—and then they would all understand her and come to beg her forgiveness, but by that time it would be too late. . . .

After supper she knelt down in the corner before the ikon and read two chapters of the Gospel. Then her maid made her bed and she got into it. Stretching herself under the white quilt, she heaved a sweet, deep sigh, as one sighs after crying, closed her eyes, and began to fall asleep.

In the morning she waked up and glanced at her watch. It was half-past nine. On the carpet near the bed was a bright, narrow streak of sunlight from a ray which came in at the window and dimly lighted up the room. Flies were buzzing behind the black curtain at the window. "It's early," thought the princess, and she closed her eyes.

Stretching and lying snug in her bed, she recalled her meeting yesterday with the doctor and all the thoughts with which she had gone to sleep the night before: she remembered she was unhappy. Then she thought of her husband living in Petersburg, her stewards, doctors, neighbours, the officials of her acquaintance . . . a long procession of familiar masculine faces passed before her imagination. She smiled and thought, if only these people could see into her heart and understand her, they would all be at her feet.

At a quarter past eleven she called her maid.

"Help me to dress, Dasha," she said languidly. "But go first and tell them to get out the horses. I must set off for Klavdia Nikolaevna's."

Going out to get into the carriage, she blinked at the glaring daylight and laughed with pleasure: it was a wonderfully fine day! As she scanned from her half-closed eyes the monks who had gathered round the steps to see her off, she nodded graciously and said:

"Goodbye, my friends! Till the day after tomorrow."

It was an agreeable surprise to her that the doctor was with the monks by the steps. His face was pale and severe.

"Princess," he said with a guilty smile, taking off his hat, "I've been waiting here a long time to see you. Forgive me, for God's sake. . . . I was carried away yesterday by an evil, vindictive feeling and I talked . . . nonsense. In short, I beg your pardon."

The princess smiled graciously, and held out her hand for him to kiss. He kissed it, turning red.

Trying to look like a bird, the princess fluttered into the carriage and nodded in all directions. There was a gay, warm, serene feeling in her heart, and she felt herself that her smile was particularly soft and friendly. As the carriage rolled towards the gates, and afterwards along the dusty road past huts and gardens, past long trains of waggons and strings of pilgrims on their way to the monastery, she still screwed up her eyes and smiled softly. She was thinking there was no higher bliss than to bring warmth, light, and joy wherever one went, to forgive injuries, to smile graciously on one's enemies. The peasants she passed bowed to her, the carriage rustled softly, clouds of dust rose from under the wheels and floated over the golden rye, and it seemed to the princess that her body was swaying not on carriage cushions but on clouds, and that she herself was like a light, transparent little cloud. . . .

"How happy I am!" she murmured, shutting her eyes. "How happy I am!"

A Dreary Story

[Written in Luka village, Sumsk region, in 1889.
First published in *Severny Vestnik*, a Russian literary magazine,
in November 1889. Revised and included in the collection
Moody People (1890). Collected in *The Wife and Other Stories* (1918).
One of Chekhov's most remarkable works,
the story is also translated as 'A Boring Story.']

FROM THE NOTEBOOK OF AN OLD MAN

I

There is in Russia an emeritus Professor Nikolay Stepanovitch, a chevalier and privy councillor; he has so many Russian and foreign decorations that when he has occasion to put them on the students nickname him "The Ikonstand." His acquaintances are of the most aristocratic; for the last twenty-five or thirty years, at any rate, there has not been one single distinguished man of learning in Russia with whom he has not been intimately acquainted. There is no one for him to make friends with nowadays; but if we turn to the past, the long list of his famous friends winds up with such names as Pirogov, Kavelin, and the poet Nekrasov, all of whom bestowed upon him a warm and sincere affection. He is a member of all the Russian and of three foreign universities. And so on, and so on. All that and a great deal more that might be said makes up what is called my "name."

That is my name as known to the public. In Russia it is known to every educated man, and abroad it is mentioned in the lecture room with the addition "honoured and distinguished." It is one of those fortunate names to abuse which or to take which in vain, in public or in print, is considered a sign of bad taste. And that is as it should be. You see, my name is closely associated with the conception of a highly distinguished man of great gifts and unquestionable usefulness. I have the industry and power of endurance of a camel, and that is important, and I have talent, which is even more important. Moreover, while I am on this subject, I am a well-educated, modest, and honest fellow. I have never poked my nose into literature or politics; I have never sought popularity in polemics with the ignorant; I have never made speeches either at public dinners or at the funerals of my friends. . . . In fact, there is no slur on my learned name, and there is no complaint one can make against it. It is fortunate.

The bearer of that name, that is I, see myself as a man of sixty-two, with a bald head, with false teeth, and with an incurable tic douloureux. I am myself as dingy and unsightly as my name is brilliant and splendid. My head and my hands tremble with weakness; my neck, as Turgenev says of one of his heroines, is like the handle of a double bass; my chest is hollow; my shoulders narrow; when I talk or lecture, my mouth turns down at one corner; when I smile, my whole face is covered with aged-looking, deathly wrinkles. There is nothing impressive about my pitiful figure; only, perhaps, when I have an attack of tic douloureux my face wears a peculiar expression, the sight of which must have roused in every one the grim and impressive thought, "Evidently that man will soon die."

I still, as in the past, lecture fairly well; I can still, as in the past, hold the attention of my listeners for a couple of hours. My fervour, the literary skill of my exposition, and my humour, almost efface the defects of my voice, though it is harsh, dry, and monotonous as a praying beggar's. I write poorly. That bit of my brain which presides over the faculty of authorship refuses to work. My memory has grown weak; there is a lack of sequence in my ideas, and when I put them on paper it always seems to me that I have lost the instinct for their organic connection; my construction is monotonous; my language is poor and timid. Often I write what I do not mean; I have forgotten the beginning when I am writing the end. Often I forget ordinary words, and I always have to waste a great deal of energy in avoiding superfluous phrases and unnecessary parentheses in my letters, both unmistakable proofs of a decline in mental activity. And it is noteworthy that the simpler the letter the more painful the effort to write it. At a scientific article I feel far more intelligent and at ease than at a letter of congratulation or a minute of proceedings. Another point: I find it easier to write German or English than to write Russian.

As regards my present manner of life, I must give a foremost place to the insomnia from which I have suffered of late. If I were asked what constituted the chief and fundamental feature of my existence now, I should answer, Insomnia. As in the past, from habit I undress and go to bed exactly at midnight. I fall asleep quickly, but before two o'clock I wake up and feel as though I had not slept at all. Sometimes I get out of bed and light a lamp. For an hour or two I walk up and down the room looking at the familiar photographs and pictures. When I am weary of walking about, I sit down to my table. I sit motionless, thinking of nothing, conscious of no inclination; if a book is lying before me, I mechanically move it closer and read it without any interest—in that way not long ago I mechanically read through in one night a whole novel, with the strange title "The Song the Lark was Singing"; or to occupy my attention I force myself to count to a thousand; or I imagine the face of one of my colleagues and begin trying to remember in what year and under what circumstances he entered the service. I like listening to sounds. Two rooms away from me my daughter Liza says something rapidly in her sleep, or my wife crosses the drawing room with a candle and invariably drops the matchbox; or a warped cupboard creaks; or the burner of the lamp suddenly begins to hum—and all these sounds, for some reason, excite me.

To lie awake at night means to be at every moment conscious of being abnormal, and so I look forward with impatience to the morning and the day when I have a right to be awake. Many wearisome hours pass before the cock crows in the yard. He is my first bringer of good tidings. As soon as he crows I know that within an hour the porter will wake up below, and, coughing angrily, will go upstairs to fetch something. And then a pale light will begin gradually glimmering at the windows, voices will sound in the street. . . .

The day begins for me with the entrance of my wife. She comes in to me in her petticoat, before she has done her hair, but after she has washed, smelling of flower-scented eau-de-Cologne, looking as though she had come in by chance. Every time she says exactly the same thing: "Excuse me, I have just come in for a minute. . . . Have you had a bad night again?"

Then she puts out the lamp, sits down near the table, and begins talking. I am no prophet, but I know what she will talk about. Every morning it is exactly the same thing. Usually, after anxious inquiries concerning my health, she suddenly mentions our son who is an officer serving at Warsaw. After the twentieth of each month we send him fifty roubles, and that serves as the chief topic of our conversation.

"Of course it is difficult for us," my wife would sigh, "but until he is completely on his own feet it is our duty to help him. The boy is among strangers, his pay is small. . . . However, if you like, next month we won't send him fifty, but forty. What do you think?"

Daily experience might have taught my wife that constantly talking of our expenses does not reduce them, but my wife refuses to learn by experience, and regularly every morning discusses our officer son, and tells me that bread, thank God, is cheaper, while sugar is a halfpenny dearer—with a tone and an air as though she were communicating interesting news.

I listen, mechanically assent, and probably because I have had a bad night, strange and inappropriate thoughts intrude themselves upon me. I gaze at my wife and wonder like a child. I ask myself in perplexity, is it possible that this old, very stout, ungainly woman, with her dull expression of petty anxiety and alarm about daily bread, with eyes dimmed by continual brooding over debts and money difficulties, who can talk of nothing but expenses and who smiles at nothing but things getting cheaper—is it possible that this woman is no other than the slender Varya whom I fell in love with so passionately for her fine, clear intelligence, for her pure soul, her beauty, and, as Othello his Desdemona, for her "sympathy" for my studies? Could that woman be no other than the Varya who had once borne me a son?

I look with strained attention into the face of this flabby, spiritless, clumsy old woman, seeking in her my Varya, but of her past self nothing is left but her anxiety over my health and her manner of calling my salary "our salary," and my cap "our cap." It is painful for me to look at her, and, to give her what little comfort I can, I let her say what she likes, and say nothing even when she passes unjust criticisms on other people or pitches into me for not having a private practice or not publishing textbooks.

Our conversation always ends in the same way. My wife suddenly remembers with dismay that I have not had my tea.

"What am I thinking about, sitting here?" she says, getting up. "The samovar has been on the table ever so long, and here I stay gossiping. My goodness! how forgetful I am growing!"

She goes out quickly, and stops in the doorway to say:

"We owe Yegor five months' wages. Did you know it? You mustn't let the servants' wages run on; how many times I have said it! It's much easier to pay ten roubles a month than fifty roubles every five months!"

As she goes out, she stops to say:

"The person I am sorriest for is our Liza. The girl studies at the Conservatoire, always mixes with people of good position, and goodness knows how she is dressed. Her fur coat is in such a state she is ashamed to show herself in the street. If she were somebody else's daughter it wouldn't matter, but of course every one knows that her father is a distinguished professor, a privy councillor."

And having reproached me with my rank and reputation, she goes away at last. That is how my day begins. It does not improve as it goes on.

As I am drinking my tea, my Liza comes in wearing her fur coat and her cap, with her music in her hand, already quite ready to go to the Conservatoire. She is two-and-twenty. She looks younger, is pretty, and rather like my wife in her young days. She kisses me tenderly on my forehead and on my hand, and says:

"Good morning, papa; are you quite well?"

As a child she was very fond of ice cream, and I used often to take her to a confectioner's. Ice cream was for her the type of everything delightful. If she wanted to praise me she would say: "You are as nice as cream, papa." We used to call one of her little fingers "pistachio ice," the next, "cream ice," the third "raspberry," and so on. Usually when she came in to say good morning to me I used to sit her on my knee, kiss her little fingers, and say:

"Creamy ice . . . pistachio . . . lemon. . . ."

And now, from old habit, I kiss Liza's fingers and mutter: "Pistachio . . . cream . . . lemon . . ." but the effect is utterly different. I am cold as ice and I am ashamed. When my daughter comes in to me and touches my forehead with her lips I start as though a bee had stung me on the head, give a forced smile, and turn my face away. Ever since I have been suffering from sleeplessness, a question sticks in my brain like a nail. My daughter often sees me, an old man and a distinguished man, blush painfully at being in debt to my footman; she sees how often anxiety over petty debts forces me to lay aside my work and to walk up and down the room for hours together, thinking; but why is it she never comes to me in secret to whisper in my ear: "Father, here is my watch, here are my bracelets, my earrings, my dresses. . . . Pawn them all; you want money . . .?" How is it that, seeing how her mother and I are placed in a false position and do our utmost to hide our poverty from people, she does not give up her expensive pleasure of music lessons? I would not accept her watch nor her bracelets, nor the sacrifice of her lessons—God forbid! That isn't what I want.

I think at the same time of my son, the officer at Warsaw. He is a clever, honest, and sober fellow. But that is not enough for me. I think if I had an old father, and if I knew there were moments when he was put to shame by his poverty, I should give up my officer's commission to somebody else, and should go out to earn my living as a workman. Such thoughts about my children poison me. What is the use of them? It is only a narrow-minded or embittered man who can harbour evil thoughts about ordinary people because they are not heroes. But enough of that!

At a quarter to ten I have to go and give a lecture to my dear boys. I dress and walk along the road which I have known for thirty years, and which has its history for me. Here is the big grey house with the chemist's shop; at this point there used to stand a little house, and in it was a beershop; in that beershop I thought out my thesis and wrote my first love letter to Varya. I wrote it in pencil, on a page headed "Historia morbi." Here there is a grocer's shop; at one time it was kept by a little Jew, who sold me cigarettes on credit; then by a fat peasant woman, who liked the students because "every one of them has a mother"; now there is a red-haired shopkeeper sitting in it, a very stolid man who drinks tea from a copper teapot. And here are the gloomy gates of the University, which have long needed doing up; I see the bored porter in his sheepskin, the broom, the drifts of snow. . . . On a boy coming fresh from the provinces and imagining that the temple of science must really be a temple, such gates cannot make a healthy impression. Altogether the dilapidated condition of the University buildings, the gloominess of the corridors, the griminess of the walls, the lack of light, the dejected aspect of the steps, the hat-stands and the benches, take a prominent position among predisposing causes in the history of Russian pessimism. . . . Here is our garden . . . I fancy it has grown neither better nor worse since I was a student. I don't like it. It would be far more sensible if there were tall pines and fine oaks growing here instead of sickly-looking lime trees, yellow acacias, and skimpy pollard lilacs. The student whose state of mind is in the majority of cases created by his surroundings, ought in the place where he is studying to see facing him at every turn nothing but what is lofty, strong and elegant. . . . God preserve him from gaunt trees, broken windows, grey walls, and doors covered with torn American leather!

When I go to my own entrance the door is flung wide open, and I am met by my colleague, contemporary, and namesake, the porter Nikolay. As he lets me in he clears his throat and says:

"A frost, your Excellency!"

Or, if my great-coat is wet:

"Rain, your Excellency!"

Then he runs on ahead of me and opens all the doors on my way. In my study he carefully takes off my fur coat, and while doing so manages to tell me some bit of University news. Thanks to the close intimacy existing between all the University porters and beadles, he knows everything that goes on in the four faculties, in the office, in the rector's private room, in the library. What does he not know? When in an evil day a rector or dean, for instance, retires, I hear him in conversation with the young porters mention the candidates for the post, explain that such a one would not be confirmed by the minister, that another would himself refuse to accept it, then drop into fantastic details concerning mysterious papers received in the office, secret conversations alleged to have taken place between the minister and the trustee, and so on. With the exception of these details, he almost always turns out to be right. His estimates of the candidates, though original, are very correct, too. If one wants to know in what year some one read his thesis, entered the service, retired, or died, then summon to your assistance the vast memory of that soldier, and he will not only tell you the year, the month and the day, but will furnish you also with the details that accompanied this or that event. Only one who loves can remember like that.

He is the guardian of the University traditions. From the porters who were his predecessors he has inherited many legends of University life, has added to that wealth much of his own gained during his time of service, and if you care to hear he will tell you many long and intimate stories. He can tell one about extraordinary sages who knew *everything*, about remarkable students who did not sleep for weeks, about numerous martyrs and victims of science; with him good triumphs over evil, the weak always vanquishes the strong, the wise man the fool, the humble the proud, the young the old. There is no need to take all these fables and legends for sterling coin; but filter them, and you will have left what is wanted: our fine traditions and the names of real heroes, recognized as such by all.

In our society the knowledge of the learned world consists of anecdotes of the extraordinary absentmindedness of certain old professors, and two or three witticisms variously ascribed to Gruber, to me, and to Babukin. For the educated public that is not much. If it loved science, learned men, and students, as Nikolay does, its literature would long ago have contained whole epics, records of sayings and doings such as, unfortunately, it cannot boast of now.

After telling me a piece of news, Nikolay assumes a severe expression, and conversation about business begins. If any outsider could at such times overhear Nikolay's free use of our terminology, he might perhaps imagine that he was a learned man disguised as a soldier. And, by the way, the rumours of the erudition of the University porters are greatly exaggerated. It is true that Nikolay knows more than a hundred Latin words, knows how to put the skeleton together, sometimes prepares the apparatus and amuses the students by some long, learned quotation, but the by no means complicated theory of the circulation of the blood, for instance, is as much a mystery to him now as it was twenty years ago.

At the table in my study, bending low over some book or preparation, sits Pyotr Ignatyevitch, my demonstrator, a modest and industrious but by no means clever man of five-and-thirty, already bald and corpulent; he works from morning to night, reads a lot, remembers well everything he has read—and in that way he is not a man, but pure gold; in all else he is a carthorse or, in other words, a learned dullard. The carthorse characteristics that show his lack of talent are these: his outlook is narrow and sharply limited by his specialty; outside his special branch he is simple as a child.

"Fancy! what a misfortune! They say Skobelev is dead."

Nikolay crosses himself, but Pyotr Ignatyevitch turns to me and asks: "What Skobelev is that?"

Another time—somewhat earlier—I told him that Professor Perov was dead. Good Pyotr Ignatyevitch asked:

"What did he lecture on?"

I believe if Patti had sung in his very ear, if a horde of Chinese had invaded Russia, if there had been an earthquake, he would not have stirred a limb, but screwing up his eye, would have gone on calmly looking through his microscope. What is he to Hecuba or Hecuba to him, in fact? I would give a good deal to see how this dry stick sleeps with his wife at night.

Another characteristic is his fanatical faith in the infallibility of science, and, above all, of everything written by the Germans. He believes in himself, in his preparations; knows the object of life, and knows nothing of the doubts and disappointments that turn the hair of talent grey. He has a slavish reverence for authorities and a complete lack of any desire for independent thought. To change his convictions is difficult, to argue with him impossible. How is one to argue with a man who is firmly persuaded that medicine is the finest of sciences, that doctors are the best of men, and that the traditions of the medical profession are superior to those of any other? Of the evil past of medicine only one tradition has been preserved—the white tie still worn by doctors; for a learned—in fact, for any educated man the only traditions that can exist are those of the University as a whole, with no distinction between medicine, law, etc. But it would be hard for Pyotr Ignatyevitch to accept these facts, and he is ready to argue with you till the day of judgment.

I have a clear picture in my mind of his future. In the course of his life he will prepare many hundreds of chemicals of exceptional purity; he will write a number of dry and very accurate memoranda, will make some dozen conscientious translations, but he won't do anything striking. To do that one must have imagination, inventiveness, the gift of insight, and Pyotr Ignatyevitch has nothing of the kind. In short, he is not a master in science, but a journeyman.

Pyotr Ignatyevitch, Nikolay, and I, talk in subdued tones. We are not quite ourselves. There is always a peculiar feeling when one hears through the doors a murmur as of the sea from the lecture-theatre. In the course of thirty years I have not grown accustomed to this feeling, and I experience it every morning. I nervously button up my coat, ask Nikolay unnecessary questions, lose my temper. . . . It is just as though I were frightened; it is not timidity, though, but something different which I can neither describe nor find a name for.

Quite unnecessarily, I look at my watch and say: "Well, it's time to go in."

And we march into the room in the following order: foremost goes Nikolay, with the chemicals and apparatus or with a chart; after him I come; and then the carthorse follows humbly, with hanging head; or, when necessary, a dead body is carried in first on a stretcher, followed by Nikolay, and so on. On my entrance the students all stand up, then they sit down, and the sound as of the sea is suddenly hushed. Stillness reigns.

I know what I am going to lecture about, but I don't know how I am going to lecture, where I am going to begin or with what I am going to end. I haven't a single sentence ready in my head. But I have only to look round the lecture hall (it is built in the form of an amphitheatre) and utter the stereotyped phrase, "Last lecture we stopped at . . ." when sentences spring up from my soul in a long string, and I am carried away by my own eloquence. I speak with irresistible rapidity and passion, and it seems as though there were no force which could check the flow of my words. To lecture well—that is, with profit to the listeners and without boring them—one must have, besides talent, experience and a special knack; one must possess a clear conception of one's own powers, of the audience to which one is lecturing, and of the subject of one's lecture. Moreover, one must be a man who knows what he is doing; one must keep a sharp lookout, and not for one second lose sight of what lies before one.

A good conductor, interpreting the thought of the composer, does twenty things at once: reads the score, waves his baton, watches the singer, makes a motion sideways, first to the drum then to the wind-instruments, and so on. I do just the same when I lecture. Before me a hundred and fifty faces, all unlike one another; three hundred eyes all looking straight into my face. My object is to dominate this many-headed monster. If every moment as I lecture I have a clear vision of the degree of its attention and its power of comprehension, it is in my power. The other foe I have to overcome is in myself. It is the infinite variety of forms, phenomena, laws, and the multitude of ideas of my own and other people's conditioned by them. Every moment I must have the skill to snatch out of that vast mass of material what is most important and necessary, and, as rapidly as my words flow, clothe my thought in a form in which it can be grasped by the monster's intelligence, and may arouse its attention, and at the same time one must keep a sharp lookout that one's thoughts are conveyed, not just as they come, but in a certain order, essential for the correct composition of the picture I wish to sketch. Further, I endeavour to make my diction literary, my definitions brief and precise, my wording, as far as possible, simple and eloquent. Every minute I have to pull myself up and remember that I have only an hour and forty minutes at my disposal. In short, one has one's work cut out. At one and the same minute one has to play the part of savant and teacher and orator, and it's a bad thing if the orator gets the upper hand of the savant or of the teacher in one, or *vice versa*.

You lecture for a quarter of an hour, for half an hour, when you notice that the students are beginning to look at the ceiling, at Pyotr Ignatyevitch; one is feeling for his handkerchief, another shifts in his seat, another smiles at his thoughts. . . . That means that their attention is flagging. Something must be done. Taking advantage of the first opportunity, I make some pun. A broad grin comes on to a hundred and fifty faces, the eyes shine brightly, the sound of the sea is audible for a brief moment. . . . I laugh too. Their attention is refreshed, and I can go on.

No kind of sport, no kind of game or diversion, has ever given me such enjoyment as lecturing. Only at lectures have I been able to abandon myself entirely to passion, and have understood that inspiration is not an invention of the poets, but exists in real life, and I imagine Hercules after the most piquant of his exploits felt just such voluptuous exhaustion as I experience after every lecture.

That was in old times. Now at lectures I feel nothing but torture. Before half an hour is over I am conscious of an overwhelming weakness in my legs and my shoulders. I sit down in my chair, but I am not accustomed to lecture sitting down; a minute later I get up and go on standing, then sit down again. There is a dryness in my mouth, my voice grows husky, my head begins to go round. . . . To conceal my condition from my audience I continually drink water, cough, often blow my nose as though I were hindered by a cold, make puns inappropriately, and in the end break off earlier than I ought to. But above all I am ashamed.

My conscience and my intelligence tell me that the very best thing I could do now would be to deliver a farewell lecture to the boys, to say my last word to them, to bless them, and give up my post to a man younger and stronger than me. But, God, be my judge, I have not manly courage enough to act according to my conscience.

Unfortunately, I am not a philosopher and not a theologian. I know perfectly well that I cannot live more than another six months; it might be supposed that I ought now to be chiefly concerned with the question of the shadowy life beyond the grave, and the visions that will visit my slumbers in the tomb. But for some reason my soul refuses to recognize these questions, though my mind is fully alive to their importance. Just as twenty, thirty years ago, so now, on the threshold of death, I am interested in nothing but science. As I yield up my last breath I shall still believe that science is the most important, the most splendid, the most essential thing in the life of man; that it always has been and will be the highest manifestation of love, and that only by means of it will man conquer himself and nature. This faith is perhaps naive and may rest on false assumptions, but it is not my fault that I believe that and nothing else; I cannot overcome in myself this belief.

But that is not the point. I only ask people to be indulgent to my weakness, and to realize that to tear from the lecture-theatre and his pupils a man who is more interested in the history of the development of the bone medulla than in the final object of creation would be equivalent to taking him and nailing him up in his coffin without waiting for him to be dead.

Sleeplessness and the consequent strain of combating increasing weakness leads to something strange in me. In the middle of my lecture tears suddenly rise in my throat, my eyes begin to smart, and I feel a passionate, hysterical desire to stretch out my hands before me and break into loud lamentation. I want to cry out in a loud voice that I, a famous man, have been sentenced by fate to the death penalty, that within some six months another man will be in control here in the lecture-theatre. I want to shriek that I am poisoned; new ideas such as I have not known before have poisoned the last days of my life, and are still stinging my brain like mosquitoes. And at that moment my position seems to me so awful that I want all my listeners to be horrified, to leap up from their seats and to rush in panic terror, with desperate screams, to the exit.

It is not easy to get through such moments.

II

After my lecture I sit at home and work. I read journals and monographs, or prepare my next lecture; sometimes I write something. I work with interruptions, as I have from time to time to see visitors.

There is a ring at the bell. It is a colleague come to discuss some business matter with me. He comes in to me with his hat and his stick, and, holding out both these objects to me, says:

"Only for a minute! Only for a minute! Sit down, *collega*! Only a couple of words."

To begin with, we both try to show each other that we are extraordinarily polite and highly delighted to see each other. I make him sit down in an easy chair, and he makes me sit down; as we do so, we cautiously pat each other on the back, touch each other's buttons, and it looks as though we were feeling each other and afraid of scorching our fingers. Both of us laugh, though we say nothing amusing. When we are seated we bow our heads towards each other and begin talking in subdued voices. However affectionately disposed we may be to one another, we cannot help adorning our conversation with all sorts of Chinese mannerisms, such as "As you so justly observed," or "I have already had the honour to inform you"; we cannot help laughing if one of us makes a joke, however unsuccessfully. When we have finished with business my colleague gets up impulsively and, waving his hat in the direction of my work, begins to say goodbye. Again we paw one another and laugh. I see him into the hall; when I assist my colleague to put on his coat, while he does all he can to decline this high honour. Then when Yegor opens the door my colleague declares that I shall catch cold, while I make a show of being ready to go even into the street with him. And when at last I go back into my study my face still goes on smiling, I suppose from inertia.

A little later another ring at the bell. Somebody comes into the hall, and is a long time coughing and taking off his things. Yegor announces a student. I tell him to ask him in. A minute later a young man of agreeable appearance comes in. For the last year he and I have been on strained relations; he answers me disgracefully at the examinations, and I mark him one. Every year I have some seven such hopefuls whom, to express it in the students' slang, I "chivy" or "floor." Those of them who fail in their examination through incapacity or illness usually bear their cross patiently and do not haggle with me; those who come to the house and haggle with me are always youths of sanguine temperament, broad natures, whose failure at examinations spoils their appetites and hinders them from visiting the opera with their usual regularity. I let the first class off easily, but the second I chivy through a whole year.

"Sit down," I say to my visitor; "what have you to tell me?"

"Excuse me, professor, for troubling you," he begins, hesitating, and not looking me in the face. "I would not have ventured to trouble you if it had not been . . . I have been up for your examination five times, and have been ploughed. . . . I beg you, be so good as to mark me for a pass, because . . ."

The argument which all the sluggards bring forward on their own behalf is always the same; they have passed well in all their subjects and have only come to grief in mine, and that is the more surprising because they have always been particularly interested in my subject and knew it so well; their failure has always been entirely owing to some incomprehensible misunderstanding.

"Excuse me, my friend," I say to the visitor; "I cannot mark you for a pass. Go and read up the lectures and come to me again. Then we shall see."

A pause. I feel an impulse to torment the student a little for liking beer and the opera better than science, and I say, with a sigh:

"To my mind, the best thing you can do now is to give up medicine altogether. If, with your abilities, you cannot succeed in passing the examination, it's evident that you have neither the desire nor the vocation for a doctor's calling."

The sanguine youth's face lengthens.

"Excuse me, professor," he laughs, "but that would be odd of me, to say the least of it. After studying for five years, all at once to give it up."

"Oh, well! Better to have lost your five years than have to spend the rest of your life in doing work you do not care for."

But at once I feel sorry for him, and I hasten to add:

"However, as you think best. And so read a little more and come again."

"When?" the idle youth asks in a hollow voice.

"When you like. Tomorrow if you like."

And in his good-natured eyes I read:

"I can come all right, but of course you will plough me again, you beast!"

"Of course," I say, "you won't know more science for going in for my examination another fifteen times, but it is training your character, and you must be thankful for that."

Silence follows. I get up and wait for my visitor to go, but he stands and looks towards the window, fingers his beard, and thinks. It grows boring.

The sanguine youth's voice is pleasant and mellow, his eyes are clever and ironical, his face is genial, though a little bloated from frequent indulgence in beer and overlong lying on the sofa; he looks as though he could tell me a lot of interesting things about the opera, about his affairs of the heart, and about comrades whom he likes. Unluckily, it is not the thing to discuss these subjects, or else I should have been glad to listen to him.

"Professor, I give you my word of honour that if you mark me for a pass I . . . I'll . . ."

As soon as we reach the "word of honour" I wave my hands and sit down to the table. The student ponders a minute longer, and says dejectedly:

"In that case, goodbye . . . I beg your pardon."

"Goodbye, my friend. Good luck to you."

He goes irresolutely into the hall, slowly puts on his outdoor things, and, going out into the street, probably ponders for some time longer; unable to think of anything, except "old devil," inwardly addressed to me, he goes into a wretched restaurant to dine and drink beer, and then home to bed. "Peace be to thy ashes, honest toiler."

A third ring at the bell. A young doctor, in a pair of new black trousers, gold spectacles, and of course a white tie, walks in. He introduces himself. I beg him to be seated, and ask what I can do for him. Not without emotion, the young devotee of science begins telling me that he has passed his examination as a doctor of medicine, and that he has now only to write his dissertation. He would like to work with me under my guidance, and he would be greatly obliged to me if I would give him a subject for his dissertation.

"Very glad to be of use to you, colleague," I say, "but just let us come to an understanding as to the meaning of a dissertation. That word is taken to mean a composition which is a product of independent creative effort. Is that not so? A work written on another man's subject and under another man's guidance is called something different. . . ."

The doctor says nothing. I fly into a rage and jump up from my seat.

"Why is it you all come to me?" I cry angrily. "Do I keep a shop? I don't deal in subjects. For the thousand and oneth time I ask you all to leave me in peace! Excuse my brutality, but I am quite sick of it!"

The doctor remains silent, but a faint flush is apparent on his cheekbones. His face expresses a profound reverence for my fame and my learning, but from his eyes I can see he feels a contempt for my voice, my pitiful figure, and my nervous gesticulation. I impress him in my anger as a queer fish.

"I don't keep a shop," I go on angrily. "And it is a strange thing! Why don't you want to be independent? Why have you such a distaste for independence?"

I say a great deal, but he still remains silent. By degrees I calm down, and of course give in. The doctor gets a subject from me for his theme not worth a halfpenny, writes under my supervision a dissertation of no use to any one, with dignity defends it in a dreary discussion, and receives a degree of no use to him.

The rings at the bell may follow one another endlessly, but I will confine my description here to four of them. The bell rings for the fourth time, and I hear familiar footsteps, the rustle of a dress, a dear voice. . . .

Eighteen years ago a colleague of mine, an oculist, died leaving a little daughter Katya, a child of seven, and sixty thousand roubles. In his will he made me the child's guardian. Till she was ten years old Katya lived with us as one of the family, then she was sent to a boarding-school, and only spent the summer holidays with us. I never had time to look after her education. I only superintended it at leisure moments, and so I can say very little about her childhood.

The first thing I remember, and like so much in remembrance, is the extraordinary trustfulness with which she came into our house and let herself be treated by the doctors, a trustfulness which was always shining in her little face. She would sit somewhere out of the way, with her face tied up, invariably watching something with attention; whether she watched me writing or turning over the pages of a book, or watched my wife bustling about, or the cook scrubbing a potato in the kitchen, or the dog playing, her eyes invariably expressed the same thought—that is, "Everything that is done in this world is nice and sensible." She was curious, and very fond of talking to me. Sometimes she would sit at the table opposite me, watching my movements and asking questions. It interested her to know what I was reading, what I did at the University, whether I was not afraid of the dead bodies, what I did with my salary.

"Do the students fight at the University?" she would ask.

"They do, dear."

"And do you make them go down on their knees?"

"Yes, I do."

And she thought it funny that the students fought and I made them go down on their knees, and she laughed. She was a gentle, patient, good child. It happened not infrequently that I saw something taken away from her, saw her punished without reason, or her curiosity repressed; at such times a look of sadness was mixed with the invariable expression of trustfulness on her face—that was all. I did not know how to take her part; only when I saw her sad I had an inclination to draw her to me and to commiserate her like some old nurse: "My poor little orphan one!"

I remember, too, that she was fond of fine clothes and of sprinkling herself with scent. In that respect she was like me. I, too, am fond of pretty clothes and nice scent.

I regret that I had not time nor inclination to watch over the rise and development of the passion which took complete possession of Katya when she was fourteen or fifteen. I mean her passionate love for the theatre. When she used to come from boarding-school and stay with us for the summer holidays, she talked of nothing with such pleasure and such warmth as of plays and actors. She bored us with her continual talk of the theatre. My wife and children would not listen to her. I was the only one who had not the courage to refuse to attend to her. When she had a longing to share her transports, she used to come into my study and say in an imploring tone:

"Nikolay Stepanovitch, do let me talk to you about the theatre!"

I pointed to the clock, and said:

"I'll give you half an hour—begin."

Later on she used to bring with her dozens of portraits of actors and actresses which she worshipped; then she attempted several times to take part in private theatricals, and the upshot of it all was that when she left school she came to me and announced that she was born to be an actress.

I had never shared Katya's inclinations for the theatre. To my mind, if a play is good there is no need to trouble the actors in order that it may make the right impression; it is enough to read it. If the play is poor, no acting will make it good.

In my youth I often visited the theatre, and now my family takes a box twice a year and carries me off for a little distraction. Of course, that is not enough to give me the right to judge of the theatre. In my opinion the theatre has become no better than it was thirty or forty years ago. Just as in the past, I can never find a glass of clean water in the corridors or foyers of the theatre. Just as in the past, the attendants fine me twenty kopecks for my fur coat, though there is nothing reprehensible in wearing a warm coat in winter. As in the past, for no sort of reason, music is played in the intervals, which adds something new and uncalled-for to the impression made by the play. As in the past, men go in the intervals and drink spirits in the buffet. If no progress can be seen in trifles, I should look for it in vain in what is more important. When an actor wrapped from head to foot in stage traditions and conventions tries to recite a simple ordinary speech, "To be or not to be," not simply, but invariably with the accompaniment of hissing and convulsive movements all over his body, or when he tries to convince me at all costs that Tchatsky, who talks so much with fools and is so fond of folly, is a very clever man, and that "Woe from Wit" is not a dull play, the stage gives me the same feeling of conventionality which bored me so much forty years ago when I was regaled with the classical howling and beating on the breast. And every time I come out of the theatre more conservative than I go in.

The sentimental and confiding public may be persuaded that the stage, even in its present form, is a school; but any one who is familiar with a school in its true sense will not be caught with that bait. I cannot say what will happen in fifty or a hundred years, but in its actual condition the theatre can serve only as an entertainment. But this entertainment is too costly to be frequently enjoyed. It robs the state of thousands of healthy and talented young men and women, who, if they had not devoted themselves to the theatre, might have been good doctors, farmers, schoolmistresses, officers; it robs the public of the evening hours—the best time for intellectual work and social intercourse. I say nothing of the waste of money and the moral damage to the spectator when he sees murder, fornication, or false witness unsuitably treated on the stage.

Katya was of an entirely different opinion. She assured me that the theatre, even in its present condition, was superior to the lecture hall, to books, or to anything in the world. The stage was a power that united in itself all the arts, and actors were missionaries. No art nor science was capable of producing so strong and so certain an effect on the soul of man as the stage, and it was with good reason that an actor of medium quality enjoys greater popularity than the greatest savant or artist. And no sort of public service could provide such enjoyment and gratification as the theatre.

And one fine day Katya joined a troupe of actors, and went off, I believe to Ufa, taking away with her a good supply of money, a store of rainbow hopes, and the most aristocratic views of her work.

Her first letters on the journey were marvellous. I read them, and was simply amazed that those small sheets of paper could contain so much youth, purity of spirit, holy innocence, and at the same time subtle and apt judgments which would have done credit to a fine masculine intellect. It was more like a rapturous paean of praise she sent me than a mere description of the Volga, the country, the towns she visited, her companions, her failures and successes; every sentence was fragrant with that confiding trustfulness I was accustomed to read in her face—and at the same time there were a great many grammatical mistakes, and there was scarcely any punctuation at all.

Before six months had passed I received a highly poetical and enthusiastic letter beginning with the words, "I have come to love . . ." This letter was accompanied by a photograph representing a young man with a shaven face, a wide-brimmed hat, and a plaid flung over his shoulder. The letters that followed were as splendid as before, but now commas and stops made their appearance in them, the grammatical mistakes disappeared, and there was a distinctly masculine flavour about them. Katya began writing to me how splendid it would be to build a great theatre somewhere on the Volga, on a cooperative system, and to attract to the enterprise the rich merchants and the steamer owners; there would be a great deal of money in it; there would be vast audiences; the actors would play on co-operative terms. . . . Possibly all this was really excellent, but it seemed to me that such schemes could only originate from a man's mind.

However that may have been, for a year and a half everything seemed to go well: Katya was in love, believed in her work, and was happy; but then I began to notice in her letters unmistakable signs of falling off. It began with Katya's complaining of her companions—this was the first and most ominous symptom; if a young scientific or literary man begins his career with bitter complaints of scientific and literary men, it is a sure sign that he is worn out and not fit for his work. Katya wrote to me that her companions did not attend the rehearsals and never knew their parts; that one could see in every one of them an utter disrespect for the public in the production of absurd plays, and in their behaviour on the stage; that for the benefit of the Actors' Fund, which they only talked about, actresses of the serious drama demeaned themselves by singing chansonettes, while tragic actors sang comic songs making fun of deceived husbands and the pregnant condition of unfaithful wives, and so on. In fact, it was amazing that all this had not yet ruined the provincial stage, and that it could still maintain itself on such a rotten and unsubstantial footing.

In answer I wrote Katya a long and, I must confess, a very boring letter. Among other things, I wrote to her:

"I have more than once happened to converse with old actors, very worthy men, who showed a friendly disposition towards me; from my conversations with them I could understand that their work was controlled not so much by their own intelligence and free choice as by fashion and the mood of the public. The best of them had had to play in their day in tragedy, in operetta, in Parisian farces, and in extravaganzas, and they always seemed equally sure that they were on the right path and that they were of use. So, as you see, the cause of the evil must be sought, not in the actors, but, more deeply, in the art itself and in the attitude of the whole of society to it."

This letter of mine only irritated Katya. She answered me:

"You and I are singing parts out of different operas. I wrote to you, not of the worthy men who showed a friendly disposition to you, but of a band of knaves who have nothing worthy about them. They are a horde of savages who have got on the stage simply because no one would have taken them elsewhere, and who call themselves artists simply because they are impudent. There are numbers of dull-witted creatures, drunkards, intriguing schemers and slanderers, but there is not one person of talent among them. I cannot tell you how bitter it is to me that the art I love has fallen into the hands of people I detest; how bitter it is that the best men look on at evil from afar, not caring to come closer, and, instead of intervening, write ponderous commonplaces and utterly useless sermons. . . ." And so on, all in the same style.

A little time passed, and I got this letter: "I have been brutally deceived. I cannot go on living. Dispose of my money as you think best. I loved you as my father and my only friend. Goodbye."

It turned out that *he*, too, belonged to the "horde of savages." Later on, from certain hints, I gathered that there had been an attempt at suicide. I believe Katya tried to poison herself. I imagine that she must have been seriously ill afterwards, as the next letter I got was from Yalta, where she had most probably been sent by the doctors. Her last letter contained a request to send her a thousand roubles to Yalta as quickly as possible, and ended with these words:

"Excuse the gloominess of this letter; yesterday I buried my child." After spending about a year in the Crimea, she returned home.

She had been about four years on her travels, and during those four years, I must confess, I had played a rather strange and unenviable part in regard to her. When in earlier days she had told me she was going on the stage, and then wrote to me of her love; when she was periodically overcome by extravagance, and I continually had to send her first one and then two thousand roubles; when she wrote to me of her intention of suicide, and then of the death of her baby, every time I lost my head, and all my sympathy for her sufferings found no expression except that, after prolonged reflection, I wrote long, boring letters which I might just as well not have written. And yet I took a father's place with her and loved her like a daughter!

Now Katya is living less than half a mile off. She has taken a flat of five rooms, and has installed herself fairly comfortably and in the taste of the day. If any one were to undertake to describe her surroundings, the most characteristic note in the picture would be indolence. For the indolent body there are soft lounges, soft stools; for indolent feet soft rugs; for indolent eyes faded, dingy, or flat colours; for the indolent soul the walls are hung with a number of cheap fans and trivial pictures, in which the originality of the execution is more conspicuous than the subject; and the room contains a multitude of little tables and shelves filled with utterly useless articles of no value, and shapeless rags in place of curtains. . . .

All this, together with the dread of bright colours, of symmetry, and of empty space, bears witness not only to spiritual indolence, but also to a corruption of natural taste. For days together Katya lies on the lounge reading, principally novels and stories. She only goes out of the house once a day, in the afternoon, to see me.

I go on working while Katya sits silent not far from me on the sofa, wrapping herself in her shawl, as though she were cold. Either because I find her sympathetic or because I was used to her frequent visits when she was a little girl, her presence does not prevent me from concentrating my attention. From time to time I mechanically ask her some question; she gives very brief replies; or, to rest for a minute, I turn round and watch her as she looks dreamily at some medical journal or review. And at such moments I notice that her face has lost the old look of confiding trustfulness. Her expression now is cold, apathetic, and absent-minded, like that of passengers who had to wait too long for a train. She is dressed, as in old days, simply and beautifully, but carelessly; her dress and her hair show visible traces of the sofas and rocking chairs in which she spends whole days at a stretch. And she has lost the curiosity she had in old days. She has ceased to ask me questions now, as though she had experienced everything in life and looked for nothing new from it.

Towards four o'clock there begins to be sounds of movement in the hall and in the drawing room. Liza has come back from the Conservatoire, and has brought some girlfriends in with her. We hear them playing on the piano, trying their voices and laughing; in the dining room Yegor is laying the table, with the clatter of crockery.

"Goodbye," said Katya. "I won't go in and see your people today. They must excuse me. I haven't time. Come and see me."

While I am seeing her to the door, she looks me up and down grimly, and says with vexation:

"You are getting thinner and thinner! Why don't you consult a doctor? I'll call at Sergey Fyodorovitch's and ask him to have a look at you."

"There's no need, Katya."

"I can't think where your people's eyes are! They are a nice lot, I must say!"

She puts on her fur coat abruptly, and as she does so two or three hairpins drop unnoticed on the floor from her carelessly arranged hair.

She is too lazy and in too great a hurry to do her hair up; she carelessly stuffs the falling curls under her hat, and goes away.

When I go into the dining room my wife asks me:

"Was Katya with you just now? Why didn't she come in to see us? It's really strange. . . ."

"Mamma," Liza says to her reproachfully, "let her alone, if she doesn't want to. We are not going down on our knees to her."

"It's very neglectful, anyway. To sit for three hours in the study without remembering our existence! But of course she must do as she likes."

Varya and Liza both hate Katya. This hatred is beyond my comprehension, and probably one would have to be a woman in order to understand it. I am ready to stake my life that of the hundred and fifty young men I see every day in the lecture-theatre, and of the hundred elderly ones I meet every week, hardly one could be found capable of understanding their hatred and aversion for Katya's past—that is, for her having been a mother without being a wife, and for her having had an illegitimate child; and at the same time I cannot recall one woman or girl of my acquaintance who would not consciously or unconsciously harbour such feelings. And this is not because woman is purer or more virtuous than man: why, virtue and purity are not very different from vice if they are not free from evil feeling. I attribute this simply to the backwardness of woman. The mournful feeling of compassion and the pang of conscience experienced by a modern man at the sight of suffering is, to my mind, far greater proof of culture and moral elevation than hatred and aversion. Woman is as tearful and as coarse in her feelings now as she was in the Middle Ages, and to my thinking those who advise that she should be educated like a man are quite right.

My wife also dislikes Katya for having been an actress, for ingratitude, for pride, for eccentricity, and for the numerous vices which one woman can always find in another.

Besides my wife and daughter and me, there are dining with us two or three of my daughter's friends and Alexandr Adolfovitch Gnekker, her admirer and suitor. He is a fair-haired young man under thirty, of medium height, very stout and broad-shouldered, with red whiskers near his ears, and little waxed moustaches which make his plump smooth face look like a toy. He is dressed in a very short reefer jacket, a flowered waistcoat, breeches very full at the top and very narrow at the ankle, with a large check pattern on them, and yellow boots without heels. He has prominent eyes like a crab's, his cravat is like a crab's neck, and I even fancy there is a smell of crab-soup about the young man's whole person. He visits us every day, but no one in my family knows anything of his origin nor of the place of his education, nor of his means of livelihood. He neither plays nor sings, but has some connection with music and singing, sells somebody's pianos somewhere, is frequently at the Conservatoire, is acquainted with all the celebrities, and is a steward at the concerts; he criticizes music with great authority, and I have noticed that people are eager to agree with him.

Rich people always have dependents hanging about them; the arts and sciences have the same. I believe there is not an art nor a science in the world free from "foreign bodies" after the style of this Mr. Gnekker. I am not a musician, and possibly I am mistaken in regard to Mr. Gnekker, of whom, indeed, I know very little. But his air of authority and the dignity with which he takes his stand beside the piano when any one is playing or singing strike me as very suspicious.

You may be ever so much of a gentleman and a privy councillor, but if you have a daughter you cannot be secure of immunity from that petty bourgeois atmosphere which is so often brought into your house and into your mood by the attentions of suitors, by matchmaking and marriage. I can never reconcile myself, for instance, to the expression of triumph on my wife's face every time Gnekker is in our company, nor can I reconcile myself to the bottles of Lafitte, port and sherry which are only brought out on his account, that he may see with his own eyes the liberal and luxurious way in which we live. I cannot tolerate the habit of spasmodic laughter Liza has picked up at the Conservatoire, and her way of screwing up her eyes whenever there are men in the room. Above all, I cannot understand why a creature utterly alien to my habits, my studies, my whole manner of life, completely different from the people I like, should come and see me every day, and every day should dine with me. My wife and my servants mysteriously whisper that he is a suitor, but still I don't understand his presence; it rouses in me the same wonder and perplexity as if they were to set a Zulu beside me at the table. And it seems strange to me, too, that my daughter, whom I am used to thinking of as a child, should love that cravat, those eyes, those soft cheeks. . . .

In the old days I used to like my dinner, or at least was indifferent about it; now it excites in me no feeling but weariness and irritation. Ever since I became an "Excellency" and one of the Deans of the Faculty my family has for some reason found it necessary to make a complete change in our menu and dining habits. Instead of the simple dishes to which I was accustomed when I was a student and when I was in practice, now they feed me with a puree with little white things like circles floating about in it, and kidneys stewed in madeira. My rank as a general and my fame have robbed me for ever of cabbage-soup and savoury pies, and goose with apple-sauce, and bream with boiled grain. They have robbed me of our maid-servant Agasha, a chatty and laughter-loving old woman, instead of whom Yegor, a dull-witted and conceited fellow with a white glove on his right hand, waits at dinner. The intervals between the courses are short, but they seem immensely long because there is nothing to occupy them. There is none of the gaiety of the old days, the spontaneous talk, the jokes, the laughter; there is nothing of mutual affection and the joy which used to animate the children, my wife, and me when in old days we met together at meals. For me, the celebrated man of science, dinner was a time of rest and reunion, and for my wife and children a fete—brief indeed, but bright and joyous—in which they knew that for half an hour I belonged, not to science, not to students, but to them alone. Our real exhilaration from one glass of wine is gone for ever, gone is Agasha, gone the bream with boiled grain, gone the uproar that greeted every little startling incident at dinner, such as the cat and dog fighting under the table, or Katya's bandage falling off her face into her soup-plate.

To describe our dinner nowadays is as uninteresting as to eat it. My wife's face wears a look of triumph and affected dignity, and her habitual expression of anxiety. She looks at our plates and says, "I see you don't care for the joint. Tell me; you don't like it, do you?" and I am obliged to answer: "There is no need for you to trouble, my dear; the meat is very nice." And she will say: "You always stand up for me, Nikolay Stepanovitch, and you never tell the truth. Why is Alexandr Adolfovitch eating so little?" And so on in the same style all through dinner. Liza laughs spasmodically and screws up her eyes. I watch them both, and it is only now at dinner that it becomes absolutely evident to me that the inner life of these two has slipped away out of my ken. I have a feeling as though I had once lived at home with a real wife and children and that now I am dining with visitors, in the house of a sham wife who is not the real one, and am looking at a Liza who is not the real Liza. A startling change has taken place in both of them; I have missed the long process by which that change was effected, and it is no wonder that I can make nothing of it. Why did that change take place? I don't know. Perhaps the whole trouble is that God has not given my wife and daughter the same strength of character as me. From childhood I have been accustomed to resisting external influences, and have steeled myself pretty thoroughly. Such catastrophes in life as fame, the rank of a general, the transition from comfort to living beyond our means, acquaintance with celebrities, etc., have scarcely affected me, and I have remained intact and unashamed; but on my wife and Liza, who have not been through the same hardening process and are weak, all this has fallen like an avalanche of snow, overwhelming them. Gnekker and the young ladies talk of fugues, of counterpoint, of singers and pianists, of Bach and Brahms, while my wife, afraid of their suspecting her of ignorance of music, smiles to them sympathetically and mutters: "That's exquisite . . . really! You don't say so! . . ." Gnekker eats with solid dignity, jests with solid dignity, and condescendingly listens to the remarks of the young ladies. From time to time he is moved to speak in bad French, and then, for some reason or other, he thinks it necessary to address me as *"Votre Excellence."*

And I am glum. Evidently I am a constraint to them and they are a constraint to me. I have never in my earlier days had a close knowledge of class antagonism, but now I am tormented by something of that sort. I am on the lookout for nothing but bad qualities in Gnekker; I quickly find them, and am fretted at the thought that a man not of my circle is sitting here as my daughter's suitor. His presence has a bad influence on me in other ways, too. As a rule, when I am alone or in the society of people I like, never think of my own achievements, or, if I do recall them, they seem to me as trivial as though I had only completed my studies yesterday; but in the presence of people like Gnekker my achievements in science seem to be a lofty mountain the top of which vanishes into the clouds, while at its foot Gnekkers are running about scarcely visible to the naked eye.

After dinner I go into my study and there smoke my pipe, the only one in the whole day, the sole relic of my old bad habit of smoking from morning till night. While I am smoking my wife comes in and sits down to talk to me. Just as in the morning, I know beforehand what our conversation is going to be about.

"I must talk to you seriously, Nikolay Stepanovitch," she begins. "I mean about Liza. . . . Why don't you pay attention to it?"

"To what?"

"You pretend to notice nothing. But that is not right. We can't shirk responsibility. . . . Gnekker has intentions in regard to Liza. . . . What do you say?"

"That he is a bad man I can't say, because I don't know him, but that I don't like him I have told you a thousand times already."

"But you can't . . . you can't!"

She gets up and walks about in excitement.

"You can't take up that attitude to a serious step," she says. "When it is a question of our daughter's happiness we must lay aside all personal feeling. I know you do not like him. . . . Very good . . . if we refuse him now, if we break it all off, how can you be sure that Liza will not have a grievance against us all her life? Suitors are not plentiful nowadays, goodness knows, and it may happen that no other match will turn up. . . . He is very much in love with Liza, and she seems to like him. . . . Of course, he has no settled position, but that can't be helped. Please God, in time he will get one. He is of good family and well off."

"Where did you learn that?"

"He told us so. His father has a large house in Harkov and an estate in the neighbourhood. In short, Nikolay Stepanovitch, you absolutely must go to Harkov."

"What for?"

"You will find out all about him there. . . . You know the professors there; they will help you. I would go myself, but I am a woman. I cannot. . . ."

"I am not going to Harkov," I say morosely.

My wife is frightened, and a look of intense suffering comes into her face.

"For God's sake, Nikolay Stepanovitch," she implores me, with tears in her voice—"for God's sake, take this burden off me! I am so worried!"

It is painful for me to look at her.

"Very well, Varya," I say affectionately, "if you wish it, then certainly I will go to Harkov and do all you want."

She presses her handkerchief to her eyes and goes off to her room to cry, and I am left alone.

A little later lights are brought in. The armchair and the lampshade cast familiar shadows that have long grown wearisome on the walls and on the floor, and when I look at them I feel as though the night had come and with it my accursed sleeplessness. I lie on my bed, then get up and walk about the room, then lie down again. As a rule it is after dinner, at the approach of evening, that my nervous excitement reaches its highest pitch. For no reason I begin crying and burying my head in the pillow. At such times I am afraid that some one may come in; I am afraid of suddenly dying; I am ashamed of my tears, and altogether there is something insufferable in my soul. I feel that I can no longer bear the sight of my lamp, of my books, of the shadows on the floor. I cannot bear the sound of the voices coming from the drawing room. Some force unseen, uncomprehended, is roughly thrusting me out of my flat. I leap up hurriedly, dress, and cautiously, that my family may not notice, slip out into the street. Where am I to go?

The answer to that question has long been ready in my brain. To Katya.

III

As a rule she is lying on the sofa or in a lounge-chair reading. Seeing me, she raises her head languidly, sits up, and shakes hands.

"You are always lying down," I say, after pausing and taking breath. "That's not good for you. You ought to occupy yourself with something."

"What?"

"I say you ought to occupy yourself in some way."

"With what? A woman can be nothing but a simple workwoman or an actress."

"Well, if you can't be a workwoman, be an actress."

She says nothing.

"You ought to get married," I say, half in jest.

"There is no one to marry. There's no reason to, either."

"You can't live like this."

"Without a husband? Much that matters; I could have as many men as I like if I wanted to."

"That's ugly, Katya."

194

"What is ugly?"

"Why, what you have just said."

Noticing that I am hurt and wishing to efface the disagreeable impression, Katya says:

"Let us go; come this way."

She takes me into a very snug little room, and says, pointing to the writing-table:

"Look . . . I have got that ready for you. You shall work here. Come here every day and bring your work with you. They only hinder you there at home. Will you work here? Will you like to?"

Not to wound her by refusing, I answer that I will work here, and that I like the room very much. Then we both sit down in the snug little room and begin talking.

The warm, snug surroundings and the presence of a sympathetic person does not, as in old days, arouse in me a feeling of pleasure, but an intense impulse to complain and grumble. I feel for some reason that if I lament and complain I shall feel better.

"Things are in a bad way with me, my dear—very bad. . . ."

"What is it?"

"You see how it is, my dear; the best and holiest right of kings is the right of mercy. And I have always felt myself a king, since I have made unlimited use of that right. I have never judged, I have been indulgent, I have readily forgiven every one, right and left. Where others have protested and expressed indignation, I have only advised and persuaded. All my life it has been my endeavour that my society should not be a burden to my family, to my students, to my colleagues, to my servants. And I know that this attitude to people has had a good influence on all who have chanced to come into contact with me. But now I am not a king. Something is happening to me that is only excusable in a slave; day and night my brain is haunted by evil thoughts, and feelings such as I never knew before are brooding in my soul. I am full of hatred, and contempt, and indignation, and loathing, and dread. I have become excessively severe, exacting, irritable, ungracious, suspicious. Even things that in old days would have provoked me only to an unnecessary jest and a good-natured laugh now arouse an oppressive feeling in me. My reasoning, too, has undergone a change: in old days I despised money; now I harbour an evil feeling, not towards money, but towards the rich as though they were to blame: in old days I hated violence and tyranny, but now I hate the men who make use of violence, as though they were alone to blame, and not all of us who do not know how to educate each other. What is the meaning of it? If these new ideas and new feelings have come from a change of convictions, what is that change due to? Can the world have grown worse and I better, or was I blind before and indifferent? If this change is the result of a general decline of physical and intellectual powers—I am ill, you know, and every day I am losing weight—my position is pitiable; it means that my new ideas are morbid and abnormal; I ought to be ashamed of them and think them of no consequence. . . ."

"Illness has nothing to do with it," Katya interrupts me; "it's simply that your eyes are opened, that's all. You have seen what in old days, for some reason, you refused to see. To my thinking, what you ought to do first of all, is to break with your family for good, and go away."

"You are talking nonsense."

"You don't love them; why should you force your feelings? Can you call them a family? Nonentities! If they died today, no one would notice their absence tomorrow."

Katya despises my wife and Liza as much as they hate her. One can hardly talk at this date of people's having a right to despise one another. But if one looks at it from Katya's standpoint and recognizes such a right, one can see she has as much right to despise my wife and Liza as they have to hate her.

"Nonentities," she goes on. "Have you had dinner today? How was it they did not forget to tell you it was ready? How is it they still remember your existence?"

"Katya," I say sternly, "I beg you to be silent."

"You think I enjoy talking about them? I should be glad not to know them at all. Listen, my dear: give it all up and go away. Go abroad. The sooner the better."

"What nonsense! What about the University?"

"The University, too. What is it to you? There's no sense in it, anyway. You have been lecturing for thirty years, and where are your pupils? Are many of them celebrated scientific men? Count them up! And to multiply the doctors who exploit ignorance and pile up hundreds of thousands for themselves, there is no need to be a good and talented man. You are not wanted."

"Good heavens! how harsh you are!" I cry in horror. "How harsh you are! Be quiet or I will go away! I don't know how to answer the harsh things you say!"

The maid comes in and summons us to tea. At the samovar our conversation, thank God, changes. After having had my grumble out, I have a longing to give way to another weakness of old age, reminiscences. I tell Katya about my past, and to my great astonishment tell her incidents which, till then, I did not suspect of being still preserved in my memory, and she listens to me with tenderness, with pride, holding her breath. I am particularly fond of telling her how I was educated in a seminary and dreamed of going to the University.

"At times I used to walk about our seminary garden . . ." I would tell her. "If from some faraway tavern the wind floated sounds of a song and the squeaking of an accordion, or a sledge with bells dashed by the garden fence, it was quite enough to send a rush of happiness, filling not only my heart, but even my stomach, my legs, my arms. . . . I would listen to the accordion or the bells dying away in the distance and imagine myself a doctor, and paint pictures, one better than another. And here, as you see, my dreams have come true. I have had more than I dared to dream of. For thirty years I have been the favourite professor, I have had splendid comrades, I have enjoyed fame and honour. I have loved, married from passionate love, have had children. In fact, looking back upon it, I see my whole life as a fine composition arranged with talent. Now all that is left to me is not to spoil the end. For that I must die like a man. If death is really a thing to dread, I must meet it as a teacher, a man of science, and a citizen of a Christian country ought to meet it, with courage and untroubled soul. But I am spoiling the end; I am sinking, I fly to you, I beg for help, and you tell me 'Sink; that is what you ought to do.'"

But here there comes a ring at the front-door. Katya and I recognize it, and say:

"It must be Mihail Fyodorovitch."

And a minute later my colleague, the philologist Mihail Fyodorovitch, a tall, well-built man of fifty, clean-shaven, with thick grey hair and black eyebrows, walks in. He is a good-natured man and an excellent comrade. He comes of a fortunate and talented old noble family which has played a prominent part in the history of literature and enlightenment. He is himself intelligent, talented, and very highly educated, but has his oddities. To a certain extent we are all odd and all queer fish, but in his oddities there is something exceptional, apt to cause anxiety among his acquaintances. I know a good many people for whom his oddities completely obscure his good qualities.

Coming in to us, he slowly takes off his gloves and says in his velvety bass:

"Good evening. Are you having tea? That's just right. It's diabolically cold."

Then he sits down to the table, takes a glass, and at once begins talking. What is most characteristic in his manner of talking is the continually jesting tone, a sort of mixture of philosophy and drollery as in Shakespeare's gravediggers. He is always talking about serious things, but he never speaks seriously. His judgments are always harsh and railing, but, thanks to his soft, even, jesting tone, the harshness and abuse do not jar upon the ear, and one soon grows used to them. Every evening he brings with him five or six anecdotes from the University, and he usually begins with them when he sits down to table.

"Oh, Lord!" he sighs, twitching his black eyebrows ironically. "What comic people there are in the world!"

"Well?" asks Katya.

"As I was coming from my lecture this morning I met that old idiot N. N—— on the stairs. . . . He was going along as usual, sticking out his chin like a horse, looking for some one to listen to his grumblings at his migraine, at his wife, and his students who won't attend his lectures. 'Oh,' I thought, 'he has seen me—I am done for now; it is all up. . . .'"

And so on in the same style. Or he will begin like this:

"I was yesterday at our friend Z. Z——'s public lecture. I wonder how it is our alma mater—don't speak of it after dark—dare display in public such noodles and patent dullards as that Z. Z—— Why, he is a European fool! Upon my word, you could not find another like him all over Europe! He lectures—can you imagine?—as though he were sucking a sugar-stick—sue, sue, sue; . . . he is in a nervous funk; he can hardly decipher his own manuscript; his poor little thoughts crawl along like a bishop on a bicycle, and, what's worse, you can never make out what he is trying to say. The deadly dulness is awful, the very flies expire. It can only be compared with the boredom in the assembly-hall at the yearly meeting when the traditional address is read—damn it!"

And at once an abrupt transition:

"Three years ago—Nikolay Stepanovitch here will remember it—I had to deliver that address. It was hot, stifling, my uniform cut me under the arms—it was deadly! I read for half an hour, for an hour, for an hour and a half, for two hours. . . . 'Come,' I thought; 'thank God, there are only ten pages left!' And at the end there were four pages that there was no need to read, and I reckoned to leave them out. 'So there are only six really,' I thought; 'that is, only six pages left to read.' But, only fancy, I chanced to glance before me, and, sitting in the front row, side by side, were a general with a ribbon on his breast and a bishop. The poor beggars were numb with boredom; they were staring with their eyes wide open to keep awake, and yet they were trying to put on an expression of attention and to pretend that they understood what I was saying and liked it. 'Well,' I thought, 'since you like it you shall have it! I'll pay you out;' so I just gave them those four pages too."

As is usual with ironical people, when he talks nothing in his face smiles but his eyes and eyebrows. At such times there is no trace of hatred or spite in his eyes, but a great deal of humour, and that peculiar fox-like slyness which is only to be noticed in very observant people. Since I am speaking about his eyes, I notice another peculiarity in them. When he takes a glass from Katya, or listens to her speaking, or looks after her as she goes out of the room for a moment, I notice in his eyes something gentle, beseeching, pure. . . .

The maid-servant takes away the samovar and puts on the table a large piece of cheese, some fruit, and a bottle of Crimean champagne—a rather poor wine of which Katya had grown fond in the Crimea. Mihail Fyodorovitch takes two packs of cards off the whatnot and begins to play patience. According to him, some varieties of patience require great concentration and attention, yet while he lays out the cards he does not leave off distracting his attention with talk. Katya watches his cards attentively, and more by gesture than by words helps him in his play. She drinks no more than a couple of wine glasses of wine the whole evening; I drink four glasses, and the rest of the bottle falls to the share of Mihail Fyodorovitch, who can drink a great deal and never get drunk.

Over our patience we settle various questions, principally of the higher order, and what we care for most of all—that is, science and learning—is more roughly handled than anything.

"Science, thank God, has outlived its day," says Mihail Fyodorovitch emphatically. "Its song is sung. Yes, indeed. Mankind begins to feel impelled to replace it by something different. It has grown on the soil of superstition, been nourished by superstition, and is now just as much the quintessence of superstition as its defunct granddames, alchemy, metaphysics, and philosophy. And, after all, what has it given to mankind? Why, the difference between the learned Europeans and the Chinese who have no science is trifling, purely external. The Chinese know nothing of science, but what have they lost thereby?"

"Flies know nothing of science, either," I observe, "but what of that?"

"There is no need to be angry, Nikolay Stepanovitch. I only say this here between ourselves . . . I am more careful than you think, and I am not going to say this in public—God forbid! The superstition exists in the multitude that the arts and sciences are superior to agriculture, commerce, superior to handicrafts. Our sect is maintained by that superstition, and it is not for you and me to destroy it. God forbid!"

After patience the younger generation comes in for a dressing too.

"Our audiences have degenerated," sighs Mihail Fyodorovitch. "Not to speak of ideals and all the rest of it, if only they were capable of work and rational thought! In fact, it's a case of 'I look with mournful eyes on the young men of today.'"

"Yes; they have degenerated horribly," Katya agrees. "Tell me, have you had one man of distinction among them for the last five or ten years?"

"I don't know how it is with the other professors, but I can't remember any among mine."

"I have seen in my day many of your students and young scientific men and many actors—well, I have never once been so fortunate as to meet—I won't say a hero or a man of talent, but even an interesting man. It's all the same grey mediocrity, puffed up with self-conceit."

All this talk of degeneration always affects me as though I had accidentally overheard offensive talk about my own daughter. It offends me that these charges are wholesale, and rest on such worn-out commonplaces, on such wordy vapourings as degeneration and absence of ideals, or on references to the splendours of the past. Every accusation, even if it is uttered in ladies' society, ought to be formulated with all possible definiteness, or it is not an accusation, but idle disparagement, unworthy of decent people.

I am an old man, I have been lecturing for thirty years, but I notice neither degeneration nor lack of ideals, and I don't find that the present is worse than the past. My porter Nikolay, whose experience of this subject has its value, says that the students of today are neither better nor worse than those of the past.

If I were asked what I don't like in my pupils of today, I should answer the question, not straight off and not at length, but with sufficient definiteness. I know their failings, and so have no need to resort to vague generalities. I don't like their smoking, using spirituous beverages, marrying late, and often being so irresponsible and careless that they will let one of their number be starving in their midst while they neglect to pay their subscriptions to the Students' Aid Society. They don't know modern languages, and they don't express themselves correctly in Russian; no longer ago than yesterday my colleague, the professor of hygiene, complained to me that he had to give twice as many lectures, because the students had a very poor knowledge of physics and were utterly ignorant of meteorology. They are readily carried away by the influence of the last new writers, even when they are not first-rate, but they take absolutely no interest in classics such as Shakespeare, Marcus Aurelius, Epictetus, or Pascal, and this inability to distinguish the great from the small betrays their ignorance of practical life more than anything. All difficult questions that have more or less a social character (for instance the migration question) they settle by studying monographs on the subject, but not by way of scientific investigation or experiment, though that method is at their disposal and is more in keeping with their calling. They gladly become ward-surgeons, assistants, demonstrators, external teachers, and are ready to fill such posts until they are forty, though independence, a sense of freedom and personal initiative, are no less necessary in science than, for instance, in art or commerce. I have pupils and listeners, but no successors and helpers, and so I love them and am touched by them, but am not proud of them. And so on, and so on. . . .

Such shortcomings, however numerous they may be, can only give rise to a pessimistic or fault-finding temper in a faint-hearted and timid man. All these failings have a casual, transitory character, and are completely dependent on conditions of life; in some ten years they will have disappeared or given place to other fresh defects, which are all inevitable and will in their turn alarm the faint-hearted. The students' sins often vex me, but that vexation is nothing in comparison with the joy I have been experiencing now for the last thirty years when I talk to my pupils, lecture to them, watch their relations, and compare them with people not of their circle.

Mihail Fyodorovitch speaks evil of everything. Katya listens, and neither of them notices into what depths the apparently innocent diversion of finding fault with their neighbours is gradually drawing them. They are not conscious how by degrees simple talk passes into malicious mockery and jeering, and how they are both beginning to drop into the habits and methods of slander.

"Killing types one meets with," says Mihail Fyodorovitch. "I went yesterday to our friend Yegor Petrovitch's, and there I found a studious gentleman, one of your medicals in his third year, I believe. Such a face! . . . in the Dobrolubov style, the imprint of profound thought on his brow; we got into talk. 'Such doings, young man,' said I. 'I've read,' said I, 'that some German—I've forgotten his name—has created from the human brain a new kind of alkaloid, idiotine.' What do you think? He believed it, and there was positively an expression of respect on his face, as though to say, 'See what we fellows can do!' And the other day I went to the theatre. I took my seat. In the next row directly in front of me were sitting two men: one of 'us fellows' and apparently a law student, the other a shaggy-looking figure, a medical student. The latter was as drunk as a cobbler. He did not look at the stage at all. He was dozing with his nose on his shirt-front. But as soon as an actor begins loudly reciting a monologue, or simply raises his voice, our friend starts, pokes his neighbour in the ribs, and asks, 'What is he saying? Is it elevating?' 'Yes,' answers one of our fellows. 'B-r-r-ravo!' roars the medical student. 'Elevating! Bravo!' He had gone to the theatre, you see, the drunken blockhead, not for the sake of art, the play, but for elevation! He wanted noble sentiments."

Katya listens and laughs. She has a strange laugh; she catches her breath in rhythmically regular gasps, very much as though she were playing the accordion, and nothing in her face is laughing but her nostrils. I grow depressed and don't know what to say. Beside myself, I fire up, leap up from my seat, and cry:

"Do leave off! Why are you sitting here like two toads, poisoning the air with your breath? Give over!"

And without waiting for them to finish their gossip I prepare to go home. And, indeed, it is high time: it is past ten.

"I will stay a little longer," says Mihail Fyodorovitch. "Will you allow me, Ekaterina Vladimirovna?"

"I will," answers Katya.

"*Bene!* In that case have up another little bottle."

They both accompany me with candles to the hall, and while I put on my fur coat, Mihail Fyodorovitch says:

"You have grown dreadfully thin and older looking, Nikolay Stepanovitch. What's the matter with you? Are you ill?"

"Yes; I am not very well."

"And you are not doing anything for it . . ." Katya puts in grimly.

"Why don't you? You can't go on like that! God helps those who help themselves, my dear fellow. Remember me to your wife and daughter, and make my apologies for not having been to see them. In a day or two, before I go abroad, I shall come to say goodbye. I shall be sure to. I am going away next week."

I come away from Katya, irritated and alarmed by what has been said about my being ill, and dissatisfied with myself. I ask myself whether I really ought not to consult one of my colleagues. And at once I imagine how my colleague, after listening to me, would walk away to the window without speaking, would think a moment, then would turn round to me and, trying to prevent my reading the truth in his face, would say in a careless tone: "So far I see nothing serious, but at the same time, *collega*, I advise you to lay aside your work. . . ." And that would deprive me of my last hope.

Who is without hope? Now that I am diagnosing my illness and prescribing for myself, from time to time I hope that I am deceived by my own illness, that I am mistaken in regard to the albumen and the sugar I find, and in regard to my heart, and in regard to the swellings I have twice noticed in the mornings; when with the fervour of the hypochondriac I look through the textbooks of therapeutics and take a different medicine every day, I keep fancying that I shall hit upon something comforting. All that is petty.

Whether the sky is covered with clouds or the moon and the stars are shining, I turn my eyes towards it every evening and think that death is taking me soon. One would think that my thoughts at such times ought to be deep as the sky, brilliant, striking. . . . But no! I think about myself, about my wife, about Liza, Gnekker, the students, people in general; my thoughts are evil, petty, I am insincere with myself, and at such times my theory of life may be expressed in the words the celebrated Araktcheev said in one of his intimate letters: "Nothing good can exist in the world without evil, and there is more evil than good." That is, everything is disgusting; there is nothing to live for, and the sixty-two years I have already lived must be reckoned as wasted. I catch myself in these thoughts, and try to persuade myself that they are accidental, temporary, and not deeply rooted in me, but at once I think:

"If so, what drives me every evening to those two toads?"

And I vow to myself that I will never go to Katya's again, though I know I shall go next evening.

Ringing the bell at the door and going upstairs, I feel that I have no family now and no desire to bring it back again. It is clear that the new Araktcheev thoughts are not casual, temporary visitors, but have possession of my whole being. With my conscience ill at ease, dejected, languid, hardly able to move my limbs, feeling as though tons were added to my weight, I get into bed and quickly drop asleep.

And then—insomnia!

IV

Summer comes on and life is changed.

One fine morning Liza comes in to me and says in a jesting tone:

"Come, your Excellency! We are ready."

My Excellency is conducted into the street, and seated in a cab. As I go along, having nothing to do, I read the signboards from right to left. The word "Traktir" reads "Ritkart"; that would just suit some baron's family: Baroness Ritkart. Farther on I drive through fields, by the graveyard, which makes absolutely no impression on me, though I shall soon lie in it; then I drive by forests and again by fields. There is nothing of interest. After two hours of driving, my Excellency is conducted into the lower storey of a summer villa and installed in a small, very cheerful little room with light blue hangings.

At night there is sleeplessness as before, but in the morning I do not put a good face upon it and listen to my wife, but lie in bed. I do not sleep, but lie in the drowsy, half-conscious condition in which you know you are not asleep, but dreaming. At midday I get up and from habit sit down at my table, but I do not work now; I amuse myself with French books in yellow covers, sent me by Katya. Of course, it would be more patriotic to read Russian authors, but I must confess I cherish no particular liking for them. With the exception of two or three of the older writers, all our literature of today strikes me as not being literature, but a special sort of home industry, which exists simply in order to be encouraged, though people do not readily make use of its products. The very best of these home products cannot be called remarkable and cannot be sincerely praised without qualification. I must say the same of all the literary novelties I have read during the last ten or fifteen years; not one of them is remarkable, and not one of them can be praised without a "but." Cleverness, a good tone, but no talent; talent, a good tone, but no cleverness; or talent, cleverness, but not a good tone.

I don't say the French books have talent, cleverness, and a good tone. They don't satisfy me, either. But they are not so tedious as the Russian, and it is not unusual to find in them the chief element of artistic creation—the feeling of personal freedom which is lacking in the Russian authors. I don't remember one new book in which the author does not try from the first page to entangle himself in all sorts of conditions and contracts with his conscience. One is afraid to speak of the naked body; another ties himself up hand and foot in psychological analysis; a third must have a "warm attitude to man"; a fourth purposely scrawls whole descriptions of nature that he may not be suspected of writing with a purpose. . . . One is bent upon being middle-class in his work, another must be a nobleman, and so on. There is intentionalness, circumspection, and self-will, but they have neither the independence nor the manliness to write as they like, and therefore there is no creativeness.

All this applies to what is called belles-lettres.

As for serious treatises in Russian on sociology, for instance, on art, and so on, I do not read them simply from timidity. In my childhood and early youth I had for some reason a terror of doorkeepers and attendants at the theatre, and that terror has remained with me to this day. I am afraid of them even now. It is said that we are only afraid of what we do not understand. And, indeed, it is very difficult to understand why doorkeepers and theatre attendants are so dignified, haughty, and majestically rude. I feel exactly the same terror when I read serious articles. Their extraordinary dignity, their bantering lordly tone, their familiar manner to foreign authors, their ability to split straws with dignity—all that is beyond my understanding; it is intimidating and utterly unlike the quiet, gentlemanly tone to which I am accustomed when I read the works of our medical and scientific writers. It oppresses me to read not only the articles written by serious Russians, but even works translated or edited by them. The pretentious, edifying tone of the preface; the redundancy of remarks made by the translator, which prevent me from concentrating my attention; the question marks and "sic" in parenthesis scattered all over the book or article by the liberal translator, are to my mind an outrage on the author and on my independence as a reader.

Once I was summoned as an expert to a circuit court; in an interval one of my fellow-experts drew my attention to the rudeness of the public prosecutor to the defendants, among whom there were two ladies of good education. I believe I did not exaggerate at all when I told him that the prosecutor's manner was no ruder than that of the authors of serious articles to one another. Their manners are, indeed, so rude that I cannot speak of them without distaste. They treat one another and the writers they criticize either with superfluous respect, at the sacrifice of their own dignity, or, on the contrary, with far more ruthlessness than I have shown in my notes and my thoughts in regard to my future son-in-law Gnekker. Accusations of irrationality, of evil intentions, and, indeed, of every sort of crime, form an habitual ornament of serious articles. And that, as young medical men are fond of saying in their monographs, is the *ultima ratio!* Such ways must infallibly have an effect on the morals of the younger generation of writers, and so I am not at all surprised that in the new works with which our literature has been enriched during the last ten or fifteen years the heroes drink too much vodka and the heroines are not over-chaste.

I read French books, and I look out of the window which is open; I can see the spikes of my garden fence, two or three scraggy trees, and beyond the fence the road, the fields, and beyond them a broad stretch of pine-wood. Often I admire a boy and girl, both flaxen-headed and ragged, who clamber on the fence and laugh at my baldness. In their shining little eyes I read, "Go up, go up, thou baldhead!" They are almost the only people who care nothing for my celebrity or my rank.

Visitors do not come to me every day now. I will only mention the visits of Nikolay and Pyotr Ignatyevitch. Nikolay usually comes to me on holidays, with some pretext of business, though really to see me. He arrives very much exhilarated, a thing which never occurs to him in the winter.

"What have you to tell me?" I ask, going out to him in the hall.

"Your Excellency!" he says, pressing his hand to his heart and looking at me with the ecstasy of a lover—"your Excellency! God be my witness! Strike me dead on the spot! *Gaudeamus egitur juventus!*"

And he greedily kisses me on the shoulder, on the sleeve, and on the buttons.

"Is everything going well?" I ask him.

"Your Excellency! So help me God! . . ."

He persists in grovelling before me for no sort of reason, and soon bores me, so I send him away to the kitchen, where they give him dinner.

Pyotr Ignatyevitch comes to see me on holidays, too, with the special object of seeing me and sharing his thoughts with me. He usually sits down near my table, modest, neat, and reasonable, and does not venture to cross his legs or put his elbows on the table. All the time, in a soft, even, little voice, in rounded bookish phrases, he tells me various, to his mind, very interesting and piquant items of news which he has read in the magazines and journals. They are all alike and may be reduced to this type: "A Frenchman has made a discovery; some one else, a German, has denounced him, proving that the discovery was made in 1870 by some American; while a third person, also a German, trumps them both by proving they both had made fools of themselves, mistaking bubbles of air for dark pigment under the microscope." Even when he wants to amuse me, Pyotr Ignatyevitch tells me things in the same lengthy, circumstantial manner as though he were defending a thesis, enumerating in detail the literary sources from which he is deriving his narrative, doing his utmost to be accurate as to the date and number of the journals and the name of every one concerned, invariably mentioning it in full—Jean Jacques Petit, never simply Petit. Sometimes he stays to dinner with us, and then during the whole of dinner-time he goes on telling me the same sort of piquant anecdotes, reducing every one at table to a state of dejected boredom. If Gnekker and Liza begin talking before him of fugues and counterpoint, Brahms and Bach, he drops his eyes modestly, and is overcome with embarrassment; he is ashamed that such trivial subjects should be discussed before such serious people as him and me.

In my present state of mind five minutes of him is enough to sicken me as though I had been seeing and hearing him for an eternity. I hate the poor fellow. His soft, smooth voice and bookish language exhaust me, and his stories stupefy me. . . . He cherishes the best of feelings for me, and talks to me simply in order to give me pleasure, and I repay him by looking at him as though I wanted to hypnotize him, and think, "Go, go, go! . . ." But he is not amenable to thought-suggestion, and sits on and on and on. . . .

While he is with me I can never shake off the thought, "It's possible when I die he will be appointed to succeed me," and my poor lecture hall presents itself to me as an oasis in which the spring is died up; and I am ungracious, silent, and surly with Pyotr Ignatyevitch, as though he were to blame for such thoughts, and not I myself. When he begins, as usual, praising up the German savants, instead of making fun of him good-humouredly, as I used to do, I mutter sullenly:

"Asses, your Germans! . . ."

That is like the late Professor Nikita Krylov, who once, when he was bathing with Pirogov at Revel and vexed at the water's being very cold, burst out with, "Scoundrels, these Germans!" I behave badly with Pyotr Ignatyevitch, and only when he is going away, and from the window I catch a glimpse of his grey hat behind the garden fence, I want to call out and say, "Forgive me, my dear fellow!"

Dinner is even drearier than in the winter. Gnekker, whom now I hate and despise, dines with us almost every day. I used to endure his presence in silence, now I aim biting remarks at him which make my wife and daughter blush. Carried away by evil feeling, I often say things that are simply stupid, and I don't know why I say them. So on one occasion it happened that I stared a long time at Gnekker, and, *a propos* of nothing, I fired off:

"An eagle may perchance swoop down below a cock,

But never will the fowl soar upwards to the clouds . . ."

And the most vexatious thing is that the fowl Gnekker shows himself much cleverer than the eagle professor. Knowing that my wife and daughter are on his side, he takes up the line of meeting my gibes with condescending silence, as though to say:

"The old chap is in his dotage; what's the use of talking to him?"

Or he makes fun of me good-naturedly. It is wonderful how petty a man may become! I am capable of dreaming all dinner-time of how Gnekker will turn out to be an adventurer, how my wife and Liza will come to see their mistake, and how I will taunt them—and such absurd thoughts at the time when I am standing with one foot in the grave!

There are now, too, misunderstandings of which in the old days I had no idea except from hearsay. Though I am ashamed of it, I will describe one that occurred the other day after dinner.

I was sitting in my room smoking a pipe; my wife came in as usual, sat down, and began saying what a good thing it would be for me to go to Harkov now while it is warm and I have free time, and there find out what sort of person our Gnekker is.

"Very good; I will go," I assented.

My wife, pleased with me, got up and was going to the door, but turned back and said:

"By the way, I have another favour to ask of you. I know you will be angry, but it is my duty to warn you. . . . Forgive my saying it, Nikolay Stepanovitch, but all our neighbours and acquaintances have begun talking about your being so often at Katya's. She is clever and well-educated; I don't deny that her company may be agreeable; but at your age and with your social position it seems strange that you should find pleasure in her society. . . . Besides, she has such a reputation that . . ."

All the blood suddenly rushed to my brain, my eyes flashed fire, I leaped up and, clutching at my head and stamping my feet, shouted in a voice unlike my own:

"Let me alone! let me alone! let me alone!"

Probably my face was terrible, my voice was strange, for my wife suddenly turned pale and began shrieking aloud in a despairing voice that was utterly unlike her own. Liza, Gnekker, then Yegor, came running in at our shouts. . . .

"Let me alone!" I cried; "let me alone! Go away!"

My legs turned numb as though they had ceased to exist; I felt myself falling into someone's arms; for a little while I still heard weeping, then sank into a swoon which lasted two or three hours.

Now about Katya; she comes to see me every day towards evening, and of course neither the neighbours nor our acquaintants can avoid noticing it. She comes in for a minute and carries me off for a drive with her. She has her own horse and a new chaise bought this summer. Altogether she lives in an expensive style; she has taken a big detached villa with a large garden, and has taken all her town retinue with her—two maids, a coachman . . . I often ask her:

"Katya, what will you live on when you have spent your father's money?"

"Then we shall see," she answers.

"That money, my dear, deserves to be treated more seriously. It was earned by a good man, by honest labour."

"You have told me that already. I know it."

At first we drive through the open country, then through the pine-wood which is visible from my window. Nature seems to me as beautiful as it always has been, though some evil spirit whispers to me that these pines and fir trees, birds, and white clouds on the sky, will not notice my absence when in three or four months I am dead. Katya loves driving, and she is pleased that it is fine weather and that I am sitting beside her. She is in good spirits and does not say harsh things.

"You are a very good man, Nikolay Stepanovitch," she says. "You are a rare specimen, and there isn't an actor who would understand how to play you. Me or Mihail Fyodorovitch, for instance, any poor actor could do, but not you. And I envy you, I envy you horribly! Do you know what I stand for? What?"

She ponders for a minute, and then asks me:

"Nikolay Stepanovitch, I am a negative phenomenon! Yes?"

"Yes," I answer.

"H'm! what am I to do?"

What answer was I to make her? It is easy to say "work," or "give your possessions to the poor," or "know yourself," and because it is so easy to say that, I don't know what to answer.

My colleagues when they teach therapeutics advise "the individual study of each separate case." One has but to obey this advice to gain the conviction that the methods recommended in the textbooks as the best and as providing a safe basis for treatment turn out to be quite unsuitable in individual cases. It is just the same in moral ailments.

But I must make some answer, and I say:

"You have too much free time, my dear; you absolutely must take up some occupation. After all, why shouldn't you be an actress again if it is your vocation?"

"I cannot!"

"Your tone and manner suggest that you are a victim. I don't like that, my dear; it is your own fault. Remember, you began with falling out with people and methods, but you have done nothing to make either better. You did not struggle with evil, but were cast down by it, and you are not the victim of the struggle, but of your own impotence. Well, of course you were young and inexperienced then; now it may all be different. Yes, really, go on the stage. You will work, you will serve a sacred art."

"Don't pretend, Nikolay Stepanovitch," Katya interrupts me. "Let us make a compact once for all; we will talk about actors, actresses, and authors, but we will let art alone. You are a splendid and rare person, but you don't know enough about art sincerely to think it sacred. You have no instinct or feeling for art. You have been hard at work all your life, and have not had time to acquire that feeling. Altogether . . . I don't like talk about art," she goes on nervously. "I don't like it! And, my goodness, how they have vulgarized it!"

"Who has vulgarized it?"

"They have vulgarized it by drunkenness, the newspapers by their familiar attitude, clever people by philosophy."

"Philosophy has nothing to do with it."

"Yes, it has. If any one philosophizes about it, it shows he does not understand it."

To avoid bitterness I hasten to change the subject, and then sit a long time silent. Only when we are driving out of the wood and turning towards Katya's villa I go back to my former question, and say:

"You have still not answered me, why you don't want to go on the stage."

"Nikolay Stepanovitch, this is cruel!" she cries, and suddenly flushes all over. "You want me to tell you the truth aloud? Very well, if . . . if you like it! I have no talent! No talent and . . . and a great deal of vanity! So there!"

After making this confession she turns her face away from me, and to hide the trembling of her hands tugs violently at the reins.

As we are driving towards her villa we see Mihail Fyodorovitch walking near the gate, impatiently awaiting us.

"That Mihail Fyodorovitch again!" says Katya with vexation. "Do rid me of him, please! I am sick and tired of him . . . bother him!"

Mihail Fyodorovitch ought to have gone abroad long ago, but he puts off going from week to week. Of late there have been certain changes in him. He looks, as it were, sunken, has taken to drinking until he is tipsy, a thing which never used to happen to him, and his black eyebrows are beginning to turn grey. When our chaise stops at the gate he does not conceal his joy and his impatience. He fussily helps me and Katya out, hurriedly asks questions, laughs, rubs his hands, and that gentle, imploring, pure expression, which I used to notice only in his eyes, is now suffused all over his face. He is glad and at the same time he is ashamed of his gladness, ashamed of his habit of spending every evening with Katya. And he thinks it necessary to explain his visit by some obvious absurdity such as: "I was driving by, and I thought I would just look in for a minute."

We all three go indoors; first we drink tea, then the familiar packs of cards, the big piece of cheese, the fruit, and the bottle of Crimean champagne are put upon the table. The subjects of our conversation are not new; they are just the same as in the winter. We fall foul of the University, the students, and literature and the theatre; the air grows thick and stifling with evil speaking, and poisoned by the breath, not of two toads as in the winter, but of three. Besides the velvety baritone laugh and the giggle like the gasp of a concertina, the maid who waits upon us hears an unpleasant cracked "He, he!" like the chuckle of a general in a vaudeville.

V

There are terrible nights with thunder, lightning, rain, and wind, such as are called among the people "sparrow nights." There has been one such night in my personal life.

I woke up after midnight and leaped suddenly out of bed. It seemed to me for some reason that I was just immediately going to die. Why did it seem so? I had no sensation in my body that suggested my immediate death, but my soul was oppressed with terror, as though I had suddenly seen a vast menacing glow of fire.

I rapidly struck a light, drank some water straight out of the decanter, then hurried to the open window. The weather outside was magnificent.

There was a smell of hay and some other very sweet scent. I could see the spikes of the fence, the gaunt, drowsy trees by the window, the road, the dark streak of woodland, there was a serene, very bright moon in the sky and not a single cloud, perfect stillness, not one leaf stirring. I felt that everything was looking at me and waiting for me to die. . . .

It was uncanny. I closed the window and ran to my bed. I felt for my pulse, and not finding it in my wrist, tried to find it in my temple, then in my chin, and again in my wrist, and everything I touched was cold and clammy with sweat. My breathing came more and more rapidly, my body was shivering, all my inside was in commotion; I had a sensation on my face and on my bald head as though they were covered with spiders' webs.

What should I do? Call my family? No; it would be no use. I could not imagine what my wife and Liza would do when they came in to me.

I hid my head under the pillow, closed my eyes, and waited and waited. . . . My spine was cold; it seemed to be drawn inwards, and I felt as though death were coming upon me stealthily from behind.

"Kee-vee! kee-vee!" I heard a sudden shriek in the night's stillness, and did not know where it was—in my breast or in the street—"Kee-vee! kee-vee!"

"My God, how terrible!" I would have drunk some more water, but by then it was fearful to open my eyes and I was afraid to raise my head. I was possessed by unaccountable animal terror, and I cannot understand why I was so frightened: was it that I wanted to live, or that some new unknown pain was in store for me?

Upstairs, overhead, some one moaned or laughed. I listened. Soon afterwards there was a sound of footsteps on the stairs. Some one came hurriedly down, then went up again. A minute later there was a sound of steps downstairs again; some one stopped near my door and listened.

"Who is there?" I cried.

The door opened. I boldly opened my eyes, and saw my wife. Her face was pale and her eyes were tear-stained.

"You are not asleep, Nikolay Stepanovitch?" she asked.

"What is it?"

"For God's sake, go up and have a look at Liza; there is something the matter with her. . . ."

"Very good, with pleasure," I muttered, greatly relieved at not being alone. "Very good, this minute. . . ."

I followed my wife, heard what she said to me, and was too agitated to understand a word. Patches of light from her candle danced about the stairs, our long shadows trembled. My feet caught in the skirts of my dressing gown; I gasped for breath, and felt as though something were pursuing me and trying to catch me from behind.

"I shall die on the spot, here on the staircase," I thought. "On the spot. . . ." But we passed the staircase, the dark corridor with the Italian windows, and went into Liza's room. She was sitting on the bed in her nightdress, with her bare feet hanging down, and she was moaning.

"Oh, my God! Oh, my God!" she was muttering, screwing up her eyes at our candle. "I can't bear it."

"Liza, my child," I said, "what is it?"

Seeing me, she began crying out, and flung herself on my neck.

"My kind papa! . . ." she sobbed—"my dear, good papa . . . my darling, my pet, I don't know what is the matter with me. . . . I am miserable!"

She hugged me, kissed me, and babbled fond words I used to hear from her when she was a child.

"Calm yourself, my child. God be with you," I said. "There is no need to cry. I am miserable, too."

I tried to tuck her in; my wife gave her water, and we awkwardly stumbled by her bedside; my shoulder jostled against her shoulder, and meanwhile I was thinking how we used to give our children their bath together.

"Help her! help her!" my wife implored me. "Do something!"

What could I do? I could do nothing. There was some load on the girl's heart; but I did not understand, I knew nothing about it, and could only mutter:

"It's nothing, it's nothing; it will pass. Sleep, sleep!"

To make things worse, there was a sudden sound of dogs howling, at first subdued and uncertain, then loud, two dogs howling together. I had never attached significance to such omens as the howling of dogs or the shrieking of owls, but on that occasion it sent a pang to my heart, and I hastened to explain the howl to myself.

"It's nonsense," I thought, "the influence of one organism on another. The intensely strained condition of my nerves has infected my wife, Liza, the dog—that is all. . . . Such infection explains presentiments, forebodings. . . ."

When a little later I went back to my room to write a prescription for Liza, I no longer thought I should die at once, but only had such a weight, such a feeling of oppression in my soul that I felt actually sorry that I had not died on the spot. For a long time I stood motionless in the middle of the room, pondering what to prescribe for Liza. But the moans overhead ceased, and I decided to prescribe nothing, and yet I went on standing there. . . .

There was a deathlike stillness, such a stillness, as some author has expressed it, "it rang in one's ears." Time passed slowly; the streaks of moonlight on the window-sill did not shift their position, but seemed as though frozen. . . . It was still some time before dawn.

But the gate in the fence creaked, some one stole in and, breaking a twig from one of those scraggy trees, cautiously tapped on the window with it.

"Nikolay Stepanovitch," I heard a whisper. "Nikolay Stepanovitch."

I opened the window, and fancied I was dreaming: under the window, huddled against the wall, stood a woman in a black dress, with the moonlight bright upon her, looking at me with great eyes. Her face was pale, stern, and weird-looking in the moonlight, like marble, her chin was quivering.

"It is I," she said—"I . . . Katya."

In the moonlight all women's eyes look big and black, all people look taller and paler, and that was probably why I had not recognized her for the first minute.

"What is it?"

"Forgive me!" she said. "I suddenly felt unbearably miserable . . . I couldn't stand it, so came here. There was a light in your window and . . . and I ventured to knock. . . . I beg your pardon. Ah! if you knew how miserable I am! What are you doing just now?"

"Nothing. . . . I can't sleep."

"I had a feeling that there was something wrong, but that is nonsense."

Her brows were lifted, her eyes shone with tears, and her whole face was lighted up with the familiar look of trustfulness which I had not seen for so long.

"Nikolay Stepanovitch," she said imploringly, stretching out both hands to me, "my precious friend, I beg you, I implore you. . . . If you don't despise my affection and respect for you, consent to what I ask of you."

"What is it?"

"Take my money from me!"

"Come! what an idea! What do I want with your money?"

"You'll go away somewhere for your health. . . . You ought to go for your health. Will you take it? Yes? Nikolay Stepanovitch darling, yes?"

She looked greedily into my face and repeated: "Yes, you will take it?"

"No, my dear, I won't take it," I said. "Thank you."

She turned her back upon me and bowed her head. Probably I refused her in a tone which made further conversation about money impossible.

"Go home to bed," I said. "We will see each other tomorrow."

"So you don't consider me your friend?" she asked dejectedly.

"I don't say that. But your money would be no use to me now."

"I beg your pardon . . ." she said, dropping her voice a whole octave. "I understand you . . . to be indebted to a person like me . . . a retired actress. . . . But, goodbye. . . ."

And she went away so quickly that I had not time even to say goodbye.

VI

I am in Harkov.

As it would be useless to contend against my present mood and, indeed, beyond my power, I have made up my mind that the last days of my life shall at least be irreproachable externally. If I am unjust in regard to my wife and daughter, which I fully recognize, I will try and do as she wishes; since she wants me to go to Harkov, I go to Harkov. Besides, I have become of late so indifferent to everything that it is really all the same to me where I go, to Harkov, or to Paris, or to Berditchev.

I arrived here at midday, and have put up at the hotel not far from the cathedral. The train was jolting, there were draughts, and now I am sitting on my bed, holding my head and expecting tic douloureux. I ought to have gone today to see some professors of my acquaintance, but I have neither strength nor inclination.

The old corridor attendant comes in and asks whether I have brought my bed linen. I detain him for five minutes, and put several questions to him about Gnekker, on whose account I have come here. The attendant turns out to be a native of Harkov; he knows the town like the fingers of his hand, but does not remember any household of the surname of Gnekker. I question him about the estate—the same answer.

The clock in the corridor strikes one, then two, then three. . . . These last months in which I am waiting for death seem much longer than the whole of my life. And I have never before been so ready to resign myself to the slowness of time as now. In the old days, when one sat in the station and waited for a train, or presided in an examination room, a quarter of an hour would seem an eternity. Now I can sit all night on my bed without moving, and quite unconcernedly reflect that tomorrow will be followed by another night as long and colourless, and the day after tomorrow.

In the corridor it strikes five, six, seven. . . . It grows dark.

There is a dull pain in my cheek, the tic beginning. To occupy myself with thoughts, I go back to my old point of view, when I was not so indifferent, and ask myself why I, a distinguished man, a privy councillor, am sitting in this little hotel room, on this bed with the unfamiliar grey quilt. Why am I looking at that cheap tin washing-stand and listening to the whirr of the wretched clock in the corridor? Is all this in keeping with my fame and my lofty position? And I answer these questions with a jeer. I am amused by the naivete with which I used in my youth to exaggerate the value of renown and of the exceptional position which celebrities are supposed to enjoy. I am famous, my name is pronounced with reverence, my portrait has been both in the *Niva* and in the *Illustrated News of the World*; I have read my biography even in a German magazine. And what of all that? Here I am sitting utterly alone in a strange town, on a strange bed, rubbing my aching cheek with my hand. . . . Domestic worries, the hard-heartedness of creditors, the rudeness of the railway servants, the inconveniences of the passport system, the expensive and unwholesome food in the refreshment rooms, the general rudeness and coarseness in social intercourse—all this, and a great deal more which would take too long to reckon up, affects me as much as any working man who is famous only in his alley. In what way, does my exceptional position find expression? Admitting that I am celebrated a thousand times over, that I am a hero of whom my country is proud. They publish bulletins of my illness in every paper, letters of sympathy come to me by post from my colleagues, my pupils, the general public; but all that does not prevent me from dying in a strange bed, in misery, in utter loneliness. Of course, no one is to blame for that; but I in my foolishness dislike my popularity. I feel as though it had cheated me.

At ten o'clock I fall asleep, and in spite of the tic I sleep soundly, and should have gone on sleeping if I had not been awakened. Soon after one came a sudden knock at the door.

"Who is there?"

"A telegram."

"You might have waited till tomorrow," I say angrily, taking the telegram from the attendant. "Now I shall not get to sleep again."

"I am sorry. Your light was burning, so I thought you were not asleep."

I tear open the telegram and look first at the signature. From my wife.

"What does she want?"

"Gnekker was secretly married to Liza yesterday. Return."

I read the telegram, and my dismay does not last long. I am dismayed, not by what Liza and Gnekker have done, but by the indifference with which I hear of their marriage. They say philosophers and the truly wise are indifferent. It is false: indifference is the paralysis of the soul; it is premature death.

I go to bed again, and begin trying to think of something to occupy my mind. What am I to think about? I feel as though everything had been thought over already and there is nothing which could hold my attention now.

When daylight comes I sit up in bed with my arms round my knees, and to pass the time I try to know myself. "Know thyself" is excellent and useful advice; it is only a pity that the ancients never thought to indicate the means of following this precept.

When I have wanted to understand somebody or myself I have considered, not the actions, in which everything is relative, but the desires.

"Tell me what you want, and I will tell you what manner of man you are."

And now I examine myself: what do I want?

I want our wives, our children, our friends, our pupils, to love in us, not our fame, not the brand and not the label, but to love us as ordinary men. Anything else? I should like to have had helpers and successors. Anything else? I should like to wake up in a hundred years' time and to have just a peep out of one eye at what is happening in science. I should have liked to have lived another ten years . . . What further? Why, nothing further. I think and think, and can think of nothing more. And however much I might think, and however far my thoughts might travel, it is clear to me that there is nothing vital, nothing of great importance in my desires. In my passion for science, in my desire to live, in this sitting on a strange bed, and in this striving to know myself—in all the thoughts, feelings, and ideas I form about everything, there is no common bond to connect it all into one whole. Every feeling and every thought exists apart in me; and in all my criticisms of science, the theatre, literature, my pupils, and in all the pictures my imagination draws, even the most skilful analyst could not find what is called a general idea, or the god of a living man.

And if there is not that, then there is nothing.

In a state so poverty-stricken, a serious ailment, the fear of death, the influences of circumstance and men were enough to turn upside down and scatter in fragments all which I had once looked upon as my theory of life, and in which I had seen the meaning and joy of my existence. So there is nothing surprising in the fact that I have over-shadowed the last months of my life with thoughts and feelings only worthy of a slave and barbarian, and that now I am indifferent and take no heed of the dawn. When a man has not in him what is loftier and mightier than all external impressions a bad cold is really enough to upset his equilibrium and make him begin to see an owl in every bird, to hear a dog howling in every sound. And all his pessimism or optimism with his thoughts great and small have at such times significance as symptoms and nothing more.

I am vanquished. If it is so, it is useless to think, it is useless to talk. I will sit and wait in silence for what is to come.

In the morning the corridor attendant brings me tea and a copy of the local newspaper. Mechanically I read the advertisements on the first page, the leading article, the extracts from the newspapers and journals, the chronicle of events. . . . In the latter I find, among other things, the following paragraph: "Our distinguished savant, Professor Nikolay Stepanovitch So-and-so, arrived yesterday in Harkov, and is staying in the So-and-so Hotel."

Apparently, illustrious names are created to live on their own account, apart from those that bear them. Now my name is promenading tranquilly about Harkov; in another three months, printed in gold letters on my monument, it will shine bright as the sun itself, while I shall be already under the moss.

A light tap at the door. Somebody wants me.

"Who is there? Come in."

The door opens, and I step back surprised and hurriedly wrap my dressing gown round me. Before me stands Katya.

"How do you do?" she says, breathless with running upstairs. "You didn't expect me? I have come here, too. . . . I have come, too!"

She sits down and goes on, hesitating and not looking at me.

"Why don't you speak to me? I have come, too . . . today. . . . I found out that you were in this hotel, and have come to you."

"Very glad to see you," I say, shrugging my shoulders, "but I am surprised. You seem to have dropped from the skies. What have you come for?"

"Oh . . . I've simply come."

Silence. Suddenly she jumps up impulsively and comes to me.

"Nikolay Stepanovitch," she says, turning pale and pressing her hands on her bosom—"Nikolay Stepanovitch, I cannot go on living like this! I cannot! For God's sake tell me quickly, this minute, what I am to do! Tell me, what am I to do?"

"What can I tell you?" I ask in perplexity. "I can do nothing."

"Tell me, I beseech you," she goes on, breathing hard and trembling all over. "I swear that I cannot go on living like this. It's too much for me!"

She sinks on a chair and begins sobbing. She flings her head back, wrings her hands, taps with her feet; her hat falls off and hangs bobbing on its elastic; her hair is ruffled.

"Help me! help me!" she implores me. "I cannot go on!"

She takes her handkerchief out of her travelling-bag, and with it pulls out several letters, which fall from her lap to the floor. I pick them up, and on one of them I recognize the handwriting of Mihail Fyodorovitch and accidentally read a bit of a word "passionat . . ."

"There is nothing I can tell you, Katya," I say.

"Help me!" she sobs, clutching at my hand and kissing it. "You are my father, you know, my only friend! You are clever, educated; you have lived so long; you have been a teacher! Tell me, what am I to do?"

"Upon my word, Katya, I don't know. . . ."

I am utterly at a loss and confused, touched by her sobs, and hardly able to stand.

"Let us have lunch, Katya," I say, with a forced smile. "Give over crying."

And at once I add in a sinking voice:

"I shall soon be gone, Katya. . . ."

"Only one word, only one word!" she weeps, stretching out her hands to me.

"What am I to do?"

"You are a queer girl, really . . ." I mutter. "I don't understand it! So sensible, and all at once crying your eyes out. . . ."

A silence follows. Katya straightens her hair, puts on her hat, then crumples up the letters and stuffs them in her bag—and all this deliberately, in silence. Her face, her bosom, and her gloves are wet with tears, but her expression now is cold and forbidding. . . . I look at her, and feel ashamed that I am happier than she. The absence of what my philosophic colleagues call a general idea I have detected in myself only just before death, in the decline of my days, while the soul of this poor girl has known and will know no refuge all her life, all her life!

"Let us have lunch, Katya," I say.

"No, thank you," she answers coldly. Another minute passes in silence. "I don't like Harkov," I say; "it's so grey here—such a grey town."

"Yes, perhaps. . . . It's ugly. I am here not for long, passing through. I am going on today."

"Where?"

"To the Crimea . . . that is, to the Caucasus."

"Oh! For long?"

"I don't know."

Katya gets up, and, with a cold smile, holds out her hand without looking at me.

I want to ask her, "Then, you won't be at my funeral?" but she does not look at me; her hand is cold and, as it were, strange. I escort her to the door in silence. She goes out, walks down the long corridor without looking back; she knows that I am looking after her, and most likely she will look back at the turn.

No, she did not look back. I've seen her black dress for the last time: her steps have died away. Farewell, my treasure!

Gusev

[First published in 1890.
Collected in *The Witch and Other Stories* (1918).]

I

It was getting dark; it would soon be night.

Gusev, a discharged soldier, sat up in his hammock and said in an undertone:

"I say, Pavel Ivanitch. A soldier at Sutchan told me: while they were sailing a big fish came into collision with their ship and stove a hole in it."

The nondescript individual whom he was addressing, and whom everyone in the ship's hospital called Pavel Ivanitch, was silent, as though he had not heard.

And again a stillness followed . . . The wind frolicked with the rigging, the screw throbbed, the waves lashed, the hammocks creaked, but the ear had long ago become accustomed to these sounds, and it seemed that everything around was asleep and silent. It was dreary. The three invalids—two soldiers and a sailor—who had been playing cards all the day were asleep and talking in their dreams.

It seemed as though the ship were beginning to rock. The hammock slowly rose and fell under Gusev, as though it were heaving a sigh, and this was repeated once, twice, three times. . . . Something crashed on to the floor with a clang: it must have been a jug falling down.

"The wind has broken loose from its chain . . ." said Gusev, listening.

This time Pavel Ivanitch cleared his throat and answered irritably:

"One minute a vessel's running into a fish, the next, the wind's breaking loose from its chain. Is the wind a beast that it can break loose from its chain?"

"That's how christened folk talk."

"They are as ignorant as you are then. They say all sorts of things. One must keep a head on one's shoulders and use one's reason. You are a senseless creature."

Pavel Ivanitch was subject to seasickness. When the sea was rough he was usually ill-humoured, and the merest trifle would make him irritable. And in Gusev's opinion there was absolutely nothing to be vexed about. What was there strange or wonderful, for instance, in the fish or in the wind's breaking loose from its chain? Suppose the fish were as big as a mountain and its back were as hard as a sturgeon: and in the same way, supposing that away yonder at the end of the world there stood great stone walls and the fierce winds were chained up to the walls . . . if they had not broken loose, why did they tear about all over the sea like maniacs, and struggle to escape like dogs? If they were not chained up, what did become of them when it was calm?

Gusev pondered for a long time about fishes as big as a mountain and stout, rusty chains, then he began to feel dull and thought of his native place to which he was returning after five years' service in the East. He pictured an immense pond covered with snow. . . . On one side of the pond the red-brick building of the potteries with a tall chimney and clouds of black smoke; on the other side—a village. . . . His brother Alexey comes out in a sledge from the fifth yard from the end; behind him sits his little son Vanka in big felt over-boots, and his little girl Akulka, also in big felt boots. Alexey has been drinking, Vanka is laughing, Akulka's face he could not see, she had muffled herself up.

"You never know, he'll get the children frozen . . ." thought Gusev. "Lord send them sense and judgment that they may honour their father and mother and not be wiser than their parents."

"They want re-soleing," a delirious sailor says in a bass voice. "Yes, yes!"

Gusev's thoughts break off, and instead of a pond there suddenly appears apropos of nothing a huge bull's head without eyes, and the horse and sledge are not driving along, but are whirling round and round in a cloud of smoke. But still he was glad he had seen his own folks. He held his breath from delight, shudders ran all over him, and his fingers twitched.

"The Lord let us meet again," he muttered feverishly, but he at once opened his eyes and sought in the darkness for water.

He drank and lay back, and again the sledge was moving, then again the bull's head without eyes, smoke, clouds. . . . And so on till daybreak.

II

The first outline visible in the darkness was a blue circle—the little round window; then little by little Gusev could distinguish his neighbour in the next hammock, Pavel Ivanitch. The man slept sitting up, as he could not breathe lying down. His face was grey, his nose was long and sharp, his eyes looked huge from the terrible thinness of his face, his temples were sunken, his beard was skimpy, his hair was long. . . . Looking at him you could not make out of what class he was, whether he were a gentleman, a merchant, or a peasant. Judging from his expression and his long hair he might have been a hermit or a lay brother in a monastery—but if one listened to what he said it seemed that he could not be a monk. He was worn out by his cough and his illness and by the stifling heat, and breathed with difficulty, moving his parched lips. Noticing that Gusev was looking at him he turned his face towards him and said:

"I begin to guess. . . . Yes. . . . I understand it all perfectly now."

"What do you understand, Pavel Ivanitch?"

"I'll tell you. . . . It has always seemed to me strange that terribly ill as you are you should be here in a steamer where it is so hot and stifling and we are always being tossed up and down, where, in fact, everything threatens you with death; now it is all clear to me. . . . Yes. . . . Your doctors put you on the steamer to get rid of you. They get sick of looking after poor brutes like you. . . . You don't pay them anything, they have a bother with you, and you damage their records with your deaths—so, of course, you are brutes! It's not difficult to get rid of you. . . . All that is necessary is, in the first place, to have no conscience or humanity, and, secondly, to deceive the steamer authorities. The first condition need hardly be considered, in that respect we are artists; and one can always succeed in the second with a little practice. In a crowd of four hundred healthy soldiers and sailors half a dozen sick ones are not conspicuous;

well, they drove you all on to the steamer, mixed you with the healthy ones, hurriedly counted you over, and in the confusion nothing amiss was noticed, and when the steamer had started they saw that there were paralytics and consumptives in the last stage lying about on the deck. . . ."

Gusev did not understand Pavel Ivanitch; but supposing he was being blamed, he said in self-defence:

"I lay on the deck because I had not the strength to stand; when we were unloaded from the barge on to the ship I caught a fearful chill."

"It's revolting," Pavel Ivanitch went on. "The worst of it is they know perfectly well that you can't last out the long journey, and yet they put you here. Supposing you get as far as the Indian Ocean, what then? It's horrible to think of it. . . . And that's their gratitude for your faithful, irreproachable service!"

Pavel Ivanitch's eyes looked angry; he frowned contemptuously and said, gasping:

"Those are the people who ought to be plucked in the newspapers till the feathers fly in all directions."

The two sick soldiers and the sailor were awake and already playing cards. The sailor was half reclining in his hammock, the soldiers were sitting near him on the floor in the most uncomfortable attitudes. One of the soldiers had his right arm in a sling, and the hand was swathed up in a regular bundle so that he held his cards under his right arm or in the crook of his elbow while he played with the left. The ship was rolling heavily. They could not stand up, nor drink tea, nor take their medicines.

"Were you an officer's servant?" Pavel Ivanitch asked Gusev.

"Yes, an officer's servant."

"My God, my God!" said Pavel Ivanitch, and he shook his head mournfully. "To tear a man out of his home, drag him twelve thousand miles away, then to drive him into consumption and . . . and what is it all for, one wonders? To turn him into a servant for some Captain Kopeikin or midshipman Dirka! How logical!"

"It's not hard work, Pavel Ivanitch. You get up in the morning and clean the boots, get the samovar, sweep the rooms, and then you have nothing more to do. The lieutenant is all the day drawing plans, and if you like you can say your prayers, if you like you can read a book or go out into the street. God grant everyone such a life."

"Yes, very nice, the lieutenant draws plans all the day and you sit in the kitchen and pine for home. . . . Plans indeed! . . . It is not plans that matter, but a human life. Life is not given twice, it must be treated mercifully."

"Of course, Pavel Ivanitch, a bad man gets no mercy anywhere, neither at home nor in the army, but if you live as you ought and obey orders, who has any need to insult you? The officers are educated gentlemen, they understand. . . . In five years I was never once in prison, and I was never struck a blow, so help me God, but once."

"What for?"

"For fighting. I have a heavy hand, Pavel Ivanitch. Four Chinamen came into our yard; they were bringing firewood or something, I don't remember. Well, I was bored and I knocked them about a bit, one's nose began bleeding, damn the fellow. . . . The lieutenant saw it through the little window, he was angry and gave me a box on the ear."

"Foolish, pitiful man . . ." whispered Pavel Ivanitch. "You don't understand anything."

He was utterly exhausted by the tossing of the ship and closed his eyes; his head alternately fell back and dropped forward on his breast. Several times he tried to lie down but nothing came of it; his difficulty in breathing prevented it.

"And what did you hit the four Chinamen for?" he asked a little while afterwards.

"Oh, nothing. They came into the yard and I hit them."

And a stillness followed. . . . The card-players had been playing for two hours with enthusiasm and loud abuse of one another, but the motion of the ship overcame them, too; they threw aside the cards and lay down. Again Gusev saw the big pond, the brick building, the village. . . . Again the sledge was coming along, again Vanka was laughing and Akulka, silly little thing, threw open her fur coat and stuck her feet out, as much as to say: "Look, good people, my snowboots are not like Vanka's, they are new ones."

"Five years old, and she has no sense yet," Gusev muttered in delirium. "Instead of kicking your legs you had better come and get your soldier uncle a drink. I will give you something nice."

Then Andron with a flintlock gun on his shoulder was carrying a hare he had killed, and he was followed by the decrepit old Jew Isaitchik, who offers to barter the hare for a piece of soap; then the black calf in the shed, then Domna sewing at a shirt and crying about something, and then again the bull's head without eyes, black smoke. . . .

Overhead someone gave a loud shout, several sailors ran by, they seemed to be dragging something bulky over the deck, something fell with a crash. Again they ran by. . . . Had something gone wrong? Gusev raised his head, listened, and saw that the two soldiers and the sailor were playing cards again; Pavel Ivanitch was sitting up moving his lips. It was stifling, one hadn't strength to breathe, one was thirsty, the water was warm, disgusting. The ship heaved as much as ever.

Suddenly something strange happened to one of the soldiers playing cards. . . . He called hearts diamonds, got muddled in his score, and dropped his cards, then with a frightened, foolish smile looked round at all of them.

"I shan't be a minute, mates, I'll . . ." he said, and lay down on the floor.

Everybody was amazed. They called to him, he did not answer.

"Stephan, maybe you are feeling bad, eh?" the soldier with his arm in a sling asked him. "Perhaps we had better bring the priest, eh?"

"Have a drink of water, Stepan . . ." said the sailor. "Here, lad, drink."

"Why are you knocking the jug against his teeth?" said Gusev angrily. "Don't you see, turnip head?"

"What?"

"What?" Gusev repeated, mimicking him. "There is no breath in him, he is dead! That's what! What nonsensical people, Lord have mercy on us . . .!"

III

The ship was not rocking and Pavel Ivanitch was more cheerful. He was no longer ill-humoured. His face had a boastful, defiant, mocking expression. He looked as though he wanted to say: "Yes, in a minute I will tell you something that will make you split your sides with laughing." The little round window was open and a soft breeze was blowing on Pavel Ivanitch. There was a sound of voices, of the plash of oars in the water. . . . Just under the little window someone began droning in a high, unpleasant voice: no doubt it was a Chinaman singing.

"Here we are in the harbour," said Pavel Ivanitch, smiling ironically. "Only another month and we shall be in Russia. Well, worthy gentlemen and warriors! I shall arrive at Odessa and from there go straight to Harkov. In Harkov I have a friend, a literary man. I shall go to him and say, 'Come, old man, put aside your horrid subjects, ladies' amours and the beauties of nature, and show up human depravity.'"

For a minute he pondered, then said:

"Gusev, do you know how I took them in?"

"Took in whom, Pavel Ivanitch?"

"Why, these fellows. . . . You know that on this steamer there is only a first-class and a third-class, and they only allow peasants—that is the rift-raft—to go in the third. If you have got on a reefer jacket and have the faintest resemblance to a gentleman or a bourgeois you must go first-class, if you please. You must fork out five hundred roubles if you die for it. Why, I ask, have you made such a rule? Do you want to raise the prestige of educated Russians thereby? Not a bit of it. We don't let you go third-class simply because a decent person can't go third-class; it is very horrible and disgusting. Yes, indeed. I am very grateful for such solicitude for decent people's welfare. But in any case, whether it is nasty there or nice, five hundred roubles I haven't got. I haven't pilfered government money. I haven't exploited the natives, I haven't trafficked in contraband, I have flogged no one to death, so judge whether I have the right to travel first-class and even less to reckon myself of the educated class? But you won't catch them with logic. . . . One has to resort to deception. I put on a workman's coat and high boots, I assumed a drunken, servile mug and went to the agents: 'Give us a little ticket, your honour,' said I. . . ."

"Why, what class do you belong to?" asked a sailor.

"Clerical. My father was an honest priest, he always told the great ones of the world the truth to their faces; and he had a great deal to put up with in consequence."

Pavel Ivanitch was exhausted with talking and gasped for breath, but still went on:

"Yes, I always tell people the truth to their faces. I am not afraid of anyone or anything. There is a vast difference between me and all of you in that respect. You are in darkness, you are blind, crushed; you see nothing and what you do see you don't understand. . . . You are told the wind breaks loose from its chain, that you are beasts, Petchenyegs, and you believe it; they punch you in the neck, you kiss their hands; some animal in a sable-lined coat robs you and then tips you fifteen kopecks and you: 'Let me kiss your hand, sir.' You are pariahs, pitiful people. . . . I am a different sort. My eyes are open, I see it all as clearly as a hawk or an eagle when it floats over the earth, and I understand it all. I am a living protest. I see irresponsible tyranny—I protest. I see cant and hypocrisy—I protest. I see swine triumphant—I protest. And I cannot be suppressed, no Spanish Inquisition can make me hold my tongue. No. . . . Cut out my tongue and I would protest in dumb show; shut me up in a cellar—I will shout from it to be heard half a mile away, or I will starve myself to death that they may have another weight on their black consciences. Kill me and I will haunt them with my ghost. All my acquaintances say to me: 'You are a most insufferable person, Pavel Ivanitch.' I am proud of such a reputation. I have served three years in the far East, and I shall be remembered there for a hundred years: I had rows with everyone. My friends write to me from Russia, 'Don't come back,' but here I am going back to spite them . . . yes. . . . That is life as I understand it. That is what one can call life."

Gusev was looking at the little window and was not listening. A boat was swaying on the transparent, soft, turquoise water all bathed in hot, dazzling sunshine. In it there were naked Chinamen holding up cages with canaries and calling out:

"It sings, it sings!"

Another boat knocked against the first; the steam cutter darted by. And then there came another boat with a fat Chinaman sitting in it, eating rice with little sticks.

Languidly the water heaved, languidly the white seagulls floated over it.

"I should like to give that fat fellow one in the neck," thought Gusev, gazing at the stout Chinaman, with a yawn.

He dozed off, and it seemed to him that all nature was dozing, too. Time flew swiftly by; imperceptibly the day passed, imperceptibly the darkness came on. . . . The steamer was no longer standing still, but moving on further.

IV

Two days passed, Pavel Ivanitch lay down instead of sitting up; his eyes were closed, his nose seemed to have grown sharper.

"Pavel Ivanitch," Gusev called to him. "Hey, Pavel Ivanitch."

Pavel Ivanitch opened his eyes and moved his lips.

"Are you feeling bad?"

"No . . . it's nothing . . ." answered Pavel Ivanitch, gasping. "Nothing; on the contrary—I am rather better. . . . You see I can lie down. I am a little easier. . . ."

"Well, thank God for that, Pavel Ivanitch."

"When I compare myself with you I am sorry for you . . . poor fellow. My lungs are all right, it is only a stomach cough. . . . I can stand hell, let alone the Red Sea. Besides I take a critical attitude to my illness and to the medicines they give me for it. While you . . . you are in darkness. . . . It's hard for you, very, very hard!"

The ship was not rolling, it was calm, but as hot and stifling as a bath-house; it was not only hard to speak but even hard to listen. Gusev hugged his knees, laid his head on them and thought of his home. Good heavens, what a relief it was to think of snow and cold in that stifling heat! You drive in a sledge, all at once the horses take fright at something and bolt. . . . Regardless of the road, the ditches, the ravines, they dash like mad things, right through the village, over the pond by the pottery works, out across the open fields. "Hold on," the pottery hands and the peasants shout, meeting them. "Hold on." But why? Let the keen, cold wind beat in one's face and bite one's hands; let the lumps of snow, kicked up by the horses' hoofs, fall on one's cap, on one's back, down one's collar, on one's chest; let the runners ring on the snow, and the traces and the sledge be smashed, deuce take them one and all! And how delightful when the sledge upsets and you go flying full tilt into a drift, face downwards in the snow, and then you get up white all over with icicles on your moustaches; no cap, no gloves, your belt undone. . . . People laugh, the dogs bark. . . .

Pavel Ivanitch half opened one eye, looked at Gusev with it, and asked softly:

"Gusev, did your commanding officer steal?"

"Who can tell, Pavel Ivanitch! We can't say, it didn't reach us."

And after that a long time passed in silence. Gusev brooded, muttered something in delirium, and kept drinking water; it was hard for him to talk and hard to listen, and he was afraid of being talked to. An hour passed, a second, a third; evening came on, then night, but he did not notice it. He still sat dreaming of the frost.

There was a sound as though someone came into the hospital, and voices were audible, but a few minutes passed and all was still again.

"The Kingdom of Heaven and eternal peace," said the soldier with his arm in a sling. "He was an uncomfortable man."

"What?" asked Gusev. "Who?"

"He is dead, they have just carried him up."

"Oh, well," muttered Gusev, yawning, "the Kingdom of Heaven be his."

"What do you think?" the soldier with his arm in a sling asked Gusev. "Will he be in the Kingdom of Heaven or not?"

"Who is it you are talking about?"

"Pavel Ivanitch."

"He will be . . . he suffered so long. And there is another thing, he belonged to the clergy, and the priests always have a lot of relations. Their prayers will save him."

The soldier with the sling sat down on a hammock near Gusev and said in an undertone:

"And you, Gusev, are not long for this world. You will never get to Russia."

"Did the doctor or his assistant say so?" asked Gusev.

"It isn't that they said so, but one can see it. . . . One can see directly when a man's going to die. You don't eat, you don't drink; it's dreadful to see how thin you've got. It's consumption, in fact. I say it, not to upset you, but because maybe you would like to have the sacrament and extreme unction. And if you have any money you had better give it to the senior officer."

"I haven't written home . . ." Gusev sighed. "I shall die and they won't know."

"They'll hear of it," the sick sailor brought out in a bass voice. "When you die they will put it down in the *Gazette*, at Odessa they will send in a report to the commanding officer there and he will send it to the parish or somewhere. . . ."

Gusev began to be uneasy after such a conversation and to feel a vague yearning. He drank water—it was not that; he dragged himself to the window and breathed the hot, moist air—it was not that; he tried to think of home, of the frost—it was not that. . . . At last it seemed to him one minute longer in the ward and he would certainly expire.

"It's stifling, mates . . ." he said. "I'll go on deck. Help me up, for Christ's sake."

"All right," assented the soldier with the sling. "I'll carry you, you can't walk, hold on to my neck."

Gusev put his arm round the soldier's neck, the latter put his unhurt arm round him and carried him up. On the deck sailors and time-expired soldiers were lying asleep side by side; there were so many of them it was difficult to pass.

"Stand down," the soldier with the sling said softly. "Follow me quietly, hold on to my shirt. . . ."

It was dark. There was no light on deck, nor on the masts, nor anywhere on the sea around. At the furthest end of the ship the man on watch was standing perfectly still like a statue, and it looked as though he were asleep. It seemed as though the steamer were abandoned to itself and were going at its own will.

"Now they will throw Pavel Ivanitch into the sea," said the soldier with the sling. "In a sack and then into the water."

"Yes, that's the rule."

"But it's better to lie at home in the earth. Anyway, your mother comes to the grave and weeps."

"Of course."

There was a smell of hay and of dung. There were oxen standing with drooping heads by the ship's rail. One, two, three; eight of them! And there was a little horse. Gusev put out his hand to stroke it, but it shook its head, showed its teeth, and tried to bite his sleeve.

"Damned brute . . ." said Gusev angrily.

The two of them, he and the soldier, threaded their way to the head of the ship, then stood at the rail and looked up and down. Overhead deep sky, bright stars, peace and stillness, exactly as at home in the village, below darkness and disorder. The tall waves were resounding, no one could tell why. Whichever wave you looked at each one was trying to rise higher than all the rest and to chase and crush the next one; after it a third as fierce and hideous flew noisily, with a glint of light on its white crest.

The sea has no sense and no pity. If the steamer had been smaller and not made of thick iron, the waves would have crushed it to pieces without the slightest compunction, and would have devoured all the people in it with no distinction of saints or sinners. The steamer had the same cruel and meaningless expression. This monster with its huge beak was dashing onwards, cutting millions of waves in its path; it had no fear of the darkness nor the wind, nor of space, nor of solitude, caring for nothing, and if the ocean had its people, this monster would have crushed them, too, without distinction of saints or sinners.

"Where are we now?" asked Gusev.

"I don't know. We must be in the ocean."

"There is no sight of land . . ."

"No indeed! They say we shan't see it for seven days."

The two soldiers watched the white foam with the phosphorus light on it and were silent, thinking. Gusev was the first to break the silence.

"There is nothing to be afraid of," he said, "only one is full of dread as though one were sitting in a dark forest; but if, for instance, they let a boat down on to the water this minute and an officer ordered me to go a hundred miles over the sea to catch fish, I'd go. Or, let's say, if a Christian were to fall into the water this minute, I'd go in after him. A German or a Chinaman I wouldn't save, but I'd go in after a Christian."

"And are you afraid to die?"

"Yes. I am sorry for the folks at home. My brother at home, you know, isn't steady; he drinks, he beats his wife for nothing, he does not honour his parents. Everything will go to ruin without me, and father and my old mother will be begging their bread, I shouldn't wonder. But my legs won't bear me, brother, and it's hot here. Let's go to sleep."

V

Gusev went back to the ward and got into his hammock. He was again tormented by a vague craving, and he could not make out what he wanted. There was an oppression on his chest, a throbbing in his head, his mouth was so dry that it was difficult for him to move his tongue. He dozed, and murmured in his sleep, and, worn out with nightmares, his cough, and the stifling heat, towards morning he fell into a sound sleep. He dreamed that they were just taking the bread out of the oven in the barracks and he climbed into the stove and had a steam bath in it, lashing himself with a bunch of birch twigs. He slept for two days, and at midday on the third two sailors came down and carried him out.

He was sewn up in sailcloth and to make him heavier they put with him two iron weights. Sewn up in the sailcloth he looked like a carrot or a radish: broad at the head and narrow at the feet. . . . Before sunset they brought him up to the deck and put him on a plank; one end of the plank lay on the side of the ship, the other on a box, placed on a stool. Round him stood the soldiers and the officers with their caps off.

"Blessed be the Name of the Lord . . ." the priest began. "As it was in the beginning, is now, and ever shall be."

"Amen," chanted three sailors.

The soldiers and the officers crossed themselves and looked away at the waves. It was strange that a man should be sewn up in sailcloth and should soon be flying into the sea. Was it possible that such a thing might happen to anyone?

The priest strewed earth upon Gusev and bowed down. They sang "Eternal Memory."

The man on watch duty tilted up the end of the plank, Gusev slid off and flew head foremost, turned a somersault in the air and splashed into the sea. He was covered with foam and for a moment looked as though he were wrapped in lace, but the minute passed and he disappeared in the waves.

He went rapidly towards the bottom. Did he reach it? It was said to be three miles to the bottom. After sinking sixty or seventy feet, he began moving more and more slowly, swaying rhythmically, as though he were hesitating and, carried along by the current, moved more rapidly sideways than downwards.

Then he was met by a shoal of the fish called harbour pilots. Seeing the dark body the fish stopped as though petrified, and suddenly turned round and disappeared. In less than a minute they flew back swift as an arrow to Gusev, and began zigzagging round him in the water.

After that another dark body appeared. It was a shark. It swam under Gusev with dignity and no show of interest, as though it did not notice him, and sank down upon its back, then it turned belly upwards, basking in the warm, transparent water and languidly opened its jaws with two rows of teeth. The harbour pilots are delighted, they stop to see what will come next. After playing a little with the body the shark nonchalantly puts its jaws under it, cautiously touches it with its teeth, and the sailcloth is rent its full length from head to foot; one of the weights falls out and frightens the harbour pilots, and striking the shark on the ribs goes rapidly to the bottom.

Overhead at this time the clouds are massed together on the side where the sun is setting; one cloud like a triumphal arch, another like a lion, a third like a pair of scissors. . . . From behind the clouds a broad, green shaft of light pierces through and stretches to the middle of the sky; a little later another, violet-coloured, lies beside it; next that, one of gold, then one rose-coloured. . . . The sky turns a soft lilac. Looking at this gorgeous, enchanted sky, at first the ocean scowls, but soon it, too, takes tender, joyous, passionate colours for which it is hard to find a name in human speech.

Peasant Wives

[First published in No. 5502 issue of *Novoye Vremya*,
a Russian newspaper, in 1891. First translated in English in 1908
by R. E. C. Long, titled 'Women.' Later collected in
The Witch and Other Stories (1918). One of Chekhov's brillant tales,
it was among Leo Tolstoy's personal list of Chekhov's best stories.]

In the village of Reybuzh, just facing the church, stands a two-storeyed house with a stone foundation and an iron roof. In the lower storey the owner himself, Filip Ivanov Kashin, nicknamed Dyudya, lives with his family, and on the upper floor, where it is apt to be very hot in summer and very cold in winter, they put up government officials, merchants, or landowners, who chance to be travelling that way. Dyudya rents some bits of land, keeps a tavern on the highroad, does a trade in tar, honey, cattle, and jackdaws, and has already something like eight thousand roubles put by in the bank in the town.

His elder son, Fyodor, is head engineer in the factory, and, as the peasants say of him, he has risen so high in the world that he is quite out of reach now. Fyodor's wife, Sofya, a plain, ailing woman, lives at home at her father-in-law's. She is for ever crying, and every Sunday she goes over to the hospital for medicine. Dyudya's second son, the hunchback Alyoshka, is living at home at his father's. He has only lately been married to Varvara, whom they singled out for him from a poor family. She is a handsome young woman, smart and buxom. When officials or merchants put up at the house, they always insist on having Varvara to bring in the samovar and make their beds.

One June evening when the sun was setting and the air was full of the smell of hay, of steaming dung-heaps and new milk, a plain-looking cart drove into Dyudya's yard with three people in it: a man of about thirty in a canvas suit, beside him a little boy of seven or eight in a long black coat with big bone buttons, and on the driver's seat a young fellow in a red shirt.

The young fellow took out the horses and led them out into the street to walk them up and down a bit, while the traveller washed, said a prayer, turning towards the church, then spread a rug near the cart and sat down with the boy to supper. He ate without haste, sedately, and Dyudya, who had seen a good many travellers in his time, knew him from his manners for a businesslike man, serious and aware of his own value.

Dyudya was sitting on the step in his waistcoat without a cap on, waiting for the visitor to speak first. He was used to hearing all kinds of stories from the travellers in the evening, and he liked listening to them before going to bed. His old wife, Afanasyevna, and his daughter-in-law Sofya, were milking in the cowshed. The other daughter-in-law, Varvara, was sitting at the open window of the upper storey, eating sunflower seeds.

"The little chap will be your son, I'm thinking?" Dyudya asked the traveller.

"No; adopted. An orphan. I took him for my soul's salvation."

They got into conversation. The stranger seemed to be a man fond of talking and ready of speech, and Dyudya learned from him that he was from the town, was of the tradesman class, and had a house of his own, that his name was Matvey Savitch, that he was on his way now to look at some gardens that he was renting from some German colonists, and that the boy's name was Kuzka. The evening was hot and close, no one felt inclined for sleep. When it was getting dark and pale stars began to twinkle here and there in the sky, Matvey Savitch began to tell how he had come by Kuzka. Afanasyevna and Sofya stood a little way off, listening. Kuzka had gone to the gate.

"It's a complicated story, old man," began Matvey Savitch, "and if I were to tell you all just as it happened, it would take all night and more. Ten years ago in a little house in our street, next door to me, where now there's a tallow and oil factory, there was living an old widow, Marfa Semyonovna Kapluntsev, and she had two sons: one was a guard on the railway, but the other, Vasya, who was just my own age, lived at home with his mother. Old Kapluntsev had kept five pair of horses and sent carriers all over the town; his widow had not given up the business, but managed the carriers as well as her husband had done, so that some days they would bring in as much as five roubles from their rounds.

"The young fellow, too, made a trifle on his own account. He used to breed fancy pigeons and sell them to fanciers; at times he would stand for hours on the roof, waving a broom in the air and whistling; his pigeons were right up in the clouds, but it wasn't enough for him, and he'd want them to go higher yet. Siskins and starlings, too, he used to catch, and he made cages for sale. All trifles, but, mind you, he'd pick up some ten roubles a month over such trifles. Well, as time went on, the old lady lost the use of her legs and took to her bed. In consequence of which event the house was left without a woman to look after it, and that's for all the world like a man without an eye. The old lady bestirred herself and made up her mind to marry Vasya. They called in a matchmaker at once, the women got to talking of one thing and another, and Vasya went off to have a look at the girls. He picked out Mashenka, a widow's daughter. They made up their minds without loss of time and in a week it was all settled. The girl was a little slip of a thing, seventeen, but fair-skinned and pretty-looking, and like a lady in all her ways; and a decent dowry with her, five hundred roubles, a cow, a bed. . . . Well, the old lady—it seemed as though she had known it was coming—three days after the wedding, departed to the Heavenly Jerusalem where is neither sickness nor sighing. The young people gave her a good funeral and began their life together. For just six months they got on splendidly, and then all of a sudden another misfortune. It never rains but it pours: Vasya was summoned to the recruiting office to draw lots for the service. He was taken, poor chap, for a soldier, and not even granted exemption. They shaved his head and packed him off to Poland. It was God's will; there was nothing to be done. When he said goodbye to his wife in the yard, he bore it all right; but as he glanced up at the hay-loft and his pigeons for the last time, he burst out crying. It was pitiful to see him.

"At first Mashenka got her mother to stay with her, that she mightn't be dull all alone; she stayed till the baby—this very Kuzka here—was born, and then she went off to Oboyan to another married daughter's and left Mashenka alone with the baby. There were five peasants—the carriers—a drunken saucy lot; horses, too, and dray-carts to see to, and then the fence would be broken or the soot afire in the chimney—jobs beyond a woman, and through our being neighbours, she got into the way of turning to me for every little thing. . . . Well, I'd go over, set things to rights, and give advice. . . . Naturally, not without going indoors, drinking a cup of tea and having a little chat with her. I was a young fellow, intellectual, and fond of talking on all sorts of subjects; she, too, was well-bred and educated. She was always neatly dressed, and in summer she walked out with a sunshade. Sometimes I would begin upon religion or politics with her, and she was flattered and would entertain me with tea and jam. . . . In a word, not to make a long story of it, I must tell you, old man, a year had not passed before the Evil One, the enemy of all mankind, confounded me. I began to notice that any day I didn't go to see her, I seemed out of sorts and dull. And I'd be continually making up something that I must see her about: 'It's high time,' I'd say to myself, 'to put the double windows in for the winter,' and the whole day I'd idle away over at her place putting in the windows and take good care to leave a couple of them over for the next day too.

"'I ought to count over Vasya's pigeons, to see none of them have strayed,' and so on. I used always to be talking to her across the fence, and in the end I made a little gate in the fence so as not to have to go so far round. From womankind comes much evil into the world and every kind of abomination. Not we sinners only; even the saints themselves have been led astray by them. Mashenka did not try to keep me at a distance. Instead of thinking of her husband and being on her guard, she fell in love with me. I began to notice that she was dull without me, and was always walking to and fro by the fence looking into my yard through the cracks.

"My brains were going round in my head in a sort of frenzy. On Thursday in Holy Week I was going early in the morning—it was scarcely light—to market. I passed close by her gate, and the Evil One was by me—at my elbow. I looked—she had a gate with open trellis work at the top—and there she was, up already, standing in the middle of the yard, feeding the ducks. I could not restrain myself, and I called her name. She came up and looked at me through the trellis. . . . Her little face was white, her eyes soft and sleepy-looking. . . . I liked her looks immensely, and I began paying her compliments, as though we were not at the gate, but just as one does on namedays, while she blushed, and laughed, and kept looking straight into my eyes without winking. . . . I lost all sense and began to declare my love to her. . . . She opened the gate, and from that morning we began to live as man and wife. . . ."

The hunchback Alyoshka came into the yard from the street and ran out of breath into the house, not looking at any one. A minute later he ran out of the house with a concertina. Jingling some coppers in his pocket, and cracking sunflower seeds as he ran, he went out at the gate.

"And who's that, pray?" asked Matvey Savitch.

"My son Alexey," answered Dyudya. "He's off on a spree, the rascal. God has afflicted him with a hump, so we are not very hard on him."

"And he's always drinking with the other fellows, always drinking," sighed Afanasyevna. "Before Carnival we married him, thinking he'd be steadier, but there! he's worse than ever."

"It's been no use. Simply keeping another man's daughter for nothing," said Dyudya.

Somewhere behind the church they began to sing a glorious, mournful song. The words they could not catch and only the voices could be heard—two tenors and a bass. All were listening; there was complete stillness in the yard. . . . Two voices suddenly broke off with a loud roar of laughter, but the third, a tenor, still sang on, and took so high a note that every one instinctively looked upwards, as though the voice had soared to heaven itself.

Varvara came out of the house, and screening her eyes with her hand, as though from the sun, she looked towards the church.

"It's the priest's sons with the schoolmaster," she said.

Again all the three voices began to sing together. Matvey Savitch sighed and went on:

"Well, that's how it was, old man. Two years later we got a letter from Vasya from Warsaw. He wrote that he was being sent home sick. He was ill. By that time I had put all that foolishness out of my head, and I had a fine match picked out all ready for me, only I didn't know how to break it off with my sweetheart. Every day I'd make up my mind to have it out with Mashenka, but I didn't know how to approach her so as not to have a woman's screeching about my ears. The letter freed my hands. I read it through with Mashenka; she turned white as a sheet, while I said to her: 'Thank God; now,' says I, 'you'll be a married woman again.' But says she: 'I'm not going to live with him.' 'Why, isn't he your husband?' said I. 'Is

240

it an easy thing? . . . I never loved him and I married him not of my own free will. My mother made me.' 'Don't try to get out of it, silly,' said I, 'but tell me this: were you married to him in church or not?' 'I was married,' she said, 'but it's you that I love, and I will stay with you to the day of my death. Folks may jeer. I don't care. . . .' 'You're a Christian woman,' said I, 'and have read the Scriptures; what is written there?'

"Once married, with her husband she must live," said Dyudya.

"'Man and wife are one flesh. We have sinned,' I said, 'you and I, and it is enough; we must repent and fear God. We must confess it all to Vasya,' said I; 'he's a quiet fellow and soft—he won't kill you. And indeed,' said I, 'better to suffer torments in this world at the hands of your lawful master than to gnash your teeth at the dread Seat of Judgment.' The wench wouldn't listen; she stuck to her silly, 'It's you I love!' and nothing more could I get out of her.

"Vasya came back on the Saturday before Trinity, early in the morning. From my fence I could see everything; he ran into the house, and came back a minute later with Kuzka in his arms, and he was laughing and crying all at once; he was kissing Kuzka and looking up at the hay-loft, and hadn't the heart to put the child down, and yet he was longing to go to his pigeons. He was always a soft sort of chap—sentimental. That day passed off very well, all quiet and proper. They had begun ringing the church bells for the evening service, when the thought struck me: 'Tomorrow's Trinity Sunday; how is it they are not decking the gates and the fence with green? Something's wrong,' I thought. I went over to them. I peeped in, and there he was, sitting on the floor in the middle of the room, his eyes staring like a drunken man's, the tears streaming down his cheeks and his hands shaking; he was pulling cracknels, necklaces, gingerbread nuts, and all sorts of little presents out of his bundle and flinging them on the floor. Kuzka—he was three years old—was crawling on the floor, munching the gingerbreads, while Mashenka stood by the stove, white and shivering all over, muttering: 'I'm not your wife; I can't live with you,' and all sorts of foolishness. I bowed down at Vasya's feet, and said: 'We have sinned against you, Vassily Maximitch; forgive us, for Christ's sake!' Then I got up and spoke to Mashenka: 'You, Marya Semyonovna, ought now to wash Vassily Maximitch's feet and drink the water. Do you be an obedient wife to him, and pray to God for me, that He in His mercy may forgive my transgression.' It came to me like an inspiration from an angel of Heaven;

I gave her solemn counsel and spoke with such feeling that my own tears flowed too. And so two days later Vasya comes to me: 'Matyusha,' says he, 'I forgive you and my wife; God have mercy on you! She was a soldier's wife, a young thing all alone; it was hard for her to be on her guard. She's not the first, nor will she be the last. Only,' he says, 'I beg you to behave as though there had never been anything between you, and to make no sign, while I,' says he, 'will do my best to please her in every way, so that she may come to love me again.' He gave me his hand on it, drank a cup of tea, and went away more cheerful.

"'Well,' thought I, 'thank God!' and I did feel glad that everything had gone off so well. But no sooner had Vasya gone out of the yard, when in came Mashenka. Ah! What I had to suffer! She hung on my neck, weeping and praying: 'For God's sake, don't cast me off; I can't live without you!'"

"The vile hussy!" sighed Dyudya.

"I swore at her, stamped my foot, and dragging her into the passage, I fastened the door with the hook. 'Go to your husband,' I cried. 'Don't shame me before folks. Fear God!' And every day there was a scene of that sort.

"One morning I was standing in my yard near the stable cleaning a bridle. All at once I saw her running through the little gate into my yard, with bare feet, in her petticoat, and straight towards me; she clutched at the bridle, getting all smeared with the pitch, and shaking and weeping, she cried: 'I can't stand him; I loathe him; I can't bear it! If you don't love me, better kill me!' I was angry, and I struck her twice with the bridle, but at that instant Vasya ran in at the gate, and in a despairing voice he shouted: 'Don't beat her! Don't beat her!' But he ran up himself, and waving his arms, as though he were mad, he let fly with his fists at her with all his might, then flung her on the ground and kicked her. I tried to defend her, but he snatched up the reins and thrashed her with them, and all the while, like a colt's whinny, he went: 'He—he—he!'"

"I'd take the reins and let you feel them," muttered Varvara, moving away; "murdering our sister, the damned brutes! . . ."

"Hold your tongue, you jade!" Dyudya shouted at her.

"'He—he—he!'" Matvey Savitch went on. "A carrier ran out of his yard; I called to my workman, and the three of us got Mashenka away from him and carried her home in our arms. The disgrace of it! The same day I went over in the evening to see how things were. She was lying in bed, all wrapped up in bandages, nothing but her eyes and nose to be seen; she was looking at the ceiling. I said: 'Good evening, Marya Semyonovna!' She did not speak. And Vasya was sitting in the next room, his head in his hands, crying and saying: 'Brute that I am! I've ruined my life! O God, let me die!' I sat for half an hour by Mashenka and gave her a good talking-to. I tried to frighten her a bit. 'The righteous,' said I, 'after this life go to Paradise, but you will go to a Gehenna of fire, like all adulteresses. Don't strive against your husband, go and lay yourself at his feet.' But never a word from her; she didn't so much as bJlink an eyelid, for all the world as though I were talking to a post. The next day Vasya fell ill with something like cholera, and in the evening I heard that he was dead. Well, so they buried him, and Mashenka did not go to the funeral; she didn't care to show her shameless face and her bruises. And soon there began to be talk all over the district that Vasya had not died a natural death, that Mashenka had made away with him. It got to the ears of the police; they had Vasya dug up and cut open, and in his stomach they found arsenic. It was clear he had been poisoned; the police came and took Mashenka away, and with her the innocent Kuzka. They were put in prison. . . . The woman had gone too far—God punished her. . . . Eight months later they tried her. She sat, I remember, on a low stool, with a little white kerchief on her head, wearing a grey gown, and she was so thin, so pale, so sharp-eyed it made one sad to look at her. Behind her stood a soldier with a gun. She would not confess her guilt. Some in the court said she had poisoned her husband and others declared he had poisoned himself for grief. I was one of the witnesses. When they questioned me, I told the whole truth according to my oath. 'Hers,' said I, 'is the guilt. It's no good to conceal it; she did not love her husband, and she had a will of her own. . . .' The trial began in the morning and towards night they passed this sentence: to send her to hard labour in Siberia for thirteen years. After that sentence Mashenka remained three months longer in prison. I went to see her, and from Christian charity I took her a little tea and sugar. But as soon as she set eyes on me she began to shake all over, wringing her hands and muttering: 'Go away! go away!' And Kuzka she clasped to her as though she were afraid I would take him away. 'See,' said I, 'what you have come to! Ah, Masha, Masha! you would not listen to me when I gave you good advice, and now you must repent it. You are yourself to blame,' said I; 'blame yourself!' I was giving her good counsel, but she:

'Go away, go away!' huddling herself and Kuzka against the wall, and trembling all over.

"When they were taking her away to the chief town of our province, I walked by the escort as far as the station and slipped a rouble into her bundle for my soul's salvation. But she did not get as far as Siberia. . . . She fell sick of fever and died in prison."

"Live like a dog and you must die a dog's death," said Dyudya.

"Kuzka was sent back home. . . . I thought it over and took him to bring up. After all—though a convict's child—still he was a living soul, a Christian. . . . I was sorry for him. I shall make him my clerk, and if I have no children of my own, I'll make a merchant of him. Wherever I go now, I take him with me; let him learn his work."

All the while Matvey Savitch had been telling his story, Kuzka had sat on a little stone near the gate. His head propped in both hands, he gazed at the sky, and in the distance he looked in the dark like a stump of wood.

"Kuzka, come to bed," Matvey Savitch bawled to him.

"Yes, it's time," said Dyudya, getting up; he yawned loudly and added: "Folks will go their own way, and that's what comes of it."

Over the yard the moon was floating now in the heavens; she was moving one way, while the clouds beneath moved the other way; the clouds were disappearing into the darkness, but still the moon could be seen high above the yard.

Matvey Savitch said a prayer, facing the church, and saying goodnight, he lay down on the ground near his cart. Kuzka, too, said a prayer, lay down in the cart, and covered himself with his little overcoat; he made himself a little hole in the hay so as to be more comfortable, and curled up so that his elbows looked like knees. From the yard Dyudya could be seen lighting a candle in his room below, putting on his spectacles and standing in the corner with a book. He was a long while reading and crossing himself.

The travellers fell asleep. Afanasyevna and Sofya came up to the cart and began looking at Kuzka.

"The little orphan's asleep," said the old woman. "He's thin and frail, nothing but bones. No mother and no one to care for him properly."

"My Grishutka must be two years older," said Sofya. "Up at the factory he lives like a slave without his mother. The foreman beats him, I dare say. When I looked at this poor mite just now, I thought of my own Grishutka, and my heart went cold within me."

A minute passed in silence.

"Doesn't remember his mother, I suppose," said the old woman.

"How could he remember?"

And big tears began dropping from Sofya's eyes.

"He's curled himself up like a cat," she said, sobbing and laughing with tenderness and sorrow. . . . "Poor motherless mite!"

Kuzka started and opened his eyes. He saw before him an ugly, wrinkled, tear-stained face, and beside it another, aged and toothless, with a sharp chin and hooked nose, and high above them the infinite sky with the flying clouds and the moon. He cried out in fright, and Sofya, too, uttered a cry; both were answered by the echo, and a faint stir passed over the stifling air; a watchman tapped somewhere near, a dog barked. Matvey Savitch muttered something in his sleep and turned over on the other side.

Late at night when Dyudya and the old woman and the neighbouring watchman were all asleep, Sofya went out to the gate and sat down on the bench. She felt stifled and her head ached from weeping. The street was a wide and long one; it stretched for nearly two miles to the right and as far to the left, and the end of it was out of sight. The moon was now not over the yard, but behind the church. One side of the street was flooded with moonlight, while the other side lay in black shadow. The long shadows of the poplars and the starling-cotes stretched right across the street, while the church cast a broad shadow, black and terrible that enfolded Dyudya's gates and half his house. The street was still and deserted. From time to time the strains of music floated faintly from the end of the street—Alyoshka, most likely, playing his concertina.

Someone moved in the shadow near the church enclosure, and Sofya could not make out whether it were a man or a cow, or perhaps merely a big bird rustling in the trees. But then a figure stepped out of the shadow, halted, and said something in a man's voice, then vanished down the turning by the church. A little later, not three yards from the gate, another figure came into sight; it walked straight from the church to the gate and stopped short, seeing Sofya on the bench.

"Varvara, is that you?" said Sofya.

"And if it were?"

It was Varvara. She stood still a minute, then came up to the bench and sat down.

"Where have you been?" asked Sofya.

Varvara made no answer.

"You'd better mind you don't get into trouble with such goings-on, my girl," said Sofya. "Did you hear how Mashenka was kicked and lashed with the reins? You'd better look out, or they'll treat you the same."

"Well, let them!"

Varvara laughed into her kerchief and whispered:

"I have just been with the priest's son."

"Nonsense!"

"I have!"

"It's a sin!" whispered Sofya.

"Well, let it be. . . . What do I care? If it's a sin, then it is a sin, but better be struck dead by thunder than live like this. I'm young and strong, and I've a filthy crooked hunchback for a husband, worse than Dyudya himself, curse him! When I was a girl, I hadn't bread to eat, or a shoe to my foot, and to get away from that wretchedness I was tempted by Alyoshka's money, and got caught like a fish in a net, and I'd rather have a viper for my bedfellow than that scurvy Alyoshka. And what's your life? It makes me sick to look at it. Your Fyodor sent you packing from the factory and he's taken up with another woman. They have robbed you of your boy and made a slave of him. You work like a horse, and never hear a kind word. I'd rather pine all my days an old maid, I'd rather get half a rouble from the priest's son, I'd rather beg my bread, or throw myself into the well . . ."

"It's a sin!" whispered Sofya again.

"Well, let it be."

Somewhere behind the church the same three voices, two tenors and a bass, began singing again a mournful song. And again the words could not be distinguished.

"They are not early to bed," Varvara said, laughing.

And she began telling in a whisper of her midnight walks with the priest's son, and of the stories he had told her, and of his comrades, and of the fun she had with the travellers who stayed in the house. The mournful song stirred a longing for life and freedom. Sofya began to laugh; she thought it sinful and terrible and sweet to hear about, and she felt envious and sorry that she, too, had not been a sinner when she was young and pretty.

In the churchyard they heard twelve strokes beaten on the watchman's board.

"It's time we were asleep," said Sofya, getting up, "or, maybe, we shall catch it from Dyudya."

They both went softly into the yard.

"I went away without hearing what he was telling about Mashenka," said Varvara, making herself a bed under the window.

"She died in prison, he said. She poisoned her husband."

Varvara lay down beside Sofya a while, and said softly:

"I'd make away with my Alyoshka and never regret it."

"You talk nonsense; God forgive you."

When Sofya was just dropping asleep, Varvara, coming close, whispered in her ear:

"Let us get rid of Dyudya and Alyoshka!"

Sofya started and said nothing. Then she opened her eyes and gazed a long while steadily at the sky.

"People would find out," she said.

"No, they wouldn't. Dyudya's an old man, it's time he did die; and they'd say Alyoshka died of drink."

"I'm afraid . . . God would chastise us."

"Well, let Him. . . ."

Both lay awake thinking in silence.

"It's cold," said Sofya, beginning to shiver all over. "It will soon be morning. . . . Are you asleep?"

"No. . . . Don't you mind what I say, dear," whispered Varvara; "I get so mad with the damned brutes, I don't know what I do say. Go to sleep, or it will be daylight directly. . . . Go to sleep."

Both were quiet and soon they fell asleep.

Earlier than all woke the old woman. She waked up Sofya and they went together into the cowshed to milk the cows. The hunchback Alyoshka came in hopelessly drunk without his concertina; his breast and knees had been in the dust and straw—he must have fallen down in the road. Staggering, he went into the cowshed, and without undressing he rolled into a sledge and began to snore at once. When first the crosses on the church and then the windows were flashing in the light of the rising sun, and shadows stretched across the yard over the dewy grass from the trees and the top of the well, Matvey Savitch jumped up and began hurrying about:

"Kuzka! get up!" he shouted. "It's time to put in the horses! Look sharp!"

The bustle of morning was beginning. A young Jewess in a brown gown with flounces led a horse into the yard to drink. The pulley of the well creaked plaintively, the bucket knocked as it went down. . . .

Kuzka, sleepy, tired, covered with dew, sat up in the cart, lazily putting on his little overcoat, and listening to the drip of the water from the bucket into the well as he shivered with the cold.

"Auntie!" shouted Matvey Savitch to Sofya, "tell my lad to hurry up and to harness the horses!"

And Dyudya at the same instant shouted from the window:

"Sofya, take a farthing from the Jewess for the horse's drink! They're always in here, the mangy creatures!"

In the street sheep were running up and down, baaing; the peasant women were shouting at the shepherd, while he played his pipes, cracked his whip, or answered them in a thick sleepy bass. Three sheep strayed into the yard, and not finding the gate again, pushed at the fence.

Varvara was waked by the noise, and bundling her bedding up in her arms, she went into the house.

"You might at least drive the sheep out!" the old woman bawled after her, "my lady!"

"I dare say! As if I were going to slave for you Herods!" muttered Varvara, going into the house.

Dyudya came out of the house with his accounts in his hands, sat down on the step, and began reckoning how much the traveller owed him for the night's lodging, oats, and watering his horses.

"You charge pretty heavily for the oats, my good man," said Matvey Savitch.

"If it's too much, don't take them. There's no compulsion, merchant."

When the travellers were ready to start, they were detained for a minute. Kuzka had lost his cap.

"Little swine, where did you put it?" Matvey Savitch roared angrily. "Where is it?"

Kuzka's face was working with terror; he ran up and down near the cart, and not finding it there, ran to the gate and then to the shed. The old woman and Sofya helped him look.

"I'll pull your ears off!" yelled Matvey Savitch. "Dirty brat!"

The cap was found at the bottom of the cart.

Kuzka brushed the hay off it with his sleeve, put it on, and timidly he crawled into the cart, still with an expression of terror on his face as though he were afraid of a blow from behind.

Matvey Savitch crossed himself. The driver gave a tug at the reins and the cart rolled out of the yard.

Ward No. 6

[First published in the November 1892 issue of
Russkaya Mysl (Russian Thought), a Russian magazine.
Included in the collection *The Horse-Stealers and Other Stories* (1921).]

I

In the hospital yard there stands a small lodge surrounded by a perfect forest of burdocks, nettles, and wild hemp. Its roof is rusty, the chimney is tumbling down, the steps at the front-door are rotting away and overgrown with grass, and there are only traces left of the stucco. The front of the lodge faces the hospital; at the back it looks out into the open country, from which it is separated by the grey hospital fence with nails on it. These nails, with their points upwards, and the fence, and the lodge itself, have that peculiar, desolate, God-forsaken look which is only found in our hospital and prison buildings.

If you are not afraid of being stung by the nettles, come by the narrow footpath that leads to the lodge, and let us see what is going on inside. Opening the first door, we walk into the entry. Here along the walls and by the stove every sort of hospital rubbish lies littered about. Mattresses, old tattered dressing gowns, trousers, blue striped shirts, boots and shoes no good for anything—all these remnants are piled up in heaps, mixed up and crumpled, mouldering and giving out a sickly smell.

The porter, Nikita, an old soldier wearing rusty good-conduct stripes, is always lying on the litter with a pipe between his teeth. He has a grim, surly, battered-looking face, overhanging eyebrows which give him the expression of a sheep-dog of the steppes, and a red nose; he is short and looks thin and scraggy, but he is of imposing deportment and his fists are vigorous. He belongs to the class of simple-hearted, practical, and dull-witted people, prompt in carrying out orders, who like discipline better than anything in the world, and so are convinced that it is their duty to beat people. He showers blows on the face, on the chest, on the back, on whatever comes first, and is convinced that there would be no order in the place if he did not.

Next you come into a big, spacious room which fills up the whole lodge except for the entry. Here the walls are painted a dirty blue, the ceiling is as sooty as in a hut without a chimney—it is evident that in the winter the stove smokes and the room is full of fumes. The windows are disfigured by iron gratings on the inside. The wooden floor is grey and full of splinters. There is a stench of sour cabbage, of smouldering wicks, of bugs, and of ammonia, and for the first minute this stench gives you the impression of having walked into a menagerie.

There are bedsteads screwed to the floor. Men in blue hospital dressing gowns, and wearing nightcaps in the old style, are sitting and lying on them. These are the lunatics.

There are five of them in all here. Only one is of the upper class, the rest are all artisans. The one nearest the door—a tall, lean workman with shining red whiskers and tear-stained eyes—sits with his head propped on his hand, staring at the same point. Day and night he grieves, shaking his head, sighing and smiling bitterly. He takes a part in conversation and usually makes no answer to questions; he eats and drinks mechanically when food is offered him. From his agonizing, throbbing cough, his thinness, and the flush on his cheeks, one may judge that he is in the first stage of consumption. Next to him is a little, alert, very lively old man, with a pointed beard and curly black hair like a negro's. By day he walks up and down the ward from window to window, or sits on his bed, cross-legged like a Turk, and, ceaselessly as a bullfinch whistles, softly sings and titters. He shows his childish gaiety and lively character at night also when he gets up to say his prayers—that is, to beat himself on the chest with his fists, and to scratch with his fingers at the door. This is the Jew Moiseika, an imbecile, who went crazy twenty years ago when his hat factory was burnt down.

And of all the inhabitants of Ward No. 6, he is the only one who is allowed to go out of the lodge, and even out of the yard into the street.

He has enjoyed this privilege for years, probably because he is an old inhabitant of the hospital—a quiet, harmless imbecile, the buffoon of the town, where people are used to seeing him surrounded by boys and dogs. In his wretched gown, in his absurd night-cap, and in slippers, sometimes with bare legs and even without trousers, he walks about the streets, stopping at the gates and little shops, and begging for a copper. In one place they will give him some kvass, in another some bread, in another a copper, so that he generally goes back to the ward feeling rich and well fed. Everything that he brings back Nikita takes from him for his own benefit. The soldier does this roughly, angrily turning the Jew's pockets inside out, and calling God to witness that he will not let him go into the street again, and that breach of the regulations is worse to him than anything in the world.

Moiseika likes to make himself useful. He gives his companions water, and covers them up when they are asleep; he promises each of them to bring him back a kopeck, and to make him a new cap; he feeds with a spoon his neighbour on the left, who is paralyzed. He acts in this way, not from compassion nor from any considerations of a humane kind, but through imitation, unconsciously dominated by Gromov, his neighbour on the right hand.

Ivan Dmitritch Gromov, a man of thirty-three, who is a gentleman by birth, and has been a court usher and provincial secretary, suffers from the mania of persecution. He either lies curled up in bed, or walks from corner to corner as though for exercise; he very rarely sits down. He is always excited, agitated, and overwrought by a sort of vague, undefined expectation. The faintest rustle in the entry or shout in the yard is enough to make him raise his head and begin listening: whether they are coming for him, whether they are looking for him. And at such times his face expresses the utmost uneasiness and repulsion.

I like his broad face with its high cheekbones, always pale and unhappy, and reflecting, as though in a mirror, a soul tormented by conflict and long-continued terror. His grimaces are strange and abnormal, but the delicate lines traced on his face by profound, genuine suffering show intelligence and sense, and there is a warm and healthy light in his eyes. I like the man himself, courteous, anxious to be of use, and extraordinarily gentle to everyone except Nikita. When anyone drops a button or a spoon, he jumps up from his bed quickly and picks it up; every day he says good morning to his companions, and when he goes to bed he wishes them goodnight.

Besides his continually overwrought condition and his grimaces, his madness shows itself in the following way also. Sometimes in the evenings he wraps himself in his dressing gown, and, trembling all over, with his teeth chattering, begins walking rapidly from corner to corner and between the bedsteads. It seems as though he is in a violent fever. From the way he suddenly stops and glances at his companions, it can be seen that he is longing to say something very important, but, apparently reflecting that they would not listen, or would not understand him, he shakes his head impatiently and goes on pacing up and down. But soon the desire to speak gets the upper hand of every consideration, and he will let himself go and speak fervently and passionately. His talk is disordered and feverish like delirium, disconnected, and not always intelligible, but, on the other hand, something extremely fine may be felt in it, both in the words and the voice. When he talks you recognize in him the lunatic and the man. It is difficult to reproduce on paper his insane talk. He speaks of the baseness of mankind, of violence trampling on justice, of the glorious life which will one day be upon earth, of the window-gratings, which remind him every minute of the stupidity and cruelty of oppressors. It makes a disorderly, incoherent potpourri of themes old but not yet out of date.

II

Some twelve or fifteen years ago an official called Gromov, a highly respectable and prosperous person, was living in his own house in the principal street of the town. He had two sons, Sergey and Ivan. When Sergey was a student in his fourth year he was taken ill with galloping consumption and died, and his death was, as it were, the first of a whole series of calamities which suddenly showered on the Gromov family. Within a week of Sergey's funeral the old father was put on trial for fraud and misappropriation, and he died of typhoid in the prison hospital soon afterwards. The house, with all their belongings, was sold by auction, and Ivan Dmitritch and his mother were left entirely without means.

Hitherto in his father's lifetime, Ivan Dmitritch, who was studying in the University of Petersburg, had received an allowance of sixty or seventy roubles a month, and had had no conception of poverty; now he had to make an abrupt change in his life. He had to spend his time from morning to night giving lessons for next to nothing, to work at copying, and with all that to go hungry, as all his earnings were sent to keep his mother. Ivan Dmitritch could not stand such a life; he lost heart and strength, and, giving up the university, went home.

Here, through interest, he obtained the post of teacher in the district school, but could not get on with his colleagues, was not liked by the boys, and soon gave up the post. His mother died. He was for six months without work, living on nothing but bread and water; then he became a court usher. He kept this post until he was dismissed owing to his illness.

He had never even in his young student days given the impression of being perfectly healthy. He had always been pale, thin, and given to catching cold; he ate little and slept badly. A single glass of wine went to his head and made him hysterical. He always had a craving for society, but, owing to his irritable temperament and suspiciousness, he never became very intimate with anyone, and had no friends. He always spoke with contempt of his fellow-townsmen, saying that their coarse ignorance and sleepy animal existence seemed to him loathsome and horrible. He spoke in a loud tenor, with heat, and invariably either with scorn and indignation, or with wonder and enthusiasm, and always with perfect sincerity. Whatever one talked to him about he always brought it round to the same subject: that life was dull and stifling in the town; that the townspeople had no lofty interests, but lived a dingy, meaningless life, diversified by violence, coarse profligacy, and hypocrisy; that scoundrels were well fed and clothed, while honest men lived from hand to mouth; that they needed schools, a progressive local paper, a theatre, public lectures, the co-ordination of the intellectual elements; that society must see its failings and be horrified. In his criticisms of people he laid on the colours thick, using only black and white, and no fine shades; mankind was divided for him into honest men and scoundrels: there was nothing in between. He always spoke with passion and enthusiasm of women and of love, but he had never been in love.

In spite of the severity of his judgments and his nervousness, he was liked, and behind his back was spoken of affectionately as Vanya. His innate refinement and readiness to be of service, his good breeding, his moral purity, and his shabby coat, his frail appearance and family misfortunes, aroused a kind, warm, sorrowful feeling. Moreover, he was well educated and well read; according to the townspeople's notions, he knew everything, and was in their eyes something like a walking encyclopedia.

He had read a great deal. He would sit at the club, nervously pulling at his beard and looking through the magazines and books; and from his face one could see that he was not reading, but devouring the pages without giving himself time to digest what he read. It must be supposed that reading was one of his morbid habits, as he fell upon anything that came into his hands with equal avidity, even last year's newspapers and calendars. At home he always read lying down.

III

One autumn morning Ivan Dmitritch, turning up the collar of his greatcoat and splashing through the mud, made his way by side-streets and back lanes to see some artisan, and to collect some payment that was owing. He was in a gloomy mood, as he always was in the morning. In one of the side-streets he was met by two convicts in fetters and four soldiers with rifles in charge of them. Ivan Dmitritch had very often met convicts before, and they had always excited feelings of compassion and discomfort in him; but now this meeting made a peculiar, strange impression on him. It suddenly seemed to him for some reason that he, too, might be put into fetters and led through the mud to prison like that. After visiting the artisan, on the way home he met near the post office a police superintendent of his acquaintance, who greeted him and walked a few paces along the street with him, and for some reason this seemed to him suspicious. At home he could not get the convicts or the soldiers with their rifles out of his head all day, and an unaccountable inward agitation prevented him from reading or concentrating his mind. In the evening he did not light his lamp, and at night he could not sleep, but kept thinking that he might be arrested, put into fetters, and thrown into prison. He did not know of any harm he had done, and could be certain that he would never be guilty of murder, arson, or theft in the future either; but was it not easy to commit a crime by accident, unconsciously, and was not false witness always possible, and, indeed, miscarriage of justice? It was not without good reason that the agelong experience of the simple people teaches that beggary and prison are ills none can be safe from. A judicial mistake is very possible as legal proceedings are conducted nowadays, and there is nothing to be wondered at in it. People who have an official, professional relation to other men's sufferings—for instance, judges, police officers, doctors—in course of time, through habit, grow so callous that they cannot, even if they wish it, take any but a formal attitude to their clients; in this respect they are not different from the peasant who slaughters sheep and calves in the back-yard, and does not notice the blood. With this formal, soulless attitude to human personality the judge needs but one thing—time—in order to deprive an innocent man of all rights of property, and to condemn him to penal servitude. Only the time spent on performing certain formalities for which the judge is paid his salary, and then—it is all over. Then you may look in vain for justice and protection in this dirty, wretched little town a hundred and fifty miles from a railway station! And, indeed, is it not absurd even to think of justice when every kind of violence is accepted by society as a rational and consistent necessity, and every act of mercy—for instance, a verdict of acquittal—calls forth a perfect outburst of dissatisfied and revengeful feeling?

In the morning Ivan Dmitritch got up from his bed in a state of horror, with cold perspiration on his forehead, completely convinced that he might be arrested any minute. Since his gloomy thoughts of yesterday had haunted him so long, he thought, it must be that there was some truth in them. They could not, indeed, have come into his mind without any grounds whatever.

A policeman walking slowly passed by the windows: that was not for nothing. Here were two men standing still and silent near the house. Why were they silent? And agonizing days and nights followed for Ivan Dmitritch. Everyone who passed by the windows or came into the yard seemed to him a spy or a detective. At midday the chief of the police usually drove down the street with a pair of horses; he was going from his estate near the town to the police department; but Ivan Dmitritch fancied every time that he was driving especially quickly, and that he had a peculiar expression: it was evident that he was in haste to announce that there was a very important criminal in the town. Ivan Dmitritch started at every ring at the bell and knock at the gate, and was agitated whenever he came upon anyone new at his landlady's; when he met police officers and gendarmes he smiled and began whistling so as to seem unconcerned. He could not sleep for whole nights in succession expecting to be arrested, but he snored loudly and sighed as though in deep sleep, that his landlady might think he was asleep; for if he could not sleep it meant that he was tormented by the stings of conscience—what a piece of evidence! Facts and common sense persuaded him that all these terrors were nonsense and morbidity, that if one looked at the matter more broadly there was nothing really terrible in arrest and imprisonment—so long as the conscience is at ease; but the more sensibly and logically he reasoned, the more acute and agonizing his mental distress became. It might be compared with the story of a hermit who tried to cut a dwelling-place for himself in a virgin forest; the more zealously he worked with his axe, the thicker the forest grew. In the end Ivan Dmitritch, seeing it was useless, gave up reasoning altogether, and abandoned himself entirely to despair and terror.

He began to avoid people and to seek solitude. His official work had been distasteful to him before: now it became unbearable to him. He was afraid they would somehow get him into trouble, would put a bribe in his pocket unnoticed and then denounce him, or that he would accidentally make a mistake in official papers that would appear to be fraudulent, or would lose other people's money. It is strange that his imagination had never at other times been so agile and inventive as now, when every day he thought of thousands of different reasons for being seriously anxious over his freedom and honour; but, on the other hand, his interest in the outer world, in books in particular, grew sensibly fainter, and his memory began to fail him.

In the spring when the snow melted there were found in the ravine near the cemetery two half-decomposed corpses—the bodies of an old woman and a boy bearing the traces of death by violence. Nothing was talked of but these bodies and their unknown murderers. That people might not think he had been guilty of the crime, Ivan Dmitritch walked about the streets, smiling, and when he met acquaintances he turned pale, flushed, and began declaring that there was no greater crime than the murder of the weak and defenceless. But this duplicity soon exhausted him, and after some reflection he decided that in his position the best thing to do was to hide in his landlady's cellar. He sat in the cellar all day and then all night, then another day, was fearfully cold, and waiting till dusk, stole secretly like a thief back to his room. He stood in the middle of the room till daybreak, listening without stirring. Very early in the morning, before sunrise, some workmen came into the house. Ivan Dmitritch knew perfectly well that they had come to mend the stove in the kitchen, but terror told him that they were police officers disguised as workmen. He slipped stealthily out of the flat, and, overcome by terror, ran along the street without his cap and coat. Dogs raced after him barking, a peasant shouted somewhere behind him, the wind whistled in his ears, and it seemed to Ivan Dmitritch that the force and violence of the whole world was massed together behind his back and was chasing after him.

He was stopped and brought home, and his landlady sent for a doctor. Doctor Andrey Yefimitch, of whom we shall have more to say hereafter, prescribed cold compresses on his head and laurel drops, shook his head, and went away, telling the landlady he should not come again, as one should not interfere with people who are going out of their minds. As he had not the means to live at home and be nursed, Ivan Dmitritch was soon sent to the hospital, and was there put into the ward for venereal patients. He could not sleep at night, was full of whims and fancies, and disturbed the patients, and was soon afterwards, by Andrey Yefimitch's orders, transferred to Ward No. 6.

Within a year Ivan Dmitritch was completely forgotten in the town, and his books, heaped up by his landlady in a sledge in the shed, were pulled to pieces by boys.

IV

Ivan Dmitritch's neighbour on the left hand is, as I have said already, the Jew Moiseika; his neighbour on the right hand is a peasant so rolling in fat that he is almost spherical, with a blankly stupid face, utterly devoid of thought. This is a motionless, gluttonous, unclean animal who has long ago lost all powers of thought or feeling. An acrid, stifling stench always comes from him.

Nikita, who has to clean up after him, beats him terribly with all his might, not sparing his fists; and what is dreadful is not his being beaten—that one can get used to—but the fact that this stupefied creature does not respond to the blows with a sound or a movement, nor by a look in the eyes, but only sways a little like a heavy barrel.

The fifth and last inhabitant of Ward No. 6 is a man of the artisan class who had once been a sorter in the post office, a thinnish, fair little man with a good-natured but rather sly face. To judge from the clear, cheerful look in his calm and intelligent eyes, he has some pleasant idea in his mind, and has some very important and agreeable secret. He has under his pillow and under his mattress something that he never shows anyone, not from fear of its being taken from him and stolen, but from modesty. Sometimes he goes to the window, and turning his back to his companions, puts something on his breast, and bending his head, looks at it; if you go up to him at such a moment, he is overcome with confusion and snatches something off his breast. But it is not difficult to guess his secret.

"Congratulate me," he often says to Ivan Dmitritch; "I have been presented with the Stanislav order of the second degree with the star. The second degree with the star is only given to foreigners, but for some reason they want to make an exception for me," he says with a smile, shrugging his shoulders in perplexity. "That I must confess I did not expect."

"I don't understand anything about that," Ivan Dmitritch replies morosely.

"But do you know what I shall attain to sooner or later?" the former sorter persists, screwing up his eyes slyly. "I shall certainly get the Swedish 'Polar Star.' That's an order it is worth working for, a white cross with a black ribbon. It's very beautiful."

Probably in no other place is life so monotonous as in this ward. In the morning the patients, except the paralytic and the fat peasant, wash in the entry at a big tab and wipe themselves with the skirts of their dressing gowns; after that they drink tea out of tin mugs which Nikita brings them out of the main building. Everyone is allowed one mugful. At midday they have soup made out of sour cabbage and boiled grain, in the evening their supper consists of grain left from dinner. In the intervals they lie down, sleep, look out of window, and walk from one corner to the other. And so every day. Even the former sorter always talks of the same orders.

Fresh faces are rarely seen in Ward No. 6. The doctor has not taken in any new mental cases for a long time, and the people who are fond of visiting lunatic asylums are few in this world. Once every two months Semyon Lazaritch, the barber, appears in the ward. How he cuts the patients' hair, and how Nikita helps him to do it, and what a trepidation the lunatics are always thrown into by the arrival of the drunken, smiling barber, we will not describe.

No one even looks into the ward except the barber. The patients are condemned to see day after day no one but Nikita.

A rather strange rumour has, however, been circulating in the hospital of late.

It is rumoured that the doctor has begun to visit Ward No. 6.

V

A strange rumour!

Dr. Andrey Yefimitch Ragin is a strange man in his way. They say that when he was young he was very religious, and prepared himself for a clerical career, and that when he had finished his studies at the high school in 1863 he intended to enter a theological academy, but that his father, a surgeon and doctor of medicine, jeered at him and declared point-blank that he would disown him if he became a priest. How far this is true I don't know, but Andrey Yefimitch himself has more than once confessed that he has never had a natural bent for medicine or science in general.

However that may have been, when he finished his studies in the medical faculty he did not enter the priesthood. He showed no special devoutness, and was no more like a priest at the beginning of his medical career than he is now.

His exterior is heavy—coarse like a peasant's, his face, his beard, his flat hair, and his coarse, clumsy figure, suggest an overfed, intemperate, and harsh innkeeper on the highroad. His face is surly-looking and covered with blue veins, his eyes are little and his nose is red. With his height and broad shoulders he has huge hands and feet; one would think that a blow from his fist would knock the life out of anyone, but his step is soft, and his walk is cautious and insinuating; when he meets anyone in a narrow passage he is always the first to stop and make way, and to say, not in a bass, as one would expect, but in a high, soft tenor: "I beg your pardon!" He has a little swelling on his neck which prevents him from wearing stiff starched collars, and so he always goes about in soft linen or cotton shirts. Altogether he does not dress like a doctor. He wears the same suit for ten years, and the new clothes, which he usually buys at a Jewish shop, look as shabby and crumpled on him as his old ones; he sees patients and dines and pays visits all in the same coat; but this is not due to niggardliness, but to complete carelessness about his appearance.

When Andrey Yefimitch came to the town to take up his duties the "institution founded to the glory of God" was in a terrible condition. One could hardly breathe for the stench in the wards, in the passages, and in the courtyards of the hospital. The hospital servants, the nurses, and their children slept in the wards together with the patients. They complained that there was no living for beetles, bugs, and mice. The surgical wards were never free from erysipelas. There were only two scalpels and not one thermometer in the whole hospital; potatoes were kept in the baths. The superintendent, the housekeeper, and the medical assistant robbed the patients, and of the old doctor, Andrey Yefimitch's predecessor, people declared that he secretly sold the hospital alcohol, and that he kept a regular harem consisting of nurses and female patients. These disorderly proceedings were perfectly well known in the town, and were even exaggerated, but people took them calmly; some justified them on the ground that there were only peasants and working men in the hospital, who could not be dissatisfied, since they were much worse off at home than in the hospital—they couldn't be fed on woodcocks! Others said in excuse that the town alone, without help from the Zemstvo, was not equal to maintaining a good hospital; thank God for having one at all, even a poor one. And the newly formed Zemstvo did not open infirmaries either in the town or the neighbourhood, relying on the fact that the town already had its hospital.

After looking over the hospital Andrey Yefimitch came to the conclusion that it was an immoral institution and extremely prejudicial to the health of the townspeople. In his opinion the most sensible thing that could be done was to let out the patients and close the hospital. But he reflected that his will alone was not enough to do this, and that it would be useless; if physical and moral impurity were driven out of one place, they would only move to another; one must wait for it to wither away of itself. Besides, if people open a hospital and put up with having it, it must be because they need it; superstition and all the nastiness and abominations of daily life were necessary, since in process of time they worked out to something sensible, just as manure turns into black earth. There was nothing on earth so good that it had not something nasty about its first origin.

When Andrey Yefimitch undertook his duties he was apparently not greatly concerned about the irregularities at the hospital. He only asked the attendants and nurses not to sleep in the wards, and had two cupboards of instruments put up; the superintendent, the housekeeper, the medical assistant, and the erysipelas remained unchanged.

Andrey Yefimitch loved intelligence and honesty intensely, but he had no strength of will nor belief in his right to organize an intelligent and honest life about him. He was absolutely unable to give orders, to forbid things, and to insist. It seemed as though he had taken a vow never to raise his voice and never to make use of the imperative. It was difficult for him to say "Fetch" or "Bring"; when he wanted his meals he would cough hesitatingly and say to the cook, "How about tea? . . ." or "How about dinner? . . ." To dismiss the superintendent or to tell him to leave off stealing, or to abolish the unnecessary parasitic post altogether, was absolutely beyond his powers. When Andrey Yefimitch was deceived or flattered, or accounts he knew to be cooked were brought him to sign, he would turn as red as a crab and feel guilty, but yet he would sign the accounts. When the patients complained to him of being hungry or of the roughness of the nurses, he would be confused and mutter guiltily: "Very well, very well, I will go into it later. . . . Most likely there is some misunderstanding . . ."

At first Andrey Yefimitch worked very zealously. He saw patients every day from morning till dinner-time, performed operations, and even attended confinements. The ladies said of him that he was attentive and clever at diagnosing diseases, especially those of women and children. But in process of time the work unmistakably wearied him by its monotony and obvious uselessness. Today one sees thirty patients, and tomorrow they have increased to thirty-five, the next day forty, and so on from day to day, from year to year, while the mortality in the town did not decrease and the patients did not leave off coming. To be any real help to forty patients between morning and dinner was not physically possible, so it could but lead to deception. If twelve thousand patients were seen in a year it meant, if one looked at it simply, that twelve thousand men were deceived. To put those who were seriously ill into wards, and to treat them according to the principles of science, was impossible, too, because though there were principles there was no science; if he were to put aside philosophy and pedantically follow the rules as other doctors did, the things above all necessary were cleanliness and ventilation instead of dirt, wholesome nourishment instead of broth made of stinking, sour cabbage, and good assistants instead of thieves; and, indeed, why hinder people dying if death is the normal and legitimate end of everyone? What is gained if some shopkeeper or clerk lives an extra five or ten years? If the aim of medicine is by drugs to alleviate suffering, the question forces itself on one: why alleviate it? In the first place, they say that suffering leads man to perfection; and in the second, if mankind really learns to alleviate its sufferings with pills and drops, it will completely abandon religion and philosophy, in which it has hitherto found not merely protection from all sorts of trouble, but even happiness. Pushkin suffered terrible agonies before his death, poor Heine lay paralyzed for several years; why, then, should not some Andrey Yefimitch or Matryona Savishna be ill, since their lives had nothing of importance in them, and would have been entirely empty and like the life of an amoeba except for suffering?

Oppressed by such reflections, Andrey Yefimitch relaxed his efforts and gave up visiting the hospital every day.

VI

His life was passed like this. As a rule he got up at eight o'clock in the morning, dressed, and drank his tea. Then he sat down in his study to read, or went to the hospital. At the hospital the out-patients were sitting in the dark, narrow little corridor waiting to be seen by the doctor. The nurses and the attendants, tramping with their boots over the brick floors, ran by them; gaunt-looking patients in dressing gowns passed; dead bodies and vessels full of filth were carried by; the children were crying, and there was a cold draught. Andrey Yefimitch knew that such surroundings were torture to feverish, consumptive, and impressionable patients; but what could be done? In the consulting room he was met by his assistant, Sergey Sergeyitch—a fat little man with a plump, well-washed shaven face, with soft, smooth manners, wearing a new loosely cut suit, and looking more like a senator than a medical assistant. He had an immense practice in the town, wore a white tie, and considered himself more proficient than the doctor, who had no practice. In the corner of the consulting room there stood a large ikon in a shrine with a heavy lamp in front of it, and near it a candle-stand with a white cover on it. On the walls hung portraits of bishops, a view of the Svyatogorsky Monastery, and wreaths of dried cornflowers. Sergey Sergeyitch was religious, and liked solemnity and decorum. The ikon had been put up at his expense; at his instructions some one of the patients read the hymns of praise in the consulting room on Sundays, and after the reading Sergey Sergeyitch himself went through the wards with a censer and burned incense.

There were a great many patients, but the time was short, and so the work was confined to the asking of a few brief questions and the administration of some drugs, such as castor-oil or volatile ointment. Andrey Yefimitch would sit with his cheek resting in his hand, lost in thought and asking questions mechanically. Sergey Sergeyitch sat down too, rubbing his hands, and from time to time putting in his word.

"We suffer pain and poverty," he would say, "because we do not pray to the merciful God as we should. Yes!"

Andrey Yefimitch never performed any operation when he was seeing patients; he had long ago given up doing so, and the sight of blood upset him. When he had to open a child's mouth in order to look at its throat, and the child cried and tried to defend itself with its little hands, the noise in his ears made his head go round and brought tears to his eyes. He would make haste to prescribe a drug, and motion to the woman to take the child away.

He was soon wearied by the timidity of the patients and their incoherence, by the proximity of the pious Sergey Sergeyitch, by the portraits on the walls, and by his own questions which he had asked over and over again for twenty years. And he would go away after seeing five or six patients. The rest would be seen by his assistant in his absence.

With the agreeable thought that, thank God, he had no private practice now, and that no one would interrupt him, Andrey Yefimitch sat down to the table immediately on reaching home and took up a book. He read a great deal and always with enjoyment. Half his salary went on buying books, and of the six rooms that made up his abode three were heaped up with books and old magazines. He liked best of all works on history and philosophy; the only medical publication to which he subscribed was *The Doctor*, of which he always read the last pages first. He would always go on reading for several hours without a break and without being weary. He did not read as rapidly and impulsively as Ivan

Dmitritch had done in the past, but slowly and with concentration, often pausing over a passage which he liked or did not find intelligible. Near the books there always stood a decanter of vodka, and a salted cucumber or a pickled apple lay beside it, not on a plate, but on the baize tablecloth. Every half-hour he would pour himself out a glass of vodka and drink it without taking his eyes off the book. Then without looking at it he would feel for the cucumber and bite off a bit.

At three o'clock he would go cautiously to the kitchen door; cough, and say, "Daryushka, what about dinner?"

After his dinner—a rather poor and untidily served one—Andrey Yefimitch would walk up and down his rooms with his arms folded, thinking. The clock would strike four, then five, and still he would be walking up and down thinking. Occasionally the kitchen door would creak, and the red and sleepy face of Daryushka would appear.

"Andrey Yefimitch, isn't it time for you to have your beer?" she would ask anxiously.

"No, it's not time yet . . ." he would answer. "I'll wait a little. . . . I'll wait a little . . ."

Towards the evening the postmaster, Mihail Averyanitch, the only man in town whose society did not bore Andrey Yefimitch, would come in. Mihail Averyanitch had once been a very rich landowner, and had served in the calvary, but had come to ruin, and was forced by poverty to take a job in the post office late in life. He had a hale and hearty appearance, luxuriant grey whiskers, the manners of a well-bred man, and a loud, pleasant voice. He was good-natured and emotional, but hot-tempered. When anyone in the post office made a protest, expressed disagreement, or even began to argue, Mihail Averyanitch would turn crimson, shake all over, and shout in a voice of thunder, "Hold your tongue!" so that the post office had long enjoyed the reputation of an institution which it was terrible to visit. Mihail Averyanitch liked and respected Andrey Yefimitch for his culture and the loftiness of his soul; he treated the other inhabitants of the town superciliously, as though they were his subordinates.

"Here I am," he would say, going in to Andrey Yefimitch. "Good evening, my dear fellow! I'll be bound, you are getting sick of me, aren't you?"

"On the contrary, I am delighted," said the doctor. "I am always glad to see you."

The friends would sit on the sofa in the study and for some time would smoke in silence.

"Daryushka, what about the beer?" Andrey Yefimitch would say.

They would drink their first bottle still in silence, the doctor brooding and Mihail Averyanitch with a gay and animated face, like a man who has something very interesting to tell. The doctor was always the one to begin the conversation.

"What a pity," he would say quietly and slowly, not looking his friend in the face (he never looked anyone in the face)—"what a great pity it is that there are no people in our town who are capable of carrying on intelligent and interesting conversation, or care to do so. It is an immense privation for us. Even the educated class do not rise above vulgarity; the level of their development, I assure you, is not a bit higher than that of the lower orders."

"Perfectly true. I agree."

"You know, of course," the doctor went on quietly and deliberately, "that everything in this world is insignificant and uninteresting except the higher spiritual manifestations of the human mind. Intellect draws a sharp line between the animals and man, suggests the divinity of the latter, and to some extent even takes the place of the immortality which does not exist. Consequently the intellect is the only possible source of enjoyment. We see and hear of no trace of intellect about us, so we are deprived of enjoyment. We have books, it is true, but that is not at all the same as living talk and converse. If you will allow me to make a not quite apt comparison: books are the printed score, while talk is the singing."

"Perfectly true."

A silence would follow. Daryushka would come out of the kitchen and with an expression of blank dejection would stand in the doorway to listen, with her face propped on her fist.

"Eh!" Mihail Averyanitch would sigh. "To expect intelligence of this generation!"

And he would describe how wholesome, entertaining, and interesting life had been in the past. How intelligent the educated class in Russia used to be, and what lofty ideas it had of honour and friendship; how they used to lend money without an IOU, and it was thought a disgrace not to give a helping hand to a comrade in need; and what campaigns, what adventures, what skirmishes, what comrades, what women! And the Caucasus, what a marvellous country! The wife of a battalion commander, a queer woman, used to put on an officer's uniform and drive off into the mountains in the evening, alone, without a guide. It was said that she had a love affair with some princeling in the native village.

"Queen of Heaven, Holy Mother . . ." Daryushka would sigh.

"And how we drank! And how we ate! And what desperate liberals we were!"

Andrey Yefimitch would listen without hearing; he was musing as he sipped his beer.

"I often dream of intellectual people and conversation with them," he said suddenly, interrupting Mihail Averyanitch. "My father gave me an excellent education, but under the influence of the ideas of the sixties made me become a doctor. I believe if I had not obeyed him then, by now I should have been in the very centre of the intellectual movement. Most likely I should have become a member of some university. Of course, intellect, too, is transient and not eternal, but you know why I cherish a partiality for it. Life is a vexatious trap; when a thinking man reaches maturity and attains to full consciousness he cannot help feeling that he is in a trap from which there is no escape. Indeed, he is summoned without his choice by fortuitous circumstances from non-existence into life . . . what for? He tries to find out the meaning and object of his existence; he is told nothing, or he is told absurdities; he knocks and it is not opened to him; death comes to him—also without his choice. And so, just as in prison men held together by common misfortune feel more at ease when they are together, so one does not notice the trap in life when people with a bent for analysis and generalization meet together and pass their time in the interchange of proud and free ideas. In that sense the intellect is the source of an enjoyment nothing can replace."

"Perfectly true."

Not looking his friend in the face, Andrey Yefimitch would go on, quietly and with pauses, talking about intellectual people and conversation with them, and Mihail Averyanitch would listen attentively and agree: "Perfectly true."

"And you do not believe in the immortality of the soul?" he would ask suddenly.

"No, honoured Mihail Averyanitch; I do not believe it, and have no grounds for believing it."

"I must own I doubt it too. And yet I have a feeling as though I should never die. Oh, I think to myself: 'Old fogey, it is time you were dead!' But there is a little voice in my soul says: 'Don't believe it; you won't die.'"

Soon after nine o'clock Mihail Averyanitch would go away. As he put on his fur coat in the entry he would say with a sigh:

"What a wilderness fate has carried us to, though, really! What's most vexatious of all is to have to die here. Ech! . . ."

VII

After seeing his friend out Andrey Yefimitch would sit down at the table and begin reading again. The stillness of the evening, and afterwards of the night, was not broken by a single sound, and it seemed as though time were standing still and brooding with the doctor over the book, and as though there were nothing in existence but the books and the lamp with the green shade. The doctor's coarse peasant-like face was gradually lighted up by a smile of delight and enthusiasm over the progress of the human intellect. Oh, why is not man immortal? he thought. What is the good of the brain centres and convolutions, what is the good of sight, speech, self-consciousness, genius, if it is all destined to depart into the soil, and in the end to grow cold together with the earth's crust, and then for millions of years to fly with the earth round the sun with no meaning and no object? To do that there was no need at all to draw man with his lofty, almost godlike intellect out of non-existence, and then, as though in mockery, to turn him into clay. The transmutation of substances! But what cowardice to comfort oneself with that cheap substitute for immortality! The unconscious processes that take place in nature are lower even than the stupidity of man, since in stupidity there is, anyway, consciousness and will, while in those processes there is absolutely nothing. Only the coward who has more fear of death than dignity can comfort himself with the fact that his body will in time live again in the grass, in the stones, in the toad. To find one's immortality in the transmutation of substances is as strange as to prophesy a brilliant future for the case after a precious violin has been broken and become useless.

When the clock struck, Andrey Yefimitch would sink back into his chair and close his eyes to think a little. And under the influence of the fine ideas of which he had been reading he would, unawares, recall his past and his present. The past was hateful—better not to think of it. And it was the same in the present as in the past. He knew that at the very time when his thoughts were floating together with the cooling earth round the sun, in the main building beside his abode people were suffering in sickness and physical impurity: someone perhaps could not sleep and was making war upon the insects, someone was being infected by erysipelas, or moaning over too tight a bandage; perhaps the patients were playing cards with the nurses and drinking vodka. According to the yearly return, twelve thousand people had been deceived; the whole hospital rested as it had done twenty years ago on thieving, filth, scandals, gossip, on gross quackery, and, as before, it was an immoral institution extremely injurious to the health of the inhabitants. He knew that Nikita knocked the patients about behind the barred windows of Ward No. 6, and that Moiseika went about the town every day begging alms.

On the other hand, he knew very well that a magical change had taken place in medicine during the last twenty-five years. When he was studying at the university he had fancied that medicine would soon be overtaken by the fate of alchemy and metaphysics; but now when he was reading at night the science of medicine touched him and excited his wonder, and even enthusiasm. What unexpected brilliance, what a revolution! Thanks to the antiseptic system operations were performed such as the great Pirogov had considered impossible even *in spe*. Ordinary Zemstvo doctors were venturing to perform the resection of the kneecap; of abdominal operations only one per cent. was fatal; while stone was considered such a trifle that they did not even write about it. A radical cure for syphilis had been discovered. And the theory of heredity, hypnotism, the discoveries of Pasteur and of Koch, hygiene based on statistics, and the work of Zemstvo doctors!

Psychiatry with its modern classification of mental diseases, methods of diagnosis, and treatment, was a perfect Elborus in comparison with what had been in the past. They no longer poured cold water on the heads of lunatics nor put strait-waistcoats upon them; they treated them with humanity, and even, so it was stated in the papers, got up balls and entertainments for them. Andrey Yefimitch knew that with modern tastes and views such an abomination as Ward No. 6 was possible only a hundred and fifty miles from a railway in a little town where the mayor and all the town council were half-illiterate tradesmen who looked upon the doctor as an oracle who must be believed without any criticism even if he had poured molten lead into their mouths; in any other place the public and the newspapers would long ago have torn this little Bastille to pieces.

"But, after all, what of it?" Andrey Yefimitch would ask himself, opening his eyes. "There is the antiseptic system, there is Koch, there is Pasteur, but the essential reality is not altered a bit; ill-health and mortality are still the same. They get up balls and entertainments for the mad, but still they don't let them go free; so it's all nonsense and vanity, and there is no difference in reality between the best Vienna clinic and my hospital." But depression and a feeling akin to envy prevented him from feeling indifferent; it must have been owing to exhaustion. His heavy head sank on to the book, he put his hands under his face to make it softer, and thought: "I serve in a pernicious institution and receive a salary from people whom I am deceiving. I am not honest, but then, I of myself am nothing, I am only part of an inevitable social evil: all local officials are pernicious and receive their salary for doing nothing. . . . And so for my dishonesty it is not I who am to blame, but the times. . . . If I had been born two hundred years later I should have been different . . ."

When it struck three he would put out his lamp and go into his bedroom; he was not sleepy.

VIII

Two years before, the Zemstvo in a liberal mood had decided to allow three hundred roubles a year to pay for additional medical service in the town till the Zemstvo hospital should be opened, and the district doctor, Yevgeny Fyodoritch Hobotov, was invited to the town to assist Andrey Yefimitch. He was a very young man—not yet thirty—tall and dark, with broad cheekbones and little eyes; his forefathers had probably come from one of the many alien races of Russia. He arrived in the town without a farthing, with a small portmanteau, and a plain young woman whom he called his cook. This woman had a baby at the breast. Yevgeny Fyodoritch used to go about in a cap with a peak, and in high boots, and in the winter wore a sheepskin. He made great friends with Sergey Sergeyitch, the medical assistant, and with the treasurer, but held aloof from the other

270

officials, and for some reason called them aristocrats. He had only one book in his lodgings, "The Latest Prescriptions of the Vienna Clinic for 1881." When he went to a patient he always took this book with him. He played billiards in the evening at the club: he did not like cards. He was very fond of using in conversation such expressions as "endless bobbery," "canting soft soap," "shut up with your finicking . . ."

He visited the hospital twice a week, made the round of the wards, and saw out-patients. The complete absence of antiseptic treatment and the cupping roused his indignation, but he did not introduce any new system, being afraid of offending Andrey Yefimitch. He regarded his colleague as a sly old rascal, suspected him of being a man of large means, and secretly envied him. He would have been very glad to have his post.

IX

On a spring evening towards the end of March, when there was no snow left on the ground and the starlings were singing in the hospital garden, the doctor went out to see his friend the postmaster as far as the gate. At that very moment the Jew Moiseika, returning with his booty, came into the yard. He had no cap on, and his bare feet were thrust into goloshes; in his hand he had a little bag of coppers.

"Give me a kopeck!" he said to the doctor, smiling, and shivering with cold. Andrey Yefimitch, who could never refuse anyone anything, gave him a ten-kopeck piece.

"How bad that is!" he thought, looking at the Jew's bare feet with their thin red ankles. "Why, it's wet."

And stirred by a feeling akin both to pity and disgust, he went into the lodge behind the Jew, looking now at his bald head, now at his ankles. As the doctor went in, Nikita jumped up from his heap of litter and stood at attention.

"Good day, Nikita," Andrey Yefimitch said mildly. "That Jew should be provided with boots or something, he will catch cold."

"Certainly, your honour. I'll inform the superintendent."

"Please do; ask him in my name. Tell him that I asked."

The door into the ward was open. Ivan Dmitritch, lying propped on his elbow on the bed, listened in alarm to the unfamiliar voice, and suddenly recognized the doctor. He trembled all over with anger, jumped up, and with a red and wrathful face, with his eyes starting out of his head, ran out into the middle of the road.

"The doctor has come!" he shouted, and broke into a laugh. "At last! Gentlemen, I congratulate you. The doctor is honouring us with a visit! Cursed reptile!" he shrieked, and stamped in a frenzy such as had never been seen in the ward before. "Kill the reptile! No, killing's too good. Drown him in the midden-pit!"

Andrey Yefimitch, hearing this, looked into the ward from the entry and asked gently: "What for?"

"What for?" shouted Ivan Dmitritch, going up to him with a menacing air and convulsively wrapping himself in his dressing gown. "What for? Thief!" he said with a look of repulsion, moving his lips as though he would spit at him. "Quack! hangman!"

"Calm yourself," said Andrey Yefimitch, smiling guiltily. "I assure you I have never stolen anything; and as to the rest, most likely you greatly exaggerate. I see you are angry with me. Calm yourself, I beg, if you can, and tell me coolly what are you angry for?"

"What are you keeping me here for?"

"Because you are ill."

"Yes, I am ill. But you know dozens, hundreds of madmen are walking about in freedom because your ignorance is incapable of distinguishing them from the sane. Why am I and these poor wretches to be shut up here like scapegoats for all the rest? You, your assistant, the superintendent, and all your hospital rabble, are immeasurably inferior to every one of us morally; why then are we shut up and you not? Where's the logic of it?"

"Morality and logic don't come in, it all depends on chance. If anyone is shut up he has to stay, and if anyone is not shut up he can walk about, that's all. There is neither morality nor logic in my being a doctor and your being a mental patient, there is nothing but idle chance."

"That twaddle I don't understand . . ." Ivan Dmitritch brought out in a hollow voice, and he sat down on his bed.

Moiseika, whom Nikita did not venture to search in the presence of the doctor, laid out on his bed pieces of bread, bits of paper, and little bones, and, still shivering with cold, began rapidly in a sing-song voice saying something in Yiddish. He most likely imagined that he had opened a shop.

"Let me out," said Ivan Dmitritch, and his voice quivered.

"I cannot."

"But why, why?"

"Because it is not in my power. Think, what use will it be to you if I do let you out? Go. The townspeople or the police will detain you or bring you back."

"Yes, yes, that's true," said Ivan Dmitritch, and he rubbed his forehead. "It's awful! But what am I to do, what?"

Andrey Yefimitch liked Ivan Dmitritch's voice and his intelligent young face with its grimaces. He longed to be kind to the young man and soothe him; he sat down on the bed beside him, thought, and said:

"You ask me what to do. The very best thing in your position would be to run away. But, unhappily, that is useless. You would be taken up. When society protects itself from the criminal, mentally deranged, or otherwise inconvenient people, it is invincible. There is only one thing left for you: to resign yourself to the thought that your presence here is inevitable."

"It is no use to anyone."

"So long as prisons and madhouses exist someone must be shut up in them. If not you, I. If not I, some third person. Wait till in the distant future prisons and madhouses no longer exist, and there will be neither bars on the windows nor hospital gowns. Of course, that time will come sooner or later."

Ivan Dmitritch smiled ironically.

"You are jesting," he said, screwing up his eyes. "Such gentlemen as you and your assistant Nikita have nothing to do with the future, but you may be sure, sir, better days will come! I may express myself cheaply, you may laugh, but the dawn of a new life is at hand; truth and justice will triumph, and—our turn will come! I shall not live to see it, I shall perish, but some people's great-grandsons will see it. I greet them with all my heart and rejoice, rejoice with them! Onward! God be your help, friends!"

With shining eyes Ivan Dmitritch got up, and stretching his hands towards the window, went on with emotion in his voice:

"From behind these bars I bless you! Hurrah for truth and justice! I rejoice!"

"I see no particular reason to rejoice," said Andrey Yefimitch, who thought Ivan Dmitritch's movement theatrical, though he was delighted

273

by it. "Prisons and madhouses there will not be, and truth, as you have just expressed it, will triumph; but the reality of things, you know, will not change, the laws of nature will still remain the same. People will suffer pain, grow old, and die just as they do now. However magnificent a dawn lighted up your life, you would yet in the end be nailed up in a coffin and thrown into a hole."

"And immortality?"

"Oh, come, now!"

"You don't believe in it, but I do. Somebody in Dostoevsky or Voltaire said that if there had not been a God men would have invented him. And I firmly believe that if there is no immortality the great intellect of man will sooner or later invent it."

"Well said," observed Andrey Yefimitch, smiling with pleasure; "its a good thing you have faith. With such a belief one may live happily even shut up within walls. You have studied somewhere, I presume?"

"Yes, I have been at the university, but did not complete my studies."

"You are a reflecting and a thoughtful man. In any surroundings you can find tranquillity in yourself. Free and deep thinking which strives for the comprehension of life, and complete contempt for the foolish bustle of the world—those are two blessings beyond any that man has ever known. And you can possess them even though you lived behind threefold bars. Diogenes lived in a tub, yet he was happier than all the kings of the earth."

"Your Diogenes was a blockhead," said Ivan Dmitritch morosely. "Why do you talk to me about Diogenes and some foolish comprehension of life?" he cried, growing suddenly angry and leaping up. "I love life; I love it passionately. I have the mania of persecution, a continual agonizing terror; but I have moments when I am overwhelmed by the thirst for life, and then I am afraid of going mad. I want dreadfully to live, dreadfully!"

He walked up and down the ward in agitation, and said, dropping his voice:

"When I dream I am haunted by phantoms. People come to me, I hear voices and music, and I fancy I am walking through woods or by the seashore, and I long so passionately for movement, for interests. . . . Come, tell me, what news is there?" asked Ivan Dmitritch; "what's happening?"

"Do you wish to know about the town or in general?"

"Well, tell me first about the town, and then in general."

"Well, in the town it is appallingly dull. . . . There's no one to say a word to, no one to listen to. There are no new people. A young doctor called Hobotov has come here recently."

"He had come in my time. Well, he is a low cad, isn't he?"

"Yes, he is a man of no culture. It's strange, you know. . . . Judging by every sign, there is no intellectual stagnation in our capital cities; there is a movement—so there must be real people there too; but for some reason they always send us such men as I would rather not see. It's an unlucky town!"

"Yes, it is an unlucky town," sighed Ivan Dmitritch, and he laughed. "And how are things in general? What are they writing in the papers and reviews?"

It was by now dark in the ward. The doctor got up, and, standing, began to describe what was being written abroad and in Russia, and the tendency of thought that could be noticed now. Ivan Dmitritch listened attentively and put questions, but suddenly, as though recalling something terrible, clutched at his head and lay down on the bed with his back to the doctor.

"What's the matter?" asked Andrey Yefimitch.

"You will not hear another word from me," said Ivan Dmitritch rudely. "Leave me alone."

"Why so?"

"I tell you, leave me alone. Why the devil do you persist?"

Andrey Yefimitch shrugged his shoulders, heaved a sigh, and went out. As he crossed the entry he said: "You might clear up here, Nikita . . . there's an awfully stuffy smell."

"Certainly, your honour."

"What an agreeable young man!" thought Andrey Yefimitch, going back to his flat. "In all the years I have been living here I do believe he is the first I have met with whom one can talk. He is capable of reasoning and is interested in just the right things."

While he was reading, and afterwards, while he was going to bed, he kept thinking about Ivan Dmitritch, and when he woke next morning he remembered that he had the day before made the acquaintance of an intelligent and interesting man, and determined to visit him again as soon as possible.

X

Ivan Dmitritch was lying in the same position as on the previous day, with his head clutched in both hands and his legs drawn up. His face was not visible.

"Good day, my friend," said Andrey Yefimitch. "You are not asleep, are you?"

"In the first place, I am not your friend," Ivan Dmitritch articulated into the pillow; "and in the second, your efforts are useless; you will not get one word out of me."

"Strange," muttered Andrey Yefimitch in confusion. "Yesterday we talked peacefully, but suddenly for some reason you took offence and broke off all at once. . . . Probably I expressed myself awkwardly, or perhaps gave utterance to some idea which did not fit in with your convictions. . . ."

"Yes, a likely idea!" said Ivan Dmitritch, sitting up and looking at the doctor with irony and uneasiness. His eyes were red. "You can go and spy and probe somewhere else, it's no use your doing it here. I knew yesterday what you had come for."

"A strange fancy," laughed the doctor. "So you suppose me to be a spy?"

"Yes, I do. . . . A spy or a doctor who has been charged to test me—it's all the same—"

"Oh excuse me, what a queer fellow you are really!"

The doctor sat down on the stool near the bed and shook his head reproachfully.

"But let us suppose you are right," he said, "let us suppose that I am treacherously trying to trap you into saying something so as to betray you to the police. You would be arrested and then tried. But would you be any worse off being tried and in prison than you are here? If you are banished to a settlement, or even sent to penal servitude, would it be worse than being shut up in this ward? I imagine it would be no worse. . . . What, then, are you afraid of?"

These words evidently had an effect on Ivan Dmitritch. He sat down quietly.

It was between four and five in the afternoon—the time when Andrey Yefimitch usually walked up and down his rooms, and Daryushka asked whether it was not time for his beer. It was a still, bright day.

"I came out for a walk after dinner, and here I have come, as you see," said the doctor. "It is quite spring."

"What month is it? March?" asked Ivan Dmitritch.

"Yes, the end of March."

"Is it very muddy?"

"No, not very. There are already paths in the garden."

"It would be nice now to drive in an open carriage somewhere into the country," said Ivan Dmitritch, rubbing his red eyes as though he were just awake, "then to come home to a warm, snug study, and . . . and to have a decent doctor to cure one's headache. . . . It's so long since I have lived like a human being. It's disgusting here! Insufferably disgusting!"

After his excitement of the previous day he was exhausted and listless, and spoke unwillingly. His fingers twitched, and from his face it could be seen that he had a splitting headache.

"There is no real difference between a warm, snug study and this ward," said Andrey Yefimitch. "A man's peace and contentment do not lie outside a man, but in himself."

"What do you mean?"

"The ordinary man looks for good and evil in external things—that is, in carriages, in studies—but a thinking man looks for it in himself."

"You should go and preach that philosophy in Greece, where it's warm and fragrant with the scent of pomegranates, but here it is not suited to the climate. With whom was it I was talking of Diogenes? Was it with you?"

"Yes, with me yesterday."

"Diogenes did not need a study or a warm habitation; it's hot there without. You can lie in your tub and eat oranges and olives. But bring him to Russia to live: he'd be begging to be let indoors in May, let alone December. He'd be doubled up with the cold."

"No. One can be insensible to cold as to every other pain. Marcus Aurelius says: 'A pain is a vivid idea of pain; make an effort of will to change that idea, dismiss it, cease to complain, and the pain will disappear.' That is true. The wise man, or simply the reflecting, thoughtful man, is distinguished precisely by his contempt for suffering; he is always contented and surprised at nothing."

"Then I am an idiot, since I suffer and am discontented and surprised at the baseness of mankind."

"You are wrong in that; if you will reflect more on the subject you will understand how insignificant is all that external world that agitates us. One must strive for the comprehension of life, and in that is true happiness."

"Comprehension . . ." repeated Ivan Dmitritch frowning. "External, internal. . . . Excuse me, but I don't understand it. I only know," he said, getting up and looking angrily at the doctor—"I only know that God has created me of warm blood and nerves, yes, indeed! If organic tissue is capable of life it must react to every stimulus. And I do! To pain I respond with tears and outcries, to baseness with indignation, to filth with loathing. To my mind, that is just what is called life. The lower the organism, the less sensitive it is, and the more feebly it reacts to stimulus; and the higher it is, the more responsively and vigorously it reacts to reality. How is it you don't know that? A doctor, and not know such trifles! To despise suffering, to be always contented, and to be surprised at nothing, one must reach this condition"—and Ivan Dmitritch pointed to the peasant who was a mass of fat—"or to harden oneself by suffering to such a point that one loses all sensibility to it—that is, in other words, to cease to live. You must excuse me, I am not a sage or a philosopher," Ivan Dmitritch continued with irritation, "and I don't understand anything about it. I am not capable of reasoning."

"On the contrary, your reasoning is excellent."

"The Stoics, whom you are parodying, were remarkable people, but their doctrine crystallized two thousand years ago and has not advanced, and will not advance, an inch forward, since it is not practical or living. It had a success only with the minority which spends its life in savouring all sorts of theories and ruminating over them; the majority did not understand it. A doctrine which advocates indifference to wealth and to the comforts of life, and a contempt for suffering and death, is quite unintelligible to the vast majority of men, since that majority has never known wealth or the comforts of life; and to despise suffering would mean to it despising life itself, since the whole existence of man is made up of the sensations of hunger, cold, injury, and a Hamlet-like dread of death. The whole of life lies in these sensations; one may be oppressed by it, one may hate it, but one cannot despise it. Yes, so, I repeat, the doctrine of the Stoics can never have a future; from the beginning of time up to today you see continually increasing the struggle, the sensibility to pain, the capacity of responding to stimulus."

Ivan Dmitritch suddenly lost the thread of his thoughts, stopped, and rubbed his forehead with vexation.

"I meant to say something important, but I have lost it," he said. "What was I saying? Oh, yes! This is what I mean: one of the Stoics sold himself into slavery to redeem his neighbour, so, you see, even a Stoic did react to stimulus, since, for such a generous act as the destruction of oneself for the sake of one's neighbour, he must have had a soul capable of pity and indignation. Here in prison I have forgotten everything I have learned, or else I could have recalled something else. Take Christ, for instance: Christ responded to reality by weeping, smiling, being sorrowful and moved to wrath, even overcome by misery. He did not go to meet His sufferings with a smile, He did not despise death, but prayed in the Garden of Gethsemane that this cup might pass Him by."

Ivan Dmitritch laughed and sat down.

"Granted that a man's peace and contentment lie not outside but in himself," he said, "granted that one must despise suffering and not be surprised at anything, yet on what ground do you preach the theory? Are you a sage? A philosopher?"

"No, I am not a philosopher, but everyone ought to preach it because it is reasonable."

"No, I want to know how it is that you consider yourself competent to judge of 'comprehension,' contempt for suffering, and so on. Have you ever suffered? Have you any idea of suffering? Allow me to ask you, were you ever thrashed in your childhood?"

"No, my parents had an aversion for corporal punishment."

"My father used to flog me cruelly; my father was a harsh, sickly Government clerk with a long nose and a yellow neck. But let us talk of you. No one has laid a finger on you all your life, no one has scared you nor beaten you; you are as strong as a bull. You grew up under your father's wing and studied at his expense, and then you dropped at once into a sinecure. For more than twenty years you have lived rent free with heating, lighting, and service all provided, and had the right to work how you pleased and as much as you pleased, even to do nothing. You were naturally a flabby, lazy man, and so you have tried to arrange your life so that nothing should disturb you or make you move. You have handed over your work to the assistant and the rest of the rabble while you sit in peace and warmth, save money, read, amuse yourself with reflections, with all

279

sorts of lofty nonsense, and" (Ivan Dmitritch looked at the doctor's red nose) "with boozing; in fact, you have seen nothing of life, you know absolutely nothing of it, and are only theoretically acquainted with reality; you despise suffering and are surprised at nothing for a very simple reason: vanity of vanities, the external and the internal, contempt for life, for suffering and for death, comprehension, true happiness—that's the philosophy that suits the Russian sluggard best. You see a peasant beating his wife, for instance. Why interfere? Let him beat her, they will both die sooner or later, anyway; and, besides, he who beats injures by his blows, not the person he is beating, but himself. To get drunk is stupid and unseemly, but if you drink you die, and if you don't drink you die. A peasant woman comes with toothache . . . well, what of it? Pain is the idea of pain, and besides 'there is no living in this world without illness; we shall all die, and so, go away, woman, don't hinder me from thinking and drinking vodka.' A young man asks advice, what he is to do, how he is to live; anyone else would think before answering, but you have got the answer ready: strive for 'comprehension' or for true happiness. And what is that fantastic 'true happiness'? There's no answer, of course. We are kept here behind barred windows, tortured, left to rot; but that is very good and reasonable, because there is no difference at all between this ward and a warm, snug study. A convenient philosophy. You can do nothing, and your conscience is clear, and you feel you are wise. . . . No, sir, it is not philosophy, it's not thinking, it's not breadth of vision, but laziness, fakirism, drowsy stupefaction. Yes," cried Ivan Dmitritch, getting angry again, "you despise suffering, but I'll be bound if you pinch your finger in the door you will howl at the top of your voice."

"And perhaps I shouldn't howl," said Andrey Yefimitch, with a gentle smile.

"Oh, I dare say! Well, if you had a stroke of paralysis, or supposing some fool or bully took advantage of his position and rank to insult you in public, and if you knew he could do it with impunity, then you would understand what it means to put people off with comprehension and true happiness."

"That's original," said Andrey Yefimitch, laughing with pleasure and rubbing his hands. "I am agreeably struck by your inclination for drawing generalizations, and the sketch of my character you have just drawn is simply brilliant. I must confess that talking to you gives me great pleasure. Well, I've listened to you, and now you must graciously listen to me."

XI

The conversation went on for about an hour longer, and apparently made a deep impression on Andrey Yefimitch. He began going to the ward every day. He went there in the mornings and after dinner, and often the dusk of evening found him in conversation with Ivan Dmitritch. At first Ivan Dmitritch held aloof from him, suspected him of evil designs, and openly expressed his hostility. But afterwards he got used to him, and his abrupt manner changed to one of condescending irony.

Soon it was all over the hospital that the doctor, Andrey Yefimitch, had taken to visiting Ward No. 6. No one—neither Sergey Sergevitch, nor Nikita, nor the nurses—could conceive why he went there, why he stayed there for hours together, what he was talking about, and why he did not write prescriptions. His actions seemed strange. Often Mihail Averyanitch did not find him at home, which had never happened in the past, and Daryushka was greatly perturbed, for the doctor drank his beer now at no definite time, and sometimes was even late for dinner.

One day—it was at the end of June—Dr. Hobotov went to see Andrey Yefimitch about something. Not finding him at home, he proceeded to look for him in the yard; there he was told that the old doctor had gone to see the mental patients. Going into the lodge and stopping in the entry, Hobotov heard the following conversation:

"We shall never agree, and you will not succeed in converting me to your faith," Ivan Dmitritch was saying irritably; "you are utterly ignorant of reality, and you have never known suffering, but have only like a leech fed beside the sufferings of others, while I have been in continual suffering from the day of my birth till today. For that reason, I tell you frankly, I consider myself superior to you and more competent in every respect. It's not for you to teach me."

"I have absolutely no ambition to convert you to my faith," said Andrey Yefimitch gently, and with regret that the other refused to understand him. "And that is not what matters, my friend; what matters is not that you have suffered and I have not. Joy and suffering are passing; let us leave them, never mind them. What matters is that you and I think; we see in each other people who are capable of thinking and reasoning, and that is a common bond between us however different our views. If you knew, my friend, how sick I am of the universal senselessness, ineptitude, stupidity, and with what delight I always talk with you! You are an intelligent man, and I enjoyed your company."

Hobotov opened the door an inch and glanced into the ward; Ivan Dmitritch in his night-cap and the doctor Andrey Yefimitch were sitting side by side on the bed. The madman was grimacing, twitching, and convulsively wrapping himself in his gown, while the doctor sat motionless with bowed head, and his face was red and look helpless and sorrowful. Hobotov shrugged his shoulders, grinned, and glanced at Nikita. Nikita shrugged his shoulders too.

Next day Hobotov went to the lodge, accompanied by the assistant. Both stood in the entry and listened.

"I fancy our old man has gone clean off his chump!" said Hobotov as he came out of the lodge.

"Lord have mercy upon us sinners!" sighed the decorous Sergey Sergeyitch, scrupulously avoiding the puddles that he might not muddy his polished boots. "I must own, honoured Yevgeny Fyodoritch, I have been expecting it for a long time."

XII

After this Andrey Yefimitch began to notice a mysterious air in all around him. The attendants, the nurses, and the patients looked at him inquisitively when they met him, and then whispered together. The superintendent's little daughter Masha, whom he liked to meet in the hospital garden, for some reason ran away from him now when he went up with a smile to stroke her on the head. The postmaster no longer said, "Perfectly true," as he listened to him, but in unaccountable confusion muttered, "Yes, yes, yes . . ." and looked at him with a grieved and thoughtful expression; for some reason he took to advising his friend to give up vodka and beer, but as a man of delicate feeling he did not say this directly, but hinted it, telling him first about the commanding officer of his battalion, an excellent man, and then about the priest of the regiment, a capital fellow, both of whom drank and fell ill, but on giving up drinking completely regained their health. On two or three occasions Andrey Yefimitch was visited by his colleague Hobotov, who also advised him to give up spirituous liquors, and for no apparent reason recommended him to take bromide.

In August Andrey Yefimitch got a letter from the mayor of the town asking him to come on very important business. On arriving at the town hall at the time fixed, Andrey Yefimitch found there the military commander, the superintendent of the district school, a member of the town council, Hobotov, and a plump, fair gentleman who was introduced to him as a doctor. This doctor, with a Polish surname difficult to pronounce, lived at a pedigree stud-farm twenty miles away, and was now on a visit to the town.

"There's something that concerns you," said the member of the town council, addressing Andrey Yefimitch after they had all greeted one another and sat down to the table. "Here Yevgeny Fyodoritch says that there is not room for the dispensary in the main building, and that it ought to be transferred to one of the lodges. That's of no consequence—of course it can be transferred, but the point is that the lodge wants doing up."

"Yes, it would have to be done up," said Andrey Yefimitch after a moment's thought. "If the corner lodge, for instance, were fitted up as a dispensary, I imagine it would cost at least five hundred roubles. An unproductive expenditure!"

Everyone was silent for a space.

"I had the honour of submitting to you ten years ago," Andrey Yefimitch went on in a low voice, "that the hospital in its present form is a luxury for the town beyond its means. It was built in the forties, but things were different then. The town spends too much on unnecessary buildings and superfluous staff. I believe with a different system two model hospitals might be maintained for the same money."

"Well, let us have a different system, then!" the member of the town council said briskly.

"I have already had the honour of submitting to you that the medical department should be transferred to the supervision of the Zemstvo."

"Yes, transfer the money to the Zemstvo and they will steal it," laughed the fair-haired doctor.

"That's what it always comes to," the member of the council assented, and he also laughed.

Andrey Yefimitch looked with apathetic, lustreless eyes at the fair-haired doctor and said: "One should be just."

Again there was silence. Tea was brought in. The military commander, for some reason much embarrassed, touched Andrey Yefimitch's hand across the table and said: "You have quite forgotten us, doctor. But of course you are a hermit: you don't play cards and don't like women. You would be dull with fellows like us."

They all began saying how boring it was for a decent person to live in such a town. No theatre, no music, and at the last dance at the club there had been about twenty ladies and only two gentlemen. The young men did not dance, but spent all the time crowding round the refreshment bar or playing cards.

Not looking at anyone and speaking slowly in a low voice, Andrey Yefimitch began saying what a pity, what a terrible pity it was that the townspeople should waste their vital energy, their hearts, and their minds on cards and gossip, and should have neither the power nor the inclination to spend their time in interesting conversation and reading, and should refuse to take advantage of the enjoyments of the mind. The mind alone was interesting and worthy of attention, all the rest was low and petty. Hobotov listened to his colleague attentively and suddenly asked:

"Andrey Yefimitch, what day of the month is it?"

Having received an answer, the fair-haired doctor and he, in the tone of examiners conscious of their lack of skill, began asking Andrey Yefimitch what was the day of the week, how many days there were in the year, and whether it was true that there was a remarkable prophet living in Ward No. 6.

In response to the last question Andrey Yefimitch turned rather red and said: "Yes, he is mentally deranged, but he is an interesting young man."

They asked him no other questions.

When he was putting on his overcoat in the entry, the military commander laid a hand on his shoulder and said with a sigh:

"It's time for us old fellows to rest!"

As he came out of the hall, Andrey Yefimitch understood that it had been a committee appointed to enquire into his mental condition. He recalled the questions that had been asked him, flushed crimson, and for some reason, for the first time in his life, felt bitterly grieved for medical science.

"My God . . ." he thought, remembering how these doctors had just examined him; "why, they have only lately been hearing lectures on mental pathology; they had passed an examination—what's the explanation of this crass ignorance? They have not a conception of mental pathology!"

And for the first time in his life he felt insulted and moved to anger.

In the evening of the same day Mihail Averyanitch came to see him. The postmaster went up to him without waiting to greet him, took him by both hands, and said in an agitated voice:

"My dear fellow, my dear friend, show me that you believe in my genuine affection and look on me as your friend!" And preventing Andrey Yefimitch from speaking, he went on, growing excited: "I love you for your culture and nobility of soul. Listen to me, my dear fellow. The rules of their profession compel the doctors to conceal the truth from you, but I blurt out the plain truth like a soldier. You are not well! Excuse me, my dear fellow, but it is the truth; everyone about you has been noticing it for a long time. Dr. Yevgeny Fyodoritch has just told me that it is essential for you to rest and distract your mind for the sake of your health. Perfectly true! Excellent! In a day or two I am taking a holiday and am going away for a sniff of a different atmosphere. Show that you are a friend to me, let us go together! Let us go for a jaunt as in the good old days."

"I feel perfectly well," said Andrey Yefimitch after a moment's thought. "I can't go away. Allow me to show you my friendship in some other way."

To go off with no object, without his books, without his Daryushka, without his beer, to break abruptly through the routine of life, established for twenty years—the idea for the first minute struck him as wild and fantastic, but he remembered the conversation at the Zemstvo committee and the depressing feelings with which he had returned home, and the thought of a brief absence from the town in which stupid people looked on him as a madman was pleasant to him.

"And where precisely do you intend to go?" he asked.

"To Moscow, to Petersburg, to Warsaw. . . . I spent the five happiest years of my life in Warsaw. What a marvellous town! Let us go, my dear fellow!"

XIII

A week later it was suggested to Andrey Yefimitch that he should have a rest—that is, send in his resignation—a suggestion he received with indifference, and a week later still, Mihail Averyanitch and he were sitting in a posting carriage driving to the nearest railway station. The days were cool and bright, with a blue sky and a transparent distance. They were two days driving the hundred and fifty miles to the railway station, and stayed two nights on the way. When at the posting station the glasses given them for their tea had not been properly washed, or the drivers were slow in harnessing the horses, Mihail Averyanitch would turn crimson, and quivering all over would shout:

"Hold your tongue! Don't argue!"

And in the carriage he talked without ceasing for a moment, describing his campaigns in the Caucasus and in Poland. What adventures he had had, what meetings! He talked loudly and opened his eyes so wide with wonder that he might well be thought to be lying. Moreover, as he talked he breathed in Andrey Yefimitch's face and laughed into his ear. This bothered the doctor and prevented him from thinking or concentrating his mind.

In the train they travelled, from motives of economy, third-class in a non-smoking compartment. Half the passengers were decent people. Mihail Averyanitch soon made friends with everyone, and moving from one seat to another, kept saying loudly that they ought not to travel by these appalling lines. It was a regular swindle! A very different thing riding on a good horse: one could do over seventy miles a day and feel fresh and well after it. And our bad harvests were due to the draining of the Pinsk marshes; altogether, the way things were done was dreadful. He got excited, talked loudly, and would not let others speak. This endless chatter to the accompaniment of loud laughter and expressive gestures wearied Andrey Yefimitch.

"Which of us is the madman?" he thought with vexation. "I, who try not to disturb my fellow-passengers in any way, or this egoist who thinks that he is cleverer and more interesting than anyone here, and so will leave no one in peace?"

In Moscow Mihail Averyanitch put on a military coat without epaulettes and trousers with red braid on them. He wore a military cap and overcoat in the street, and soldiers saluted him. It seemed to Andrey Yefimitch, now, that his companion was a man who had flung away all that was good and kept only what was bad of all the characteristics of a country gentleman that he had once possessed. He liked to be waited on even when it was quite unnecessary. The matches would be lying before him on the table, and he would see them and shout to the waiter to give him the matches; he did not hesitate to appear before a maidservant in nothing but his underclothes; he used the familiar mode of address to all footmen indiscriminately, even old men, and when he was angry called them fools and blockheads. This, Andrey Yefimitch thought, was like a gentleman, but disgusting.

First of all Mihail Averyanitch led his friend to the Iversky Madonna. He prayed fervently, shedding tears and bowing down to the earth, and when he had finished, heaved a deep sigh and said:

"Even though one does not believe it makes one somehow easier when one prays a little. Kiss the ikon, my dear fellow."

Andrey Yefimitch was embarrassed and he kissed the image, while Mihail Averyanitch pursed up his lips and prayed in a whisper, and again tears came into his eyes. Then they went to the Kremlin and looked there at the Tsar-cannon and the Tsar-bell, and even touched them with their fingers, admired the view over the river, visited St. Saviour's and the Rumyantsev museum.

They dined at Tyestov's. Mihail Averyanitch looked a long time at the menu, stroking his whiskers, and said in the tone of a gourmand accustomed to dine in restaurants:

"We shall see what you give us to eat today, angel!"

XIV

The doctor walked about, looked at things, ate and drank, but he had all the while one feeling: annoyance with Mihail Averyanitch. He longed to have a rest from his friend, to get away from him, to hide himself, while the friend thought it was his duty not to let the doctor move a step away from him, and to provide him with as many distractions as possible. When there was nothing to look at he entertained him with conversation. For two days Andrey Yefimitch endured it, but on the third he announced to his friend that he was ill and wanted to stay at home for the whole day; his friend replied that in that case he would stay too—that really he needed rest, for he was run off his legs already. Andrey Yefimitch lay on the sofa, with his face to the back, and clenching his teeth, listened to his friend, who assured him with heat that sooner or later France would certainly thrash Germany, that there were a great many scoundrels in Moscow, and that it was impossible to judge of a horse's quality by its outward appearance. The doctor began to have a buzzing in his ears and palpitations of the heart, but out of delicacy could not bring himself to beg his friend to go away or hold his tongue. Fortunately Mihail Averyanitch grew weary of sitting in the hotel room, and after dinner he went out for a walk.

As soon as he was alone Andrey Yefimitch abandoned himself to a feeling of relief. How pleasant to lie motionless on the sofa and to know that one is alone in the room! Real happiness is impossible without solitude. The fallen angel betrayed God probably because he longed for solitude, of which the angels know nothing. Andrey Yefimitch wanted to think about what he had seen and heard during the last few days, but he could not get Mihail Averyanitch out of his head.

"Why, he has taken a holiday and come with me out of friendship, out of generosity," thought the doctor with vexation; "nothing could be worse than this friendly supervision. I suppose he is good-natured and generous and a lively fellow, but he is a bore. An insufferable bore. In the same way there are people who never say anything but what is clever and good, yet one feels that they are dull-witted people."

For the following days Andrey Yefimitch declared himself ill and would not leave the hotel room; he lay with his face to the back of the sofa, and suffered agonies of weariness when his friend entertained him with conversation, or rested when his friend was absent. He was vexed with himself for having come, and with his friend, who grew every day more talkative and more free-and-easy; he could not succeed in attuning his thoughts to a serious and lofty level.

"This is what I get from the real life Ivan Dmitritch talked about," he thought, angry at his own pettiness. "It's of no consequence, though. . . . I shall go home, and everything will go on as before. . . ."

It was the same thing in Petersburg too; for whole days together he did not leave the hotel room, but lay on the sofa and only got up to drink beer.

Mihail Averyanitch was all haste to get to Warsaw.

"My dear man, what should I go there for?" said Andrey Yefimitch in an imploring voice. "You go alone and let me get home! I entreat you!"

"On no account," protested Mihail Averyanitch. "It's a marvellous town."

Andrey Yefimitch had not the strength of will to insist on his own way, and much against his inclination went to Warsaw. There he did not leave the hotel room, but lay on the sofa, furious with himself, with his friend, and with the waiters, who obstinately refused to understand Russian; while Mihail Averyanitch, healthy, hearty, and full of spirits as usual, went about the town from morning to night, looking for his old acquaintances. Several times he did not return home at night. After one night spent in some unknown haunt he returned home early in the morning, in a violently excited condition, with a red face and tousled hair. For a long time he walked up and down the rooms muttering something to himself, then stopped and said:

"Honour before everything."

After walking up and down a little longer he clutched his head in both hands and pronounced in a tragic voice: "Yes, honour before everything! Accursed be the moment when the idea first entered my head to visit this Babylon! My dear friend," he added, addressing the doctor, "you may despise me, I have played and lost; lend me five hundred roubles!"

Andrey Yefimitch counted out five hundred roubles and gave them to his friend without a word. The latter, still crimson with shame and anger, incoherently articulated some useless vow, put on his cap, and went out. Returning two hours later he flopped into an easy chair, heaved a loud sigh, and said:

"My honour is saved. Let us go, my friend; I do not care to remain another hour in this accursed town. Scoundrels! Austrian spies!"

By the time the friends were back in their own town it was November, and deep snow was lying in the streets. Dr. Hobotov had Andrey Yefimitch's post; he was still living in his old lodgings, waiting for Andrey Yefimitch to arrive and clear out of the hospital apartments. The plain woman whom he called his cook was already established in one of the lodges.

Fresh scandals about the hospital were going the round of the town. It was said that the plain woman had quarrelled with the superintendent, and that the latter had crawled on his knees before her begging forgiveness. On the very first day he arrived Andrey Yefimitch had to look out for lodgings.

"My friend," the postmaster said to him timidly, "excuse an indiscreet question: what means have you at your disposal?"

Andrey Yefimitch, without a word, counted out his money and said: "Eighty-six roubles."

"I don't mean that," Mihail Averyanitch brought out in confusion, misunderstanding him; "I mean, what have you to live on?"

"I tell you, eighty-six roubles . . . I have nothing else."

Mihail Averyanitch looked upon the doctor as an honourable man, yet he suspected that he had accumulated a fortune of at least twenty thousand. Now learning that Andrey Yefimitch was a beggar, that he had nothing to live on he was for some reason suddenly moved to tears and embraced his friend.

XV

Andrey Yefimitch now lodged in a little house with three windows. There were only three rooms besides the kitchen in the little house. The doctor lived in two of them which looked into the street, while Daryushka and the landlady with her three children lived in the third room and the kitchen. Sometimes the landlady's lover, a drunken peasant who was rowdy and reduced the children and Daryushka to terror, would come for the night. When he arrived and established himself in the kitchen and demanded vodka, they all felt very uncomfortable, and the doctor would be moved by pity to take the crying children into his room and let them lie on his floor, and this gave him great satisfaction.

He got up as before at eight o'clock, and after his morning tea sat down to read his old books and magazines: he had no money for new ones. Either because the books were old, or perhaps because of the change in his surroundings, reading exhausted him, and did not grip his attention as before. That he might not spend his time in idleness he made a detailed catalogue of his books and gummed little labels on their backs, and this mechanical, tedious work seemed to him more interesting than reading. The monotonous, tedious work lulled his thoughts to sleep in some unaccountable way, and the time passed quickly while he thought of nothing. Even sitting in the kitchen, peeling potatoes with Daryushka or picking over the buckwheat grain, seemed to him interesting. On Saturdays and Sundays he went to church. Standing near the wall and half closing his eyes, he listened to the singing and thought of his father, of his mother, of the university, of the religions of the world; he felt calm and melancholy, and as he went out of the church afterwards he regretted that the service was so soon over. He went twice to the hospital to talk to Ivan Dmitritch. But on both occasions Ivan Dmitritch was unusually excited and ill-humoured; he bade the doctor leave him in peace, as he had long been sick of empty chatter, and declared, to make up for all his sufferings, he asked from the damned scoundrels only one favour—solitary confinement. Surely they would not refuse him even that? On both occasions when Andrey Yefimitch was taking leave of him and wishing him goodnight, he answered rudely and said:

"Go to hell!"

And Andrey Yefimitch did not know now whether to go to him for the third time or not. He longed to go.

In old days Andrey Yefimitch used to walk about his rooms and think in the interval after dinner, but now from dinner-time till evening tea he lay on the sofa with his face to the back and gave himself up to trivial thoughts which he could not struggle against. He was mortified that after more than twenty years of service he had been given neither a pension nor any assistance. It is true that he had not done his work honestly, but, then, all who are in the Service get a pension without distinction whether they are honest or not. Contemporary justice lies precisely in the bestowal of grades, orders, and pensions, not for moral qualities or capacities, but for service whatever it may have been like. Why was he alone to be an exception? He had no money at all. He was ashamed to pass by the shop and look at the woman who owned it. He owed thirty-two roubles for beer already. There was money owing to the landlady also. Daryushka sold old clothes and books on the sly, and told lies to the landlady, saying that the doctor was just going to receive a large sum of money.

He was angry with himself for having wasted on travelling the thousand roubles he had saved up. How useful that thousand roubles would have been now! He was vexed that people would not leave him in peace. Hobotov thought it his duty to look in on his sick colleague from time to time. Everything about him was revolting to Andrey Yefimitch—his well-fed face and vulgar, condescending tone, and his use of the word "colleague," and his high top-boots; the most revolting thing was that he thought it was his duty to treat Andrey Yefimitch, and thought that he really was treating him. On every visit he brought a bottle of bromide and rhubarb pills.

Mihail Averyanitch, too, thought it his duty to visit his friend and entertain him. Every time he went in to Andrey Yefimitch with an affectation of ease, laughed constrainedly, and began assuring him that he was looking very well today, and that, thank God, he was on the highroad to recovery, and from this it might be concluded that he looked on his friend's condition as hopeless. He had not yet repaid his Warsaw debt, and was overwhelmed by shame; he was constrained, and so tried to laugh louder and talk more amusingly. His anecdotes and descriptions seemed endless now, and were an agony both to Andrey Yefimitch and himself.

In his presence Andrey Yefimitch usually lay on the sofa with his face to the wall, and listened with his teeth clenched; his soul was oppressed with rankling disgust, and after every visit from his friend he felt as though this disgust had risen higher, and was mounting into his throat.

To stifle petty thoughts he made haste to reflect that he himself, and Hobotov, and Mihail Averyanitch, would all sooner or later perish without leaving any trace on the world. If one imagined some spirit flying by the earthly globe in space in a million years he would see nothing but clay and bare rocks. Everything—culture and the moral law—would pass away and not even a burdock would grow out of them. Of what consequence was shame in the presence of a shopkeeper, of what consequence was the insignificant Hobotov or the wearisome friendship of Mihail Averyanitch? It was all trivial and nonsensical.

But such reflections did not help him now. Scarcely had he imagined the earthly globe in a million years, when Hobotov in his high top-boots or Mihail Averyanitch with his forced laugh would appear from behind a bare rock, and he even heard the shamefaced whisper: "The Warsaw debt. . . . I will repay it in a day or two, my dear fellow, without fail. . . ."

XVI

One day Mihail Averyanitch came after dinner when Andrey Yefimitch was lying on the sofa. It so happened that Hobotov arrived at the same time with his bromide. Andrey Yefimitch got up heavily and sat down, leaning both arms on the sofa.

"You have a much better colour today than you had yesterday, my dear man," began Mihail Averyanitch. "Yes, you look jolly. Upon my soul, you do!"

"It's high time you were well, dear colleague," said Hobotov, yawning. "I'll be bound, you are sick of this bobbery."

"And we shall recover," said Mihail Averyanitch cheerfully. "We shall live another hundred years! To be sure!"

"Not a hundred years, but another twenty," Hobotov said reassuringly. "It's all right, all right, colleague; don't lose heart. . . . Don't go piling it on!"

"We'll show what we can do," laughed Mihail Averyanitch, and he slapped his friend on the knee. "We'll show them yet! Next summer, please God, we shall be off to the Caucasus, and we will ride all over it on horseback—trot, trot, trot! And when we are back from the Caucasus I shouldn't wonder if we will all dance at the wedding." Mihail Averyanitch gave a sly wink. "We'll marry you, my dear boy, we'll marry you. . . ."

Andrey Yefimitch felt suddenly that the rising disgust had mounted to his throat, his heart began beating violently.

"That's vulgar," he said, getting up quickly and walking away to the window. "Don't you understand that you are talking vulgar nonsense?"

He meant to go on softly and politely, but against his will he suddenly clenched his fists and raised them above his head.

"Leave me alone," he shouted in a voice unlike his own, blushing crimson and shaking all over. "Go away, both of you!"

Mihail Averyanitch and Hobotov got up and stared at him first with amazement and then with alarm.

"Go away, both!" Andrey Yefimitch went on shouting. "Stupid people! Foolish people! I don't want either your friendship or your medicines, stupid man! Vulgar! Nasty!"

Hobotov and Mihail Averyanitch, looking at each other in bewilderment, staggered to the door and went out. Andrey Yefimitch snatched up the bottle of bromide and flung it after them; the bottle broke with a crash on the door-frame.

"Go to the devil!" he shouted in a tearful voice, running out into the passage. "To the devil!"

When his guests were gone Andrey Yefimitch lay down on the sofa, trembling as though in a fever, and went on for a long while repeating: "Stupid people! Foolish people!"

When he was calmer, what occurred to him first of all was the thought that poor Mihail Averyanitch must be feeling fearfully ashamed and depressed now, and that it was all dreadful. Nothing like this had ever happened to him before. Where was his intelligence and his tact? Where was his comprehension of things and his philosophical indifference?

The doctor could not sleep all night for shame and vexation with himself, and at ten o'clock next morning he went to the post office and apologized to the postmaster.

"We won't think again of what has happened," Mihail Averyanitch, greatly touched, said with a sigh, warmly pressing his hand. "Let bygones be bygones. Lyubavkin," he suddenly shouted so loud that all the postmen and other persons present started, "hand a chair; and you wait," he shouted to a peasant woman who was stretching out a registered letter to him through the grating. "Don't you see that I am busy? We will not remember the past," he went on, affectionately addressing Andrey Yefimitch; "sit down, I beg you, my dear fellow."

For a minute he stroked his knees in silence, and then said:

"I have never had a thought of taking offence. Illness is no joke, I understand. Your attack frightened the doctor and me yesterday, and we had a long talk about you afterwards. My dear friend, why won't you treat your illness seriously? You can't go on like this. . . . Excuse me speaking openly as a friend," whispered Mihail Averyanitch. "You live in the most unfavourable surroundings, in a crowd, in uncleanliness, no one to look after you, no money for proper treatment. . . . My dear friend, the doctor and I implore you with all our hearts, listen to our advice: go into the hospital! There you will have wholesome food and attendance and treatment. Though, between ourselves, Yevgeny Fyodoritch is *mauvais ton*, yet he does understand his work, you can fully rely upon him. He has promised me he will look after you."

Andrey Yefimitch was touched by the postmaster's genuine sympathy and the tears which suddenly glittered on his cheeks.

"My honoured friend, don't believe it!" he whispered, laying his hand on his heart; "don't believe them. It's all a sham. My illness is only that in twenty years I have only found one intelligent man in the whole town, and he is mad. I am not ill at all, it's simply that I have got into an enchanted circle which there is no getting out of. I don't care; I am ready for anything."

"Go into the hospital, my dear fellow."

"I don't care if it were into the pit."

"Give me your word, my dear man, that you will obey Yevgeny Fyodoritch in everything."

"Certainly I will give you my word. But I repeat, my honoured friend, I have got into an enchanted circle. Now everything, even the genuine sympathy of my friends, leads to the same thing—to my ruin. I am going to my ruin, and I have the manliness to recognize it."

"My dear fellow, you will recover."

"What's the use of saying that?" said Andrey Yefimitch, with irritation. "There are few men who at the end of their lives do not experience what I am experiencing now. When you are told that you have something such as diseased kidneys or enlarged heart, and you begin being treated for it, or are told you are mad or a criminal—that is, in fact, when people suddenly turn their attention to you—you may be sure you have got into an enchanted circle from which you will not escape. You will try to escape and make things worse. You had better give in, for no human efforts can save you. So it seems to me."

Meanwhile the public was crowding at the grating. That he might not be in their way, Andrey Yefimitch got up and began to take leave. Mihail Averyanitch made him promise on his honour once more, and escorted him to the outer door.

Towards evening on the same day Hobotov, in his sheepskin and his high top-boots, suddenly made his appearance, and said to Andrey Yefimitch in a tone as though nothing had happened the day before:

"I have come on business, colleague. I have come to ask you whether you would not join me in a consultation. Eh?"

Thinking that Hobotov wanted to distract his mind with an outing, or perhaps really to enable him to earn something, Andrey Yefimitch put on his coat and hat, and went out with him into the street. He was glad of the opportunity to smooth over his fault of the previous day and to be reconciled, and in his heart thanked Hobotov, who did not even allude to yesterday's scene and was evidently sparing him. One would never have expected such delicacy from this uncultured man.

"Where is your invalid?" asked Andrey Yefimitch.

"In the hospital. . . . I have long wanted to show him to you. A very interesting case."

They went into the hospital yard, and going round the main building, turned towards the lodge where the mental cases were kept, and all this, for some reason, in silence. When they went into the lodge Nikita as usual jumped up and stood at attention.

"One of the patients here has a lung complication." Hobotov said in an undertone, going into the yard with Andrey Yefimitch. "You wait here, I'll be back directly. I am going for a stethoscope."

And he went away.

XVII

It was getting dusk. Ivan Dmitritch was lying on his bed with his face thrust unto his pillow; the paralytic was sitting motionless, crying quietly and moving his lips. The fat peasant and the former sorter were asleep. It was quiet.

Andrey Yefimitch sat down on Ivan Dmitritch's bed and waited. But half an hour passed, and instead of Hobotov, Nikita came into the ward with a dressing gown, some underlinen, and a pair of slippers in a heap on his arm.

"Please change your things, your honour," he said softly. "Here is your bed; come this way," he added, pointing to an empty bedstead which had obviously recently been brought into the ward. "It's all right; please God, you will recover."

Andrey Yefimitch understood it all. Without saying a word he crossed to the bed to which Nikita pointed and sat down; seeing that Nikita was standing waiting, he undressed entirely and he felt ashamed. Then he put on the hospital clothes; the drawers were very short, the shirt was long, and the dressing gown smelt of smoked fish.

"Please God, you will recover," repeated Nikita, and he gathered up Andrey Yefimitch's clothes into his arms, went out, and shut the door after him.

"No matter . . ." thought Andrey Yefimitch, wrapping himself in his dressing gown in a shamefaced way and feeling that he looked like a convict in his new costume. "It's no matter. . . . It does not matter whether it's a dress-coat or a uniform or this dressing gown."

But how about his watch? And the notebook that was in the side-pocket? And his cigarettes? Where had Nikita taken his clothes? Now perhaps to the day of his death he would not put on trousers, a waistcoat, and high boots. It was all somehow strange and even incomprehensible at first. Andrey Yefimitch was even now convinced that there was no difference between his landlady's house and Ward No. 6, that everything in this world was nonsense and vanity of vanities. And yet his hands were trembling, his feet were cold, and he was filled with dread at the thought that soon Ivan Dmitritch would get up and see that he was in a dressing gown. He got up and walked across the room and sat down again.

Here he had been sitting already half an hour, an hour, and he was miserably sick of it: was it really possible to live here a day, a week, and even years like these people? Why, he had been sitting here, had walked about and sat down again; he could get up and look out of window and walk from corner to corner again, and then what? Sit so all the time, like a post, and think? No, that was scarcely possible.

Andrey Yefimitch lay down, but at once got up, wiped the cold sweat from his brow with his sleeve and felt that his whole face smelt of smoked fish. He walked about again.

"It's some misunderstanding . . ." he said, turning out the palms of his hands in perplexity. "It must be cleared up. There is a misunderstanding."

Meanwhile Ivan Dmitritch woke up; he sat up and propped his cheeks on his fists. He spat. Then he glanced lazily at the doctor, and apparently for the first minute did not understand; but soon his sleepy face grew malicious and mocking.

"Aha! so they have put you in here, too, old fellow?" he said in a voice husky from sleepiness, screwing up one eye. "Very glad to see you. You sucked the blood of others, and now they will suck yours. Excellent!"

"It's a misunderstanding . . ." Andrey Yefimitch brought out, frightened by Ivan Dmitritch's words; he shrugged his shoulders and repeated: "It's some misunderstanding."

Ivan Dmitritch spat again and lay down.

"Cursed life," he grumbled, "and what's bitter and insulting, this life will not end in compensation for our sufferings, it will not end with apotheosis as it would in an opera, but with death; peasants will come and drag one's dead body by the arms and the legs to the cellar. Ugh! Well, it does not matter. . . . We shall have our good time in the other world. . . . I shall come here as a ghost from the other world and frighten these reptiles. I'll turn their hair grey."

Moiseika returned, and, seeing the doctor, held out his hand.

"Give me one little kopeck," he said.

XVIII

Andrey Yefimitch walked away to the window and looked out into the open country. It was getting dark, and on the horizon to the right a cold crimson moon was mounting upwards. Not far from the hospital fence, not much more than two hundred yards away, stood a tall white house shut in by a stone wall. This was the prison.

"So this is real life," thought Andrey Yefimitch, and he felt frightened.

The moon and the prison, and the nails on the fence, and the faraway flames at the bone-charring factory were all terrible. Behind him there was the sound of a sigh. Andrey Yefimitch looked round and saw a man with glittering stars and orders on his breast, who was smiling and slyly winking. And this, too, seemed terrible.

Andrey Yefimitch assured himself that there was nothing special about the moon or the prison, that even sane persons wear orders, and that everything in time will decay and turn to earth, but he was suddenly overcome with desire; he clutched at the grating with both hands and shook it with all his might. The strong grating did not yield.

Then that it might not be so dreadful he went to Ivan Dmitritch's bed and sat down.

"I have lost heart, my dear fellow," he muttered, trembling and wiping away the cold sweat, "I have lost heart."

"You should be philosophical," said Ivan Dmitritch ironically.

"My God, my God. . . . Yes, yes. . . . You were pleased to say once that there was no philosophy in Russia, but that all people, even the paltriest, talk philosophy. But you know the philosophizing of the paltriest does not harm anyone," said Andrey Yefimitch in a tone as if he wanted to cry and complain. "Why, then, that malignant laugh, my friend, and how can these paltry creatures help philosophizing if they are not satisfied? For an intelligent, educated man, made in God's image, proud and loving freedom, to have no alternative but to be a doctor in a filthy, stupid, wretched little town, and to spend his whole life among bottles, leeches, mustard plasters! Quackery, narrowness, vulgarity! Oh, my God!"

"You are talking nonsense. If you don't like being a doctor you should have gone in for being a statesman."

"I could not, I could not do anything. We are weak, my dear friend. . . . I used to be indifferent. I reasoned boldly and soundly, but at the first coarse touch of life upon me I have lost heart. . . . Prostration. . . . We are weak, we are poor creatures . . . and you, too, my dear friend, you are intelligent, generous, you drew in good impulses with your mother's milk, but you had hardly entered upon life when you were exhausted and fell ill. . . . Weak, weak!"

Andrey Yefimitch was all the while at the approach of evening tormented by another persistent sensation besides terror and the feeling of resentment. At last he realized that he was longing for a smoke and for beer.

"I am going out, my friend," he said. "I will tell them to bring a light; I can't put up with this. . . . I am not equal to it. . . ."

Andrey Yefimitch went to the door and opened it, but at once Nikita jumped up and barred his way.

"Where are you going? You can't, you can't!" he said. "It's bedtime."

"But I'm only going out for a minute to walk about the yard," said Andrey Yefimitch.

"You can't, you can't; it's forbidden. You know that yourself."

"But what difference will it make to anyone if I do go out?" asked Andrey Yefimitch, shrugging his shoulders. "I don't understand. Nikita, I must go out!" he said in a trembling voice. "I must."

"Don't be disorderly, it's not right," Nikita said peremptorily.

"This is beyond everything," Ivan Dmitritch cried suddenly, and he jumped up. "What right has he not to let you out? How dare they keep us here? I believe it is clearly laid down in the law that no one can be deprived of freedom without trial! It's an outrage! It's tyranny!"

"Of course it's tyranny," said Andrey Yefimitch, encouraged by Ivan Dmitritch's outburst. "I must go out, I want to. He has no right! Open, I tell you."

"Do you hear, you dull-witted brute?" cried Ivan Dmitritch, and he banged on the door with his fist. "Open the door, or I will break it open! Torturer!"

"Open the door," cried Andrey Yefimitch, trembling all over; "I insist!"

"Talk away!" Nikita answered through the door, "talk away. . . ."

"Anyhow, go and call Yevgeny Fyodoritch! Say that I beg him to come for a minute!"

"His honour will come of himself tomorrow."

"They will never let us out," Ivan Dmitritch was going on meanwhile. "They will leave us to rot here! Oh, Lord, can there really be no hell in the next world, and will these wretches be forgiven? Where is justice? Open the door, you wretch! I am choking!" he cried in a hoarse voice, and flung himself upon the door. "I'll dash out my brains, murderers!"

Nikita opened the door quickly, and roughly with both his hands and his knee shoved Andrey Yefimitch back, then swung his arm and punched him in the face with his fist. It seemed to Andrey Yefimitch as though a huge salt wave enveloped him from his head downwards and dragged him to the bed; there really was a salt taste in his mouth: most likely the blood was running from his teeth. He waved his arms as though he were trying to swim out and clutched at a bedstead, and at the same moment felt Nikita hit him twice on the back.

Ivan Dmitritch gave a loud scream. He must have been beaten too.

Then all was still, the faint moonlight came through the grating, and a shadow like a net lay on the floor. It was terrible. Andrey Yefimitch lay and held his breath: he was expecting with horror to be struck again. He felt as though someone had taken a sickle, thrust it into him, and turned it round several times in his breast and bowels. He bit the pillow from pain and clenched his teeth, and all at once through the chaos in his brain there flashed the terrible unbearable thought that these people, who seemed now like black shadows in the moonlight, had to endure such pain day by day for years. How could it have happened that for more than twenty years he had not known it and had refused to know it? He knew nothing of pain, had no conception of it, so he was not to blame, but his conscience, as inexorable and as rough as Nikita, made him turn cold from the crown of his head to his heels. He leaped up, tried to cry out with all his might, and to run in haste to kill Nikita, and then Hobotov, the superintendent and the assistant, and then himself; but no sound came from his chest, and his legs would not obey him. Gasping for breath, he tore at the dressing gown and the shirt on his breast, rent them, and fell senseless on the bed.

XIX

Next morning his head ached, there was a droning in his ears and a feeling of utter weakness all over. He was not ashamed at recalling his weakness the day before. He had been cowardly, had even been afraid of the moon, had openly expressed thoughts and feelings such as he had not expected in himself before; for instance, the thought that the paltry people who philosophized were really dissatisfied. But now nothing mattered to him.

He ate nothing; he drank nothing. He lay motionless and silent.

"It is all the same to me," he thought when they asked him questions. "I am not going to answer. . . . It's all the same to me."

After dinner Mihail Averyanitch brought him a quarter pound of tea and a pound of fruit pastilles. Daryushka came too and stood for a whole hour by the bed with an expression of dull grief on her face. Dr. Hobotov visited him. He brought a bottle of bromide and told Nikita to fumigate the ward with something.

Towards evening Andrey Yefimitch died of an apoplectic stroke. At first he had a violent shivering fit and a feeling of sickness; something revolting as it seemed, penetrating through his whole body, even to his finger-tips, strained from his stomach to his head and flooded his eyes and ears. There was a greenness before his eyes. Andrey Yefimitch understood that his end had come, and remembered that Ivan Dmitritch, Mihail Averyanitch, and millions of people believed in immortality. And what if it really existed? But he did not want immortality—and he thought of it only for one instant. A herd of deer, extraordinarily beautiful and graceful, of which he had been reading the day before, ran by him; then a peasant woman stretched out her hand to him with a registered letter. . . . Mihail Averyanitch said something, then it all vanished, and Andrey Yefimitch sank into oblivion for ever.

The hospital porters came, took him by his arms and legs, and carried him away to the chapel.

There he lay on the table, with open eyes, and the moon shed its light upon him at night. In the morning Sergey Sergeyitch came, prayed piously before the crucifix, and closed his former chief's eyes.

Next day Andrey Yefimitch was buried. Mihail Averyanitch and Daryushka were the only people at the funeral.

In Exile

[First published in *Vsemirnaya Illustratsiya*, a Russian
weekly magazine, on May 9, 1892. Revised and included in
the collection *Novellas and Stories* (1894).
Collected in *The Schoolmistress and Other Stories* (1918).]

Old semyon, nicknamed Canny, and a young Tatar, whom no one knew
by name, were sitting on the riverbank by the campfire; the other three
ferrymen were in the hut. Semyon, an old man of sixty, lean and toothless,
but broad shouldered and still healthy-looking, was drunk; he would
have gone in to sleep long before, but he had a bottle in his pocket and he
was afraid that the fellows in the hut would ask him for vodka. The Tatar
was ill and weary, and wrapping himself up in his rags was describing
how nice it was in the Simbirsk province, and what a beautiful and clever
wife he had left behind at home. He was not more than twenty five, and
now by the light of the campfire, with his pale and sick, mournful face,
he looked like a boy.

"To be sure, it is not paradise here," said Canny. "You can see for
yourself, the water, the bare banks, clay, and nothing else. . . . Easter
has long passed and yet there is ice on the river, and this morning there
was snow . . ."

"It's bad! it's bad!" said the Tatar, and looked round him in terror.

The dark, cold river was flowing ten paces away; it grumbled, lapped
against the hollow clay banks and raced on swiftly towards the faraway
sea. Close to the bank there was the dark blur of a big barge, which the
ferrymen called a "karbos." Far away on the further bank, lights, dying
down and flickering up again, zigzagged like little snakes; they were

burning last year's grass. And beyond the little snakes there was darkness again. There little icicles could be heard knocking against the barge. It was damp and cold. . . .

The Tatar glanced at the sky. There were as many stars as at home, and the same blackness all round, but something was lacking. At home in the Simbirsk province the stars were quite different, and so was the sky.

"It's bad! it's bad!" he repeated.

"You will get used to it," said Semyon, and he laughed. "Now you are young and foolish, the milk is hardly dry on your lips, and it seems to you in your foolishness that you are more wretched than anyone; but the time will come when you will say to yourself: 'I wish no one a better life than mine.' You look at me. Within a week the floods will be over and we shall set up the ferry; you will all go wandering off about Siberia while I shall stay and shall begin going from bank to bank. I've been going like that for twenty-two years, day and night. The pike and the salmon are under the water while I am on the water. And thank God for it, I want nothing; God give everyone such a life."

The Tatar threw some dry twigs on the campfire, lay down closer to the blaze, and said:

"My father is a sick man. When he dies my mother and wife will come here. They have promised."

"And what do you want your wife and mother for?" asked Canny. "That's mere foolishness, my lad. It's the devil confounding you, damn his soul! Don't you listen to him, the cursed one. Don't let him have his way. He is at you about the women, but you spite him; say, 'I don't want them!' He is on at you about freedom, but you stand up to him and say: 'I don't want it!' I want nothing, neither father nor mother, nor wife, nor freedom, nor post, nor paddock; I want nothing, damn their souls!"

Semyon took a pull at the bottle and went on:

"I am not a simple peasant, not of the working class, but the son of a deacon, and when I was free I lived at Kursk; I used to wear a frockcoat, and now I have brought myself to such a pass that I can sleep naked on the ground and eat grass. And I wish no one a better life. I want nothing and I am afraid of nobody, and the way I look at it is that there is nobody richer and freer than I am. When they sent me here from Russia from the first day I stuck it out; I want nothing! The devil was at me about my wife and about my home and about freedom, but I told him: 'I want nothing.' I stuck to it, and here you see I live well, and I don't complain, and if anyone gives way to the devil and listens to him, if but once, he is lost, there is no salvation for him: he is sunk in the bog to the crown of his head and will never get out.

"It is not only a foolish peasant like you, but even gentlemen, well-educated people, are lost. Fifteen years ago they sent a gentleman here from Russia. He hadn't shared something with his brothers and had forged something in a will. They did say he was a prince or a baron, but maybe he was simply an official—who knows? Well, the gentleman arrived here, and first thing he bought himself a house and land in Muhortinskoe. 'I want to live by my own work,' says he, 'in the sweat of my brow, for I am not a gentleman now,' says he, 'but a settler.' 'Well,' says I, 'God help you, that's the right thing.' He was a young man then, busy and careful; he used to mow himself and catch fish and ride sixty miles on horseback. Only this is what happened: from the very first year he took to riding to Gyrino for the post; he used to stand on my ferry and sigh: 'Ech, Semyon, how long it is since they sent me any money from home!' 'You don't want money, Vassily Sergeyitch,' says I. 'What use is it to you? You cast away the past, and forget it as though it had never been at all, as though it had been a dream, and begin to live anew. Don't listen to the devil,' says I; 'he will bring you to no good, he'll draw you into a snare. Now you want money,' says I, 'but in a very little while you'll be wanting something else, and then more and more. If you want to be happy,' says I, the chief thing is not to want anything. Yes. . . . If,' says I, 'if Fate has wronged you and me cruelly it's no good asking for her favour and bowing down to her, but you despise her and laugh at her, or else she will laugh at you.' That's what I said to him. . . .

"Two years later I ferried him across to this side, and he was rubbing his hands and laughing. 'I am going to Gyrino to meet my wife,' says he. 'She was sorry for me,' says he; 'she has come. She is good and kind.' And he was breathless with joy. So a day later he came with his wife. A beautiful young lady in a hat; in her arms was a baby girl. And lots of luggage of all sorts. And my Vassily Sergeyitch was fussing round her; he couldn't take his eyes off her and couldn't say enough in praise of her. 'Yes, brother Semyon, even in Siberia people can live!' 'Oh, all right,' thinks I, 'it will be a different tale presently.' And from that time forward he went almost every week to inquire whether money had not come from

Russia. He wanted a lot of money. 'She is losing her youth and beauty here in Siberia for my sake,' says he, 'and sharing my bitter lot with me, and so I ought,' says he, 'to provide her with every comfort. . . .'

"To make it livelier for the lady he made acquaintance with the officials and all sorts of riff-raff. And of course he had to give food and drink to all that crew, and there had to be a piano and a shaggy lapdog on the sofa—plague take it! . . . Luxury, in fact, self-indulgence. The lady did not stay with him long. How could she? The clay, the water, the cold, no vegetables for you, no fruit. All around you ignorant and drunken people and no sort of manners, and she was a spoilt lady from Petersburg or Moscow. . . . To be sure she moped. Besides, her husband, say what you like, was not a gentleman now, but a settler—not the same rank.

"Three years later, I remember, on the eve of the Assumption, there was shouting from the further bank. I went over with the ferry, and what do I see but the lady, all wrapped up, and with her a young gentleman, an official. A sledge with three horses. . . . I ferried them across here, they got in and away like the wind. They were soon lost to sight. And towards morning Vassily Sergeyitch galloped down to the ferry. 'Didn't my wife come this way with a gentleman in spectacles, Semyon?' 'She did,' said I; 'you may look for the wind in the fields!' He galloped in pursuit of them. For five days and nights he was riding after them. When I ferried him over to the other side afterwards, he flung himself on the ferry and beat his head on the boards of the ferry and howled. 'So that's how it is,' says I. I laughed, and reminded him 'people can live even in Siberia!' And he beat his head harder than ever. . . .

"Then he began longing for freedom. His wife had slipped off to Russia, and of course he was drawn there to see her and to get her away from her lover. And he took, my lad, to galloping almost every day, either to the post or the town to see the commanding officer; he kept sending in petitions for them to have mercy on him and let him go back home; and he used to say that he had spent some two hundred roubles on telegrams alone. He sold his land and mortgaged his house to the Jews. He grew grey and bent, and yellow in the face, as though he was in consumption. If he talked to you he would go, khee—khee—khee . . . and there were tears in his eyes. He kept rushing about like this with petitions for eight years, but now he has grown brighter and more cheerful again: he has found another whim to give way to. You see, his daughter has grown up. He looks at her, and she is the apple of his eye. And to tell the truth she is all right, good-looking, with black eyebrows and a lively disposition. Every Sunday he used to ride with her to church in Gyrino. They used to stand on the ferry, side by side, she would laugh and he could not take his eyes off her. 'Yes, Semyon,' says he, 'people can live even in Siberia. Even in Siberia there is happiness. Look,' says he, 'what a daughter I have got! I warrant you wouldn't find another like her for a thousand versts round.' 'Your daughter is all right,' says I, 'that's true, certainly.' But to myself I thought: 'Wait a bit, the wench is young, her blood is dancing, she wants to live, and there is no life here.' And she did begin to pine, my lad. . . . She faded and faded, and now she can hardly crawl about. Consumption.

"So you see what Siberian happiness is, damn its soul! You see how people can live in Siberia. . . . He has taken to going from one doctor to another and taking them home with him. As soon as he hears that two or three hundred miles away there is a doctor or a sorcerer, he will drive to fetch him. A terrible lot of money he spent on doctors, and to my thinking he had better have spent the money on drink. . . . She'll die just the same. She is certain to die, and then it will be all over with him. He'll hang himself from grief or run away to Russia—that's a sure thing. He'll run away and they'll catch him, then he will be tried, sent to prison, he will have a taste of the lash. . . ."

"Good! good!" said the Tatar, shivering with cold.

"What is good?" asked Canny.

"His wife, his daughter. . . . What of prison and what of sorrow!—anyway, he did see his wife and his daughter. . . . You say, want nothing. But 'nothing' is bad! His wife lived with him three years—that was a gift from God. 'Nothing' is bad, but three years is good. How not understand?"

Shivering and hesitating, with effort picking out the Russian words of which he knew but few, the Tatar said that God forbid one should fall sick and die in a strange land, and be buried in the cold and dark earth; that if his wife came to him for one day, even for one hour, that for such happiness he would be ready to bear any suffering and to thank God. Better one day of happiness than nothing.

Then he described again what a beautiful and clever wife he had left at home. Then, clutching his head in both hands, he began crying and assuring Semyon that he was not guilty, and was suffering for nothing.

His two brothers and an uncle had carried off a peasant's horses, and had beaten the old man till he was half dead, and the commune had not judged fairly, but had contrived a sentence by which all the three brothers were sent to Siberia, while the uncle, a rich man, was left at home.

"You will get used to it!" said Semyon.

The Tatar was silent, and stared with tear-stained eyes at the fire; his face expressed bewilderment and fear, as though he still did not understand why he was here in the darkness and the wet, beside strangers, and not in the Simbirsk province.

Canny lay near the fire, chuckled at something, and began humming a song in an undertone.

"What joy has she with her father?" he said a little later. "He loves her and he rejoices in her, that's true; but, mate, you must mind your ps and qs with him, he is a strict old man, a harsh old man. And young wenches don't want strictness. They want petting and ha-ha-ha! and ho-ho-ho! and scent and pomade. Yes. . . . Ech! life, life," sighed Semyon, and he got up heavily. "The vodka is all gone, so it is time to sleep. Eh? I am going, my lad. . . ."

Left alone, the Tatar put on more twigs, lay down and stared at the fire; he began thinking of his own village and of his wife. If his wife could only come for a month, for a day; and then if she liked she might go back again. Better a month or even a day than nothing. But if his wife kept her promise and came, what would he have to feed her on? Where could she live here?

"If there were not something to eat, how could she live?" the Tatar asked aloud.

He was paid only ten kopecks for working all day and all night at the oar; it is true that travellers gave him tips for tea and for vodkas but the men shared all they received among themselves, and gave nothing to the Tatar, but only laughed at him. And from poverty he was hungry, cold, and frightened. . . . Now, when his whole body was aching and shivering, he ought to go into the hut and lie down to sleep; but he had nothing to cover him there, and it was colder than on the riverbank; here he had nothing to cover him either, but at least he could make up the fire. . . .

In another week, when the floods were quite over and they set the ferry going, none of the ferrymen but Semyon would be wanted, and the Tatar would begin going from village to village begging for alms and for work. His wife was only seventeen; she was beautiful, spoilt, and shy; could she possibly go from village to village begging alms with her face unveiled? No, it was terrible even to think of that. . . .

It was already getting light; the barge, the bushes of willow on the water, and the waves could be clearly discerned, and if one looked round there was the steep clay slope; at the bottom of it the hut thatched with dingy brown straw, and the huts of the village lay clustered higher up. The cocks were already crowing in the village.

The rusty red clay slope, the barge, the river, the strange, unkind people, hunger, cold, illness, perhaps all that was not real. Most likely it was all a dream, thought the Tatar. He felt that he was asleep and heard his own snoring. . . . Of course he was at home in the Simbirsk province, and he had only to call his wife by name for her to answer; and in the next room was his mother. . . . What terrible dreams there are, though! What are they for? The Tatar smiled and opened his eyes. What river was this, the Volga?

Snow was falling.

"Boat!" was shouted on the further side. "Boat!"

The Tatar woke up, and went to wake his mates and row over to the other side. The ferrymen came on to the riverbank, putting on their torn sheepskins as they walked, swearing with voices husky from sleepiness and shivering from the cold. On waking from their sleep, the river, from which came a breath of piercing cold, seemed to strike them as revolting and horrible. They jumped into the barge without hurrying themselves. . . . The Tatar and the three ferrymen took the long, broad-bladed oars, which in the darkness looked like the claws of crabs; Semyon leaned his stomach against the tiller. The shout on the other side still continued, and two shots were fired from a revolver, probably with the idea that the ferrymen were asleep or had gone to the pot-house in the village.

"All right, you have plenty of time," said Semyon in the tone of a man convinced that there was no necessity in this world to hurry—that it would lead to nothing, anyway.

The heavy, clumsy barge moved away from the bank and floated between the willow-bushes, and only the willows slowly moving back showed that the barge was not standing still but moving. The ferrymen swung the oars evenly in time; Semyon lay with his stomach on the tiller and, describing a semicircle in the air, flew from one side to the other. In the darkness it looked as though the men were sitting on some antediluvian animal with long paws, and were moving on it through a cold, desolate land, the land of which one sometimes dreams in nightmares.

They passed beyond the willows and floated out into the open. The creak and regular splash of the oars was heard on the further shore, and a shout came: "Make haste! make haste!"

Another ten minutes passed, and the barge banged heavily against the landing-stage.

"And it keeps sprinkling and sprinkling," muttered Semyon, wiping the snow from his face; "and where it all comes from God only knows."

On the bank stood a thin man of medium height in a jacket lined with fox fur and in a white lambskin cap. He was standing at a little distance from his horses and not moving; he had a gloomy, concentrated expression, as though he were trying to remember something and angry with his untrustworthy memory. When Semyon went up to him and took off his cap, smiling, he said:

"I am hastening to Anastasyevka. My daughter's worse again, and they say that there is a new doctor at Anastasyevka."

They dragged the carriage on to the barge and floated back. The man whom Semyon addressed as Vassily Sergeyitch stood all the time motionless, tightly compressing his thick lips and staring off into space; when his coachman asked permission to smoke in his presence he made no answer, as though he had not heard. Semyon, lying with his stomach on the tiller, looked mockingly at him and said:

"Even in Siberia people can live—can li-ive!"

There was a triumphant expression on Canny's face, as though he had proved something and was delighted that things had happened as he had foretold. The unhappy helplessness of the man in the foxskin coat evidently afforded him great pleasure.

"It's muddy driving now, Vassily Sergeyitch," he said when the horses were harnessed again on the bank. "You should have put off going for another fortnight, when it will be drier. Or else not have gone at all. . . . If any good would come of your going—but as you know yourself, people have been driving about for years and years, day and night, and it's always been no use. That's the truth."

Vassily Sergeyitch tipped him without a word, got into his carriage and drove off.

"There, he has galloped off for a doctor!" said Semyon, shrinking from the cold. "But looking for a good doctor is like chasing the wind in the fields or catching the devil by the tail, plague take your soul! What a queer chap, Lord forgive me a sinner!"

The Tatar went up to Canny, and, looking at him with hatred and repulsion, shivering, and mixing Tatar words with his broken Russian, said: "He is good . . . good; but you are bad! You are bad! The gentleman is a good soul, excellent, and you are a beast, bad! The gentleman is alive, but you are a dead carcass. . . . God created man to be alive, and to have joy and grief and sorrow; but you want nothing, so you are not alive, you are stone, clay! A stone wants nothing and you want nothing. You are a stone, and God does not love you, but He loves the gentleman!"

Everyone laughed; the Tatar frowned contemptuously, and with a wave of his hand wrapped himself in his rags and went to the campfire. The ferrymen and Semyon sauntered to the hut.

"It's cold," said one ferryman huskily as he stretched himself on the straw with which the damp clay floor was covered.

"Yes, it's not warm," another assented. "It's a dog's life. . . ."

They all lay down. The door was thrown open by the wind and the snow drifted into the hut; nobody felt inclined to get up and shut the door: they were cold, and it was too much trouble.

"I am all right," said Semyon as he began to doze. "I wouldn't wish anyone a better life."

"You are a tough one, we all know. Even the devils won't take you!"

Sounds like a dog's howling came from outside.

"What's that? Who's there?"

"It's the Tatar crying."

"I say. . . . He's a queer one!"

"He'll get u-used to it!" said Semyon, and at once fell asleep.

The others were soon asleep too. The door remained unclosed.

After the Theatre

[First published in 1892.
Collected in *The Schoolmistress and Other Stories* (1918).]

Nadya Zelenin had just come back with her mamma from the theatre where she had seen a performance of "Yevgeny Onyegin." As soon as she reached her own room she threw off her dress, let down her hair, and in her petticoat and white dressing-jacket hastily sat down to the table to write a letter like Tatyana's.

"I love you," she wrote, "but you do not love me, do not love me!"

She wrote it and laughed.

She was only sixteen and did not yet love anyone. She knew that an officer called Gorny and a student called Gruzdev loved her, but now after the opera she wanted to be doubtful of their love. To be unloved and unhappy—how interesting that was. There is something beautiful, touching, and poetical about it when one loves and the other is indifferent. Onyegin was interesting because he was not in love at all, and Tatyana was fascinating because she was so much in love; but if they had been equally in love with each other and had been happy, they would perhaps have seemed dull.

"Leave off declaring that you love me," Nadya went on writing, thinking of Gorny. "I cannot believe it. You are very clever, cultivated, serious, you have immense talent, and perhaps a brilliant future awaits you, while I am an uninteresting girl of no importance, and you know very well that I should be only a hindrance in your life. It is true that you were attracted by me and thought you had found your ideal in me, but that was a mistake, and now you are asking yourself in despair: 'Why did I meet that girl?' And only your goodness of heart prevents you from owning it to yourself. . . ."

Nadya felt sorry for herself, she began to cry, and went on:

"It is hard for me to leave my mother and my brother, or I should take a nun's veil and go whither chance may lead me. And you would be left free and would love another. Oh, if I were dead!"

She could not make out what she had written through her tears; little rainbows were quivering on the table, on the floor, on the ceiling, as though she were looking through a prism. She could not write, she sank back in her easy chair and fell to thinking of Gorny.

My God! how interesting, how fascinating men were! Nadya recalled the fine expression, ingratiating, guilty, and soft, which came into the officer's face when one argued about music with him, and the effort he made to prevent his voice from betraying his passion. In a society where cold haughtiness and indifference are regarded as signs of good breeding and gentlemanly bearing, one must conceal one's passions. And he did try to conceal them, but he did not succeed, and everyone knew very well that he had a passionate love of music. The endless discussions about music and the bold criticisms of people who knew nothing about it kept him always on the strain; he was frightened, timid, and silent. He played the piano magnificently, like a professional pianist, and if he had not been in the army he would certainly have been a famous musician.

The tears on her eyes dried. Nadya remembered that Gorny had declared his love at a Symphony concert, and again downstairs by the hatstand where there was a tremendous draught blowing in all directions.

"I am very glad that you have at last made the acquaintance of Gruzdev, our student friend," she went on writing. "He is a very clever man, and you will be sure to like him. He came to see us yesterday and stayed till two o'clock. We were all delighted with him, and I regretted that you had not come. He said a great deal that was remarkable."

Nadya laid her arms on the table and leaned her head on them, and her hair covered the letter. She recalled that the student, too, loved her, and that he had as much right to a letter from her as Gorny. Wouldn't it be better after all to write to Gruzdev? There was a stir of joy in her bosom for no reason whatever; at first the joy was small, and rolled in her bosom like an india-rubber ball; then it became more massive, bigger, and rushed like a wave. Nadya forgot Gorny and Gruzdev; her thoughts were in a tangle and her joy grew and grew; from her bosom it passed into her arms and legs, and it seemed as though a light, cool breeze were breathing on her head and ruffling her hair. Her shoulders quivered with subdued laughter, the table and the lamp chimney shook, too, and tears from her eyes splashed on the letter. She could not stop laughing, and to prove to herself that she was not laughing about nothing she made haste to think of something funny.

"What a funny poodle," she said, feeling as though she would choke with laughter. "What a funny poodle!"

She thought how, after tea the evening before, Gruzdev had played with Maxim the poodle, and afterwards had told them about a very intelligent poodle who had run after a crow in the yard, and the crow had looked round at him and said: "Oh, you scamp!"

The poodle, not knowing he had to do with a learned crow, was fearfully confused and retreated in perplexity, then began barking. . . .

"No, I had better love Gruzdev," Nadya decided, and she tore up the letter to Gorny.

She fell to thinking of the student, of his love, of her love; but the thoughts in her head insisted on flowing in all directions, and she thought about everything—about her mother, about the street, about the pencil, about the piano. . . . She thought of them joyfully, and felt that everything was good, splendid, and her joy told her that this was not all, that in a little while it would be better still. Soon it would be spring, summer, going with her mother to Gorbiki. Gorny would come for his furlough, would walk about the garden with her and make love to her. Gruzdev would come too. He would play croquet and skittles with her, and would tell her wonderful things. She had a passionate longing for the garden, the darkness, the pure sky, the stars. Again her shoulders shook with laughter, and it seemed to her that there was a scent of wormwood in the room and that a twig was tapping at the window.

She went to her bed, sat down, and not knowing what to do with the immense joy which filled her with yearning, she looked at the holy image hanging at the back of her bed, and said:

"Oh, Lord God! Oh, Lord God!"

The Black Monk

[Written in 1893 in the village of Melikhovo. First published in the January 1894 issue of *The Artist*, a Russian literary magazine. Collected in *The Lady with the Dog and Other Stories* (1917).]

I

Andrey Vassilitch Kovrin, who held a master's degree at the University, had exhausted himself, and had upset his nerves. He did not send for a doctor, but casually, over a bottle of wine, he spoke to a friend who was a doctor, and the latter advised him to spend the spring and summer in the country. Very opportunely a long letter came from Tanya Pesotsky, who asked him to come and stay with them at Borissovka. And he made up his mind that he really must go.

To begin with—that was in April—he went to his own home, Kovrinka, and there spent three weeks in solitude; then, as soon as the roads were in good condition, he set off, driving in a carriage, to visit Pesotsky, his former guardian, who had brought him up, and was a horticulturist well known all over Russia. The distance from Kovrinka to Borissovka was reckoned only a little over fifty miles. To drive along a soft road in May in a comfortable carriage with springs was a real pleasure.

Pesotsky had an immense house with columns and lions, off which the stucco was peeling, and with a footman in swallow-tails at the entrance. The old park, laid out in the English style, gloomy and severe, stretched for almost three-quarters of a mile to the river, and there ended in a steep, precipitous clay bank, where pines grew with bare roots that looked like shaggy paws; the water shone below with an unfriendly gleam, and the peewits flew up with a plaintive cry, and there one always felt that one must sit down and write a ballad. But near the house itself, in the courtyard and orchard, which together with the nurseries covered ninety acres, it was all life and gaiety even in bad weather. Such marvellous roses, lilies, camellias; such tulips of all possible shades, from glistening white to sooty black—such a wealth of flowers, in fact, Kovrin had never seen anywhere as at Pesotsky's. It was only the beginning of spring, and the real glory of the flower beds was still hidden away in the hot-houses. But even the flowers along the avenues, and here and there in the flower beds, were enough to make one feel, as one walked about the garden, as though one were in a realm of tender colours, especially in the early morning when the dew was glistening on every petal.

What was the decorative part of the garden, and what Pesotsky contemptuously spoke of as rubbish, had at one time in his childhood given Kovrin an impression of fairyland.

Every sort of caprice, of elaborate monstrosity and mockery at Nature was here. There were espaliers of fruit trees, a pear tree in the shape of a pyramidal poplar, spherical oaks and lime trees, an apple tree in the shape of an umbrella, plum trees trained into arches, crests, candelabra, and even into the number 1862—the year when Pesotsky first took up horticulture. One came across, too, lovely, graceful trees with strong, straight stems like palms, and it was only by looking intently that one could recognise these trees as gooseberries or currants. But what made the garden most cheerful and gave it a lively air, was the continual coming and going in it, from early morning till evening; people with wheelbarrows, shovels, and watering-cans swarmed round the trees and bushes, in the avenues and the flower beds, like ants. . . .

Kovrin arrived at Pesotsky's at ten o'clock in the evening. He found Tanya and her father, Yegor Semyonitch, in great anxiety. The clear starlight sky and the thermometer foretold a frost towards morning, and meanwhile Ivan Karlovitch, the gardener, had gone to the town, and they had no one to rely upon. At supper they talked of nothing but the morning frost, and it was settled that Tanya should not go to bed, and between twelve and one should walk through the garden, and see that everything was done properly, and Yegor Semyonitch should get up at three o'clock or even earlier.

Kovrin sat with Tanya all the evening, and after midnight went out with her into the garden. It was cold. There was a strong smell of burning already in the garden. In the big orchard, which was called the commercial garden, and which brought Yegor Semyonitch several thousand clear profit, a thick, black, acrid smoke was creeping over the ground and, curling around the trees, was saving those thousands from the frost. Here the trees were arranged as on a chessboard, in straight and regular rows like ranks of soldiers, and this severe pedantic regularity, and the fact that all the trees were of the same size, and had tops and trunks all exactly alike, made them look monotonous and even dreary. Kovrin and Tanya walked along the rows where fires of dung, straw, and all sorts of refuse were smouldering, and from time to time they were met by labourers who wandered in the smoke like shadows. The only trees in flower were the cherries, plums, and certain sorts of apples, but the whole garden was plunged in smoke, and it was only near the nurseries that Kovrin could breathe freely.

"Even as a child I used to sneeze from the smoke here," he said, shrugging his shoulders, "but to this day I don't understand how smoke can keep off frost."

"Smoke takes the place of clouds when there are none . . ." answered Tanya.

"And what do you want clouds for?"

"In overcast and cloudy weather there is no frost."

"You don't say so."

He laughed and took her arm. Her broad, very earnest face, chilled with the frost, with her delicate black eyebrows, the turned-up collar of her coat, which prevented her moving her head freely, and the whole of her thin, graceful figure, with her skirts tucked up on account of the dew, touched him.

"Good heavens! she is grown up," he said. "When I went away from here last, five years ago, you were still a child. You were such a thin, longlegged creature, with your hair hanging on your shoulders; you used to wear short frocks, and I used to tease you, calling you a heron. . . . What time does!"

"Yes, five years!" sighed Tanya. "Much water has flowed since then. Tell me, Andryusha, honestly," she began eagerly, looking him in the face: "do you feel strange with us now? But why do I ask you? You are a man, you live your own interesting life, you are somebody. . . . To grow apart is so natural! But however that may be, Andryusha, I want you to think of us as your people. We have a right to that."

"I do, Tanya."

"On your word of honour?"

"Yes, on my word of honour."

"You were surprised this evening that we have so many of your photographs. You know my father adores you. Sometimes it seems to me that he loves you more than he does me. He is proud of you. You are a clever, extraordinary man, you have made a brilliant career for yourself, and he is persuaded that you have turned out like this because he brought you up. I don't try to prevent him from thinking so. Let him."

Dawn was already beginning, and that was especially perceptible from the distinctness with which the coils of smoke and the tops of the trees began to stand out in the air.

"It's time we were asleep, though," said Tanya, "and it's cold, too." She took his arm. "Thank you for coming, Andryusha. We have only uninteresting acquaintances, and not many of them. We have only the garden, the garden, the garden, and nothing else. Standards, half-standards," she laughed. "Aports, Reinettes, Borovinkas, budded stocks, grafted stocks. . . . All, all our life has gone into the garden. I never even dream of anything but apples and pears. Of course, it is very nice and useful, but sometimes one longs for something else for variety. I remember that when you used to come to us for the summer holidays, or simply a visit, it always seemed to be fresher and brighter in the house, as though the covers had been taken off the lustres and the furniture. I was only a little girl then, but yet I understood it."

She talked a long while and with great feeling. For some reason the idea came into his head that in the course of the summer he might grow fond of this little, weak, talkative creature, might be carried away and fall in love; in their position it was so possible and natural! This thought touched and amused him; he bent down to her sweet, preoccupied face and hummed softly:

> "'Onyegin, I won't conceal it;
> I madly love Tatiana. . . .'"

By the time they reached the house, Yegor Semyonitch had got up. Kovrin did not feel sleepy; he talked to the old man and went to the garden with him. Yegor Semyonitch was a tall, broad-shouldered, corpulent man, and he suffered from asthma, yet he walked so fast that it was hard work to hurry after him. He had an extremely preoccupied air; he was always hurrying somewhere, with an expression that suggested that if he were one minute late all would be ruined!

"Here is a business, brother . . ." he began, standing still to take breath. "On the surface of the ground, as you see, is frost; but if you raise the thermometer on a stick fourteen feet above the ground, there it is warm. . . . Why is that?"

"I really don't know," said Kovrin, and he laughed.

"H'm! . . . One can't know everything, of course. . . . However large the intellect may be, you can't find room for everything in it. I suppose you still go in chiefly for philosophy?"

"Yes, I lecture in psychology; I am working at philosophy in general."

"And it does not bore you?"

"On the contrary, it's all I live for."

"Well, God bless you! . . ." said Yegor Semyonitch, meditatively stroking his grey whiskers. "God bless you! . . . I am delighted about you . . . delighted, my boy. . . ."

But suddenly he listened, and, with a terrible face, ran off and quickly disappeared behind the trees in a cloud of smoke.

"Who tied this horse to an apple tree?" Kovrin heard his despairing, heart-rending cry. "Who is the low scoundrel who has dared to tie this horse to an apple tree? My God, my God! They have ruined everything; they have spoilt everything; they have done everything filthy, horrible, and abominable. The orchard's done for, the orchard's ruined. My God!"

When he came back to Kovrin, his face looked exhausted and mortified.

"What is one to do with these accursed people?" he said in a tearful voice, flinging up his hands. "Styopka was carting dung at night, and tied the horse to an apple tree! He twisted the reins round it, the rascal, as tightly as he could, so that the bark is rubbed off in three places. What do you think of that! I spoke to him and he stands like a post and only blinks his eyes. Hanging is too good for him."

Growing calmer, he embraced Kovrin and kissed him on the cheek.

"Well, God bless you! . . . God bless you! . . ." he muttered. "I am very glad you have come. Unutterably glad. . . . Thank you."

Then, with the same rapid step and preoccupied face, he made the round of the whole garden, and showed his former ward all his greenhouses and hot-houses, his covered-in garden, and two apiaries which he called the marvel of our century.

While they were walking the sun rose, flooding the garden with brilliant light. It grew warm. Foreseeing a long, bright, cheerful day, Kovrin recollected that it was only the beginning of May, and that he had before him a whole summer as bright, cheerful, and long; and suddenly there stirred in his bosom a joyous, youthful feeling, such as he used to experience in his childhood, running about in that garden. And he hugged the old man and kissed him affectionately. Both of them, feeling touched, went indoors and drank tea out of old-fashioned china cups, with cream and satisfying krendels made with milk and eggs; and these trifles reminded Kovrin again of his childhood and boyhood. The delightful present was blended with the impressions of the past that stirred within him; there was a tightness at his heart; yet he was happy.

He waited till Tanya was awake and had coffee with her, went for a walk, then went to his room and sat down to work. He read attentively, making notes, and from time to time raised his eyes to look out at the open windows or at the fresh, still dewy flowers in the vases on the table; and again he dropped his eyes to his book, and it seemed to him as though every vein in his body was quivering and fluttering with pleasure.

II

In the country he led just as nervous and restless a life as in town. He read and wrote a great deal, he studied Italian, and when he was out for a walk, thought with pleasure that he would soon sit down to work again. He slept so little that every one wondered at him; if he accidentally dozed for half an hour in the daytime, he would lie awake all night, and, after a sleepless night, would feel cheerful and vigorous as though nothing had happened.

He talked a great deal, drank wine, and smoked expensive cigars. Very often, almost every day, young ladies of neighbouring families would come to the Pesotskys', and would sing and play the piano with Tanya; sometimes a young neighbour who was a good violinist would come, too. Kovrin listened with eagerness to the music and singing, and was exhausted by it, and this showed itself by his eyes closing and his head falling to one side.

One day he was sitting on the balcony after evening tea, reading. At the same time, in the drawing room, Tanya taking soprano, one of the young ladies a contralto, and the young man with his violin, were practising a well-known serenade of Braga's. Kovrin listened to the words—they were Russian—and could not understand their meaning. At last, leaving his book and listening attentively, he understood: a maiden, full of sick fancies, heard one night in her garden mysterious sounds, so strange and lovely that she was obliged to recognise them as a holy harmony which is unintelligible to us mortals, and so flies back to heaven. Kovrin's eyes began to close. He got up, and in exhaustion walked up and down the drawing room, and then the dining room. When the singing was over he took Tanya's arm, and with her went out on the balcony.

"I have been all day thinking of a legend," he said. "I don't remember whether I have read it somewhere or heard it, but it is a strange and almost grotesque legend. To begin with, it is somewhat obscure. A thousand years ago a monk, dressed in black, wandered about the desert, somewhere in Syria or Arabia. . . . Some miles from where he was, some fisherman saw another black monk, who was moving slowly over the surface of a lake. This second monk was a mirage. Now forget all the laws of optics, which the legend does not recognise, and listen to the rest. From that mirage there was cast another mirage, then from that other a third, so that the image of the black monk began to be repeated endlessly from one layer of the atmosphere to another. So that he was seen at one time in Africa, at another in Spain, then in Italy, then in the Far North. . . . Then he passed out of the atmosphere of the earth, and now he is wandering all over the universe, still never coming into conditions in which he might disappear. Possibly he may be seen now in Mars or in some star of the Southern Cross. But, my dear, the real point on which the whole legend hangs lies in the fact that, exactly a thousand years from the day when the monk walked in the desert, the mirage will return to the atmosphere of the earth again and will appear to men. And it seems that the thousand years is almost up. . . . According to the legend, we may look out for the black monk today or tomorrow."

"A queer mirage," said Tanya, who did not like the legend.

"But the most wonderful part of it all," laughed Kovrin, "is that I simply cannot recall where I got this legend from. Have I read it somewhere? Have I heard it? Or perhaps I dreamed of the black monk. I swear I don't remember. But the legend interests me. I have been thinking about it all day."

Letting Tanya go back to her visitors, he went out of the house, and, lost in meditation, walked by the flower beds. The sun was already setting. The flowers, having just been watered, gave forth a damp, irritating fragrance. Indoors they began singing again, and in the distance the violin had the effect of a human voice. Kovrin, racking his brains to remember where he had read or heard the legend, turned slowly towards the park, and unconsciously went as far as the river. By a little path that ran along the steep bank, between the bare roots, he went down to the water, disturbed the peewits there and frightened two ducks. The last rays of the setting sun still threw light here and there on the gloomy pines, but it was quite dark on the surface of the river. Kovrin crossed to the other side by the narrow bridge. Before him lay a wide field covered with young rye not yet in blossom. There was no living habitation, no living soul in the distance, and it seemed as though the little path, if one went along it, would take one to the unknown, mysterious place where the sun had just gone down, and where the evening glow was flaming in immensity and splendour.

"How open, how free, how still it is here!" thought Kovrin, walking along the path. "And it feels as though all the world were watching me, hiding and waiting for me to understand it. . . ."

But then waves began running across the rye, and a light evening breeze softly touched his uncovered head. A minute later there was another gust of wind, but stronger—the rye began rustling, and he heard behind him the hollow murmur of the pines. Kovrin stood still in amazement. From the horizon there rose up to the sky, like a whirlwind or a waterspout, a tall black column. Its outline was indistinct, but from the first instant it could be seen that it was not standing still, but moving with fearful rapidity, moving straight towards Kovrin, and the nearer it came the smaller and the more distinct it was. Kovrin moved aside into the rye to make way for it, and only just had time to do so.

A monk, dressed in black, with a grey head and black eyebrows, his arms crossed over his breast, floated by him. . . . His bare feet did not touch the earth. After he had floated twenty feet beyond him, he looked round at Kovrin, and nodded to him with a friendly but sly smile. But what a pale, fearfully pale, thin face! Beginning to grow larger again, he flew across the river, collided noiselessly with the clay bank and pines, and passing through them, vanished like smoke.

"Why, you see," muttered Kovrin, "there must be truth in the legend."

Without trying to explain to himself the strange apparition, glad that he had succeeded in seeing so near and so distinctly, not only the monk's black garments, but even his face and eyes, agreeably excited, he went back to the house.

In the park and in the garden people were moving about quietly, in the house they were playing—so he alone had seen the monk. He had an intense desire to tell Tanya and Yegor Semyonitch, but he reflected that they would certainly think his words the ravings of delirium, and that would frighten them; he had better say nothing.

He laughed aloud, sang, and danced the mazurka; he was in high spirits, and all of them, the visitors and Tanya, thought he had a peculiar look, radiant and inspired, and that he was very interesting.

III

After supper, when the visitors had gone, he went to his room and lay down on the sofa: he wanted to think about the monk. But a minute later Tanya came in.

"Here, Andryusha; read father's articles," she said, giving him a bundle of pamphlets and proofs. "They are splendid articles. He writes capitally."

"Capitally, indeed!" said Yegor Semyonitch, following her and smiling constrainedly; he was ashamed. "Don't listen to her, please; don't read them! Though, if you want to go to sleep, read them by all means; they are a fine soporific."

"I think they are splendid articles," said Tanya, with deep conviction. "You read them, Andryusha, and persuade father to write oftener. He could write a complete manual of horticulture."

Yegor Semyonitch gave a forced laugh, blushed, and began uttering the phrases usually made use of by an embarrassed author. At last he began to give way.

"In that case, begin with Gaucher's article and these Russian articles," he muttered, turning over the pamphlets with a trembling hand, "or else you won't understand. Before you read my objections, you must know what I am objecting to. But it's all nonsense . . . tiresome stuff. Besides, I believe it's bedtime."

Tanya went away. Yegor Semyonitch sat down on the sofa by Kovrin and heaved a deep sigh.

"Yes, my boy . . ." he began after a pause. "That's how it is, my dear lecturer. Here I write articles, and take part in exhibitions, and receive medals. . . . Pesotsky, they say, has apples the size of a head, and Pesotsky, they say, has made his fortune with his garden. In short, 'Kotcheby is rich and glorious.' But one asks oneself: what is it all for? The garden is certainly fine, a model. It's not really a garden, but a regular institution, which is of the greatest public importance because it marks, so to say, a new era in Russian agriculture and Russian industry. But, what's it for? What's the object of it?"

"The fact speaks for itself."

"I do not mean in that sense. I meant to ask: what will happen to the garden when I die? In the condition in which you see it now, it would not be maintained for one month without me. The whole secret of success lies not in its being a big garden or a great number of labourers being employed in it, but in the fact that I love the work. Do you understand? I love it perhaps more than myself. Look at me; I do everything myself. I work from morning to night: I do all the grafting myself, the pruning myself, the planting myself. I do it all myself: when any one helps me I am jealous and irritable till I am rude. The whole secret lies in loving it—that is, in the sharp eye of the master; yes, and in the master's hands, and in the feeling that makes one, when one goes anywhere for an hour's visit, sit, ill at ease, with one's heart far away, afraid that something may have happened in the garden. But when I die, who will look after it? Who will work? The gardener? The labourers? Yes? But I will tell you, my dear fellow, the worst enemy in the garden is not a hare, not a cockchafer, and not the frost, but any outside person."

"And Tanya?" asked Kovrin, laughing. "She can't be more harmful than a hare? She loves the work and understands it."

"Yes, she loves it and understands it. If after my death the garden goes to her and she is the mistress, of course nothing better could be wished. But if, which God forbid, she should marry," Yegor Semyonitch whispered, and looked with a frightened look at Kovrin, "that's just it. If she marries and children come, she will have no time to think about the garden. What I fear most is: she will marry some fine gentleman, and he will be greedy, and he will let the garden to people who will run it for profit, and everything will go to the devil the very first year! In our work females are the scourge of God!"

Yegor Semyonitch sighed and paused for a while.

"Perhaps it is egoism, but I tell you frankly: I don't want Tanya to get married. I am afraid of it! There is one young dandy comes to see us, bringing his violin and scraping on it; I know Tanya will not marry him, I know it quite well; but I can't bear to see him! Altogether, my boy, I am very queer. I know that."

Yegor Semyonitch got up and walked about the room in excitement, and it was evident that he wanted to say something very important, but could not bring himself to it.

"I am very fond of you, and so I am going to speak to you openly," he decided at last, thrusting his hands into his pockets. "I deal plainly with certain delicate questions, and say exactly what I think, and I cannot endure so-called hidden thoughts. I will speak plainly: you are the only man to whom I should not be afraid to marry my daughter. You are a clever man with a good heart, and would not let my beloved work go to ruin; and the chief reason is that I love you as a son, and I am proud of you. If Tanya and you could get up a romance somehow, then—well! I should be very glad and even happy. I tell you this plainly, without mincing matters, like an honest man."

Kovrin laughed. Yegor Semyonitch opened the door to go out, and stood in the doorway.

"If Tanya and you had a son, I would make a horticulturist of him," he said, after a moment's thought. "However, this is idle dreaming. Goodnight."

Left alone, Kovrin settled himself more comfortably on the sofa and took up the articles. The title of one was "On Intercropping"; of another, "A few Words on the Remarks of Monsieur Z. concerning the Trenching of the Soil for a New Garden"; a third, "Additional Matter concerning Grafting with a Dormant Bud"; and they were all of the same sort. But what a restless, jerky tone! What nervous, almost hysterical passion!

Here was an article, one would have thought, with most peaceable and impersonal contents: the subject of it was the Russian Antonovsky Apple. But Yegor Semyonitch began it with "Audiatur altera pars," and finished it with "Sapienti sat"; and between these two quotations a perfect torrent of venomous phrases directed "at the learned ignorance of our recognised horticultural authorities, who observe Nature from the height of their university chairs," or at Monsieur Gaucher, "whose success has been the work of the vulgar and the dilettanti." And then followed an inappropriate, affected, and insincere regret that peasants who stole fruit and broke the branches could not nowadays be flogged.

"It is beautiful, charming, healthy work, but even in this there is strife and passion," thought Kovrin, "I suppose that everywhere and in all careers men of ideas are nervous, and marked by exaggerated sensitiveness. Most likely it must be so."

He thought of Tanya, who was so pleased with Yegor Semyonitch's articles. Small, pale, and so thin that her shoulder-blades stuck out, her eyes, wide and open, dark and intelligent, had an intent gaze, as though looking for something. She walked like her father with a little hurried step. She talked a great deal and was fond of arguing, accompanying every phrase, however insignificant, with expressive mimicry and gesticulation. No doubt she was nervous in the extreme.

Kovrin went on reading the articles, but he understood nothing of them, and flung them aside. The same pleasant excitement with which he had earlier in the evening danced the mazurka and listened to the music was now mastering him again and rousing a multitude of thoughts. He got up and began walking about the room, thinking about the black monk. It occurred to him that if this strange, supernatural monk had appeared to him only, that meant that he was ill and had reached the point of having hallucinations. This reflection frightened him, but not for long.

"But I am all right, and I am doing no harm to any one; so there is no harm in my hallucinations," he thought; and he felt happy again.

He sat down on the sofa and clasped his hands round his head. Restraining the unaccountable joy which filled his whole being, he then paced up and down again, and sat down to his work. But the thought that he read in the book did not satisfy him. He wanted something gigantic, unfathomable, stupendous. Towards morning he undressed and reluctantly went to bed: he ought to sleep.

When he heard the footsteps of Yegor Semyonitch going out into the garden, Kovrin rang the bell and asked the footman to bring him some wine. He drank several glasses of Lafitte, then wrapped himself up, head and all; his consciousness grew clouded and he fell asleep.

IV

Yegor Semyonitch and Tanya often quarrelled and said nasty things to each other.

They quarrelled about something that morning. Tanya burst out crying and went to her room. She would not come down to dinner nor to tea. At first Yegor Semyonitch went about looking sulky and dignified, as though to give every one to understand that for him the claims of justice and good order were more important than anything else in the world; but he could not keep it up for long, and soon sank into depression. He walked about the park dejectedly, continually sighing: "Oh, my God! My God!" and at dinner did not eat a morsel. At last, guilty and conscience-stricken, he knocked at the locked door and called timidly:

"Tanya! Tanya!"

And from behind the door came a faint voice, weak with crying but still determined:

"Leave me alone, if you please."

The depression of the master and mistress was reflected in the whole household, even in the labourers working in the garden. Kovrin was absorbed in his interesting work, but at last he, too, felt dreary and uncomfortable. To dissipate the general ill-humour in some way, he made up his mind to intervene, and towards evening he knocked at Tanya's door. He was admitted.

"Fie, fie, for shame!" he began playfully, looking with surprise at Tanya's tear-stained, woebegone face, flushed in patches with crying. "Is it really so serious? Fie, fie!"

"But if you knew how he tortures me!" she said, and floods of scalding tears streamed from her big eyes. "He torments me to death," she went on, wringing her hands. "I said nothing to him . . . nothing . . . I only said that there was no need to keep . . . too many labourers . . . if we could hire them by the day when we wanted them. You know . . . you know the labourers have been doing nothing for a whole week. . . . I . . . I . . . only said that, and he shouted and . . . said . . . a lot of horrible insulting things to me. What for?"

"There, there," said Kovrin, smoothing her hair. "You've quarrelled with each other, you've cried, and that's enough. You must not be angry for long—that's wrong . . . all the more as he loves you beyond everything."

"He has . . . has spoiled my whole life," Tanya went on, sobbing. "I hear nothing but abuse and . . . insults. He thinks I am of no use in the house. Well! He is right. I shall go away tomorrow; I shall become a telegraph clerk. . . . I don't care. . . ."

"Come, come, come. . . . You mustn't cry, Tanya. You mustn't, dear. . . . You are both hot-tempered and irritable, and you are both to blame. Come along; I will reconcile you."

Kovrin talked affectionately and persuasively, while she went on crying, twitching her shoulders and wringing her hands, as though some terrible misfortune had really befallen her. He felt all the sorrier for her because her grief was not a serious one, yet she suffered extremely. What trivialities were enough to make this little creature miserable for a whole day, perhaps for her whole life! Comforting Tanya, Kovrin thought that, apart from this girl and her father, he might hunt the world over and would not find people who would love him as one of themselves, as one of their kindred. If it had not been for those two he might very likely, having lost his father and mother in early childhood, never to the day of his death have known what was meant by genuine affection and that naïve, uncritical love which is only lavished on very close blood relations; and he felt that the nerves of this weeping, shaking girl responded to his half-sick, overstrained nerves like iron to a magnet. He never could have loved a healthy, strong, rosy-cheeked woman, but pale, weak, unhappy Tanya attracted him.

And he liked stroking her hair and her shoulders, pressing her hand and wiping away her tears. . . . At last she left off crying. She went on for a long time complaining of her father and her hard, insufferable life in that house, entreating Kovrin to put himself in her place; then she began, little by little, smiling, and sighing that God had given her such a bad temper. At last, laughing aloud, she called herself a fool, and ran out of the room.

When a little later Kovrin went into the garden, Yegor Semyonitch and Tanya were walking side by side along an avenue as though nothing had happened, and both were eating rye bread with salt on it, as both were hungry.

V

Glad that he had been so successful in the part of peacemaker, Kovrin went into the park. Sitting on a garden seat, thinking, he heard the rattle of a carriage and a feminine laugh—visitors were arriving. When the shades of evening began falling on the garden, the sounds of the violin and singing voices reached him indistinctly, and that reminded him of the black monk. Where, in what land or in what planet, was that optical absurdity moving now?

Hardly had he recalled the legend and pictured in his imagination the dark apparition he had seen in the rye-field, when, from behind a pine tree exactly opposite, there came out noiselessly, without the slightest rustle, a man of medium height with uncovered grey head, all in black, and barefooted like a beggar, and his black eyebrows stood out conspicuously on his pale, death-like face. Nodding his head graciously, this beggar or pilgrim came noiselessly to the seat and sat down, and Kovrin recognised him as the black monk.

For a minute they looked at one another, Kovrin with amazement, and the monk with friendliness, and, just as before, a little slyness, as though he were thinking something to himself.

"But you are a mirage," said Kovrin. "Why are you here and sitting still? That does not fit in with the legend."

"That does not matter," the monk answered in a low voice, not immediately turning his face towards him. "The legend, the mirage, and I are all the products of your excited imagination. I am a phantom."

"Then you don't exist?" said Kovrin.

"You can think as you like," said the monk, with a faint smile. "I exist in your imagination, and your imagination is part of nature, so I exist in nature."

"You have a very old, wise, and extremely expressive face, as though you really had lived more than a thousand years," said Kovrin. "I did not know that my imagination was capable of creating such phenomena. But why do you look at me with such enthusiasm? Do you like me?"

"Yes, you are one of those few who are justly called the chosen of God. You do the service of eternal truth. Your thoughts, your designs, the marvellous studies you are engaged in, and all your life, bear the Divine, the heavenly stamp, seeing that they are consecrated to the rational and the beautiful—that is, to what is eternal."

"You said 'eternal truth.' . . . But is eternal truth of use to man and within his reach, if there is no eternal life?"

"There is eternal life," said the monk.

"Do you believe in the immortality of man?"

"Yes, of course. A grand, brilliant future is in store for you men. And the more there are like you on earth, the sooner will this future be realised. Without you who serve the higher principle and live in full understanding and freedom, mankind would be of little account; developing in a natural way, it would have to wait a long time for the end of its earthly history. You will lead it some thousands of years earlier into the kingdom of eternal truth—and therein lies your supreme service. You are the incarnation of the blessing of God, which rests upon men."

"And what is the object of eternal life?" asked Kovrin.

"As of all life—enjoyment. True enjoyment lies in knowledge, and eternal life provides innumerable and inexhaustible sources of knowledge, and in that sense it has been said: 'In My Father's house there are many mansions.'"

"If only you knew how pleasant it is to hear you!" said Kovrin, rubbing his hands with satisfaction.

"I am very glad."

"But I know that when you go away I shall be worried by the question of your reality. You are a phantom, an hallucination. So I am mentally deranged, not normal?"

"What if you are? Why trouble yourself? You are ill because you have overworked and exhausted yourself, and that means that you have sacrificed your health to the idea, and the time is near at hand when you will give up life itself to it. What could be better? That is the goal towards which all divinely endowed, noble natures strive."

"If I know I am mentally affected, can I trust myself?"

"And are you sure that the men of genius, whom all men trust, did not see phantoms, too? The learned say now that genius is allied to madness. My friend, healthy and normal people are only the common herd. Reflections upon the neurasthenia of the age, nervous exhaustion and degeneracy, et cetera, can only seriously agitate those who place the object of life in the present—that is, the common herd."

"The Romans used to say: *Mens sana in corpore sano*."

"Not everything the Greeks and the Romans said is true. Exaltation, enthusiasm, ecstasy—all that distinguishes prophets, poets, martyrs for the idea, from the common folk—is repellent to the animal side of man—that is, his physical health. I repeat, if you want to be healthy and normal, go to the common herd."

"Strange that you repeat what often comes into my mind," said Kovrin. "It is as though you had seen and overheard my secret thoughts. But don't let us talk about me. What do you mean by 'eternal truth'?"

The monk did not answer. Kovrin looked at him and could not distinguish his face. His features grew blurred and misty. Then the monk's head and arms disappeared; his body seemed merged into the seat and the evening twilight, and he vanished altogether.

"The hallucination is over," said Kovrin; and he laughed. "It's a pity."

He went back to the house, light-hearted and happy. The little the monk had said to him had flattered, not his vanity, but his whole soul, his whole being. To be one of the chosen, to serve eternal truth, to stand in the ranks of those who could make mankind worthy of the kingdom of God some thousands of years sooner—that is, to free men from some thousands of years of unnecessary struggle, sin, and suffering; to sacrifice to the idea everything—youth, strength, health; to be ready to die for the common weal—what an exalted, what a happy lot! He recalled his past—pure, chaste, laborious; he remembered what he had learned himself and what he had taught to others, and decided that there was no exaggeration in the monk's words.

Tanya came to meet him in the park: she was by now wearing a different dress.

"Are you here?" she said. "And we have been looking and looking for you. . . . But what is the matter with you?" she asked in wonder, glancing at his radiant, ecstatic face and eyes full of tears. "How strange you are, Andryusha!"

"I am pleased, Tanya," said Kovrin, laying his hand on her shoulders. "I am more than pleased: I am happy. Tanya, darling Tanya, you are an extraordinary, nice creature. Dear Tanya, I am so glad, I am so glad!"

He kissed both her hands ardently, and went on:

"I have just passed through an exalted, wonderful, unearthly moment. But I can't tell you all about it or you would call me mad and not believe me. Let us talk of you. Dear, delightful Tanya! I love you, and am used to loving you. To have you near me, to meet you a dozen times a day, has become a necessity of my existence; I don't know how I shall get on without you when I go back home."

"Oh," laughed Tanya, "you will forget about us in two days. We are humble people and you are a great man."

"No; let us talk in earnest!" he said. "I shall take you with me, Tanya. Yes? Will you come with me? Will you be mine?"

"Come," said Tanya, and tried to laugh again, but the laugh would not come, and patches of colour came into her face.

She began breathing quickly and walked very quickly, but not to the house, but further into the park.

"I was not thinking of it . . . I was not thinking of it," she said, wringing her hands in despair.

And Kovrin followed her and went on talking, with the same radiant, enthusiastic face:

"I want a love that will dominate me altogether; and that love only you, Tanya, can give me. I am happy! I am happy!"

She was overwhelmed, and huddling and shrinking together, seemed ten years older all at once, while he thought her beautiful and expressed his rapture aloud:

"How lovely she is!"

VI

Learning from Kovrin that not only a romance had been got up, but that there would even be a wedding, Yegor Semyonitch spent a long time in pacing from one corner of the room to the other, trying to conceal his agitation. His hands began trembling, his neck swelled and turned purple, he ordered his racing droshky and drove off somewhere. Tanya, seeing how he lashed the horse, and seeing how he pulled his cap over his ears, understood what he was feeling, shut herself up in her room, and cried the whole day.

In the hot-houses the peaches and plums were already ripe; the packing and sending off of these tender and fragile goods to Moscow took a great deal of care, work, and trouble. Owing to the fact that the summer was very hot and dry, it was necessary to water every tree, and a great deal of time and labour was spent on doing it. Numbers of caterpillars made their appearance, which, to Kovrin's disgust, the labourers and even Yegor Semyonitch and Tanya squashed with their fingers. In spite of all that, they had already to book autumn orders for fruit and trees, and to carry on a great deal of correspondence. And at the very busiest time, when no one seemed to have a free moment, the work of the fields carried off more than half their labourers from the garden. Yegor Semyonitch, sunburnt, exhausted, ill-humoured, galloped from the fields to the garden and back again; cried that he was being torn to pieces, and that he should put a bullet through his brains.

Then came the fuss and worry of the trousseau, to which the Pesotskys attached a good deal of importance. Every one's head was in a whirl from the snipping of the scissors, the rattle of the sewing-machine, the smell of hot irons, and the caprices of the dressmaker, a huffy and nervous lady. And, as ill-luck would have it, visitors came every day, who had to be entertained, fed, and even put up for the night. But all this hard labour passed unnoticed as though in a fog. Tanya felt that love and happiness had taken her unawares, though she had, since she was fourteen, for some reason been convinced that Kovrin would marry her and no one else. She was bewildered, could not grasp it, could not believe herself. . . . At one minute such joy would swoop down upon her that she longed to fly away to the clouds and there pray to God, at another moment she would remember that in August she would have to part from her home and leave her father; or, goodness knows why, the idea would occur to her that she was worthless—insignificant and unworthy of a great man like Kovrin—and she would go to her room, lock herself in, and cry bitterly for several hours. When there were visitors, she would suddenly fancy that Kovrin looked extraordinarily handsome, and that all the women were in love with him and envying her, and her soul was filled with pride and rapture, as though she had vanquished the whole world; but he had only to smile politely at any young lady for her to be trembling with jealousy, to retreat to her room—and tears again. These new sensations mastered her completely; she helped her father mechanically, without noticing peaches, caterpillars or labourers, or how rapidly the time was passing.

It was almost the same with Yegor Semyonitch. He worked from morning till night, was always in a hurry, was irritable, and flew into rages, but all of this was in a sort of spellbound dream. It seemed as though there were two men in him: one was the real Yegor Semyonitch, who was moved to indignation, and clutched his head in despair when he heard of some irregularity from Ivan Karlovitch the gardener; and another—not the real one—who seemed as though he were half drunk, would interrupt a business conversation at half a word, touch the gardener on the shoulder, and begin muttering:

"Say what you like, there is a great deal in blood. His mother was a wonderful woman, most high-minded and intelligent. It was a pleasure to look at her good, candid, pure face; it was like the face of an angel. She drew splendidly, wrote verses, spoke five foreign languages, sang. . . . Poor thing! she died of consumption.-The Kingdom of Heaven be hers."

The unreal Yegor Semyonitch sighed, and after a pause went on:

"When he was a boy and growing up in my house, he had the same angelic face, good and candid. The way he looks and talks and moves is as soft and elegant as his mother's. And his intellect! We were always struck with his intelligence. To be sure, it's not for nothing he's a Master of Arts! It's not for nothing! And wait a bit, Ivan Karlovitch, what will he be in ten years' time? He will be far above us!"

But at this point the real Yegor Semyonitch, suddenly coming to himself, would make a terrible face, would clutch his head and cry:

"The devils! They have spoilt everything! They have ruined everything! They have spoilt everything! The garden's done for, the garden's ruined!"

Kovrin, meanwhile, worked with the same ardour as before, and did not notice the general commotion. Love only added fuel to the flames. After every talk with Tanya he went to his room, happy and triumphant, took up his book or his manuscript with the same passion with which he had just kissed Tanya and told her of his love. What the black monk had told him of the chosen of God, of eternal truth, of the brilliant future of mankind and so on, gave peculiar and extraordinary significance to his work, and filled his soul with pride and the consciousness of his own exalted consequence. Once or twice a week, in the park or in the house, he met the black monk and had long conversations with him, but this did not alarm him, but, on the contrary, delighted him, as he was now firmly persuaded that such apparitions only visited the elect few who rise up above their fellows and devote themselves to the service of the idea.

One day the monk appeared at dinner-time and sat in the dining room window. Kovrin was delighted, and very adroitly began a conversation with Yegor Semyonitch and Tanya of what might be of interest to the monk; the black-robed visitor listened and nodded his head graciously, and Yegor Semyonitch and Tanya listened, too, and smiled gaily without suspecting that Kovrin was not talking to them but to his hallucination.

Imperceptibly the fast of the Assumption was approaching, and soon after came the wedding, which, at Yegor Semyonitch's urgent desire, was celebrated with "a flourish"—that is, with senseless festivities that lasted for two whole days and nights. Three thousand roubles' worth of food and drink was consumed, but the music of the wretched hired band, the noisy toasts, the scurrying to and fro of the footmen, the uproar and crowding, prevented them from appreciating the taste of the expensive wines and wonderful delicacies ordered from Moscow.

VII

One long winter night Kovrin was lying in bed, reading a French novel. Poor Tanya, who had headaches in the evenings from living in town, to which she was not accustomed, had been asleep a long while, and, from time to time, articulated some incoherent phrase in her restless dreams.

It struck three o'clock. Kovrin put out the light and lay down to sleep, lay for a long time with his eyes closed, but could not get to sleep because, as he fancied, the room was very hot and Tanya talked in her sleep. At half-past four he lighted the candle again, and this time he saw the black monk sitting in an armchair near the bed.

"Good morning," said the monk, and after a brief pause he asked: "What are you thinking of now?"

"Of fame," answered Kovrin. "In the French novel I have just been reading, there is a description of a young *savant*, who does silly things and pines away through worrying about fame. I can't understand such anxiety."

"Because you are wise. Your attitude towards fame is one of indifference, as towards a toy which no longer interests you."

"Yes, that is true."

"Renown does not allure you now. What is there flattering, amusing, or edifying in their carving your name on a tombstone, then time rubbing off the inscription together with the gilding? Moreover, happily there are too many of you for the weak memory of mankind to be able to retain your names."

"Of course," assented Kovrin. "Besides, why should they be remembered? But let us talk of something else. Of happiness, for instance. What is happiness?"

When the clock struck five, he was sitting on the bed, dangling his feet to the carpet, talking to the monk:

"In ancient times a happy man grew at last frightened of his happiness—it was so great!—and to propitiate the gods he brought as a sacrifice his favourite ring. Do you know, I, too, like Polykrates, begin to be uneasy of my happiness. It seems strange to me that from morning to night I feel nothing but joy; it fills my whole being and smothers all other feelings. I don't know what sadness, grief, or boredom is. Here I am not asleep; I suffer from sleeplessness, but I am not dull. I say it in earnest; I begin to feel perplexed."

"But why?" the monk asked in wonder. "Is joy a supernatural feeling? Ought it not to be the normal state of man? The more highly a man is developed on the intellectual and moral side, the more independent he is, the more pleasure life gives him. Socrates, Diogenes, and Marcus Aurelius, were joyful, not sorrowful. And the Apostle tells us: 'Rejoice continually'; 'Rejoice and be glad.'"

"But will the gods be suddenly wrathful?" Kovrin jested; and he laughed. "If they take from me comfort and make me go cold and hungry, it won't be very much to my taste."

Meanwhile Tanya woke up and looked with amazement and horror at her husband. He was talking, addressing the armchair, laughing and gesticulating; his eyes were gleaming, and there was something strange in his laugh.

"Andryusha, whom are you talking to?" she asked, clutching the hand he stretched out to the monk. "Andryusha! Whom?"

"Oh! Whom?" said Kovrin in confusion. "Why, to him. . . . He is sitting here," he said, pointing to the black monk.

"There is no one here . . . no one! Andryusha, you are ill!"

Tanya put her arm round her husband and held him tight, as though protecting him from the apparition, and put her hand over his eyes.

"You are ill!" she sobbed, trembling all over. "Forgive me, my precious, my dear one, but I have noticed for a long time that your mind is clouded in some way. . . . You are mentally ill, Andryusha. . . ."

Her trembling infected him, too. He glanced once more at the armchair, which was now empty, felt a sudden weakness in his arms and legs, was frightened, and began dressing.

"It's nothing, Tanya; it's nothing," he muttered, shivering. "I really am not quite well . . . it's time to admit that."

"I have noticed it for a long time . . . and father has noticed it," she said, trying to suppress her sobs. "You talk to yourself, smile somehow strangely . . . and can't sleep. Oh, my God, my God, save us!" she said in terror. "But don't be frightened, Andryusha; for God's sake don't be frightened. . . ."

She began dressing, too. Only now, looking at her, Kovrin realised the danger of his position—realised the meaning of the black monk and his conversations with him. It was clear to him now that he was mad.

Neither of them knew why they dressed and went into the dining room: she in front and he following her. There they found Yegor Semyonitch standing in his dressing gown and with a candle in his hand. He was staying with them, and had been awakened by Tanya's sobs.

"Don't be frightened, Andryusha," Tanya was saying, shivering as though in a fever; "don't be frightened. . . . Father, it will all pass over . . . it will all pass over. . . ."

Kovrin was too much agitated to speak. He wanted to say to his father-in-law in a playful tone: "Congratulate me; it appears I have gone out of my mind"; but he could only move his lips and smile bitterly.

At nine o'clock in the morning they put on his jacket and fur coat, wrapped him up in a shawl, and took him in a carriage to a doctor.

VIII

Summer had come again, and the doctor advised their going into the country. Kovrin had recovered; he had left off seeing the black monk, and he had only to get up his strength. Staying at his father-in-law's, he drank a great deal of milk, worked for only two hours out of the twenty-four, and neither smoked nor drank wine.

On the evening before Elijah's Day they had an evening service in the house. When the deacon was handing the priest the censer the immense old room smelt like a graveyard, and Kovrin felt bored. He went out into the garden. Without noticing the gorgeous flowers, he walked about the garden, sat down on a seat, then strolled about the park; reaching the river, he went down and then stood lost in thought, looking at the water. The sullen pines with their shaggy roots, which had seen him a year before so young, so joyful and confident, were not whispering now, but standing mute and motionless, as though they did not recognise him. And, indeed, his head was closely cropped, his beautiful long hair was gone, his step was lagging, his face was fuller and paler than last summer.

He crossed by the footbridge to the other side. Where the year before there had been rye the oats stood, reaped, and lay in rows. The sun had set and there was a broad stretch of glowing red on the horizon, a sign of windy weather next day. It was still. Looking in the direction from which the year before the black monk had first appeared, Kovrin stood for twenty minutes, till the evening glow had begun to fade. . . .

When, listless and dissatisfied, he returned home the service was over. Yegor Semyonitch and Tanya were sitting on the steps of the verandah, drinking tea. They were talking of something, but, seeing Kovrin, ceased at once, and he concluded from their faces that their talk had been about him.

"I believe it is time for you to have your milk," Tanya said to her husband.

"No, it is not time yet . . ." he said, sitting down on the bottom step. "Drink it yourself; I don't want it."

Tanya exchanged a troubled glance with her father, and said in a guilty voice:

"You notice yourself that milk does you good."

"Yes, a great deal of good!" Kovrin laughed. "I congratulate you: I have gained a pound in weight since Friday." He pressed his head tightly in his hands and said miserably: "Why, why have you cured me? Preparations of bromide, idleness, hot baths, supervision, cowardly consternation at every mouthful, at every step—all this will reduce me at last to idiocy. I went out of my mind, I had megalomania; but then I was cheerful, confident, and even happy; I was interesting and original. Now I have become more sensible and stolid, but I am just like every one else: I am—mediocrity; I am weary of life. . . . Oh, how cruelly you have treated

337

me! . . . I saw hallucinations, but what harm did that do to any one? I ask, what harm did that do any one?"

"Goodness knows what you are saying!" sighed Yegor Semyonitch. "It's positively wearisome to listen to it."

"Then don't listen."

The presence of other people, especially Yegor Semyonitch, irritated Kovrin now; he answered him drily, coldly, and even rudely, never looked at him but with irony and hatred, while Yegor Semyonitch was overcome with confusion and cleared his throat guiltily, though he was not conscious of any fault in himself. At a loss to understand why their charming and affectionate relations had changed so abruptly, Tanya huddled up to her father and looked anxiously in his face; she wanted to understand and could not understand, and all that was clear to her was that their relations were growing worse and worse every day, that of late her father had begun to look much older, and her husband had grown irritable, capricious, quarrelsome and uninteresting. She could not laugh or sing; at dinner she ate nothing; did not sleep for nights together, expecting something awful, and was so worn out that on one occasion she lay in a dead faint from dinner-time till evening. During the service she thought her father was crying, and now while the three of them were sitting together on the terrace she made an effort not to think of it.

"How fortunate Buddha, Mahomed, and Shakespeare were that their kind relations and doctors did not cure them of their ecstasy and their inspiration," said Kovrin. "If Mahomed had taken bromide for his nerves, had worked only two hours out of the twenty-four, and had drunk milk, that remarkable man would have left no more trace after him than his dog. Doctors and kind relations will succeed in stupefying mankind, in making mediocrity pass for genius and in bringing civilisation to ruin. If only you knew," Kovrin said with annoyance, "how grateful I am to you."

He felt intense irritation, and to avoid saying too much, he got up quickly and went into the house. It was still, and the fragrance of the tobacco plant and the marvel of Peru floated in at the open window. The moonlight lay in green patches on the floor and on the piano in the big dark dining room. Kovrin remembered the raptures of the previous summer when there had been the same scent of the marvel of Peru and the moon had shone in at the window. To bring back the mood of last year he went quickly to his study, lighted a strong cigar, and told the footman to bring him some wine. But the cigar left a bitter and disgusting taste in his mouth, and the wine had not the same flavour as it had the year before. And so great is the effect of giving up a habit, the cigar and the two gulps of wine made him giddy, and brought on palpitations of the heart, so that he was obliged to take bromide.

Before going to bed, Tanya said to him:

"Father adores you. You are cross with him about something, and it is killing him. Look at him; he is ageing, not from day to day, but from hour to hour. I entreat you, Andryusha, for God's sake, for the sake of your dead father, for the sake of my peace of mind, be affectionate to him."

"I can't, I don't want to."

"But why?" asked Tanya, beginning to tremble all over. "Explain why."

"Because he is antipathetic to me, that's all," said Kovrin carelessly; and he shrugged his shoulders. "But we won't talk about him: he is your father."

"I can't understand, I can't," said Tanya, pressing her hands to her temples and staring at a fixed point. "Something incomprehensible, awful, is going on in the house. You have changed, grown unlike yourself. . . . You, clever, extraordinary man as you are, are irritated over trifles, meddle in paltry nonsense. . . . Such trivial things excite you, that sometimes one is simply amazed and can't believe that it is you. Come, come, don't be angry, don't be angry," she went on, kissing his hands, frightened of her own words. "You are clever, kind, noble. You will be just to father. He is so good."

"He is not good; he is just good-natured. Burlesque old uncles like your father, with well-fed, good-natured faces, extraordinarily hospitable and queer, at one time used to touch me and amuse me in novels and in farces and in life; now I dislike them. They are egoists to the marrow of their bones. What disgusts me most of all is their being so well-fed, and that purely bovine, purely hoggish optimism of a full stomach."

Tanya sat down on the bed and laid her head on the pillow.

"This is torture," she said, and from her voice it was evident that she was utterly exhausted, and that it was hard for her to speak. "Not one moment of peace since the winter. . . . Why, it's awful! My God! I am wretched."

"Oh, of course, I am Herod, and you and your father are the innocents. Of course."

His face seemed to Tanya ugly and unpleasant. Hatred and an ironical expression did not suit him. And, indeed, she had noticed before that there was something lacking in his face, as though ever since his hair had been cut his face had changed, too. She wanted to say something wounding to him, but immediately she caught herself in this antagonistic feeling, she was frightened and went out of the bedroom.

IX

Kovrin received a professorship at the University. The inaugural address was fixed for the second of December, and a notice to that effect was hung up in the corridor at the University. But on the day appointed he informed the students' inspector, by telegram, that he was prevented by illness from giving the lecture.

He had hæmorrhage from the throat. He was often spitting blood, but it happened two or three times a month that there was a considerable loss of blood, and then he grew extremely weak and sank into a drowsy condition. This illness did not particularly frighten him, as he knew that his mother had lived for ten years or longer suffering from the same disease, and the doctors assured him that there was no danger, and had only advised him to avoid excitement, to lead a regular life, and to speak as little as possible.

In January again his lecture did not take place owing to the same reason, and in February it was too late to begin the course. It had to be postponed to the following year.

By now he was living not with Tanya, but with another woman, who was two years older than he was, and who looked after him as though he were a baby. He was in a calm and tranquil state of mind; he readily gave in to her, and when Varvara Nikolaevna—that was the name of his friend—decided to take him to the Crimea, he agreed, though he had a presentiment that no good would come of the trip.

They reached Sevastopol in the evening and stopped at an hotel to rest and go on the next day to Yalta. They were both exhausted by the journey. Varvara Nikolaevna had some tea, went to bed and was soon asleep. But Kovrin did not go to bed. An hour before starting for the station, he had received a letter from Tanya, and had not brought himself to open it, and now it was lying in his coat pocket, and the thought of it excited him disagreeably. At the bottom of his heart he genuinely considered now that his marriage to Tanya had been a mistake. He was glad that their separation was final, and the thought of that woman who in the end had turned into a living relic, still walking about though everything seemed dead in her except her big, staring, intelligent eyes—the thought of her roused in him nothing but pity and disgust with himself. The handwriting on the envelope reminded him how cruel and unjust he had been two years before, how he had worked off his anger at his spiritual emptiness, his boredom, his loneliness, and his dissatisfaction with life by revenging himself on people in no way to blame. He remembered, also, how he had torn up his dissertation and all the articles he had written during his illness, and how he had thrown them out of window, and the bits of paper had fluttered in the wind and caught on the trees and flowers. In every line of them he saw strange, utterly groundless pretension, shallow defiance, arrogance, megalomania; and they made him feel as though he were reading a description of his vices. But when the last manuscript had been torn up and sent flying out of window, he felt, for some reason, suddenly bitter and angry; he went to his wife and said a great many unpleasant things to her. My God, how he had tormented her! One day, wanting to cause her pain, he told her that her father had played a very unattractive part in their romance, that he had asked him to marry her. Yegor Semyonitch accidentally overheard this, ran into the room, and, in his despair, could not utter a word, could only stamp and make a strange, bellowing sound as though he had lost the power of speech, and Tanya, looking at her father, had uttered a heart-rending shriek and had fallen into a swoon. It was hideous.

All this came back into his memory as he looked at the familiar writing. Kovrin went out on to the balcony; it was still warm weather and there was a smell of the sea. The wonderful bay reflected the moonshine and the lights, and was of a colour for which it was difficult to find a name. It was a soft and tender blending of dark blue and green; in places the water was like blue vitriol, and in places it seemed as though the moonlight were liquefied and filling the bay instead of water. And what harmony of colours, what an atmosphere of peace, calm, and sublimity!

In the lower storey under the balcony the windows were probably open, for women's voices and laughter could be heard distinctly. Apparently there was an evening party.

Kovrin made an effort, tore open the envelope, and, going back into his room, read:

"My father is just dead. I owe that to you, for you have killed him. Our garden is being ruined; strangers are managing it already—that is, the very thing is happening that poor father dreaded. That, too, I owe to you. I hate you with my whole soul, and I hope you may soon perish. Oh, how wretched I am! Insufferable anguish is burning my soul. . . . My curses on you. I took you for an extraordinary man, a genius; I loved you, and you have turned out a madman. . . ."

Kovrin could read no more, he tore up the letter and threw it away. He was overcome by an uneasiness that was akin to terror. Varvara Nikolaevna was asleep behind the screen, and he could hear her breathing. From the lower storey came the sounds of laughter and women's voices, but he felt as though in the whole hotel there were no living soul but him. Because Tanya, unhappy, broken by sorrow, had cursed him in her letter and hoped for his perdition, he felt eerie and kept glancing hurriedly at the door, as though he were afraid that the uncomprehended force which two years before had wrought such havoc in his life and in the life of those near him might come into the room and master him once more.

He knew by experience that when his nerves were out of hand the best thing for him to do was to work. He must sit down to the table and force himself, at all costs, to concentrate his mind on some one thought. He took from his red portfolio a manuscript containing a sketch of a small work of the nature of a compilation, which he had planned in case he should find it dull in the Crimea without work. He sat down to the table and began working at this plan, and it seemed to him that his calm, peaceful, indifferent mood was coming back. The manuscript with the sketch even led him to meditation on the vanity of the world. He thought how much life exacts for the worthless or very commonplace blessings it can give a man. For instance, to gain, before forty, a university chair, to be an ordinary professor, to expound ordinary and second-hand thoughts in dull, heavy, insipid language— in fact, to gain the position of a mediocre learned man, he, Kovrin, had had to study for fifteen years, to work day and night, to endure a terrible mental illness, to experience an unhappy marriage, and to do a great number of stupid and unjust things which it would have been pleasant not to remember. Kovrin recognised clearly, now, that he was a mediocrity, and readily resigned himself to it, as he considered that every man ought to be satisfied with what he is.

The plan of the volume would have soothed him completely, but the torn letter showed white on the floor and prevented him from concentrating his attention. He got up from the table, picked up the pieces of the letter and threw them out of window, but there was a light wind blowing from the sea, and the bits of paper were scattered on the windowsill. Again he was overcome by uneasiness akin to terror, and he felt as though in the whole hotel there were no living soul but himself. . . . He went out on the balcony. The bay, like a living thing, looked at him with its multitude of light blue, dark blue, turquoise and fiery eyes, and seemed beckoning to him. And it really was hot and oppressive, and it would not have been amiss to have a bathe.

Suddenly in the lower storey under the balcony a violin began playing, and two soft feminine voices began singing. It was something familiar. The song was about a maiden, full of sick fancies, who heard one night in her garden mysterious sounds, so strange and lovely that she was obliged to recognise them as a holy harmony which is unintelligible to us mortals, and so flies back to heaven. . . . Kovrin caught his breath and there was a pang of sadness at his heart, and a thrill of the sweet, exquisite delight he had so long forgotten began to stir in his breast.

A tall black column, like a whirlwind or a waterspout, appeared on the further side of the bay. It moved with fearful rapidity across the bay, towards the hotel, growing smaller and darker as it came, and Kovrin only just had time to get out of the way to let it pass. . . . The monk with bare grey head, black eyebrows, barefoot, his arms crossed over his breast, floated by him, and stood still in the middle of the room.

"Why did you not believe me?" he asked reproachfully, looking affectionately at Kovrin. "If you had believed me then, that you were a genius, you would not have spent these two years so gloomily and so wretchedly."

Kovrin already believed that he was one of God's chosen and a genius; he vividly recalled his conversations with the monk in the past and tried to speak, but the blood flowed from his throat on to his breast, and not knowing what he was doing, he passed his hands over his breast, and his cuffs were soaked with blood. He tried to call Varvara Nikolaevna, who was asleep behind the screen; he made an effort and said:

"Tanya!"

He fell on the floor, and propping himself on his arms, called again: "Tanya!"

He called Tanya, called to the great garden with the gorgeous flowers sprinkled with dew, called to the park, the pines with their shaggy roots, the rye-field, his marvellous learning, his youth, courage, joy—called to life, which was so lovely. He saw on the floor near his face a great pool of blood, and was too weak to utter a word, but an unspeakable, infinite happiness flooded his whole being. Below, under the balcony, they were playing the serenade, and the black monk whispered to him that he was a genius, and that he was dying only because his frail human body had lost its balance and could no longer serve as the mortal garb of genius.

When Varvara Nikolaevna woke up and came out from behind the screen, Kovrin was dead, and a blissful smile was set upon his face.

Rothschild's Fiddle

[First published in February 1894 in *Russkiye Vedomosti*,
a Russian liberal daily newspaper. The story was adapted for
an opera by Veniamin Fleishman. Also translated as
'Rothchild's Violin.' Included in *The Chorus Girl and Other Stories* (1920).]

The town was a little one, worse than a village, and it was inhabited by scarcely any but old people who died with an infrequency that was really annoying. In the hospital and in the prison fortress very few coffins were needed. In fact business was bad. If Yakov Ivanov had been an undertaker in the chief town of the province he would certainly have had a house of his own, and people would have addressed him as Yakov Matveyitch; here in this wretched little town people called him simply Yakov; his nickname in the street was for some reason Bronze, and he lived in a poor way like a humble peasant, in a little old hut in which there was only one room, and in this room he and Marfa, the stove, a double bed, the coffins, his bench, and all their belongings were crowded together.

Yakov made good, solid coffins. For peasants and working people he made them to fit himself, and this was never unsuccessful, for there were none taller and stronger than he, even in the prison, though he was seventy. For gentry and for women he made them to measure, and used an iron foot-rule for the purpose. He was very unwilling to take orders for children's coffins, and made them straight off without measurements, contemptuously, and when he was paid for the work he always said:

"I must confess I don't like trumpery jobs."

Apart from his trade, playing the fiddle brought him in a small income.

The Jews' orchestra conducted by Moisey Ilyitch Shahkes, the tinsmith, who took more than half their receipts for himself, played as a rule at weddings in the town. As Yakov played very well on the fiddle, especially Russian songs, Shahkes sometimes invited him to join the orchestra at a fee of half a rouble a day, in addition to tips from the visitors. When Bronze sat in the orchestra first of all his face became crimson and perspiring; it was hot, there was a suffocating smell of garlic, the fiddle squeaked, the double bass wheezed close to his right ear, while the flute wailed at his left, played by a gaunt, red-haired Jew who had a perfect network of red and blue veins all over his face, and who bore the name of the famous millionaire Rothschild. And this accursed Jew contrived to play even the liveliest things plaintively. For no apparent reason Yakov little by little became possessed by hatred and contempt for the Jews, and especially for Rothschild; he began to pick quarrels with him, rail at him in unseemly language and once even tried to strike him, and Rothschild was offended and said, looking at him ferociously:

"If it were not that I respect you for your talent, I would have sent you flying out of the window."

Then he began to weep. And because of this Yakov was not often asked to play in the orchestra; he was only sent for in case of extreme necessity in the absence of one of the Jews.

Yakov was never in a good temper, as he was continually having to put up with terrible losses. For instance, it was a sin to work on Sundays or Saints' days, and Monday was an unlucky day, so that in the course of the year there were some two hundred days on which, whether he liked it or not, he had to sit with his hands folded. And only think, what a loss that meant. If anyone in the town had a wedding without music, or if Shahkes did not send for Yakov, that was a loss, too. The superintendent of the prison was ill for two years and was wasting away, and Yakov was impatiently waiting for him to die, but the superintendent went away to the chief town of the province to be doctored, and there took and died. There's a loss for you, ten roubles at least, as there would have been an expensive coffin to make, lined with brocade. The thought of his losses haunted Yakov, especially at night; he laid his fiddle on the bed beside him, and when all sorts of nonsensical ideas came into his mind he touched a string; the fiddle gave out a sound in the darkness, and he felt better.

On the sixth of May of the previous year Marfa had suddenly been taken ill. The old woman's breathing was laboured, she drank a great deal of water, and she staggered as she walked, yet she lighted the stove in the morning and even went herself to get water. Towards evening she lay down. Yakov played his fiddle all day; when it was quite dark he took the book in which he used every day to put down his losses, and, feeling dull, he began adding up the total for the year. It came to more than a thousand roubles. This so agitated him that he flung the reckoning beads down, and trampled them under his feet. Then he picked up the reckoning beads, and again spent a long time clicking with them and heaving deep, strained sighs. His face was crimson and wet with perspiration. He thought that if he had put that lost thousand roubles in the bank, the interest for a year would have been at least forty roubles, so that forty roubles was a loss too. In fact, wherever one turned there were losses and nothing else.

"Yakov!" Marfa called unexpectedly. "I am dying."

He looked round at his wife. Her face was rosy with fever, unusually bright and joyful-looking. Bronze, accustomed to seeing her face always pale, timid, and unhappy-looking, was bewildered. It looked as if she really were dying and were glad that she was going away for ever from that hut, from the coffins, and from Yakov. . . . And she gazed at the ceiling and moved her lips, and her expression was one of happiness, as though she saw death as her deliverer and were whispering with him.

It was daybreak; from the windows one could see the flush of dawn. Looking at the old woman, Yakov for some reason reflected that he had not once in his life been affectionate to her, had had no feeling for her, had never once thought to buy her a kerchief, or to bring her home some dainty from a wedding, but had done nothing but shout at her, scold her for his losses, shake his fists at her; it is true he had never actually beaten her, but he had frightened her, and at such times she had always been numb with terror. Why, he had forbidden her to drink tea because they spent too much without that, and she drank only hot water. And he understood why she had such a strange, joyful face now, and he was overcome with dread.

As soon as it was morning he borrowed a horse from a neighbour and took Marfa to the hospital. There were not many patients there, and so he had not long to wait, only three hours. To his great satisfaction the patients were not being received by the doctor, who was himself ill, but by the assistant, Maxim Nikolaitch, an old man of whom everyone in the town used to say that, though he drank and was quarrelsome, he knew more than the doctor.

"I wish you good day," said Yakov, leading his old woman into the consulting room. "You must excuse us, Maxim Nikolaitch, we are always troubling you with our trumpery affairs. Here you see my better half is ailing, the partner of my life, as they say, excuse the expression. . . ."

Knitting his grizzled brows and stroking his whiskers the assistant began to examine the old woman, and she sat on a stool, a wasted, bent figure with a sharp nose and open mouth, looking like a bird that wants to drink.

"H—m . . . Ah! . . ." the assistant said slowly, and he heaved a sigh. "Influenza and possibly fever. There's typhus in the town now. Well, the old woman has lived her life, thank God. . . . How old is she?"

"She'll be seventy in another year, Maxim Nikolaitch."

"Well, the old woman has lived her life, it's time to say goodbye."

"You are quite right in what you say, of course, Maxim Nikolaitch," said Yakov, smiling from politeness, "and we thank you feelingly for your kindness, but allow me to say every insect wants to live."

"To be sure," said the assistant, in a tone which suggested that it depended upon him whether the woman lived or died. "Well, then, my good fellow, put a cold compress on her head, and give her these powders twice a day, and so goodbye. Bonjour."

From the expression of his face Yakov saw that it was a bad case, and that no sort of powders would be any help; it was clear to him that Marfa would die very soon, if not today, tomorrow. He nudged the assistant's elbow, winked at him, and said in a low voice:

"If you would just cup her, Maxim Nikolaitch."

"I have no time, I have no time, my good fellow. Take your old woman and go in God's name. Goodbye."

"Be so gracious," Yakov besought him. "You know yourself that if, let us say, it were her stomach or her inside that were bad, then powders or drops, but you see she had got a chill! In a chill the first thing is to let blood, Maxim Nikolaitch."

But the assistant had already sent for the next patient, and a peasant woman came into the consulting room with a boy.

"Go along! go along," he said to Yakov, frowning. "It's no use to—"

"In that case put on leeches, anyway! Make us pray for you for ever."

The assistant flew into a rage and shouted:

"You speak to me again! You blockhead. . . ."

Yakov flew into a rage too, and he turned crimson all over, but he did not utter a word. He took Marfa on his arm and led her out of the room. Only when they were sitting in the cart he looked morosely and ironically at the hospital, and said:

"A nice set of artists they have settled here! No fear, but he would have cupped a rich man, but even a leech he grudges to the poor. The Herods!"

When they got home and went into the hut, Marfa stood for ten minutes holding on to the stove. It seemed to her that if she were to lie down Yakov would talk to her about his losses, and scold her for lying down and not wanting to work. Yakov looked at her drearily and thought that tomorrow was St. John the Divine's, and next day St. Nikolay the Wonder-worker's, and the day after that was Sunday, and then Monday, an unlucky day. For four days he would not be able to work, and most likely Marfa would die on one of those days; so he would have to make the coffin today. He picked up his iron rule, went up to the old woman and took her measure. Then she lay down, and he crossed himself and began making the coffin.

When the coffin was finished Bronze put on his spectacles and wrote in his book: "Marfa Ivanov's coffin, two roubles, forty kopecks."

And he heaved a sigh. The old woman lay all the time silent with her eyes closed. But in the evening, when it got dark, she suddenly called the old man.

"Do you remember, Yakov," she asked, looking at him joyfully. "Do you remember fifty years ago God gave us a little baby with flaxen hair? We used always to be sitting by the river then, singing songs . . . under the willows," and laughing bitterly, she added: "The baby girl died."

Yakov racked his memory, but could not remember the baby or the willows.

"It's your fancy," he said.

The priest arrived; he administered the sacrament and extreme unction. Then Marfa began muttering something unintelligible, and towards morning she died. Old women, neighbours, washed her, dressed her, and laid her in the coffin. To avoid paying the sacristan, Yakov read the psalms over the body himself, and they got nothing out of him for the grave, as the grave-digger was a crony of his. Four peasants carried the coffin to the graveyard, not for money, but from respect. The coffin was followed by old women, beggars, and a couple of crazy saints, and the people who met it crossed themselves piously. . . . And Yakov was very much pleased that it was so creditable, so decorous, and so cheap, and no offence to anyone. As he took his last leave of Marfa he touched the coffin and thought: "A good piece of work!"

But as he was going back from the cemetery he was overcome by acute depression. He didn't feel quite well: his breathing was laboured and feverish, his legs felt weak, and he had a craving for drink. And thoughts of all sorts forced themselves on his mind. He remembered again that all his life he had never felt for Marfa, had never been affectionate to her. The fifty-two years they had lived in the same hut had dragged on a long, long time, but it had somehow happened that in all that time he had never once thought of her, had paid no attention to her, as though she had been a cat or a dog. And yet, every day, she had lighted the stove, had cooked and baked, had gone for the water, had chopped the wood, had slept with him in the same bed, and when he came home drunk from the weddings always reverently hung his fiddle on the wall and put him to bed, and all this in silence, with a timid, anxious expression.

Rothschild, smiling and bowing, came to meet Yakov.

"I was looking for you, uncle," he said. "Moisey Ilyitch sends you his greetings and bids you come to him at once."

Yakov felt in no mood for this. He wanted to cry.

"Leave me alone," he said, and walked on.

"How can you," Rothschild said, fluttered, running on in front. "Moisey Ilyitch will be offended! He bade you come at once!"

Yakov was revolted at the Jew's gasping for breath and blinking, and having so many red freckles on his face. And it was disgusting to look at his green coat with black patches on it, and all his fragile, refined figure.

"Why are you pestering me, garlic?" shouted Yakov. "Don't persist!"

The Jew got angry and shouted too:

"Not so noisy, please, or I'll send you flying over the fence!"

"Get out of my sight!" roared Yakov, and rushed at him with his fists. "One can't live for you scabby Jews!"

Rothschild, half dead with terror, crouched down and waved his hands over his head, as though to ward off a blow; then he leapt up and ran away as fast as his legs could carry him: as he ran he gave little skips and kept clasping his hands, and Yakov could see how his long thin spine wriggled. Some boys, delighted at the incident, ran after him shouting "Jew! Jew!" Some dogs joined in the chase barking. Someone burst into a roar of laughter, then gave a whistle; the dogs barked with even more noise and unanimity. Then a dog must have bitten Rothschild, as a desperate, sickly scream was heard.

Yakov went for a walk on the grazing ground, then wandered on at random in the outskirts of the town, while the street boys shouted:

"Here's Bronze! Here's Bronze!"

He came to the river, where the curlews floated in the air uttering shrill cries and the ducks quacked. The sun was blazing hot, and there was a glitter from the water, so that it hurt the eyes to look at it. Yakov walked by a path along the bank and saw a plump, rosy-cheeked lady come out of the bathing-shed, and thought about her: "Ugh! you otter!"

Not far from the bathing-shed boys were catching crayfish with bits of meat; seeing him, they began shouting spitefully, "Bronze! Bronze!" And then he saw an old spreading willow tree with a big hollow in it, and a crow's nest on it. . . . And suddenly there rose up vividly in Yakov's memory a baby with flaxen hair, and the willow tree Marfa had spoken of. Why, that is it, the same willow-tree-green, still, and sorrowful. . . . How old it has grown, poor thing!

He sat down under it and began to recall the past. On the other bank, where now there was the water meadow, in those days there stood a big birchwood, and yonder on the bare hillside that could be seen on the horizon an old, old pine forest used to be a bluish patch in the distance. Big boats used to sail on the river. But now it was all smooth and unruffled, and on the other bank there stood now only one birch tree, youthful and slender like a young lady, and there was nothing on the river but ducks and geese, and it didn't look as though there had ever been boats on it. It seemed as though even the geese were fewer than of old. Yakov shut his eyes, and in his imagination huge flocks of white geese soared, meeting one another.

He wondered how it had happened that for the last forty or fifty years of his life he had never once been to the river, or if he had been by it he had not paid attention to it. Why, it was a decent sized river, not a trumpery one; he might have gone in for fishing and sold the fish to merchants, officials, and the bar-keeper at the station, and then have put money in the bank; he might have sailed in a boat from one house to another, playing the fiddle, and people of all classes would have paid to hear him; he might have tried getting big boats afloat again—that would be better than making coffins; he might have bred geese, killed them and sent them in the winter to Moscow. Why, the feathers alone would very likely mount up to ten roubles in the year. But he had wasted his time, he had done nothing of this. What losses! Ah! What losses! And if he had gone in for all those things at once—catching fish and playing the fiddle, and running boats and killing geese—what a fortune he would have made! But nothing of this had happened, even in his dreams; life had passed uselessly without any pleasure, had been wasted for nothing, not even a pinch of snuff; there was nothing left in front, and if one looked back—there was nothing there but losses, and such terrible ones, it made one cold all over. And why was it a man could not live so as to avoid these losses and misfortunes? One wondered why they had cut down the birch copse and the pine forest. Why was he walking with no reason on the grazing ground? Why do people always do what isn't needful? Why had Yakov all his life scolded, bellowed, shaken his fists, ill-treated his wife, and, one might ask, what necessity was there for him to frighten and insult the Jew that day? Why did people in general hinder each other from living? What losses were due to it! what terrible losses! If it were not for hatred and malice people would get immense benefit from one another.

In the evening and the night he had visions of the baby, of the willow, of fish, of slaughtered geese, and Marfa looking in profile like a bird that wants to drink, and the pale, pitiful face of Rothschild, and faces moved down from all sides and muttered of losses. He tossed from side to side, and got out of bed five times to play the fiddle.

In the morning he got up with an effort and went to the hospital. The same Maxim Nikolaitch told him to put a cold compress on his head, and gave him some powders, and from his tone and expression of face Yakov realized that it was a bad case and that no powders would be any use. As he went home afterwards, he reflected that death would be nothing but a benefit; he would not have to eat or drink, or pay taxes or offend people, and, as a man lies in his grave not for one year but for hundreds and thousands, if one reckoned it up the gain would be enormous. A man's life meant loss: death meant gain. This reflection was, of course, a just one, but yet it was bitter and mortifying; why was the order of the world so strange, that life, which is given to man only once, passes away without benefit?

He was not sorry to die, but at home, as soon as he saw his fiddle, it sent a pang to his heart and he felt sorry. He could not take the fiddle with him to the grave, and now it would be left forlorn, and the same thing would happen to it as to the birch copse and the pine forest. Everything in this world was wasted and would be wasted! Yakov went out of the hut and sat in the doorway, pressing the fiddle to his bosom. Thinking of his wasted, profitless life, he began to play, he did not know what, but it was plaintive and touching, and tears trickled down his cheeks. And the harder he thought, the more mournfully the fiddle wailed.

The latch clicked once and again, and Rothschild appeared at the gate. He walked across half the yard boldly, but seeing Yakov he stopped short, and seemed to shrink together, and probably from terror, began making signs with his hands as though he wanted to show on his fingers what o'clock it was.

"Come along, it's all right," said Yakov in a friendly tone, and he beckoned him to come up. "Come along!"

Looking at him mistrustfully and apprehensively, Rothschild began to advance, and stopped seven feet off.

"Be so good as not to beat me," he said, ducking. "Moisey Ilyitch has sent me again. 'Don't be afraid,' he said; 'go to Yakov again and tell him,' he said, 'we can't get on without him.' There is a wedding on Wednesday. . . . Ye—es! Mr. Shapovalov is marrying his daughter to a good man. . . . And it will be a grand wedding, oo-oo!" added the Jew, screwing up one eye.

"I can't come," said Yakov, breathing hard. "I'm ill, brother."

And he began playing again, and the tears gushed from his eyes on to the fiddle. Rothschild listened attentively, standing sideways to him and folding his arms on his chest. The scared and perplexed expression on his face, little by little, changed to a look of woe and suffering; he rolled his eyes as though he were experiencing an agonizing ecstasy, and articulated, "Vachhh!" and tears slowly ran down his cheeks and trickled on his greenish coat.

And Yakov lay in bed all the rest of the day grieving. In the evening, when the priest confessing him asked, Did he remember any special sin he had committed? straining his failing memory he thought again of Marfa's unhappy face, and the despairing shriek of the Jew when the dog bit him, and said, hardly audibly, "Give the fiddle to Rothschild."

"Very well," answered the priest.

And now everyone in the town asks where Rothschild got such a fine fiddle. Did he buy it or steal it? Or perhaps it had come to him as a pledge. He gave up the flute long ago, and now plays nothing but the fiddle. As plaintive sounds flow now from his bow, as came once from his flute, but when he tries to repeat what Yakov played, sitting in the doorway, the effect is something so sad and sorrowful that his audience weep, and he himself rolls his eyes and articulates "Vachhh! . . ." And this new air was so much liked in the town that the merchants and officials used to be continually sending for Rothschild and making him play it over and over again a dozen times.

The Student

[Written in Yalta. First published in *Russkie Vedomosti*,
a Russian newspaper, on April 16, 1894. First published
in English in the collection *The Witch and Other Stories* (1918).
Chekhov's personal favourite, it is one of his shortest stories.]

At first the weather was fine and still. The thrushes were calling, and in the swamps close by something alive droned pitifully with a sound like blowing into an empty bottle. A snipe flew by, and the shot aimed at it rang out with a gay, resounding note in the spring air. But when it began to get dark in the forest a cold, penetrating wind blew inappropriately from the east, and everything sank into silence. Needles of ice stretched across the pools, and it felt cheerless, remote, and lonely in the forest. There was a whiff of winter.

Ivan Velikopolsky, the son of a sacristan, and a student of the clerical academy, returning home from shooting, walked all the time by the path in the water-side meadow. His fingers were numb and his face was burning with the wind. It seemed to him that the cold that had suddenly come on had destroyed the order and harmony of things, that nature itself felt ill at ease, and that was why the evening darkness was falling more rapidly than usual. All around it was deserted and peculiarly gloomy. The only light was one gleaming in the widows' gardens near the river; the village, over three miles away, and everything in the distance all round was plunged in the cold evening mist. The student remembered that, as he went out from the house, his mother was sitting barefoot on the floor in the entry, cleaning the samovar, while his father lay on the stove coughing; as it was Good Friday nothing had been cooked, and the student was terribly hungry. And now, shrinking from the cold, he thought that just such a wind had blown in the days of Rurik and in the time of Ivan the Terrible and Peter, and in their time there had been just the same desperate poverty and hunger, the same thatched roofs with holes in them, ignorance, misery, the same desolation around, the same darkness, the same feeling of oppression—all these had existed, did exist, and would exist, and the lapse of a thousand years would make life no better. And he did not want to go home.

The gardens were called the widows' because they were kept by two widows, mother and daughter. A camp fire was burning brightly with a crackling sound, throwing out light far around on the ploughed earth. The widow Vasilisa, a tall, fat old woman in a man's coat, was standing by and looking thoughtfully into the fire; her daughter Lukerya, a little pock-marked woman with a stupid-looking face, was sitting on the ground, washing a caldron and spoons. Apparently they had just had supper. There was a sound of men's voices; it was the labourers watering their horses at the river.

"Here you have winter back again," said the student, going up to the camp fire. "Good evening."

Vasilisa started, but at once recognized him and smiled cordially.

"I did not know you; God bless you," she said.

"You'll be rich."

They talked. Vasilisa, a woman of experience, who had been in service with the gentry, first as a wet-nurse, afterwards as a children's nurse, expressed herself with refinement, and a soft, sedate smile never left her face; her daughter Lukerya, a village peasant woman, who had been beaten by her husband, simply screwed up her eyes at the student and said nothing, and she had a strange expression like that of a deaf mute.

"At just such a fire the Apostle Peter warmed himself," said the student, stretching out his hands to the fire, "so it must have been cold then, too. Ah, what a terrible night it must have been, granny! An utterly dismal long night!"

He looked round at the darkness, shook his head abruptly and asked:

"No doubt you have been at the reading of the Twelve Gospels?"

"Yes, I have," answered Vasilisa.

"If you remember at the Last Supper Peter said to Jesus, 'I am ready to go with Thee into darkness and unto death.' And our Lord answered him thus: 'I say unto thee, Peter, before the cock croweth thou wilt have denied Me thrice.' After the supper Jesus went through the agony of death in the garden and prayed, and poor Peter was weary in spirit and faint, his eyelids were heavy and he could not struggle against sleep. He fell asleep. Then you heard how Judas the same night kissed Jesus and betrayed Him to His tormentors. They took Him bound to the high priest and beat Him, while Peter, exhausted, worn out with misery and alarm, hardly awake, you know, feeling that something awful was just going to happen on earth, followed behind. . . . He loved Jesus passionately, intensely, and now he saw from far off how He was beaten . . ."

Lukerya left the spoons and fixed an immovable stare upon the student.

"They came to the high priest's," he went on; "they began to question Jesus, and meantime the labourers made a fire in the yard as it was cold, and warmed themselves. Peter, too, stood with them near the fire and warmed himself as I am doing. A woman, seeing him, said: 'He was with Jesus, too'—that is as much as to say that he, too, should be taken to be questioned. And all the labourers that were standing near the fire must have looked sourly and suspiciously at him, because he was confused and said: 'I don't know Him.' A little while after again someone recognized him as one of Jesus' disciples and said: 'Thou, too, art one of them,' but again he denied it. And for the third time someone turned to him: 'Why, did I not see thee with Him in the garden today?' For the third time he denied it. And immediately after that time the cock crowed, and Peter, looking from afar off at Jesus, remembered the words He had said to him in the evening. . . . He remembered, he came to himself, went out of the yard and wept bitterly—bitterly. In the Gospel it is written: 'He went out and wept bitterly.' I imagine it: the still, still, dark, dark garden, and in the stillness, faintly audible, smothered sobbing . . ."

The student sighed and sank into thought. Still smiling, Vasilisa suddenly gave a gulp, big tears flowed freely down her cheeks, and she screened her face from the fire with her sleeve as though ashamed of her tears, and Lukerya, staring immovably at the student, flushed crimson, and her expression became strained and heavy like that of someone enduring intense pain.

The labourers came back from the river, and one of them riding a horse was quite near, and the light from the fire quivered upon him.

The student said goodnight to the widows and went on. And again the darkness was about him and his fingers began to be numb. A cruel wind was blowing, winter really had come back and it did not feel as though Easter would be the day after tomorrow.

Now the student was thinking about Vasilisa: since she had shed tears all that had happened to Peter the night before the Crucifixion must have some relation to her. . . .

He looked round. The solitary light was still gleaming in the darkness and no figures could be seen near it now. The student thought again that if Vasilisa had shed tears, and her daughter had been troubled, it was evident that what he had just been telling them about, which had happened nineteen centuries ago, had a relation to the present—to both women, to the desolate village, to himself, to all people. The old woman had wept, not because he could tell the story touchingly, but because Peter was near to her, because her whole being was interested in what was passing in Peter's soul.

And joy suddenly stirred in his soul, and he even stopped for a minute to take breath. "The past," he thought, "is linked with the present by an unbroken chain of events flowing one out of another." And it seemed to him that he had just seen both ends of that chain; that when he touched one end the other quivered.

When he crossed the river by the ferry boat and afterwards, mounting the hill, looked at his village and towards the west where the cold crimson sunset lay a narrow streak of light, he thought that truth and beauty which had guided human life there in the garden and in the yard of the high priest had continued without interruption to this day, and had evidently always been the chief thing in human life and in all earthly life, indeed; and the feeling of youth, health, vigour—he was only twenty-two—and the inexpressible sweet expectation of happiness, of unknown mysterious happiness, took possession of him little by little, and life seemed to him enchanting, marvellous, and full of lofty meaning.

'Anna on the Neck'

[First published on October 22, 1895,
in *Russkiye Vedomosti*, a Russian liberal daily newspaper.
Collected in *The Party and Other Stories* (1917).]

I

After the wedding they had not even light refreshments; the happy pair simply drank a glass of champagne, changed into their travelling things, and drove to the station. Instead of a gay wedding ball and supper, instead of music and dancing, they went on a journey to pray at a shrine a hundred and fifty miles away. Many people commended this, saying that Modest Alexeitch was a man high up in the service and no longer young, and that a noisy wedding might not have seemed quite suitable; and music is apt to sound dreary when a government official of fifty-two marries a girl who is only just eighteen. People said, too, that Modest Alexeitch, being a man of principle, had arranged this visit to the monastery expressly in order to make his young bride realize that even in marriage he put religion and morality above everything.

The happy pair were seen off at the station. The crowd of relations and colleagues in the service stood, with glasses in their hands, waiting for the train to start to shout "Hurrah!" and the bride's father, Pyotr Leontyitch, wearing a top-hat and the uniform of a teacher, already drunk and very pale, kept craning towards the window, glass in hand and saying in an imploring voice:

"Anyuta! Anya, Anya! one word!"

Anna bent out of the window to him, and he whispered something to her, enveloping her in a stale smell of alcohol, blew into her ear—she could make out nothing—and made the sign of the cross over her face, her bosom, and her hands; meanwhile he was breathing in gasps and tears were shining in his eyes. And the schoolboys, Anna's brothers, Petya and Andrusha, pulled at his coat from behind, whispering in confusion:

"Father, hush! . . . Father, that's enough. . . ."

When the train started, Anna saw her father run a little way after the train, staggering and spilling his wine, and what a kind, guilty, pitiful face he had:

"Hurra—ah!" he shouted.

The happy pair were left alone. Modest Alexeitch looked about the compartment, arranged their things on the shelves, and sat down, smiling, opposite his young wife. He was an official of medium height, rather stout and puffy, who looked exceedingly well nourished, with long whiskers and no moustache. His clean-shaven, round, sharply defined chin looked like the heel of a foot. The most characteristic point in his face was the absence of moustache, the bare, freshly shaven place, which gradually passed into the fat cheeks, quivering like jelly. His deportment was dignified, his movements were deliberate, his manner was soft.

"I cannot help remembering now one circumstance," he said, smiling. "When, five years ago, Kosorotov received the order of St. Anna of the second grade, and went to thank His Excellency, His Excellency expressed himself as follows: 'So now you have three Annas: one in your buttonhole and two on your neck.' And it must be explained that at that time Kosorotov's wife, a quarrelsome and frivolous person, had just returned to him, and that her name was Anna. I trust that when I receive the Anna of the second grade His Excellency will not have occasion to say the same thing to me."

He smiled with his little eyes. And she, too, smiled, troubled at the thought that at any moment this man might kiss her with his thick damp lips, and that she had no right to prevent his doing so. The soft movements of his fat person frightened her; she felt both fear and disgust. He got up, without haste took off the order from his neck, took off his coat and waistcoat, and put on his dressing gown.

"That's better," he said, sitting down beside Anna.

Anna remembered what agony the wedding had been, when it had seemed to her that the priest, and the guests, and every one in church had been looking at her sorrowfully and asking why, why was she, such a sweet, nice girl, marrying such an elderly, uninteresting gentleman. Only that morning she was delighted that everything had been satisfactorily arranged, but at the time of the wedding, and now in the railway carriage, she felt cheated, guilty, and ridiculous. Here she had married a rich man and yet she had no money, her wedding-dress had been bought on credit, and when her father and brothers had been saying goodbye, she could see from their faces that they had not a farthing. Would they have any supper that day? And tomorrow? And for some reason it seemed to her that her father and the boys were sitting tonight hungry without her, and feeling the same misery as they had the day after their mother's funeral.

"Oh, how unhappy I am!" she thought. "Why am I so unhappy?"

With the awkwardness of a man with settled habits, unaccustomed to deal with women, Modest Alexeitch touched her on the waist and patted her on the shoulder, while she went on thinking about money, about her mother and her mother's death. When her mother died, her father, Pyotr Leontyitch, a teacher of drawing and writing in the high school, had taken to drink, impoverishment had followed, the boys had not had boots or goloshes, their father had been hauled up before the magistrate, the warrant officer had come and made an inventory of the furniture. . . . What a disgrace! Anna had had to look after her drunken father, darn her brothers' stockings, go to market, and when she was complimented on her youth, her beauty, and her elegant manners, it seemed to her that every one was looking at her cheap hat and the holes in her boots that were inked over. And at night there had been tears and a haunting dread that her father would soon, very soon, be dismissed from the school for his weakness, and that he would not survive it, but would die, too, like their mother. But ladies of their acquaintance had taken the matter in hand and looked about for a good match for Anna. This Modest Alexevitch, who was neither young nor good-looking but had money, was soon found. He had a hundred thousand in the bank and the family estate, which he had let on lease. He was a man of principle and stood well with His Excellency; it would be nothing to him, so they told Anna, to get a note from His Excellency to the directors of the high school, or even to the Education Commissioner, to prevent Pyotr Leontyitch from being dismissed.

While she was recalling these details, she suddenly heard strains of music which floated in at the window, together with the sound of voices. The train was stopping at a station. In the crowd beyond the platform an accordion and a cheap squeaky fiddle were being briskly played, and the sound of a military band came from beyond the villas and the tall birches and poplars that lay bathed in the moonlight; there must have been a dance in the place. Summer visitors and townspeople, who used to come out here by train in fine weather for a breath of fresh air, were parading up and down on the platform. Among them was the wealthy owner of all the summer villas—a tall, stout, dark man called Artynov. He had prominent eyes and looked like an Armenian. He wore a strange costume; his shirt was unbuttoned, showing his chest; he wore high boots with spurs, and a black cloak hung from his shoulders and dragged on the ground like a train. Two boar-hounds followed him with their sharp noses to the ground.

Tears were still shining in Anna's eyes, but she was not thinking now of her mother, nor of money, nor of her marriage; but shaking hands with schoolboys and officers she knew, she laughed gaily and said quickly:

"How do you do? How are you?"

She went out on to the platform between the carriages into the moonlight, and stood so that they could all see her in her new splendid dress and hat.

"Why are we stopping here?" she asked.

"This is a junction. They are waiting for the mail train to pass."

Seeing that Artynov was looking at her, she screwed up her eyes coquettishly and began talking aloud in French; and because her voice sounded so pleasant, and because she heard music and the moon was reflected in the pond, and because Artynov, the notorious Don Juan and spoiled child of fortune, was looking at her eagerly and with curiosity, and because every one was in good spirits—she suddenly felt joyful, and when the train started and the officers of her acquaintance saluted her, she was humming the polka the strains of which reached her from the military band playing beyond the trees; and she returned to her compartment feeling as though it had been proved to her at the station that she would certainly be happy in spite of everything.

The happy pair spent two days at the monastery, then went back to town. They lived in a rent-free flat. When Modest Alexevitch had gone to the office, Anna played the piano, or shed tears of depression, or lay down on a couch and read novels or looked through fashion papers. At dinner Modest Alexevitch ate a great deal and talked about politics, about appointments, transfers, and promotions in the service, about the necessity of hard work, and said that, family life not being a pleasure but a duty, if you took care of the kopecks the roubles would take care of themselves, and that he put religion and morality before everything else in the world. And holding his knife in his fist as though it were a sword, he would say:

"Every one ought to have his duties!"

And Anna listened to him, was frightened, and could not eat, and she usually got up from the table hungry. After dinner her husband lay down for a nap and snored loudly, while Anna went to see her own people. Her father and the boys looked at her in a peculiar way, as though just before she came in they had been blaming her for having married for money a tedious, wearisome man she did not love; her rustling skirts, her bracelets, and her general air of a married lady, offended them and made them uncomfortable. In her presence they felt a little embarrassed and did not know what to talk to her about; but yet they still loved her as before, and were not used to having dinner without her. She sat down with them to cabbage soup, porridge, and fried potatoes, smelling of mutton dripping. Pyotr Leontyitch filled his glass from the decanter with a trembling hand and drank it off hurriedly, greedily, with repulsion, then poured out a second glass and then a third. Petya and Andrusha, thin, pale boys with big eyes, would take the decanter and say desperately:

"You mustn't, father. . . . Enough, father. . . ."

And Anna, too, was troubled and entreated him to drink no more; and he would suddenly fly into a rage and beat the table with his fists:

"I won't allow any one to dictate to me!" he would shout. "Wretched boys! wretched girl! I'll turn you all out!"

But there was a note of weakness, of good-nature in his voice, and no one was afraid of him. After dinner he usually dressed in his best. Pale, with a cut on his chin from shaving, craning his thin neck, he would stand for half an hour before the glass, prinking, combing his hair, twisting his black moustache, sprinkling himself with scent, tying his cravat in a bow; then he would put on his gloves and his top-hat, and go off to give his private lessons. Or if it was a holiday he would stay at home and paint, or play the harmonium, which wheezed and growled; he would try to wrest from it pure harmonious sounds and would sing to it; or would storm at the boys:

"Wretches! Good-for-nothing boys! You have spoiled the instrument!"

In the evening Anna's husband played cards with his colleagues, who lived under the same roof in the government quarters. The wives of these gentlemen would come in—ugly, tastelessly dressed women, as coarse as cooks—and gossip would begin in the flat as tasteless and unattractive as the ladies themselves. Sometimes Modest Alexevitch would take Anna to the theatre. In the intervals he would never let her stir a step from his side, but walked about arm in arm with her through the corridors and the foyer. When he bowed to some one, he immediately whispered to Anna: "A civil councillor . . . visits at His Excellency's"; or, "A man of means . . . has a house of his own." When they passed the buffet Anna had a great longing for something sweet; she was fond of chocolate and apple cakes, but she had no money, and she did not like to ask her husband. He would take a pear, pinch it with his fingers, and ask uncertainly:

"How much?"

"Twenty-five kopecks!"

"I say!" he would reply, and put it down; but as it was awkward to leave the buffet without buying anything, he would order some seltzer-water and drink the whole bottle himself, and tears would come into his eyes. And Anna hated him at such times.

And suddenly flushing crimson, he would say to her rapidly:

"Bow to that old lady!"

"But I don't know her."

"No matter. That's the wife of the director of the local treasury! Bow, I tell you," he would grumble insistently. "Your head won't drop off."

Anna bowed and her head certainly did not drop off, but it was agonizing. She did everything her husband wanted her to, and was furious with herself for having let him deceive her like the veriest idiot. She had only married him for his money, and yet she had less money now than before her marriage. In old days her father would sometimes give her twenty kopecks, but now she had not a farthing.

To take money by stealth or ask for it, she could not; she was afraid of her husband, she trembled before him. She felt as though she had been afraid of him for years. In her childhood the director of the high school had always seemed the most impressive and terrifying force in the world, sweeping down like a thunderstorm or a steam-engine ready to crush her; another similar force of which the whole family talked, and of which they were for some reason afraid, was His Excellency; then there were a dozen others, less formidable, and among them the teachers at the high school, with shaven upper lips, stern, implacable; and now finally, there was Modest Alexeitch, a man of principle, who even resembled the director in the face. And in Anna's imagination all these forces blended together into one, and, in the form of a terrible, huge white bear, menaced the weak and erring such as her father. And she was afraid to say anything in opposition to her husband, and gave a forced smile, and tried to make a show of pleasure when she was coarsely caressed and defiled by embraces that excited her terror. Only once Pyotr Leontyitch had the temerity to ask for a loan of fifty roubles in order to pay some very irksome debt, but what an agony it had been!

"Very good; I'll give it to you," said Modest Alexeitch after a moment's thought; "but I warn you I won't help you again till you give up drinking. Such a failing is disgraceful in a man in the government service! I must remind you of the well-known fact that many capable people have been ruined by that passion, though they might possibly, with temperance, have risen in time to a very high position."

And long-winded phrases followed: "inasmuch as . . .," "following upon which proposition . . .," "in view of the aforesaid contention . . ."; and Pyotr Leontyitch was in agonies of humiliation and felt an intense craving for alcohol.

And when the boys came to visit Anna, generally in broken boots and threadbare trousers, they, too, had to listen to sermons.

"Every man ought to have his duties!" Modest Alexeitch would say to them.

And he did not give them money. But he did give Anna bracelets, rings, and brooches, saying that these things would come in useful for a rainy day. And he often unlocked her drawer and made an inspection to see whether they were all safe.

Meanwhile winter came on. Long before Christmas there was an announcement in the local papers that the usual winter ball would take place on the twenty-ninth of December in the Hall of Nobility. Every evening after cards Modest Alexeitch was excitedly whispering with his colleagues' wives and glancing at Anna, and then paced up and down the room for a long while, thinking. At last, late one evening, he stood still, facing Anna, and said:

"You ought to get yourself a ball dress. Do you understand? Only please consult Marya Grigoryevna and Natalya Kuzminishna."

And he gave her a hundred roubles. She took the money, but she did not consult any one when she ordered the ball dress; she spoke to no one but her father, and tried to imagine how her mother would have dressed for a ball. Her mother had always dressed in the latest fashion and had always taken trouble over Anna, dressing her elegantly like a doll, and had taught her to speak French and dance the mazurka superbly (she had been a governess for five years before her marriage). Like her mother, Anna could make a new dress out of an old one, clean gloves with benzine, hire jewels; and, like her mother, she knew how to screw up her eyes, lisp, assume graceful attitudes, fly into raptures when necessary, and throw a mournful and enigmatic look into her eyes. And from her father she had inherited the dark colour of her hair and eyes, her highly-strung nerves, and the habit of always making herself look her best.

When, half an hour before setting off for the ball, Modest Alexeitch went into her room without his coat on, to put his order round his neck before her pier-glass, dazzled by her beauty and the splendour of her fresh, ethereal dress, he combed his whiskers complacently and said:

"So that's what my wife can look like . . . so that's what you can look like! Anyuta!" he went on, dropping into a tone of solemnity, "I have made your fortune, and now I beg you to do something for mine. I beg you to get introduced to the wife of His Excellency! For God's sake, do! Through her I may get the post of senior reporting clerk!"

They went to the ball. They reached the Hall of Nobility, the entrance with the hall porter. They came to the vestibule with the hat-stands, the fur coats; footmen scurrying about, and ladies with low necks putting up their fans to screen themselves from the draughts. There was a smell of gas and of soldiers. When Anna, walking upstairs on her husband's arm, heard the music and saw herself full length in the looking-glass in the full glow of the lights, there was a rush of joy in her heart, and she felt the same presentiment of happiness as in the moonlight at the station. She walked in proudly, confidently, for the first time feeling herself not a girl but a lady, and unconsciously imitating her mother in her walk and in her manner. And for the first time in her life she felt rich and free. Even her husband's presence did not oppress her, for as she crossed the threshold of the hall she had guessed instinctively that the proximity of an old husband did not detract from her in the least, but, on the contrary, gave her that shade of piquant mystery that is so attractive to men. The orchestra was already playing and the dances had begun. After their flat Anna was overwhelmed by the lights, the bright colours, the music, the noise, and looking round the room, thought, "Oh, how lovely!" She at once distinguished in the crowd all her acquaintances, every one she had met before at parties or on picnics—all the officers, the teachers, the lawyers, the officials, the landowners, His Excellency, Artynov, and the ladies of the highest standing, dressed up and very *décollettées*, handsome and ugly, who had already taken up their positions in the stalls and pavilions of the charity bazaar, to begin selling things for the benefit of the poor. A huge officer in epaulettes—she had been introduced to him in Staro-Kievsky Street when she was a schoolgirl, but now she could not remember his name—seemed to spring from out of the ground, begging her for a waltz, and she flew away from her husband, feeling as though she were floating away in a sailing-boat in a violent storm, while her husband was left far away on the shore. She danced passionately, with fervour, a waltz, then a polka and a quadrille, being snatched by one partner as soon as she was left by another, dizzy with music and the noise, mixing Russian with French, lisping, laughing, and with no thought of her husband or anything else. She excited great admiration among the men—that was evident, and indeed it could not have been otherwise; she was breathless with excitement, felt thirsty, and convulsively clutched her fan. Pyotr Leontyitch, her father, in a crumpled dress-coat that smelt of benzine, came up to her, offering her a plate of pink ice.

"You are enchanting this evening," he said, looking at her rapturously, "and I have never so much regretted that you were in such a hurry to get married. . . . What was it for? I know you did it for our sake, but . . ." With a shaking hand he drew out a roll of notes and said: "I got the money for my lessons today, and can pay your husband what I owe him."

She put the plate back into his hand, and was pounced upon by some one and borne off to a distance. She caught a glimpse over her partner's shoulder of her father gliding over the floor, putting his arm round a lady and whirling down the ballroom with her.

"How sweet he is when he is sober!" she thought.

She danced the mazurka with the same huge officer; he moved gravely, as heavily as a dead carcase in a uniform, twitched his shoulders and his chest, stamped his feet very languidly—he felt fearfully disinclined to dance. She fluttered round him, provoking him by her beauty, her bare neck; her eyes glowed defiantly, her movements were passionate, while he became more and more indifferent, and held out his hands to her as graciously as a king.

"Bravo, bravo!" said people watching them.

But little by little the huge officer, too, broke out; he grew lively, excited, and, overcome by her fascination, was carried away and danced lightly, youthfully, while she merely moved her shoulders and looked slyly at him as though she were now the queen and he were her slave; and at that moment it seemed to her that the whole room was looking at them, and that everybody was thrilled and envied them. The huge officer had hardly had time to thank her for the dance, when the crowd suddenly parted and the men drew themselves up in a strange way, with their hands at their sides.

His Excellency, with two stars on his dress-coat, was walking up to her. Yes, His Excellency was walking straight towards her, for he was staring directly at her with a sugary smile, while he licked his lips as he always did when he saw a pretty woman.

"Delighted, delighted . . ." he began. "I shall order your husband to be clapped in a lock-up for keeping such a treasure hidden from us till now. I've come to you with a message from my wife," he went on, offering her his arm. "You must help us. . . . M-m-yes. . . . We ought to give you the prize for beauty as they do in America. . . . M-m-yes. . . . The Americans. . . . My wife is expecting you impatiently."

He led her to a stall and presented her to a middle-aged lady, the lower part of whose face was disproportionately large, so that she looked as though she were holding a big stone in her mouth.

"You must help us," she said through her nose in a sing-song voice. "All the pretty women are working for our charity bazaar, and you are the only one enjoying yourself. Why won't you help us?"

She went away, and Anna took her place by the cups and the silver samovar. She was soon doing a lively trade. Anna asked no less than a rouble for a cup of tea, and made the huge officer drink three cups. Artynov, the rich man with prominent eyes, who suffered from asthma, came up, too; he was not dressed in the strange costume in which Anna had seen him in the summer at the station, but wore a dress-coat like every one else. Keeping his eyes fixed on Anna, he drank a glass of champagne and paid a hundred roubles for it, then drank some tea and gave another hundred—all this without saying a word, as he was short of breath through asthma. . . . Anna invited purchasers and got money out of them, firmly convinced by now that her smiles and glances could not fail to afford these people great pleasure. She realized now that she was created exclusively for this noisy, brilliant, laughing life, with its music, its dancers, its adorers, and her old terror of a force that was sweeping down upon her and menacing to crush her seemed to her ridiculous: she was afraid of no one now, and only regretted that her mother could not be there to rejoice at her success.

Pyotr Leontyitch, pale by now but still steady on his legs, came up to the stall and asked for a glass of brandy. Anna turned crimson, expecting him to say something inappropriate (she was already ashamed of having such a poor and ordinary father); but he emptied his glass, took ten roubles out of his roll of notes, flung it down, and walked away with dignity without uttering a word. A little later she saw him dancing in the grand chain, and by now he was staggering and kept shouting something, to the great confusion of his partner; and Anna remembered how at the ball three years before he had staggered and shouted in the same way, and it had ended in the police-sergeant's taking him home to bed, and next day the director had threatened to dismiss him from his post. How inappropriate that memory was!

When the samovars were put out in the stalls and the exhausted ladies handed over their takings to the middle-aged lady with the stone in her mouth, Artynov took Anna on his arm to the hall where supper was served to all who had assisted at the bazaar. There were some twenty people at supper, not more, but it was very noisy. His Excellency proposed a toast:

"In this magnificent dining room it will be appropriate to drink to the success of the cheap dining rooms, which are the object of today's bazaar."

The brigadier-general proposed the toast: "To the power by which even the artillery is vanquished," and all the company clinked glasses with the ladies. It was very, very gay.

When Anna was escorted home it was daylight and the cooks were going to market. Joyful, intoxicated, full of new sensations, exhausted, she undressed, dropped into bed, and at once fell asleep. . . .

It was past one in the afternoon when the servant waked her and announced that M. Artynov had called. She dressed quickly and went down into the drawing room. Soon after Artynov, His Excellency called to thank her for her assistance in the bazaar. With a sugary smile, chewing his lips, he kissed her hand, and asking her permission to come again, took his leave, while she remained standing in the middle of the drawing room, amazed, enchanted, unable to believe that this change in her life, this marvellous change, had taken place so quickly; and at that moment Modest Alexeitch walked in . . . and he, too, stood before her now with the same ingratiating, sugary, cringingly respectful expression which she was accustomed to see on his face in the presence of the great and powerful; and with rapture, with indignation, with contempt, convinced that no harm would come to her from it, she said, articulating distinctly each word:

"Be off, you blockhead!"

From this time forward Anna never had one day free, as she was always taking part in picnics, expeditions, performances. She returned home every day after midnight, and went to bed on the floor in the drawing room, and afterwards used to tell every one, touchingly, how she slept under flowers. She needed a very great deal of money, but she was no longer afraid of Modest Alexeitch, and spent his money as though it were her own; and she did not ask, did not demand it, simply sent him in the bills. "Give bearer two hundred roubles," or "Pay one hundred roubles at once."

At Easter Modest Alexeitch received the Anna of the second grade. When he went to offer his thanks, His Excellency put aside the paper he was reading and settled himself more comfortably in his chair.

"So now you have three Annas," he said, scrutinizing his white hands and pink nails—"one on your buttonhole and two on your neck."

Modest Alexeitch put two fingers to his lips as a precaution against laughing too loud and said:

"Now I have only to look forward to the arrival of a little Vladimir. I make bold to beg your Excellency to stand godfather."

He was alluding to Vladimir of the fourth grade, and was already imagining how he would tell everywhere the story of this pun, so happy in its readiness and audacity, and he wanted to say something equally happy, but His Excellency was buried again in his newspaper, and merely gave him a nod.

And Anna went on driving about with three horses, going out hunting with Artynov, playing in one-act dramas, going out to supper, and was more and more rarely with her own family; they dined now alone. Pyotr Leontyitch was drinking more heavily than ever; there was no money, and the harmonium had been sold long ago for debt. The boys did not let him go out alone in the street now, but looked after him for fear he might fall down; and whenever they met Anna driving in Staro-Kievsky Street with a pair of horses and Artynov on the box instead of a coachman, Pyotr Leontyitch took off his top-hat, and was about to shout to her, but Petya and Andrusha took him by the arm, and said imploringly:

"You mustn't, father. Hush, father!"

An Artist's Story

[First published under the title 'The House with the Mezzanine,'
subtitled 'An Artist's Story,' in *Russkaya Mysl* (*Russian Thought*),
a Russian magazine, in April 1896.
Collected in *The Darling and Other Stories* (1916).]

I

It was six or seven years ago when I was living in one of the districts
of the province of T——, on the estate of a young landowner called
Byelokurov, who used to get up very early, wear a peasant tunic, drink
beer in the evenings, and continually complain to me that he never met
with sympathy from any one. He lived in the lodge in the garden, and I
in the old seigniorial house, in a big room with columns, where there was
no furniture except a wide sofa on which I used to sleep, and a table on
which I used to lay out patience. There was always, even in still weather,
a droning noise in the old Amos stoves, and in thunderstorms the whole
house shook and seemed to be cracking into pieces; and it was rather
terrifying, especially at night, when all the ten big windows were suddenly
lit up by lightning.

Condemned by destiny to perpetual idleness, I did absolutely nothing.
For hours together I gazed out of window at the sky, at the birds, at the
avenue, read everything that was brought me by post, slept. Sometimes I
went out of the house and wandered about till late in the evening.

One day as I was returning home, I accidentally strayed into a place I
did not know. The sun was already sinking, and the shades of evening lay
across the flowering rye. Two rows of old, closely planted, very tall fir trees

stood like two dense walls forming a picturesque, gloomy avenue. I easily climbed over the fence and walked along the avenue, slipping over the fir-needles which lay two inches deep on the ground. It was still and dark, and only here and there on the high tree-tops the vivid golden light quivered and made rainbows in the spiders' webs. There was a strong, almost stifling smell of resin. Then I turned into a long avenue of limes. Here, too, all was desolation and age; last year's leaves rusted mournfully under my feet and in the twilight shadows lurked between the trees. From the old orchard on the right came the faint, reluctant note of the golden oriole, who must have been old too. But at last the limes ended. I walked by an old white house of two storeys with a terrace, and there suddenly opened before me a view of a courtyard, a large pond with a bathing-house, a group of green willows, and a village on the further bank, with a high, narrow belfry on which there glittered a cross reflecting the setting sun.

For a moment it breathed upon me the fascination of something near and very familiar, as though I had seen that landscape at some time in my childhood.

At the white stone gates which led from the yard to the fields, old-fashioned solid gates with lions on them, were standing two girls. One of them, the elder, a slim, pale, very handsome girl with a perfect haystack of chestnut hair and a little obstinate mouth, had a severe expression and scarcely took notice of me, while the other, who was still very young, not more than seventeen or eighteen, and was also slim and pale, with a large mouth and large eyes, looked at me with astonishment as I passed by, said something in English, and was overcome with embarrassment. And it seemed to me that these two charming faces, too, had long been familiar to me. And I returned home feeling as though I had had a delightful dream.

One morning soon afterwards, as Byelokurov and I were walking near the house, a carriage drove unexpectedly into the yard, rustling over the grass, and in it was sitting one of those girls. It was the elder one. She had come to ask for subscriptions for some villagers whose cottages had been burnt down. Speaking with great earnestness and precision, and not looking at us, she told us how many houses in the village of Siyanovo had been burnt, how many men, women, and children were left homeless, and what steps were proposed, to begin with, by the Relief Committee, of which she was now a member. After handing us the subscription list for our signatures, she put it away and immediately began to take leave of us.

"You have quite forgotten us, Pyotr Petrovitch," she said to Byelokurov as she shook hands with him. "Do come, and if Monsieur N. (she mentioned my name) cares to make the acquaintance of admirers of his work, and will come and see us, mother and I will be delighted."

I bowed.

When she had gone Pyotr Petrovitch began to tell me about her. The girl was, he said, of good family, and her name was Lidia Voltchaninov, and the estate on which she lived with her mother and sister, like the village on the other side of the pond, was called Shelkovka. Her father had once held an important position in Moscow, and had died with the rank of privy councillor. Although they had ample means, the Voltchaninovs lived on their estate summer and winter without going away. Lidia was a teacher in the Zemstvo school in her own village, and received a salary of twenty-five roubles a month. She spent nothing on herself but her salary, and was proud of earning her own living.

"An interesting family," said Byelokurov. "Let us go over one day. They will be delighted to see you."

One afternoon on a holiday we thought of the Voltchaninovs, and went to Shelkovka to see them. They—the mother and two daughters—were at home. The mother, Ekaterina Pavlovna, who at one time had been handsome, but now, asthmatic, depressed, vague, and over-feeble for her years, tried to entertain me with conversation about painting. Having heard from her daughter that I might come to Shelkovka, she had hurriedly recalled two or three of my landscapes which she had seen in exhibitions in Moscow, and now asked what I meant to express by them. Lidia, or as they called her Lida, talked more to Byelokurov than to me. Earnest and unsmiling, she asked him why he was not on the Zemstvo, and why he had not attended any of its meetings.

"It's not right, Pyotr Petrovitch," she said reproachfully. "It's not right. It's too bad."

"That's true, Lida—that's true," the mother assented. "It isn't right."

"Our whole district is in the hands of Balagin," Lida went on, addressing me. "He is the chairman of the Zemstvo Board, and he has distributed all the posts in the district among his nephews and sons-in-law; and he does as he likes. He ought to be opposed. The young men ought to make a strong party, but you see what the young men among us are like. It's a shame, Pyotr Petrovitch!"

The younger sister, Genya, was silent while they were talking of the Zemstvo. She took no part in serious conversation. She was not looked upon as quite grown up by her family, and, like a child, was always called by the nickname of Misuce, because that was what she had called her English governess when she was a child. She was all the time looking at me with curiosity, and when I glanced at the photographs in the album, she explained to me: "That's uncle . . . that's god-father," moving her finger across the photograph. As she did so she touched me with her shoulder like a child, and I had a close view of her delicate, undeveloped chest, her slender shoulders, her plait, and her thin little body tightly drawn in by her sash.

We played croquet and lawn tennis, we walked about the garden, drank tea, and then sat a long time over supper. After the huge empty room with columns, I felt, as it were, at home in this small snug house where there were no oleographs on the walls and where the servants were spoken to with civility. And everything seemed to me young and pure, thanks to the presence of Lida and Misuce, and there was an atmosphere of refinement over everything. At supper Lida talked to Byelokurov again of the Zemstvo, of Balagin, and of school libraries. She was an energetic, genuine girl, with convictions, and it was interesting to listen to her, though she talked a great deal and in a loud voice—perhaps because she was accustomed to talking at school. On the other hand, Pyotr Petrovitch, who had retained from his student days the habit of turning every conversation into an argument, was tedious, flat, long-winded, and unmistakably anxious to appear clever and advanced. Gesticulating, he upset a sauce-boat with his sleeve, making a huge pool on the tablecloth, but no one except me appeared to notice it.

It was dark and still as we went home.

"Good breeding is shown, not by not upsetting the sauce, but by not noticing it when somebody else does," said Byelokurov, with a sigh. "Yes, a splendid, intellectual family! I've dropped out of all decent society; it's dreadful how I've dropped out of it! It's all through work, work, work!"

He talked of how hard one had to work if one wanted to be a model farmer. And I thought what a heavy, sluggish fellow he was! Whenever he talked of anything serious he articulated "Er-er" with intense effort, and worked just as he talked—slowly, always late and behind-hand. I had little faith in his business capacity if only from the fact that when I gave him letters to post he carried them about in his pocket for weeks together.

"The hardest thing of all," he muttered as he walked beside me—"the hardest thing of all is that, work as one may, one meets with no sympathy from any one. No sympathy!"

II

I took to going to see the Voltchaninovs. As a rule I sat on the lower step of the terrace; I was fretted by dissatisfaction with myself; I was sorry at the thought of my life passing so rapidly and uninterestingly, and felt as though I would like to tear out of my breast the heart which had grown so heavy. And meanwhile I heard talk on the terrace, the rustling of dresses, the pages of a book being turned. I soon grew accustomed to the idea that during the day Lida received patients, gave out books, and often went into the village with a parasol and no hat, and in the evening talked aloud of the Zemstvo and schools. This slim, handsome, invariably austere girl, with her small well-cut mouth, always said dryly when the conversation turned on serious subjects:

"That's of no interest to you."

She did not like me. She disliked me because I was a landscape painter and did not in my pictures portray the privations of the peasants, and that, as she fancied, I was indifferent to what she put such faith in. I remember when I was travelling on the banks of Lake Baikal, I met a Buriat girl on horseback, wearing a shirt and trousers of blue Chinese canvas; I asked her if she would sell me her pipe. While we talked she looked contemptuously at my European face and hat, and in a moment she was bored with talking to me; she shouted to her horse and galloped on. And in just the same way Lida despised me as an alien. She never outwardly expressed her dislike for me, but I felt it, and sitting on the lower step of the terrace, I felt irritated, and said that doctoring peasants when one was not a doctor was deceiving them, and that it was easy to be benevolent when one had six thousand acres.

Meanwhile her sister Misuce had no cares, and spent her life in complete idleness just as I did. When she got up in the morning she immediately took up a book and sat down to read on the terrace in a deep armchair, with her feet hardly touching the ground, or hid herself with her book in the lime avenue, or walked out into the fields. She spent the whole day reading, poring greedily over her book, and only from the tired, dazed look in her eyes and the extreme paleness of her face one could divine how this continual reading exhausted her brain. When I arrived she would flush a little, leave her book, and looking into my face with her big eyes, would tell me eagerly of anything that had happened—for instance, that the chimney had been on fire in the servants' hall, or that one of the men had caught a huge fish in the pond. On ordinary days she usually went about in a light blouse and a dark blue skirt. We went for walks together, picked cherries for making jam, went out in the boat. When she jumped up to reach a cherry or sculled in the boat, her thin, weak arms showed through her transparent sleeves. Or I painted a sketch, and she stood beside me watching rapturously.

One Sunday at the end of July I came to the Voltchaninovs about nine o'clock in the morning. I walked about the park, keeping a good distance from the house, looking for white mushrooms, of which there was a great number that summer, and noting their position so as to come and pick them afterwards with Genya. There was a warm breeze. I saw Genya and her mother both in light holiday dresses coming home from church, Genya holding her hat in the wind. Afterwards I heard them having tea on the terrace.

For a careless person like me, trying to find justification for my perpetual idleness, these holiday mornings in our country-houses in the summer have always had a particular charm. When the green garden, still wet with dew, is all sparkling in the sun and looks radiant with happiness, when there is a scent of mignonette and oleander near the house, when the young people have just come back from church and are having breakfast in the garden, all so charmingly dressed and gay, and one knows that all these healthy, well-fed, handsome people are going to do nothing the whole long day, one wishes that all life were like that. Now, too, I had the same thought, and walked about the garden prepared to walk about like that, aimless and unoccupied, the whole day, the whole summer.

Genya came out with a basket; she had a look in her face as though she knew she would find me in the garden, or had a presentiment of it. We gathered mushrooms and talked, and when she asked a question she walked a little ahead so as to see my face.

"A miracle happened in the village yesterday," she said. "The lame woman Pelagea has been ill the whole year. No doctors or medicines did her any good; but yesterday an old woman came and whispered something over her, and her illness passed away."

"That's nothing much," I said. "You mustn't look for miracles only among sick people and old women. Isn't health a miracle? And life itself? Whatever is beyond understanding is a miracle."

"And aren't you afraid of what is beyond understanding?"

"No. Phenomena I don't understand I face boldly, and am not overwhelmed by them. I am above them. Man ought to recognise himself as superior to lions, tigers, stars, superior to everything in nature, even what seems miraculous and is beyond his understanding, or else he is not a man, but a mouse afraid of everything."

Genya believed that as an artist I knew a very great deal, and could guess correctly what I did not know. She longed for me to initiate her into the domain of the Eternal and the Beautiful—into that higher world in which, as she imagined, I was quite at home. And she talked to me of God, of the eternal life, of the miraculous. And I, who could never admit that my self and my imagination would be lost forever after death, answered: "Yes, men are immortal"; "Yes, there is eternal life in store for us." And she listened, believed, and did not ask for proofs.

As we were going home she stopped suddenly and said:

"Our Lida is a remarkable person—isn't she? I love her very dearly, and would be ready to give my life for her any minute. But tell me"—Genya touched my sleeve with her finger—"tell me, why do you always argue with her? Why are you irritated?"

"Because she is wrong."

Genya shook her head and tears came into her eyes.

"How incomprehensible that is!" she said. At that minute Lida had just returned from somewhere, and standing with a whip in her hand, a slim, beautiful figure in the sunlight, at the steps, she was giving some orders to one of the men. Talking loudly, she hurriedly received two or three sick villagers; then with a busy and anxious face she walked about the rooms, opening one cupboard after another, and went upstairs. It was a long time before they could find her and call her to dinner, and she came in when we had finished our soup. All these tiny details I remember with tenderness, and that whole day I remember vividly, though nothing special happened. After dinner Genya lay in a long armchair reading, while I sat upon the bottom step of the terrace. We were silent. The whole sky was overcast with clouds, and it began to spot with fine rain. It was hot; the wind had dropped, and it seemed as though the day would never end. Ekaterina Pavlovna came out on the terrace, looking drowsy and carrying a fan.

"Oh, mother," said Genya, kissing her hand, "it's not good for you to sleep in the day."

They adored each other. When one went into the garden, the other would stand on the terrace, and, looking towards the trees, call "Aa— oo, Genya!" or "Mother, where are you?" They always said their prayers together, and had the same faith; and they understood each other perfectly even when they did not speak. And their attitude to people was the same. Ekaterina Pavlovna, too, grew quickly used to me and fond of me, and when I did not come for two or three days, sent to ask if I were well. She, too, gazed at my sketches with enthusiasm, and with the same openness and readiness to chatter as Misuce, she told me what had happened, and confided to me her domestic secrets.

She had a perfect reverence for her elder daughter. Lida did not care for endearments, she talked only of serious matters; she lived her life apart, and to her mother and sister was as sacred and enigmatic a person as the admiral, always sitting in his cabin, is to the sailors.

"Our Lida is a remarkable person," the mother would often say. "Isn't she?"

Now, too, while it was drizzling with rain, we talked of Lida.

"She is a remarkable girl," said her mother, and added in an undertone, like a conspirator, looking about her timidly: "You wouldn't easily find another like her; only, do you know, I am beginning to be a little uneasy. The school, the dispensary, books—all that's very good, but why go to extremes? She is three-and-twenty, you know; it's time for her to think seriously of herself. With her books and her dispensary she will find life has slipped by without having noticed it. . . . She must be married."

Genya, pale from reading, with her hair disarranged, raised her head and said as it were to herself, looking at her mother:

"Mother, everything is in God's hands."

And again she buried herself in her book.

Byelokurov came in his tunic and embroidered shirt. We played croquet and tennis, then when it got dark, sat a long time over supper and talked again about schools, and about Balagin, who had the whole district under his thumb. As I went away from the Voltchaninovs that evening,

I carried away the impression of a long, long idle day, with a melancholy consciousness that everything ends in this world, however long it may be.

Genya saw us out to the gate, and perhaps because she had been with me all day, from morning till night, I felt dull without her, and that all that charming family were near and dear to me, and for the first time that summer I had a yearning to paint.

"Tell me, why do you lead such a dreary, colourless life?" I asked Byelokurov as I went home. "My life is dreary, difficult, and monotonous because I am an artist, a strange person. From my earliest days I've been wrung by envy, self-dissatisfaction, distrust in my work. I'm always poor, I'm a wanderer, but you—you're a healthy, normal man, a landowner, and a gentleman. Why do you live in such an uninteresting way? Why do you get so little out of life? Why haven't you, for instance, fallen in love with Lida or Genya?"

"You forget that I love another woman," answered Byelokurov.

He was referring to Liubov Ivanovna, the lady who shared the lodge with him. Every day I saw this lady, very plump, rotund, and dignified, not unlike a fat goose, walking about the garden, in the Russian national dress and beads, always carrying a parasol; and the servant was continually calling her in to dinner or to tea. Three years before she had taken one of the lodges for a summer holiday, and had settled down at Byelokurov's apparently forever. She was ten years older than he was, and kept a sharp hand over him, so much so that he had to ask her permission when he went out of the house. She often sobbed in a deep masculine note, and then I used to send word to her that if she did not leave off, I should give up my rooms there; and she left off.

When we got home Byelokurov sat down on the sofa and frowned thoughtfully, and I began walking up and down the room, conscious of a soft emotion as though I were in love. I wanted to talk about the Voltchaninovs.

"Lida could only fall in love with a member of the Zemstvo, as devoted to schools and hospitals as she is," I said. "Oh, for the sake of a girl like that one might not only go into the Zemstvo, but even wear out iron shoes, like the girl in the fairy tale. And Misuce? What a sweet creature she is, that Misuce!"

Byelokurov, drawling out "Er—er," began a long-winded disquisition on the malady of the age—pessimism. He talked confidently, in a tone that suggested that I was opposing him. Hundreds of miles of desolate, monotonous, burnt-up steppe cannot induce such deep depression as one man when he sits and talks, and one does not know when he will go.

"It's not a question of pessimism or optimism," I said irritably; "its simply that ninety-nine people out of a hundred have no sense."

Byelokurov took this as aimed at himself, was offended, and went away.

III

"The prince is staying at Malozyomovo, and he asks to be remembered to you," said Lida to her mother. She had just come in, and was taking off her gloves. "He gave me a great deal of interesting news .... He promised to raise the question of a medical relief centre at Malozyomovo again at the provincial assembly, but he says there is very little hope of it." And turning to me, she said: "Excuse me, I always forget that this cannot be interesting to you."

I felt irritated.

"Why not interesting to me?" I said, shrugging my shoulders. "You do not care to know my opinion, but I assure you the question has great interest for me."

"Yes?"

"Yes. In my opinion a medical relief centre at Malozyomovo is quite unnecessary."

My irritation infected her; she looked at me, screwing up her eyes, and asked:

"What is necessary? Landscapes?"

"Landscapes are not, either. Nothing is."

She finished taking off her gloves, and opened the newspaper, which had just been brought from the post. A minute later she said quietly, evidently restraining herself:

"Last week Anna died in childbirth, and if there had been a medical relief centre near, she would have lived. And I think even landscape-painters ought to have some opinions on the subject."

"I have a very definite opinion on that subject, I assure you," I answered; and she screened herself with the newspaper, as though unwilling to listen to me. "To my mind, all these schools, dispensaries, libraries, medical relief centres, under present conditions, only serve to aggravate the bondage of the people. The peasants are fettered by a great chain, and you do not break the chain, but only add fresh links to it—that's my view of it."

She raised her eyes to me and smiled ironically, and I went on trying to formulate my leading idea.

"What matters is not that Anna died in childbirth, but that all these Annas, Mavras, Pelageas, toil from early morning till dark, fall ill from working beyond their strength, all their lives tremble for their sick and hungry children, all their lives are being doctored, and in dread of death and disease, fade and grow old early, and die in filth and stench. Their children begin the same story over again as soon as they grow up, and so it goes on for hundreds of years and milliards of men live worse than beasts—in continual terror, for a mere crust of bread. The whole horror of their position lies in their never having time to think of their souls, of their image and semblance. Cold, hunger, animal terror, a burden of toil, like avalanches of snow, block for them every way to spiritual activity—that is, to what distinguishes man from the brutes and what is the only thing which makes life worth living. You go to their help with hospitals and schools, but you don't free them from their fetters by that; on the contrary, you bind them in closer bonds, as, by introducing new prejudices, you increase the number of their wants, to say nothing of the fact that they've got to pay the Zemstvo for drugs and books, and so toil harder than ever."

"I am not going to argue with you," said Lida, putting down the paper. "I've heard all that before. I will only say one thing: one cannot sit with one's hands in one's lap. It's true that we are not saving humanity, and perhaps we make a great many mistakes; but we do what we can, and we are right. The highest and holiest task for a civilised being is to serve his neighbours, and we try to serve them as best we can. You don't like it, but one can't please every one."

"That's true, Lida," said her mother—"that's true."

In Lida's presence she was always a little timid, and looked at her nervously as she talked, afraid of saying something superfluous or inopportune. And she never contradicted her, but always assented: "That's true, Lida—that's true."

"Teaching the peasants to read and write, books of wretched precepts and rhymes, and medical relief centres, cannot diminish either ignorance or the death-rate, just as the light from your windows cannot light up this huge garden," said I. "You give nothing. By meddling in these people's lives you only create new wants in them, and new demands on their labour."

"Ach! Good heavens! But one must do something!" said Lida with vexation, and from her tone one could see that she thought my arguments worthless and despised them.

"The people must be freed from hard physical labour," said I. "We must lighten their yoke, let them have time to breathe, that they may not spend all their lives at the stove, at the wash-tub, and in the fields, but may also have time to think of their souls, of God—may have time to develop their spiritual capacities. The highest vocation of man is spiritual activity—the perpetual search for truth and the meaning of life. Make coarse animal labour unnecessary for them, let them feel themselves free, and then you will see what a mockery these dispensaries and books are. Once a man recognises his true vocation, he can only be satisfied by religion, science, and art, and not by these trifles."

"Free them from labour?" laughed Lida. "But is that possible?"

"Yes. Take upon yourself a share of their labour. If all of us, townspeople and country people, all without exception, would agree to divide between us the labour which mankind spends on the satisfaction of their physical needs, each of us would perhaps need to work only for two or three hours a day. Imagine that we all, rich and poor, work only for three hours a day, and the rest of our time is free. Imagine further that in order to depend even less upon our bodies and to labour less, we invent machines to replace our work, we try to cut down our needs to the minimum. We would harden ourselves and our children that they should not be afraid of hunger and cold, and that we shouldn't be continually trembling for their health like Anna, Mavra, and Pelagea. Imagine that we don't doctor ourselves, don't keep dispensaries, tobacco factories, distilleries—what a lot of free time would be left us after all! All of us together would devote our leisure to science and art. Just as the peasants sometimes work, the whole community together mending the roads, so all of us, as a community, would search for truth and the meaning of life, and I am convinced that the truth would be discovered very quickly; man would escape from this continual, agonising, oppressive dread of death, and even from death itself."

"You contradict yourself, though," said Lida. "You talk about science, and are yourself opposed to elementary education."

"Elementary education when a man has nothing to read but the signs on public houses and sometimes books which he cannot understand—such education has existed among us since the times of Rurik; Gogol's Petrushka has been reading for ever so long, yet as the village was in the days of Rurik so it has remained. What is needed is not elementary education, but freedom for a wide development of spiritual capacities. What are wanted are not schools, but universities."

"You are opposed to medicine, too."

"Yes. It would be necessary only for the study of diseases as natural phenomena, and not for the cure of them. If one must cure, it should not be diseases, but the causes of them. Remove the principal cause—physical labour, and then there will be no disease. I don't believe in a science that cures disease," I went on excitedly. "When science and art are real, they aim not at temporary private ends, but at eternal and universal—they seek for truth and the meaning of life, they seek for God, for the soul, and when they are tied down to the needs and evils of the day, to dispensaries and libraries, they only complicate and hamper life. We have plenty of doctors, chemists, lawyers, plenty of people can read and write, but we are quite without biologists, mathematicians, philosophers, poets. The whole of our intelligence, the whole of our spiritual energy, is spent on satisfying temporary, passing needs. Scientific men, writers, artists, are hard at work; thanks to them, the conveniences of life are multiplied from day to day. Our physical demands increase, yet truth is still a long way off, and man still remains the most rapacious and dirty animal; everything is tending to the degeneration of the majority of mankind, and the loss forever of all fitness for life. In such conditions an artist's work has no meaning, and the more talented he is, the stranger and the more unintelligible is his position, as when one looks into it, it is evident that he is working for the amusement of a rapacious and unclean animal, and is supporting the existing order. And I don't care to work and I won't work. . . . Nothing is any use; let the earth sink to perdition!"

"Misuce, go out of the room!" said Lida to her sister, apparently thinking my words pernicious to the young girl.

Genya looked mournfully at her mother and sister, and went out of the room.

"These are the charming things people say when they want to justify their indifference," said Lida. "It is easier to disapprove of schools and hospitals, than to teach or heal."

"That's true, Lida—that's true," the mother assented.

"You threaten to give up working," said Lida. "You evidently set a high value on your work. Let us give up arguing; we shall never agree, since I put the most imperfect dispensary or library of which you have just spoken so contemptuously on a higher level than any landscape." And turning at once to her mother, she began speaking in quite a different tone: "The prince is very much changed, and much thinner than when he was with us last. He is being sent to Vichy."

She told her mother about the prince in order to avoid talking to me. Her face glowed, and to hide her feeling she bent low over the table as though she were short-sighted, and made a show of reading the newspaper. My presence was disagreeable to her. I said goodbye and went home.

IV

It was quite still out of doors; the village on the further side of the pond was already asleep; there was not a light to be seen, and only the stars were faintly reflected in the pond. At the gate with the lions on it Genya was standing motionless, waiting to escort me.

"Every one is asleep in the village," I said to her, trying to make out her face in the darkness, and I saw her mournful dark eyes fixed upon me. "The publican and the horse-stealers are asleep, while we, well-bred people, argue and irritate each other."

It was a melancholy August night—melancholy because there was already a feeling of autumn; the moon was rising behind a purple cloud, and it shed a faint light upon the road and on the dark fields of winter corn by the sides. From time to time a star fell. Genya walked beside me along the road, and tried not to look at the sky, that she might not see the falling stars, which for some reason frightened her.

"I believe you are right," she said, shivering with the damp night air. "If people, all together, could devote themselves to spiritual ends, they would soon know everything."

"Of course. We are higher beings, and if we were really to recognise the whole force of human genius and lived only for higher ends, we should in the end become like gods. But that will never be—mankind will degenerate till no traces of genius remain."

When the gates were out of sight, Genya stopped and shook hands with me.

"Goodnight," she said, shivering; she had nothing but her blouse over her shoulders and was shrinking with cold. "Come tomorrow."

I felt wretched at the thought of being left alone, irritated and dissatisfied with myself and other people; and I, too, tried not to look at the falling stars. "Stay another minute," I said to her, "I entreat you."

I loved Genya. I must have loved her because she met me when I came and saw me off when I went away; because she looked at me tenderly and enthusiastically. How touchingly beautiful were her pale face, slender neck, slender arms, her weakness, her idleness, her reading. And intelligence? I suspected in her intelligence above the average. I was fascinated by the breadth of her views, perhaps because they were different from those of the stern, handsome Lida, who disliked me. Genya liked me, because I was an artist. I had conquered her heart by my talent, and had a passionate desire to paint for her sake alone; and I dreamed of her as of my little queen who with me would possess those trees, those fields, the mists, the dawn, the exquisite and beautiful scenery in the midst of which I had felt myself hopelessly solitary and useless.

"Stay another minute," I begged her. "I beseech you."

I took off my overcoat and put it over her chilly shoulders; afraid of looking ugly and absurd in a man's overcoat, she laughed, threw it off, and at that instant I put my arms round her and covered her face, shoulders, and hands with kisses.

"Till tomorrow," she whispered, and softly, as though afraid of breaking upon the silence of the night, she embraced me. "We have no secrets from one another. I must tell my mother and my sister at once. . . . It's so dreadful! Mother is all right; mother likes you—but Lida!"

She ran to the gates.

"Goodbye!" she called.

And then for two minutes I heard her running. I did not want to go home, and I had nothing to go for. I stood still for a little time hesitating, and made my way slowly back, to look once more at the house in which she lived, the sweet, simple old house, which seemed to be watching me from the windows of its upper storey, and understanding all about it. I walked by the terrace, sat on the seat by the tennis ground, in the dark under the old elm tree, and looked from there at the house. In the windows of the top storey where Misuce slept there appeared a bright light, which changed to a soft green—they had covered the lamp with the shade. Shadows began to move. . . . I was full of tenderness, peace, and satisfaction with myself—satisfaction at having been able to be carried away by my feelings and having fallen in love, and at the same time I felt uncomfortable at the thought that only a few steps away from me, in one of the rooms of that house there was Lida, who disliked and perhaps hated me. I went on sitting there wondering whether Genya would come out; I listened and fancied I heard voices talking upstairs.

About an hour passed. The green light went out, and the shadows were no longer visible. The moon was standing high above the house, and lighting up the sleeping garden and the paths; the dahlias and the roses in front of the house could be seen distinctly, and looked all the same colour. It began to grow very cold. I went out of the garden, picked up my coat on the road, and slowly sauntered home.

When next day after dinner I went to the Voltchaninovs, the glass door into the garden was wide open. I sat down on the terrace, expecting Genya every minute, to appear from behind the flower beds on the lawn, or from one of the avenues, or that I should hear her voice from the house. Then I walked into the drawing room, the dining room. There was not a soul to be seen. From the dining room I walked along the long corridor to the hall and back. In this corridor there were several doors, and through one of them I heard the voice of Lida:

"'God . . . sent . . . a crow,'" she said in a loud, emphatic voice, probably dictating—"'God sent a crow a piece of cheese. . . . A crow . . . a piece of cheese.' . . . Who's there?" she called suddenly, hearing my steps.

"It's I."

"Ah! Excuse me, I cannot come out to you this minute; I'm giving Dasha her lesson."

"Is Ekaterina Pavlovna in the garden?"

"No, she went away with my sister this morning to our aunt in the province of Penza. And in the winter they will probably go abroad," she added after a pause. "'God sent . . . the crow . . . a piece . . . of cheese.' . . . Have you written it?"

I went into the hall, and stared vacantly at the pond and the village, and the sound reached me of "A piece of cheese. . . . God sent the crow a piece of cheese."

And I went back by the way I had come here for the first time—first from the yard into the garden past the house, then into the avenue of lime trees. . . . At this point I was overtaken by a small boy who gave me a note:

"I told my sister everything and she insists on my parting from you," I read. "I could not wound her by disobeying. God will give you happiness. Forgive me. If only you knew how bitterly my mother and I are crying!"

Then there was the dark fir avenue, the broken-down fence. . . . On the field where then the rye was in flower and the corncrakes were calling, now there were cows and hobbled horses. On the slope there were bright green patches of winter corn. A sober workaday feeling came over me and I felt ashamed of all I had said at the Voltchaninovs', and felt bored with life as I had been before. When I got home, I packed and set off that evening for Petersburg.

****

I never saw the Voltchaninovs again. Not long ago, on my way to the Crimea, I met Byelokurov in the train. As before, he was wearing a jerkin and an embroidered shirt, and when I asked how he was, he replied that, God be praised, he was well. We began talking. He had sold his old estate and bought another smaller one, in the name of Liubov Ivanovna. He could tell me little about the Voltchaninovs. Lida, he said, was still living in Shelkovka and teaching in the school; she had by degrees succeeded in gathering round her a circle of people sympathetic to her who made a strong party, and at the last election had turned out Balagin, who had till then had the whole district under his thumb. About Genya he only told me that she did not live at home, and that he did not know where she was.

I am beginning to forget the old house, and only sometimes when I am painting or reading I suddenly, apropos of nothing, remember the green light in the window, the sound of my footsteps as I walked home through the fields in the night, with my heart full of love, rubbing my hands in the cold. And still more rarely, at moments when I am sad and depressed by loneliness, I have dim memories, and little by little I begin to feel that she is thinking of me, too—that she is waiting for me, and that we shall meet. . . .

Misuce, where are you?

The Schoolmistress

[Written in November 1897 in Nice, France.
First published on December 21, 1897, in *Russkiye Vedomosti*,
a Russian liberal daily newspaper. Also translated as 'In the Cart.'
Collected in *The Schoolmistress and Other Stories* (1918).]

At half-past eight they drove out of the town.

The highroad was dry, a lovely April sun was shining warmly, but the snow was still lying in the ditches and in the woods. Winter, dark, long, and spiteful, was hardly over; spring had come all of a sudden. But neither the warmth nor the languid transparent woods, warmed by the breath of spring, nor the black flocks of birds flying over the huge puddles that were like lakes, nor the marvelous fathomless sky, into which it seemed one would have gone away so joyfully, presented anything new or interesting to Marya Vassilyevna who was sitting in the cart. For thirteen years she had been schoolmistress, and there was no reckoning how many times during all those years she had been to the town for her salary; and whether it were spring as now, or a rainy autumn evening, or winter, it was all the same to her, and she always—invariably—longed for one thing only, to get to the end of her journey as quickly as could be.

She felt as though she had been living in that part of the country for ages and ages, for a hundred years, and it seemed to her that she knew every stone, every tree on the road from the town to her school. Her past was here, her present was here, and she could imagine no other future than the school, the road to the town and back again, and again the school and again the road. . . .

She had got out of the habit of thinking of her past before she became a schoolmistress, and had almost forgotten it. She had once had a father and mother; they had lived in Moscow in a big flat near the Red Gate, but of all that life there was left in her memory only something vague and fluid like a dream. Her father had died when she was ten years old, and her mother had died soon after. . . . She had a brother, an officer; at first they used to write to each other, then her brother had given up answering her letters, he had got out of the way of writing. Of her old belongings, all that was left was a photograph of her mother, but it had grown dim from the dampness of the school, and now nothing could be seen but the hair and the eyebrows.

When they had driven a couple of miles, old Semyon, who was driving, turned round and said:

"They have caught a government clerk in the town. They have taken him away. The story is that with some Germans he killed Alexeyev, the Mayor, in Moscow."

"Who told you that?"

"They were reading it in the paper, in Ivan Ionov's tavern."

And again they were silent for a long time. Marya Vassilyevna thought of her school, of the examination that was coming soon, and of the girl and four boys she was sending up for it. And just as she was thinking about the examination, she was overtaken by a neighbouring landowner called Hanov in a carriage with four horses, the very man who had been examiner in her school the year before. When he came up to her he recognized her and bowed.

"Good morning," he said to her. "You are driving home, I suppose."

This Hanov, a man of forty with a listless expression and a face that showed signs of wear, was beginning to look old, but was still handsome and admired by women. He lived in his big homestead alone, and was not in the service; and people used to say of him that he did nothing at home but walk up and down the room whistling, or play chess with his old footman. People said, too, that he drank heavily. And indeed at the examination the year before the very papers he brought with him smelt of wine and scent. He had been dressed all in new clothes on that occasion, and Marya Vassilyevna thought him very attractive, and all the while she sat beside him she had felt embarrassed. She was accustomed to see frigid and sensible examiners at the school, while this one did not remember a single prayer, or know what to ask questions about, and was exceedingly courteous and delicate, giving nothing but the highest marks.

"I am going to visit Bakvist," he went on, addressing Marya Vassilyevna, "but I am told he is not at home."

They turned off the highroad into a by-road to the village, Hanov leading the way and Semyon following. The four horses moved at a walking pace, with effort dragging the heavy carriage through the mud. Semyon tacked from side to side, keeping to the edge of the road, at one time through a snowdrift, at another through a pool, often jumping out of the cart and helping the horse. Marya Vassilyevna was still thinking about the school, wondering whether the arithmetic questions at the examination would be difficult or easy. And she felt annoyed with the Zemstvo board at which she had found no one the day before. How unbusiness-like! Here she had been asking them for the last two years to dismiss the watchman, who did nothing, was rude to her, and hit the schoolboys; but no one paid any attention. It was hard to find the president at the office, and when one did find him he would say with tears in his eyes that he hadn't a moment to spare; the inspector visited the school at most once in three years, and knew nothing whatever about his work, as he had been in the Excise Duties Department, and had received the post of school inspector through influence. The School Council met very rarely, and there was no knowing where it met; the school guardian was an almost illiterate peasant, the head of a tanning business, unintelligent, rude, and a great friend of the watchman's—and goodness knows to whom she could appeal with complaints or inquiries. . . .

"He really is handsome," she thought, glancing at Hanov.

The road grew worse and worse. . . . They drove into the wood. Here there was no room to turn round, the wheels sank deeply in, water splashed and gurgled through them, and sharp twigs struck them in the face.

"What a road!" said Hanov, and he laughed.

The schoolmistress looked at him and could not understand why this queer man lived here. What could his money, his interesting appearance, his refined bearing do for him here, in this mud, in this God-forsaken, dreary place? He got no special advantages out of life, and here, like Semyon, was driving at a jog-trot on an appalling road and enduring the same discomforts. Why live here if one could live in Petersburg or abroad? And one would have thought it would be nothing for a rich man like him to make a good road instead of this bad one, to avoid enduring this misery and seeing the despair on the faces of his coachman and Semyon; but he only laughed, and apparently did not mind, and wanted no better life. He was kind, soft, naive, and he did not understand this coarse life, just as at the examination he did not know the prayers. He subscribed nothing to the schools but globes, and genuinely regarded himself as a useful person and a prominent worker in the cause of popular education. And what use were his globes here?

"Hold on, Vassilyevna!" said Semyon.

The cart lurched violently and was on the point of upsetting; something heavy rolled on to Marya Vassilyevna's feet—it was her parcel of purchases. There was a steep ascent uphill through the clay; here in the winding ditches rivulets were gurgling. The water seemed to have gnawed away the road; and how could one get along here! The horses breathed hard. Hanov got out of his carriage and walked at the side of the road in his long overcoat. He was hot.

"What a road!" he said, and laughed again. "It would soon smash up one's carriage."

"Nobody obliges you to drive about in such weather," said Semyon surlily. "You should stay at home."

"I am dull at home, grandfather. I don't like staying at home."

Beside old Semyon he looked graceful and vigorous, but yet in his walk there was something just perceptible which betrayed in him a being already touched by decay, weak, and on the road to ruin. And all at once there was a whiff of spirits in the wood. Marya Vassilyevna was filled with dread and pity for this man going to his ruin for no visible cause or reason, and it came into her mind that if she had been his wife or sister she would have devoted her whole life to saving him from ruin. His wife! Life was so ordered that here he was living in his great house alone, and she was living in a God-forsaken village alone, and yet for some reason the mere thought that he and she might be close to one another and equals seemed impossible and absurd. In reality, life was arranged and human relations were complicated so utterly beyond all understanding that when one thought about it one felt uncanny and one's heart sank.

"And it is beyond all understanding," she thought, "why God gives beauty, this graciousness, and sad, sweet eyes to weak, unlucky, useless people—why they are so charming."

"Here we must turn off to the right," said Hanov, getting into his carriage. "Goodbye! I wish you all things good!"

And again she thought of her pupils, of the examination, of the watchman, of the School Council; and when the wind brought the sound of the retreating carriage these thoughts were mingled with others. She longed to think of beautiful eyes, of love, of the happiness which would never be. . . .

His wife? It was cold in the morning, there was no one to heat the stove, the watchman disappeared; the children came in as soon as it was light, bringing in snow and mud and making a noise: it was all so inconvenient, so comfortless. Her abode consisted of one little room and the kitchen close by. Her head ached every day after her work, and after dinner she had heartburn. She had to collect money from the school-children for wood and for the watchman, and to give it to the school guardian, and then to entreat him—that overfed, insolent peasant—for God's sake to send her wood. And at night she dreamed of examinations, peasants, snowdrifts. And this life was making her grow old and coarse, making her ugly, angular, and awkward, as though she were made of lead. She was always afraid, and she would get up from her seat and not venture to sit down in the presence of a member of the Zemstvo or the school guardian. And she used formal, deferential expressions when she spoke of any one of them. And no one thought her attractive, and life was passing drearily, without affection, without friendly sympathy, without interesting acquaintances. How awful it would have been in her position if she had fallen in love!

"Hold on, Vassilyevna!"

Again a sharp ascent uphill. . . .

She had become a schoolmistress from necessity, without feeling any vocation for it; and she had never thought of a vocation, of serving the cause of enlightenment; and it always seemed to her that what was most important in her work was not the children, nor enlightenment, but the examinations. And what time had she for thinking of vocation, of serving the cause of enlightenment? Teachers, badly paid doctors, and their assistants, with their terribly hard work, have not even the comfort of thinking that they are serving an idea or the people, as their heads are always stuffed with thoughts of their daily bread, of wood for the fire, of bad roads, of illnesses. It is a hard-working, an uninteresting life, and only silent, patient cart-horses like Mary Vassilyevna could put up with it for long; the lively, nervous, impressionable people who talked about vocation and serving the idea were soon weary of it and gave up the work.

Semyon kept picking out the driest and shortest way, first by a meadow, then by the backs of the village huts; but in one place the peasants would not let them pass, in another it was the priest's land and they could not cross it, in another Ivan Ionov had bought a plot from the landowner and had dug a ditch round it. They kept having to turn back.

They reached Nizhneye Gorodistche. Near the tavern on the dung-strewn earth, where the snow was still lying, there stood wagons that had brought great bottles of crude sulphuric acid. There were a great many people in the tavern, all drivers, and there was a smell of vodka, tobacco, and sheepskins. There was a loud noise of conversation and the banging of the swing-door. Through the wall, without ceasing for a moment, came the sound of a concertina being played in the shop. Marya Vassilyevna sat down and drank some tea, while at the next table peasants were drinking vodka and beer, perspiring from the tea they had just swallowed and the stifling fumes of the tavern.

"I say, Kuzma!" voices kept shouting in confusion. "What there!" "The Lord bless us!" "Ivan Dementyitch, I can tell you that!" "Look out, old man!"

A little pock-marked man with a black beard, who was quite drunk, was suddenly surprised by something and began using bad language.

"What are you swearing at, you there?" Semyon, who was sitting some way off, responded angrily. "Don't you see the young lady?"

"The young lady!" someone mimicked in another corner.

"Swinish crow!"

"We meant nothing . . ." said the little man in confusion. "I beg your pardon. We pay with our money and the young lady with hers. Good morning!"

"Good morning," answered the schoolmistress.

"And we thank you most feelingly."

Marya Vassilyevna drank her tea with satisfaction, and she, too, began turning red like the peasants, and fell to thinking again about firewood, about the watchman. . . .

"Stay, old man," she heard from the next table, "it's the schoolmistress from Vyazovye. . . . We know her; she's a good young lady."

"She's all right!"

The swing-door was continually banging, some coming in, others going out. Marya Vassilyevna sat on, thinking all the time of the same things, while the concertina went on playing and playing. The patches of sunshine had been on the floor, then they passed to the counter, to the wall, and disappeared altogether; so by the sun it was past midday. The peasants at the next table were getting ready to go. The little man, somewhat unsteadily, went up to Marya Vassilyevna and held out his hand to her; following his example, the others shook hands, too, at parting, and went out one after another, and the swing-door squeaked and slammed nine times.

"Vassilyevna, get ready," Semyon called to her.

They set off. And again they went at a walking pace.

"A little while back they were building a school here in their Nizhneye Gorodistche," said Semyon, turning round. "It was a wicked thing that was done!"

"Why, what?"

"They say the president put a thousand in his pocket, and the school guardian another thousand in his, and the teacher five hundred."

"The whole school only cost a thousand. It's wrong to slander people, grandfather. That's all nonsense."

"I don't know . . . I only tell you what folks say."

But it was clear that Semyon did not believe the schoolmistress. The peasants did not believe her. They always thought she received too large a salary, twenty-one roubles a month (five would have been enough), and that of the money that she collected from the children for the firewood and the watchman the greater part she kept for herself. The guardian thought the same as the peasants, and he himself made a profit off the firewood and received payments from the peasants for being a guardian— without the knowledge of the authorities.

The forest, thank God! was behind them, and now it would be flat, open ground all the way to Vyazovye, and there was not far to go now. They had to cross the river and then the railway line, and then Vyazovye was in sight.

"Where are you driving?" Marya Vassilyevna asked Semyon. "Take the road to the right to the bridge."

"Why, we can go this way as well. It's not deep enough to matter."

"Mind you don't drown the horse."

"What?"

"Look, Hanov is driving to the bridge," said Marya Vassilyevna, seeing the four horses far away to the right. "It is he, I think."

"It is. So he didn't find Bakvist at home. What a pig-headed fellow he is. Lord have mercy upon us! He's driven over there, and what for? It's fully two miles nearer this way."

They reached the river. In the summer it was a little stream easily crossed by wading. It usually dried up in August, but now, after the spring floods, it was a river forty feet in breadth, rapid, muddy, and cold; on the bank and right up to the water there were fresh tracks of wheels, so it had been crossed here.

"Go on!" shouted Semyon angrily and anxiously, tugging violently at the reins and jerking his elbows as a bird does its wings. "Go on!"

The horse went on into the water up to his belly and stopped, but at once went on again with an effort, and Marya Vassilyevna was aware of a keen chilliness in her feet.

"Go on!" she, too, shouted, getting up. "Go on!"

They got out on the bank.

"Nice mess it is, Lord have mercy upon us!" muttered Semyon, setting straight the harness. "It's a perfect plague with this Zemstvo. . . ."

Her shoes and goloshes were full of water, the lower part of her dress and of her coat and one sleeve were wet and dripping: the sugar and flour had got wet, and that was worst of all, and Marya Vassilyevna could only clasp her hands in despair and say:

"Oh, Semyon, Semyon! How tiresome you are really! . . ."

The barrier was down at the railway crossing. A train was coming out of the station. Marya Vassilyevna stood at the crossing waiting till it should pass, and shivering all over with cold. Vyazovye was in sight now, and the school with the green roof, and the church with its crosses flashing in the evening sun: and the station windows flashed too, and a pink smoke rose from the engine . . . and it seemed to her that everything was trembling with cold.

Here was the train; the windows reflected the gleaming light like the crosses on the church: it made her eyes ache to look at them. On the little platform between two first-class carriages a lady was standing, and Marya Vassilyevna glanced at her as she passed. Her mother! What a resemblance! Her mother had had just such luxuriant hair, just such a brow and bend of the head. And with amazing distinctness, for the first time in those thirteen years, there rose before her mind a vivid picture of her mother, her father, her brother, their flat in Moscow, the aquarium with little fish, everything to the tiniest detail; she heard the sound of the piano, her father's voice; she felt as she had been then, young, good-looking, well-dressed, in a bright warm room among her own people. A feeling of joy and happiness suddenly came over her, she pressed her hands to her temples in an ecstacy, and called softly, beseechingly:

"Mother!"

And she began crying, she did not know why. Just at that instant Hanov drove up with his team of four horses, and seeing him she imagined happiness such as she had never had, and smiled and nodded to him as an equal and a friend, and it seemed to her that her happiness, her triumph, was glowing in the sky and on all sides, in the windows and on the trees. Her father and mother had never died, she had never been a schoolmistress, it was a long, tedious, strange dream, and now she had awakened. . . .

"Vassilyevna, get in!"

And at once it all vanished. The barrier was slowly raised. Marya Vassilyevna, shivering and numb with cold, got into the cart. The carriage with the four horses crossed the railway line; Semyon followed it. The signalman took off his cap.

"And here is Vyazovye. Here we are."

Peasants

[First published in the April 1897 issue of
Russkaya Mysl (*Russian Thought*), a Russian magazine.
Collected in *The Witch and Other Stories* (1918).
The story was considered the "greatest piece of literature"
and continues to remain his masterpiece.]

I

Nikolay Tchikildyeev, a waiter in the Moscow hotel, Slavyansky Bazaar, was taken ill. His legs went numb and his gait was affected, so that on one occasion, as he was going along the corridor, he tumbled and fell down with a tray full of ham and peas. He had to leave his job. All his own savings and his wife's were spent on doctors and medicines; they had nothing left to live upon. He felt dull with no work to do, and he made up his mind he must go home to the village. It is better to be ill at home, and living there is cheaper; and it is a true saying that the walls of home are a help.

He reached Zhukovo towards evening. In his memories of childhood he had pictured his home as bright, snug, comfortable. Now, going into the hut, he was positively frightened; it was so dark, so crowded, so unclean. His wife Olga and his daughter Sasha, who had come with him, kept looking in bewilderment at the big untidy stove, which filled up almost half the hut and was black with soot and flies. What lots of flies! The stove was on one side, the beams lay slanting on the walls, and it looked as though the hut were just going to fall to pieces. In the corner, facing the door, under the holy images, bottle labels and newspaper cuttings were stuck on the walls instead of pictures. The poverty, the poverty! Of the grown-up people there were none at home; all were at work at the harvest. On the stove was sitting a white-headed girl of eight, unwashed and apathetic; she did not even glance at them as they came in. On the floor a white cat was rubbing itself against the oven fork.

"Puss, puss!" Sasha called to her. "Puss!"

"She can't hear," said the little girl; "she has gone deaf."

"How is that?"

"Oh, she was beaten."

Nikolay and Olga realized from the first glance what life was like here, but said nothing to one another; in silence they put down their bundles, and went out into the village street. Their hut was the third from the end, and seemed the very poorest and oldest-looking; the second was not much better; but the last one had an iron roof, and curtains in the windows. That hut stood apart, not enclosed; it was a tavern. The huts were in a single row, and the whole of the little village—quiet and dreamy, with willows, elders, and mountain-ash trees peeping out from the yards—had an attractive look.

Beyond the peasants homesteads there was a slope down to the river, so steep and precipitous that huge stones jutted out bare here and there through the clay. Down the slope, among the stones and holes dug by the potters, ran winding paths; bits of broken pottery, some brown, some red, lay piled up in heaps, and below there stretched a broad, level, bright green meadow, from which the hay had been already carried, and in which the peasants' cattle were wandering. The river, three-quarters of a mile from the village, ran twisting and turning, with beautiful leafy banks; beyond it was again a broad meadow, a herd of cattle, long strings of white geese; then, just as on the near side, a steep ascent uphill, and on the top of the hill a hamlet, and a church with five domes, and at a little distance the manor-house.

"It's lovely here in your parts!" said Olga, crossing herself at the sight of the church. "What space, oh Lord!"

Just at that moment the bell began ringing for service (it was Saturday evening). Two little girls, down below, who were dragging up a pail of water, looked round at the church to listen to the bell.

"At this time they are serving the dinners at the Slavyansky Bazaar," said Nikolay dreamily.

Sitting on the edge of the slope, Nikolay and Olga watched the sun setting, watched the gold and crimson sky reflected in the river, in the church windows, and in the whole air—which was soft and still and unutterably pure as it never was in Moscow. And when the sun had set the flocks and herds passed, bleating and lowing; geese flew across from the further side of the river, and all sank into silence; the soft light died away in the air, and the dusk of evening began quickly moving down upon them.

Meanwhile Nikolay's father and mother, two gaunt, bent, toothless old people, just of the same height, came back. The women—the sisters-in-law Marya and Fyokla—who had been working on the landowner's estate beyond the river, arrived home, too. Marya, the wife of Nikolay's brother Kiryak, had six children, and Fyokla, the wife of Nikolay's brother Denis—who had gone for a soldier—had two; and when Nikolay, going into the hut, saw all the family, all those bodies big and little moving about on the lockers, in the hanging cradles and in all the corners, and when he saw the greed with which the old father and the women ate the black bread, dipping it in water, he realized he had made a mistake in coming here, sick, penniless, and with a family, too—a great mistake!

"And where is Kiryak?" he asked after they had exchanged greetings.

"He is in service at the merchant's," answered his father; "a keeper in the woods. He is not a bad peasant, but too fond of his glass."

"He is no great help!" said the old woman tearfully. "Our men are a grievous lot; they bring nothing into the house, but take plenty out. Kiryak drinks, and so does the old man; it is no use hiding a sin; he knows his way to the tavern. The Heavenly Mother is wroth."

In honour of the visitors they brought out the samovar. The tea smelt of fish; the sugar was grey and looked as though it had been nibbled; cockroaches ran to and fro over the bread and among the crockery. It was disgusting to drink, and the conversation was disgusting, too—about nothing but poverty and illnesses. But before they had time to empty their first cups there came a loud, prolonged, drunken shout from the yard:

"Ma-arya!"

"It looks as though Kiryak were coming," said the old man. "Speak of the devil."

All were hushed. And again, soon afterwards, the same shout, coarse and drawn-out as though it came out of the earth:

"Ma-arya!"

Marya, the elder sister-in-law, turned pale and huddled against the stove, and it was strange to see the look of terror on the face of the strong, broad-shouldered, ugly woman. Her daughter, the child who had been sitting on the stove and looked so apathetic, suddenly broke into loud weeping.

"What are you howling for, you plague?" Fyokla, a handsome woman, also strong and broad-shouldered, shouted to her. "He won't kill you, no fear!"

From his old father Nikolay learned that Marya was afraid to live in the forest with Kiryak, and that when he was drunk he always came for her, made a row, and beat her mercilessly.

"Ma-arya!" the shout sounded close to the door.

"Protect me, for Christ's sake, good people!" faltered Marya, breathing as though she had been plunged into very cold water. "Protect me, kind people. . . ."

All the children in the hut began crying, and looking at them, Sasha, too, began to cry. They heard a drunken cough, and a tall, black-bearded peasant wearing a winter cap came into the hut, and was the more terrible because his face could not be seen in the dim light of the little lamp. It was Kiryak. Going up to his wife, he swung his arm and punched her in the face with his fist. Stunned by the blow, she did not utter a sound, but sat down, and her nose instantly began bleeding.

"What a disgrace! What a disgrace!" muttered the old man, clambering up on to the stove. "Before visitors, too! It's a sin!"

The old mother sat silent, bowed, lost in thought; Fyokla rocked the cradle.

Evidently conscious of inspiring fear, and pleased at doing so, Kiryak seized Marya by the arm, dragged her towards the door, and bellowed like an animal in order to seem still more terrible; but at that moment he suddenly caught sight of the visitors and stopped.

"Oh, they have come," he said, letting his wife go; "my own brother and his family. . . ."

Staggering and opening wide his red, drunken eyes, he said his prayer before the image and went on:

"My brother and his family have come to the parental home . . . from Moscow, I suppose. The great capital Moscow, to be sure, the mother of cities. . . . Excuse me."

He sank down on the bench near the samovar and began drinking tea, sipping it loudly from the saucer in the midst of general silence. . . . He drank off a dozen cups, then reclined on the bench and began snoring.

They began going to bed. Nikolay, as an invalid, was put on the stove with his old father; Sasha lay down on the floor, while Olga went with the other women into the barn.

"Aye, aye, dearie," she said, lying down on the hay beside Marya; "you won't mend your trouble with tears. Bear it in patience, that is all. It is written in the Scriptures: 'If anyone smite thee on the right cheek, offer him the left one also.' . . . Aye, aye, dearie."

Then in a low sing-song murmur she told them about Moscow, about her own life, how she had been a servant in furnished lodgings.

"And in Moscow the houses are big, built of brick," she said; "and there are ever so many churches, forty times forty, dearie; and they are all gentry in the houses, so handsome and so proper!"

Marya told her that she had not only never been in Moscow, but had not even been in their own district town; she could not read or write, and knew no prayers, not even "Our Father." Both she and Fyokla, the other sister-in-law, who was sitting a little way off listening, were extremely ignorant and could understand nothing. They both disliked their husbands; Marya was afraid of Kiryak, and whenever he stayed with her she was shaking with fear, and always got a headache from the fumes of vodka and tobacco with which he reeked. And in answer to the question whether she did not miss her husband, Fyokla answered with vexation:

"Miss him!"

They talked a little and sank into silence.

It was cool, and a cock crowed at the top of his voice near the barn, preventing them from sleeping. When the bluish morning light was already peeping through all the crevices, Fyokla got up stealthily and went out, and then they heard the sound of her bare feet running off somewhere.

II

Olga went to church, and took Marya with her. As they went down the path towards the meadow both were in good spirits. Olga liked the wide view, and Marya felt that in her sister-in-law she had someone near and akin to her. The sun was rising. Low down over the meadow floated a drowsy hawk. The river looked gloomy; there was a haze hovering over it here and there, but on the further bank a streak of light already stretched across the hill. The church was gleaming, and in the manor garden the rooks were cawing furiously.

"The old man is all right," Marya told her, "but Granny is strict; she is continually nagging. Our own grain lasted till Carnival. We buy flour now at the tavern. She is angry about it; she says we eat too much."

"Aye, aye, dearie! Bear it in patience, that is all. It is written: 'Come unto Me, all ye that labour and are heavy laden.'"

Olga spoke sedately, rhythmically, and she walked like a pilgrim woman, with a rapid, anxious step. Every day she read the gospel, read it aloud like a deacon; a great deal of it she did not understand, but the words of the gospel moved her to tears, and words like "for as much as" and "verily" she pronounced with a sweet flutter at her heart. She believed in God, in the Holy Mother, in the Saints; she believed one must not offend anyone in the world—not simple folks, nor Germans, nor gypsies, nor Jews—and woe even to those who have no compassion on the beasts. She believed this was written in the Holy Scriptures; and so, when she pronounced phrases from Holy Writ, even though she did not understand them, her face grew softened, compassionate, and radiant.

"What part do you come from?" Marya asked her.

"I am from Vladimir. Only I was taken to Moscow long ago, when I was eight years old."

They reached the river. On the further side a woman was standing at the water's edge, undressing.

"It's our Fyokla," said Marya, recognizing her. "She has been over the river to the manor yard. To the stewards. She is a shameless hussy and foul-mouthed—fearfully!"

Fyokla, young and vigorous as a girl, with her black eyebrows and her loose hair, jumped off the bank and began splashing the water with her feet, and waves ran in all directions from her.

"Shameless—dreadfully!" repeated Marya.

The river was crossed by a rickety little bridge of logs, and exactly below it in the clear, limpid water was a shoal of broad-headed mullets. The dew was glistening on the green bushes that looked into the water. There was a feeling of warmth; it was comforting! What a lovely morning! And how lovely life would have been in this world, in all likelihood, if it were not for poverty, horrible, hopeless poverty, from which one can find no refuge! One had only to look round at the village to remember vividly all that had happened the day before, and the illusion of happiness which seemed to surround them vanished instantly.

They reached the church. Marya stood at the entrance, and did not dare to go farther. She did not dare to sit down either. Though they only began ringing for mass between eight and nine, she remained standing the whole time.

While the gospel was being read the crowd suddenly parted to make way for the family from the great house. Two young girls in white frocks and wide-brimmed hats walked in; with them a chubby, rosy boy in a sailor suit. Their appearance touched Olga; she made up her mind from the first glance that they were refined, well-educated, handsome people. Marya looked at them from under her brows, sullenly, dejectedly, as though they were not human beings coming in, but monsters who might crush her if she did not make way for them.

And every time the deacon boomed out something in his bass voice she fancied she heard "Ma-arya!" and she shuddered.

III

The arrival of the visitors was already known in the village, and directly after mass a number of people gathered together in the hut. The Leonytchevs and Matvyeitchevs and the Ilyitchovs came to inquire about their relations who were in service in Moscow. All the lads of Zhukovo who could read and write were packed off to Moscow and hired out as butlers or waiters (while from the village on the other side of the river the boys all became bakers), and that had been the custom from the days of serfdom long ago when a certain Luka Ivanitch, a peasant from Zhukovo, now a legendary figure, who had been a waiter in one of the Moscow clubs, would take none but his fellow-villagers into his service, and found jobs for them in taverns and restaurants; and from that time the village of Zhukovo was always called among the inhabitants of the surrounding districts Slaveytown. Nikolay had been taken to Moscow when he was eleven, and Ivan Makaritch, one of the Matvyeitchevs, at that time a headwaiter in the "Hermitage" garden, had put him into a situation. And now, addressing the Matvyeitchevs, Nikolay said emphatically:

"Ivan Makaritch was my benefactor, and I am bound to pray for him day and night, as it is owing to him I have become a good man."

"My good soul!" a tall old woman, the sister of Ivan Makaritch, said tearfully, "and not a word have we heard about him, poor dear."

"In the winter he was in service at Omon's, and this season there was a rumour he was somewhere out of town, in gardens. . . . He has aged! In old days he would bring home as much as ten roubles a day in the summertime, but now things are very quiet everywhere. The old man frets."

The women looked at Nikolay's feet, shod in felt boots, and at his pale face, and said mournfully:

"You are not one to get on, Nikolay Osipitch; you are not one to get on! No, indeed!"

And they all made much of Sasha. She was ten years old, but she was little and very thin, and might have been taken for no more than seven. Among the other little girls, with their sunburnt faces and roughly cropped hair, dressed in long faded smocks, she with her white little face, with her big dark eyes, with a red ribbon in her hair, looked funny, as though she were some little wild creature that had been caught and brought into the hut.

"She can read, too," Olga said in her praise, looking tenderly at her daughter. "Read a little, child!" she said, taking the gospel from the corner. "You read, and the good Christian people will listen."

The testament was an old and heavy one in leather binding, with dog's-eared edges, and it exhaled a smell as though monks had come into the hut. Sasha raised her eyebrows and began in a loud rhythmic chant:

"'And the angel of the Lord . . . appeared unto Joseph, saying unto him: Rise up, and take the Babe and His mother.'"

"The Babe and His mother," Olga repeated, and flushed all over with emotion.

"'And flee into Egypt . . . and tarry there until such time as . . .'"

At the word "tarry" Olga could not refrain from tears. Looking at her, Marya began to whimper, and after her Ivan Makaritch's sister. The old father cleared his throat, and bustled about to find something to give his granddaughter, but, finding nothing, gave it up with a wave of his hand. And when the reading was over the neighbours dispersed to their homes, feeling touched and very much pleased with Olga and Sasha.

As it was a holiday, the family spent the whole day at home. The old woman, whom her husband, her daughters-in-law, her grandchildren all alike called Granny, tried to do everything herself; she heated the stove and set the samovar with her own hands, even waited at the midday meal, and then complained that she was worn out with work. And all the time she was uneasy for fear someone should eat a piece too much, or that her husband and daughters-in-law would sit idle. At one time she would hear the tavern-keeper's geese going at the back of the huts to her kitchen garden, and she would run out of the hut with a long stick and spend half an hour screaming shrilly by her cabbages, which were as gaunt and scraggy as herself; at another time she fancied that a crow had designs on her chickens, and she rushed to attack it with loud words of abuse. She was cross and grumbling from morning till night. And often she raised such an outcry that passers-by stopped in the street.

She was not affectionate towards the old man, reviling him as a lazy-bones and a plague. He was not a responsible, reliable peasant, and perhaps if she had not been continually nagging at him he would not have worked at all, but would have simply sat on the stove and talked. He talked to his son at great length about certain enemies of his, complained of the insults he said he had to put up with every day from the neighbours, and it was tedious to listen to him.

"Yes," he would say, standing with his arms akimbo, "yes. . . . A week after the Exaltation of the Cross I sold my hay willingly at thirty kopecks a pood. . . . Well and good. . . . So you see I was taking the hay in the morning with a good will; I was interfering with no one. In an unlucky hour I see the village elder, Antip Syedelnikov, coming out of the tavern. 'Where are you taking it, you ruffian?' says he, and takes me by the ear."

Kiryak had a fearful headache after his drinking bout, and was ashamed to face his brother.

"What vodka does! Ah, my God!" he muttered, shaking his aching head. "For Christ's sake, forgive me, brother and sister; I'm not happy myself."

As it was a holiday, they bought a herring at the tavern and made a soup of the herring's head. At midday they all sat down to drink tea, and went on drinking it for a long time, till they were all perspiring; they looked positively swollen from the tea-drinking, and after it began sipping the broth from the herring's head, all helping themselves out of one bowl. But the herring itself Granny had hidden.

In the evening a potter began firing pots on the ravine. In the meadow below the girls got up a choral dance and sang songs. They played the concertina. And on the other side of the river a kiln for baking pots was lighted, too, and the girls sang songs, and in the distance the singing sounded soft and musical. The peasants were noisy in and about the tavern. They were singing with drunken voices, each on his own account, and swearing at one another, so that Olga could only shudder and say:

"Oh, holy Saints!"

She was amazed that the abuse was incessant, and those who were loudest and most persistent in this foul language were the old men who were so near their end. And the girls and children heard the swearing, and were not in the least disturbed by it, and it was evident that they were used to it from their cradles.

It was past midnight, the kilns on both sides of the river were put out, but in the meadow below and in the tavern the merrymaking still went on. The old father and Kiryak, both drunk, walking arm-in-arm and jostling against each other's shoulders, went to the barn where Olga and Marya were lying.

"Let her alone," the old man persuaded him; "let her alone. . . . She is a harmless woman. . . . It's a sin. . . ."

"Ma-arya!" shouted Kiryak.

"Let her be. . . . It's a sin. . . . She is not a bad woman."

Both stopped by the barn and went on.

"I lo-ove the flowers of the fi-ield," the old man began singing suddenly in a high, piercing tenor. "I lo-ove to gather them in the meadows!"

Then he spat, and with a filthy oath went into the hut.

IV

Granny put Sasha by her kitchen garden and told her to keep watch that the geese did not go in. It was a hot August day. The tavern-keeper's geese could make their way into the kitchen garden by the backs of the huts, but now they were busily engaged picking up oats by the tavern, peacefully conversing together, and only the gander craned his head high as though trying to see whether the old woman were coming with her stick. The other geese might come up from below, but they were now grazing far away the other side of the river, stretched out in a long white garland about the meadow. Sasha stood about a little, grew weary, and, seeing that the geese were not coming, went away to the ravine.

There she saw Marya's eldest daughter Motka, who was standing motionless on a big stone, staring at the church. Marya had given birth to thirteen children, but she only had six living, all girls, not one boy, and the eldest was eight. Motka in a long smock was standing barefooted in the full sunshine; the sun was blazing down right on her head, but she did not notice that, and seemed as though turned to stone. Sasha stood beside her and said, looking at the church:

"God lives in the church. Men have lamps and candles, but God has little green and red and blue lamps like little eyes. At night God walks about the church, and with Him the Holy Mother of God and Saint Nikolay, thud, thud, thud! . . . And the watchman is terrified, terrified! Aye, aye, dearie," she added, imitating her mother. "And when the end of the world comes all the churches will be carried up to heaven."

"With the-ir be-ells?" Motka asked in her deep voice, drawling every syllable.

"With their bells. And when the end of the world comes the good will go to Paradise, but the angry will burn in fire eternal and unquenchable, dearie. To my mother as well as to Marya God will say: 'You never offended anyone, and for that go to the right to Paradise'; but to Kiryak and Granny He will say: 'You go to the left into the fire.' And anyone who has eaten meat in Lent will go into the fire, too."

She looked upwards at the sky, opening wide her eyes, and said:

"Look at the sky without winking, you will see angels."

Motka began looking at the sky, too, and a minute passed in silence.

"Do you see them?" asked Sasha.

"I don't," said Motka in her deep voice.

"But I do. Little angels are flying about the sky and flap, flap with their little wings as though they were gnats."

Motka thought for a little, with her eyes on the ground, and asked:

"Will Granny burn?"

"She will, dearie."

From the stone an even gentle slope ran down to the bottom, covered with soft green grass, which one longed to lie down on or to touch with one's hands . . . Sasha lay down and rolled to the bottom. Motka with a grave, severe face, taking a deep breath, lay down, too, and rolled to the bottom, and in doing so tore her smock from the hem to the shoulder.

"What fun it is!" said Sasha, delighted.

They walked up to the top to roll down again, but at that moment they heard a shrill, familiar voice. Oh, how awful it was! Granny, a toothless, bony, hunchbacked figure, with short grey hair which was fluttering in the wind, was driving the geese out of the kitchen garden with a long stick, shouting.

"They have trampled all the cabbages, the damned brutes! I'd cut your throats, thrice accursed plagues! Bad luck to you!"

She saw the little girls, flung down the stick and picked up a switch, and, seizing Sasha by the neck with her fingers, thin and hard as the gnarled branches of a tree, began whipping her. Sasha cried with pain and terror, while the gander, waddling and stretching his neck, went up to the old woman and hissed at her, and when he went back to his flock all the geese greeted him approvingly with "Ga-ga-ga!" Then Granny proceeded to whip Motka, and in this Motka's smock was torn again. Feeling in despair, and crying loudly, Sasha went to the hut to complain. Motka followed her; she, too, was crying on a deeper note, without wiping her tears, and her face was as wet as though it had been dipped in water.

"Holy Saints!" cried Olga, aghast, as the two came into the hut. "Queen of Heaven!"

Sasha began telling her story, while at the same time Granny walked in with a storm of shrill cries and abuse; then Fyokla flew into a rage, and there was an uproar in the hut.

"Never mind, never mind!" Olga, pale and upset, tried to comfort them, stroking Sasha's head. "She is your grandmother; it's a sin to be angry with her. Never mind, my child."

Nikolay, who was worn out already by the everlasting hubbub, hunger, stifling fumes, filth, who hated and despised the poverty, who was ashamed for his wife and daughter to see his father and mother, swung his legs off the stove and said in an irritable, tearful voice, addressing his mother:

"You must not beat her! You have no right to beat her!"

"You lie rotting on the stove, you wretched creature!" Fyokla shouted at him spitefully. "The devil brought you all on us, eating us out of house and home."

Sasha and Motka and all the little girls in the hut huddled on the stove in the corner behind Nikolay's back, and from that refuge listened in silent terror, and the beating of their little hearts could be distinctly heard. Whenever there is someone in a family who has long been ill, and hopelessly ill, there come painful moments when all timidly, secretly, at the bottom of their hearts long for his death; and only the children fear the death of someone near them, and always feel horrified at the thought of it. And now the children, with bated breath, with a mournful look on their faces, gazed at Nikolay and thought that he was soon to die; and they wanted to cry and to say something friendly and compassionate to him.

He pressed close to Olga, as though seeking protection, and said to her softly in a quavering voice:

"Olya darling, I can't stay here longer. It's more than I can bear. For God's sake, for Christ's sake, write to your sister Klavdia Abramovna. Let her sell and pawn everything she has; let her send us the money. We will go away from here. Oh, Lord," he went on miserably, "to have one peep at Moscow! If I could see it in my dreams, the dear place!"

And when the evening came on, and it was dark in the hut, it was so dismal that it was hard to utter a word. Granny, very ill-tempered, soaked some crusts of rye bread in a cup, and was a long time, a whole hour, sucking at them. Marya, after milking the cow, brought in a pail of milk and set it on a bench; then Granny poured it from the pail into a jug just as slowly and deliberately, evidently pleased that it was now the Fast of the Assumption, so that no one would drink milk and it would be left untouched. And she only poured out a very little in a saucer for Fyokla's baby. When Marya and she carried the jug down to the cellar Motka suddenly stirred, clambered down from the stove, and going to the bench where stood the wooden cup full of crusts, sprinkled into it some milk from the saucer.

Granny, coming back into the hut, sat down to her soaked crusts again, while Sasha and Motka, sitting on the stove, gazed at her, and they were glad that she had broken her fast and now would go to hell. They were comforted and lay down to sleep, and Sasha as she dozed off to sleep imagined the Day of Judgment: a huge fire was burning, somewhat like a potter's kiln, and the Evil One, with horns like a cow's, and black all over, was driving Granny into the fire with a long stick, just as Granny herself had been driving the geese.

V

On the day of the Feast of the Assumption, between ten and eleven in the evening, the girls and lads who were merrymaking in the meadow suddenly raised a clamour and outcry, and ran in the direction of the village; and those who were above on the edge of the ravine could not for the first moment make out what was the matter.

"Fire! Fire!" they heard desperate shouts from below. "The village is on fire!"

Those who were sitting above looked round, and a terrible and extraordinary spectacle met their eyes. On the thatched roof of one of the end cottages stood a column of flame, seven feet high, which curled round and scattered sparks in all directions as though it were a fountain. And all at once the whole roof burst into bright flame, and the crackling of the fire was audible.

The light of the moon was dimmed, and the whole village was by now bathed in a red quivering glow: black shadows moved over the ground, there was a smell of burning, and those who ran up from below were all gasping and could not speak for trembling; they jostled against each other, fell down, and they could hardly see in the unaccustomed light, and did not recognize each other. It was terrible. What seemed particularly dreadful was that doves were flying over the fire in the smoke; and in the tavern, where they did not yet know of the fire, they were still singing and playing the concertina as though there were nothing the matter.

"Uncle Semyon's on fire," shouted a loud, coarse voice.

Marya was fussing about round her hut, weeping and wringing her hands, while her teeth chattered, though the fire was a long way off at the other end of the village. Nikolay came out in high felt boots, the children ran out in their little smocks. Near the village constable's hut an iron sheet was struck. Boom, boom, boom! . . . floated through the air, and this repeated, persistent sound sent a pang to the heart and turned one cold. The old women stood with the holy ikons. Sheep, calves, cows were driven out of the back-yards into the street; boxes, sheepskins, tubs were carried out. A black stallion, who was kept apart from the drove of horses because he kicked and injured them, on being set free ran once or twice up and down the village, neighing and pawing the ground; then suddenly stopped short near a cart and began kicking it with his hind-legs.

They began ringing the bells in the church on the other side of the river.

Near the burning hut it was hot and so light that one could distinctly see every blade of grass. Semyon, a red-haired peasant with a long nose, wearing a reefer-jacket and a cap pulled down right over his ears, sat on one of the boxes which they had succeeded in bringing out: his wife was lying on her face, moaning and unconscious. A little old man of eighty, with a big beard, who looked like a gnome—not one of the villagers, though obviously connected in some way with the fire—walked about bareheaded, with a white bundle in his arms. The glare was reflected on his bald head. The village elder, Antip Syedelnikov, as swarthy and black-haired as a gypsy, went up to the hut with an axe, and hacked out the windows one after another—no one knew why—then began chopping up the roof.

"Women, water!" he shouted. "Bring the engine! Look sharp!"

The peasants, who had been drinking in the tavern just before, dragged the engine up. They were all drunk; they kept stumbling and falling down, and all had a helpless expression and tears in their eyes.

"Wenches, water!" shouted the elder, who was drunk, too. "Look sharp, wenches!"

The women and the girls ran downhill to where there was a spring, and kept hauling pails and buckets of water up the hill, and, pouring it into the engine, ran down again. Olga and Marya and Sasha and Motka all brought water. The women and the boys pumped the water; the pipe hissed, and the elder, directing it now at the door, now at the windows, held back the stream with his finger, which made it hiss more sharply still.

"Bravo, Antip!" voices shouted approvingly. "Do your best."

Antip went inside the hut into the fire and shouted from within.

"Pump! Bestir yourselves, good Christian folk, in such a terrible mischance!"

The peasants stood round in a crowd, doing nothing but staring at the fire. No one knew what to do, no one had the sense to do anything, though there were stacks of wheat, hay, barns, and piles of faggots standing all round. Kiryak and old Osip, his father, both tipsy, were standing there, too. And as though to justify his doing nothing, old Osip said, addressing the woman who lay on the ground:

"What is there to trouble about, old girl! The hut is insured—why are you taking on?"

Semyon, addressing himself first to one person and then to another, kept describing how the fire had started.

"That old man, the one with the bundle, a house-serf of General Zhukov's. . . . He was cook at our general's, God rest his soul! He came over this evening: 'Let me stay the night,' says he. . . . Well, we had a glass, to be sure. . . . The wife got the samovar—she was going to give the old fellow a cup of tea, and in an unlucky hour she set the samovar in the entrance. The sparks from the chimney must have blown straight up to the thatch; that's how it was. We were almost burnt ourselves. And the old fellow's cap has been burnt; what a shame!"

And the sheet of iron was struck indefatigably, and the bells kept ringing in the church the other side of the river. In the glow of the fire, Olga, breathless, looking with horror at the red sheep and the pink doves flying in the smoke, kept running down the hill and up again. It seemed to her that the ringing went to her heart with a sharp stab, that the fire would never be over, that Sasha was lost. . . . And when the ceiling of the hut fell in with a crash, the thought that now the whole village would be burnt made her weak and faint, and she could not go on fetching water, but sat down on the ravine, setting the pail down near her; beside her and below her, the peasant women sat wailing as though at a funeral.

Then the stewards and watchmen from the estate the other side of the river arrived in two carts, bringing with them a fire-engine. A very young student in an unbuttoned white tunic rode up on horseback. There was the thud of axes. They put a ladder to the burning framework of the house, and five men ran up it at once. Foremost of them all was the student, who was red in the face and shouting in a harsh hoarse voice, and in a tone as though putting out fires was a thing he was used to. They pulled the house to pieces, a beam at a time; they dragged away the corn, the hurdles, and the stacks that were near.

"Don't let them break it up!" cried stern voices in the crowd. "Don't let them."

Kiryak made his way up to the hut with a resolute air, as though he meant to prevent the newcomers from breaking up the hut, but one of the workmen turned him back with a blow in his neck. There was the sound of laughter, the workman dealt him another blow, Kiryak fell down, and crawled back into the crowd on his hands and knees.

Two handsome girls in hats, probably the student's sisters, came from the other side of the river. They stood a little way off, looking at the fire. The beams that had been dragged apart were no longer burning, but were smoking vigorously; the student, who was working the hose, turned the water, first on the beams, then on the peasants, then on the women who were bringing the water.

"George!" the girls called to him reproachfully in anxiety, "George!"

The fire was over. And only when they began to disperse they noticed that the day was breaking, that everyone was pale and rather dark in the face, as it always seems in the early morning when the last stars are going out. As they separated, the peasants laughed and made jokes about General Zhukov's cook and his cap which had been burnt; they already wanted to turn the fire into a joke, and even seemed sorry that it had so soon been put out.

"How well you extinguished the fire, sir!" said Olga to the student. "You ought to come to us in Moscow: there we have a fire every day."

"Why, do you come from Moscow?" asked one of the young ladies.

"Yes, miss. My husband was a waiter at the Slavyansky Bazaar. And this is my daughter," she said, indicating Sasha, who was cold and huddling up to her. "She is a Moscow girl, too."

The two young ladies said something in French to the student, and he gave Sasha a twenty-kopeck piece.

Old Father Osip saw this, and there was a gleam of hope in his face.

"We must thank God, your honour, there was no wind," he said, addressing the student, "or else we should have been all burnt up together. Your honour, kind gentlefolks," he added in embarrassment in a lower tone, "the morning's chilly . . . something to warm one . . . half a bottle to your honour's health."

Nothing was given him, and clearing his throat he slouched home. Olga stood afterwards at the end of the street and watched the two carts crossing the river by the ford and the gentlefolks walking across the meadow; a carriage was waiting for them the other side of the river. Going into the hut, she described to her husband with enthusiasm:

"Such good people! And so beautiful! The young ladies were like cherubim."

"Plague take them!" Fyokla, sleepy, said spitefully.

VI

Marya thought herself unhappy, and said that she would be very glad to die; Fyokla, on the other hand, found all this life to her taste: the poverty, the uncleanliness, and the incessant quarrelling. She ate what was given her without discrimination; slept anywhere, on whatever came to hand. She would empty the slops just at the porch, would splash them out from the doorway, and then walk barefoot through the puddle. And from the very first day she took a dislike to Olga and Nikolay just because they did not like this life.

"We shall see what you'll find to eat here, you Moscow gentry!" she said malignantly. "We shall see!"

One morning, it was at the beginning of September, Fyokla, vigorous, good-looking, and rosy from the cold, brought up two pails of water; Marya and Olga were sitting meanwhile at the table drinking tea.

"Tea and sugar," said Fyokla sarcastically. "The fine ladies!" she added, setting down the pails. "You have taken to the fashion of tea every day. You better look out that you don't burst with your tea-drinking," she went on, looking with hatred at Olga. "That's how you have come by your fat mug, having a good time in Moscow, you lump of flesh!" She swung the yoke and hit Olga such a blow on the shoulder that the two sisters-in-law could only clasp their hands and say:

"Oh, holy Saints!"

Then Fyokla went down to the river to wash the clothes, swearing all the time so loudly that she could be heard in the hut.

The day passed and was followed by the long autumn evening. They wound silk in the hut; everyone did it except Fyokla; she had gone over the river. They got the silk from a factory close by, and the whole family working together earned next to nothing, twenty kopecks a week.

"Things were better in the old days under the gentry," said the old father as he wound silk. "You worked and ate and slept, everything in its turn. At dinner you had cabbage-soup and boiled grain, and at supper the same again. Cucumbers and cabbage in plenty: you could eat to your heart's content, as much as you wanted. And there was more strictness. Everyone minded what he was about."

The hut was lighted by a single little lamp, which burned dimly and smoked. When someone screened the lamp and a big shadow fell across the window, the bright moonlight could be seen. Old Osip, speaking slowly, told them how they used to live before the emancipation; how in those very parts, where life was now so poor and so dreary, they used to hunt with harriers, greyhounds, retrievers, and when they went out as beaters the peasants were given vodka; how whole waggonloads of game used to be sent to Moscow for the young masters; how the bad were beaten with rods or sent away to the Tver estate, while the good were rewarded. And Granny told them something, too. She remembered everything, positively everything. She described her mistress, a kind, God-fearing woman, whose husband was a profligate and a rake, and all of whose daughters made unlucky marriages: one married a drunkard, another married a workman, the other eloped secretly (Granny herself, at that time a young girl, helped in the elopement), and they had all three as well as their mother died early from grief. And remembering all this, Granny positively began to shed tears.

All at once someone knocked at the door, and they all started.

"Uncle Osip, give me a night's lodging."

The little bald old man, General Zhukov's cook, the one whose cap had been burnt, walked in. He sat down and listened, then he, too, began telling stories of all sorts. Nikolay, sitting on the stove with his legs hanging down, listened and asked questions about the dishes that were prepared in the old days for the gentry. They talked of rissoles, cutlets, various soups and sauces, and the cook, who remembered everything very well, mentioned dishes that are no longer served. There was one, for instance—a dish made of bulls' eyes, which was called "waking up in the morning."

"And used you to do cutlets a la marechal?" asked Nikolay.

"No."

Nikolay shook his head reproachfully and said:

"Tut, tut! You were not much of a cook!"

The little girls sitting and lying on the stove stared down without bJlinking; it seemed as though there were a great many of them, like cherubim in the clouds. They liked the stories: they were breathless; they shuddered and turned pale with alternate rapture and terror, and they listened breathlessly, afraid to stir, to Granny, whose stories were the most interesting of all.

They lay down to sleep in silence; and the old people, troubled and excited by their reminiscences, thought how precious was youth, of which, whatever it might have been like, nothing was left in the memory but what was living, joyful, touching, and how terribly cold was death, which was not far off, better not think of it! The lamp died down. And the dusk, and the two little windows sharply defined by the moonlight, and the stillness and the creak of the cradle, reminded them for some reason that life was over, that nothing one could do would bring it back.... You doze off, you forget yourself, and suddenly someone touches your shoulder or breathes on your cheek—and sleep is gone; your body feels cramped, and thoughts of death keep creeping into your mind. You turn on the other side: death is forgotten, but old dreary, sickening thoughts of poverty, of food, of how dear flour is getting, stray through the mind, and a little later again you remember that life is over and you cannot bring it back....

"Oh, Lord!" sighed the cook.

Someone gave a soft, soft tap at the window. It must be Fyokla come back. Olga got up, and yawning and whispering a prayer, opened the door, then drew the bolt in the outer room, but no one came in; only from the street came a cold draught and a sudden brightness from the moonlight. The street, still and deserted, and the moon itself floating across the sky, could be seen at the open door.

"Who is there?" called Olga.

"I," she heard the answer—"it is I."

Near the door, crouching against the wall, stood Fyokla, absolutely naked. She was shivering with cold, her teeth were chattering, and in the bright moonlight she looked very pale, strange, and beautiful. The shadows on her, and the bright moonlight on her skin, stood out vividly, and her dark eyebrows and firm, youthful bosom were defined with peculiar distinctness.

"The ruffians over there undressed me and turned me out like this," she said. "I've come home without my clothes . . . naked as my mother bore me. Bring me something to put on."

"But go inside!" Olga said softly, beginning to shiver, too.

"I don't want the old folks to see." Granny was, in fact, already stirring and muttering, and the old father asked: "Who is there?" Olga brought her own smock and skirt, dressed Fyokla, and then both went softly into the inner room, trying not to make a noise with the door.

"Is that you, you sleek one?" Granny grumbled angrily, guessing who it was. "Fie upon you, nightwalker! . . . Bad luck to you!"

"It's all right, it's all right," whispered Olga, wrapping Fyokla up; "it's all right, dearie."

All was stillness again. They always slept badly; everyone was kept awake by something worrying and persistent: the old man by the pain in his back, Granny by anxiety and anger, Marya by terror, the children by itch and hunger. Now, too, their sleep was troubled; they kept turning over from one side to the other, talking in their sleep, getting up for a drink.

Fyokla suddenly broke into a loud, coarse howl, but immediately checked herself, and only uttered sobs from time to time, growing softer and on a lower note, until she relapsed into silence. From time to time from the other side of the river there floated the sound of the beating of the hours; but the time seemed somehow strange—five was struck and then three.

"Oh Lord!" sighed the cook.

Looking at the windows, it was difficult to tell whether it was still moonlight or whether the dawn had begun. Marya got up and went out, and she could be heard milking the cows and saying, "Stea-dy!" Granny went out, too. It was still dark in the hut, but all the objects in it could be discerned.

Nikolay, who had not slept all night, got down from the stove. He took his dress-coat out of a green box, put it on, and going to the window, stroked the sleeves and took hold of the coat-tails—and smiled. Then he carefully took off the coat, put it away in his box, and lay down again.

Marya came in again and began lighting the stove. She was evidently hardly awake, and seemed dropping asleep as she walked. Probably she had had some dream, or the stories of the night before came into her mind as, stretching luxuriously before the stove, she said:

"No, freedom is better."

VII

The master arrived—that was what they called the police inspector. When he would come and what he was coming for had been known for the last week. There were only forty households in Zhukovo, but more than two thousand roubles of arrears of rates and taxes had accumulated.

The police inspector stopped at the tavern. He drank there two glasses of tea, and then went on foot to the village elder's hut, near which a crowd of those who were in debt stood waiting. The elder, Antip Syedelnikov, was, in spite of his youth—he was only a little over thirty—strict and always on the side of the authorities, though he himself was poor and did not pay his taxes regularly. Evidently he enjoyed being elder, and liked the sense of authority, which he could only display by strictness. In the village council the peasants were afraid of him and obeyed him. It would sometimes happen that he would pounce on a drunken man in the street or near the tavern, tie his hands behind him, and put him in the lock-up. On one occasion he even put Granny in the lock-up because she went to the village council instead of Osip, and began swearing, and he kept her there for a whole day and night. He had never lived in a town or read a book, but somewhere or other had picked up various learned expressions, and loved to make use of them in conversation, and he was respected for this though he was not always understood.

When Osip came into the village elder's hut with his tax book, the police inspector, a lean old man with a long grey beard, in a grey tunic, was sitting at a table in the passage, writing something. It was clean in the hut; all the walls were dotted with pictures cut out of the illustrated papers, and in the most conspicuous place near the ikon there was a portrait of the Battenburg who was the Prince of Bulgaria. By the table stood Antip Syedelnikov with his arms folded.

"There is one hundred and nineteen roubles standing against him," he said when it came to Osip's turn. "Before Easter he paid a rouble, and he has not paid a kopeck since."

The police inspector raised his eyes to Osip and asked:

"Why is this, brother?"

"Show Divine mercy, your honour," Osip began, growing agitated. "Allow me to say last year the gentleman at Lutorydsky said to me, 'Osip,' he said, 'sell your hay . . . you sell it,' he said. Well, I had a hundred poods for sale; the women mowed it on the water-meadow. Well, we struck a bargain all right, willingly. . . ."

He complained of the elder, and kept turning round to the peasants as though inviting them to bear witness; his face flushed red and perspired, and his eyes grew sharp and angry.

"I don't know why you are saying all this," said the police inspector. "I am asking you . . . I am asking you why you don't pay your arrears. You don't pay, any of you, and am I to be responsible for you?"

"I can't do it."

"His words have no sequel, your honour," said the elder. "The Tchikildyeevs certainly are of a defective class, but if you will just ask the others, the root of it all is vodka, and they are a very bad lot. With no sort of understanding."

The police inspector wrote something down, and said to Osip quietly, in an even tone, as though he were asking him for water:

"Be off."

Soon he went away; and when he got into his cheap chaise and cleared his throat, it could be seen from the very expression of his long thin back that he was no longer thinking of Osip or of the village elder, nor of the Zhukovo arrears, but was thinking of his own affairs. Before he had gone three-quarters of a mile Antip was already carrying off the samovar from the Tchikildyeevs' cottage, followed by Granny, screaming shrilly and straining her throat:

"I won't let you have it, I won't let you have it, damn you!"

He walked rapidly with long steps, and she pursued him panting, almost falling over, a bent, ferocious figure; her kerchief slipped on to her shoulders, her grey hair with greenish lights on it was blown about in the wind. She suddenly stopped short, and like a genuine rebel, fell to beating her breast with her fists and shouting louder than ever in a sing-song voice, as though she were sobbing:

"Good Christians and believers in God! Neighbours, they have ill-treated me! Kind friends, they have oppressed me! Oh, oh! dear people, take my part."

"Granny, Granny!" said the village elder sternly, "have some sense in your head!"

It was hopelessly dreary in the Tchikildyeevs' hut without the samovar; there was something humiliating in this loss, insulting, as though the honour of the hut had been outraged. Better if the elder had carried off the table, all the benches, all the pots—it would not have seemed so empty. Granny screamed, Marya cried, and the little girls, looking at her, cried, too. The old father, feeling guilty, sat in the corner with bowed head and said nothing. And Nikolay, too, was silent. Granny loved him and was sorry for him, but now, forgetting her pity, she fell upon him with abuse, with reproaches, shaking her fist right in his face. She shouted that it was all his fault; why had he sent them so little when he boasted in his letters that he was getting fifty roubles a month at the Slavyansky Bazaar? Why had he come, and with his family, too? If he died, where was the money to come from for his funeral . . .? And it was pitiful to look at Nikolay, Olga, and Sasha.

The old father cleared his throat, took his cap, and went off to the village elder. Antip was soldering something by the stove, puffing out his cheeks; there was a smell of burning. His children, emaciated and unwashed, no better than the Tchikildyeevs, were scrambling about the floor; his wife, an ugly, freckled woman with a prominent stomach, was winding silk. They were a poor, unlucky family, and Antip was the only one who looked vigorous and handsome. On a bench there were five samovars standing in a row. The old man said his prayer to Battenburg and said:

"Antip, show the Divine mercy. Give me back the samovar, for Christ's sake!"

"Bring three roubles, then you shall have it."

"I can't do it!"

Antip puffed out his cheeks, the fire roared and hissed, and the glow was reflected in the samovar. The old man crumpled up his cap and said after a moment's thought:

"You give it me back."

The swarthy elder looked quite black, and was like a magician; he turned round to Osip and said sternly and rapidly:

"It all depends on the rural captain. On the twenty-sixth instant you can state the grounds for your dissatisfaction before the administrative session, verbally or in writing."

Osip did not understand a word, but he was satisfied with that and went home.

Ten days later the police inspector came again, stayed an hour and went away. During those days the weather had changed to cold and windy; the river had been frozen for some time past, but still there was no snow, and people found it difficult to get about. On the eve of a holiday some of the neighbours came in to Osip's to sit and have a talk. They did not light the lamp, as it would have been a sin to work, but talked in the darkness. There were some items of news, all rather unpleasant. In two or three households hens had been taken for the arrears, and had been sent to the district police station, and there they had died because no one had fed them; they had taken sheep, and while they were being driven away tied to one another, shifted into another cart at each village, one of them had died. And now they were discussing the question, who was to blame?

"The Zemstvo," said Osip. "Who else?"

"Of course it is the Zemstvo."

The Zemstvo was blamed for everything—for the arrears, and for the oppressions, and for the failure of the crops, though no one of them knew what was meant by the Zemstvo. And this dated from the time when well-to-do peasants who had factories, shops, and inns of their own were members of the Zemstvos, were dissatisfied with them, and took to swearing at the Zemstvos in their factories and inns.

They talked of God's not sending the snow; they had to bring in wood for fuel, and there was no driving nor walking in the frozen ruts. In old days fifteen to twenty years ago conversation was much more interesting in Zhukovo. In those days every old man looked as though he were treasuring some secret; as though he knew something and was expecting something. They used to talk about an edict in golden letters, about the division of lands, about new land, about treasures; they hinted at something. Now the people of Zhukovo had no mystery at all; their whole life was bare and open in the sight of all, and they could talk of nothing but poverty, food, there being no snow yet. . . .

There was a pause. Then they thought again of the hens, of the sheep, and began discussing whose fault it was.

"The Zemstvo," said Osip wearily. "Who else?"

VIII

The parish church was nearly five miles away at Kosogorovo, and the peasants only attended it when they had to do so for baptisms, weddings, or funerals; they went to the services at the church across the river. On holidays in fine weather the girls dressed up in their best and went in a crowd together to church, and it was a cheering sight to see them in their red, yellow, and green dresses cross the meadow; in bad weather they all stayed at home. They went for the sacrament to the parish church. From each of those who did not manage in Lent to go to confession in readiness for the sacrament the parish priest, going the round of the huts with the cross at Easter, took fifteen kopecks.

The old father did not believe in God, for he hardly ever thought about Him; he recognized the supernatural, but considered it was entirely the women's concern, and when religion or miracles were discussed before him, or a question were put to him, he would say reluctantly, scratching himself:

"Who can tell!"

Granny believed, but her faith was somewhat hazy; everything was mixed up in her memory, and she could scarcely begin to think of sins, of death, of the salvation of the soul, before poverty and her daily cares took possession of her mind, and she instantly forgot what she was thinking about. She did not remember the prayers, and usually in the evenings, before lying down to sleep, she would stand before the ikons and whisper:

"Holy Mother of Kazan, Holy Mother of Smolensk, Holy Mother of Troerutchitsy . . ."

Marya and Fyokla crossed themselves, fasted, and took the sacrament every year, but understood nothing. The children were not taught their prayers, nothing was told them about God, and no moral principles were instilled into them; they were only forbidden to eat meat or milk in Lent. In the other families it was much the same: there were few who believed, few who understood. At the same time everyone loved the Holy Scripture, loved it with a tender, reverent love; but they had no Bible, there was no one to read it and explain it, and because Olga sometimes read them the gospel, they respected her, and they all addressed her and Sasha as though they were superior to themselves.

For church holidays and services Olga often went to neighbouring villages, and to the district town, in which there were two monasteries and twenty-seven churches. She was dreamy, and when she was on these pilgrimages she quite forgot her family, and only when she got home again suddenly made the joyful discovery that she had a husband and daughter, and then would say, smiling and radiant:

"God has sent me blessings!"

What went on in the village worried her and seemed to her revolting. On Elijah's Day they drank, at the Assumption they drank, at the Ascension they drank. The Feast of the Intercession was the parish holiday for Zhukovo, and the peasants used to drink then for three days; they squandered on drink fifty roubles of money belonging to the Mir, and then collected more for vodka from all the households. On the first day of the feast the Tchikildyeevs killed a sheep and ate of it in the morning, at dinner-time, and in the evening; they ate it ravenously, and the children got up at night to eat more. Kiryak was fearfully drunk for three whole days; he drank up everything, even his boots and cap, and beat Marya so terribly that they had to pour water over her. And then they were all ashamed and sick.

However, even in Zhukovo, in this "Slaveytown," there was once an outburst of genuine religious enthusiasm. It was in August, when throughout the district they carried from village to village the Holy Mother, the giver of life. It was still and overcast on the day when they expected *Her* at Zhukovo. The girls set off in the morning to meet the ikon, in their bright holiday dresses, and brought Her towards the evening, in procession with the cross and with singing, while the bells pealed in the church across the river. An immense crowd of villagers and strangers flooded the street; there was noise, dust, a great crush. . . . And the old father and Granny and Kiryak—all stretched out their hands to the ikon, looked eagerly at it and said, weeping:

"Defender! Mother! Defender!"

All seemed suddenly to realize that there was not an empty void between earth and heaven, that the rich and the powerful had not taken possession of everything, that there was still a refuge from injury, from slavish bondage, from crushing, unendurable poverty, from the terrible vodka.

"Defender! Mother!" sobbed Marya. "Mother!"

But the thanksgiving service ended and the ikon was carried away, and everything went on as before; and again there was a sound of coarse drunken oaths from the tavern.

Only the well-to-do peasants were afraid of death; the richer they were the less they believed in God, and in the salvation of souls, and only through fear of the end of the world put up candles and had services said for them, to be on the safe side. The peasants who were rather poorer were not afraid of death. The old father and Granny were told to their faces that they had lived too long, that it was time they were dead, and they did not mind. They did not hinder Fyokla from saying in Nikolay's presence that when Nikolay died her husband Denis would get exemption—to return home from the army. And Marya, far from fearing death, regretted that it was so slow in coming, and was glad when her children died.

Death they did not fear, but of every disease they had an exaggerated terror. The merest trifle was enough—a stomach upset, a slight chill, and Granny would be wrapped up on the stove, and would begin moaning loudly and incessantly:

"I am dy-ing!"

The old father hurried off for the priest, and Granny received the sacrament and extreme unction. They often talked of colds, of worms, of tumours which move in the stomach and coil round to the heart. Above all, they were afraid of catching cold, and so put on thick clothes even in the summer and warmed themselves at the stove. Granny was fond of being doctored, and often went to the hospital, where she used to say she was not seventy, but fifty-eight; she supposed that if the doctor knew her real age he would not treat her, but would say it was time she died instead of taking medicine. She usually went to the hospital early in the morning, taking with her two or three of the little girls, and came back in the evening, hungry and ill-tempered—with drops for herself and ointments for the little girls. Once she took Nikolay, who swallowed drops for a fortnight afterwards, and said he felt better.

Granny knew all the doctors and their assistants and the wise men for twenty miles round, and not one of them she liked. At the Intercession, when the priest made the round of the huts with the cross, the deacon told her that in the town near the prison lived an old man who had been a medical orderly in the army, and who made wonderful cures, and advised her to try him. Granny took his advice. When the first snow fell she drove to the town and fetched an old man with a big beard, a converted Jew, in a long gown, whose face was covered with blue veins. There were outsiders at work in the hut at the time: an old tailor, in terrible spectacles, was cutting a waistcoat out of some rags, and two young men were making felt boots out of wool; Kiryak, who had been dismissed from his place for drunkenness, and now lived at home, was sitting beside the tailor mending a bridle. And it was crowded, stifling, and noisome in the hut. The converted Jew examined Nikolay and said that it was necessary to try cupping.

He put on the cups, and the old tailor, Kiryak, and the little girls stood round and looked on, and it seemed to them that they saw the disease being drawn out of Nikolay; and Nikolay, too, watched how the cups suckling at his breast gradually filled with dark blood, and felt as though there really were something coming out of him, and smiled with pleasure.

"It's a good thing," said the tailor. "Please God, it will do you good."

The Jew put on twelve cups and then another twelve, drank some tea, and went away. Nikolay began shivering; his face looked drawn, and, as the women expressed it, shrank up like a fist; his fingers turned blue. He wrapped himself up in a quilt and in a sheepskin, but got colder and colder. Towards the evening he began to be in great distress; asked to be laid on the ground, asked the tailor not to smoke; then he subsided under the sheepskin and towards morning he died.

IX

Oh, what a grim, what a long winter!

Their own grain did not last beyond Christmas, and they had to buy flour. Kiryak, who lived at home now, was noisy in the evenings, inspiring terror in everyone, and in the mornings he suffered from headache and was ashamed; and he was a pitiful sight. In the stall the starved cows bellowed day and night—a heart-rending sound to Granny and Marya. And as ill-luck would have it, there was a sharp frost all the winter, the snow drifted in high heaps, and the winter dragged on. At Annunciation there was a regular blizzard, and there was a fall of snow at Easter.

But in spite of it all the winter did end. At the beginning of April there came warm days and frosty nights. Winter would not give way, but one warm day overpowered it at last, and the streams began to flow and the birds began to sing. The whole meadow and the bushes near the river were drowned in the spring floods, and all the space between Zhukovo and the further side was filled up with a vast sheet of water, from which wild ducks rose up in flocks here and there. The spring sunset, flaming among gorgeous clouds, gave every evening something new, extraordinary, incredible—just what one does not believe in afterwards, when one sees those very colours and those very clouds in a picture.

The cranes flew swiftly, swiftly, with mournful cries, as though they were calling themselves. Standing on the edge of the ravine, Olga looked a long time at the flooded meadow, at the sunshine, at the bright church, that looked as though it had grown younger; and her tears flowed and her breath came in gasps from her passionate longing to go away, to go far away to the end of the world. It was already settled that she should go back to Moscow to be a servant, and that Kiryak should set off with her to get a job as a porter or something. Oh, to get away quickly!

As soon as it dried up and grew warm they got ready to set off. Olga and Sasha, with wallets on their backs and shoes of plaited bark on their feet, came out before daybreak: Marya came out, too, to see them on their way. Kiryak was not well, and was kept at home for another week. For the last time Olga prayed at the church and thought of her husband, and though she did not shed tears, her face puckered up and looked ugly like an old woman's. During the winter she had grown thinner and plainer, and her hair had gone a little grey, and instead of the old look of sweetness and the pleasant smile on her face, she had the resigned, mournful expression left by the sorrows she had been through, and there was something blank and irresponsive in her eyes, as though she did not hear what was said. She was sorry to part from the village and the peasants. She remembered how they had carried out Nikolay, and how a requiem had been ordered for him at almost every hut, and all had shed tears in sympathy with her grief. In the course of the summer and the winter there had been hours and days when it seemed as though these people lived worse than the beasts, and to live with them was terrible; they were coarse, dishonest, filthy, and drunken; they did not live in harmony, but quarrelled continually, because they distrusted and feared and did not respect one another. Who keeps the tavern and makes the people drunken? A peasant. Who wastes and spends on drink the funds of the commune, of the schools, of the church? A peasant. Who stole from his neighbours, set fire to their property, gave false witness at the court for a bottle of vodka? At the meetings of the Zemstvo and other local bodies, who was the first to fall foul of the peasants? A peasant. Yes, to live with them was terrible; but yet, they were human beings, they suffered and wept like human beings, and there was nothing in their lives for which one could not find excuse. Hard labour that made the whole body ache at night, the cruel winters, the scanty harvests, the overcrowding; and they had no help and none to whom they could look for help. Those of them who were a little stronger and better off could be no help, as they were themselves coarse, dishonest, drunken, and abused one another just as revoltingly; the paltriest little clerk or official treated the peasants as though they were tramps, and addressed even the village elders and church wardens as inferiors, and considered they had a right to do so. And, indeed, can any sort of help or good example be given by mercenary, greedy, depraved, and idle persons who only visit the village in order to insult, to despoil, and to terrorize? Olga remembered the pitiful, humiliated look of the old people when in the winter Kiryak had been taken to be flogged. . . . And now she felt sorry for all these people, painfully so, and as she walked on she kept looking back at the huts.

After walking two miles with them Marya said goodbye, then kneeling, and falling forward with her face on the earth, she began wailing:

"Again I am left alone. Alas, for poor me! poor, unhappy! . . ."

And she wailed like this for a long time, and for a long way Olga and Sasha could still see her on her knees, bowing down to someone at the side and clutching her head in her hands, while the rooks flew over her head.

The sun rose high; it began to get hot. Zhukovo was left far behind. Walking was pleasant. Olga and Sasha soon forgot both the village and Marya; they were gay and everything entertained them. Now they came upon an ancient barrow, now upon a row of telegraph posts running one after another into the distance and disappearing into the horizon, and the wires hummed mysteriously. Then they saw a homestead, all wreathed in green foliage; there came a scent from it of dampness, of hemp, and it seemed for some reason that happy people lived there. Then they came upon a horse's skeleton whitening in solitude in the open fields. And the larks trilled unceasingly, the corncrakes called to one another, and the landrail cried as though someone were really scraping at an old iron rail.

At midday Olga and Sasha reached a big village. There in the broad street they met the little old man who was General Zhukov's cook. He was hot, and his red, perspiring bald head shone in the sunshine. Olga and he did not recognize each other, then looked round at the same moment, recognized each other, and went their separate ways without saying a word. Stopping near the hut which looked newest and most prosperous, Olga bowed down before the open windows, and said in a loud, thin, chanting voice:

"Good Christian folk, give alms, for Christ's sake, that God's blessing may be upon you, and that your parents may be in the Kingdom of Heaven in peace eternal."

"Good Christian folk," Sasha began chanting, "give, for Christ's sake, that God's blessing, the Heavenly Kingdom . . ."

The Man in a Case

[Written in Nice, France. First published in
Russkaya Mysl (*Russian Thought*), a Russian magazine, in July 1898.
The story was the first part of *The Little Trilogy*.
It was included in *The Wife and Other Stories* (1918).]

At the furthest end of the village of Mironositskoe some belated sportsmen lodged for the night in the elder Prokofy's barn. There were two of them, the veterinary surgeon Ivan Ivanovitch and the schoolmaster Burkin. Ivan Ivanovitch had a rather strange double-barrelled surname—Tchimsha-Himalaisky—which did not suit him at all, and he was called simply Ivan Ivanovitch all over the province. He lived at a stud-farm near the town, and had come out shooting now to get a breath of fresh air. Burkin, the high-school teacher, stayed every summer at Count P——'s, and had been thoroughly at home in this district for years.

They did not sleep. Ivan Ivanovitch, a tall, lean old fellow with long moustaches, was sitting outside the door, smoking a pipe in the moonlight. Burkin was lying within on the hay, and could not be seen in the darkness.

They were telling each other all sorts of stories. Among other things, they spoke of the fact that the elder's wife, Mavra, a healthy and by no means stupid woman, had never been beyond her native village, had never seen a town nor a railway in her life, and had spent the last ten years sitting behind the stove, and only at night going out into the street.

"What is there wonderful in that!" said Burkin. "There are plenty of people in the world, solitary by temperament, who try to retreat into their shell like a hermit crab or a snail. Perhaps it is an instance of atavism, a return to the period when the ancestor of man was not yet a social animal and lived alone in his den, or perhaps it is only one of the diversities of human character—who knows? I am not a natural science man, and it is not my business to settle such questions; I only mean to say that people like Mavra are not uncommon. There is no need to look far; two months ago a man called Byelikov, a colleague of mine, the Greek master, died in our town. You have heard of him, no doubt. He was remarkable for always wearing goloshes and a warm wadded coat, and carrying an umbrella even in the very finest weather. And his umbrella was in a case, and his watch was in a case made of grey chamois leather, and when he took out his penknife to sharpen his pencil, his penknife, too, was in a little case; and his face seemed to be in a case too, because he always hid it in his turned-up collar. He wore dark spectacles and flannel vests, stuffed up his ears with cotton-wool, and when he got into a cab always told the driver to put up the hood. In short, the man displayed a constant and insurmountable impulse to wrap himself in a covering, to make himself, so to speak, a case which would isolate him and protect him from external influences. Reality irritated him, frightened him, kept him in continual agitation, and, perhaps to justify his timidity, his aversion for the actual, he always praised the past and what had never existed; and even the classical languages which he taught were in reality for him goloshes and umbrellas in which he sheltered himself from real life.

"'Oh, how sonorous, how beautiful is the Greek language!' he would say, with a sugary expression; and as though to prove his words he would screw up his eyes and, raising his finger, would pronounce 'Anthropos!'

"And Byelikov tried to hide his thoughts also in a case. The only things that were clear to his mind were government circulars and newspaper articles in which something was forbidden. When some proclamation prohibited the boys from going out in the streets after nine o'clock in the evening, or some article declared carnal love unlawful, it was to his mind clear and definite; it was forbidden, and that was enough. For him there was always a doubtful element, something vague and not fully expressed, in any sanction or permission. When a dramatic club or a reading room or a tea-shop was licensed in the town, he would shake his head and say softly:

"It is all right, of course; it is all very nice, but I hope it won't lead to anything!"

"Every sort of breach of order, deviation or departure from rule, depressed him, though one would have thought it was no business of his. If one of his colleagues was late for church or if rumours reached him of some prank of the high-school boys, or one of the mistresses was seen late in the evening in the company of an officer, he was much disturbed, and said he hoped that nothing would come of it. At the teachers' meetings he simply oppressed us with his caution, his circumspection, and his characteristic reflection on the ill-behaviour of the young people in both male and female high-schools, the uproar in the classes.

"Oh, he hoped it would not reach the ears of the authorities; oh, he hoped nothing would come of it; and he thought it would be a very good thing if Petrov were expelled from the second class and Yegorov from the fourth. And, do you know, by his sighs, his despondency, his black spectacles on his pale little face, a little face like a pole-cat's, you know, he crushed us all, and we gave way, reduced Petrov's and Yegorov's marks for conduct, kept them in, and in the end expelled them both. He had a strange habit of visiting our lodgings. He would come to a teacher's, would sit down, and remain silent, as though he were carefully inspecting something. He would sit like this in silence for an hour or two and then go away. This he called 'maintaining good relations with his colleagues'; and it was obvious that coming to see us and sitting there was tiresome to him, and that he came to see us simply because he considered it his duty as our colleague. We teachers were afraid of him. And even the headmaster was afraid of him. Would you believe it, our teachers were all intellectual, right-minded people, brought up on Turgenev and Shtchedrin, yet this little chap, who always went about with goloshes and an umbrella, had the whole high-school under his thumb for fifteen long years! High-school, indeed—he had the whole town under his thumb! Our ladies did not get up private theatricals on Saturdays for fear he should hear of it, and the clergy dared not eat meat or play cards in his presence. Under the influence of people like Byelikov we have got into the way of being afraid of everything in our town for the last ten or fifteen years. They are afraid to speak aloud, afraid to send letters, afraid to make acquaintances, afraid to read books, afraid to help the poor, to teach people to read and write. . . ."

Ivan Ivanovitch cleared his throat, meaning to say something, but first lighted his pipe, gazed at the moon, and then said, with pauses:

"Yes, intellectual, right minded people read Shtchedrin and Turgenev, Buckle, and all the rest of them, yet they knocked under and put up with it . . . that's just how it is."

"Byelikov lived in the same house as I did," Burkin went on, "on the same storey, his door facing mine; we often saw each other, and I knew how he lived when he was at home. And at home it was the same story: dressing gown, nightcap, blinds, bolts, a perfect succession of prohibitions and restrictions of all sorts, and—'Oh, I hope nothing will come of it!' Lenten fare was bad for him, yet he could not eat meat, as people might perhaps say Byelikov did not keep the fasts, and he ate freshwater fish with butter—not a Lenten dish, yet one could not say that it was meat. He did not keep a female servant for fear people might think evil of him, but had as cook an old man of sixty, called Afanasy, half-witted and given to tippling, who had once been an officer's servant and could cook after a fashion. This Afanasy was usually standing at the door with his arms folded; with a deep sigh, he would mutter always the same thing:

"'There are plenty of *them* about nowadays!'

"Byelikov had a little bedroom like a box; his bed had curtains. When he went to bed he covered his head over; it was hot and stuffy; the wind battered on the closed doors; there was a droning noise in the stove and a sound of sighs from the kitchen—ominous sighs. . . . And he felt frightened under the bed-clothes. He was afraid that something might happen, that Afanasy might murder him, that thieves might break in, and so he had troubled dreams all night, and in the morning, when we went together to the high-school, he was depressed and pale, and it was evident that the high-school full of people excited dread and aversion in his whole being, and that to walk beside me was irksome to a man of his solitary temperament.

"'They make a great noise in our classes,' he used to say, as though trying to find an explanation for his depression. 'It's beyond anything.'

"And the Greek master, this man in a case—would you believe it?—almost got married."

Ivan Ivanovitch glanced quickly into the barn, and said:

"You are joking!"

"Yes, strange as it seems, he almost got married. A new teacher of history and geography, Milhail Savvitch Kovalenko, a Little Russian, was appointed. He came, not alone, but with his sister Varinka. He was a tall, dark young man with huge hands, and one could see from his face that he had a bass voice, and, in fact, he had a voice that seemed to come out of a barrel—'boom, boom, boom!' And she was not so young, about thirty, but she, too, was tall, well-made, with black eyebrows and red cheeks—in fact, she was a regular sugar-plum, and so sprightly, so noisy; she was always singing Little Russian songs and laughing. For the least thing she would go off into a ringing laugh—'Ha-ha-ha!' We made our first thorough acquaintance with the Kovalenkos at the headmaster's name-day party. Among the glum and intensely bored teachers who came even to the name-day party as a duty we suddenly saw a new Aphrodite risen from the waves; she walked with her arms akimbo, laughed, sang, danced. . . . She sang with feeling 'The Winds do Blow,' then another song, and another, and she fascinated us all—all, even Byelikov. He sat down by her and said with a honeyed smile:

"'The Little Russian reminds one of the ancient Greek in its softness and agreeable resonance.'

"That flattered her, and she began telling him with feeling and earnestness that they had a farm in the Gadyatchsky district, and that her mamma lived at the farm, and that they had such pears, such melons, such *kabaks*! The Little Russians call pumpkins *kabaks* (i.e., pothouses), while their pothouses they call *shinki*, and they make a beetroot soup with tomatoes and aubergines in it, 'which was so nice—awfully nice!'

"We listened and listened, and suddenly the same idea dawned upon us all:

"'It would be a good thing to make a match of it,' the headmaster's wife said to me softly.

"We all for some reason recalled the fact that our friend Byelikov was not married, and it now seemed to us strange that we had hitherto failed to observe, and had in fact completely lost sight of, a detail so important in his life. What was his attitude to woman? How had he settled this vital question for himself? This had not interested us in the least till then; perhaps we had not even admitted the idea that a man who went out in all weathers in goloshes and slept under curtains could be in love.

"'He is a good deal over forty and she is thirty,' the headmaster's wife went on, developing her idea. 'I believe she would marry him.'

"All sorts of things are done in the provinces through boredom, all sorts of unnecessary and nonsensical things! And that is because what is necessary is not done at all. What need was there for instance, for us to make a match for this Byelikov, whom one could not even imagine married? The headmaster's wife, the inspector's wife, and all our high-school ladies, grew livelier and even better-looking, as though they had suddenly found a new object in life. The headmaster's wife would take a box at the theatre, and we beheld sitting in her box Varinka, with such a fan, beaming and happy, and beside her Byelikov, a little bent figure, looking as though he had been extracted from his house by pincers. I would give an evening party, and the ladies would insist on my inviting Byelikov and Varinka. In short, the machine was set in motion. It appeared that Varinka was not averse to matrimony. She had not a very cheerful life with her brother; they could do nothing but quarrel and scold one another from morning till night. Here is a scene, for instance. Kovalenko would be coming along the street, a tall, sturdy young ruffian, in an embroidered shirt, his love-locks falling on his forehead under his cap, in one hand a bundle of books, in the other a thick knotted stick, followed by his sister, also with books in her hand.

"'But you haven't read it, Mihalik!' she would be arguing loudly. 'I tell you, I swear you have not read it at all!'

"'And I tell you I have read it,' cries Kovalenko, thumping his stick on the pavement.

"'Oh, my goodness, Mihalik! why are you so cross? We are arguing about principles.'

"'I tell you that I have read it!' Kovalenko would shout, more loudly than ever.

"And at home, if there was an outsider present, there was sure to be a skirmish. Such a life must have been wearisome, and of course she must have longed for a home of her own. Besides, there was her age to be considered; there was no time left to pick and choose; it was a case of marrying anybody, even a Greek master. And, indeed, most of our young ladies don't mind whom they marry so long as they do get married. However that may be, Varinka began to show an unmistakable partiality for Byelikov.

"And Byelikov? He used to visit Kovalenko just as he did us. He would arrive, sit down, and remain silent. He would sit quiet, and Varinka would sing to him 'The Winds do Blow,' or would look pensively at him with her dark eyes, or would suddenly go off into a peal—'Ha-ha-ha!'

"Suggestion plays a great part in love affairs, and still more in getting married. Everybody—both his colleagues and the ladies—began assuring Byelikov that he ought to get married, that there was nothing left for him in life but to get married; we all congratulated him, with solemn countenances delivered ourselves of various platitudes, such as 'Marriage is a serious step.' Besides, Varinka was good-looking and interesting; she was the daughter of a civil councillor, and had a farm; and what was more, she was the first woman who had been warm and friendly in her manner to him. His head was turned, and he decided that he really ought to get married."

"Well, at that point you ought to have taken away his goloshes and umbrella," said Ivan Ivanovitch.

"Only fancy! that turned out to be impossible. He put Varinka's portrait on his table, kept coming to see me and talking about Varinka, and home life, saying marriage was a serious step. He was frequently at Kovalenko's, but he did not alter his manner of life in the least; on the contrary, indeed, his determination to get married seemed to have a depressing effect on him. He grew thinner and paler, and seemed to retreat further and further into his case.

"'I like Varvara Savvishna,' he used to say to me, with a faint and wry smile, 'and I know that every one ought to get married, but . . . you know all this has happened so suddenly. . . . One must think a little.'

"'What is there to think over?' I used to say to him. 'Get married— that is all.'

"'No; marriage is a serious step. One must first weigh the duties before one, the responsibilities . . . that nothing may go wrong afterwards. It worries me so much that I don't sleep at night. And I must confess I am afraid: her brother and she have a strange way of thinking; they look at things strangely, you know, and her disposition is very impetuous. One may get married, and then, there is no knowing, one may find oneself in an unpleasant position.'

"And he did not make an offer; he kept putting it off, to the great vexation of the headmaster's wife and all our ladies; he went on weighing his future duties and responsibilities, and meanwhile he went for a walk with Varinka almost every day—possibly he thought that this was necessary in his position—and came to see me to talk about family life. And in all probability in the end he would have proposed to her, and would have made one of those unnecessary, stupid marriages such as are made by thousands among us from being bored and having nothing to do, if it had not been for a *kolossalische scandal*. I must mention that Varinka's brother, Kovalenko, detested Byelikov from the first day of their acquaintance, and could not endure him.

"'I don't understand,' he used to say to us, shrugging his shoulders— 'I don't understand how you can put up with that sneak, that nasty phiz. Ugh! how can you live here! The atmosphere is stifling and unclean! Do you call yourselves schoolmasters, teachers? You are paltry government clerks. You keep, not a temple of science, but a department for red tape and loyal behaviour, and it smells as sour as a police-station. No, my friends; I will stay with you for a while, and then I will go to my farm and there catch crabs and teach the Little Russians. I shall go, and you can stay here with your Judas—damn his soul!'

"Or he would laugh till he cried, first in a loud bass, then in a shrill, thin laugh, and ask me, waving his hands:

"'What does he sit here for? What does he want? He sits and stares.'

"He even gave Byelikov a nickname, 'The Spider.' And it will readily be understood that we avoided talking to him of his sister's being about to marry 'The Spider.'

"And on one occasion, when the headmaster's wife hinted to him what a good thing it would be to secure his sister's future with such a reliable, universally respected man as Byelikov, he frowned and muttered:

"'It's not my business; let her marry a reptile if she likes. I don't like meddling in other people's affairs.'

"Now hear what happened next. Some mischievous person drew a caricature of Byelikov walking along in his goloshes with his trousers tucked up, under his umbrella, with Varinka on his arm; below, the inscription 'Anthropos in love.' The expression was caught to a marvel, you know. The artist must have worked for more than one night, for the teachers of both the boys' and girls' high-schools, the teachers of the seminary, the government officials, all received a copy. Byelikov received one, too. The caricature made a very painful impression on him.

"We went out together; it was the first of May, a Sunday, and all of us, the boys and the teachers, had agreed to meet at the high-school and then to go for a walk together to a wood beyond the town. We set off, and he was green in the face and gloomier than a storm cloud.

"'What wicked, ill-natured people there are!' he said, and his lips quivered.

"I felt really sorry for him. We were walking along, and all of a sudden—would you believe it?—Kovalenko came bowling along on a bicycle, and after him, also on a bicycle, Varinka, flushed and exhausted, but good-humoured and gay.

"'We are going on ahead,' she called. 'What lovely weather! Awfully lovely!'

"And they both disappeared from our sight. Byelikov turned white instead of green, and seemed petrified. He stopped short and stared at me. . . .

"'What is the meaning of it? Tell me, please!' he asked. 'Can my eyes have deceived me? Is it the proper thing for high-school masters and ladies to ride bicycles?'

"'What is there improper about it?' I said. 'Let them ride and enjoy themselves.'

"'But how can that be?' he cried, amazed at my calm. 'What are you saying?'

"And he was so shocked that he was unwilling to go on, and returned home.

"Next day he was continually twitching and nervously rubbing his hands, and it was evident from his face that he was unwell. And he left before his work was over, for the first time in his life. And he ate no dinner. Towards evening he wrapped himself up warmly, though it was quite warm weather, and sallied out to the Kovalenkos.' Varinka was out; he found her brother, however.

"'Pray sit down,' Kovalenko said coldly, with a frown. His face looked sleepy; he had just had a nap after dinner, and was in a very bad humour.

"Byelikov sat in silence for ten minutes, and then began:

"'I have come to see you to relieve my mind. I am very, very much troubled. Some scurrilous fellow has drawn an absurd caricature of me and another person, in whom we are both deeply interested. I regard it as a duty to assure you that I have had no hand in it. . . . I have given no sort of ground for such ridicule—on the contrary, I have always behaved in every way like a gentleman.'

"Kovalenko sat sulky and silent. Byelikov waited a little, and went on slowly in a mournful voice:

"'And I have something else to say to you. I have been in the service for years, while you have only lately entered it, and I consider it my duty as an older colleague to give you a warning. You ride on a bicycle, and that pastime is utterly unsuitable for an educator of youth.'

"'Why so?' asked Kovalenko in his bass.

"'Surely that needs no explanation, Mihail Savvitch—surely you can understand that? If the teacher rides a bicycle, what can you expect the pupils to do? You will have them walking on their heads next! And so long as there is no formal permission to do so, it is out of the question. I was horrified yesterday! When I saw your sister everything seemed dancing before my eyes. A lady or a young girl on a bicycle—it's awful!'

"'What is it you want exactly?'

"'All I want is to warn you, Mihail Savvitch. You are a young man, you have a future before you, you must be very, very careful in your behaviour, and you are so careless—oh, so careless! You go about in an embroidered shirt, are constantly seen in the street carrying books, and now the bicycle, too. The headmaster will learn that you and your sister ride the bicycle, and then it will reach the higher authorities. . . . Will that be a good thing?'

"'It's no business of anybody else if my sister and I do bicycle!' said Kovalenko, and he turned crimson. 'And damnation take any one who meddles in my private affairs!'

"Byelikov turned pale and got up.

"'If you speak to me in that tone I cannot continue,' he said. 'And I beg you never to express yourself like that about our superiors in my presence; you ought to be respectful to the authorities.'

"'Why, have I said any harm of the authorities?' asked Kovalenko, looking at him wrathfully. 'Please leave me alone. I am an honest man, and do not care to talk to a gentleman like you. I don't like sneaks!'

"Byelikov flew into a nervous flutter, and began hurriedly putting on his coat, with an expression of horror on his face. It was the first time in his life he had been spoken to so rudely.

"'You can say what you please,' he said, as he went out from the entry to the landing on the staircase. 'I ought only to warn you: possibly some one may have overheard us, and that our conversation may not be misunderstood and harm come of it, I shall be compelled to inform our headmaster of our conversation . . . in its main features. I am bound to do so.'

"'Inform him? You can go and make your report!'

"Kovalenko seized him from behind by the collar and gave him a push, and Byelikov rolled downstairs, thudding with his goloshes. The staircase was high and steep, but he rolled to the bottom unhurt, got up, and touched his nose to see whether his spectacles were all right. But just as he was falling down the stairs Varinka came in, and with her two ladies; they stood below staring, and to Byelikov this was more terrible than anything. I believe he would rather have broken his neck or both legs than have been an object of ridicule. 'Why, now the whole town would hear of it; it would come to the headmaster's ears, would reach the higher authorities—oh, it might lead to something! There would be another caricature, and it would all end in his being asked to resign his post. . . .

"When he got up, Varinka recognized him, and, looking at his ridiculous face, his crumpled overcoat, and his goloshes, not understanding what had happened and supposing that he had slipped down by accident, could not restrain herself, and laughed loud enough to be heard by all the flats:

"'Ha-ha-ha!'

"And this pealing, ringing 'Ha-ha-ha!' was the last straw that put an end to everything: to the proposed match and to Byelikov's earthly existence. He did not hear what Varinka said to him; he saw nothing. On reaching home, the first thing he did was to remove her portrait from the table; then he went to bed, and he never got up again.

"Three days later Afanasy came to me and asked whether we should not send for the doctor, as there was something wrong with his master. I went in to Byelikov. He lay silent behind the curtain, covered with a quilt; if one asked him a question, he said 'Yes' or 'No' and not another sound. He lay there while Afanasy, gloomy and scowling, hovered about him, sighing heavily, and smelling like a pothouse.

"A month later Byelikov died. We all went to his funeral—that is, both the high-schools and the seminary. Now when he was lying in his coffin his expression was mild, agreeable, even cheerful, as though he were glad that he had at last been put into a case which he would never leave again. Yes, he had attained his ideal! And, as though in his honour, it was dull, rainy weather on the day of his funeral, and we all wore goloshes and took our umbrellas. Varinka, too, was at the funeral, and when the coffin was lowered into the grave she burst into tears. I have noticed that Little Russian women are always laughing or crying—no intermediate mood.

"One must confess that to bury people like Byelikov is a great pleasure. As we were returning from the cemetery we wore discreet Lenten faces; no one wanted to display this feeling of pleasure—a feeling like that we had experienced long, long ago as children when our elders had gone out and we ran about the garden for an hour or two, enjoying complete freedom. Ah, freedom, freedom! The merest hint, the faintest hope of its possibility gives wings to the soul, does it not?

"We returned from the cemetery in a good humour. But not more than a week had passed before life went on as in the past, as gloomy, oppressive, and senseless—a life not forbidden by government prohibition, but not fully permitted, either: it was no better. And, indeed, though we had buried Byelikov, how many such men in cases were left, how many more of them there will be!"

"That's just how it is," said Ivan Ivanovitch and he lighted his pipe.

"How many more of them there will be!" repeated Burkin.

The schoolmaster came out of the barn. He was a short, stout man, completely bald, with a black beard down to his waist. The two dogs came out with him.

"What a moon!" he said, looking upwards.

It was midnight. On the right could be seen the whole village, a long street stretching far away for four miles. All was buried in deep silent slumber; not a movement, not a sound; one could hardly believe that nature could be so still. When on a moonlight night you see a broad village street, with its cottages, haystacks, and slumbering willows, a feeling of calm comes over the soul; in this peace, wrapped away from care, toil, and sorrow in the darkness of night, it is mild, melancholy, beautiful, and it seems as though the stars look down upon it kindly and with tenderness, and as though there were no evil on earth and all were well. On the left the open country began from the end of the village; it could be seen stretching far away to the horizon, and there was no movement, no sound in that whole expanse bathed in moonlight.

"Yes, that is just how it is," repeated Ivan Ivanovitch; "and isn't our living in town, airless and crowded, our writing useless papers, our playing *vint*—isn't that all a sort of case for us? And our spending our whole lives among trivial, fussy men and silly, idle women, our talking and our listening to all sorts of nonsense—isn't that a case for us, too? If you like, I will tell you a very edifying story."

"No; it's time we were asleep," said Burkin. "Tell it tomorrow."

They went into the barn and lay down on the hay. And they were both covered up and beginning to doze when they suddenly heard light footsteps—patter, patter.... Some one was walking not far from the barn, walking a little and stopping, and a minute later, patter, patter again.... The dogs began growling.

"That's Mavra," said Burkin.

The footsteps died away.

"You see and hear that they lie," said Ivan Ivanovitch, turning over on the other side, "and they call you a fool for putting up with their lying. You endure insult and humiliation, and dare not openly say that you are on the side of the honest and the free, and you lie and smile yourself; and all that for the sake of a crust of bread, for the sake of a warm corner, for the sake of a wretched little worthless rank in the service. No, one can't go on living like this."

"Well, you are off on another tack now, Ivan Ivanovitch," said the schoolmaster. "Let us go to sleep!"

And ten minutes later Burkin was asleep. But Ivan Ivanovitch kept sighing and turning over from side to side; then he got up, went outside again, and, sitting in the doorway, lighted his pipe.

Gooseberries

[Written in 1898 in Melikhovo. First published in the August 1898
issue of *Russkaya Mysl* (*Russian Thought*), a Russian magazine.
Collected in *The Wife and Other Stories* (1918).
The story became the second part of *The Little Trilogy*.]

The whole sky had been overcast with rain-clouds from early morning;
it was a still day, not hot, but heavy, as it is in grey dull weather when
the clouds have been hanging over the country for a long while, when
one expects rain and it does not come. Ivan Ivanovitch, the veterinary
surgeon, and Burkin, the high-school teacher, were already tired from
walking, and the fields seemed to them endless. Far ahead of them they
could just see the windmills of the village of Mironositskoe; on the right
stretched a row of hillocks which disappeared in the distance behind
the village, and they both knew that this was the bank of the river, that
there were meadows, green willows, homesteads there, and that if one
stood on one of the hillocks one could see from it the same vast plain,
telegraph-wires, and a train which in the distance looked like a crawling
caterpillar, and that in clear weather one could even see the town. Now,
in still weather, when all nature seemed mild and dreamy, Ivan Ivanovitch
and Burkin were filled with love of that countryside, and both thought
how great, how beautiful a land it was.

"Last time we were in Prokofy's barn," said Burkin, "you were about
to tell me a story."

"Yes; I meant to tell you about my brother."

Ivan Ivanovitch heaved a deep sigh and lighted a pipe to begin to
tell his story, but just at that moment the rain began. And five minutes

later heavy rain came down, covering the sky, and it was hard to tell when it would be over. Ivan Ivanovitch and Burkin stopped in hesitation; the dogs, already drenched, stood with their tails between their legs gazing at them feelingly.

"We must take shelter somewhere," said Burkin. "Let us go to Alehin's; it's close by."

"Come along."

They turned aside and walked through mown fields, sometimes going straight forward, sometimes turning to the right, till they came out on the road. Soon they saw poplars, a garden, then the red roofs of barns; there was a gleam of the river, and the view opened on to a broad expanse of water with a windmill and a white bath-house: this was Sofino, where Alehin lived.

The watermill was at work, drowning the sound of the rain; the dam was shaking. Here wet horses with drooping heads were standing near their carts, and men were walking about covered with sacks. It was damp, muddy, and desolate; the water looked cold and malignant. Ivan Ivanovitch and Burkin were already conscious of a feeling of wetness, messiness, and discomfort all over; their feet were heavy with mud, and when, crossing the dam, they went up to the barns, they were silent, as though they were angry with one another.

In one of the barns there was the sound of a winnowing machine, the door was open, and clouds of dust were coming from it. In the doorway was standing Alehin himself, a man of forty, tall and stout, with long hair, more like a professor or an artist than a landowner. He had on a white shirt that badly needed washing, a rope for a belt, drawers instead of trousers, and his boots, too, were plastered up with mud and straw. His eyes and nose were black with dust. He recognized Ivan Ivanovitch and Burkin, and was apparently much delighted to see them.

"Go into the house, gentlemen," he said, smiling; "I'll come directly, this minute."

It was a big two-storeyed house. Alehin lived in the lower storey, with arched ceilings and little windows, where the bailiffs had once lived; here everything was plain, and there was a smell of rye bread, cheap vodka, and harness. He went upstairs into the best rooms only on rare occasions, when visitors came. Ivan Ivanovitch and Burkin were met in the house by a maid-servant, a young woman so beautiful that they both stood still and looked at one another.

"You can't imagine how delighted I am to see you, my friends," said Alehin, going into the hall with them. "It is a surprise! Pelagea," he said, addressing the girl, "give our visitors something to change into. And, by the way, I will change too. Only I must first go and wash, for I almost think I have not washed since spring. Wouldn't you like to come into the bath-house? and meanwhile they will get things ready here."

Beautiful Pelagea, looking so refined and soft, brought them towels and soap, and Alehin went to the bath-house with his guests.

"It's a long time since I had a wash," he said, undressing. "I have got a nice bath-house, as you see—my father built it—but I somehow never have time to wash."

He sat down on the steps and soaped his long hair and his neck, and the water round him turned brown.

"Yes, I must say," said Ivan Ivanovitch meaningly, looking at his head.

"It's a long time since I washed . . ." said Alehin with embarrassment, giving himself a second soaping, and the water near him turned dark blue, like ink.

Ivan Ivanovitch went outside, plunged into the water with a loud splash, and swam in the rain, flinging his arms out wide. He stirred the water into waves which set the white lilies bobbing up and down; he swam to the very middle of the millpond and dived, and came up a minute later in another place, and swam on, and kept on diving, trying to touch the bottom.

"Oh, my goodness!" he repeated continually, enjoying himself thoroughly. "Oh, my goodness!" He swam to the mill, talked to the peasants there, then returned and lay on his back in the middle of the pond, turning his face to the rain. Burkin and Alehin were dressed and ready to go, but he still went on swimming and diving. "Oh, my goodness! . . ." he said. "Oh, Lord, have mercy on me! . . ."

"That's enough!" Burkin shouted to him.

They went back to the house. And only when the lamp was lighted in the big drawing room upstairs, and Burkin and Ivan Ivanovitch, attired in silk dressing gowns and warm slippers, were sitting in armchairs; and Alehin, washed and combed, in a new coat, was walking about the drawing room, evidently enjoying the feeling of warmth, cleanliness, dry clothes, and light shoes; and when lovely Pelagea, stepping noiselessly on the carpet and smiling softly, handed tea and jam on a tray—only then Ivan Ivanovitch began on his story, and it seemed as though not only Burkin and Alehin were listening, but also the ladies, young and old, and the officers who looked down upon them sternly and calmly from their gold frames.

"There are two of us brothers," he began—"I, Ivan Ivanovitch, and my brother, Nikolay Ivanovitch, two years younger. I went in for a learned profession and became a veterinary surgeon, while Nikolay sat in a government office from the time he was nineteen. Our father, Tchimsha-Himalaisky, was a kantonist, but he rose to be an officer and left us a little estate and the rank of nobility. After his death the little estate went in debts and legal expenses; but, anyway, we had spent our childhood running wild in the country. Like peasant children, we passed our days and nights in the fields and the woods, looked after horses, stripped the bark off the trees, fished, and so on. . . . And, you know, whoever has once in his life caught perch or has seen the migrating of the thrushes in autumn, watched how they float in flocks over the village on bright, cool days, he will never be a real townsman, and will have a yearning for freedom to the day of his death. My brother was miserable in the government office. Years passed by, and he went on sitting in the same place, went on writing the same papers and thinking of one and the same thing—how to get into the country. And this yearning by degrees passed into a definite desire, into a dream of buying himself a little farm somewhere on the banks of a river or a lake.

"He was a gentle, good-natured fellow, and I was fond of him, but I never sympathized with this desire to shut himself up for the rest of his life in a little farm of his own. It's the correct thing to say that a man needs no more than six feet of earth. But six feet is what a corpse needs, not a man. And they say, too, now, that if our intellectual classes are attracted to the land and yearn for a farm, it's a good thing. But these farms are just the same as six feet of earth. To retreat from town, from the struggle, from the bustle of life, to retreat and bury oneself in one's farm—it's not life, it's egoism, laziness, it's monasticism of a sort, but monasticism without good works. A man does not need six feet of earth or a farm, but the whole globe, all nature, where he can have room to display all the qualities and peculiarities of his free spirit.

"My brother Nikolay, sitting in his government office, dreamed of how he would eat his own cabbages, which would fill the whole yard with such a savoury smell, take his meals on the green grass, sleep in the sun, sit for whole hours on the seat by the gate gazing at the fields and the forest. Gardening books and the agricultural hints in calendars were his delight, his favourite spiritual sustenance; he enjoyed reading newspapers, too, but the only things he read in them were the advertisements of so many acres of arable land and a grass meadow with farm-houses and buildings, a river, a garden, a mill and millponds, for sale. And his imagination pictured the garden-paths, flowers and fruit, starling cotes, the carp in the pond, and all that sort of thing, you know. These imaginary pictures were of different kinds according to the advertisements which he came across, but for some reason in every one of them he had always to have gooseberries. He could not imagine a homestead, he could not picture an idyllic nook, without gooseberries.

"'Country life has its conveniences,' he would sometimes say. 'You sit on the verandah and you drink tea, while your ducks swim on the pond, there is a delicious smell everywhere, and . . . and the gooseberries are growing.'

"He used to draw a map of his property, and in every map there were the same things—(a) house for the family, (b) servants' quarters, (c) kitchen garden, (d) gooseberry-bushes. He lived parsimoniously, was frugal in food and drink, his clothes were beyond description; he looked like a beggar, but kept on saving and putting money in the bank. He grew fearfully avaricious. I did not like to look at him, and I used to give him something and send him presents for Christmas and Easter, but he used to save that too. Once a man is absorbed by an idea there is no doing anything with him.

"Years passed: he was transferred to another province. He was over forty, and he was still reading the advertisements in the papers and saving up. Then I heard he was married. Still with the same object of buying a farm and having gooseberries, he married an elderly and ugly widow without a trace of feeling for her, simply because she had filthy lucre. He went on living frugally after marrying her, and kept her short of food, while he put her money in the bank in his name.

"Her first husband had been a postmaster, and with him she was accustomed to pies and homemade wines, while with her second husband she did not get enough black bread; she began to pine away with this sort of life, and three years later she gave up her soul to God. And I need hardly say that my brother never for one moment imagined that he was responsible for her death. Money, like vodka, makes a man queer. In our town there was a merchant who, before he died, ordered a plateful of honey and ate up all his money and lottery tickets with the honey, so that no one might get the benefit of it. While I was inspecting cattle at a railway-station, a cattle-dealer fell under an engine and had his leg cut off. We carried him into the waiting room, the blood was flowing—it was a horrible thing—and he kept asking them to look for his leg and was very much worried about it; there were twenty roubles in the boot on the leg that had been cut off, and he was afraid they would be lost."

"That's a story from a different opera," said Burkin.

"After his wife's death," Ivan Ivanovitch went on, after thinking for half a minute, "my brother began looking out for an estate for himself. Of course, you may look about for five years and yet end by making a mistake, and buying something quite different from what you have dreamed of. My brother Nikolay bought through an agent a mortgaged estate of three hundred and thirty acres, with a house for the family, with servants' quarters, with a park, but with no orchard, no gooseberry-bushes, and no duck-pond; there was a river, but the water in it was the colour of coffee, because on one side of the estate there was a brickyard and on the other a factory for burning bones. But Nikolay Ivanovitch did not grieve much; he ordered twenty gooseberry-bushes, planted them, and began living as a country gentleman.

"Last year I went to pay him a visit. I thought I would go and see what it was like. In his letters my brother called his estate 'Tchumbaroklov Waste, alias Himalaiskoe.' I reached 'alias Himalaiskoe' in the afternoon. It was hot. Everywhere there were ditches, fences, hedges, fir trees planted in rows, and there was no knowing how to get to the yard, where to put one's horse. I went up to the house, and was met by a fat red dog that looked like a pig. It wanted to bark, but it was too lazy. The cook, a fat, barefooted woman, came out of the kitchen, and she, too, looked like a pig, and said that her master was resting after dinner. I went in to see my brother. He was sitting up in bed with a quilt over his legs; he had grown older, fatter, wrinkled; his cheeks, his nose, and his mouth all stuck out—he looked as though he might begin grunting into the quilt at any moment.

"We embraced each other, and shed tears of joy and of sadness at the thought that we had once been young and now were both grey-headed and near the grave. He dressed, and led me out to show me the estate.

"'Well, how are you getting on here?' I asked.

"'Oh, all right, thank God; I am getting on very well.'

"He was no more a poor timid clerk, but a real landowner, a gentleman. He was already accustomed to it, had grown used to it, and liked it. He ate a great deal, went to the bath-house, was growing stout, was already at law with the village commune and both factories, and was very much offended when the peasants did not call him 'Your Honour.' And he concerned himself with the salvation of his soul in a substantial, gentlemanly manner, and performed deeds of charity, not simply, but with an air of consequence. And what deeds of charity! He treated the peasants for every sort of disease with soda and castor oil, and on his name-day had a thanksgiving service in the middle of the village, and then treated the peasants to a gallon of vodka—he thought that was the thing to do. Oh, those horrible gallons of vodka! One day the fat landowner hauls the peasants up before the district captain for trespass, and next day, in honour of a holiday, treats them to a gallon of vodka, and they drink and shout 'Hurrah!' and when they are drunk bow down to his feet. A change of life for the better, and being well-fed and idle develop in a Russian the most insolent self-conceit. Nikolay Ivanovitch, who at one time in the government office was afraid to have any views of his own, now could say nothing that was not gospel truth, and uttered such truths in the tone of a prime minister. 'Education is essential, but for the peasants it is premature.' 'Corporal punishment is harmful as a rule, but in some cases it is necessary and there is nothing to take its place.'

"'I know the peasants and understand how to treat them,' he would say. 'The peasants like me. I need only to hold up my little finger and the peasants will do anything I like.'

"And all this, observe, was uttered with a wise, benevolent smile. He repeated twenty times over 'We noblemen,' 'I as a noble'; obviously he did not remember that our grandfather was a peasant, and our father a soldier. Even our surname Tchimsha-Himalaisky, in reality so incongruous, seemed to him now melodious, distinguished, and very agreeable.

"But the point just now is not he, but myself. I want to tell you about the change that took place in me during the brief hours I spent at his country place. In the evening, when we were drinking tea, the cook put on the table a plateful of gooseberries. They were not bought, but his own gooseberries, gathered for the first time since the bushes were planted.

Nikolay Ivanovitch laughed and looked for a minute in silence at the gooseberries, with tears in his eyes; he could not speak for excitement. Then he put one gooseberry in his mouth, looked at me with the triumph of a child who has at last received his favourite toy, and said:

"'How delicious!'

"And he ate them greedily, continually repeating, 'Ah, how delicious! Do taste them!'

"They were sour and unripe, but, as Pushkin says:

"'Dearer to us the falsehood that exalts

Than hosts of baser truths.'

"I saw a happy man whose cherished dream was so obviously fulfilled, who had attained his object in life, who had gained what he wanted, who was satisfied with his fate and himself. There is always, for some reason, an element of sadness mingled with my thoughts of human happiness, and, on this occasion, at the sight of a happy man I was overcome by an oppressive feeling that was close upon despair. It was particularly oppressive at night. A bed was made up for me in the room next to my brother's bedroom, and I could hear that he was awake, and that he kept getting up and going to the plate of gooseberries and taking one. I reflected how many satisfied, happy people there really are! What a suffocating force it is! You look at life: the insolence and idleness of the strong, the ignorance and brutishness of the weak, incredible poverty all about us, overcrowding, degeneration, drunkenness, hypocrisy, lying. . . . Yet all is calm and stillness in the houses and in the streets; of the fifty thousand living in a town, there is not one who would cry out, who would give vent to his indignation aloud. We see the people going to market for provisions, eating by day, sleeping by night, talking their silly nonsense, getting married, growing old, serenely escorting their dead to the cemetery; but we do not see and we do not hear those who suffer, and what is terrible in life goes on somewhere behind the scenes. . . . Everything is quiet and peaceful, and nothing protests but mute statistics: so many people gone out of their minds, so many gallons of vodka drunk, so many children dead from malnutrition. . . . And this order of things is evidently necessary; evidently the happy man only feels at ease because the unhappy bear their burdens in silence, and without that silence happiness would be impossible. It's a case of general hypnotism. There ought to be behind the door of every happy, contented man some one standing with a hammer continually reminding him with a tap that there are unhappy people; that however happy he may be, life will show him her laws sooner or later, trouble will come for him—disease, poverty, losses, and no one will see or hear, just as now he neither sees nor hears others. But there is no man with a hammer; the happy man lives at his ease, and trivial daily cares faintly agitate him like the wind in the aspen tree—and all goes well.

"That night I realized that I, too, was happy and contented," Ivan Ivanovitch went on, getting up. "I, too, at dinner and at the hunt liked to lay down the law on life and religion, and the way to manage the peasantry. I, too, used to say that science was light, that culture was essential, but for the simple people reading and writing was enough for the time. Freedom is a blessing, I used to say; we can no more do without it than without air, but we must wait a little. Yes, I used to talk like that, and now I ask, 'For what reason are we to wait?'" asked Ivan Ivanovitch, looking angrily at Burkin. "Why wait, I ask you? What grounds have we for waiting? I shall be told, it can't be done all at once; every idea takes shape in life gradually, in its due time. But who is it says that? Where is the proof that it's right? You will fall back upon the natural order of things, the uniformity of phenomena; but is there order and uniformity in the fact that I, a living, thinking man, stand over a chasm and wait for it to close of itself, or to fill up with mud at the very time when perhaps I might leap over it or build a bridge across it? And again, wait for the sake of what? Wait till there's no strength to live? And meanwhile one must live, and one wants to live!

"I went away from my brother's early in the morning, and ever since then it has been unbearable for me to be in town. I am oppressed by its peace and quiet; I am afraid to look at the windows, for there is no spectacle more painful to me now than the sight of a happy family sitting round the table drinking tea. I am old and am not fit for the struggle; I am not even capable of hatred; I can only grieve inwardly, feel irritated and vexed; but at night my head is hot from the rush of ideas, and I cannot sleep. . . . Ah, if I were young!"

Ivan Ivanovitch walked backwards and forwards in excitement, and repeated: "If I were young!"

He suddenly went up to Alehin and began pressing first one of his hands and then the other.

"Pavel Konstantinovitch," he said in an imploring voice, "don't be calm and contented, don't let yourself be put to sleep! While you are young, strong, confident, be not weary in well-doing! There is no happiness, and there ought not to be; but if there is a meaning and an object in life, that meaning and object is not our happiness, but something greater and more rational. Do good!"

And all this Ivan Ivanovitch said with a pitiful, imploring smile, as though he were asking him a personal favour.

Then all three sat in armchairs at different ends of the drawing room and were silent. Ivan Ivanovitch's story had not satisfied either Burkin or Alehin. When the generals and ladies gazed down from their gilt frames, looking in the dusk as though they were alive, it was dreary to listen to the story of the poor clerk who ate gooseberries. They felt inclined, for some reason, to talk about elegant people, about women. And their sitting in the drawing room where everything—the chandeliers in their covers, the armchairs, and the carpet under their feet—reminded them that those very people who were now looking down from their frames had once moved about, sat, drunk tea in this room, and the fact that lovely Pelagea was moving noiselessly about was better than any story.

Alehin was fearfully sleepy; he had got up early, before three o'clock in the morning, to look after his work, and now his eyes were closing; but he was afraid his visitors might tell some interesting story after he had gone, and he lingered on. He did not go into the question whether what Ivan Ivanovitch had just said was right and true. His visitors did not talk of groats, nor of hay, nor of tar, but of something that had no direct bearing on his life, and he was glad and wanted them to go on.

"It's bedtime, though," said Burkin, getting up. "Allow me to wish you goodnight."

Alehin said goodnight and went downstairs to his own domain, while the visitors remained upstairs. They were both taken for the night to a big room where there stood two old wooden beds decorated with carvings, and in the corner was an ivory crucifix. The big cool beds, which had been made by the lovely Pelagea, smelt agreeably of clean linen.

Ivan Ivanovitch undressed in silence and got into bed.

"Lord forgive us sinners!" he said, and put his head under the quilt.

His pipe lying on the table smelt strongly of stale tobacco, and Burkin could not sleep for a long while, and kept wondering where the oppressive smell came from.

The rain was pattering on the windowpanes all night.

About Love

[Written June-July 1898 in Melikhovo.
First published in the August 1898 issue of
Russkaya Mysl (*Russian Thought*), a Russian magazine.
Collected in *The Wife and Other Stories* (1918).
The story is the final part of *The Little Trilogy*.]

At lunch next day there were very nice pies, crayfish, and mutton cutlets; and while we were eating, Nikanor, the cook, came up to ask what the visitors would like for dinner. He was a man of medium height, with a puffy face and little eyes; he was close-shaven, and it looked as though his moustaches had not been shaved, but had been pulled out by the roots. Alehin told us that the beautiful Pelagea was in love with this cook. As he drank and was of a violent character, she did not want to marry him, but was willing to live with him without. He was very devout, and his religious convictions would not allow him to "live in sin"; he insisted on her marrying him, and would consent to nothing else, and when he was drunk he used to abuse her and even beat her. Whenever he got drunk she used to hide upstairs and sob, and on such occasions Alehin and the servants stayed in the house to be ready to defend her in case of necessity.

We began talking about love.

"How love is born," said Alehin, "why Pelagea does not love somebody more like herself in her spiritual and external qualities, and why she fell in love with Nikanor, that ugly snout—we all call him 'The Snout'—how far questions of personal happiness are of consequence in love—all that is known; one can take what view one likes of it. So far only one incontestable truth has been uttered about love: 'This is a great

452

mystery.' Everything else that has been written or said about love is not a conclusion, but only a statement of questions which have remained unanswered. The explanation which would seem to fit one case does not apply in a dozen others, and the very best thing, to my mind, would be to explain every case individually without attempting to generalize. We ought, as the doctors say, to individualize each case."

"Perfectly true," Burkin assented.

"We Russians of the educated class have a partiality for these questions that remain unanswered. Love is usually poeticized, decorated with roses, nightingales; we Russians decorate our loves with these momentous questions, and select the most uninteresting of them, too. In Moscow, when I was a student, I had a friend who shared my life, a charming lady, and every time I took her in my arms she was thinking what I would allow her a month for housekeeping and what was the price of beef a pound. In the same way, when we are in love we are never tired of asking ourselves questions: whether it is honourable or dishonourable, sensible or stupid, what this love is leading up to, and so on. Whether it is a good thing or not I don't know, but that it is in the way, unsatisfactory, and irritating, I do know."

It looked as though he wanted to tell some story. People who lead a solitary existence always have something in their hearts which they are eager to talk about. In town bachelors visit the baths and the restaurants on purpose to talk, and sometimes tell the most interesting things to bath attendants and waiters; in the country, as a rule, they unbosom themselves to their guests. Now from the window we could see a grey sky, trees drenched in the rain; in such weather we could go nowhere, and there was nothing for us to do but to tell stories and to listen.

"I have lived at Sofino and been farming for a long time," Alehin began, "ever since I left the University. I am an idle gentleman by education, a studious person by disposition; but there was a big debt owing on the estate when I came here, and as my father was in debt partly because he had spent so much on my education, I resolved not to go away, but to work till I paid off the debt. I made up my mind to this and set to work, not, I must confess, without some repugnance. The land here does not yield much, and if one is not to farm at a loss one must employ serf labour or hired labourers, which is almost the same thing, or put it on a peasant footing—that is, work the fields oneself and with one's family. There is no middle path. But in those days I did not go into such subtleties. I did not leave a clod of earth unturned; I gathered together all the peasants, men and women, from the neighbouring villages; the work went on at a tremendous pace. I myself ploughed and sowed and reaped, and was bored doing it, and frowned with disgust, like a village cat driven by hunger to eat cucumbers in the kitchen garden. My body ached, and I slept as I walked. At first it seemed to me that I could easily reconcile this life of toil with my cultured habits; to do so, I thought, all that is necessary is to maintain a certain external order in life. I established myself upstairs here in the best rooms, and ordered them to bring me there coffee and liquor after lunch and dinner, and when I went to bed I read every night the *Yyesnik Evropi*. But one day our priest, Father Ivan, came and drank up all my liquor at one sitting; and the *Yyesnik Evropi* went to the priest's daughters; as in the summer, especially at the haymaking, I did not succeed in getting to my bed at all, and slept in the sledge in the barn, or somewhere in the forester's lodge, what chance was there of reading? Little by little I moved downstairs, began dining in the servants' kitchen, and of my former luxury nothing is left but the servants who were in my father's service, and whom it would be painful to turn away.

"In the first years I was elected here an honourary justice of the peace. I used to have to go to the town and take part in the sessions of the congress and of the circuit court, and this was a pleasant change for me. When you live here for two or three months without a break, especially in the winter, you begin at last to pine for a black coat. And in the circuit court there were frock-coats, and uniforms, and dress-coats, too, all lawyers, men who have received a general education; I had some one to talk to. After sleeping in the sledge and dining in the kitchen, to sit in an armchair in clean linen, in thin boots, with a chain on one's waistcoat, is such luxury!

"I received a warm welcome in the town. I made friends eagerly. And of all my acquaintanceships the most intimate and, to tell the truth, the most agreeable to me was my acquaintance with Luganovitch, the vice-president of the circuit court. You both know him: a most charming personality. It all happened just after a celebrated case of incendiarism; the preliminary investigation lasted two days; we were exhausted. Luganovitch looked at me and said:

"'Look here, come round to dinner with me.'

"This was unexpected, as I knew Luganovitch very little, only officially, and I had never been to his house. I only just went to my hotel room to change and went off to dinner. And here it was my lot to meet Anna Alexyevna, Luganovitch's wife. At that time she was still very young, not more than twenty-two, and her first baby had been born just six months before. It is all a thing of the past; and now I should find it difficult to define what there was so exceptional in her, what it was in her attracted me so much; at the time, at dinner, it was all perfectly clear to me. I saw a lovely young, good, intelligent, fascinating woman, such as I had never met before; and I felt her at once some one close and already familiar, as though that face, those cordial, intelligent eyes, I had seen somewhere in my childhood, in the album which lay on my mother's chest of drawers.

"Four Jews were charged with being incendiaries, were regarded as a gang of robbers, and, to my mind, quite groundlessly. At dinner I was very much excited, I was uncomfortable, and I don't know what I said, but Anna Alexyevna kept shaking her head and saying to her husband:

"'Dmitry, how is this?'

"Luganovitch is a good-natured man, one of those simple-hearted people who firmly maintain the opinion that once a man is charged before a court he is guilty, and to express doubt of the correctness of a sentence cannot be done except in legal form on paper, and not at dinner and in private conversation.

"'You and I did not set fire to the place,' he said softly, 'and you see we are not condemned, and not in prison.'

"And both husband and wife tried to make me eat and drink as much as possible. From some trifling details, from the way they made the coffee together, for instance, and from the way they understood each other at half a word, I could gather that they lived in harmony and comfort, and that they were glad of a visitor. After dinner they played a duet on the piano; then it got dark, and I went home. That was at the beginning of spring.

"After that I spent the whole summer at Sofino without a break, and I had no time to think of the town, either, but the memory of the graceful fair-haired woman remained in my mind all those days; I did not think of her, but it was as though her light shadow were lying on my heart.

"In the late autumn there was a theatrical performance for some charitable object in the town. I went into the governor's box (I was invited to go there in the interval); I looked, and there was Anna Alexyevna

455

sitting beside the governor's wife; and again the same irresistible, thrilling impression of beauty and sweet, caressing eyes, and again the same feeling of nearness. We sat side by side, then went to the foyer.

"'You've grown thinner,' she said; 'have you been ill?'

"'Yes, I've had rheumatism in my shoulder, and in rainy weather I can't sleep.'

"'You look dispirited. In the spring, when you came to dinner, you were younger, more confident. You were full of eagerness, and talked a great deal then; you were very interesting, and I really must confess I was a little carried away by you. For some reason you often came back to my memory during the summer, and when I was getting ready for the theatre today I thought I should see you.'

"And she laughed.

"'But you look dispirited today,' she repeated; 'it makes you seem older.'

"The next day I lunched at the Luganovitchs." After lunch they drove out to their summer villa, in order to make arrangements there for the winter, and I went with them. I returned with them to the town, and at midnight drank tea with them in quiet domestic surroundings, while the fire glowed, and the young mother kept going to see if her baby girl was asleep. And after that, every time I went to town I never failed to visit the Luganovitchs. They grew used to me, and I grew used to them. As a rule I went in unannounced, as though I were one of the family.

"'Who is there?' I would hear from a faraway room, in the drawling voice that seemed to me so lovely.

"'It is Pavel Konstantinovitch,' answered the maid or the nurse.

"Anna Alexyevna would come out to me with an anxious face, and would ask every time:

"'Why is it so long since you have been? Has anything happened?'

"Her eyes, the elegant refined hand she gave me, her indoor dress, the way she did her hair, her voice, her step, always produced the same impression on me of something new and extraordinary in my life, and very important. We talked together for hours, were silent, thinking each our own thoughts, or she played for hours to me on the piano. If there were no one at home I stayed and waited, talked to the nurse, played with the child, or lay on the sofa in the study and read; and when Anna Alexyevna came back I met her in the hall, took all her parcels from her, and for some reason I carried those parcels every time with as much love, with as much solemnity, as a boy.

"There is a proverb that if a peasant woman has no troubles she will buy a pig. The Luganovitchs had no troubles, so they made friends with me. If I did not come to the town I must be ill or something must have happened to me, and both of them were extremely anxious. They were worried that I, an educated man with a knowledge of languages, should, instead of devoting myself to science or literary work, live in the country, rush round like a squirrel in a rage, work hard with never a penny to show for it. They fancied that I was unhappy, and that I only talked, laughed, and ate to conceal my sufferings, and even at cheerful moments when I felt happy I was aware of their searching eyes fixed upon me. They were particularly touching when I really was depressed, when I was being worried by some creditor or had not money enough to pay interest on the proper day. The two of them, husband and wife, would whisper together at the window; then he would come to me and say with a grave face:

"'If you really are in need of money at the moment, Pavel Konstantinovitch, my wife and I beg you not to hesitate to borrow from us.'

"And he would blush to his ears with emotion. And it would happen that, after whispering in the same way at the window, he would come up to me, with red ears, and say:

"'My wife and I earnestly beg you to accept this present.'

"And he would give me studs, a cigar-case, or a lamp, and I would send them game, butter, and flowers from the country. They both, by the way, had considerable means of their own. In early days I often borrowed money, and was not very particular about it—borrowed wherever I could—but nothing in the world would have induced me to borrow from the Luganovitchs. But why talk of it?

"I was unhappy. At home, in the fields, in the barn, I thought of her; I tried to understand the mystery of a beautiful, intelligent young woman's marrying some one so uninteresting, almost an old man (her husband was over forty), and having children by him; to understand the mystery of this uninteresting, good, simple-hearted man, who argued with such wearisome good sense, at balls and evening parties kept near the more solid people, looking listless and superfluous, with a submissive, uninterested expression, as though he had been brought there for sale,

457

who yet believed in his right to be happy, to have children by her; and I kept trying to understand why she had met him first and not me, and why such a terrible mistake in our lives need have happened.

"And when I went to the town I saw every time from her eyes that she was expecting me, and she would confess to me herself that she had had a peculiar feeling all that day and had guessed that I should come. We talked a long time, and were silent, yet we did not confess our love to each other, but timidly and jealously concealed it. We were afraid of everything that might reveal our secret to ourselves. I loved her tenderly, deeply, but I reflected and kept asking myself what our love could lead to if we had not the strength to fight against it. It seemed to be incredible that my gentle, sad love could all at once coarsely break up the even tenor of the life of her husband, her children, and all the household in which I was so loved and trusted. Would it be honourable? She would go away with me, but where? Where could I take her? It would have been a different matter if I had had a beautiful, interesting life—if, for instance, I had been struggling for the emancipation of my country, or had been a celebrated man of science, an artist or a painter; but as it was it would mean taking her from one everyday humdrum life to another as humdrum or perhaps more so. And how long would our happiness last? What would happen to her in case I was ill, in case I died, or if we simply grew cold to one another?

"And she apparently reasoned in the same way. She thought of her husband, her children, and of her mother, who loved the husband like a son. If she abandoned herself to her feelings she would have to lie, or else to tell the truth, and in her position either would have been equally terrible and inconvenient. And she was tormented by the question whether her love would bring me happiness—would she not complicate my life, which, as it was, was hard enough and full of all sorts of trouble? She fancied she was not young enough for me, that she was not industrious nor energetic enough to begin a new life, and she often talked to her husband of the importance of my marrying a girl of intelligence and merit who would be a capable housewife and a help to me—and she would immediately add that it would be difficult to find such a girl in the whole town.

"Meanwhile the years were passing. Anna Alexyevna already had two children. When I arrived at the Luganovitchs' the servants smiled cordially, the children shouted that Uncle Pavel Konstantinovitch had come, and hung on my neck; every one was overjoyed. They did not understand what was passing in my soul, and thought that I, too, was happy. Every one looked on me as a noble being. And grown-ups and children alike felt that a noble being was walking about their rooms, and that gave a peculiar charm to their manner towards me, as though in my presence their life, too, was purer and more beautiful. Anna Alexyevna and I used to go to the theatre together, always walking there; we used to sit side by side in the stalls, our shoulders touching. I would take the opera-glass from her hands without a word, and feel at that minute that she was near me, that she was mine, that we could not live without each other; but by some strange misunderstanding, when we came out of the theatre we always said goodbye and parted as though we were strangers. Goodness knows what people were saying about us in the town already, but there was not a word of truth in it all!

"In the latter years Anna Alexyevna took to going away for frequent visits to her mother or to her sister; she began to suffer from low spirits, she began to recognize that her life was spoilt and unsatisfied, and at times she did not care to see her husband nor her children. She was already being treated for neurasthenia.

"We were silent and still silent, and in the presence of outsiders she displayed a strange irritation in regard to me; whatever I talked about, she disagreed with me, and if I had an argument she sided with my opponent. If I dropped anything, she would say coldly:

"'I congratulate you.'

"If I forgot to take the opera-glass when we were going to the theatre, she would say afterwards:

"'I knew you would forget it.'

"Luckily or unluckily, there is nothing in our lives that does not end sooner or later. The time of parting came, as Luganovitch was appointed president in one of the western provinces. They had to sell their furniture, their horses, their summer villa. When they drove out to the villa, and afterwards looked back as they were going away, to look for the last time at the garden, at the green roof, every one was sad, and I realized that I had to say goodbye not only to the villa. It was arranged that at the end of August we should see Anna Alexyevna off to the Crimea, where the doctors were sending her, and that a little later Luganovitch and the children would set off for the western province.

"We were a great crowd to see Anna Alexyevna off. When she had said goodbye to her husband and her children and there was only a minute left before the third bell, I ran into her compartment to put a basket, which she had almost forgotten, on the rack, and I had to say goodbye. When our eyes met in the compartment our spiritual fortitude deserted us both; I took her in my arms, she pressed her face to my breast, and tears flowed from her eyes. Kissing her face, her shoulders, her hands wet with tears—oh, how unhappy we were!—I confessed my love for her, and with a burning pain in my heart I realized how unnecessary, how petty, and how deceptive all that had hindered us from loving was. I understood that when you love you must either, in your reasonings about that love, start from what is highest, from what is more important than happiness or unhappiness, sin or virtue in their accepted meaning, or you must not reason at all.

"I kissed her for the last time, pressed her hand, and parted for ever. The train had already started. I went into the next compartment—it was empty—and until I reached the next station I sat there crying. Then I walked home to Sofino. . . ."

While Alehin was telling his story, the rain left off and the sun came out. Burkin and Ivan Ivanovitch went out on the balcony, from which there was a beautiful view over the garden and the mill-pond, which was shining now in the sunshine like a mirror. They admired it, and at the same time they were sorry that this man with the kind, clever eyes, who had told them this story with such genuine feeling, should be rushing round and round this huge estate like a squirrel on a wheel instead of devoting himself to science or something else which would have made his life more pleasant; and they thought what a sorrowful face Anna Alexyevna must have had when he said goodbye to her in the railway-carriage and kissed her face and shoulders. Both of them had met her in the town, and Burkin knew her and thought her beautiful.

The Darling

[First published in Moscow on January 3, 1899,
in *Semya* (Family) magazine.
Collected in *The Darling and Other Stories* (1916).]

Olenka, the daughter of the retired collegiate assessor, Plemyanniakov, was sitting in her back porch, lost in thought. It was hot, the flies were persistent and teasing, and it was pleasant to reflect that it would soon be evening. Dark rainclouds were gathering from the east, and bringing from time to time a breath of moisture in the air.

Kukin, who was the manager of an open-air theatre called the Tivoli, and who lived in the lodge, was standing in the middle of the garden looking at the sky.

"Again!" he observed despairingly. "It's going to rain again! Rain every day, as though to spite me. I might as well hang myself! It's ruin! Fearful losses every day."

He flung up his hands, and went on, addressing Olenka:

"There! that's the life we lead, Olga Semyonovna. It's enough to make one cry. One works and does one's utmost, one wears oneself out, getting no sleep at night, and racks one's brain what to do for the best. And then what happens? To begin with, one's public is ignorant, boorish. I give them the very best operetta, a dainty masque, first rate music-hall artists. But do you suppose that's what they want! They don't understand anything of that sort. They want a clown; what they ask for is vulgarity. And then look at the weather! Almost every evening it rains. It started on the tenth of May, and it's kept it up all May and June. It's simply awful! The public doesn't come, but I've to pay the rent just the same, and pay the artists."

The next evening the clouds would gather again, and Kukin would say with an hysterical laugh:

"Well, rain away, then! Flood the garden, drown me! Damn my luck in this world and the next! Let the artists have me up! Send me to prison!—to Siberia!—the scaffold! Ha, ha, ha!"

And next day the same thing.

Olenka listened to Kukin with silent gravity, and sometimes tears came into her eyes. In the end his misfortunes touched her; she grew to love him. He was a small thin man, with a yellow face, and curls combed forward on his forehead. He spoke in a thin tenor; as he talked his mouth worked on one side, and there was always an expression of despair on his face; yet he aroused a deep and genuine affection in her. She was always fond of some one, and could not exist without loving. In earlier days she had loved her papa, who now sat in a darkened room, breathing with difficulty; she had loved her aunt who used to come every other year from Bryansk; and before that, when she was at school, she had loved her French master. She was a gentle, soft-hearted, compassionate girl, with mild, tender eyes and very good health. At the sight of her full rosy cheeks, her soft white neck with a little dark mole on it, and the kind, naïve smile, which came into her face when she listened to anything pleasant, men thought, "Yes, not half bad," and smiled too, while lady visitors could not refrain from seizing her hand in the middle of a conversation, exclaiming in a gush of delight, "You darling!"

The house in which she had lived from her birth upwards, and which was left her in her father's will, was at the extreme end of the town, not far from the Tivoli. In the evenings and at night she could head the band playing, and the crackling and banging of fireworks, and it seemed to her that it was Kukin struggling with his destiny, storming the entrenchments of his chief foe, the indifferent public; there was a sweet thrill at her heart, she had no desire to sleep, and when he returned home at day-break, she tapped softly at her bedroom window, and showing him only her face and one shoulder through the curtain, she gave him a friendly smile. . . .

He proposed to her, and they were married. And when he had a closer view of her neck and her plump, fine shoulders, he threw up his hands, and said:

"You darling!"

He was happy, but as it rained on the day and night of his wedding, his face still retained an expression of despair.

They got on very well together. She used to sit in his office, to look after things in the Tivoli, to put down the accounts and pay the wages. And her rosy cheeks, her sweet, naïve, radiant smile, were to be seen now at the office window, now in the refreshment bar or behind the scenes of the theatre. And already she used to say to her acquaintances that the theatre was the chief and most important thing in life and that it was only through the drama that one could derive true enjoyment and become cultivated and humane.

"But do you suppose the public understands that?" she used to say. "What they want is a clown. Yesterday we gave 'Faust Inside Out,' and almost all the boxes were empty; but if Vanitchka and I had been producing some vulgar thing, I assure you the theatre would have been packed. Tomorrow Vanitchka and I are doing 'Orpheus in Hell.' Do come."

And what Kukin said about the theatre and the actors she repeated. Like him she despised the public for their ignorance and their indifference to art; she took part in the rehearsals, she corrected the actors, she kept an eye on the behaviour of the musicians, and when there was an unfavourable notice in the local paper, she shed tears, and then went to the editor's office to set things right.

The actors were fond of her and used to call her "Vanitchka and I," and "the darling"; she was sorry for them and used to lend them small sums of money, and if they deceived her, she used to shed a few tears in private, but did not complain to her husband.

They got on well in the winter too. They took the theatre in the town for the whole winter, and let it for short terms to a Little Russian company, or to a conjurer, or to a local dramatic society. Olenka grew stouter, and was always beaming with satisfaction, while Kukin grew thinner and yellower, and continually complained of their terrible losses, although he had not done badly all the winter. He used to cough at night, and she used to give him hot raspberry tea or lime-flower water, to rub him with eau-de-Cologne and to wrap him in her warm shawls.

"You're such a sweet pet!" she used to say with perfect sincerity, stroking his hair. "You're such a pretty dear!"

Towards Lent he went to Moscow to collect a new troupe, and without him she could not sleep, but sat all night at her window, looking at the stars, and she compared herself with the hens, who are awake all night and uneasy when the cock is not in the hen-house. Kukin was detained in Moscow, and wrote that he would be back at Easter, adding some instructions about the Tivoli. But on the Sunday before Easter, late in the evening, came a sudden ominous knock at the gate; some one was hammering on the gate as though on a barrel—boom, boom, boom! The drowsy cook went flopping with her bare feet through the puddles, as she ran to open the gate.

"Please open," said some one outside in a thick bass. "There is a telegram for you."

Olenka had received telegrams from her husband before, but this time for some reason she felt numb with terror. With shaking hands she opened the telegram and read as follows:

"IVAN PETROVITCH DIED SUDDENLY TODAY. AWAITING IMMATE INSTRUCTIONS FUFUNERAL TUESDAY."

That was how it was written in the telegram—"fufuneral," and the utterly incomprehensible word "immate." It was signed by the stage manager of the operatic company.

"My darling!" sobbed Olenka. "Vanka, my precious, my darling! Why did I ever meet you! Why did I know you and love you! Your poor heartbroken Olenka is alone without you!"

Kukin's funeral took place on Tuesday in Moscow, Olenka returned home on Wednesday, and as soon as she got indoors, she threw herself on her bed and sobbed so loudly that it could be heard next door, and in the street.

"Poor darling!" the neighbours said, as they crossed themselves. "Olga Semyonovna, poor darling! How she does take on!"

Three months later Olenka was coming home from mass, melancholy and in deep mourning. It happened that one of her neighbours, Vassily Andreitch Pustovalov, returning home from church, walked back beside her. He was the manager at Babakayev's, the timber merchant's. He wore a straw hat, a white waistcoat, and a gold watch-chain, and looked more a country gentleman than a man in trade.

"Everything happens as it is ordained, Olga Semyonovna," he said gravely, with a sympathetic note in his voice; "and if any of our dear ones die, it must be because it is the will of God, so we ought have fortitude and bear it submissively."

After seeing Olenka to her gate, he said goodbye and went on. All day afterwards she heard his sedately dignified voice, and whenever she shut her eyes she saw his dark beard. She liked him very much. And apparently she had made an impression on him too, for not long afterwards an elderly lady, with whom she was only slightly acquainted, came to drink coffee with her, and as soon as she was seated at table began to talk about Pustovalov, saying that he was an excellent man whom one could thoroughly depend upon, and that any girl would be glad to marry him. Three days later Pustovalov came himself. He did not stay long, only about ten minutes, and he did not say much, but when he left, Olenka loved him—loved him so much that she lay awake all night in a perfect fever, and in the morning she sent for the elderly lady. The match was quickly arranged, and then came the wedding.

Pustovalov and Olenka got on very well together when they were married.

Usually he sat in the office till dinner-time, then he went out on business, while Olenka took his place, and sat in the office till evening, making up accounts and booking orders.

"Timber gets dearer every year; the price rises twenty per cent," she would say to her customers and friends. "Only fancy we used to sell local timber, and now Vassitchka always has to go for wood to the Mogilev district. And the freight!" she would add, covering her cheeks with her hands in horror. "The freight!"

It seemed to her that she had been in the timber trade for ages and ages, and that the most important and necessary thing in life was timber; and there was something intimate and touching to her in the very sound of words such as "baulk," "post," "beam," "pole," "scantling," "batten," "lath," "plank," etc.

At night when she was asleep she dreamed of perfect mountains of planks and boards, and long strings of wagons, carting timber somewhere far away. She dreamed that a whole regiment of six-inch beams forty feet high, standing on end, was marching upon the timber-yard; that logs, beams, and boards knocked together with the resounding crash of dry wood, kept falling and getting up again, piling themselves on each other. Olenka cried out in her sleep, and Pustovalov said to her tenderly: "Olenka, what's the matter, darling? Cross yourself!"

Her husband's ideas were hers. If he thought the room was too hot, or that business was slack, she thought the same. Her husband did not care for entertainments, and on holidays he stayed at home. She did likewise.

"You are always at home or in the office," her friends said to her. "You should go to the theatre, darling, or to the circus."

"Vassitchka and I have no time to go to theatres," she would answer sedately. "We have no time for nonsense. What's the use of these theatres?"

On Saturdays Pustovalov and she used to go to the evening service; on holidays to early mass, and they walked side by side with softened faces as they came home from church. There was a pleasant fragrance about them both, and her silk dress rustled agreeably. At home they drank tea, with fancy bread and jams of various kinds, and afterwards they ate pie. Every day at twelve o'clock there was a savoury smell of beet-root soup and of mutton or duck in their yard, and on fast-days of fish, and no one could pass the gate without feeling hungry. In the office the samovar was always boiling, and customers were regaled with tea and cracknels. Once a week the couple went to the baths and returned side by side, both red in the face.

"Yes, we have nothing to complain of, thank God," Olenka used to say to her acquaintances. "I wish every one were as well off as Vassitchka and I."

When Pustovalov went away to buy wood in the Mogilev district, she missed him dreadfully, lay awake and cried. A young veterinary surgeon in the army, called Smirnin, to whom they had let their lodge, used sometimes to come in in the evening. He used to talk to her and play cards with her, and this entertained her in her husband's absence. She was particularly interested in what he told her of his home life. He was married and had a little boy, but was separated from his wife because she had been unfaithful to him, and now he hated her and used to send her forty roubles a month for the maintenance of their son. And hearing of all this, Olenka sighed and shook her head. She was sorry for him.

"Well, God keep you," she used to say to him at parting, as she lighted him down the stairs with a candle. "Thank you for coming to cheer me up, and may the Mother of God give you health."

And she always expressed herself with the same sedateness and dignity, the same reasonableness, in imitation of her husband. As the veterinary surgeon was disappearing behind the door below, she would say:

"You know, Vladimir Platonitch, you'd better make it up with your wife. You should forgive her for the sake of your son. You may be sure the little fellow understands."

And when Pustovalov came back, she told him in a low voice about the veterinary surgeon and his unhappy home life, and both sighed and shook their heads and talked about the boy, who, no doubt, missed his father, and by some strange connection of ideas, they went up to the holy ikons, bowed to the ground before them and prayed that God would give them children.

And so the Pustovalovs lived for six years quietly and peaceably in love and complete harmony.

But behold! one winter day after drinking hot tea in the office, Vassily Andreitch went out into the yard without his cap on to see about sending off some timber, caught cold and was taken ill. He had the best doctors, but he grew worse and died after four months' illness. And Olenka was a widow once more.

"I've nobody, now you've left me, my darling," she sobbed, after her husband's funeral. "How can I live without you, in wretchedness and misery! Pity me, good people, all alone in the world!"

She went about dressed in black with long "weepers," and gave up wearing hat and gloves for good. She hardly ever went out, except to church, or to her husband's grave, and led the life of a nun. It was not till six months later that she took off the weepers and opened the shutters of the windows. She was sometimes seen in the mornings, going with her cook to market for provisions, but what went on in her house and how she lived now could only be surmised. People guessed, from seeing her drinking tea in her garden with the veterinary surgeon, who read the newspaper aloud to her, and from the fact that, meeting a lady she knew at the post-office, she said to her:

"There is no proper veterinary inspection in our town, and that's the cause of all sorts of epidemics. One is always hearing of people's getting infection from the milk supply, or catching diseases from horses and cows. The health of domestic animals ought to be as well cared for as the health of human beings."

She repeated the veterinary surgeon's words, and was of the same opinion as he about everything. It was evident that she could not live a year without some attachment, and had found new happiness in the lodge. In any one else this would have been censured, but no one could think ill of Olenka; everything she did was so natural. Neither she nor the veterinary surgeon said anything to other people of the change in their relations, and tried, indeed, to conceal it, but without success, for Olenka could not keep a secret. When he had visitors, men serving in his regiment, and she poured out tea or served the supper, she would begin talking of the cattle plague, of the foot and mouth disease, and of the municipal slaughterhouses. He was dreadfully embarrassed, and when the guests had gone, he would seize her by the hand and hiss angrily:

"I've asked you before not to talk about what you don't understand. When we veterinary surgeons are talking among ourselves, please don't put your word in. It's really annoying."

And she would look at him with astonishment and dismay, and ask him in alarm: "But, Voloditchka, what am I to talk about?"

And with tears in her eyes she would embrace him, begging him not to be angry, and they were both happy.

But this happiness did not last long. The veterinary surgeon departed, departed for ever with his regiment, when it was transferred to a distant place—to Siberia, it may be. And Olenka was left alone.

Now she was absolutely alone. Her father had long been dead, and his armchair lay in the attic, covered with dust and lame of one leg. She got thinner and plainer, and when people met her in the street they did not look at her as they used to, and did not smile to her; evidently her best years were over and left behind, and now a new sort of life had begun for her, which did not bear thinking about. In the evening Olenka sat in the porch, and heard the band playing and the fireworks popping in the Tivoli, but now the sound stirred no response. She looked into her yard without interest, thought of nothing, wished for nothing, and afterwards, when night came on she went to bed and dreamed of her empty yard. She ate and drank as it were unwillingly.

And what was worst of all, she had no opinions of any sort. She saw the objects about her and understood what she saw, but could not form any opinion about them, and did not know what to talk about. And how awful it is not to have any opinions! One sees a bottle, for instance, or the rain, or a peasant driving in his cart, but what the bottle is for, or the rain, or the peasant, and what is the meaning of it, one can't say, and could not even for a thousand roubles. When she had Kukin, or Pustovalov, or the veterinary surgeon, Olenka could explain everything, and give her opinion about anything you like, but now there was the same emptiness in her brain and in her heart as there was in her yard outside. And it was as harsh and as bitter as wormwood in the mouth.

Little by little the town grew in all directions. The road became a street, and where the Tivoli and the timber-yard had been, there were new turnings and houses. How rapidly time passes! Olenka's house grew dingy, the roof got rusty, the shed sank on one side, and the whole yard was overgrown with docks and stinging-nettles. Olenka herself had grown plain and elderly; in summer she sat in the porch, and her soul, as before, was empty and dreary and full of bitterness. In winter she sat at her window and looked at the snow. When she caught the scent of spring, or heard the chime of the church bells, a sudden rush of memories from the past came over her, there was a tender ache in her heart, and her eyes brimmed over with tears; but this was only for a minute, and then came emptiness again and the sense of the futility of life. The black kitten, Briska, rubbed against her and purred softly, but Olenka was not touched by these feline caresses. That was not what she needed. She wanted a love that would absorb her whole being, her whole soul and reason—that would give her ideas and an object in life, and would warm her old blood. And she would shake the kitten off her skirt and say with vexation:

"Get along; I don't want you!"

And so it was, day after day and year after year, and no joy, and no opinions. Whatever Mavra, the cook, said she accepted.

One hot July day, towards evening, just as the cattle were being driven away, and the whole yard was full of dust, some one suddenly knocked at the gate. Olenka went to open it herself and was dumbfounded when she looked out: she saw Smirnin, the veterinary surgeon, grey-headed, and dressed as a civilian. She suddenly remembered everything. She could not help crying and letting her head fall on his breast without uttering a word, and in the violence of her feeling she did not notice how they both walked into the house and sat down to tea.

"My dear Vladimir Platonitch! What fate has brought you?" she muttered, trembling with joy.

"I want to settle here for good, Olga Semyonovna," he told her. "I have resigned my post, and have come to settle down and try my luck on my own account. Besides, it's time for my boy to go to school. He's a big boy. I am reconciled with my wife, you know."

"Where is she?' asked Olenka.

"She's at the hotel with the boy, and I'm looking for lodgings."

"Good gracious, my dear soul! Lodgings? Why not have my house? Why shouldn't that suit you? Why, my goodness, I wouldn't take any rent!" cried Olenka in a flutter, beginning to cry again. "You live here, and the lodge will do nicely for me. Oh dear! how glad I am!"

Next day the roof was painted and the walls were whitewashed, and Olenka, with her arms akimbo walked about the yard giving directions. Her face was beaming with her old smile, and she was brisk and alert as though she had waked from a long sleep. The veterinary's wife arrived—a thin, plain lady, with short hair and a peevish expression. With her was her little Sasha, a boy of ten, small for his age, blue-eyed, chubby, with dimples in his cheeks. And scarcely had the boy walked into the yard when he ran after the cat, and at once there was the sound of his gay, joyous laugh.

"Is that your puss, auntie?" he asked Olenka. "When she has little ones, do give us a kitten. Mamma is awfully afraid of mice."

Olenka talked to him, and gave him tea. Her heart warmed and there was a sweet ache in her bosom, as though the boy had been her own child. And when he sat at the table in the evening, going over his lessons, she looked at him with deep tenderness and pity as she murmured to herself:

"You pretty pet! . . . my precious! . . . Such a fair little thing, and so clever."

"'An island is a piece of land which is entirely surrounded by water,'" he read aloud.

"An island is a piece of land," she repeated, and this was the first opinion to which she gave utterance with positive conviction after so many years of silence and dearth of ideas.

Now she had opinions of her own, and at supper she talked to Sasha's parents, saying how difficult the lessons were at the high schools, but that yet the high school was better than a commercial one, since with a high-school education all careers were open to one, such as being a doctor or an engineer.

Sasha began going to the high school. His mother departed to Harkov to her sister's and did not return; his father used to go off every day to inspect cattle, and would often be away from home for three days together, and it seemed to Olenka as though Sasha was entirely abandoned, that he was not wanted at home, that he was being starved, and she carried him off to her lodge and gave him a little room there.

And for six months Sasha had lived in the lodge with her. Every morning Olenka came into his bedroom and found him fast asleep, sleeping noiselessly with his hand under his cheek. She was sorry to wake him.

"Sashenka," she would say mournfully, "get up, darling. It's time for school."

He would get up, dress and say his prayers, and then sit down to breakfast, drink three glasses of tea, and eat two large cracknels and a half a buttered roll. All this time he was hardly awake and a little ill-humoured in consequence.

"You don't quite know your fable, Sashenka," Olenka would say, looking at him as though he were about to set off on a long journey. "What a lot of trouble I have with you! You must work and do your best, darling, and obey your teachers."

"Oh, do leave me alone!" Sasha would say.

Then he would go down the street to school, a little figure, wearing a big cap and carrying a satchel on his shoulder. Olenka would follow him noiselessly.

"Sashenka!" she would call after him, and she would pop into his hand a date or a caramel. When he reached the street where the school was, he would feel ashamed of being followed by a tall, stout woman, he would turn round and say:

"You'd better go home, auntie. I can go the rest of the way alone."

She would stand still and look after him fixedly till he had disappeared at the school-gate.

Ah, how she loved him! Of her former attachments not one had been so deep; never had her soul surrendered to any feeling so spontaneously, so disinterestedly, and so joyously as now that her maternal instincts were aroused. For this little boy with the dimple in his cheek and the big school cap, she would have given her whole life, she would have given it with joy and tears of tenderness. Why? Who can tell why?

When she had seen the last of Sasha, she returned home, contented and serene, brimming over with love; her face, which had grown younger during the last six months, smiled and beamed; people meeting her looked at her with pleasure.

"Good morning, Olga Semyonovna, darling. How are you, darling?"

"The lessons at the high school are very difficult now," she would relate at the market. "It's too much; in the first class yesterday they gave him a fable to learn by heart, and a Latin translation and a problem. You know it's too much for a little chap."

And she would begin talking about the teachers, the lessons, and the school books, saying just what Sasha said.

At three o'clock they had dinner together: in the evening they learned their lessons together and cried. When she put him to bed, she would stay a long time making the Cross over him and murmuring a prayer; then she would go to bed and dream of that faraway misty future when Sasha would finish his studies and become a doctor or an engineer, would have a big house of his own with horses and a carriage, would get married and have children. . . . She would fall asleep still thinking of the same thing, and tears would run down her cheeks from her closed eyes, while the black cat lay purring beside her: "Mrr, mrr, mrr."

Suddenly there would come a loud knock at the gate.

Olenka would wake up breathless with alarm, her heart throbbing. Half a minute later would come another knock.

"It must be a telegram from Harkov," she would think, beginning to tremble from head to foot. "Sasha's mother is sending for him from Harkov. . . . Oh, mercy on us!"

She was in despair. Her head, her hands, and her feet would turn chill, and she would feel that she was the most unhappy woman in the world. But another minute would pass, voices would be heard: it would turn out to be the veterinary surgeon coming home from the club.

"Well, thank God!" she would think.

And gradually the load in her heart would pass off, and she would feel at ease. She would go back to bed thinking of Sasha, who lay sound asleep in the next room, sometimes crying out in his sleep:

"I'll give it you! Get away! Shut up!"

At Christmas Time

[Written in December 1898. First published in
Peterburgskaya Gazeta (*St. Petersburg Gazette*),
a Russian literary newspaper, in January 1899.
Collected in *The Witch and Other Stories* (1918).]

I

"What shall I write?" said Yegor, and he dipped his pen in the ink.

Vasilisa had not seen her daughter for four years. Her daughter Yefimya had gone after her wedding to Petersburg, had sent them two letters, and since then seemed to vanish out of their lives; there had been no sight nor sound of her. And whether the old woman were milking her cow at dawn, or heating her stove, or dozing at night, she was always thinking of one and the same thing—what was happening to Yefimya, whether she were alive out yonder. She ought to have sent a letter, but the old father could not write, and there was no one to write.

But now Christmas had come, and Vasilisa could not bear it any longer, and went to the tavern to Yegor, the brother of the innkeeper's wife, who had sat in the tavern doing nothing ever since he came back from the army; people said that he could write letters very well if he were properly paid. Vasilisa talked to the cook at the tavern, then to the mistress of the house, then to Yegor himself. They agreed upon fifteen kopecks.

And now—it happened on the second day of the holidays, in the tavern kitchen—Yegor was sitting at the table, holding the pen in his hand. Vasilisa was standing before him, pondering with an expression of anxiety and woe on her face. Pyotr, her husband, a very thin old man with a brownish bald patch, had come with her; he stood looking straight before him like a blind man. On the stove a piece of pork was being braised in a saucepan; it was spurting and hissing, and seemed to be actually saying: "Flu-flu-flu." It was stifling.

"What am I to write?" Yegor asked again.

"What?" asked Vasilisa, looking at him angrily and suspiciously. "Don't worry me! You are not writing for nothing; no fear, you'll be paid for it. Come, write: 'To our dear son-in-law, Andrey Hrisanfitch, and to our only beloved daughter, Yefimya Petrovna, with our love we send a low bow and our parental blessing abiding for ever.'"

"Written; fire away."

"And we wish them a happy Christmas; we are alive and well, and I wish you the same, please the Lord . . . the Heavenly King."

Vasilisa pondered and exchanged glances with the old man.

"And I wish you the same, please the Lord the Heavenly King," she repeated, beginning to cry.

She could say nothing more. And yet before, when she lay awake thinking at night, it had seemed to her that she could not get all she had to say into a dozen letters. Since the time when her daughter had gone away with her husband much water had flowed into the sea, the old people had lived feeling bereaved, and sighed heavily at night as though they had buried their daughter. And how many events had occurred in the village since then, how many marriages and deaths! How long the winters had been! How long the nights!

"It's hot," said Yegor, unbuttoning his waistcoat. "It must be seventy degrees. What more?" he asked.

The old people were silent.

"What does your son-in-law do in Petersburg?" asked Yegor.

"He was a soldier, my good friend," the old man answered in a weak voice. "He left the service at the same time as you did. He was a soldier, and now, to be sure, he is at Petersburg at a hydropathic establishment. The doctor treats the sick with water. So he, to be sure, is house-porter at the doctor's."

"Here it is written down," said the old woman, taking a letter out of her pocket. "We got it from Yefimya, goodness knows when. Maybe they are no longer in this world."

Yegor thought a little and began writing rapidly:

"At the present time"—he wrote—"since your destiny through your own doing allotted you to the Military Career, we counsel you to look into the Code of Disciplinary Offences and Fundamental Laws of the War Office, and you will see in that law the Civilization of the Officials of the War Office."

He wrote and kept reading aloud what was written, while Vasilisa considered what she ought to write: how great had been their want the year before, how their corn had not lasted even till Christmas, how they had to sell their cow. She ought to ask for money, ought to write that the old father was often ailing and would soon no doubt give up his soul to God . . . but how to express this in words? What must be said first and what afterwards?

"Take note," Yegor went on writing, "in volume five of the Army Regulations soldier is a common noun and a proper one, a soldier of the first rank is called a general, and of the last a private. . . ."

The old man stirred his lips and said softly:

"It would be all right to have a look at the grandchildren."

"What grandchildren?" asked the old woman, and she looked angrily at him; "perhaps there are none."

"Well, but perhaps there are. Who knows?"

"And thereby you can judge," Yegor hurried on, "what is the enemy without and what is the enemy within. The foremost of our enemies within is Bacchus." The pen squeaked, executing upon the paper flourishes like fish-hooks. Yegor hastened and read over every line several times. He sat on a stool sprawling his broad feet under the table, well-fed, bursting with health, with a coarse animal face and a red bull neck. He was vulgarity itself: coarse, conceited, invincible, proud of having been born and bred in a pot-house; and Vasilisa quite understood the vulgarity, but could not express it in words, and could only look angrily and suspiciously at Yegor. Her head was beginning to ache, and her thoughts were in confusion from the sound of his voice and his unintelligible words, from the heat and the stuffiness, and she said nothing and thought nothing, but simply waited for him to finish scribbling. But the old man looked with full confidence. He believed in his old woman who had brought him there, and in Yegor; and when he had mentioned the hydropathic establishment it could be seen that he believed in the establishment and the healing efficacy of water.

Having finished the letter, Yegor got up and read the whole of it through from the beginning. The old man did not understand, but he nodded his head trustfully.

"That's all right; it is smooth . . ." he said. "God give you health. That's all right. . . ."

They laid on the table three five-kopeck pieces and went out of the tavern; the old man looked immovably straight before him as though he were blind, and perfect trustfulness was written on his face; but as Vasilisa came out of the tavern she waved angrily at the dog, and said angrily:

"Ugh, the plague."

The old woman did not sleep all night; she was disturbed by thoughts, and at daybreak she got up, said her prayers, and went to the station to send off the letter.

It was between eight and nine miles to the station.

II

Dr. B. O. Mozelweiser's hydropathic establishment worked on New Year's Day exactly as on ordinary days; the only difference was that the porter, Andrey Hrisanfitch, had on a uniform with new braiding, his boots had an extra polish, and he greeted every visitor with "A Happy New Year to you!"

It was the morning; Andrey Hrisanfitch was standing at the door, reading the newspaper. Just at ten o'clock there arrived a general, one of the habitual visitors, and directly after him the postman; Andrey Hrisanfitch helped the general off with his great-coat, and said:

"A Happy New Year to your Excellency!"

"Thank you, my good fellow; the same to you."

And at the top of the stairs the general asked, nodding towards the door (he asked the same question every day and always forgot the answer):

"And what is there in that room?"

"The massage room, your Excellency."

When the general's steps had died away Andrey Hrisanfitch looked at the post that had come, and found one addressed to himself. He tore it open, read several lines, then, looking at the newspaper, he walked without haste to his own room, which was downstairs close by at the end of the passage. His wife Yefimya was sitting on the bed, feeding her baby; another child, the eldest, was standing by, laying its curly head on her knee; a third was asleep on the bed.

Going into the room, Andrey gave his wife the letter and said:

"From the country, I suppose."

Then he walked out again without taking his eyes from the paper. He could hear Yefimya with a shaking voice reading the first lines. She read them and could read no more; these lines were enough for her. She burst into tears, and hugging her eldest child, kissing him, she began saying— and it was hard to say whether she were laughing or crying:

"It's from granny, from grandfather," she said. "From the country. . . . The Heavenly Mother, Saints and Martyrs! The snow lies heaped up under the roofs now . . . the trees are as white as white. The boys slide on little sledges . . . and dear old bald grandfather is on the stove . . . and there is a little yellow dog. . . . My own darlings!"

Andrey Hrisanfitch, hearing this, recalled that his wife had on three or four occasions given him letters and asked him to send them to the country, but some important business had always prevented him; he had not sent them, and the letters somehow got lost.

"And little hares run about in the fields," Yefimya went on chanting, kissing her boy and shedding tears. "Grandfather is kind and gentle; granny is good, too—kind-hearted. They are warm-hearted in the country, they are God-fearing . . . and there is a little church in the village; the peasants sing in the choir. Queen of Heaven, Holy Mother and Defender, take us away from here!"

Andrey Hrisanfitch returned to his room to smoke a little till there was another ring at the door, and Yefimya ceased speaking, subsided, and wiped her eyes, though her lips were still quivering. She was very much frightened of him—oh, how frightened of him! She trembled and was reduced to terror by the sound of his steps, by the look in his eyes, and dared not utter a word in his presence.

Andrey Hrisanfitch lighted a cigarette, but at that very moment there was a ring from upstairs. He put out his cigarette, and, assuming a very grave face, hastened to his front door.

The general was coming downstairs, fresh and rosy from his bath.

"And what is there in that room?" he asked, pointing to a door.

Andrey Hrisanfitch put his hands down swiftly to the seams of his trousers, and pronounced loudly:

"Charcot douche, your Excellency!"

On Official Duty

[First published in January 1899 in *Books of the Week*,
the literary supplement to the Russian literary and
political newspaper *Nedelya*. Also translated as
'On Official Business' and 'On Duty.'
Collected in *The Schoolmistress and Other Stories* (1918).]

The deputy examining magistrate and the district doctor were going to an inquest in the village of Syrnya. On the road they were overtaken by a snowstorm; they spent a long time going round and round, and arrived, not at midday, as they had intended, but in the evening when it was dark. They put up for the night at the Zemstvo hut. It so happened that it was in this hut that the dead body was lying—the corpse of the Zemstvo insurance agent, Lesnitsky, who had arrived in Syrnya three days before and, ordering the samovar in the hut, had shot himself, to the great surprise of everyone; and the fact that he had ended his life so strangely, after unpacking his eatables and laying them out on the table, and with the samovar before him, led many people to suspect that it was a case of murder; an inquest was necessary.

In the outer room the doctor and the examining magistrate shook the snow off themselves and knocked it off their boots. And meanwhile the old village constable, Ilya Loshadin, stood by, holding a little tin lamp. There was a strong smell of paraffin.

"Who are you?" asked the doctor.

"Conshtable . . ." answered the constable.

He used to spell it "conshtable" when he signed the receipts at the post office.

"And where are the witnesses?"

"They must have gone to tea, your honour."

On the right was the parlor, the travellers' or gentry's room; on the left the kitchen, with a big stove and sleeping shelves under the rafters. The doctor and the examining magistrate, followed by the constable, holding the lamp high above his head, went into the parlor. Here a still, long body covered with white linen was lying on the floor close to the table-legs. In the dim light of the lamp they could clearly see, besides the white covering, new rubber goloshes, and everything about it was uncanny and sinister: the dark walls, and the silence, and the goloshes, and the stillness of the dead body. On the table stood a samovar, cold long ago; and round it parcels, probably the eatables.

"To shoot oneself in the Zemstvo hut, how tactless!" said the doctor. "If one does want to put a bullet through one's brains, one ought to do it at home in some outhouse."

He sank on to a bench, just as he was, in his cap, his fur coat, and his felt overboots; his fellow-traveller, the examining magistrate, sat down opposite.

"These hysterical, neurasthenic people are great egoists," the doctor went on hotly. "If a neurasthenic sleeps in the same room with you, he rustles his newspaper; when he dines with you, he gets up a scene with his wife without troubling about your presence; and when he feels inclined to shoot himself, he shoots himself in a village in a Zemstvo hut, so as to give the maximum of trouble to everybody. These gentlemen in every circumstance of life think of no one but themselves! That's why the elderly so dislike our 'nervous age.'"

"The elderly dislike so many things," said the examining magistrate, yawning. "You should point out to the elder generation what the difference is between the suicides of the past and the suicides of today. In the old days the so-called gentleman shot himself because he had made away with Government money, but nowadays it is because he is sick of life, depressed. . . . Which is better?"

"Sick of life, depressed; but you must admit that he might have shot himself somewhere else."

"Such trouble!" said the constable, "such trouble! It's a real affliction. The people are very much upset, your honour; they haven't slept these three nights. The children are crying. The cows ought to be milked, but the women won't go to the stall—they are afraid . . . for fear the gentleman should appear to them in the darkness. Of course they are silly women, but some of the men are frightened too. As soon as it is dark they won't go by the hut one by one, but only in a flock together. And the witnesses too. . . ."

Dr. Startchenko, a middle-aged man in spectacles with a dark beard, and the examining magistrate Lyzhin, a fair man, still young, who had only taken his degree two years before and looked more like a student than an official, sat in silence, musing. They were vexed that they were late. Now they had to wait till morning, and to stay here for the night, though it was not yet six o'clock; and they had before them a long evening, a dark night, boredom, uncomfortable beds, beetles, and cold in the morning; and listening to the blizzard that howled in the chimney and in the loft, they both thought how unlike all this was the life which they would have chosen for themselves and of which they had once dreamed, and how far away they both were from their contemporaries, who were at that moment walking about the lighted streets in town without noticing the weather, or were getting ready for the theatre, or sitting in their studies over a book. Oh, how much they would have given now only to stroll along the Nevsky Prospect, or along Petrovka in Moscow, to listen to decent singing, to sit for an hour or so in a restaurant!

"Oo-oo-oo-oo!" sang the storm in the loft, and something outside slammed viciously, probably the signboard on the hut. "Oo-oo-oo-oo!"

"You can do as you please, but I have no desire to stay here," said Startchenko, getting up. "It's not six yet, it's too early to go to bed; I am off. Von Taunitz lives not far from here, only a couple of miles from Syrnya. I shall go to see him and spend the evening there. Constable, run and tell my coachman not to take the horses out. And what are you going to do?" he asked Lyzhin.

"I don't know; I expect I shall go to sleep."

The doctor wrapped himself in his fur coat and went out. Lyzhin could hear him talking to the coachman and the bells beginning to quiver on the frozen horses. He drove off.

"It is not nice for you, sir, to spend the night in here," said the constable; "come into the other room. It's dirty, but for one night it won't matter. I'll get a samovar from a peasant and heat it directly. I'll heap up some hay for you, and then you go to sleep, and God bless you, your honour."

A little later the examining magistrate was sitting in the kitchen drinking tea, while Loshadin, the constable, was standing at the door talking. He was an old man about sixty, short and very thin, bent and white, with a naive smile on his face and watery eyes, and he kept smacking with his lips as though he were sucking a sweetmeat. He was wearing a short sheepskin coat and high felt boots, and held his stick in his hands all the time. The youth of the examining magistrate aroused his compassion, and that was probably why he addressed him familiarly.

"The elder gave orders that he was to be informed when the police superintendent or the examining magistrate came," he said, "so I suppose I must go now. . . . It's nearly three miles to the *volost*, and the storm, the snowdrifts, are something terrible—maybe one won't get there before midnight. Ough! how the wind roars!"

"I don't need the elder," said Lyzhin. "There is nothing for him to do here."

He looked at the old man with curiosity, and asked:

"Tell me, grandfather, how many years have you been constable?"

"How many? Why, thirty years. Five years after the Freedom I began going as constable, that's how I reckon it. And from that time I have been going every day since. Other people have holidays, but I am always going. When it's Easter and the church bells are ringing and Christ has risen, I still go about with my bag—to the treasury, to the post, to the police superintendent's lodgings, to the rural captain, to the tax inspector, to the municipal office, to the gentry, to the peasants, to all orthodox Christians. I carry parcels, notices, tax papers, letters, forms of different sorts, circulars, and to be sure, kind gentleman, there are all sorts of forms nowadays, so as to note down the numbers—yellow, white, and red— and every gentleman or priest or well-to-do peasant must write down a dozen times in the year how much he has sown and harvested, how many quarters or poods he has of rye, how many of oats, how many of hay, and what the weather's like, you know, and insects, too, of all sorts. To be sure you can write what you like, it's only a regulation, but one must go and give out the notices and then go again and collect them. Here, for instance, there's no need to cut open the gentleman; you know yourself it's a silly thing, it's only dirtying your hands, and here you have been put to trouble, your honour; you have come because it's the regulation; you can't help it. For thirty years I have been going round according to regulation. In the summer it is all right, it is warm and dry; but in winter and autumn it's uncomfortable. At times I have been almost drowned and almost frozen; all sorts of things have happened—wicked people set on me in the forest and took away my bag; I have been beaten, and I have been before a court of law."

"What were you accused of?"

"Of fraud."

"How do you mean?"

"Why, you see, Hrisanf Grigoryev, the clerk, sold the contractor some boards belonging to someone else—cheated him, in fact. I was mixed up in it. They sent me to the tavern for vodka; well, the clerk did not share with me—did not even offer me a glass; but as through my poverty I was—in appearance, I mean—not a man to be relied upon, not a man of any worth, we were both brought to trial; he was sent to prison, but, praise God! I was acquitted on all points. They read a notice, you know, in the court. And they were all in uniforms—in the court, I mean. I can tell you, your honour, my duties for anyone not used to them are terrible, absolutely killing; but to me it is nothing. In fact, my feet ache when I am not walking. And at home it is worse for me. At home one has to heat the stove for the clerk in the *volost* office, to fetch water for him, to clean his boots."

"And what wages do you get?" Lyzhin asked.

"Eighty-four roubles a year."

"I'll bet you get other little sums coming in. You do, don't you?"

"Other little sums? No, indeed! Gentlemen nowadays don't often give tips. Gentlemen nowadays are strict, they take offense at anything. If you bring them a notice they are offended, if you take off your cap before them they are offended. 'You have come to the wrong entrance,' they say. 'You are a drunkard,' they say. 'You smell of onion; you are a blockhead; you are the son of a bitch.' There are kind-hearted ones, of course; but what does one get from them? They only laugh and call one all sorts of names. Mr. Altuhin, for instance, he is a good-natured gentleman; and if you look at him he seems sober and in his right mind, but so soon as he sees me he shouts and does not know what he means himself. He gave me such a name 'You,' said he . . .'" The constable uttered some word, but in such a low voice that it was impossible to make out what he said.

"What?" Lyzhin asked. "Say it again."

"'Administration,'" the constable repeated aloud. "He has been calling me that for a long while, for the last six years. 'Hullo, Administration!' But I don't mind; let him, God bless him! Sometimes a lady will send one a glass of vodka and a bit of pie and one drinks to her health. But peasants give more; peasants are more kind-hearted, they have the fear of God in their hearts: one will give a bit of bread, another a drop of cabbage soup, another will stand one a glass. The village elders treat one to tea in the tavern. Here the witnesses have gone to their tea. 'Loshadin,' they said, 'you stay here and keep watch for us,' and they gave me a kopeck each. You see, they are frightened, not being used to it, and yesterday they gave me fifteen kopecks and offered me a glass."

"And you, aren't you frightened?"

"I am, sir; but of course it is my duty, there is no getting away from it. In the summer I was taking a convict to the town, and he set upon me and gave me such a drubbing! And all around were fields, forest—how could I get away from him? It's just the same here. I remember the gentleman, Mr. Lesnitsky, when he was so high, and I knew his father and mother. I am from the village of Nedoshtchotova, and they, the Lesnitsky family, were not more than three-quarters of a mile from us and less than that, their ground next to ours, and Mr. Lesnitsky had a sister, a God-fearing and tender-hearted lady. Lord keep the soul of Thy servant Yulya, eternal memory to her! She was never married, and when she was dying she divided all her property; she left three hundred acres to the monastery, and six hundred to the commune of peasants of Nedoshtchotova to commemorate her soul; but her brother hid the will, they do say burnt it in the stove, and took all this land for himself. He thought, to be sure, it was for his benefit; but—nay, wait a bit, you won't get on in the world through injustice, brother. The gentleman did not go to confession for twenty years after. He kept away from the church, to be sure, and died impenitent. He burst. He was a very fat man, so he burst lengthways. Then everything was taken from the young master, from Seryozha, to pay the debts—everything there was. Well, he had not gone very far in his studies, he couldn't do anything, and the president of the Rural Board, his uncle—'I'll take him'—Seryozha, I mean—thinks he, 'for an agent; let him collect the insurance, that's not a difficult job,' and the gentleman was young and proud, he wanted to be living on a bigger scale and in better style and with more freedom. To be sure it was a come-down for him to be jolting about the district in a wretched cart and talking to the peasants; he would walk and keep looking on the ground, looking on the ground and saying nothing; if you called his name right in his ear, 'Sergey Sergeyitch!' he would look round like this, 'Eh?' and look down on the ground again, and now you see he has laid hands on himself. There's no sense in it, your honour, it's not right, and there's no making out what's the meaning of it, merciful Lord! Say your father was rich and you are poor; it is mortifying, there's no doubt about it, but there, you must make up your mind to it. I used to live in good style, too; I had two horses, your honour, three cows, I used to keep twenty head of sheep; but the time has come, and I am left with nothing but a wretched bag, and even that is not mine but Government property. And now in our Nedoshtchotova, if the truth is to be told, my house is the worst of the lot. Makey had four footmen, and now Makey is a footman himself. Petrak had four labourers, and now Petrak is a labourer himself."

"How was it you became poor?" asked the examining magistrate.

"My sons drink terribly. I could not tell you how they drink, you wouldn't believe it."

Lyzhin listened and thought how he, Lyzhin, would go back sooner or later to Moscow, while this old man would stay here for ever, and would always be walking and walking. And how many times in his life he would come across such battered, unkempt old men, not "men of any worth," in whose souls fifteen kopecks, glasses of vodka, and a profound belief that you can't get on in this life by dishonesty, were equally firmly rooted.

Then he grew tired of listening, and told the old man to bring him some hay for his bed, There was an iron bedstead with a pillow and a quilt in the traveller's room, and it could be fetched in; but the dead man had been lying by it for nearly three days (and perhaps sitting on it just before his death), and it would be disagreeable to sleep upon it now. . . .

"It's only half-past seven," thought Lyzhin, glancing at his watch. "How awful it is!"

He was not sleepy, but having nothing to do to pass away the time, he lay down and covered himself with a rug. Loshadin went in and out several times, clearing away the tea-things; smacking his lips and sighing, he kept tramping round the table; at last he took his little lamp and went out, and, looking at his long, gray-headed, bent figure from behind, Lyzhin thought:

"Just like a magician in an opera."

It was dark. The moon must have been behind the clouds, as the windows and the snow on the window-frames could be seen distinctly.

"Oo-oo-oo!" sang the storm, "Oo-oo-oo-oo!"

"Ho-ho-ly sa-aints!" wailed a woman in the loft, or it sounded like it. "Ho-ho-ly sa-aints!"

"B-booh!" something outside banged against the wall. "Trah!"

The examining magistrate listened: there was no woman up there, it was the wind howling. It was rather cold, and he put his fur coat over his rug. As he got warm he thought how remote all this—the storm, and the hut, and the old man, and the dead body lying in the next room—how remote it all was from the life he desired for himself, and how alien it all was to him, how petty, how uninteresting. If this man had killed himself in Moscow or somewhere in the neighbourhood, and he had had to hold an inquest on him there, it would have been interesting, important, and perhaps he might even have been afraid to sleep in the next room to the corpse. Here, nearly a thousand miles from Moscow, all this was seen somehow in a different light; it was not life, they were not human beings, but something only existing "according to the regulation," as Loshadin said; it would leave not the faintest trace in the memory, and would be forgotten as soon as he, Lyzhin, drove away from Syrnya. The fatherland, the real Russia, was Moscow, Petersburg; but here he was in the provinces, the colonies. When one dreamed of playing a leading part, of becoming a popular figure, of being, for instance, examining magistrate in particularly important cases or prosecutor in a circuit court, of being a society lion, one always thought of Moscow. To live, one must be in Moscow; here one cared for nothing, one grew easily resigned to one's insignificant position, and only expected one thing of life—to get away quickly, quickly. And Lyzhin mentally moved about the Moscow streets, went into the familiar houses, met his kindred, his comrades, and there was a sweet pang at his heart at the thought that he was only twenty-six, and that if in five or ten years he could break away from here and get to Moscow, even then it would not be too late and he would still have a whole life before him. And as he sank into unconsciousness, as his thoughts began to be confused, he imagined the long corridor of the court at Moscow, himself delivering a speech, his sisters, the orchestra which for some reason kept droning: "Oo-oo-oo-oo! Oo-oooo-oo!"

"Booh! Trah!" sounded again. "Booh!"

And he suddenly recalled how one day, when he was talking to the bookkeeper in the little office of the Rural Board, a thin, pale gentleman with black hair and dark eyes walked in; he had a disagreeable look in his eyes such as one sees in people who have slept too long after dinner, and it spoilt his delicate, intelligent profile; and the high boots he was wearing did not suit him, but looked clumsy. The bookkeeper had introduced him: "This is our insurance agent."

"So that was Lesnitsky . . . this same man," Lyzhin reflected now.

He recalled Lesnitsky's soft voice, imagined his gait, and it seemed to him that someone was walking beside him now with a step like Lesnitsky's.

All at once he felt frightened, his head turned cold.

"Who's there?" he asked in alarm.

"The conshtable!"

"What do you want here?"

"I have come to ask, your honour—you said this evening that you did not want the elder, but I am afraid he may be angry. He told me to go to him. Shouldn't I go?"

"That's enough, you bother me," said Lyzhin with vexation, and he covered himself up again.

"He may be angry. . . . I'll go, your honour. I hope you will be comfortable," and Loshadin went out.

In the passage there was coughing and subdued voices. The witnesses must have returned.

"We'll let those poor beggars get away early tomorrow . . ." thought the examining magistrate; "we'll begin the inquest as soon as it is daylight."

He began sinking into forgetfulness when suddenly there were steps again, not timid this time but rapid and noisy. There was the slam of a door, voices, the scratching of a match. . . .

"Are you asleep? Are you asleep?" Dr. Startchenko was asking him hurriedly and angrily as he struck one match after another; he was covered with snow, and brought a chill air in with him. "Are you asleep? Get up! Let us go to Von Taunitz's. He has sent his own horses for you. Come along. There, at any rate, you will have supper, and sleep like a human being. You see I have come for you myself. The horses are splendid, we shall get there in twenty minutes."

"And what time is it now?"

"A quarter past ten."

Lyzhin, sleepy and discontented, put on his felt overboots, his fur-lined coat, his cap and hood, and went out with the doctor. There was not a very sharp frost, but a violent and piercing wind was blowing and driving along the street the clouds of snow which seemed to be racing away in terror: high drifts were heaped up already under the fences and at the doorways. The doctor and the examining magistrate got into the sledge, and the white coachman bent over them to button up the cover. They were both hot.

"Ready!"

They drove through the village. "Cutting a feathery furrow," thought the examining magistrate, listlessly watching the action of the trace horse's legs. There were lights in all the huts, as though it were the eve of a great holiday: the peasants had not gone to bed because they were afraid of the dead body. The coachman preserved a sullen silence, probably he had felt dreary while he was waiting by the Zemstvo hut, and now he, too, was thinking of the dead man.

"At the Von Taunitz's," said Startchenko, "they all set upon me when they heard that you were left to spend the night in the hut, and asked me why I did not bring you with me."

As they drove out of the village, at the turning the coachman suddenly shouted at the top of his voice: "Out of the way!"

They caught a glimpse of a man: he was standing up to his knees in the snow, moving off the road and staring at the horses. The examining magistrate saw a stick with a crook, and a beard and a bag, and he fancied that it was Loshadin, and even fancied that he was smiling. He flashed by and disappeared.

The road ran at first along the edge of the forest, then along a broad forest clearing; they caught glimpses of old pines and a young birch copse, and tall, gnarled young oak trees standing singly in the clearings where the wood had lately been cut; but soon it was all merged in the clouds of snow. The coachman said he could see the forest; the examining magistrate could see nothing but the trace horse. The wind blew on their backs.

All at once the horses stopped.

"Well, what is it now?" asked Startchenko crossly.

The coachman got down from the box without a word and began running round the sledge, treading on his heels; he made larger and larger circles, getting further and further away from the sledge, and it looked as though he were dancing; at last he came back and began to turn off to the right.

"You've got off the road, eh?" asked Startchenko.

"It's all ri-ight. . . ."

Then there was a little village and not a single light in it. Again the forest and the fields. Again they lost the road, and again the coachman got down from the box and danced round the sledge. The sledge flew along a dark avenue, flew swiftly on. And the heated trace horse's hoofs knocked against the sledge. Here there was a fearful roaring sound from the trees, and nothing could be seen, as though they were flying on into space; and all at once the glaring light at the entrance and the windows flashed upon their eyes, and they heard the good-natured, drawn-out barking of dogs. They had arrived.

While they were taking off their fur coats and their felt boots below, "Un Petit Verre de Clicquot" was being played upon the piano overhead, and they could hear the children beating time with their feet. Immediately on going in they were aware of the snug warmth and special smell of the old apartments of a mansion where, whatever the weather outside, life is so warm and clean and comfortable.

"That's capital!" said Von Taunitz, a fat man with an incredibly thick neck and with whiskers, as he shook the examining magistrate's hand. "That's capital! You are very welcome, delighted to make your acquaintance. We are colleagues to some extent, you know. At one time I was deputy prosecutor; but not for long, only two years. I came here to look after the estate, and here I have grown old—an old fogey, in fact. You are very welcome," he went on, evidently restraining his voice so as not to speak too loud; he was going upstairs with his guests. "I have no wife, she's dead. But here, I will introduce my daughters," and turning round, he shouted down the stairs in a voice of thunder: "Tell Ignat to have the sledge ready at eight o'clock tomorrow morning."

His four daughters, young and pretty girls, all wearing grey dresses and with their hair done up in the same style, and their cousin, also young and attractive, with her children, were in the drawing room. Startchenko, who knew them already, began at once begging them to sing something, and two of the young ladies spent a long time declaring they could not sing and that they had no music; then the cousin sat down to the piano, and with trembling voices, they sang a duet from "The Queen of Spades."

Again "Un Petit Verre de Clicquot" was played, and the children skipped about, beating time with their feet. And Startchenko pranced about too. Everybody laughed.

Then the children said goodnight and went off to bed. The examining magistrate laughed, danced a quadrille, flirted, and kept wondering whether it was not all a dream? The kitchen of the Zemstvo hut, the heap of hay in the corner, the rustle of the beetles, the revolting poverty-stricken surroundings, the voices of the witnesses, the wind, the snow storm, the danger of being lost; and then all at once this splendid, brightly lighted room, the sounds of the piano, the lovely girls, the curly-headed children, the gay, happy laughter—such a transformation seemed to him like a fairy tale, and it seemed incredible that such transitions were possible at the distance of some two miles in the course of one hour. And dreary thoughts prevented him from enjoying himself, and he kept thinking this was not life here, but bits of life fragments, that everything here was accidental, that one could draw no conclusions from it; and he even felt sorry for these girls, who were living and would end their lives in the wilds, in a province far away from the centre of culture, where nothing is accidental, but everything is in accordance with reason and law, and where, for instance, every suicide is intelligible, so that one can explain why it has happened and what is its significance in the general scheme of things. He imagined that if the life surrounding him here in the wilds were not intelligible to him, and if he did not see it, it meant that it did not exist at all.

At supper the conversation turned on Lesnitsky.

"He left a wife and child," said Startchenko. "I would forbid neurasthenics and all people whose nervous system is out of order to marry, I would deprive them of the right and possibility of multiplying their kind. To bring into the world nervous, invalid children is a crime."

"He was an unfortunate young man," said Von Taunitz, sighing gently and shaking his head. "What a lot one must suffer and think about before one brings oneself to take one's own life . . . a young life! Such a misfortune may happen in any family, and that is awful. It is hard to bear such a thing, insufferable. . . ."

And all the girls listened in silence with grave faces, looking at their father. Lyzhin felt that he, too, must say something, but he couldn't think of anything, and merely said:

"Yes, suicide is an undesirable phenomenon."

He slept in a warm room, in a soft bed covered with a quilt under which there were fine clean sheets, but for some reason did not feel comfortable: perhaps because the doctor and Von Taunitz were, for a long time, talking in the adjoining room, and overhead he heard, through the ceiling and in the stove, the wind roaring just as in the Zemstvo hut, and as plaintively howling: "Oo-oo-oo-oo!"

Von Taunitz's wife had died two years before, and he was still unable to resign himself to his loss and, whatever he was talking about, always mentioned his wife; and there was no trace of a prosecutor left about him now.

"Is it possible that I may some day come to such a condition?" thought Lyzhin, as he fell asleep, still hearing through the wall his host's subdued, as it were bereaved, voice.

The examining magistrate did not sleep soundly. He felt hot and uncomfortable, and it seemed to him in his sleep that he was not at Von Taunitz's, and not in a soft clean bed, but still in the hay at the Zemstvo hut, hearing the subdued voices of the witnesses; he fancied that Lesnitsky was close by, not fifteen paces away. In his dreams he remembered how the insurance agent, black-haired and pale, wearing dusty high boots, had come into the bookkeeper's office. "This is our insurance agent. . . ."

Then he dreamed that Lesnitsky and Loshadin the constable were walking through the open country in the snow, side by side, supporting each other; the snow was whirling about their heads, the wind was blowing on their backs, but they walked on, singing: "We go on, and on, and on. . . ."

The old man was like a magician in an opera, and both of them were singing as though they were on the stage:

"We go on, and on, and on! . . . You are in the warmth, in the light and snugness, but we are walking in the frost and the storm, through the deep snow. . . . We know nothing of ease, we know nothing of joy. . . . We bear all the burden of this life, yours and ours. . . . Oo-oo-oo! We go on, and on, and on. . . ."

Lyzhin woke and sat up in bed. What a confused, bad dream! And why did he dream of the constable and the agent together? What nonsense! And now while Lyzhin's heart was throbbing violently and he was sitting on his bed, holding his head in his hands, it seemed to him that there really was something in common between the lives of the insurance agent and the constable. Don't they really go side by side holding each other up? Some tie unseen, but significant and essential, existed between them, and even between them and Von Taunitz and between all men—all men; in this life, even in the remotest desert, nothing is accidental, everything is full of one common idea, everything has one soul, one aim, and to understand it it is not enough to think, it is not enough to reason, one must have also, it seems, the gift of insight into life, a gift which is evidently not bestowed on all. And the unhappy man who had broken down, who had killed himself—the "neurasthenic," as the doctor called him—and the old peasant who spent every day of his life going from one man to another, were only accidental, were only fragments of life for one who thought of his own life as accidental, but were parts of one organism—marvelous and rational—for one who thought of his own life as part of that universal whole and understood it. So thought Lyzhin, and it was a thought that had long lain hidden in his soul, and only now it was unfolded broadly and clearly to his consciousness.

He lay down and began to drop asleep; and again they were going along together, singing: "We go on, and on, and on. . . . We take from life what is hardest and bitterest in it, and we leave you what is easy and joyful; and sitting at supper, you can coldly and sensibly discuss why we suffer and perish, and why we are not as sound and as satisfied as you."

What they were singing had occurred to his mind before, but the thought was somewhere in the background behind his other thoughts, and flickered timidly like a faraway light in foggy weather. And he felt that this suicide and the peasant's sufferings lay upon his conscience, too; to resign himself to the fact that these people, submissive to their fate, should take up the burden of what was hardest and gloomiest in life—how awful it was! To accept this, and to desire for himself a life full of light and movement among happy and contented people, and to be continually dreaming of such, means dreaming of fresh suicides of men crushed by toil and anxiety, or of men weak and outcast whom people only talk of sometimes at supper with annoyance or mockery, without going to their help. . . . And again:

"We go on, and on, and on . . ." as though someone were beating with a hammer on his temples.

491

He woke early in the morning with a headache, roused by a noise; in the next room Von Taunitz was saying loudly to the doctor:

"It's impossible for you to go now. Look what's going on outside. Don't argue, you had better ask the coachman; he won't take you in such weather for a million."

"But it's only two miles," said the doctor in an imploring voice.

"Well, if it were only half a mile. If you can't, then you can't. Directly you drive out of the gates it is perfect hell, you would be off the road in a minute. Nothing will induce me to let you go, you can say what you like."

"It's bound to be quieter towards evening," said the peasant who was heating the stove.

And in the next room the doctor began talking of the rigorous climate and its influence on the character of the Russian, of the long winters which, by preventing movement from place to place, hinder the intellectual development of the people; and Lyzhin listened with vexation to these observations and looked out of window at the snow drifts which were piled on the fence. He gazed at the white dust which covered the whole visible expanse, at the trees which bowed their heads despairingly to right and then to left, listened to the howling and the banging, and thought gloomily:

"Well, what moral can be drawn from it? It's a blizzard and that is all about it. . . ."

At midday they had lunch, then wandered aimlessly about the house; they went to the windows.

"And Lesnitsky is lying there," thought Lyzhin, watching the whirling snow, which raced furiously round and round upon the drifts. "Lesnitsky is lying there, the witnesses are waiting. . . ."

They talked of the weather, saying that the snowstorm usually lasted two days and nights, rarely longer. At six o'clock they had dinner, then they played cards, sang, danced; at last they had supper. The day was over, they went to bed.

In the night, towards morning, it all subsided. When they got up and looked out of window, the bare willows with their weakly drooping branches were standing perfectly motionless; it was dull and still, as though nature now were ashamed of its orgy, of its mad nights, and the license it had given to its passions. The horses, harnessed tandem, had been waiting at the front door since five o'clock in the morning. When it was fully daylight the doctor and the examining magistrate put on their fur coats and felt boots, and, saying goodbye to their host, went out.

At the steps beside the coachman stood the familiar figure of the constable, Ilya Loshadin, with an old leather bag across his shoulder and no cap on his head, covered with snow all over, and his face was red and wet with perspiration. The footman who had come out to help the gentlemen and cover their legs looked at him sternly and said:

"What are you standing here for, you old devil? Get away!"

"Your honour, the people are anxious," said Loshadin, smiling naively all over his face, and evidently pleased at seeing at last the people he had waited for so long. "The people are very uneasy, the children are crying. . . . They thought, your honour, that you had gone back to the town again. Show us the heavenly mercy, our benefactors! . . ."

The doctor and the examining magistrate said nothing, got into the sledge, and drove to Syrnya.

The Lady with the Dog

[Written in 1899 in Yalta. First published in *Russkaya Mysl*
(*Russian Thought*), a Russian magazine, in December 1899.
First published in English in 1903. One of Chekhov's most
celebrated stories, it has been adapted for stage time and again.]

I

It was said that a new person had appeared on the sea-front: a lady with
a little dog. Dmitri Dmitritch Gurov, who had by then been a fortnight
at Yalta, and so was fairly at home there, had begun to take an interest
in new arrivals. Sitting in Verney's pavilion, he saw, walking on the sea-
front, a fair-haired young lady of medium height, wearing a *béret*; a white
Pomeranian dog was running behind her.

And afterwards he met her in the public gardens and in the square
several times a day. She was walking alone, always wearing the same *béret*,
and always with the same white dog; no one knew who she was, and every
one called her simply "the lady with the dog."

"If she is here alone without a husband or friends, it wouldn't be
amiss to make her acquaintance," Gurov reflected.

He was under forty, but he had a daughter already twelve years
old, and two sons at school. He had been married young, when he was
a student in his second year, and by now his wife seemed half as old
again as he. She was a tall, erect woman with dark eyebrows, staid and
dignified, and, as she said of herself, intellectual. She read a great deal,
used phonetic spelling, called her husband, not Dmitri, but Dimitri, and
he secretly considered her unintelligent, narrow, inelegant, was afraid of

her, and did not like to be at home. He had begun being unfaithful to her long ago—had been unfaithful to her often, and, probably on that account, almost always spoke ill of women, and when they were talked about in his presence, used to call them "the lower race."

It seemed to him that he had been so schooled by bitter experience that he might call them what he liked, and yet he could not get on for two days together without "the lower race." In the society of men he was bored and not himself, with them he was cold and uncommunicative; but when he was in the company of women he felt free, and knew what to say to them and how to behave; and he was at ease with them even when he was silent. In his appearance, in his character, in his whole nature, there was something attractive and elusive which allured women and disposed them in his favour; he knew that, and some force seemed to draw him, too, to them.

Experience often repeated, truly bitter experience, had taught him long ago that with decent people, especially Moscow people—always slow to move and irresolute—every intimacy, which at first so agreeably diversifies life and appears a light and charming adventure, inevitably grows into a regular problem of extreme intricacy, and in the long run the situation becomes unbearable. But at every fresh meeting with an interesting woman this experience seemed to slip out of his memory, and he was eager for life, and everything seemed simple and amusing.

One evening he was dining in the gardens, and the lady in the *béret* came up slowly to take the next table. Her expression, her gait, her dress, and the way she did her hair told him that she was a lady, that she was married, that she was in Yalta for the first time and alone, and that she was dull there. . . . The stories told of the immorality in such places as Yalta are to a great extent untrue; he despised them, and knew that such stories were for the most part made up by persons who would themselves have been glad to sin if they had been able; but when the lady sat down at the next table three paces from him, he remembered these tales of easy conquests, of trips to the mountains, and the tempting thought of a swift, fleeting love affair, a romance with an unknown woman, whose name he did not know, suddenly took possession of him.

He beckoned coaxingly to the Pomeranian, and when the dog came up to him he shook his finger at it. The Pomeranian growled: Gurov shook his finger at it again.

The lady looked at him and at once dropped her eyes.

"He doesn't bite," she said, and blushed.

"May I give him a bone?" he asked; and when she nodded he asked courteously, "Have you been long in Yalta?"

"Five days."

"And I have already dragged out a fortnight here."

There was a brief silence.

"Time goes fast, and yet it is so dull here!" she said, not looking at him.

"That's only the fashion to say it is dull here. A provincial will live in Belyov or Zhidra and not be dull, and when he comes here it's 'Oh, the dulness! Oh, the dust!' One would think he came from Grenada."

She laughed. Then both continued eating in silence, like strangers, but after dinner they walked side by side; and there sprang up between them the light jesting conversation of people who are free and satisfied, to whom it does not matter where they go or what they talk about. They walked and talked of the strange light on the sea: the water was of a soft warm lilac hue, and there was a golden streak from the moon upon it. They talked of how sultry it was after a hot day. Gurov told her that he came from Moscow, that he had taken his degree in Arts, but had a post in a bank; that he had trained as an opera-singer, but had given it up, that he owned two houses in Moscow. . . . And from her he learnt that she had grown up in Petersburg, but had lived in S—— since her marriage two years before, that she was staying another month in Yalta, and that her husband, who needed a holiday too, might perhaps come and fetch her. She was not sure whether her husband had a post in a Crown Department or under the Provincial Council—and was amused by her own ignorance. And Gurov learnt, too, that she was called Anna Sergeyevna.

Afterwards he thought about her in his room at the hotel—thought she would certainly meet him next day; it would be sure to happen. As he got into bed he thought how lately she had been a girl at school, doing lessons like his own daughter; he recalled the diffidence, the angularity, that was still manifest in her laugh and her manner of talking with a stranger. This must have been the first time in her life she had been alone in surroundings in which she was followed, looked at, and spoken to merely from a secret motive which she could hardly fail to guess. He recalled her slender, delicate neck, her lovely grey eyes.

"There's something pathetic about her, anyway," he thought, and fell asleep.

II

A week had passed since they had made acquaintance. It was a holiday. It was sultry indoors, while in the street the wind whirled the dust round and round, and blew people's hats off. It was a thirsty day, and Gurov often went into the pavilion, and pressed Anna Sergeyevna to have syrup and water or an ice. One did not know what to do with oneself.

In the evening when the wind had dropped a little, they went out on the groyne to see the steamer come in. There were a great many people walking about the harbour; they had gathered to welcome some one, bringing bouquets. And two peculiarities of a well-dressed Yalta crowd were very conspicuous: the elderly ladies were dressed like young ones, and there were great numbers of generals.

Owing to the roughness of the sea, the steamer arrived late, after the sun had set, and it was a long time turning about before it reached the groyne. Anna Sergeyevna looked through her lorgnette at the steamer and the passengers as though looking for acquaintances, and when she turned to Gurov her eyes were shining. She talked a great deal and asked disconnected questions, forgetting next moment what she had asked; then she dropped her lorgnette in the crush.

The festive crowd began to disperse; it was too dark to see people's faces. The wind had completely dropped, but Gurov and Anna Sergeyevna still stood as though waiting to see someone else come from the steamer. Anna Sergeyevna was silent now, and sniffed the flowers without looking at Gurov.

"The weather is better this evening," he said. "Where shall we go now? Shall we drive somewhere?"

She made no answer.

Then he looked at her intently, and all at once put his arm round her and kissed her on the lips, and breathed in the moisture and the fragrance of the flowers; and he immediately looked round him, anxiously wondering whether any one had seen them.

"Let us go to your hotel," he said softly. And both walked quickly.

The room was close and smelt of the scent she had bought at the Japanese shop. Gurov looked at her and thought: "What different people one meets in the world!" From the past he preserved memories of careless, good-natured women, who loved cheerfully and were grateful to him for the happiness he gave them, however brief it might be; and of women like his wife who loved without any genuine feeling, with superfluous phrases, affectedly, hysterically, with an expression that suggested that it was not love nor passion, but something more significant; and of two or three others, very beautiful, cold women, on whose faces he had caught a glimpse of a rapacious expression—an obstinate desire to snatch from life more than it could give, and these were capricious, unreflecting, domineering, unintelligent women not in their first youth, and when Gurov grew cold to them their beauty excited his hatred, and the lace on their linen seemed to him like scales.

But in this case there was still the diffidence, the angularity of inexperienced youth, an awkward feeling; and there was a sense of consternation as though some one had suddenly knocked at the door. The attitude of Anna Sergeyevna—"the lady with the dog"—to what had happened was somehow peculiar, very grave, as though it were her fall— so it seemed, and it was strange and inappropriate. Her face dropped and faded, and on both sides of it her long hair hung down mournfully; she mused in a dejected attitude like "the woman who was a sinner" in an old-fashioned picture.

"It's wrong," she said. "You will be the first to despise me now."

There was a watermelon on the table. Gurov cut himself a slice and began eating it without haste. There followed at least half an hour of silence.

Anna Sergeyevna was touching; there was about her the purity of a good, simple woman who had seen little of life. The solitary candle burning on the table threw a faint light on her face, yet it was clear that she was very unhappy.

"How could I despise you?" asked Gurov. "You don't know what you are saying."

"God forgive me," she said, and her eyes filled with tears. "It's awful."

"You seem to feel you need to be forgiven."

"Forgiven? No. I am a bad, low woman; I despise myself and don't attempt to justify myself. It's not my husband but myself I have deceived. And not only just now; I have been deceiving myself for a long time. My husband may be a good, honest man, but he is a flunkey! I don't know what he does there, what his work is, but I know he is a flunkey! I was twenty when I was married to him. I have been tormented by curiosity; I wanted something better. 'There must be a different sort of life,' I said to myself. I wanted to live! To live, to live! . . . I was fired by curiosity . . . you don't understand it, but, I swear to God, I could not control myself; something happened to me: I could not be restrained. I told my husband I was ill, and came here. . . . And here I have been walking about as though I were dazed, like a mad creature; . . . and now I have become a vulgar, contemptible woman whom any one may despise."

Gurov felt bored already, listening to her. He was irritated by the naïve tone, by this remorse, so unexpected and inopportune; but for the tears in her eyes, he might have thought she was jesting or playing a part.

"I don't understand," he said softly. "What is it you want?"

She hid her face on his breast and pressed close to him.

"Believe me, believe me, I beseech you . . ." she said. "I love a pure, honest life, and sin is loathsome to me. I don't know what I am doing. Simple people say: 'The Evil One has beguiled me.' And I may say of myself now that the Evil One has beguiled me."

"Hush, hush! . . ." he muttered.

He looked at her fixed, scared eyes, kissed her, talked softly and affectionately, and by degrees she was comforted, and her gaiety returned; they both began laughing.

Afterwards when they went out there was not a soul on the sea-front. The town with its cypresses had quite a deathlike air, but the sea still broke noisily on the shore; a single barge was rocking on the waves, and a lantern was blinking sleepily on it.

They found a cab and drove to Oreanda.

"I found out your surname in the hall just now: it was written on the board—Von Diderits," said Gurov. "Is your husband a German?"

"No; I believe his grandfather was a German, but he is an Orthodox Russian himself."

At Oreanda they sat on a seat not far from the church, looked down at the sea, and were silent. Yalta was hardly visible through the morning mist; white clouds stood motionless on the mountain-tops. The leaves did not stir on the trees, grasshoppers chirruped, and the monotonous hollow sound of the sea rising up from below, spoke of the peace, of the eternal sleep awaiting us. So it must have sounded when there was no Yalta, no Oreanda here; so it sounds now, and it will sound as indifferently and monotonously when we are all no more. And in this constancy, in this complete indifference to the life and death of each of us, there lies hid, perhaps, a pledge of our eternal salvation, of the unceasing movement of life upon earth, of unceasing progress towards perfection. Sitting beside a young woman who in the dawn seemed so lovely, soothed and spellbound in these magical surroundings—the sea, mountains, clouds, the open sky—Gurov thought how in reality everything is beautiful in this world when one reflects: everything except what we think or do ourselves when we forget our human dignity and the higher aims of our existence.

A man walked up to them—probably a keeper—looked at them and walked away. And this detail seemed mysterious and beautiful, too. They saw a steamer come from Theodosia, with its lights out in the glow of dawn.

"There is dew on the grass," said Anna Sergeyevna, after a silence.

"Yes. It's time to go home."

They went back to the town.

Then they met every day at twelve o'clock on the sea-front, lunched and dined together, went for walks, admired the sea. She complained that she slept badly, that her heart throbbed violently; asked the same questions, troubled now by jealousy and now by the fear that he did not respect her sufficiently. And often in the square or gardens, when there was no one near them, he suddenly drew her to him and kissed her passionately. Complete idleness, these kisses in broad daylight while he looked round in dread of some one's seeing them, the heat, the smell of the sea, and the continual passing to and fro before him of idle, well-dressed, well-fed people, made a new man of him; he told Anna Sergeyevna how beautiful she was, how fascinating. He was impatiently passionate, he would not move a step away from her, while she was often pensive and continually urged him to confess that he did not respect her, did not love her in the least, and thought of her as nothing but a common woman. Rather late almost every evening they drove somewhere out of town, to Oreanda or to the waterfall; and the expedition was always a success, the scenery invariably impressed them as grand and beautiful.

They were expecting her husband to come, but a letter came from him, saying that there was something wrong with his eyes, and he entreated his wife to come home as quickly as possible. Anna Sergeyevna made haste to go.

"It's a good thing I am going away," she said to Gurov. "It's the finger of destiny!"

She went by coach and he went with her. They were driving the whole day. When she had got into a compartment of the express, and when the second bell had rung, she said:

"Let me look at you once more . . . look at you once again. That's right."

She did not shed tears, but was so sad that she seemed ill, and her face was quivering.

"I shall remember you . . . think of you," she said. "God be with you; be happy. Don't remember evil against me. We are parting forever—it must be so, for we ought never to have met. Well, God be with you."

The train moved off rapidly, its lights soon vanished from sight, and a minute later there was no sound of it, as though everything had conspired together to end as quickly as possible that sweet delirium, that madness. Left alone on the platform, and gazing into the dark distance, Gurov listened to the chirrup of the grasshoppers and the hum of the telegraph wires, feeling as though he had only just waked up. And he thought, musing, that there had been another episode or adventure in his life, and it, too, was at an end, and nothing was left of it but a memory. . . . He was moved, sad, and conscious of a slight remorse. This young woman whom he would never meet again had not been happy with him; he was genuinely warm and affectionate with her, but yet in his manner, his tone, and his caresses there had been a shade of light irony, the coarse condescension of a happy man who was, besides, almost twice her age. All the time she had called him kind, exceptional, lofty; obviously he had seemed to her different from what he really was, so he had unintentionally deceived her. . . .

Here at the station was already a scent of autumn; it was a cold evening.

"It's time for me to go north," thought Gurov as he left the platform. "High time!"

III

At home in Moscow everything was in its winter routine; the stoves were heated, and in the morning it was still dark when the children were having breakfast and getting ready for school, and the nurse would light the lamp for a short time. The frosts had begun already. When the first snow has fallen, on the first day of sledge-driving it is pleasant to see the white earth, the white roofs, to draw soft, delicious breath, and the season brings back the days of one's youth. The old limes and birches, white with hoar-frost, have a good-natured expression; they are nearer to one's heart than cypresses and palms, and near them one doesn't want to be thinking of the sea and the mountains.

Gurov was Moscow born; he arrived in Moscow on a fine frosty day, and when he put on his fur coat and warm gloves, and walked along Petrovka, and when on Saturday evening he heard the ringing of the bells, his recent trip and the places he had seen lost all charm for him. Little by little he became absorbed in Moscow life, greedily read three newspapers a day, and declared he did not read the Moscow papers on principle! He already felt a longing to go to restaurants, clubs, dinner-parties, anniversary celebrations, and he felt flattered at entertaining distinguished lawyers and artists, and at playing cards with a professor at the doctors' club. He could already eat a whole plateful of salt fish and cabbage.

In another month, he fancied, the image of Anna Sergeyevna would be shrouded in a mist in his memory, and only from time to time would visit him in his dreams with a touching smile as others did. But more than a month passed, real winter had come, and everything was still clear in his memory as though he had parted with Anna Sergeyevna only the day before. And his memories glowed more and more vividly. When in the evening stillness he heard from his study the voices of his children, preparing their lessons, or when he listened to a song or the organ at the restaurant, or the storm howled in the chimney, suddenly everything would rise up in his memory: what had happened on the groyne, and the early morning with the mist on the mountains, and the steamer coming from Theodosia, and the kisses. He would pace a long time about his room, remembering it all and smiling; then his memories passed into dreams, and in his fancy the past was mingled with what was to come. Anna Sergeyevna did not visit him in dreams, but followed him about everywhere like a shadow and haunted him. When he shut his eyes he saw her as though she were living before him, and she seemed to him lovelier, younger, tenderer than she was; and he imagined himself finer than he had been in Yalta. In the evenings she peeped out at him from the bookcase, from the fireplace, from the corner—he heard her breathing, the caressing rustle of her dress. In the street he watched the women, looking for some one like her.

He was tormented by an intense desire to confide his memories to some one. But in his home it was impossible to talk of his love, and he had no one outside; he could not talk to his tenants nor to any one at the bank. And what had he to talk of? Had he been in love, then? Had there been anything beautiful, poetical, or edifying or simply interesting in his relations with Anna Sergeyevna? And there was nothing for him but to talk vaguely of love, of woman, and no one guessed what it meant; only his wife twitched her black eyebrows, and said:

"The part of a lady-killer does not suit you at all, Dimitri."

One evening, coming out of the doctors' club with an official with whom he had been playing cards, he could not resist saying:

"If only you knew what a fascinating woman I made the acquaintance of in Yalta!"

The official got into his sledge and was driving away, but turned suddenly and shouted:

"Dmitri Dmitritch!"

"What?"

"You were right this evening: the sturgeon was a bit too strong!"

These words, so ordinary, for some reason moved Gurov to indignation, and struck him as degrading and unclean. What savage manners, what people! What senseless nights, what uninteresting, uneventful days! The rage for card-playing, the gluttony, the drunkenness, the continual talk always about the same thing. Useless pursuits and conversations always about the same things absorb the better part of one's time, the better part of one's strength, and in the end there is left a life grovelling and curtailed, worthless and trivial, and there is no escaping or getting away from it—just as though one were in a madhouse or a prison.

Gurov did not sleep all night, and was filled with indignation. And he had a headache all next day. And the next night he slept badly; he sat up in bed, thinking, or paced up and down his room. He was sick of his children, sick of the bank; he had no desire to go anywhere or to talk of anything.

In the holidays in December he prepared for a journey, and told his wife he was going to Petersburg to do something in the interests of a young friend—and he set off for S——. What for? He did not very well know himself. He wanted to see Anna Sergeyevna and to talk with her—to arrange a meeting, if possible.

He reached S—— in the morning, and took the best room at the hotel, in which the floor was covered with grey army cloth, and on the table was an inkstand, grey with dust and adorned with a figure on horseback, with its hat in its hand and its head broken off. The hotel porter gave him the necessary information; Von Diderits lived in a house of his own in Old Gontcharny Street—it was not far from the hotel: he was rich and lived in good style, and had his own horses; every one in the town knew him. The porter pronounced the name "Dridirits."

Gurov went without haste to Old Gontcharny Street and found the house. Just opposite the house stretched a long grey fence adorned with nails.

"One would run away from a fence like that," thought Gurov, looking from the fence to the windows of the house and back again.

He considered: today was a holiday, and the husband would probably be at home. And in any case it would be tactless to go into the house and upset her. If he were to send her a note it might fall into her husband's hands, and then it might ruin everything. The best thing was to trust to chance. And he kept walking up and down the street by the fence, waiting for the chance. He saw a beggar go in at the gate and dogs fly at him; then an hour later he heard a piano, and the sounds were faint and indistinct. Probably it was Anna Sergeyevna playing. The front door suddenly opened, and an old woman came out, followed by the familiar white Pomeranian. Gurov was on the point of calling to the dog, but his heart began beating violently, and in his excitement he could not remember the dog's name.

He walked up and down, and loathed the grey fence more and more, and by now he thought irritably that Anna Sergeyevna had forgotten him, and was perhaps already amusing herself with someone else, and that that was very natural in a young woman who had nothing to look at from morning till night but that confounded fence. He went back to his hotel room and sat for a long while on the sofa, not knowing what to do, then he had dinner and a long nap.

"How stupid and worrying it is!" he thought when he woke and looked at the dark windows: it was already evening. "Here I've had a good sleep for some reason. What shall I do in the night?"

He sat on the bed, which was covered by a cheap grey blanket, such as one sees in hospitals, and he taunted himself in his vexation:

"So much for the lady with the dog . . . so much for the adventure. . . . You're in a nice fix. . . ."

That morning at the station a poster in large letters had caught his eye. "The Geisha" was to be performed for the first time. He thought of this and went to the theatre.

"It's quite possible she may go to the first performance," he thought.

The theatre was full. As in all provincial theatres, there was a fog above the chandelier, the gallery was noisy and restless; in the front row the local dandies were standing up before the beginning of the performance, with their hands behind them; in the Governor's box the Governor's daughter, wearing a boa, was sitting in the front seat, while the Governor himself lurked modestly behind the curtain with only his hands visible; the orchestra was a long time tuning up; the stage curtain swayed. All the time the audience were coming in and taking their seats Gurov looked at them eagerly.

Anna Sergeyevna, too, came in. She sat down in the third row, and when Gurov looked at her his heart contracted, and he understood clearly that for him there was in the whole world no creature so near, so precious, and so important to him; she, this little woman, in no way remarkable, lost in a provincial crowd, with a vulgar lorgnette in her hand, filled his whole life now, was his sorrow and his joy, the one happiness that he now desired for himself, and to the sounds of the inferior orchestra, of the wretched provincial violins, he thought how lovely she was. He thought and dreamed.

A young man with small side-whiskers, tall and stooping, came in with Anna Sergeyevna and sat down beside her; he bent his head at every step and seemed to be continually bowing. Most likely this was the husband whom at Yalta, in a rush of bitter feeling, she had called a flunkey. And there really was in his long figure, his side-whiskers, and the small bald patch on his head, something of the flunkey's obsequiousness; his smile was sugary, and in his buttonhole there was some badge of distinction like the number on a waiter.

During the first interval the husband went away to smoke; she remained alone in her stall. Gurov, who was sitting in the stalls, too, went up to her and said in a trembling voice, with a forced smile:

"Good evening."

She glanced at him and turned pale, then glanced again with horror, unable to believe her eyes, and tightly gripped the fan and the lorgnette in her hands, evidently struggling with herself not to faint. Both were silent. She was sitting, he was standing, frightened by her confusion and not venturing to sit down beside her. The violins and the flute began tuning up. He felt suddenly frightened; it seemed as though all the people in the boxes were looking at them. She got up and went quickly to the door; he followed her, and both walked senselessly along passages, and up and down stairs, and figures in legal, scholastic, and civil service uniforms, all wearing badges, flitted before their eyes. They caught glimpses of ladies, of fur coats hanging on pegs; the draughts blew on them, bringing a smell of stale tobacco. And Gurov, whose heart was beating violently, thought:

"Oh, heavens! Why are these people here and this orchestra! . . ."

And at that instant he recalled how when he had seen Anna Sergeyevna off at the station he had thought that everything was over and they would never meet again. But how far they were still from the end!

On the narrow, gloomy staircase over which was written "To the Amphitheatre," she stopped.

"How you have frightened me!" she said, breathing hard, still pale and overwhelmed. "Oh, how you have frightened me! I am half dead. Why have you come? Why?"

"But do understand, Anna, do understand . . ." he said hastily in a low voice. "I entreat you to understand. . . ."

She looked at him with dread, with entreaty, with love; she looked at him intently, to keep his features more distinctly in her memory.

"I am so unhappy," she went on, not heeding him. "I have thought of nothing but you all the time; I live only in the thought of you. And I wanted to forget, to forget you; but why, oh, why, have you come?"

On the landing above them two schoolboys were smoking and looking down, but that was nothing to Gurov; he drew Anna Sergeyevna to him, and began kissing her face, her cheeks, and her hands.

"What are you doing, what are you doing!" she cried in horror, pushing him away. "We are mad. Go away today; go away at once. . . . I beseech you by all that is sacred, I implore you. . . . There are people coming this way!"

Some one was coming up the stairs.

"You must go away," Anna Sergeyevna went on in a whisper. "Do you hear, Dmitri Dmitritch? I will come and see you in Moscow. I have never been happy; I am miserable now, and I never, never shall be happy, never! Don't make me suffer still more! I swear I'll come to Moscow. But now let us part. My precious, good, dear one, we must part!"

She pressed his hand and began rapidly going downstairs, looking round at him, and from her eyes he could see that she really was unhappy. Gurov stood for a little while, listened, then, when all sound had died away, he found his coat and left the theatre.

IV

And Anna Sergeyevna began coming to see him in Moscow. Once in two or three months she left S——, telling her husband that she was going to consult a doctor about an internal complaint—and her husband believed her, and did not believe her. In Moscow she stayed at the Slaviansky Bazaar hotel, and at once sent a man in a red cap to Gurov. Gurov went to see her, and no one in Moscow knew of it.

Once he was going to see her in this way on a winter morning (the messenger had come the evening before when he was out). With him walked his daughter, whom he wanted to take to school: it was on the way. Snow was falling in big wet flakes.

"It's three degrees above freezing-point, and yet it is snowing," said Gurov to his daughter. "The thaw is only on the surface of the earth; there is quite a different temperature at a greater height in the atmosphere."

"And why are there no thunderstorms in the winter, father?"

He explained that, too. He talked, thinking all the while that he was going to see her, and no living soul knew of it, and probably never would know. He had two lives: one, open, seen and known by all who cared to know, full of relative truth and of relative falsehood, exactly like the lives of his friends and acquaintances; and another life running its course in secret. And through some strange, perhaps accidental, conjunction of circumstances, everything that was essential, of interest and of value to him, everything in which he was sincere and did not deceive himself, everything that made the kernel of his life, was hidden from other people; and all that was false in him, the sheath in which he hid himself to conceal the truth—such, for instance, as his work in the bank, his discussions at the club, his "lower race," his presence with his wife at anniversary festivities—all that was open. And he judged of others by himself, not believing in what he saw, and always believing that every man had his real, most interesting life under the cover of secrecy and under the cover of night. All personal life rested on secrecy, and possibly it was partly on that account that civilised man was so nervously anxious that personal privacy should be respected.

After leaving his daughter at school, Gurov went on to the Slaviansky Bazaar. He took off his fur coat below, went upstairs, and softly knocked at the door. Anna Sergeyevna, wearing his favourite grey dress, exhausted by the journey and the suspense, had been expecting him since the evening before. She was pale; she looked at him, and did not smile, and he had hardly come in when she fell on his breast. Their kiss was slow and prolonged, as though they had not met for two years.

"Well, how are you getting on there?" he asked. "What news?"

"Wait; I'll tell you directly. . . . I can't talk."

She could not speak; she was crying. She turned away from him, and pressed her handkerchief to her eyes.

"Let her have her cry out. I'll sit down and wait," he thought, and he sat down in an armchair.

Then he rang and asked for tea to be brought him, and while he drank his tea she remained standing at the window with her back to him. She was crying from emotion, from the miserable consciousness that their life was so hard for them; they could only meet in secret, hiding themselves from people, like thieves! Was not their life shattered?

"Come, do stop!" he said.

It was evident to him that this love of theirs would not soon be over, that he could not see the end of it. Anna Sergeyevna grew more and more attached to him. She adored him, and it was unthinkable to say to her that it was bound to have an end some day; besides, she would not have believed it!

He went up to her and took her by the shoulders to say something affectionate and cheering, and at that moment he saw himself in the looking-glass.

His hair was already beginning to turn grey. And it seemed strange to him that he had grown so much older, so much plainer during the last few years. The shoulders on which his hands rested were warm and quivering. He felt compassion for this life, still so warm and lovely, but probably already not far from beginning to fade and wither like his own. Why did she love him so much? He always seemed to women different from what he was, and they loved in him not himself, but the man created by their imagination, whom they had been eagerly seeking all their lives; and afterwards, when they noticed their mistake, they loved him all the same. And not one of them had been happy with him. Time passed, he had made their acquaintance, got on with them, parted, but he had never once loved; it was anything you like, but not love.

And only now when his head was grey he had fallen properly, really in love—for the first time in his life.

Anna Sergeyevna and he loved each other like people very close and akin, like husband and wife, like tender friends; it seemed to them that fate itself had meant them for one another, and they could not understand why he had a wife and she a husband; and it was as though they were a pair of birds of passage, caught and forced to live in different cages. They forgave each other for what they were ashamed of in their past, they forgave everything in the present, and felt that this love of theirs had changed them both.

In moments of depression in the past he had comforted himself with any arguments that came into his mind, but now he no longer cared for arguments; he felt profound compassion, he wanted to be sincere and tender. . . .

"Don't cry, my darling," he said. "You've had your cry; that's enough. . . . Let us talk now, let us think of some plan."

Then they spent a long while taking counsel together, talked of how to avoid the necessity for secrecy, for deception, for living in different towns and not seeing each other for long at a time. How could they be free from this intolerable bondage?

"How? How?" he asked, clutching his head. "How?"

And it seemed as though in a little while the solution would be found, and then a new and splendid life would begin; and it was clear to both of them that they had still a long, long road before them, and that the most complicated and difficult part of it was only just beginning.

The Bishop

[First published in the April 1902 issue of
Zhurnal Dlya Vsekh, a Russian magazine.
Collected in *The Bishop and Other Stories* (1919).]

I

The evening service was being celebrated on the eve of Palm Sunday in the Old Petrovsky Convent. When they began distributing the palm it was close upon ten o'clock, the candles were burning dimly, the wicks wanted snuffing; it was all in a sort of mist. In the twilight of the church the crowd seemed heaving like the sea, and to Bishop Pyotr, who had been unwell for the last three days, it seemed that all the faces—old and young, men's and women's—were alike, that everyone who came up for the palm had the same expression in his eyes. In the mist he could not see the doors; the crowd kept moving and looked as though there were no end to it. The female choir was singing, a nun was reading the prayers for the day.

How stifling, how hot it was! How long the service went on! Bishop Pyotr was tired. His breathing was laboured and rapid, his throat was parched, his shoulders ached with weariness, his legs were trembling. And it disturbed him unpleasantly when a religious maniac uttered occasional shrieks in the gallery. And then all of a sudden, as though in a dream or delirium, it seemed to the bishop as though his own mother Marya Timofyevna, whom he had not seen for nine years, or some old woman just like his mother, came up to him out of the crowd, and, after taking a palm branch from him, walked away looking at him all the while good-humouredly with a kind, joyful smile until she was lost in the crowd. And for some reason tears flowed down his face. There was peace in his heart, everything was well, yet he kept gazing fixedly towards the left choir, where the prayers were being read, where in the dusk of evening you could not recognize anyone, and—wept. Tears glistened on his face and on his beard. Here someone close at hand was weeping, then someone else farther away, then others and still others, and little by little the church was filled with soft weeping. And a little later, within five minutes, the nuns' choir was singing; no one was weeping and everything was as before.

Soon the service was over. When the bishop got into his carriage to drive home, the gay, melodious chime of the heavy, costly bells was filling the whole garden in the moonlight. The white walls, the white crosses on the tombs, the white birch trees and black shadows, and the faraway moon in the sky exactly over the convent, seemed now living their own life, apart and incomprehensible, yet very near to man. It was the beginning of April, and after the warm spring day it turned cool; there was a faint touch of frost, and the breath of spring could be felt in the soft, chilly air. The road from the convent to the town was sandy, the horses had to go at a walking pace, and on both sides of the carriage in the brilliant, peaceful moonlight there were people trudging along home from church through the sand. And all was silent, sunk in thought; everything around seemed kindly, youthful, akin, everything—trees and sky and even the moon, and one longed to think that so it would be always.

At last the carriage drove into the town and rumbled along the principal street. The shops were already shut, but at Erakin's, the millionaire shopkeeper's, they were trying the new electric lights, which flickered brightly, and a crowd of people were gathered round. Then came wide, dark, deserted streets, one after another; then the highroad, the open country, the fragrance of pines. And suddenly there rose up before the bishop's eyes a white turreted wall, and behind it a tall belfry in the full moonlight, and beside it five shining, golden cupolas: this was the Pankratievsky Monastery, in which Bishop Pyotr lived. And here, too, high above the monastery, was the silent, dreamy moon. The carriage drove in at the gate, crunching over the sand; here and there in the moonlight there were glimpses of dark monastic figures, and there was the sound of footsteps on the flag-stones. . . .

"You know, your holiness, your mamma arrived while you were away," the lay brother informed the bishop as he went into his cell.

"My mother? When did she come?"

"Before the evening service. She asked first where you were and then she went to the convent."

"Then it was her I saw in the church, just now! Oh, Lord!"

And the bishop laughed with joy.

"She bade me tell your holiness," the lay brother went on, "that she would come tomorrow. She had a little girl with her—her grandchild, I suppose. They are staying at Ovsyannikov's inn."

"What time is it now?"

"A little after eleven."

"Oh, how vexing!"

The bishop sat for a little while in the parlour, hesitating, and as it were refusing to believe it was so late. His arms and legs were stiff, his head ached. He was hot and uncomfortable. After resting a little he went into his bedroom, and there, too, he sat a little, still thinking of his mother; he could hear the lay brother going away, and Father Sisoy coughing the other side of the wall. The monastery clock struck a quarter.

The bishop changed his clothes and began reading the prayers before sleep. He read attentively those old, long familiar prayers, and at the same time thought about his mother. She had nine children and about forty grandchildren. At one time, she had lived with her husband, the deacon, in a poor village; she had lived there a very long time from the age of seventeen to sixty. The bishop remembered her from early childhood, almost from the age of three, and—how he had loved her! Sweet, precious childhood, always fondly remembered! Why did it, that long-past time that could never return, why did it seem brighter, fuller, and more festive than it had really been? When in his childhood or youth he had been ill, how tender and sympathetic his mother had been! And now his prayers mingled with the memories, which gleamed more and more brightly like a flame, and the prayers did not hinder his thinking of his mother.

When he had finished his prayers he undressed and lay down, and at once, as soon as it was dark, there rose before his mind his dead father, his mother, his native village Lesopolye . . . the creak of wheels, the bleat of sheep, the church bells on bright summer mornings, the gypsies under the window—oh, how sweet to think of it! He remembered the priest of Lesopolye, Father Simeon—mild, gentle, kindly; he was a lean little man, while his son, a divinity student, was a huge fellow and talked in a roaring bass voice. The priest's son had flown into a rage with the cook and abused her: "Ah, you Jehud's ass!" and Father Simeon overhearing it, said not a word, and was only ashamed because he could not remember where such an ass was mentioned in the Bible. After him the priest at Lesopolye had been Father Demyan, who used to drink heavily, and at times drank till he saw green snakes, and was even nicknamed Demyan Snakeseer. The schoolmaster at Lesopolye was Matvey Nikolaitch, who had been a divinity student, a kind and intelligent man, but he, too, was a drunkard; he never beat the schoolchildren, but for some reason he always had hanging on his wall a bunch of birch-twigs, and below it an utterly meaningless inscription in Latin: "Betula kinderbalsamica secuta." He had a shaggy black dog whom he called Syntax.

And his holiness laughed. Six miles from Lesopolye was the village Obnino with a wonder-working ikon. In the summer they used to carry the ikon in procession about the neighbouring villages and ring the bells the whole day long; first in one village and then in another, and it used to seem to the bishop then that joy was quivering in the air, and he (in those days his name was Pavlusha) used to follow the ikon, bareheaded and barefoot, with naïve faith, with a naïve smile, infinitely happy. In Obnino, he remembered now, there were always a lot of people, and the priest there, Father Alexey, to save time during mass, used to make his deaf nephew Ilarion read the names of those for whose health or whose souls' peace prayers were asked. Ilarion used to read them, now and then getting a five or ten kopeck piece for the service, and only when he was grey and bald, when life was nearly over, he suddenly saw written on one of the pieces of paper: "What a fool you are, Ilarion." Up to fifteen at least Pavlusha was undeveloped and idle at his lessons, so much so that they thought of taking him away from the clerical school and putting him into a shop; one day, going to the post at Obnino for letters, he had stared a long time at the post-office clerks and asked: "Allow me to ask, how do you get your salary, every month or every day?"

His holiness crossed himself and turned over on the other side, trying to stop thinking and go to sleep.

"My mother has come," he remembered and laughed.

The moon peeped in at the window, the floor was lighted up, and there were shadows on it. A cricket was chirping. Through the wall Father Sisoy was snoring in the next room, and his aged snore had a sound that suggested loneliness, forlornness, even vagrancy. Sisoy had once been housekeeper to the bishop of the diocese, and was called now "the former Father Housekeeper"; he was seventy years old, he lived in a monastery twelve miles from the town and stayed sometimes in the town, too. He had come to the Pankratievsky Monastery three days before, and the bishop had kept him that he might talk to him at his leisure about matters of business, about the arrangements here. . . .

At half-past one they began ringing for matins. Father Sisoy could be heard coughing, muttering something in a discontented voice, then he got up and walked barefoot about the rooms.

"Father Sisoy," the bishop called.

Sisoy went back to his room and a little later made his appearance in his boots, with a candle; he had on his cassock over his underclothes and on his head was an old faded skull-cap.

"I can't sleep," said the bishop, sitting up. "I must be unwell. And what it is I don't know. Fever!"

"You must have caught cold, your holiness. You must be rubbed with tallow." Sisoy stood a little and yawned. "O Lord, forgive me, a sinner."

"They had the electric lights on at Erakin's today," he said; "I don't like it!"

Father Sisoy was old, lean, bent, always dissatisfied with something, and his eyes were angry-looking and prominent as a crab's.

"I don't like it," he said, going away. "I don't like it. Bother it!"

II

Next day, Palm Sunday, the bishop took the service in the cathedral in the town, then he visited the bishop of the diocese, then visited a very sick old lady, the widow of a general, and at last drove home. Between one and two o'clock he had welcome visitors dining with him—his mother and his niece Katya, a child of eight years old. All dinner-time the spring sunshine was streaming in at the windows, throwing bright light on the white tablecloth and on Katya's red hair. Through the double windows they could hear the noise of the rooks and the notes of the starlings in the garden.

514

"It is nine years since we have met," said the old lady. "And when I looked at you in the monastery yesterday, good Lord! you've not changed a bit, except maybe you are thinner and your beard is a little longer. Holy Mother, Queen of Heaven! Yesterday at the evening service no one could help crying. I, too, as I looked at you, suddenly began crying, though I couldn't say why. His Holy Will!"

And in spite of the affectionate tone in which she said this, he could see she was constrained as though she were uncertain whether to address him formally or familiarly, to laugh or not, and that she felt herself more a deacon's widow than his mother. And Katya gazed without bElinking at her uncle, his holiness, as though trying to discover what sort of a person he was. Her hair sprang up from under the comb and the velvet ribbon and stood out like a halo; she had a turned-up nose and sly eyes. The child had broken a glass before sitting down to dinner, and now her grandmother, as she talked, moved away from Katya first a wineglass and then a tumbler. The bishop listened to his mother and remembered how many, many years ago she used to take him and his brothers and sisters to relations whom she considered rich; in those days she was taken up with the care of her children, now with her grandchildren, and she had brought Katya. . . .

"Your sister, Varenka, has four children," she told him; "Katya, here, is the eldest. And your brother-in-law Father Ivan fell sick, God knows of what, and died three days before the Assumption; and my poor Varenka is left a beggar."

"And how is Nikanor getting on?" the bishop asked about his eldest brother.

"He is all right, thank God. Though he has nothing much, yet he can live. Only there is one thing: his son, my grandson Nikolasha, did not want to go into the Church; he has gone to the university to be a doctor. He thinks it is better; but who knows! His Holy Will!"

"Nikolasha cuts up dead people," said Katya, spilling water over her knees.

"Sit still, child," her grandmother observed calmly, and took the glass out of her hand. "Say a prayer, and go on eating."

"How long it is since we have seen each other!" said the bishop, and he tenderly stroked his mother's hand and shoulder; "and I missed you abroad, mother, I missed you dreadfully."

"Thank you."

"I used to sit in the evenings at the open window, lonely and alone; often there was music playing, and all at once I used to be overcome with homesickness and felt as though I would give everything only to be at home and see you."

His mother smiled, beamed, but at once she made a grave face and said:

"Thank you."

His mood suddenly changed. He looked at his mother and could not understand how she had come by that respectfulness, that timid expression of face: what was it for? And he did not recognize her. He felt sad and vexed. And then his head ached just as it had the day before; his legs felt fearfully tired, and the fish seemed to him stale and tasteless; he felt thirsty all the time. . . .

After dinner two rich ladies, landowners, arrived and sat for an hour and a half in silence with rigid countenances; the archimandrite, a silent, rather deaf man, came to see him about business. Then they began ringing for vespers; the sun was setting behind the wood and the day was over. When he returned from church, he hurriedly said his prayers, got into bed, and wrapped himself up as warm as possible.

It was disagreeable to remember the fish he had eaten at dinner. The moonlight worried him, and then he heard talking. In an adjoining room, probably in the parlour, Father Sisoy was talking politics:

"There's war among the Japanese now. They are fighting. The Japanese, my good soul, are the same as the Montenegrins; they are the same race. They were under the Turkish yoke together."

And then he heard the voice of Marya Timofyevna:

"So, having said our prayers and drunk tea, we went, you know, to Father Yegor at Novokatnoye, so . . ."

And she kept on saying, "having had tea" or "having drunk tea," and it seemed as though the only thing she had done in her life was to drink tea.

The bishop slowly, languidly, recalled the seminary, the academy. For three years he had been Greek teacher in the seminary: by that time he could not read without spectacles. Then he had become a monk; he had been made a school inspector. Then he had defended his thesis for his degree. When he was thirty-two he had been made rector of the seminary, and consecrated archimandrite: and then his life had been so easy, so pleasant; it seemed so long, so long, no end was in sight. Then he had begun to be ill, had grown very thin and almost blind, and by the advice of the doctors had to give up everything and go abroad.

"And what then?" asked Sisoy in the next room.

"Then we drank tea . . ." answered Marya Timofyevna.

"Good gracious, you've got a green beard," said Katya suddenly in surprise, and she laughed.

The bishop remembered that the grey-headed Father Sisoy's beard really had a shade of green in it, and he laughed.

"God have mercy upon us, what we have to put up with with this girl!" said Sisoy, aloud, getting angry. "Spoilt child! Sit quiet!"

The bishop remembered the perfectly new white church in which he had conducted the services while living abroad, he remembered the sound of the warm sea. In his flat he had five lofty light rooms; in his study he had a new writing-table, lots of books. He had read a great deal and often written. And he remembered how he had pined for his native land, how a blind beggar woman had played the guitar under his window every day and sung of love, and how, as he listened, he had always for some reason thought of the past. But eight years had passed and he had been called back to Russia, and now he was a suffragan bishop, and all the past had retreated far away into the mist as though it were a dream. . . .

Father Sisoy came into the bedroom with a candle.

"I say!" he said, wondering, "are you asleep already, your holiness?"

"What is it?"

"Why, it's still early, ten o'clock or less. I bought a candle today; I wanted to rub you with tallow."

"I am in a fever . . ." said the bishop, and he sat up. "I really ought to have something. My head is bad. . . ."

Sisoy took off the bishop's shirt and began rubbing his chest and back with tallow.

"That's the way . . . that's the way . . ." he said. "Lord Jesus Christ . . . that's the way. I walked to the town today; I was at what's-his-name's—the chief priest Sidonsky's. . . . I had tea with him. I don't like him. Lord Jesus Christ. . . . That's the way. I don't like him."

III

The bishop of the diocese, a very fat old man, was ill with rheumatism or gout, and had been in bed for over a month. Bishop Pyotr went to see him almost every day, and saw all who came to ask his help. And now that he was unwell he was struck by the emptiness, the triviality of everything which they asked and for which they wept; he was vexed at their ignorance, their timidity; and all this useless, petty business oppressed him by the mass of it, and it seemed to him that now he understood the diocesan bishop, who had once in his young days written on "The Doctrines of the Freedom of the Will," and now seemed to be all lost in trivialities, to have forgotten everything, and to have no thoughts of religion. The bishop must have lost touch with Russian life while he was abroad; he did not find it easy; the peasants seemed to him coarse, the women who sought his help dull and stupid, the seminarists and their teachers uncultivated and at times savage. And the documents coming in and going out were reckoned by tens of thousands; and what documents they were! The higher clergy in the whole diocese gave the priests, young and old, and even their wives and children, marks for their behaviour—a five, a four, and sometimes even a three; and about this he had to talk and to read and write serious reports. And there was positively not one minute to spare; his soul was troubled all day long, and the bishop was only at peace when he was in church.

He could not get used, either, to the awe which, through no wish of his own, he inspired in people in spite of his quiet, modest disposition. All the people in the province seemed to him little, scared, and guilty when he looked at them. Everyone was timid in his presence, even the old chief priests; everyone "flopped" at his feet, and not long previously an old lady, a village priest's wife who had come to consult him, was so overcome by awe that she could not utter a single word, and went empty away. And he, who could never in his sermons bring himself to speak ill of people, never reproached anyone because he was so sorry for them, was moved to fury with the people who came to consult him, lost his temper and flung their petitions on the floor. The whole time he had been here, not one person had spoken to him genuinely, simply, as to a human being; even his old mother seemed now not the same! And why, he wondered, did she chatter away to Sisoy and laugh so much; while with him, her son, she was grave and usually silent and constrained, which did not suit her at all. The only person who behaved freely with him and said what he meant was old Sisoy, who had spent his whole life in the presence of bishops and had outlived eleven of them. And so the bishop was at ease with him, although, of course, he was a tedious and nonsensical man.

After the service on Tuesday, his holiness Pyotr was in the diocesan bishop's house receiving petitions there; he got excited and angry, and then drove home. He was as unwell as before; he longed to be in bed, but he had hardly reached home when he was informed that a young merchant called Erakin, who subscribed liberally to charities, had come to see him about a very important matter. The bishop had to see him. Erakin stayed about an hour, talked very loud, almost shouted, and it was difficult to understand what he said.

"God grant it may," he said as he went away. "Most essential! According to circumstances, your holiness! I trust it may!"

After him came the Mother Superior from a distant convent. And when she had gone they began ringing for vespers. He had to go to church.

In the evening the monks sang harmoniously, with inspiration. A young priest with a black beard conducted the service; and the bishop, hearing of the Bridegroom who comes at midnight and of the Heavenly Mansion adorned for the festival, felt no repentance for his sins, no tribulation, but peace at heart and tranquillity. And he was carried back in thought to the distant past, to his childhood and youth, when, too, they used to sing of the Bridegroom and of the Heavenly Mansion; and now that past rose up before him—living, fair, and joyful as in all likelihood it never had been. And perhaps in the other world, in the life to come, we shall think of the distant past, of our life here, with the same feeling. Who knows? The bishop was sitting near the altar. It was dark; tears flowed down his face. He thought that here he had attained everything a man in his position could attain; he had faith and yet everything was not clear, something was lacking still. He did not want to die; and he still felt that he had missed what was most important, something of which he had dimly dreamed in the past; and he was troubled by the same hopes for the future as he had felt in childhood, at the academy and abroad.

"How well they sing today!" he thought, listening to the singing. "How nice it is!"

IV

On Thursday he celebrated mass in the cathedral; it was the Washing of Feet. When the service was over and the people were going home, it was sunny, warm; the water gurgled in the gutters, and the unceasing trilling of the larks, tender, telling of peace, rose from the fields outside the town. The trees were already awakening and smiling a welcome, while above them the infinite, fathomless blue sky stretched into the distance, God knows whither.

On reaching home his holiness drank some tea, then changed his clothes, lay down on his bed, and told the lay brother to close the shutters on the windows. The bedroom was darkened. But what weariness, what pain in his legs and his back, a chill heavy pain, what a noise in his ears! He had not slept for a long time—for a very long time, as it seemed to him now, and some trifling detail which haunted his brain as soon as his eyes were closed prevented him from sleeping. As on the day before, sounds reached him from the adjoining rooms through the walls, voices, the jingle of glasses and teaspoons. . . . Marya Timofyevna was gaily telling Father Sisoy some story with quaint turns of speech, while the latter answered in a grumpy, ill-humoured voice: "Bother them! Not likely! What next!" And the bishop again felt vexed and then hurt that with other people his old mother behaved in a simple, ordinary way, while with him, her son, she was shy, spoke little, and did not say what she meant, and even, as he fancied, had during all those three days kept trying in his presence to find an excuse for standing up, because she was embarrassed at sitting before him. And his father? He, too, probably, if he had been living, would not have been able to utter a word in the bishop's presence. . . .

Something fell down on the floor in the adjoining room and was broken; Katya must have dropped a cup or a saucer, for Father Sisoy suddenly spat and said angrily:

"What a regular nuisance the child is! Lord forgive my transgressions! One can't provide enough for her."

Then all was quiet, the only sounds came from outside. And when the bishop opened his eyes he saw Katya in his room, standing motionless, staring at him. Her red hair, as usual, stood up from under the comb like a halo.

"Is that you, Katya?" he asked. "Who is it downstairs who keeps opening and shutting a door?"

"I don't hear it," answered Katya; and she listened.

"There, someone has just passed by."

"But that was a noise in your stomach, uncle."

He laughed and stroked her on the head.

"So you say Cousin Nikolasha cuts up dead people?" he asked after a pause.

"Yes, he is studying."

"And is he kind?"

"Oh, yes, he's kind. But he drinks vodka awfully."

"And what was it your father died of?"

"Papa was weak and very, very thin, and all at once his throat was bad. I was ill then, too, and brother Fedya; we all had bad throats. Papa died, uncle, and we got well."

Her chin began quivering, and tears gleamed in her eyes and trickled down her cheeks.

"Your holiness," she said in a shrill voice, by now weeping bitterly, "uncle, mother and all of us are left very wretched. . . . Give us a little money . . . do be kind . . . uncle darling. . . ."

He, too, was moved to tears, and for a long time was too much touched to speak. Then he stroked her on the head, patted her on the shoulder and said:

"Very good, very good, my child. When the holy Easter comes, we will talk it over. . . . I will help you. . . . I will help you. . . ."

His mother came in quietly, timidly, and prayed before the ikon. Noticing that he was not sleeping, she said:

"Won't you have a drop of soup?"

"No, thank you," he answered, "I am not hungry."

"You seem to be unwell, now I look at you. I should think so; you may well be ill! The whole day on your legs, the whole day. . . . And, my goodness, it makes one's heart ache even to look at you! Well, Easter is not far off; you will rest then, please God. Then we will have a talk, too, but now I'm not going to disturb you with my chatter. Come along, Katya; let his holiness sleep a little."

And he remembered how once very long ago, when he was a boy, she had spoken exactly like that, in the same jestingly respectful tone, with a Church dignitary. . . . Only from her extraordinarily kind eyes and the timid, anxious glance she stole at him as she went out of the room could one have guessed that this was his mother. He shut his eyes and seemed to sleep, but twice heard the clock strike and Father Sisoy coughing the other side of the wall. And once more his mother came in and looked timidly at him for a minute. Someone drove up to the steps, as he could hear, in a coach or in a chaise. Suddenly a knock, the door slammed, the lay brother came into the bedroom.

"Your holiness," he called.

"Well?"

"The horses are here; it's time for the evening service."

"What o'clock is it?"

"A quarter past seven."

He dressed and drove to the cathedral. During all the "Twelve Gospels" he had to stand in the middle of the church without moving, and the first gospel, the longest and the most beautiful, he read himself. A mood of confidence and courage came over him. That first gospel, "Now is the Son of Man glorified," he knew by heart; and as he read he raised his eyes from time to time, and saw on both sides a perfect sea of lights and heard the splutter of candles, but, as in past years, he could not see the people, and it seemed as though these were all the same people as had been round him in those days, in his childhood and his youth; that they would always be the same every year and till such time as God only knew.

His father had been a deacon, his grandfather a priest, his great-grandfather a deacon, and his whole family, perhaps from the days when Christianity had been accepted in Russia, had belonged to the priesthood; and his love for the Church services, for the priesthood, for the peal of the bells, was deep in him, ineradicable, innate. In church, particularly when he took part in the service, he felt vigorous, of good cheer, happy. So it was now. Only when the eighth gospel had been read, he felt that his voice had grown weak, even his cough was inaudible. His head had begun to ache intensely, and he was troubled by a fear that he might fall down. And his legs were indeed quite numb, so that by degrees he ceased to feel them and could not understand how or on what he was standing, and why he did not fall. . . .

It was a quarter to twelve when the service was over. When he reached home, the bishop undressed and went to bed at once without even saying his prayers. He could not speak and felt that he could not have stood up. When he had covered his head with the quilt he felt a sudden longing to be abroad, an insufferable longing! He felt that he would give his life not to see those pitiful cheap shutters, those low ceilings, not to smell that heavy monastery smell. If only there were one person to whom he could have talked, have opened his heart!

For a long while he heard footsteps in the next room and could not tell whose they were. At last the door opened, and Sisoy came in with a candle and a tea-cup in his hand.

"You are in bed already, your holiness?" he asked. "Here I have come to rub you with spirit and vinegar. A thorough rubbing does a great deal of good. Lord Jesus Christ! . . . That's the way . . . that's the way. . . . I've just been in our monastery. . . . I don't like it. I'm going away from here tomorrow, your holiness; I don't want to stay longer. Lord Jesus Christ. . . . That's the way. . . ."

Sisoy could never stay long in the same place, and he felt as though he had been a whole year in the Pankratievsky Monastery. Above all, listening to him it was difficult to understand where his home was, whether he cared for anyone or anything, whether he believed in God. . . . He did not know himself why he was a monk, and, indeed, he did not think about it, and the time when he had become a monk had long passed out of his memory; it seemed as though he had been born a monk.

"I'm going away tomorrow; God be with them all."

"I should like to talk to you. . . . I can't find the time," said the bishop softly with an effort. "I don't know anything or anybody here. . . ."

"I'll stay till Sunday if you like; so be it, but I don't want to stay longer. I am sick of them!"

"I ought not to be a bishop," said the bishop softly. "I ought to have been a village priest, a deacon . . . or simply a monk. . . . All this oppresses me . . . oppresses me."

"What? Lord Jesus Christ. . . . That's the way. Come, sleep well, your holiness! . . . What's the good of talking? It's no use. Goodnight!"

The bishop did not sleep all night. And at eight o'clock in the morning he began to have hemorrhage from the bowels. The lay brother was alarmed, and ran first to the archimandrite, then for the monastery doctor, Ivan Andreyitch, who lived in the town. The doctor, a stout old man with a long grey beard, made a prolonged examination of the bishop, and kept shaking his head and frowning, then said:

"Do you know, your holiness, you have got typhoid?"

After an hour or so of hemorrhage the bishop looked much thinner, paler, and wasted; his face looked wrinkled, his eyes looked bigger, and he seemed older, shorter, and it seemed to him that he was thinner, weaker, more insignificant than any one, that everything that had been had retreated far, far away and would never go on again or be repeated.

"How good," he thought, "how good!"

His old mother came. Seeing his wrinkled face and his big eyes, she was frightened, she fell on her knees by the bed and began kissing his face, his shoulders, his hands. And to her, too, it seemed that he was thinner, weaker, and more insignificant than anyone, and now she forgot that he was a bishop, and kissed him as though he were a child very near and very dear to her.

"Pavlusha, darling," she said; "my own, my darling son! . . . Why are you like this? Pavlusha, answer me!"

Katya, pale and severe, stood beside her, unable to understand what was the matter with her uncle, why there was such a look of suffering on her grandmother's face, why she was saying such sad and touching things. By now he could not utter a word, he could understand nothing, and he imagined he was a simple ordinary man, that he was walking quickly, cheerfully through the fields, tapping with his stick, while above him was the open sky bathed in sunshine, and that he was free now as a bird and could go where he liked!

"Pavlusha, my darling son, answer me," the old woman was saying. "What is it? My own!"

"Don't disturb his holiness," Sisoy said angrily, walking about the room. "Let him sleep . . . what's the use . . . it's no good. . . ."

Three doctors arrived, consulted together, and went away again. The day was long, incredibly long, then the night came on and passed slowly, slowly, and towards morning on Saturday the lay brother went in to the old mother who was lying on the sofa in the parlour, and asked her to go into the bedroom: the bishop had just breathed his last.

Next day was Easter Sunday. There were forty-two churches and six monasteries in the town; the sonorous, joyful clang of the bells hung over the town from morning till night unceasingly, setting the spring air aquiver; the birds were singing, the sun was shining brightly. The big market square was noisy, swings were going, barrel organs were playing, accordions were squeaking, drunken voices were shouting. After midday people began driving up and down the principal street.

In short, all was merriment, everything was satisfactory, just as it had been the year before, and as it will be in all likelihood next year.

A month later a new suffragan bishop was appointed, and no one thought anything more of Bishop Pyotr, and afterwards he was completely forgotten. And only the dead man's old mother, who is living today with her son-in-law the deacon in a remote little district town, when she goes out at night to bring her cow in and meets other women at the pasture, begins talking of her children and her grandchildren, and says that she had a son a bishop, and this she says timidly, afraid that she may not be believed. . . .

And, indeed, there are some who do not believe her.

Betrothed

[Written in 1903. First published in the December 1903
issue of *Zhurnal Dlya Vsekh*, a Russian magazine. Also translated as
'The Fiancée.' Collected in *The Schoolmaster and Other Stories* (1921).
It is Chekhov's last completed story.]

I

It was ten o'clock in the evening and the full moon was shining over
the garden. In the Shumins' house an evening service celebrated at the
request of the grandmother, Marfa Mihalovna, was just over, and now
Nadya—she had gone into the garden for a minute—could see the table
being laid for supper in the dining room, and her grandmother bustling
about in her gorgeous silk dress; Father Andrey, a chief priest of the
cathedral, was talking to Nadya's mother, Nina Ivanovna, and now in the
evening light through the window her mother for some reason looked
very young; Andrey Andreitch, Father Andrey's son, was standing by
listening attentively.

It was still and cool in the garden, and dark peaceful shadows
lay on the ground. There was a sound of frogs croaking, far, far away
beyond the town. There was a feeling of May, sweet May! One drew
deep breaths and longed to fancy that not here but far away under the
sky, above the trees, far away in the open country, in the fields and the
woods, the life of spring was unfolding now, mysterious, lovely, rich
and holy beyond the understanding of weak, sinful man. And for some
reason one wanted to cry.

She, Nadya, was already twenty-three. Ever since she was sixteen she had been passionately dreaming of marriage and at last she was engaged to Andrey Andreitch, the young man who was standing on the other side of the window; she liked him, the wedding was already fixed for July 7, and yet there was no joy in her heart, she was sleeping badly, her spirits drooped. . . . She could hear from the open windows of the basement where the kitchen was the hurrying servants, the clatter of knives, the banging of the swing door; there was a smell of roast turkey and pickled cherries, and for some reason it seemed to her that it would be like that all her life, with no change, no end to it.

Some one came out of the house and stood on the steps; it was Alexandr Timofeitch, or, as he was always called, Sasha, who had come from Moscow ten days before and was staying with them. Years ago a distant relation of the grandmother, a gentleman's widow called Marya Petrovna, a thin, sickly little woman who had sunk into poverty, used to come to the house to ask for assistance. She had a son Sasha. It used for some reason to be said that he had talent as an artist, and when his mother died Nadya's grandmother had, for the salvation of her soul, sent him to the Komissarovsky school in Moscow; two years later he went into the school of painting, spent nearly fifteen years there, and only just managed to scrape through the leaving examination in the section of architecture. He did not set up as an architect, however, but took a job at a lithographer's. He used to come almost every year, usually very ill, to stay with Nadya's grandmother to rest and recover.

He was wearing now a frock-coat buttoned up, and shabby canvas trousers, crumpled into creases at the bottom. And his shirt had not been ironed and he had somehow all over a look of not being fresh. He was very thin, with big eyes, long thin fingers and a swarthy bearded face, and all the same he was handsome. With the Shumins he was like one of the family, and in their house felt he was at home. And the room in which he lived when he was there had for years been called Sasha's room. Standing on the steps he saw Nadya, and went up to her.

"It's nice here," he said.

"Of course it's nice, you ought to stay here till the autumn."

"Yes, I expect it will come to that. I dare say I shall stay with you till September."

He laughed for no reason, and sat down beside her.

"I'm sitting gazing at mother," said Nadya. "She looks so young from here! My mother has her weaknesses, of course," she added, after a pause, "but still she is an exceptional woman."

"Yes, she is very nice . . ." Sasha agreed. "Your mother, in her own way of course, is a very good and sweet woman, but . . . how shall I say? I went early this morning into your kitchen and there I found four servants sleeping on the floor, no bedsteads, and rags for bedding, stench, bugs, beetles . . . it is just as it was twenty years ago, no change at all. Well, Granny, God bless her, what else can you expect of Granny? But your mother speaks French, you know, and acts in private theatricals. One would think she might understand."

As Sasha talked, he used to stretch out two long wasted fingers before the listener's face.

"It all seems somehow strange to me here, now I am out of the habit of it," he went on. "There is no making it out. Nobody ever does anything. Your mother spends the whole day walking about like a duchess, Granny does nothing either, nor you either. And your Andrey Andreitch never does anything either."

Nadya had heard this the year before and, she fancied, the year before that too, and she knew that Sasha could not make any other criticism, and in old days this had amused her, but now for some reason she felt annoyed.

"That's all stale, and I have been sick of it for ages," she said and got up. "You should think of something a little newer."

He laughed and got up too, and they went together toward the house. She, tall, handsome, and well-made, beside him looked very healthy and smartly dressed; she was conscious of this and felt sorry for him and for some reason awkward.

"And you say a great deal you should not," she said. "You've just been talking about my Andrey, but you see you don't know him."

"My Andrey. . . . Bother him, your Andrey. I am sorry for your youth."

They were already sitting down to supper as the young people went into the dining room. The grandmother, or Granny as she was called in the household, a very stout, plain old lady with bushy eyebrows and a little moustache, was talking loudly, and from her voice and manner of speaking it could be seen that she was the person of most importance in the house. She owned rows of shops in the market, and the old-fashioned house with columns and the garden, yet she prayed every morning that God might save her from ruin and shed tears as she did so. Her daughter-in-law, Nadya's mother, Nina Ivanovna, a fair-haired woman tightly laced in, with a pince-nez, and diamonds on every finger, Father Andrey, a lean, toothless old man whose face always looked as though he were just going to say something amusing, and his son, Andrey Andreitch, a stout and handsome young man with curly hair looking like an artist or an actor, were all talking of hypnotism.

"You will get well in a week here," said Granny, addressing Sasha. "Only you must eat more. What do you look like!" she sighed. "You are really dreadful! You are a regular prodigal son, that is what you are."

"After wasting his father's substance in riotous living," said Father Andrey slowly, with laughing eyes. "He fed with senseless beasts."

"I like my dad," said Andrey Andreitch, touching his father on the shoulder. "He is a splendid old fellow, a dear old fellow."

Everyone was silent for a space. Sasha suddenly burst out laughing and put his dinner napkin to his mouth.

"So you believe in hypnotism?" said Father Andrey to Nina Ivanovna.

"I cannot, of course, assert that I believe," answered Nina Ivanovna, assuming a very serious, even severe, expression; "but I must own that there is much that is mysterious and incomprehensible in nature."

"I quite agree with you, though I must add that religion distinctly curtails for us the domain of the mysterious."

A big and very fat turkey was served. Father Andrey and Nina Ivanovna went on with their conversation. Nina Ivanovna's diamonds glittered on her fingers, then tears began to glitter in her eyes, she grew excited.

"Though I cannot venture to argue with you," she said, "you must admit there are so many insoluble riddles in life!"

"Not one, I assure you."

After supper Andrey Andreitch played the fiddle and Nina Ivanovna accompanied him on the piano. Ten years before he had taken his degree at the university in the Faculty of Arts, but had never held any post, had no definite work, and only from time to time took part in concerts for charitable objects; and in the town he was regarded as a musician.

Andrey Andreitch played; they all listened in silence. The samovar was boiling quietly on the table and no one but Sasha was drinking tea.

Then when it struck twelve a violin string suddenly broke; everyone laughed, bustled about, and began saying goodbye.

After seeing her fiancé out, Nadya went upstairs where she and her mother had their rooms (the lower storey was occupied by the grandmother). They began putting the lights out below in the dining room, while Sasha still sat on drinking tea. He always spent a long time over tea in the Moscow style, drinking as much as seven glasses at a time. For a long time after Nadya had undressed and gone to bed she could hear the servants clearing away downstairs and Granny talking angrily. At last everything was hushed, and nothing could be heard but Sasha from time to time coughing on a bass note in his room below.

II

When Nadya woke up it must have been two o'clock, it was beginning to get light. A watchman was tapping somewhere far away. She was not sleepy, and her bed felt very soft and uncomfortable. Nadya sat up in her bed and fell to thinking as she had done every night in May. Her thoughts were the same as they had been the night before, useless, persistent thoughts, always alike, of how Andrey Andreitch had begun courting her and had made her an offer, how she had accepted him and then little by little had come to appreciate the kindly, intelligent man. But for some reason now when there was hardly a month left before the wedding, she began to feel dread and uneasiness as though something vague and oppressive were before her.

"Tick-tock, tick-tock . . ." the watchman tapped lazily. ". . . Tick-tock."

Through the big old-fashioned window she could see the garden and at a little distance bushes of lilac in full flower, drowsy and lifeless from the cold; and the thick white mist was floating softly up to the lilac, trying to cover it. Drowsy rooks were cawing in the faraway trees.

"My God, why is my heart so heavy?"

Perhaps every girl felt the same before her wedding. There was no knowing! Or was it Sasha's influence? But for several years past Sasha had been repeating the same thing, like a copybook, and when he talked he seemed naïve and queer. But why was it she could not get Sasha out of her head? Why was it?

The watchman left off tapping for a long while. The birds were twittering under the windows and the mist had disappeared from the garden. Everything was lighted up by the spring sunshine as by a smile. Soon the whole garden, warm and caressed by the sun, returned to life, and dewdrops like diamonds glittered on the leaves and the old neglected garden on that morning looked young and gaily decked.

Granny was already awake. Sasha's husky cough began. Nadya could hear them below, setting the samovar and moving the chairs. The hours passed slowly, Nadya had been up and walking about the garden for a long while and still the morning dragged on.

At last Nina Ivanovna appeared with a tear-stained face, carrying a glass of mineral water. She was interested in spiritualism and homeopathy, read a great deal, was fond of talking of the doubts to which she was subject, and to Nadya it seemed as though there were a deep mysterious significance in all that.

Now Nadya kissed her mother and walked beside her.

"What have you been crying about, mother?" she asked.

"Last night I was reading a story in which there is an old man and his daughter. The old man is in some office and his chief falls in love with his daughter. I have not finished it, but there was a passage which made it hard to keep from tears," said Nina Ivanovna and she sipped at her glass. "I thought of it this morning and shed tears again."

"I have been so depressed all these days," said Nadya after a pause. "Why is it I don't sleep at night!"

"I don't know, dear. When I can't sleep I shut my eyes very tightly, like this, and picture to myself Anna Karenin moving about and talking, or something historical from the ancient world. . . ."

Nadya felt that her mother did not understand her and was incapable of understanding. She felt this for the first time in her life, and it positively frightened her and made her want to hide herself; and she went away to her own room.

At two o'clock they sat down to dinner. It was Wednesday, a fast day, and so vegetable soup and bream with boiled grain were set before Granny.

To tease Granny Sasha ate his meat soup as well as the vegetable soup. He was making jokes all through dinner-time, but his jests were laboured and invariably with a moral bearing, and the effect was not at all amusing when before making some witty remark he raised his very long, thin, deathly-looking fingers; and when one remembered that he was very ill and would probably not be much longer in this world, one felt sorry for him and ready to weep.

After dinner Granny went off to her own room to lie down. Nina Ivanovna played on the piano for a little, and then she too went away.

"Oh, dear Nadya!" Sasha began his usual afternoon conversation, "if only you would listen to me! If only you would!"

She was sitting far back in an old-fashioned armchair, with her eyes shut, while he paced slowly about the room from corner to corner.

"If only you would go to the university," he said. "Only enlightened and holy people are interesting, it's only they who are wanted. The more of such people there are, the sooner the Kingdom of God will come on earth. Of your town then not one stone will be left, everything will be blown up from the foundations, everything will be changed as though by magic. And then there will be immense, magnificent houses here, wonderful gardens, marvellous fountains, remarkable people. . . . But that's not what matters most. What matters most is that the crowd, in our sense of the word, in the sense in which it exists now—that evil will not exist then, because every man will believe and every man will know what he is living for and no one will seek moral support in the crowd. Dear Nadya, darling girl, go away! Show them all that you are sick of this stagnant, grey, sinful life. Prove it to yourself at least!"

"I can't, Sasha, I'm going to be married."

"Oh nonsense! What's it for!"

They went out into the garden and walked up and down a little.

"And however that may be, my dear girl, you must think, you must realize how unclean, how immoral this idle life of yours is," Sasha went on. "Do understand that if, for instance, you and your mother and your grandmother do nothing, it means that someone else is working for you, you are eating up someone else's life, and is that clean, isn't it filthy?"

Nadya wanted to say "Yes, that is true"; she wanted to say that she understood, but tears came into her eyes, her spirits drooped, and shrinking into herself she went off to her room.

Towards evening Andrey Andreitch arrived and as usual played the fiddle for a long time. He was not given to much talk as a rule, and was fond of the fiddle, perhaps because one could be silent while playing. At eleven o'clock when he was about to go home and had put on his greatcoat, he embraced Nadya and began greedily kissing her face, her shoulders, and her hands.

"My dear, my sweet, my charmer," he muttered. "Oh how happy I am! I am beside myself with rapture!"

And it seemed to her as though she had heard that long, long ago, or had read it somewhere . . . in some old tattered novel thrown away long ago. In the dining room Sasha was sitting at the table drinking tea with the saucer poised on his five long fingers; Granny was laying out patience; Nina Ivanovna was reading. The flame crackled in the ikon lamp and everything, it seemed, was quiet and going well. Nadya said goodnight, went upstairs to her room, got into bed and fell asleep at once. But just as on the night before, almost before it was light, she woke up. She was not sleepy, there was an uneasy, oppressive feeling in her heart. She sat up with her head on her knees and thought of her fiancé and her marriage. . . . She for some reason remembered that her mother had not loved her father and now had nothing and lived in complete dependence on her mother-in-law, Granny. And however much Nadya pondered she could not imagine why she had hitherto seen in her mother something special and exceptional, how it was she had not noticed that she was a simple, ordinary, unhappy woman.

And Sasha downstairs was not asleep, she could hear him coughing. He is a queer, naïve man, thought Nadya, and in all his dreams, in all those marvellous gardens and wonderful fountains one felt there was something absurd. But for some reason in his naïveté, in this very absurdity there was something so beautiful that as soon as she thought of the possibility of going to the university, it sent a cold thrill through her heart and her bosom and flooded them with joy and rapture.

"But better not think, better not think . . ." she whispered. "I must not think of it."

"Tick-tock," tapped the watchman somewhere far away. "Tick-tock . . . tick-tock. . . ."

III

In the middle of June Sasha suddenly felt bored and made up his mind to return to Moscow.

"I can't exist in this town," he said gloomily. "No water supply, no drains! It disgusts me to eat at dinner; the filth in the kitchen is incredible. . . ."

"Wait a little, prodigal son!" Granny tried to persuade him, speaking for some reason in a whisper, "the wedding is to be on the seventh."

"I don't want to."

"You meant to stay with us until September!"

"But now, you see, I don't want to. I must get to work."

The summer was grey and cold, the trees were wet, everything in the garden looked dejected and uninviting, it certainly did make one long to get to work. The sound of unfamiliar women's voices was heard downstairs and upstairs, there was the rattle of a sewing machine in Granny's room, they were working hard at the trousseau. Of fur coats alone, six were provided for Nadya, and the cheapest of them, in Granny's words, had cost three hundred roubles! The fuss irritated Sasha; he stayed in his own room and was cross, but everyone persuaded him to remain, and he promised not to go before the first of July.

Time passed quickly. On St. Peter's day Andrey Andreitch went with Nadya after dinner to Moscow Street to look once more at the house which had been taken and made ready for the young couple some time before. It was a house of two storeys, but so far only the upper floor had been furnished. There was in the hall a shining floor painted and parqueted, there were Viennese chairs, a piano, a violin stand; there was a smell of paint. On the wall hung a big oil painting in a gold frame—a naked lady and beside her a purple vase with a broken handle.

"An exquisite picture," said Andrey Andreitch, and he gave a respectful sigh. "It's the work of the artist Shismatchevsky."

Then there was the drawing room with the round table, and a sofa and easy chairs upholstered in bright blue. Above the sofa was a big photograph of Father Andrey wearing a priest's velvet cap and decorations. Then they went into the dining room in which there was a sideboard; then into the bedroom; here in the half dusk stood two bedsteads side by side, and it looked as though the bedroom had been decorated with the idea that it would always be very agreeable there and could not possibly be anything else. Andrey Andreitch led Nadya about the rooms, all the while keeping his arm round her waist; and she felt weak and conscience-stricken. She hated all the rooms, the beds, the easy chairs; she was nauseated by the naked lady. It was clear to her now that she had ceased to love Andrey Andreitch or perhaps had never loved him at all; but how to say this and to whom to say it and with what object she

534

did not understand, and could not understand, though she was thinking about it all day and all night. . . . He held her round the waist, talked so affectionately, so modestly, was so happy, walking about this house of his; while she saw nothing in it all but vulgarity, stupid, naïve, unbearable vulgarity, and his arm round her waist felt as hard and cold as an iron hoop. And every minute she was on the point of running away, bursting into sobs, throwing herself out of a window. Andrey Andreitch led her into the bathroom and here he touched a tap fixed in the wall and at once water flowed.

"What do you say to that?" he said, and laughed. "I had a tank holding two hundred gallons put in the loft, and so now we shall have water."

They walked across the yard and went out into the street and took a cab. Thick clouds of dust were blowing, and it seemed as though it were just going to rain.

"You are not cold?" said Andrey Andreitch, screwing up his eyes at the dust.

She did not answer.

"Yesterday, you remember, Sasha blamed me for doing nothing," he said, after a brief silence. "Well, he is right, absolutely right! I do nothing and can do nothing. My precious, why is it? Why is it that the very thought that I may some day fix a cockade on my cap and go into the government service is so hateful to me? Why do I feel so uncomfortable when I see a lawyer or a Latin master or a member of the Zemstvo? O Mother Russia! O Mother Russia! What a burden of idle and useless people you still carry! How many like me are upon you, long-suffering Mother!"

And from the fact that he did nothing he drew generalizations, seeing in it a sign of the times.

"When we are married let us go together into the country, my precious; there we will work! We will buy ourselves a little piece of land with a garden and a river, we will labour and watch life. Oh, how splendid that will be!"

He took off his hat, and his hair floated in the wind, while she listened to him and thought: "Good God, I wish I were home!"

When they were quite near the house they overtook Father Andrey.

"Ah, here's father coming," cried Andrey Andreitch, delighted, and he waved his hat. "I love my dad really," he said as he paid the cabman. "He's a splendid old fellow, a dear old fellow."

Nadya went into the house, feeling cross and unwell, thinking that there would be visitors all the evening, that she would have to entertain them, to smile, to listen to the fiddle, to listen to all sorts of nonsense, and to talk of nothing but the wedding.

Granny, dignified, gorgeous in her silk dress, and haughty as she always seemed before visitors, was sitting before the samovar. Father Andrey came in with his sly smile.

"I have the pleasure and blessed consolation of seeing you in health," he said to Granny, and it was hard to tell whether he was joking or speaking seriously.

IV

The wind was beating on the window and on the roof; there was a whistling sound, and in the stove the house spirit was plaintively and sullenly droning his song. It was past midnight; everyone in the house had gone to bed, but no one was asleep, and it seemed all the while to Nadya as though they were playing the fiddle below. There was a sharp bang; a shutter must have been torn off. A minute later Nina Ivanovna came in in her nightgown, with a candle.

"What was the bang, Nadya?" she asked.

Her mother, with her hair in a single plait and a timid smile on her face, looked older, plainer, smaller on that stormy night. Nadya remembered that quite a little time ago she had thought her mother an exceptional woman and had listened with pride to the things she said; and now she could not remember those things, everything that came into her mind was so feeble and useless.

In the stove was the sound of several bass voices in chorus, and she even heard "O-o-o my G-o-od!" Nadya sat on her bed, and suddenly she clutched at her hair and burst into sobs.

"Mother, mother, my own," she said. "If only you knew what is happening to me! I beg you, I beseech you, let me go away! I beseech you!"

"Where?" asked Nina Ivanovna, not understanding, and she sat down on the bedstead. "Go where?"

For a long while Nadya cried and could not utter a word.

"Let me go away from the town," she said at last. "There must not and will not be a wedding, understand that! I don't love that man . . . I can't even speak about him."

"No, my own, no!" Nina Ivanovna said quickly, terribly alarmed. "Calm yourself—it's just because you are in low spirits. It will pass, it often happens. Most likely you have had a tiff with Andrey; but lovers' quarrels always end in kisses!"

"Oh, go away, mother, oh, go away," sobbed Nadya.

"Yes," said Nina Ivanovna after a pause, "it's not long since you were a baby, a little girl, and now you are engaged to be married. In nature there is a continual transmutation of substances. Before you know where you are you will be a mother yourself and an old woman, and will have as rebellious a daughter as I have."

"My darling, my sweet, you are clever you know, you are unhappy," said Nadya. "You are very unhappy; why do you say such very dull, commonplace things? For God's sake, why?"

Nina Ivanovna tried to say something, but could not utter a word; she gave a sob and went away to her own room. The bass voices began droning in the stove again, and Nadya felt suddenly frightened. She jumped out of bed and went quickly to her mother. Nina Ivanovna, with tear-stained face, was lying in bed wrapped in a pale blue quilt and holding a book in her hands.

"Mother, listen to me!" said Nadya. "I implore you, do understand! If you would only understand how petty and degrading our life is. My eyes have been opened, and I see it all now. And what is your Andrey Andreitch? Why, he is not intelligent, mother! Merciful heavens, do understand, mother, he is stupid!"

Nina Ivanovna abruptly sat up.

"You and your grandmother torment me," she said with a sob. "I want to live! to live," she repeated, and twice she beat her little fist upon her bosom. "Let me be free! I am still young, I want to live, and you have made me an old woman between you!"

She broke into bitter tears, lay down and curled up under the quilt, and looked so small, so pitiful, so foolish. Nadya went to her room, dressed, and sitting at the window fell to waiting for the morning. She sat all night thinking, while someone seemed to be tapping on the shutters and whistling in the yard.

In the morning Granny complained that the wind had blown down all the apples in the garden, and broken down an old plum tree. It was grey, murky, cheerless, dark enough for candles; everyone complained of the cold, and the rain lashed on the windows. After tea Nadya went into Sasha's room and without saying a word knelt down before an armchair in the corner and hid her face in her hands.

"What is it?" asked Sasha.

"I can't . . ." she said. "How I could go on living here before, I can't understand, I can't conceive! I despise the man I am engaged to, I despise myself, I despise all this idle, senseless existence."

"Well, well," said Sasha, not yet grasping what was meant. "That's all right . . . that's good."

"I am sick of this life," Nadya went on. "I can't endure another day here. Tomorrow I am going away. Take me with you for God's sake!"

For a minute Sasha looked at her in astonishment; at last he understood and was delighted as a child. He waved his arms and began pattering with his slippers as though he were dancing with delight.

"Splendid," he said, rubbing his hands. "My goodness, how fine that is!"

And she stared at him without bBlinking, with adoring eyes, as though spellbound, expecting every minute that he would say something important, something infinitely significant; he had told her nothing yet, but already it seemed to her that something new and great was opening before her which she had not known till then, and already she gazed at him full of expectation, ready to face anything, even death.

"I am going tomorrow," he said after a moment's thought. "You come to the station to see me off. . . . I'll take your things in my portmanteau, and I'll get your ticket, and when the third bell rings you get into the carriage, and we'll go off. You'll see me as far as Moscow and then go on to Petersburg alone. Have you a passport?"

"Yes."

"I can promise you, you won't regret it," said Sasha, with conviction. "You will go, you will study, and then go where fate takes you. When you turn your life upside down everything will be changed. The great thing is to turn your life upside down, and all the rest is unimportant. And so we will set off tomorrow?"

"Oh yes, for God's sake!"

It seemed to Nadya that she was very much excited, that her heart was heavier than ever before, that she would spend all the time till she went away in misery and agonizing thought; but she had hardly gone upstairs and lain down on her bed when she fell asleep at once, with traces of tears and a smile on her face, and slept soundly till evening.

V

A cab had been sent for. Nadya in her hat and overcoat went upstairs to take one more look at her mother, at all her belongings. She stood in her own room beside her still warm bed, looked about her, then went slowly in to her mother. Nina Ivanovna was asleep; it was quite still in her room. Nadya kissed her mother, smoothed her hair, stood still for a couple of minutes . . . then walked slowly downstairs.

It was raining heavily. The cabman with the hood pulled down was standing at the entrance, drenched with rain.

"There is not room for you, Nadya," said Granny, as the servants began putting in the luggage. "What an idea to see him off in such weather! You had better stop at home. Goodness, how it rains!"

Nadya tried to say something, but could not. Then Sasha helped Nadya in and covered her feet with a rug. Then he sat down beside her.

"Good luck to you! God bless you!" Granny cried from the steps. "Mind you write to us from Moscow, Sasha!"

"Right. Goodbye, Granny."

"The Queen of Heaven keep you!"

"Oh, what weather!" said Sasha.

It was only now that Nadya began to cry. Now it was clear to her that she certainly was going, which she had not really believed when she was saying goodbye to Granny, and when she was looking at her mother. Goodbye, town! And she suddenly thought of it all: Andrey, and his father and the new house and the naked lady with the vase; and it all no longer frightened her, nor weighed upon her, but was naïve and trivial and continually retreated further away. And when they got into the railway carriage and the train began to move, all that past which had been so big and serious shrank up into something tiny, and a vast wide future which till then had scarcely been noticed began unfolding before her. The rain pattered on the carriage windows, nothing could be seen but the green fields, telegraph posts with birds sitting on the wires flitted by, and joy made her hold her breath; she thought that she was going to freedom, going to study, and this was just like what used, ages ago, to be called going off to be a free Cossack.

She laughed and cried and prayed all at once.

"It's a-all right," said Sasha, smiling. "It's a-all right."

VI

Autumn had passed and winter, too, had gone. Nadya had begun to be very homesick and thought every day of her mother and her grandmother; she thought of Sasha too. The letters that came from home were kind and gentle, and it seemed as though everything by now were forgiven and forgotten. In May after the examinations she set off for home in good health and high spirits, and stopped on the way at Moscow to see Sasha. He was just the same as the year before, with the same beard and unkempt hair, with the same large beautiful eyes, and he still wore the same coat and canvas trousers; but he looked unwell and worried, he seemed both older and thinner, and kept coughing, and for some reason he struck Nadya as grey and provincial.

"My God, Nadya has come!" he said, and laughed gaily. "My darling girl!"

They sat in the printing room, which was full of tobacco smoke, and smelt strongly, stiflingly of Indian ink and paint; then they went to his room, which also smelt of tobacco and was full of the traces of spitting; near a cold samovar stood a broken plate with dark paper on it, and there were masses of dead flies on the table and on the floor. And everything showed that Sasha ordered his personal life in a slovenly way and lived anyhow, with utter contempt for comfort, and if anyone began talking to him of his personal happiness, of his personal life, of affection for him, he would not have understood and would have only laughed.

"It is all right, everything has gone well," said Nadya hurriedly. "Mother came to see me in Petersburg in the autumn; she said that Granny is not angry, and only keeps going into my room and making the sign of the cross over the walls."

Sasha looked cheerful, but he kept coughing, and talked in a cracked voice, and Nadya kept looking at him, unable to decide whether he really were seriously ill or whether it were only her fancy.

"Dear Sasha," she said, "you are ill."

"No, it's nothing, I am ill, but not very . . ."

"Oh, dear!" cried Nadya, in agitation. "Why don't you go to a doctor? Why don't you take care of your health? My dear, darling Sasha," she said, and tears gushed from her eyes and for some reason there rose before her imagination Andrey Andreitch and the naked lady with the vase, and all her past which seemed now as far away as her childhood; and she began crying because Sasha no longer seemed to her so novel, so cultured, and so interesting as the year before. "Dear Sasha, you are very, very ill . . . I would do anything to make you not so pale and thin. I am so indebted to you! You can't imagine how much you have done for me, my good Sasha! In reality you are now the person nearest and dearest to me."

They sat on and talked, and now, after Nadya had spent a winter in Petersburg, Sasha, his works, his smile, his whole figure had for her a suggestion of something out of date, old-fashioned, done with long ago and perhaps already dead and buried.

"I am going down the Volga the day after tomorrow," said Sasha, "and then to drink koumiss. I mean to drink koumiss. A friend and his wife are going with me. His wife is a wonderful woman; I am always at her, trying to persuade her to go to the university. I want her to turn her life upside down."

After having talked they drove to the station. Sasha got her tea and apples; and when the train began moving and he waved his handkerchief at her, smiling, it could be seen even from his legs that he was very ill and would not live long.

Nadya reached her native town at midday. As she drove home from the station the streets struck her as very wide and the houses very small and squat; there were no people about, she met no one but the German piano-tuner in a rusty greatcoat. And all the houses looked as though they were covered with dust. Granny, who seemed to have grown quite old, but was as fat and plain as ever, flung her arms round Nadya and cried for a long time with her face on Nadya's shoulder, unable to tear herself away. Nina Ivanovna looked much older and plainer and seemed shrivelled up, but was still tightly laced, and still had diamonds flashing on her fingers.

"My darling," she said, trembling all over, "my darling!"

Then they sat down and cried without speaking. It was evident that both mother and grandmother realized that the past was lost and gone, never to return; they had now no position in society, no prestige as before, no right to invite visitors; so it is when in the midst of an easy careless life the police suddenly burst in at night and made a search, and it turns out that the head of the family has embezzled money or committed forgery—and goodbye then to the easy careless life for ever!

Nadya went upstairs and saw the same bed, the same windows with naïve white curtains, and outside the windows the same garden, gay and noisy, bathed in sunshine. She touched the table, sat down and sank into thought. And she had a good dinner and drank tea with delicious rich cream; but something was missing, there was a sense of emptiness in the rooms and the ceilings were so low. In the evening she went to bed, covered herself up and for some reason it seemed to her to be funny lying in this snug, very soft bed.

Nina Ivanovna came in for a minute; she sat down as people who feel guilty sit down, timidly, and looking about her.

"Well, tell me, Nadya," she enquired after a brief pause, "are you contented? Quite contented?"

"Yes, mother."

Nina Ivanovna got up, made the sign of the cross over Nadya and the windows.

"I have become religious, as you see," she said. "You know I am studying philosophy now, and I am always thinking and thinking. . . . And many things have become as clear as daylight to me. It seems to me that what is above all necessary is that life should pass as it were through a prism."

"Tell me, mother, how is Granny in health?"

"She seems all right. When you went away that time with Sasha and the telegram came from you, Granny fell on the floor as she read it; for three days she lay without moving. After that she was always praying and crying. But now she is all right again."

She got up and walked about the room.

"Tick-tock," tapped the watchman. "Tick-tock, tick-tock. . . ."

"What is above all necessary is that life should pass as it were through a prism," she said; "in other words, that life in consciousness should be analyzed into its simplest elements as into the seven primary colours, and each element must be studied separately."

What Nina Ivanovna said further and when she went away, Nadya did not hear, as she quickly fell asleep.

May passed; June came. Nadya had grown used to being at home. Granny busied herself about the samovar, heaving deep sighs. Nina Ivanovna talked in the evenings about her philosophy; she still lived in the house like a poor relation, and had to go to Granny for every farthing. There were lots of flies in the house, and the ceilings seemed to become lower and lower. Granny and Nina Ivanovna did not go out in the streets for fear of meeting Father Andrey and Andrey Andreitch. Nadya walked about the garden and the streets, looked at the grey fences, and it seemed to her that everything in the town had grown old, was out of date and was only waiting either for the end, or for the beginning of something young and fresh. Oh, if only that new, bright life would come more quickly—that life in which one will be able to face one's fate boldly and directly, to know that one is right, to be light-hearted and free! And sooner or later such a life will come. The time will come when of Granny's house, where things are so arranged that the four servants can only live in one room in filth in the basement— the time will come when of that house not a trace will remain, and it will be forgotten, no one will remember it. And Nadya's only entertainment was from the boys next door; when she walked about the garden they knocked on the fence and shouted in mockery: "Betrothed! Betrothed!"

A letter from Sasha arrived from Saratov. In his gay dancing handwriting he told them that his journey on the Volga had been a complete success, but that he had been taken rather ill in Saratov, had lost his voice, and had been for the last fortnight in the hospital. She knew what that meant, and she was overwhelmed with a foreboding that was like a conviction. And it vexed her that this foreboding and the thought of Sasha did not distress her so much as before. She had a passionate desire for life, longed to be in Petersburg, and her friendship with Sasha seemed now sweet but something far, far away! She did not sleep all night, and in the morning sat at the window, listening. And she did in fact hear voices below; Granny, greatly agitated, was asking questions rapidly. Then some one began crying. . . . When Nadya went downstairs Granny was standing in the corner, praying before the ikon and her face was tearful. A telegram lay on the table.

For some time Nadya walked up and down the room, listening to Granny's weeping; then she picked up the telegram and read it.

It announced that the previous morning Alexandr Timofeitch, or more simply, Sasha, had died at Saratov of consumption.

Granny and Nina Ivanovna went to the church to order a memorial service, while Nadya went on walking about the rooms and thinking. She recognized clearly that her life had been turned upside down as Sasha wished; that here she was, alien, isolated, useless and that everything here was useless to her; that all the past had been torn away from her and vanished as though it had been burnt up and the ashes scattered to the winds. She went into Sasha's room and stood there for a while.

"Goodbye, dear Sasha," she thought, and before her mind rose the vista of a new, wide, spacious life, and that life, still obscure and full of mysteries, beckoned her and attracted her.

She went upstairs to her own room to pack, and next morning said goodbye to her family, and full of life and high spirits left the town—as she supposed for ever.